A Girl Like You

A Girl Like You

Maureen Lindley

B L O O M S B U R Y
LONDON · NEW DELHI · NEW YORK · SYDNEY

First published in Great Britain 2013

Copyright © 2013 by Maureen Lindley

The moral right of the author has been asserted

No part of this book may be used or reproduced in any manner whatsoever
without written permission from the Publisher except in the case of brief
quotations embodied in critical articles or reviews

Bloomsbury Publishing Plc
50 Bedford Square
London
WC1B 3DP

www.bloomsbury.com

Bloomsbury Publishing, London, New Delhi, New York and Sydney

A CIP catalogue record for this book is available from the British Library

ISBN 978 1 4088 0231 1

10 9 8 7 6 5 4 3 2 1

Printed and bound in Great Britain by CPI Group (UK) Ltd, Croydon CR0 4YY

MIX
Paper from
responsible sources
FSC
www.fsc.org
FSC® C020471

To Clive, with my love

There will be no armed uprising of Japanese . . .
For the most part local Japanese are loyal to the United
    States . . .
Their family life is disciplined and honourable.
The children are obedient and the girls virtuous . . .
[The Nisei] show a pathetic eagerness to be Americans.
There is a remarkable even extraordinary degree of loyalty
    among this suspect group.

—SPECIAL AGENT CURTIS MUNSON—SENT TO THE WEST
COAST TO INVESTIGATE THE LOYALTY OF THE JAPANESE-
AMERICANS—REPORTING TO PRESIDENT ROOSEVELT
IN NOVEMBER 1941; HIS REPORT WAS IGNORED
AND KEPT SECRET BY THE GOVERNMENT

I'm for catching every Japanese in America, Alaska, and
Hawaii now and putting them in concentration camps . . .
Damn them! Let's get rid of them now!

—CONGRESSMAN JOHN RANKIN, CONGRESSIONAL
RECORD, DECEMBER 15, 1941

I am for the immediate removal of every Japanese on the West
Coast to a point deep in the interior. I don't mean a nice part
of the interior either. Herd 'em up. Pack 'em off and give 'em
the inside room in the badlands. Let 'em be pinched, hurt,
hungry and up against it.

—HENRY MCLEMORE, SYNDICATED COLUMNIST
OF HEARST NEWSPAPERS

CONTENTS

THIRD BASE

1939
Angelina, rural California coast

SCHOOL LETS OUT at three o'clock in Angelina. Its pupils pour through the narrow portal of its door, milk from a jug, water from the tap. Their freedom shouts can be heard at the bus station half a mile away.

The white kids regularly hang around, the boys to throw ball to basket and, while they're at it, obscenities to the girls. And the girls, feigning indifference, to flick their hair and play jacks and jump rope. Only the Japanese pupils take off for home as though they are in a race.

All innocent from the smutty talk of the play yard, Satomi Baker, blooming toward beauty in her fourteenth year, and her friend Lily Morton are in the habit of parading themselves, pulling up their cute white socks, undoing the top button of their cotton dresses. They think they know all there is to know about sex and the "dirty thing" the boys want to get up to with them. The threat of it makes the flirting irresistible.

Satomi's the best at jumping rope, she's higher and faster than any of the other girls.

Californian oranges, fifty cents a pack.
Californian oranges, tap me on the back.

"Quick, Lily, jump in." The rope whistles, whipping up the air. It scares Lily a bit.

"No, let's play jacks, it's cooler."

It's early summer in Angelina, a sweltering, burning-up summer, so hot that even breathing comes hard. The heat haze hasn't let up for a month. It hangs in the sky, rocking gently like the spectral sails of a big old ship, allowing only occasional flashes of blue a look in.

"It's closing in," Satomi says to Lily. "Ghosts all around us."

"More like damp sheets on washing day," Lily says flatly. Satomi's fancies disturb her. It's all that reading that does it, she guesses.

"You should put your hair up in a band, in a real high ponytail, like mine," she advises, tossing her own dull brown tassel. "It'll make you feel cooler."

"It'll make my eyes slant, Lily, you know that."

"Oh, yeah, I forgot." Lily smirks, pleased to have hit the aimed-for spot.

"Oh, sure, Lily, you forgot."

It seems to Satomi that things are never going to cool down. The humidity clouds the shine on her black oxfords, takes the starch out of her dresses so that they never feel clean or crisp enough. At night the swampy air seeps through her window, scenting her room with a curious blend of sweet and rotten. That and the mosquitoes' whine make it hard to sleep. Her father says the earth is so parched he swears he can hear it cracking.

All the crops in her father's fields are tinted brown—"rusting up," is how her mother puts it. And even though the tomatoes are ripening, they need so much water that it's unlikely to be a profitable year.

What with the heat and the thought of small returns, it doesn't take much to get Aaron Baker riled. Satomi has been treading on eggshells around him for weeks.

"Never known a girl who needed to wash so much," he protests.

"Your mother and I need water too, you know. Guess you never give a thought to that."

Satomi rolls her eyes to heaven, she doesn't want to hear. She considers her father's moans beyond reason. It takes only small things that go wrong to set him at odds with the world. And things are always going wrong in farming: not enough rain, too many bugs, bad seed, the catalogue of his complaints is endless. Now, on top of everything, he has to bring water in by the tankload and the tiniest bit of spillage makes him sick to his stomach.

"Hey, turn the spigot off, boy, it's overflowing," he complains to the tank driver.

"Getting to it, Mr. Baker, it's no more than half a cup, though, can't judge it any nearer."

"Half a cup to you, twenty cents to me."

"It's only a little puddle, Aaron, just a little puddle," his wife Tamura soothes.

Why can't he listen to Satomi's mother? He ought to listen to Tamura, she talks sense, but he just can't seem to manage it. Satomi suspects that his nature is as much a trial to himself as to everybody else. She thinks it nags at him like a sore tooth reacting to any kind of sweetness so that he is never at ease.

Lily says, with that arch look of hers, that Aaron is good-looking—"cute," is how she puts it.

"Can't see it myself," Satomi says, screwing up her face.

She finds no softness either in her father's looks or his character. He has the sort of face that on the movie screen would suit both villain and hero—strong, she guesses. He is big and muscular, with something driven about him, something that takes charge. His thick flaxen hair, cropped short so that he needn't bother with it, sprouts from his head like wheat stubble. His eyes, a shade between gray and blue, look at the world through dusty lashes, and are closed to all but his wife. He doesn't court friendship, thinks his neighbors untrustworthy and his daughter a burden.

"I'm not going to tell you again. Get up earlier and get your chores done before school. The world wasn't made to wait around for you."

"I had homework, Father, and anyway, I—"

"No excuses girl. I've had it with your answering back. Do your chores or . . ."

Her mother pleads her case with little success.

"Please, Aaron, ease up on her a little. She's young yet and she doesn't get an easy ride anywhere."

"You had to work when you were young, Tamura. We've all got to pull our weight. Nobody gets an easy ride. If it's the Japanese part of her you're referring to, well, it's the best part, if you ask me."

"He sure is disappointed that I'm not a boy," Satomi says, sighing, to her mother.

"All men want a son to walk tall at their side," Tamura says. "He loves you, though."

Despite the fact that the farm is modestly successful, that he is known to grow the best tomatoes in the area, something is eating him up. It's said locally that he is a hard man to like, not that you'd want to, him married to a Jap, and cocky, to boot.

Tamura is a different sort altogether, kind and charming, filled to the brim with the desire to please. Aaron is her world and she obeys him in most things, but she doesn't have the heart to chastise Satomi.

"Farming is hard on us all," she excuses him.

Tamura would like to have given Aaron a son, it's hard to disappoint, but such a child as Satomi was surely meant to be.

She had wanted to call her daughter Elena, after her neighbor Elena Kaplan, a good woman, her constant and only true friend in Angelina. Elena nurtures their friendship, despite the fact that her husband Hal is always shouting at her about it. He doesn't care for foreigners, especially those who make out that they are Americans, as if you can't see those slant eyes, that yellow skin.

"I'm putting my foot down, Elena, you hear? Keep your distance from the Baker woman, she's not our sort."

Aaron, a little jealous of Tamura's affection for Elena, doesn't encourage the friendship either. He had objected to naming the child after their neighbor.

"Just because a neighbor helps with the birth, Tamura, it doesn't mean you have to name your children for her." He had laughed to emphasize the point.

"No, but it's a beautiful name, Aaron, a beautiful American name. It will help her fit in around here."

"Can't see what's so good about fitting in. In any case, Satomi's a better name, honey. I looked it up, it means wise and beautiful. Don't see how anyone can complain at that."

It doesn't please him, though, that as his daughter grows, the wise bit, if it is there at all, loses out to her stubbornness. She is willful, too ready to stand her ground against him.

"She'll get there, you can't expect the young to be wise," Tamura says.

"Well, she's sure taking her time."

Unlike his wife's character, his daughter's is without humility. As far as he is concerned her beauty is flawed. He lives in a permanent low hum of irritation with her that sets him on edge in her presence. So he doesn't much mind that she does her best to stay out of his.

"I can't see us having more," he had repeated often in the weeks after Satomi's birth.

"Oh, but one child hardly makes a family, Aaron. And with luck the next one could be a boy."

But, wounded by her husband's disappointment, by his lack of interest in their daughter, Tamura didn't push it. She feared another daughter herself, Aaron's renewed displeasure.

"Only fools trust in luck, Tamura. Best not to risk it."

"Satomi is perfect, though. Isn't she just perfect?"

"No one's perfect, honey. I'll give you she's pretty, as babies go. Look, the truth is we can't afford to feed mouths that will never do fieldwork. It's just plain stupid not to learn from experience. It's not a good world to bring kids into anyway." He hadn't believed it himself, knew that he was irked by the demands on Tamura from Satomi that took precedence over his own.

From the moment of the child's first piercing bawl, he had been aware of losing a part of Tamura. The years haven't lessened his jealousy, it's a constant, tacking his stomach like a rat in a cage, it won't let him settle. He has never been good at sharing.

Resentment as much as prudence drove him into Angelina to stock up with a good supply of what, since he was twelve years old, he has daintily referred to as "French letters." Let others leave it up to nature, to what they liked to call "God's will." God meddles in too much, if you asked him. It wasn't up for debate, nothing he could do about Satomi, but he'd have no others at Tamura's breast.

"Well, I have a beautiful daughter and a good husband. What more should a wife ask for?" Tamura said dutifully.

"Nothing, I guess, honey. That's a good way to look at it."

In her early motherhood Tamura had radiated a maternal glow that Aaron found disturbing. He didn't want her spreading like those wives in Angelina, getting all round and shapeless like half-filled cotton sacks, getting satisfied.

A second-generation Japanese-American, Tamura is pretty in a picture-perfect sort of way, fine skin, eyes like little drops of molasses, lips like the crimson bows that you sometimes see on Christmas trees. There's something of a girl about her, a fragile narrowness that brings out a fierceness in him, the need to protect her. He would kill for her if he had to.

He thinks his wife the most beautiful thing he has ever seen, but Satomi as she grows is a girl whose reality is not clouded by love. She thinks her mother's face a little too round to grant her true beauty, her style too old-fashioned. She feels mean for thinking it, for, after all, isn't love supposed to be blind? Shouldn't every daughter think her mother beautiful?

Guilt sneaks into her dreams, messing her up, so that she questions whether she is normal, whether she loves her mother at all. But she can't help agreeing with Lily that beauty is blond.

"Can't get away from it," Lily declares. "Who would you rather be, Jean Harlow or Joan Crawford? See, no contest."

Satomi, smoothing her own dark hair, thinks that Lily is right as usual, nothing beats gold hair, nothing in the world.

In the steaming nights, marooned on the island of her sweat-drenched sheets, she has plenty of time to muse on such things. She longs to read the storybooks that her teacher Mr. Beck loans her, *Little Women*, *Huckleberry Finn*, *Tom Sawyer*.

"Good American literature," he says. "Can't go wrong with that."

Mr. Beck doesn't lend his books to just anybody, you have to be special, someone who is going places.

But reading in the dim glow of her bulb attracts the moths, the big brown kind that her mother says chew up cotton by the pound, so that the linen has to be rinsed in camphor, a hand-blistering chore that her father has made hers.

She hates the thick-bodied things fluttering around her room, the sickening sound of their powdery wings blistering on the bulb.

"Mama, come," she had called as a child, "come get them."
And Tamura had come flying, catching them in her cupped hands,
launching them through the open window, laughing her sweet
laugh.

Tamura had been her world then, her beauty never in question.
When had it changed? When had she begun to flush with shame
at her mother's black eyes, her own shrinking heart?

She isn't a child anymore, though, can't call on her mother for
every little thing. In the heat, as darkness falls, a longing for those
few minutes before dawn when the light precedes the sun, precious minutes that have a little coolness in them, brings on a miserable sense of waiting.

"Stop fussing about the heat girl," Aaron says. "What difference
does it make to you? It's me that's got to find the money for water.
In any case, it stands to reason the rain can't hold off for much
longer. I can smell it coming, any day now. Yeah, I can smell it."

Aaron is pretty much on the ball when it comes to the weather.
He says his nose as much as his eyes tells him what's around the
corner; it's the farmer's gift. And it's true that there is the faintest
smell of brimstone on the air, but it has been coming and going
for days now, signifying nothing, it seems to her. Her father's just
wishful-thinking, the mean streak in him anticipating free water.

She doesn't feel like waiting until he is proved right. She has a
longing to hold her head under the water tap in their yard, to soak
her hair through to the scalp, let it drip-dry over her body. She
imagines her tangled thoughts rolling away with the water, imagines a silvery stream seeping through the litter of fallen pine needles at the road's edge, leaving her cool at last. But Aaron has
forbidden her to use the tap. It's out of bounds to her until the rain
comes and tops up the well.

"You can't be trusted to be careful with it. Your mother will
bring the water in, she never spills a drop."

"Too scared to, I guess," she had risked.

She had moved fast so that his slap caught her at the side of her head—fingers, no palm, hardly a slap at all. Still, she resented it, thought him a bully.

"If he forbids it, it's a surefire thing you're gonna do it," Lily challenged.

"If he catches me I'll get more than a slap. Don't know if it's worth the risk."

"Oh, sure, the risk. Never stopped you before."

It's hotter than ever the night before the longed-for storm finally rides in. So hot that the drenched air muffles the fox's bark and forces the moths to fly low. Satomi can hear them flapping against the wall by the quince bush. All the windows in the house are open, which hardly makes a difference, but Aaron, hoping to catch what little through-breeze might come, has left their bedroom door ajar.

Barefoot and halfway down the dark corridor, she catches sight of Aaron and Tamura in their bedroom. Aaron, in his work shirt and coveralls, is sitting on the edge of the bed unlacing his boots. Tamura is undressing, with her back to the door. In the shadowy passageway Satomi stands silent, staring. It seems to her that it isn't her mother she sees in the candlelight but the girl Tamura, who until this moment has been hidden from her.

Her mother's body, so delicate that she looks as if she might still be in her girlhood, is covered in little granules of sweat as though she has been sifted with sugar. With the red bow of her lips hidden, she looks all black and white, the cadence of her hair a dark cloud on the skin of her back, which in the candle's yielding light appears surprisingly pale.

Satomi sees her mother's beauty again, sees in her movements a sureness she had never noticed before. It occurs to her that the Bakers in reality are two, not three at all.

"Ah, Tamura." Aaron's voice is hoarse, surely too tender to be his. "Blow out the candles, would you?"

Tamura answers in Japanese, soft, all-giving words that Satomi automatically translates to, *Yes, my love.*

Her mother blows out the candles and in the dark her parents are entirely lost to her. She feels like crying, but doesn't know why. Her father, it seems, can claim the girl in Tamura at his will, peel away the layer of mother, of wife, even, and under his hands make her as burdenless as a bird. As though to confirm this, in the moment before she turns from their door she hears her father murmur, "Oh, my girl, my girl."

Back in her room, she picks up her hairbrush and starts to count, tugging the bristles through her hair, creating knots where there had been none, until her scalp burns with the force of it. She is aiming for a hundred but knows by the time she reaches twelve that she isn't going to make it. It hurts that there are things in life that she doesn't have a hold on, that she is out of the loop, way out.

Damn them all, she would go to the tap, do what she wants. Passing a moth that has fluttered to the floor seeking out the cooler air, she stamps on it with her bare foot. The sticky feel of its innards on her skin is revolting. She lets out an "Aargh" of disgust. Something close to remorse stirs in her.

The run of rusty water comes warm at first, then deliciously cool. It feels good being out in the dark yard, angry enough not to care if Aaron hears and comes after her. It hurts, though, that she is nobody's girl, that she is alone in the world.

Unable to keep from her mind the picture of her parents together in theirs, she scrubs at her skin, the skin that Lily says shines like gasoline. Lily has a cruel streak, but she never bucks the truth, you have to give her that. She kicks the tap and hears it creak.

Her parents' room, like her own, has always seemed ordinary to her, but this night it has become another place entirely, a shining mystical place, exclusive to them. Vivid in every detail, it's a picture she can't shake from her mind, her mother's silk robe carelessly spilled around the bed, their shadows moving on the wall, the little cloud of cluster flies bombing the candle, and the dark starless sky soft beyond the open window. It's their heated night, their hooting owl, their everything. She is overcome with childish jealousy.

Next morning, as she passes their room, she sees that the curtains are drawn against the light, the bed made, everything neat and tidy as usual, but somehow not as usual. Her mother's silk robe, the one with pink butterflies embroidered on it, is folded now across the chair. For the first time she notices that there are dark little moths scattered here and there among the butterflies. She doesn't like them.

With newly critical eyes, she sees the patched bedspread, the peeling paintwork, and the motes of dust like fireflies in the air. Nothing feels familiar anymore. Her world has shifted somehow, as though some small link from her senses to her brain has been broken.

"Damn—damn—damn," she curses. "It's too damned hot."

At breakfast she is sullen, out of sorts. Her father has already left for the fields; she must have slept later than usual.

"Guess I'm in trouble with him again, huh?" she says sulkily.

For once Tamura doesn't rush to Aaron's defense. "You slept well, Satomi, that's good. You've been sleeping so badly lately."

She tries to ignore her mother's sweet smile, but it has already caused a small fracture in her heart. Still, she isn't ready to be placated.

"Can't say I slept that well. Nobody's gonna get much sleep around here until this damned weather breaks."

"Please, Satomi, don't curse, you know your father won't have cursing in the house."

Hurt by her daughter's mood, Tamura turns from her, busying herself with making her *ocha*, the green tea that reminds her of home. She is fragile when it comes to love, has never resigned herself to the ups and downs of family life. As a child she had taken every little slight to heart, and nothing much has changed in the years since. Aaron knows it, so he is careful around her, gathering her up in her injured moments, telling her boastfully that she is safe with him.

"You take too much to heart," he says. "Don't let people get to you so easily."

He can't bear to see her hurt, wants to protect her from everything that the rotten world throws at her. She is the flower on the dung heap, the only pure thing he knows. And she has given up everything to be with him, a man she might never have met had he not one day by mistake taken her brother's bicycle from outside her family's grocery store in the suburbs of Honolulu.

When he returned it with the briefest of apologies, he saw Tamura in all her acquiescent beauty, lowered eyes, soft voice, and knew that he must have her.

She saw a big blue-eyed American, golden-haired and smelling sweetly of milk, and knew that he would. In an instant, Hawaii and the life she lived with her family became secondary to her need to respond to Aaron's call.

Putting down a larger than usual portion of the morning breakfast rice in front of Satomi, Tamura smiles forgivingly.

"The storm is sure to break soon." She touches her daughter's shining hair, notices the dark beneath her eyes, the way she won't look at her.

"I don't want *asagohan*. I want an American breakfast."

"I will make you eggs. It will only take a minute. Sometimes I feel like an American breakfast too."

"I'm bringing Lily back after school, Mother. We're paired up on a nature assignment," Satomi lies, hoping to annoy.

"Oh, Satomi, that's not a good idea. You know your father doesn't like Lily."

"He doesn't like anyone."

"Well—that's not— Anyway, you know what I mean."

And she did, they both knew that Aaron didn't care to know folks. When Tamura had taken him home to meet her parents, she had despaired at his offhand manner, his lack of desire to impress. They had known that their families would disapprove, had known since childhood the divide, where they were expected to draw the line between their races. But Aaron could have tried, might have made an effort.

For Tamura's parents, though, it hadn't so much been a dislike of Aaron that had angered them, but of the idea of their daughter marrying out of her race, her culture. Her mother couldn't believe that she would do such a thing, and had beaten her for even considering it.

"White boys are fine as friends, but not to marry. You are Japanese, be proud of it. If you do this we will all be lost to you. You will not be welcome in your own home. Your father will never speak to you again. Just think of it, a daughter not able to be in her father's presence, the disgrace of it might kill you."

Tamura did think of it. But she couldn't believe that her papa wouldn't come to love Aaron as she did. It hurt her beyond measure when, in the days before she left home to join Aaron, her father neither spoke to nor looked at her.

Aaron's mother, an unforgiving woman of harsh judgments, had snarled that the shame of him marrying a Jap was something she would never be able to live down.

"They're our cane-cutters, we don't marry them."

"Well, she's sweeter than our sugar, Ma. So get used to it, we're getting married."

"Can't say our family is perfect, Aaron, but none of them have ever sunk so low as to marry a Jap. Good God, boy, you'll be speaking pidgin next."

He saw the disgust on her face, suppressed the urge to slap her. "I reckon I'm getting the better of the deal, Ma."

"You've just been taken in by a pretty face, that's all. I'm telling you now, Aaron, that I don't care to know any half-and-half grandchildren. The truth is I just couldn't bring myself to touch them."

The idea to leave Hawaii had been Aaron's. Tamura, with her family's back turned to her, had agreed to it; if their people wouldn't accept them, they would give them up and set out in life as though newborn. They would let go both family and religion, his Christian, hers Buddhist, and be enough in everything for each other.

"We'll make the same sacrifices," he said. "That way we won't be able to blame each other in the future. We don't need anyone but ourselves to get along."

But equal as it seemed, it was not the same sacrifice. For Tamura it fought against her obedient nature and was all pain. The letting go of her family inflicted a wound that would never heal. Yet without knowing why, Aaron was pleased to do it. He walked away as though he had from the first been a cuckoo in the alien nest of his parents' home. He walked away a free man.

They had married in a civil ceremony, with strangers for witnesses, and had instantly left Hawaii for California, where Aaron used his savings to buy ten acres of Depression-cheap land on the outskirts of the small town of Angelina.

"Your father never looked back, but sometimes I still cry for my mother," Tamura told Satomi. "Love makes you do things that you never thought you were capable of."

But Satomi thought their desertion of their families heartless. If they needed only each other, where did that leave her?

The eggs are cooked just as she likes them, but as usual Tamura has made too many and she can't finish them. In any case it is too hot to eat, too hot to think, even.

"Don't bring Lily home," Tamura pleads. "No point in stirring up trouble."

Aaron thinks Lily sly, says that he doesn't like the way she looks down her nose at people.

"Don't know what she thinks she's got that makes her better than us. A scrawny scrap of a thing like her."

Satomi had rushed to the protection of her friendship with Lily.

"She's my best friend, Father. She's the only one who doesn't mind being friends with a Jap."

"I've warned you about that word before. I don't want to hear it from you ever again."

Jap, Jap, Jap, she had repeated in her mind, feeling heartsick.

Neither the eggs nor Tamura's pandering satisfy. She can't shake the feeling that her mother has betrayed her in some way, that she has shown herself to be an unreliable ally. Yet once out of the house, try as she might to hold on to it, her bad mood drifts away on the little breeze that fetches up a half a mile or so from the schoolhouse.

She senses it first on the nape of her neck, a delicious lick on the run of red where the sun has found her out. Walking backward, so that it's fresh on her face, she doesn't hear the distant thunder, but the faint smell of metal in the air tells her that at last the storm is coming. Aaron as usual has gotten it right.

She lingers at the roadside waiting for it, not caring that it will make her late. The light is eerie now, a hoary gray, the sun hunkered behind the clouds. And then the first drops fall big as pebbles, soaking her through so that her nipples and the line of her panties can be seen through the thin cotton of her dress.

In the cool air that follows the downpour her body seems to reconnect with her mind, and, being her father's daughter, her own immediate concerns take over. She tells herself that she doesn't care about anything, doesn't care about being on the outside, about being a Jap, about not being blond. But suddenly she is restless, can't wait to grow up, to pursue whatever that intimate thing is that is between her parents. She wants a magical room of her own, territory to feel included in.

School is out of the question. She can't be bothered to spar with kids who are little more than babies compared to her. Her teacher, Mr. Beck will raise his eyes at yet another absence. He won't mark it in the truant book, though, she knows that; knows it like she pretends not to know that he stares at her in lessons, lolling back in his chair, wetting his lips with his long pale tongue.

She'll go skinny-dipping in the river, feel the weeds between her toes. There will be nobody to spy on her at this time of day. She'll wade out to where there's still a bit of deep and submerge herself. After, she will lie on the sandy bank, light up, and practice blowing smoke rings.

In the years that followed the burning summer, Satomi glimpsed no other life on the horizon for herself.

"It's the same boring old road," she complained to Lily. "No bends or corners to turn, no surprises ahead, just straight on."

"Same old, same old," Lily agreed.

Satomi read and read, and laughed and argued with Lily, and fought her enemies, and attempted through her behavior not to be Mr. Beck's favorite. She swam alone in the river, slipping under the deep water, holding her breath until she felt like bursting. She hid from her father's demands in the pine woods with her book and her roll-up cigarettes.

Life was marked only by the smallest of things. A surprising flurry of snow one January, followed by a summer of glut that didn't please Aaron; too many tomatoes on the market meant the price went low and set his mood to match. And once, as she slept, an earth tremor came in the night and cracked their windows, putting Tamura's hens in a panic. But small concerns aside, the road went on, straight for as far as the eye could see.

Toward her fourteenth birthday she started her monthly bleeds and was told by Tamura that she was a woman now. It didn't feel like it to her. She still had to go to school, still had to dance to Aaron's tune.

Her first bra came around the same time as the bleeding and, seeing it hanging on the line, Aaron teased that it looked like a catapult for peanuts. She never hung it where he could see it again.

Her first kiss came too. Tom Broadbent, a boy with lizard eyes and an uninhibited nature, pushed her up against the school wall and pressed his dry lips to hers for a second or two. She had thought kissing would be better than that, something soft and tingly, something delicious, something like nothing else.

"He kisses everyone," Lily said contemptuously, jealous that on both counts, bra and kiss, Satomi had gotten there first.

Among Angelina's large white community, its small Japanese one, there is no one like her, no other half-and-half in the area. She'd ditch the Japanese half if she could. It takes the shine off how great it is to be an American somehow. The thought that she might be the only one in the world is too scary to think about. Lily says that there must be others the same, though.

"Don't get to thinking you're an original, Sati. Sure to be some like you in the city."

"Guess you're right, Lily. Guess nobody's a one-off."

What would she do without Lily telling it as it is? Lily's the reason she doesn't play truant more often, Lily and the fact that school's not so bad. At least it's an escape from her rule-bound home, a place to be disobedient in without feeling she's hurting her mother.

While slavishly following Satomi's bad habits, Lily thinks herself an original, a cut above the rest. Satomi thinks her fine too, and together they revel in being the risky girls, the ones who took up smoking first—took to cursing like the boys. The schoolyard rings with cursing. "Fuck" is the boys' favorite; "damn," the girls'.

If Mr. Beck catches them at it, the punishment is ten strokes with a brass-edged ruler on the palm of the hand. The devilish thing inflicts sooty blood blisters where the corner of it whips at the skin. Satomi wears hers like a badge of honor.

"Hey, Satomi, who gave you those love bites?" the boys taunt her.

"Come over here and get some more, I've never tasted a Jap."

"With a face like yours you never will." She's sewn up tight against their calls, too tight to let a bunch of no-hopers unstitch her.

There's one, though, whom she isn't immune to, so that on a truant afternoon lazing by the river, when the heat had seeped into her brain, turning her thoughts to mush, when even the birds seemed to be sleeping, she let Artie Goodwin, the best-looking boy in the school, get to second base with her.

In a torment of jealousy over Artie and not knowing her advice was already too late, Lily set down the rules for Satomi in a voice of doom.

"Don't let him get past first base," she ordered, staring Satomi feverishly in the eye. "That's just kissing. I guess that can't do much harm. Second base is kissing and touching over clothes, that's okay if you are going steady, which you aren't, are you?"

"Could if I wanted, Lily."

"Well, whatever, third base is out of bounds. They want to kiss and touch you under your clothes, ugh! Anyway, if you let them do it, it means you're a tramp."

"I can guess what a home run is."

"Home run is sex. Never allow a boy a home run, it could ruin you for life."

Lily's cousin Dorothy had allowed Davey Cromer a home run, and he had bolted when she got pregnant.

"Everyone knew that Dorothy wasn't good enough for him," Lily said. "His family being the biggest pea growers in the area an all. And that's no more than the truth."

Dorothy is the bogeyman in Lily's family, held up to the girls to show them what will happen if they let their morals lapse.

"Anyway, Sati, I don't know what you see in Artie, he's always strutting around like the 'big I am,' and you're not the only one he flirts with."

"Yeah, maybe so, but he sure is good-looking, you have to agree."

"I guess. If you like the pretty-boy type."

Lily tries not to let her jealousy show on her face. Satomi Baker is supposed to be her best friend, after all. She doesn't want people thinking that Sati has won the prize that she's desperate for herself.

"Guess you two ain't such good friends as you thought, eh, Lily?" smirk the girls whose friendship she has shunned. She hates that they know, in that way that girls know, that she's keen on Artie herself.

It's her own fault, she guesses. She chose Satomi as her best friend with the idea of showing everyone that she was something pretty special herself. Lily Morton isn't one to follow the herd.

You can't tell her what to do. Truth is, though, she wishes she had never set eyes on Satomi. Satomi is hard work, and now the worst has happened and Satomi has Artie. If only Artie hadn't been so cute, so curly-haired and fondant-lipped, she wouldn't ache so.

"Guess he likes Japs," the girls jeer. "Why else would he favor her over you, Lily?"

"Sex, for sure." She hadn't been able to stop herself from saying it. Well, it was no more than the truth, boys were always out for sex, and Artie knew he wouldn't get a sniff at it with a respectable girl like her. Never mind that she pouts her lips and crosses her legs in that come-and-get-it way whenever he glances at her.

In her daydreams Lily has Satomi running away from home, or dying quickly from some rare disease. She pictures disfiguring scabs, bad breath, sees herself comforting Artie, him falling for her.

In those daydreams Lily stars as the beauty; in reality she worries that her lips might be a bit too thin, her legs too up-and-down. She likes the dainty little maps of freckles across her cheeks, though, comforts herself that, better late than never, her breasts have started to grow. And one day she swears to God she is going to dye her mousy hair bright blond; then let Satomi watch out.

And I am white, after all, just like Artie, she reminds God in her prayers. *It would be better all around.*

Jealous she may be, but Lily knows that however much the boys might puppydog after Satomi, she will never be the one for keeps. You can't take a half-caste home to your mother and say this is the one. All she has to do is play the waiting game. Artie's bound to come to his senses.

"I don't think we can be friends if you go to third base with Artie," Lily threatens. "They'll tar me with the same brush as you, and I don't want people thinking I'm like my cousin. They'll say it runs in the family."

"Fine, Lily, I'll let you know when the time comes. You can drop me then."

But Lily will never drop her. They'll be best friends forever, she's sure of it. And Lily's advice is meant well, she's only trying to help, to save her from herself. It seems to Satomi that Lily knows the rules for everything. She marvels at how she lists them with such confidence:

"Red shoes are common."

"Eating in the street is cheap."

"Never, ever wear white after Labor Day."

Lily likes to think that one day she will have the kind of life where the rules matter. She gathers in the little nuggets of what she thinks of as wisdom, from advertisements, and the radio, and from the hand-me-down magazines her mother is given by the undertaker's wife she cleans for. She plans never to break the rules herself, they are as true for her as though she has read them in the Bible. She holds dear to the belief of the inexperienced, that there is such a thing as natural justice. Follow the rules and reap the rewards, is her motto.

Despite Lily's misgivings, Satomi longs for red shoes, finds seductive the idea that a home run might change things forever. Change is good, isn't it? Why wait for things to happen? Left to their own devices, they might never.

Those thrilling embraces, the weight of Artie as they lay together in the woods, the smell of leaf mold and fern in the air, keep from her mind Lily's warnings and the tale of Dorothy's downfall. She may not be ready to allow a home run, but everything else is up for grabs.

"Oh, God, you smell so good," Artie croons as he lights two cigarettes with one match shielded in his hand against the breeze. "You've got to give me some sugar."

"Oh, you get plenty of sugar, Artie."

"You know what I mean, Sati. Sure you do."

He takes a long drag on his cigarette, letting the smoke escape through his nose, and hands hers to her in the way he has seen it done in the movies.

"I want us to go all the way. You know I'm going to marry you, no matter what anyone says."

"Oh, that's big of you, Artie. But don't count on me saying yes."

"Come on, course you will. Guys like me don't come by the dozen."

"Hmm."

She isn't even sure that she likes Artie that much, but his embraces excite her, they induce the sweetest tingling of her skin, and strange little leaps of longing that keep her blood singing. Lured by the meaty bulk of his body, the urgency in him, it's hard sometimes not to go all the way. But it's her own fears, not Lily's, that stop her. She may not like it, but there's something of her father in her that won't bend. Artie can go his own sweet way if he wants. It's her rules or no game.

"What's so great about Artie Goodwin?" one boy after another asks. "He's soft as shit. You want more than that, don't you?"

"I don't want any of you, that's for sure."

"Who says we're asking?"

"Oh, you're asking."

She and Artie figure big in the schoolyard gossip. Her reputation is taking a hit, while his remains intact. She may have Jap in her, but she's a looker, and he's just doing what guys do.

"They think they know what's going on," she tells Lily. "Boy, do they have vivid imaginations."

"Can't blame 'em for getting ideas," Lily says caustically. "You and Artie gotta be getting up to something in those woods."

"Yeah, swimming and smoking." She grins. "Real wicked, eh?"

These days, though, when Artie puts his hand up her skirt, she lets it wander until it reaches the soft skin at the top of her thigh, lets him pull a little on the leg elastic of her panties. The sense she has that she might be carried away and let it happen feels dangerous and exciting.

"Don't be a tease, Sati, nobody likes a tease," Artie pants.

"I'm not teasing, I'm serious."

"I'm serious too, pretty damn serious."

"Pretty damn serious, pretty damn serious," she mimics, until, red in the face, Artie rolls sulkily away from her.

"I don't know what makes you think you're so fine. I could have any girl I want, you know?"

She guesses it's the truth. He's a charmer for sure. A charmer with a rolling swagger, and the sort of hard body that stirs up girls' insides, gives them that dull ache.

"Think yourself lucky, Sati," he says. "You've got your drawback, that's for sure. I'm out on a limb, with you for a sweetheart."

Despite Artie's misgivings, he is relieved and a little alarmed when on her fifteenth birthday she accepts his class ring. You can never be sure how Sati will react to things. That day, though, as if she is rewarding him, she lets him unbutton her blouse and pull her brassiere straps down from her shoulders. She lets him cup her breasts with his farm-boy hands.

He closes his eyes, feeling as though he is sinking into himself, into a sweet safe place. It feels so good he could cry, but all he says is, "They're great, really great."

Letting Artie touch her bare breasts feels to her like giving a child one sweet too many. You feel generous and it keeps them quiet for a bit, but sugar gets them excited and you know you'll pay for it later. For sure the more Artie gets, the more he wants.

She won't tell Lily, no point in getting her in a stew. She'll show her the ring and say it's nothing serious. It's going steady but just for now.

Artie, though, can't keep his mouth shut. "You ain't seen nothing like them," he tells the boys. "Not a girl here to match them. Round and firm, and the scent of her like those big red apples. It's enough to drive you nuts."

"Hand her over when you've finished," they joke crudely.

"She's out of your league," he boasts.

"Yeah, from another fuckin' continent."

Much as Artie thinks himself a catch, the big mover and shaker, his school reports confirm that he is lazy, middling at pretty much everything he takes on.

Artie's trouble, Mr. Beck writes in his neat handwriting, *is that he is ambitious without being dedicated. He expects things to be handed to him on a plate. He must learn that effort brings success, or he will continue to fail.*

Artie laughs at the reports. What does a dried-up old guy like Mr. Beck know, anyway?

Mr. Beck, though, is a fine judge of boys, he knows what he's talking about. Satomi too senses Artie's weakness. He's full of want, but too lazy to work at things.

"Life doesn't owe you," she says when Artie annoys her with his boasts, when he tells her what a big success he's going to be once he gets to the city.

Artie's all for getting out of Angelina. He wants the big city, the hustle and bustle, lights and music. He wants the chance of a life that doesn't include dirt under his fingernails. And he wants the prize of Satomi Baker, wants her to give in, to go all the way. He feels lucky, he's good looking with that "it" thing going on, life owes him, he's just waiting for it to pay up.

Artie might not be Mr. Beck's favorite, but he's popular among his classmates. In his sixteenth year, he's the best-looking, the tallest, the funniest, the most popular. If his friends want him along, it means that Satomi comes too.

"See, Sati, whatever you say, you're just as popular as me."

"Oh, sure, Artie, course I am."

But as cool as she likes to think herself about Artie, life is better with him than without. Him wanting her, when the girls who excluded her want him, makes a sort of balance. Even Lily's jealousy, her little digs, can't spoil the fun she has with Artie.

"Let's not go to school today. I'll write your note, you write mine."

"Artie, it'll be the third time this month. We won't get away with it for much longer."

"Who cares, we'll be leaving soon anyway. You have to do what you want in life, enjoy it while you can."

On their way to the woods they steal soft-shell peas from Cromer's fields near the water hole, fruit from the orchards, sinking their teeth into ripe peaches, and the sweet red strawberries that set themselves at the woods' edge. There is something of the waning summer in those fruits, something lush and fertile and close to decay.

"A smoke before or after?" Artie asks.

"After what, for heaven's sake?"

"A swim, I suppose, after a swim."

It's Artie, not her, who squeals at their submersion into the cold river; Artie who won't swim out to the deep because he might get caught up in the weeds that grow there. She can't help but sneer as she grins and swims out past him.

"Chicken."

"Fool."

They smoke Lucky Strikes when they can get them, roll-ups when they can't. She likes the roll-ups better. The ritual of opening the little tin of tobacco, the crisp feel of the white tissue, the earthy smell as they light up, unclenches some tautness in her.

She knows what he means by "after," of course. It's what Lily with her mouth all twisted up calls "making out."

"You'll get yourself a reputation," Lily warns. "You don't want that, do you?"

"Thought I already had one." Satomi winks at her outraged friend.

Much as Artie wants to be with her, he doesn't care for the woods, they are too feral for his liking. He has a deep fear of snakes, of all wild things. The slightest rustle in the undergrowth has him jumping.

"No animals in the city," he says. "Just jazz clubs and bars and the streets all lit up. And coffee shops on every corner and the latest movies, no measuring out the water, no having to eat the bruised crop that you can't sell."

"Yeah, I know, all the men are handsome and all the girls pretty and dressed up smart all the time," she can't help teasing him, even though the pictures Artie conjures up are exciting.

But Artie's dreams are not hers. She hasn't worked hers out yet. Unlike him, she loves the woods, the sweet green stillness of them, the strange shadows that play there, and the mossy scent that stays in the air for days after a storm. They are lovely to her in every season.

In her childhood years she had played in them, never afraid to be by herself under the lacy canopy of the tall ghost pines. She loves the way the light filters through their needles, the clean scent of them. And in winter, when the wind sweeps through their boughs, their creaking moans keep her from being lonely. Angelina's woods hold only magic for her.

Once, at dusk, she had seen a fox in them. It had stood big as a dog, alert but motionless by the porcelainberry bush that was hung with poisonous drupes. Its thick musky smell had come to her on the breeze before she saw it staring, working out whether she posed a threat or not. She had held the creature's gaze with a pounding heart, the hairs on her arms standing on end, amazed and scared at its closeness. It had turned its head from her, sniffing the air, and then, looking back, had given her a wild stare before trotting away.

"Don't mention it to your father," Tamura advised. "He will want to shoot it, you will only get upset. He has to protect the chickens, of course, but . . ."

In the woods' cool clearings she picks armfuls of the rough apple mint that grows around the base of the big sitting rocks and that must be strewn on the packing-shed floor to keep the rats out.

"Better mice than rats any day," Aaron says.

And in the early morning when the light is new and the scent of the juniper like incense on the air, her mother sends her to pick mushrooms in their season. Tamura calls the little flesh-colored cups "*kinoko*," the children of the trees.

Torn between love and embarrassment, Satomi secretly delights in her mother's little sayings. In later years she will know that her heart lived in her mother, she will regret not having hugged to her childhood self the unique charm of Tamura.

All her life she will be drawn to woods, but none of them will ever quite match up to the fragrant forest of Angelina, where she and Artie practiced how to be grown-up together.

"You're exotic, that's what you are," Artie says, as though complimenting her, as though isn't he just the clever one to give that description to her.

Without knowing why, she doesn't like the sound of "exotic." The word has too much heat in it, a low sort of intimacy. It isn't the first time she has been called that, and it doesn't feel like flattery to her.

Mr. Beck, a man torn between duty and impropriety when it comes to Satomi, told her once that he found her exotic.

"Know what 'exotic' means, Satomi?"

"Different, I guess."

"It means someone not native to a country. Someone poles apart from yourself."

"I'm as American as you, Mr. Beck."

"I meant it as a compliment, girl. Learn how to take a compliment."

But she can't take Mr. Beck's advice seriously. It isn't impartial, that's for sure. For one thing, he is unreliable, one minute singling her out for his favors, the next picking on her for punishment. He trembles more than she does when giving her ten strokes on the palm of each hand, his odd smile disturbing her more than the pain he inflicts. He is always including himself in her world, flattering her, intervening in her fights, touching her. She wishes he would get off her case.

"You know, Satomi, you have a kinda disturbing beauty, the kind that could get you into trouble. It sure can open things up for you, but it can cut you out of them too. My advice to you would be to study hard, so that you aren't tempted to rely on it."

"Thanks, Mr. Beck, that's good advice, I guess."

But without effort she is always somewhere near the top of the class. English comes easy, but she wings her way in math, copying Lily's neatly worked-out sums. Lily sure knows how to count.

"Why waste your time on schoolwork?" Artie says. "Your looks are as good as currency."

She can't see it herself. Some crooked thing inside won't let her see it.

If mirrors could talk, hers would say, *This is who you are. You have your mother's long eyes, only wider and a little lighter, more the color of the bark of the Bryony that grows wild by the sheds; your hair is long*

*and thick, and looks black unless you are standing next to your mother, where
in the comparison it is dark, dark brown. You have your father's lips,
cushion-full and faintly tinted as though with salmonberry. And your skin,
the color of white tea, is smooth and finely pored. Your flaws are the stubborn set to your mouth, that look of refusal that stalks your eyes.*

If offered the choice, instead of her dark eyes, her mother's
smile, she would have chosen to look fuller, lush, and plumped up
like those freckled Californian girls. A regular American.

"There are many different kinds of Americans," Tamura says,
catching sight of Satomi posing in front of the mirror, a yellow
scarf draped as hair on her head. "Ask your Japanese friends at
school. They are as American as your father, as Lily. We are all
good Americans."

She doesn't have the heart to tell Tamura that she rarely speaks
to the Japanese pupils. She doesn't care to, and they don't mix that
much, don't seek her out. Apart from Saturdays when she and Lily
see them on their way to their Japanese-language lessons, they are
rarely met outside of school. Even when the carnival came to town,
when the Ferris wheel beckoned and the sweet smell of cotton
candy got all jumbled up in your head with the fairground music
and the strutting boys, they were nowhere to be seen.

In any case, Tamura herself hardly talks to the Japanese. She
may give a greeting when she sees them in town, but she never
stops to talk. It would be pointless making friends; Aaron wouldn't
like it, no matter if they are Japanese or not. Even on the rare occasions when Elena comes he is put in a bad mood for hours.

At school with Lily, Satomi talks the latest talk, chews gum,
and thinks American thoughts. At home, in the vine-covered
wooden house that sits back from the single-track road, a mile or
so from town, there is no escaping the Japanese half of her. She
knows the rules of both her worlds, moves between them with
what seems like ease. Yet something in her struggles to find out

which life she is playacting. It never occurs to her that it might be both.

In their small community, the Bakers stand out. Feeling neither fish nor fowl, it's hard to know where to place themselves. The Japanese feel uneasy with them, advise their children to keep their distance. They've heard the gossip, judge Satomi's behavior as *haji*. She brings shame on her family, a thing not to be borne. They're schooled in family loyalty over the individual, in ritualistic good manners, so obedience is second nature to them. What kind of girl goes alone to the river with a boy after all?

The whites made their judgments on the Bakers the moment they hit town. If anything, they have grown more suspicious of them, of Aaron in particular.

"I hear they eat raw fish. Snake too when they can get it."

"It don't seem natural somehow, marrying an Oriental. God only knows what goes on in that house, what kinda life an American has to live under that roof."

"It makes me sick just thinking about it."

Scoffing at the idea of Japanese-Americans, *has the world gone mad?*, the townsfolk pump each other up, spew their dislike of anything Oriental into Angelina's ether.

"One look and you can tell they ain't trustworthy."

"You ain't never gonna find a Jap doctor, no matter how much you try to educate them. Don't tell me that's not the truth."

Lately the irritant of having the Japanese around is grating nearer the bone. Japan is playing up, making itself felt, and not in a friendly way either. The townspeople have been holding their breath, waiting for trouble for months. Now they hear that the bastards are after their oil. Roosevelt is right. Why should America sell them oil? Why should America do anything to help them out?

The handful of liberals in town warn against sanctions.

"Only months to go before they run out of oil," they say. "They'll sure enough get aggressive then."

"Let them. They'll soon find out who's boss."

Immersed in his own world, the hostility of his neighbors hardly impinges on Aaron. He shrugs it off with an indifference that ruffles their feathers. He would have chosen to be Japanese if he could. Not the modern Japanese-American man that he feels is losing status, but the old-century kind, undisputed head of the family, obeyed in all things. He is entirely seduced by the idea of a strong man complemented by a subservient woman, a female who needs to rely on him. In Tamura he has found her, the girl who kneels before him smelling sweetly of rose oil, and eager to please.

"Do it this way, honey," he says, just to see the admiration in her eyes. "It's easy when you know how." Or, "I'll have coffee now," so that he might hear her answer, "Yes, Aaron, I will get it right away."

You can't put a price on being master in your own home. He doesn't need anyone or anything else to complete his world.

Tamura, though, is more sociable. She works at being liked, attempting to defuse rudeness with her sweet smile, her obliging nature. It hurts Satomi to see her trying so childishly to please.

"Your father reminds me of my own," Tamura tells her in a whisper, fearful of bringing her family into the conversation, into their home, where it is an unspoken rule that they are not to be mentioned.

"I know that he is stern, but he is fair. And he is full of pride, and that is how a man should be. How else should a woman know who to be herself? I hope that one day you'll find a husband as splendid as your father."

Tamura knows how to be a wife, she learned it from her mother, learned how to meet a husband's needs before he knew he had them. At night when his work is done, his dinner eaten, she massages Aaron's shoulders, easing those muscles that he has asked too much of during the day. Dressed in her silky wrap, she sits at his feet, the dark fringe of her eyelashes shadowing her downy cheeks. She keeps the coffee coming and his Camel cigarettes lit, while he reads, a day late, his mail-sent copy of the *Los Angeles Times*.

Satomi thinks of those long night hours, the ones her mother calls *the moon hours*, as being endless and boring, full of her father's demands, of which it seems to her there are far too many.

Aaron makes his regulations on the hoof. One day they are to pack the tomatoes this way, the next another—he decides randomly, and nothing is up for debate. Only he can make or break them.

"Dinner at the same time every day, honey, we know where we stand that way."

He means exactly the same time each day. If Satomi is a minute late to the table, her meal goes in the trash. The girl has to learn who is important in the house, who waits for whom, who comes first.

"That's the last *wagashi* cake," Tamura warns nervously. "Best keep it for your father, you know how much he loves them."

Inside the house Satomi has to wear the rough dust jackets that Tamura makes for her from twice-soaked flour sacks. The twine spurs in the weave scratch at her skin, leaving pinpricks of red on her arms.

"Yuck, they smell. I hate them," she moans to Tamura. "It's humiliating, like we're peasants or something."

"I will give them an extra rinse. Just wear them to please your father. He doesn't ask much of you, and they save your dresses."

"It doesn't matter how many times you rinse them, they still smell like throw-up. Nobody I know has to wear such stupid things."

It's sandals only in the house. Aaron likes the sound of wood on wood. Satomi likes the sound too, but would never admit to it.

"Please, Satomi, put your hair up before your father comes home," Tamura pleads, weary with having to appease them both.

In the times when she hates her father more than she cares to soothe her mother, she fights him on every rule, standing her ground, until Aaron, tired of the argument, picks her up as though she weighs nothing, as though she is nothing. He throws her on her bed, locking her in as he leaves.

It's easy to escape her locked bedroom, hardly a jump at all from the crumbling window ledge. Outside with her book and her roll-ups, she sits with her back to the wall of the house, reading and smoking, one ear listening for Aaron's heavy footfall along the hall. He is stubborn and it can be hours before he relents, before she hears him and she has to scramble back through the window and wait for the key to turn in the lock of her door.

"Can't abide all his rules," she tells Lily, shaking her hair loose, letting it spill around her shoulders in the way that Aaron has forbidden and her teacher Mr. Beck thinks unladylike. It's the latest fashion and all the white girls are trying out the style.

"It makes us look older. Like movie stars," Lily says hopefully.

Tamura too finds her own ways to skirt around Aaron's rules, especially his ban on religion.

"Stories for simpletons," he says. "That's all the Bible is, that's all any creed is. We don't need religion in this house to tell us what's right."

As though in compensation for the loss of hers, Tamura concocts little ceremonies out of the offerings she makes to the birds that come to her kitchen door. She kneels to set the crumbs down, her body bowed in remembered prayer, her eyes closed as she loses herself in the ritual. The small thrill of disobedience that accompanies the act never fails to please.

It would have pained Aaron to see her kneeling so, to know that she is thinking of her family in Hawaii, remembering the life she lived there. As far as he is concerned Tamura and he might as well be one person, sharing the same desires, needing only each other to be whole. She came with him willingly, after all, gave herself over as women must. Men take wives, wives give allegiance, and new families are made, it isn't something to be questioned.

If truth were known, he is glad that Tamura's people are not part of their lives. He couldn't have borne the intrusion of them. Propelled by his trusted inner compass, he keeps to the unquestioned path, defending himself against the idea that his wife might desire anything more than he provides for her.

Town is one of the few places where Tamura is able to express her choices without Aaron's eye on her. He doesn't care for the place: the bank four times a year, the odd visit for tractor parts, are enough for him. The year that he opened his bank account, his first season in profit, he had received a lukewarm invitation to join the local farmers' cooperative and had declined.

"Just an excuse to gabble and guzzle beer," he told Tamura.

With Satomi in tow, Tamura goes to Angelina once every couple weeks, driving the old farm truck as smoothly as the worn gears allow, just as Aaron has taught her. She picks up the farm's supplies and her regular order of *asahi* rice to make the *donburi* with tuna that he says calms his digestion.

To Satomi's relief her mother always dresses in Western clothes on their outings, smart nipped-in jackets and skirts cut on the bias that skim her slim calves. She is a fine dressmaker and doctors her old patterns to keep up with the latest styles.

"Too short for decency," is Aaron's habitual comment.

She wears the neatest little hats, feathered and netted creations that give her an air of sophistication. Satomi's favorite, yet the one she suffers most embarrassment from, is a downy affair that sits on Tamura's head at a rakish angle, bringing to mind a tiny bird preparing for flight.

Some women have a thing for shoes, for others it's ribbons or lipstick, but hats are Tamura's weakness. The moment one sits on her head her spirits are lifted, the color rises in her cheeks.

The townsfolk think she is putting on airs, while Aaron frets that she is making herself look ridiculous. He doesn't care much for the clothes, but he hates the hats. Something about them makes him think of the world outside that he doesn't want to know. Tamura wastes no time in changing as soon as she returns home.

"You look uncomfortable," he says pointedly before she is even through the door. "All done up like a parcel." It irks him that where her hats are concerned she won't bend to his will. It's a woman's thing, he guesses.

Tamura orders the little creations from the dress shop's catalogue when the annual sale makes them a bargain. She buys her dressmaking fabrics there too. With its pretensions to French fashion, the shop is always their first port of call in Angelina.

"How fine that striped cotton is, Satomi. You need a new dress. I have a lovely pattern at home, puff sleeves and a bow at the waist. You've never seen anything so pretty."

"I'm not a child. Puffs and bows are for the elementary kids."

"But bows are so pretty. You never like anything pretty."

Tamura is right. Satomi has a horror of pretty, of puff sleeves and bows and complicated stitching. She likes plain cotton, simple shapes.

"Might as well be a boy," Lily tells her. "There's nothing as flattering as a frill."

Artie agrees with Lily, he would like a frill or two, a ribbon, perhaps, in Satomi's dark hair. It's the way girls are meant to be, after all.

In Mr. Taylor's drugstore they drink bubblegum sodas at the wooden counter and buy bags of mixed candies, strings of licorice, fruit sours, and mallow twists that they eat in the truck on their way home.

"You sure do like your candies," Mr. Taylor says, opening the pack and adding one or two for goodwill. There's something about Tamura that he likes, and it's only good business, after all.

In the town's general store Tamura is reminded of the one she grew up in. The smell of rice and ripe apples, of candied fruits and peppercorns, returns her momentarily to her happy childhood. She likes to linger there breathing it all in, stretching out the time in buying sealing wax and rubber bands, things that she has no real need of.

Her English is perfect, her manners so fine that she often gets a smile from the shopkeepers despite themselves. It is one thing to disapprove of her, *the Jap wife*, when she isn't there, hard not to like her when she is.

So that Satomi might be fluent in both languages, she has spoken Japanese to her since her baby years. It pleases her that her daughter speaks the language of her own people so well, even though the rhythm of her American phrasing grates a little.

"It's a mother's duty to pass on such things," she says. "Perhaps you will do it for your own daughter one day."

"I'm not planning on having children. Lily says kids are nothing but trouble. I agree with her."

"Oh, never mind Lily. You'll want them when you meet the right man. We all do."

Her eyes track Satomi's long stride, she listens to her daughter's words, and notes her restlessness with trepidation. Teaching Satomi Japanese has been a rare success; all else has failed. It isn't in the girl's nature to fade gracefully into the background, or to move modestly. She is always in a hurry, eating her food quickly, racing through her tasks.

"Can't see why that girl's so gingered up all the time. More boy than girl in her, if you ask me," is Aaron's take on it.

But although she never quite achieves the graceful body language of her mother, or the sweet tempo of Tamura's voice, although a stranger might not have recognized the two as mother and daughter, there are things that are inherent. Sometimes she will turn her head just like Tamura, her hand brushing away the hair from her face in the same arresting movement. And often, if Aaron isn't looking, he can hardly tell which one of them it is that he can hear laughing.

Like her mother, she can put her hair up without pins in one flowing movement and make a gleaming knot of it that sits nest-like on the nape of her neck. She has watched Tamura do it since infancy and guesses that it is one of those skills that, like skipping, once learned is never forgotten.

Mother and daughter are not obviously alike, but for all Tamura's shyness, her gentle nature, there is a core of stubbornness in her makeup that is reflected in Satomi's. It shows itself in her refusal to see that Satomi will never become the daughter her father expects her to be. It's only a question of time, she thinks obstinately, it will sort itself in time.

"Slow down, take smaller steps," she begs.

If what Aaron wanted wasn't so important to her, she might see the spring of yearning in Satomi, the character that is already made. She might recognize in her daughter the bit of her husband's nature that she admires so much.

Lately on their drives home, sneaking glances at Satomi's full breasts, her tiny waist, and her long shapely legs, she muses on the fact that her daughter is hardly a child anymore. In no time at all she will be a young woman, lost to her. No doubt she will want to escape from under Aaron the first chance she gets.

Tamura's longing for more children has never left her. Over the years since Satomi's birth, she has ached for them. The thought now of losing her only one is made more painful for her by the absence of those others that never came.

"You don't call me Mama anymore," she says wistfully. "It's always Mother these days."

"I'm not a child anymore."

"No, but you are not a woman yet either."

THE DRAFT

IN THE FALL of 1940, Aaron receives his draft registration card. He has been expecting it, and even in the face of Tamura's apprehension he can't get vexed about it.

"It ain't gonna come to much, honey," he assures her. "They're just ratcheting up the numbers."

Talk of a spat with Japan has been around for months, but Aaron thinks it's all hot air. He reads the warmongering articles in the *Los Angeles Times* as though they are works of fiction, written to stir up the readers, to keep them buying the paper for the next thrilling installment.

"We'll have to show them who's boss pretty soon" is a regular brag in Angelina, but somehow Aaron's imagination won't stretch to the possibility of what might be heading his way. It's hard for him to accept that something he hasn't ordered himself might influence his life.

In Angelina, though, the moment those draft cards sat on mantelpieces, the Baker family took on the stink of the enemy. Try as they might to ignore it, the family couldn't fail to notice the now-open hostility shown toward them.

"Something's changed, that's for sure," Aaron says. "I notice they're not turning our business away, though. They're just a bunch of hypocrites, always got to have someone to blame when things ain't going their way."

For Satomi the teasing at school has developed an uglier edge. Her fellow pupils strut around, mouthing off to her the things they have heard being said at home.

"Think we don't know you're a yella spy?" they taunt. "We don't want your kind here."

She fights her way through it. "As if I give a damn," she says to Artie. "Sure, it's tough, but not as tough as it is for the Japanese kids. They're getting it bad."

"We're gonna whip you good," the boys threaten them. "Don't you Japs know you can't beat Americans?"

"We are Americans." But their words are drowned in waves of jeering laughter.

"Looking like the enemy doesn't make them the enemy," Satomi insists to Lily. "Don't let me see you joining in the baiting."

To her own surprise, coming across the school bully Mike Loder, who is twisting the arm of a Japanese girl who hasn't made way for him in the hall, she finds herself ready, wanting to act.

Mike's voice is high, pumped up with a venomous hatred. He is so full of himself that he might as well be thumping his chest with his fists. *Look at how important I am compared to you.*

"Stand aside next time, Jap. Get it?" He is leering into the girl's face, his own fat one shining with sweat and excitement.

"Why should she, Mike? You stand aside." Satomi grabs at his shirt, pulling him away from the girl. "What's so special about you?"

"Keep out of this. Keep your half-caste nose out of it." He shoves her hard so that she stumbles, hitting the side of a locker, grazing her arm, and banging her cheekbone on its metal edge.

After, she can't remember how it happened, what had propelled her fist into Mike's face, or the pain she felt when he returned the blow. She remembers, though, feeling good, not caring that she is in for it with Mr. Beck. Something about her action, her getting involved, has made her feel that she is safe in her own hands.

Aaron, checking the bruises on her cheek, the raw graze on her arm, says it's no big deal.

"You've had worse," he says. "Still, that kid needs a lesson."

Next day she is embarrassed to see him at the school gates.

"Start walking home, girl. I'll catch you up in the truck."

Outside the gate she waits and sees him buttonhole Mike Loder, hears his voice steady and menacing.

"See this fist, boy?"

"Yes, Mr. Baker." Mike's pigeon eyes look wary, his voice little more than a squeak.

"You touch my girl again, any girl, you're gonna see it close up."

Mike hangs his head, studying the ground, shucking his foot against a broken bit of asphalt. He thinks he might just kick out, get a good hit at Old Man Baker's shin before running off. He's not sure he can pull that off, though, and he has had enough of mixing it with the Bakers.

"Tell your father to come and see me if he's got a problem with that," Aaron calls to Mike's retreating back.

Hanging a left at the gate, Mike glares at her but he doesn't say anything. He doesn't say anything at home either. His brothers would only sneer at him for letting a girl get a punch in.

Even Mr. Beck has caught the fear. "I'm pretty sure there's going to be a war," he tells the class. "But you don't need to worry none. It won't take long to see them off. We've got right on our side and no Japs are going to set foot on American soil."

He attempts to keep his voice from shaking and fails. He is a patriot, after all, and loves his country. "We all love America," he says, not looking at Satomi's bruised face, or at the Japanese students who sit in his class with blank expressions and lowered eyes.

"Guess Mr. Beck doesn't like you so much anymore," Lily whispers, hoping that soon it will be the same with Artie.

After his little speech, Mr. Beck keeps Satomi in with the pretense of talking to her about her grades.

"You have to understand," he says, warily looking around before offering her a cigarette, staring at her in that squirm-making way. "You're gonna have to choose where you stand. I'd cut any ties you have with the Japanese if I were you."

She takes the cigarette and he lights it for her with a proprietary air. He'd like to be the one to always light her cigarettes.

"You want me to cut ties with my mother, Mr. Beck?"

"Well, no, of course I didn't mean that. I just meant you should choose your friends carefully."

"Are you my friend, Mr. Beck?" Her heartbeat amps up a notch, it seems too bold a thing to ask.

"I'd like to be." He touches her cheek lightly, leaning in so that she can smell his sweat, see the moisture beading above his top lip.

"Well, if you are, then I reckon you shouldn't make out like we're the enemy."

"We?"

"Us Japs."

She's judging him, ticking him off. He's a little amused, stirred by her. It's been a long time since a woman got pert with him. But he can't favor her anymore, the time is coming when he will have to kill his desire for the girl, stop keeping her in his sights. She isn't the only one who must choose who to play with.

As things worsen between the United States and Japan, Angelina closes ranks. What few friendships some of the locals have enjoyed with their Japanese neighbors go stone cold, as though they had never been.

Tamura, painfully sensitive to people's attitudes, refuses to go into town. She misses her outings with Satomi but she feels safer at home.

"I'll go when things simmer down," she promises. "No point in asking for trouble."

While they wait for things to *simmer down*, Satomi picks up the provisions after school, not pausing for the grocery clerk to say thank you, which he rarely does, and then only when from habit it slips out. She stares down those who are rude to her, never the first to look away. She holds her head up at the overt name-calling, wanting to smash them all, to put her fists into their smug faces as she had into Mike Loder's. She minds for herself, but cares more for her mother.

"Who in their right mind could think of my mother as the enemy?" she asks Lily. "I mean, Tamura Baker, Japanese spy, can you see it?"

"Well, I guess some might, not me, of course, but some," Lily answers halfheartedly. "I guess it'll pass soon enough," she adds without conviction.

"Can't say it surprises me," Aaron says. "It comes on the back of a century of hate for Orientals. They're just plain scared, and now that Japan is playing up, they're telling themselves that they were right all along."

The Stars and Stripes begin to flutter on every porch. The talk is all of patriotism and keeping America *safe for Americans*.

"They can wrap themselves in the flag as much as they like," Aaron says. "It don't make them more American than us."

For Tamura, the thought that Aaron might be taken from her fills her with fear. She can't imagine her life without him. She has forgotten what it is to be herself in the world. So it comes as a shock when at breakfast one morning he appears in a clean shirt and his kept-for best pants, and, as though it has just occurred to him out of the blue, tells them casually that he is going to volunteer that very day.

"I'm not waiting on some guy I've never met to crook his finger and tell me to up sticks."

"But Aaron, it may never happen. Even if there is a war, they are going to need farmers to keep the land going. Please don't go, wait a bit. Wait for a couple of months at least."

"Look, Tamura, it will be best for us all if I'm one of the first to volunteer. They can hardly feel bad about you and Satomi if I'm out there doing my duty, now, can they? Wherever they send me, it will likely only be for a few months."

It's the only time that Satomi has heard her parents arguing, although it is more like pleading on Tamura's part. Aaron, though, is not to be swayed, not even by her mother's tears. For herself she can't help feeling a run of excitement at the idea of life without Aaron on her case.

It upsets Aaron seeing Tamura so anxious, but he just can't bear the idea of being summoned by a higher authority to do their bidding. The way things are moving they are going to get him one way or the other anyway. He might as well make sure that it's his way.

He volunteers for the Navy, a strange choice, Satomi thinks, for a farmer, but then you can never second-guess Aaron.

Tamura isn't surprised. "Your father has always loved boats, loved being near the water," she says. "Hawaii does that to you."

In the week before he leaves, he stacks the woodshed to the roof with logs, cleans out the well, and adds Tamura's name to the bank account.

"You two will manage fine," he says. "The best part of the harvest is in, after all. And Satomi, I expect you to pull your weight, help your mother."

Tamura watches Aaron walk down the path, not slowing, not looking back, as he swings onto the road. While he's still in her sights she feels lonely. She stays at the window long after the dust from his heels has settled back to earth, as though he might think better of it and turn for home.

Satomi watches him too, thinking how Aaron being one of the first to volunteer will shut the kids up at school.

"See your father's still at home," she will say. "Guess he's not ready to fight for America, huh?"

"Don't cry, Mama," she soothes, putting her arm around Tamura. He'll be back before you know it. And I'm still here."

Aaron had talked himself into the idea that he was doing something grand, something that would involve muscle and guns, but before he knows it, he finds himself back in Hawaii as a battleship cook. He can't work out how that happened. He had written Hawaii as his birthplace on the Navy forms, adding beneath it that for personal reasons it was the only posting he didn't want.

Tamura laughs through her tears. As far as she is aware, Aaron has never cooked a thing in his life.

"How can he be a cook? Your father has never made himself a meal, never even brewed his own coffee."

"Guess the crew will find that out soon enough," Satomi says, doubled up with laughter. The thought of her father peeling vegetables and making omelets is just ridiculous.

In his first letter home, although it wasn't to be read on the page, both wife and daughter sensed Aaron's regret at his decision to enlist.

Life in the ship's galley is a sight easier than that of a farmer. The food's not bad although the tomatoes that have to be chopped by the sack full aren't a patch on ours. They have no scent, nothing of the earth about them. The ship has the same problem with rats as we do, only they're bigger here, less scared of humans. Two days in and we were all taken off board while they fumigated the holds and cabins with poisonous gas. They say two whiffs of the stuff can fell a man, so I'm not breathing deep for a while.

He writes that Hawaii seems different to him, not the least bit like home anymore.

I don't intend looking up family. No point in dredging up dirt, so you needn't worry on that score. In any case guys get moved on all the time, I'm hoping not to be stationed here for long.

Tamura had harbored a faint hope that Aaron, back in their old territory, might relent, try to make amends with their families.

"I should have known," she says to Satomi. "Your father wasn't built for bending."

His letters begin to arrive two, sometimes three a week, his big scrawl filling page after page with what seems to them to be ramblings about nothing much, the weather, the ship's menus, how it's never quiet on board. Tamura wants to hear that he is missing her, missing home, wants him to tell her that she is doing well keeping things going on the farm. But Aaron's feelings are nowhere to be read in his letters; something stops him from saying what he feels, from pouring his heart out to her. He can't admit that he has made a mistake. He feels himself a fool for having volunteered in the first place. Good Lord, what had he been thinking? Life is harder for him in the Navy than he makes out to Tamura. He hates being in such close contact with other men, hearing them snore and sleep-talk at night, smelling the sweaty

animal scent of them. He thinks he sees in them the look of the
migrant worker, the look of men who are rootless. But really what
he sees, what he can't make any sense of, are men who haven't
chosen the land, men so unlike himself that he will never feel at
ease with them. He mimics their language, laughs at their jokes,
attempts to be a regular kind of guy, it's easier that way.

"Hey, Aaron, you got a pass for tonight? Real pretty girls at the
Pearl Bar."

"Another time, maybe. Things to do."

He has no use for the white-trash girls with their caked-on
makeup and sprayed-stiff hair that you can buy for a buck or two
at the Pearl.

"Yeah, we know, another letter to write, eh? You'll have to
show us a photo sometime soon. She must be some looker, to keep
you on the hop like that."

It's only when the bunks around him lay empty that he can let
go. He thinks then of Tamura, of the soft planes of her face, the
pools of her eyes, and the feather-weight of her body on his. He
takes his small comfort in the privacy of his narrow bunk, a moment's relief, and only a faint echo of what he so badly craves.

He has thought better about showing a photograph of Tamura
around. Perhaps it's not such a good idea to tell his so-called shipmates that his wife is Japanese. They wouldn't understand, and
he can't bear the thought of exposing Tamura to their crude
comments.

Some of the guys stick pictures of their wives on their lockers,
and then have to take the jokes, the wolf whistles and the mockery
that the good-looking ones will soon be sending "Dear John"
letters. Let them think him secretive, he'll sail through his time,
let the wind take him, keep his family to himself.

In the moments before sleep he closes his eyes and imagines
himself working his fields. He summons up the cool fragrance of

green tomatoes as they ripen in the sun. It's a source of pride for
him that he can tell what stage his crop is at simply by the smell.
First comes the sharp trace of green in the flower, the scent of
cologne, then as the fruit buds a smell as close to pickle as you'll
get, and then the ready-for-picking, full-blown peachy perfume
that fills the packing shed for days.

Finding it hard to take orders, to have his days dictated by time
sheets, he begins sending his own orders home, long lists of instructions for Tamura and Satomi, lists that comfort him and irritate them.

> Make sure you clean out the rain barrels right down to the
> bottom. The water will turn brackish if you don't. And
> Tamura, I know you don't like it but the traps must be set in
> the packing sheds. We'll be overrun if you don't. Get Satomi
> to do it and tell her to be sure to get rid of the dead ones. And
> don't forget to order the fertilizer in good time, and . . .

Once a letter is stamped and posted, his mind empties for a bit,
and he feels at ease. But a day or so later he has thought up a whole
new list of things for them to do. He dreads the idea of returning
to the farm and finding it neglected. You can't blame them, but
women aren't up to the job, they won't see what's needed, and
Tamura has never been strong.

Encouraged by the tone of the headlines in the *Los Angeles Times*,
the folks in Angelina figure that war with Japan is a surefire thing.
The men are already being called up, and those who haven't received their papers are rushing to volunteer before they are summoned. No one wants to be thought unwilling, unpatriotic.

The town seems half empty without them. Old men see their
sons off with fear in their eyes, young fathers leave their families

with trepidation. The land is left to the ministrations of grandfa-
thers, schoolboys, and the women.

The old men gather together in the farmers' cooperative, feeling themselves in charge, half alive again. War is the main topic of
conversation. The threat from Japan is changing things, taking
away the routine of their lives, their ease of mind. Angelina's Japanese take the brunt of their anger.

"The whole damn lot of them got a secret allegiance to Japan."

"When push comes to shove they can't be trusted."

Lily, on the lookout for an excuse to ditch Satomi, is half sick
with having to make-believe that Satomi is her best friend. She
doesn't share her home-packed lunches with her anymore, refusing Tamura's fish and rice balls that she is usually greedy for.

"Can't stomach fish anymore. Guess I'm allergic or something."

Lily's mother has warned that Japs can't be trusted not to put
something in the food. It's better to be safe than sorry.

"That's a shame, you loved them so much," Satomi says without sympathy. She knows what's going on with Lily, all right.

"Yeah, well, things change, I guess."

"I'm the same person, Lily."

"I know that, Sati." Lily stares her down. "I'm only talking
about fish balls."

Despite that Lily is being weird, despite that she's getting a
rougher ride at school, Satomi is enjoying life without Aaron
around. It's easy now to get her own way, tempting to take advantage of her mother's gentle nature. She likes home better without
her father in it, that's for sure. She can hardly remember his rules
now, smoking as she does without a thought to being caught, leaving her hair down, getting behind with her chores. Every now and
then, though, she hears Tamura sigh in her bed, and she suffers the
loss of Aaron herself, the fear that life is shifting too quickly.

Things with Artie are still on, although she never knows where she stands with him these days. He is offhand with her at school, making out that things have changed between them, but full-on with her when it is just the two of them.

"No point in us riling people up, they're doing enough of that themselves."

"They are morons, Artie, all of them."

"Yeah, well, fuck 'em, eh?"

Artie likes it better with Aaron away too. He calls at the farm with the excuse that he has come to help Satomi and Tamura with the chores.

"Now that you don't have a man around," he preens.

He sits around the place, watching Satomi pile the wood up in the lean-to, clean out the sheds, and stack the tomato boxes, talking to her all the while. He doesn't mind releasing the dead rats from the traps, though.

"Girls shouldn't have to," he says as he practices flinging them across the fields, seeing how far he can make them fly.

In the seed store that stinks of the rats, a thicker sort of mousy, he kisses her, long, passionate kisses, the way he thinks girls like to be kissed. He gets a kick from the risk that Mrs. Baker might come looking for them, see his hands all over Satomi. He likes to think he might be a man with the power to shock. He pushes Satomi up against the wall, his hands wandering under her dress, wanting it so bad that he thinks sometimes of forcing her.

"Come on, Sati, don't hold out. Let's do it now." She is driving him crazy, getting him hot, and doing it on purpose, most like. "When are you gonna say yes, plenty of girls would have by now."

"I guess that I'm not one of them, then. Take your ring back, if you want, give it to someone else." She is tiring of Artie, if she's honest. She doesn't like the way he ignores her at school, thinks it cowardly.

"Who knows, maybe I will."

"Fine with me, Artie, just say the word."

Christ, he could have any girl he wants, why does it have to be Satomi Baker? If only she would say yes, they could do it and maybe he could forget about her, move on. Lily, for one, is panting for it.

Tamura makes them lemonade, laughs at Artie's jokes, and is kinder to him than Satomi is. She likes having him around the place, he livens things up, makes her feel that they are still part of the world, part of Angelina. She watches Satomi and Artie dance on the scrub of earth outside the kitchen door, to the records that Artie brings over, "In the Mood," and his favorite, "Down Argentina Way." Artie has rhythm, she thinks, that free vulgar sort of American rhythm. He spins Satomi into him, pushing her away, pulling her near, showing off his fancy footwork. He can boogie with the best of them.

"Come on, Mrs. Baker, give it a try," he offers.

She longs to but always refuses. She is too shy, contained in the way that Japanese females are. Modest, her mother would say. And what would Aaron have thought? He wouldn't approve of her entertaining Artie, that's for sure. She doesn't have the heart or the energy to forbid his visits, though. Artie is fun, and Satomi needs someone of her own age around. Lily, it seems, has deserted. She hopes, though, that Artie isn't the one for Satomi. There is nothing of Aaron's steel in the boy.

While her mother sleeps, Satomi stays up in the moon hours, driving the old truck over the farm, parking up behind the sheds, smoking and gazing at the skating stars. She imagines that if she concentrates on them long enough, their energy, which seems to her to be in some mysterious way linked to her own destiny, will somehow enter her bloodstream and a different kind of life will begin.

The waiting for that different life would be fine if only the thought of war didn't prey on her mind so much, if only she didn't fear Japan. The schoolyard talk is full of lurid descriptions of the cruelties that the Japanese *bastards* will inflict if they get the upper hand. Panic rises in her chest when she thinks about *the yellow peril*.

The occasional blink of a plane's taillight heading off into the night sets her to imagining foreign lands, lives lived more excitingly than her own. One day maybe something wonderful will happen and she will be on that plane. She will see deserts, and beaches with pink sand, and all the places Mr. Beck has told them about in geography.

"You're not the only one who wants to get out," she tells Artie. "I'm not going to get stuck in Angelina for the rest of my life. I want to see the world too."

"We could go to Los Angeles," Artie offers. "It's got to be the best place on earth."

"Who told you that?"

"Oh, people talk, things get around. No place on earth like Los Angeles, they say."

"You don't want to travel far, then, Artie?"

"No need."

In the space when she is not thinking about letting Artie go, or of the Japs coming to get them, she takes the time to notice that the house is unpleasantly quiet without Aaron, that the fields are weedy at the edges, that her mother is filled with sadness.

Tamura has become listless, as though while waiting for Aaron's return she has gone into slow motion. She works the land every day, exhausting labor even with Satomi's help. Yet without shirts to wash and boots to clean, she feels at a loss. Being a creature of habit, she cooks the same meals, serves them on the same day of the week that Aaron had insisted on. But she can't be bothered with the finer details and the meals seem flavorless to Satomi.

"No more soba noodles, please, Mama. You don't like them much, I hate them, what's the point?"

But as though bad luck will follow if she doesn't, as though some link between her and Aaron will be severed, Tamura goes on making the noodles that only Aaron likes. The velvety dough sticks to her hands, little flecks of it settle in her hair like snow-flakes. It's a messy business, familiar and somehow comforting.

"Fat white worms, horrible soft gloopy things," Satomi complains to Artie. "I just can't bring myself to swallow them. Can't think why Father likes them so much."

She longs for hamburger, for steak, but never asks for them.

Used to having Aaron to guide her, Tamura turns to Satomi for confirmation of every decision she makes. It seems to Satomi that overnight mother and daughter roles have been reversed. Tamura is letting go, happy for her to be in charge.

When she notices that her mother has started squinting, she has to force Tamura to town for the sight test with the visiting optician. The steel-rimmed prescription glasses that Tamura receives a month later make her look older than her forty years.

"I won't wear them in front of your father." She grimaces into the mirror. "They make me look like my mother."

"Well, your mother sure must have been pretty," Satomi soothes. "Was she?"

Tamura doesn't answer. Since Aaron left it seems more important than ever to her to stick to his rules, to the pact they had made all those years ago. *The old families*, as Aaron has labeled them, as though they are some long-lost ancient dynasty, must remain in the past.

With twenty-twenty vision restored, Tamura sets about polishing.

"Why didn't you tell me things were getting so dusty?"

"I didn't notice, Mother."

"Oh, Satomi, what kind of wife will you make?" she despairs.

Lily hasn't been herself of late. She's been moody and more than a bit offhand with Satomi. Satomi's not taking her moods seriously. Lily will come around soon enough. Angelina being on alert must be as upsetting for Lily as it is for her. They'll ride the troubles out, still be friends when everything settles down.

Since they had smiled at each other on day one of first grade, their friendship has been steady, unbreakable, she thinks. So everything that happens on a Sunday morning in Miss Ray's after-service needlework class, as she blanket-stitches around her piece of patchwork for the wall hanging of GOD SEES ALL, comes as a shock.

Lily had talked her into joining the class in the first place, so that Miss Ray, who likes to save souls, would see that she was doing her best to bring Satomi into the fold.

"Everyone should do their bit for the church," Lily had coaxed. "And you get grape juice and a pretzel twist, two if you're lucky. You should really be a churchgoer, but I guess Miss Ray will let you off on account of your mother being, well, you know."

Satomi did know, but as usual with Lily she didn't push it. Lily didn't mean anything by it, it was just her way. The class wasn't so bad, it got her out of chores for a bit, and she never saw Artie on a Sunday anyway, what with his family being holy-rolling-religious.

"God and duty first," was Mr. Goodwin's fatherly advice to Artie. "Good Christians go to church with their people on Sundays."

"Yeah, good boring Christians," Artie complained. "Nothing but Bible reading and silence, it drives me nuts."

Just before it's time to return their needles and cottons to the pine chest marked PATCHWORK, Mr. Beck, dressed in his black Sunday-best suit, reels through the big pine door.

"Miss Ray, Miss Ray," he repeats at full volume on his way up the aisle, letting the door bang loudly behind him.

"Careful, Mr. Beck." Miss Ray extends her arm uselessly as he rushes toward her, knocking over the pattern stand, sending her book of patchwork pictures flying.

The class erupts in laughter as Mr. Beck cups his palm against Miss Ray's cheek and whispers something in her ear.

A note lands on Satomi's lap. "Pass it on," a voice whispers.

He loves her. Pass it on, it says.

They can tell the news is big by the way Miss Ray's eyes widen and go dark. Mr. Beck sure has the jitters about something. His body is shaking, his mouth twitching nervously, and he doesn't know what to do with his hands, which flutter about like the big white butterflies that come every year at pea-cropping time. He places one of them on Miss Ray's shoulder as though to steady her, to steady himself.

Satomi catches Lily's eye and smiles. Lily shrugs her shoulders, looks hostile.

"Time to go home now, girls," Miss Ray says in a high shaky voice, raising her arms in the air as though she is about to conduct an orchestra. "Be quick, now, your parents will be expecting you."

Outside the church hall Satomi catches up with Lily.

"What do you think it's all about, Lily?" she asks. "Mr. Beck and Miss Ray all fired up like that."

"Well, they ain't getting married, so I reckon we must be at war with the Japs."

Forgetting for once that "ain't" is common, Lily turns from her, her voice hard, dismissive.

Of course Lily is right. It can't be anything else. Satomi swallows hard, her mouth dry, she doesn't have enough spit and it hurts a bit. She looks down the street as though hoards of the enemy might already be on the march there.

A bunch of girls pass her, silent in their wondering, staring at her with narrowing eyes. They purse their lips, stiffen their shoulders, and start for home in huddled clusters keeping close for comfort. Mr. Beck has unnerved them. The Japs could already be nearby, in the bushes, perhaps, waiting for them on the road home.

"No need to make it a war between us," Satomi calls to Lily's retreating back. "Guess I'll see you tomorrow."

She starts for home. Perhaps her mother would know what it is all about.

Lily, running to catch up with the girls who are walking her way, links arms with one of them, keeping her back straight, her head tilted as though she is sniffing the air. If the news turns out to be war, then she has the best excuse ever to dump Satomi. Artie would have to do the same.

From the day that the Japanese bombed Pearl Harbor, she never spoke to Satomi again.

PEARL HARBOR

THEY HEAR THE president's speech on the radio, his voice
steady above the background sounds of flashbulbs flaring:

Yesterday, December the seventh, 1941, a date which will
live in infamy—the United States of America was suddenly
and deliberately attacked by naval and air forces of Japan.

The attack yesterday on the Hawaiian Islands has caused
severe damage to American naval and military forces. I regret
to tell you that many American lives have been lost.

As though standing at attention, Satomi and Tamura have positioned themselves a little apart from each other. Tamura is trembling, sheet-white, her head bowed. Satomi, returned to the
childhood habit she had when trying to figure things out, chews
at her lower lip. She's attempting to understand the president, to
make sense of his words, but her thoughts keep returning to Aaron.
She can't stop picturing him all burned up, hurting.

Reaching out, she takes Tamura's hand and squeezes it. Tamura
dares not look at her, dares not have her own fears mirrored in her
daughter's eyes. She has stopped listening to the radio and is form-
ing her own story in her mind. Of course Aaron is alive, wounded

maybe, in a hospital perhaps, but alive. They will hear from him soon, be able to count themselves among the lucky.

The day is tepid, warm enough for the time of year, but a chill has seeped through Satomi so that she has hunched her shoulders, as though bracing herself against a bitter wind. She lets go Tamura's hand and turns the volume up to full.

> Last night Japanese forces attacked Hong Kong.
> Last night Japanese forces attacked Guam.
> Last night Japanese forces attacked the Philippine Islands.
> Last night the Japanese attacked Midway Islands.
> I ask that the Congress declare that since the unprovoked and dastardly attack by Japan, a state of war has existed between the United States and the Japanese Empire.

In the moment that Aaron catches fire, Tamura is hauling bags of fertilizer onto the trailer, priding herself on how neatly she is stacking them. She has been working the fields for a couple of hours already, thinking that Aaron on Hawaiian time will still be sleeping. With luck he will be home for Christmas. He has written saying as much, although he advises against counting on it.

> Once the government's got you, you can't count on anything. I guess even if I make it home it won't be much of a break. I"ll need to catch up on things. Guess there's plenty that needs catching up on. You can't neglect the land for long before it starts paying you back.

She allows herself a moment of satisfaction. He is going to be surprised for sure when he sees how good the land is looking, despite the fact that she hasn't gotten around to the weeds that margin the fields, some of them so pretty in their flower that she hardly thinks of them as weeds at all. He should have more faith in her.

She pictures him walking up the road to their farm, smart now in his uniform, a rare smile on his face. The image sets an alarm off in her, so that she loses the rhythm of her task for a bit. In working the land she has neglected the house. Things are not as Aaron likes them, as he will expect them to be. She determines that she will clear her head and get on with the chores she has let go.

She will wash the floors, clear the bindweed from around the kitchen door, make jams and jellies, and pickles from the bruised cucumbers. She will pound the rice for Aaron's favorite soup. She will make sure that everything is just as he likes it. With Aaron home, life will return to normal, the awful uncertainty in her will lift. She will be her old self again.

An hour or so later, standing to stretch her back, she sees Elena Kaplan running down the field toward her as though her life depends on it.

Tamura's spectacles aren't so great with distances, things tend to blur, but who else can it be but Elena. Something is wrong, though, that's for sure. Only a child hurtles at that speed for the fun of it. It's a while before her friend's red hair, her wide shoulders, come into focus.

"Oh, Tamura!" Elena exclaims. "It's just so awful."

"Awful?" Tamura scans Elena's face, looking for the familiar signs of Hal's brutality, but can see only fading bruises from his last beating. One must be due, she guesses, he likes to keep them regular just so she knows she can rely on them.

You don't know, do you?" Elena says, pained at the sight of Tamura's innocent smile. "Oh, God, you don't know," she moves to Tamura's side and puts an arm around her shoulders.

Hal had relayed the news of the bombing to her, shouting it

through the window as she was hoeing the soil in her vegetable plot.

"Bad news, and worse to come," he called, beckoning her into the house. "If it wasn't for this damn leg of mine, I'd make those sorry bastards pay."

Elena is sick of hearing Hal go on about his polio-damaged leg. He blames his slight limp for everything that goes wrong in his life, for the bad luck that follows him, even as some sort of sick excuse for knocking the stuffing out of her whenever he feels like it.

"This is just about the last straw," he raged. "Don't let me catch you mixing with them down the hill anymore, you hear? From now on, you remember where your loyalties lie."

She was scared witless of him but already planning to disobey. Disobeying him is the only thing that keeps her sane. Just the thought of the meanness in him, his big ham hands itching to lash out, makes her stomach sink, but no way is Hal Kaplan going to choose her friends for her.

Hal's first beating had been on their wedding night, when, stinking of beer and rough with drink, he had shoved her face-down on the bed and attempted to mount her. She had pushed him away, desiring something more romantic, something more loving. She had learned her lesson that night. In Hal Kaplan's bed he called the shots.

"I'm going to town," he said. "Need to talk it over with the men. Don't know when I'll be back."

Before the growl of his pickup had faded she was running down the field to Tamura. How could she not go to her sweet neighbor at such a time? Over the years, Tamura had shown herself to be a true friend. She remembered the comfort Tamura had given when Hal, third day into a drinking binge, had blamed her for their not conceiving a child and beaten her until her face had swollen to the size of a pumpkin. Tamura had bathed her wounds, stitching with cotton and a small-eyed needle the deep split that had exposed her jawbone. The scar is still there, neat as anything, Tamura's tiny stitches a thin white tattoo on Elena's brown face. Tamura Baker doesn't judge, she just sets about making things better.

"It's a terrible shock, Tamura. You had better sit down. Let's go in, I will make you some tea."

There's a ringing in Tamura's head as she tries to make sense of Elena's news, a heaviness working its way from her feet, which seem too leaden to move, up to her stomach. Something painfully hot is tiding around her heart, churning things up.

"That Japan should do such a thing," she muses, feeling oddly betrayed. "It can't be true."

"I'll wait with you until Satomi comes home. She will look after you. The news has been too much for you. You need your girl."

"There's no need, Elena. It's terrible news, the worst I've ever heard, but Aaron can't be dead. I would know if he was. I promise you, I would know if he was."

"Your father is not dead," she repeats often and too brightly in the hours after the president's broadcast. "It's a good sign that we have heard nothing, bad news never keeps you waiting."

Satomi thinks of Mr. Beck arriving at Miss Ray's class with the bad news. It had certainly reached Angelina without much of a pause. And here only a day later they are at war. Perhaps her mother is right. Perhaps good news is a sluggish traveler.

She stays close to Tamura, brewing endless cups of tea, wandering aimlessly around the land with her, shaken at her mother's seeming lack of emotion. Her own emotions run the gambit through fear for her father's life to the sickening hurt at Lily's betrayal. They don't compare, she knows—the loss of a friend, after all, being nothing to the loss of a father—but still it eats away at her. The sight of Lily's retreating back yesterday had something of triumph in it, some pleasure in her cruelty. How could she ever have thought Lily Morton a true friend?

She tries to fight off the hurt, but no matter how she attempts to dismiss it, the nasty feel of it won't budge. She holds herself together, not crying, keeping her tears stored for Aaron in case it should come to that.

"She is a foolish girl," Tamura says. "Not made for true friendship."

As always, Satomi takes the initiative with Artie. She waits for him at the school gate, ignoring the catcalls of her fellow pupils, and gives him back his class ring before he can summon the courage to ask for it.

"You might as well have this, Artie. I'm never coming back to school, that's for sure. And we were never going to make it anyway. Chalk and cheese."

Artie makes a pretense of not wanting to take the ring. Not much of one, but a try, at least.

"It's just for now," he says sheepishly, dropping it into his shirt pocket. "You can have it back when things die down a bit." He pats the pocket to let her know he is keeping it safe for her.

"Don't sweat it, Artie. You and me, it was just a kid's thing. I'm not a kid anymore."

"Maybe." He shifts his weight from one foot to the other.

She can tell that he is relieved that she has made it easy for him. Well, she had known all along that he didn't have what it takes. Still, his obvious relief hurts, sets up something steely in her.

"See you around, then," he says, turning from her. His brother has been called to the Army, and he wants to get on with the business of hating the Japs without having to pussyfoot around her. She was never going to put out anyway.

With an odd mixture of dread and relief Satomi sees the telegraph boy—not a boy at all, but Mr. Stedall, who is forty if he is a day—appear in the small plot of garden at the back of the house.

She taps Tamura lightly on the shoulder to draw her attention to his arrival. Tamura stands to face him, leaving the weeding they have been doing to keep busy, to keep the waiting at bay. Since Tamura won't allow the possibility of Aaron's death to be spoken of, despite that it is the text of their nightmares, the constant thought in their minds, they have run out of things to say to each other.

"Sorry to give you this, Mrs. Baker," Mr. Stedall says, offering the telegram. "Bad news, I'm afraid. Guess you know what it is."

Tamura looks toward the horizon as though something there, something far, far away, has caught her attention. She keeps her hands at her side, her body still. She has always liked Mr. Stedall, but the desire to please has left her, she can't bring herself to smile.

"Mrs. Baker . . ."

She shakes her head, as though saying no, as though she can dismiss Mr. Stedall, he is an illusion, he isn't really there, standing in her garden waving the telegram at her. She doesn't want to touch the ugly thing, see the stupid words written, so that she has to believe them. She isn't ready to give up on hope.

Satomi, feeling a run of shame and pity at Tamura's cowardice, takes the telegram from Mr. Stedall's trembling hand. He moves away from her, looking at her inquisitively, as though she might be about to faint away, fall perhaps into his arms.

"You can go now, Mr. Stedall," she says quietly. "I'm guessing that you don't need an answer."

A week or so after the telegram a letter from the Navy arrives. Satomi opens it, begins to read it out loud, but Tamura will have none of it.

"Stop, I don't want to hear it. Throw it away, Satomi. I know what I know."

"It's the truth, Mama. You know it is."

But Tamura doesn't want the truth. She wants sweet lies, the comfort of fantasy. The sight of the telegram had been bad enough, but somehow the letter, the leaf-thinness of it, the official Navy stamp, is worse. Taking to her bed, she buries herself under the sweaty shade of her sheets and attempts to fool herself into believing that Aaron is alive, that the *knowing* she talks about is real.

With her mother out of it, Satomi rereads the letter with absolute attention to every word. It speaks of the Navy's regret, says that Aaron had been a brave seaman who had lost his life in the defense of his country. Because so many had died that day, the Navy had to bury them quickly, laying them in death alongside the shipmates they had stood beside in life. The services had been dignified and each man had been named in them. Plot numbers and details would be sent to the families as soon as possible.

She thinks of all the relatives of those who died alongside Aaron in the attack on the harbor, receiving the same letter. A thousand paper missiles with only the deceased's names to distinguish one from another.

She thinks of her father's parents, whom she is not allowed to speak of. Do they know their son is dead, buried close to them in Hawaii? Probably not. Her mother must write to them when she feels better, it's only fair.

Bringing her father's face to mind, the sound of his voice, she attempts tears for him, but there's just a burning in her eyes, a lasso tightening in her chest. Her eyes water, not with the generous streams she owes him, but with bitter little salt courses that dry before they reach her cheeks.

With Tamura lost in denial, she takes to running the place on her own. She feeds the hens, collects their eggs, cleans out the sheds, and makes a tasteless version of Tamura's onion soup. She boils rice, beans, eggs, but Tamura refuses to eat. There is something dangerous in her mother's rebuttal of food, something that threatens them both.

Each morning she sits on the edge of Tamura's bed, the letter in her hand, freshly made tea on the bedside table.

"I don't want to hear it," Tamura whines, putting her hands over her ears.

"You must, Mama. You know you must."

"Why must I?"

"Because it is right that you should. Because it's childish not to." She can't help being irritated with Tamura. She is the mother, after all.

Eventually the morning comes when Tamura, emerging from under the covers, is ready. Hunger has finally won out. She sips her tea, nibbles at a thin slice of toast, and watches Satomi take the letter from its envelope. Her eyes are shadowed and bloodshot, strands of her black hair are stuck to her forehead, she hasn't washed for a week, and she smells musty. She looks a little mad.

"Tell me again, why I must hear it?" she asks.

"Because Father would want you to, because you are his wife, because it will comfort you. It says that Father was brave."

"I don't need them to tell me that. I have always known it."

Remembering back to the day that Aaron had accidentally driven the prong of a pitchfork clean through his foot, leaving as he withdrew it a hole the size of a fifty-cent piece, Satomi knows that it is true too. He had been brave then as the blood pumped hot from his foot, concerned more for his wife, who couldn't stop weeping as she had delicately cleaned and dressed the deep wound.

"It's a bit of blood, that's all, nothing to fret about," he had said, stroking Tamura's hair, looking skeptical as she had applied a thick poultice of yarrow to the gaping gash. Catching her father's eye,

Satomi had cut her smile before Tamura saw it. Neither of them had much faith in her mother's homemade remedies.

The memory of that day, the three of them together in the warm kitchen, the way her father had given her a comforting wink, both healed and hurt. The wound had closed, but forever after Aaron had sported a red starburst of broken veins just above the joint of his smallest toe. And suddenly at last, with the thought of that scar being burned away, of Aaron being burned away, her tears come, taking her by surprise, falls of them that she can't hold back.

"I wish that I could have been a son for him," she sobs to Tamura, who nods her head in what Satomi takes for agreement.

Silently promising Aaron, wherever he might be, that she will always look after Tamura, she hopes with all her heart that in his last moments he hadn't looked up and seen the red sun of Japan on the wings of the attacking planes. That he hadn't at the end lost his love of things Japanese.

In the days that follow Tamura's revival, Satomi listens to the radio, attempting to engage with the world. It's hard to know what to think about America being at war with Japan. She's on America's side, of course, but still that the enemy should be Japan, that her father's murderers should be Japanese, is strange to think of.

Despite the loss of Aaron, the reports of troops massing, the talk of *our boys in uniform*, it's hard in her isolation to actually feel at war. It might be easier to accept if she could hear the sound of distant gunfire, if she had Lily and Artie to talk it over with, to be scared with.

In the books she has read, war usually takes place on some distant plain, men's stuff, the women left to wait and worry. Heroes rally in the thick of it, some come back to figure in their women's lives, some like her father are lost from the plot. Now there's no one left for her and Tamura to wait for. Impossible as it seems, their lives must go on without Aaron.

They haven't the energy for making new agendas. She refuses to go to school, but still the crops must be tended, the sheds kept in order, the hens fed. Birds still sing in the trees, there is no need to run for cover.

Tamura now speaks of Japan as though it is a wicked relation that she is ashamed of. Japan has abandoned her, just as she now abandons it. Her loyalty to Aaron requires no less of her. Japan killed Aaron, it is beyond forgiveness.

"Thank God I'm an American," she says, as though to convince herself. "Thank God that we are an American family."

Satomi senses the conflict in her mother. Tamura is a child of both America and Japan. She is a democrat in the grasp of tradition, a Westerner with the blood of Japan in her veins.

The fact that Aaron isn't ever coming home, not even in a coffin, fights against the reality of his death. Still desperate for it not to be true, Tamura annoyingly continues to suggest unlikely possibilities.

"He could have been wounded, not killed. He might have lost his memory, forgotten his name."

"No, that can't be so, Mama. They buried Father, they had a service."

Tamura's stubbornness is both pitiable and exasperating. Her mother's insistence on hope when they both know that there is none seems unnervingly infantile to her. But Tamura's stubbornness is not about accepting Aaron's death any longer, it's about putting life on hold for a while, about learning to accept a different future than the one she had planned with Aaron. It's about the necessity she feels to stay loyal to who she was when Aaron was alive, to remain the American wife that he made her.

Now that Aaron has gone she must launch herself into widowhood, something she has no idea how to do, something that holds only revulsion for her. She thinks of her mother, her papa, her brother, and knows now that she will never see them again. No matter how much it hurts, she will be true to Aaron. For as long as she lives she will never break their agreement. It will just be her and Satomi. They must be enough for each other now. But everything is a struggle, so that there are times when she feels as though she is suffocating.

"I can't breathe," she wails. "It's as though I'm drowning."

Satomi puts her arms around Tamura, holds her close until her mother calms and pulls away.

"It will get better, Mama. It has to get better."

"It would help if someone would tell us how he died. I'm still waiting for someone to tell us whether he suffered or not."

They had heard about the burnings, the ships on fire, men and metal littering the water. How could he not have suffered?

Satomi can hardly bear Tamura's pain. Her smiling girlish mother has disappeared, perhaps for good. And it's not so different for her. She has never been so sad or so scared herself. They are alone, haven't spoken to anyone for days. Even Elena has stayed away, her absence serving to heighten their fears about going to town.

"It will be Hal, not Elena," Satomi consoles Tamura. "He'll be on her case more than ever now."

Nothing and everything has changed. They work their way through the days, the same chores, the same fieldwork, an infestation of roaches that draws little emotion from them. They feel strangely empty, ghosts going about the business of the living.

Tamura's nightmares are so bad that she has begun to fear sleep. She screams out in them as though she is being burned up herself, so that Satomi runs to her, shaking her awake, bringing her back to a reality that is as hateful to her as her dreams.

And then Mr. Stedall calls again with a letter from a man who had served alongside Aaron. Some of their questions are answered. Others, though, are posed that will never find an answer.

Dear Mrs. Baker,

I hope that it is okay me writing you. My name is Milton Howley, Milt for short. I don't want to stir things up but I thought that you would want to know how Aaron was at the end. I worked alongside him in the ship's kitchen and I guess that you could say we were friends. He was a pretty good cook and had a good sense of humor.

I was on shore about to return to the ship when the attack happened, so I was saved. Guess I was luckier than most that day. Anyway, I met the nurse who treated him on the dock, and she was of the opinion that I should write and tell you that he didn't suffer.

Aaron was blasted into the drink in the first wave of the attack. One of those Jap bombs set fire to our magazine and sunk our ship like a stone. I reckon he must have been unconscious before he was fished out of the water. The nurse I spoke of treated his burns with tannic jelly, but I think that he had already gone by then. So you see he couldn't have known much about it.

Only the officers were sent home to their families for burial, so Aaron was buried in Oahu Cemetery along with his shipmates in a very fine service. There's a cross with his name marking the plot, so it won't be hard to find when you come. Some of the locals put flowers from their gardens on the graves, red poinsettias and hibiscus I'm told. I'm not much of a plant man myself but I thought that you might want to know that. Aaron was a good buddy and I will miss him, not more than you and your daughter Elena of course, but I sure will miss him. I'm clear in my mind that we'll make those lousy Japs pay for what they did, have no fears on that score.

I pray for you both.

Respectfully yours
Milton Howley

"Elena! His daughter Elena! Why would Father have said that?"

"'Lousy Japs'?" Tamura shakes her head in disbelief. "Didn't Aaron tell him I am Japanese?" She gave a soft little mewl at the thought of being denied by Aaron.

"I guess not." Satomi kisses Tamura's cheek, her forehead. "Perhaps it was easier for him that way, Mama. What with all the talk and bad feeling around."

"I thought that he was proud of us."

"He wasn't ashamed of us. You know he wasn't ashamed of us. It was probably just less hassle for him that way."

"I wanted to call you Elena, you know, but he wouldn't have it." Tamura is wailing now. "He was firm that it had to be a Japanese name. He wanted it to be a Japanese name."

"There you are, then, Mama. It must have been just a way for him to get through. You know how mean people can be."

But in explaining it away to Tamura, she can't understand it herself. Aaron's denial of her name, of her, makes her question if she ever really knew him. For her father, of all people, to hide his Japanese family from his white shipmates went against everything she had always believed him to be.

No matter that she and Tamura agree that Milt Howley hadn't really known Aaron, that he couldn't have been a close friend, the hurt of it won't go away. The thought of it wakes her in the night, wounds her throughout the day.

"For one thing," Tamura says, outraged, "your father never

mentioned this Milt person in his letters, and I think that this 'good cook, good sense of humor' proves that they were never really close. I loved your father, but no one who knew him could say that he had a good sense of humor."

"No, you're right. Father never saw the funny side of things."

Neither of them wants to go on questioning who it is that they have lost, who it is that they are grieving for. They dredge up every memory of Aaron that they can and improve on it. While they are holding in mind the good husband that he had been, he is becoming in legend the good father that he had not been.

"Saint Aaron," Satomi says under her breath, without malice.

She has begun to care for her mother in the knowledge that she is the stronger of the two, but not strong enough, she thinks. It's no fun being in charge, she wants her old mother back. Under Tamura's steel-rimmed spectacles her eyes have lost their light, they are like dull little buttons. She looks but doesn't see. She hardly smiles at all these days, and she won't talk about the future.

"Let's be still for a while, Satomi. Live quietly in the day."

But since the day that those of her mother's blood had killed her father, the future looms as never before. She is full of fear for what might be ahead of them. Despite what happened to Aaron, no doubt they are outcasts now. Both are nervous about testing the water in town.

"It may not be so bad, Mama. And we can't hide out here forever."

Satomi doesn't feel as brave as she sounds. She doesn't believe Angelina will allow her to be the daughter of a hero, and they won't accept Tamura as the wife of one, that's for sure. Aaron's death, she thinks, will weigh light on the scales against the guilt of Tamura's race.

Rising at first light, going to bed with the dark, they are eager after the day to be out of each other's company, to stop for a few hours the pretense that they can continue as they are. They never discuss whether they can run the farm profitably without Aaron, whether they should sell up and find a new way to live.

"I've finished with school, thank God," Satomi insists, hoping that Tamura might find the parent in herself and encourage her to return.

"That's fine, Satomi. You're grown-up now, I guess."

After years of wanting it she longs now not to be grown-up, to be instead a helpless child, to have decisions made for her. But even in the face of their need Tamura seems incapable of action. They are running out of everything, living on hen eggs and their dwindling supply of rice.

"At least we still have eggs," Tamura says disinterestedly.

The hens, though, as if they know Tamura has given up on them, have taken to laying sporadically, and some days not at all.

"Even your cockerel can hardly be bothered to crow," Satomi says.

"They're not used to you, that's all," Tamura says. "It's no good just throwing the feed at them, you have to talk to them, encourage them."

"They want you back, Mama. They'll start laying again as soon as they hear your voice."

She herself misses the sweet bell of Tamura's voice singing the nursery songs of her childhood to her farmyard audience.

Neither of them can bear the idea of wringing a neck or two for the pot.

"Your father always said he couldn't understand it. Two squeamish farm girls. But I just can't do it. Those surprised little eyes, their warm feathers. I just can't."

"We're too soft," Satomi says in despair.

If they needed an excuse not to go to town, it comes in the form of Elena summoning them on the horn of Hal's truck, calling to them from the passenger seat, the bulk of Hal restless at the wheel.

"Give it a week or two, Tamura. People ain't making much sense at the moment. You're better off at home."

Satomi moves toward the truck. "Can you buy us some rice, some flour, Elena?"

Hal's face reddens with anger; he puts his foot down on the gas and the pickup starts rolling forward.

"Damn it, Elena, I said you could wave," he growls. "No way are you gonna do their marketing for them." He leans across her and begins winding up the window.

"Best you keep to yourselves," he shouts. "Elena's got enough on her plate with her own work."

If it was up to him he'd send them all back to Japan, or better still cull the lot of them. His wife is too soft, her judgment when it comes to their Jap neighbor way off.

As the truck hauls away, Satomi runs to the coop, picks up the nearest hen, and wrings its neck.

In the aftermath of December seventh, the town speaks with one voice. All Japanese are spies or saboteurs. No exceptions. Over the weeks leading up to Christmas, Angelina's Japanese do their best to hide themselves away. No Japanese child attends school, their parents rely for their meals on their stored supplies and what they can grow. Best to steer clear of Main Street for a while.

Those of the second and third generations begin to question their routines. Perhaps they don't need to go to their Japanese-language classes with Mr. Sakatani. Japanese is the language of the enemy, after all. Perhaps their mothers should choose fried chicken over sushi more often.

Mr. Beck, lacking drama in his own life and with an audience of white faces before him, is free to fire up his class with his own outrage. His lurid description of what happened at Pearl Harbor, the details he goes into of explosions and of good Christian

Americans innocently saying their prayers that Sunday morning before the attack, thrills his pupils in much the same way that his reading of Longfellow's "Paul Revere's Ride" had the year before. *Listen my children and you shall hear . . .*

Their teacher's righteous fury, his gory descriptions of shrapnel slicing through skin, of human balls of fire, heats their blood, invites them to accept that only Americans can be trusted to act honorably.

With shaking voice he raises his hand and quotes Franklin Delano Roosevelt.

December seventh, 1941, is a date that will live in infamy.

Artie, listening to Mr. Beck's ravings, suffers a twinge when he thinks that now he has to think of Satomi as the enemy. Mr. Beck has advised him to stay away from her, Japanese blood is Japanese blood, and that's that.

"If ever there was a time to choose sides, Artie, it's now," he counsels, as much to himself as to Artie.

Artie doesn't want to stay away, though. He wants to tell her that he is sorry for taking the ring back, that he'd just gotten caught up in the action, that she's not to blame for the attack. He thinks about her all the time, daydreams about running away with her after the war. They could pretend that she is Italian or something, she could get away with that easy. And now that Mr. Baker is dead she needs a guy around, a guy like him.

But he's in a fix with Lily. According to her they are going steady now, which is odd because he isn't sure how that came about, how suddenly his class ring is on her finger.

"This is for you, Artie," she had said, fixing a REMEMBER PEARL HARBOR pin on his shirt. I guess you should let me wear your class ring for the time being. Just so people know you're not hankering after Satomi. We've all got to pull together now."

"I guess that's the way to go, at least till things quieten down," he had said, handing over the ring, thinking that a week or two should get the message over. But Lily's showing no signs of handing the ring back, even though he's given enough hints.

From the moment she trapped him, he's had to put up with the feel of her pushing up against him, following him around as though they are meant to be together. It's not doing his reputation any good. She's no Satomi, and although he'd go there, no way would it be more than once. He's in a different league than Lily Morton, after all.

Artie rolls his eyes, crosses his fingers, and hopes for the best. But, propelled into war, the town isn't about to quiet down anytime soon. Along with the rest of America it's obsessed with Japan, with the nature of the beast that had attacked them. The radio comes at it from every angle, so that no other news gets a look in. Angelina, though, scarcely needs the rest of America's righteous anger to lend oxygen to the flame of its own fury.

Satomi listens in too, as fascinated as anyone. She doesn't know how things are going to change for her and Tamura, but she knows enough now to be afraid.

"I don't want to hear it anymore," Tamura says, sick at heart. "Keep that crackling thing in your room if you want."

She does want, needs to be in touch. Her world has narrowed down to the quiet house, the lonely fields. She has the sensation that Tamura is shrinking too. She seems shorter, thinner, the frown lines between her eyebrows deepening by the day.

She feels older herself, an equal to Tamura. If it wasn't for the sound of the Kaplans' pickup coming and going, they could believe themselves to be the last people in California.

Without school, without Lily, without town, where is she meant to place herself? Who is she now that Aaron is dead other than a girl with one parent, one Japanese parent?

Aaron's newspaper still comes in the mail, its pages filled with eyewitness accounts of the raid, photographs of the destroyed port, of felled sailors. She examines every picture in detail, as though she might find her father somewhere in them among the debris. *I know, I know,* she thinks with her stomach muscles clenching, *something must be done, we must have movement.* Tamura must be pulled back from the edge, they must face town, attempt to live normally.

On a day when long white clouds string the sky and the sun sits hazy in its field of blue so that everything looks new, she gathers up the books Mr. Beck has lent her, and on the pretext of going for a walk heads to the outskirts of town, where he lodges with the pharmacist's widow in a double-fronted weatherboard.

The old house is less imposing than she remembers it. Yellowing nets droop at the windows, the gate hangs crooked on its broken latch. Weeds crowd the grass so that the once-smooth turf is now more meadow than lawn. Despite its former style, its pretensions, now in its fading there is something of the shack about it. The wavering she had felt at calling on Mr. Beck unannounced slips from her.

Skirting an old incense cedar that leans toward the house at an unsettling angle, she takes the creaking steps two by two, and is assailed by the faint whiff of mold coming off an ancient cane rocker. Just the place for Mr. Beck, she thinks, substantial, but peeling.

Long before her ring is answered, she hears a slow shuffle along the hall, a heavy sighing.

"You wait here, girl," the widow says. "Sit on the porch if you like."

She doesn't sit, she wants to be standing when Mr. Beck comes.

"I'm returning your books," she says when he does. "I've finished with school, no time for it anymore; my mother can't manage the land on her own."

"Did you read them all?" he asks, taking the string-tied bundle from her, careful not to let his hand touch hers.

"All but *Little Women*. I never got around to that one."

"Ah. So what now, Satomi?"

"You tell me, Mr. Beck. Any suggestions?"

"Well, a girl like you wasn't made for farming, that's for sure. I'd head east if I were you, before things get worse 'round here."

"And leave our land, leave my mother?"

"It's a problem, I can see that."

Mr. Beck tries not to think about Satomi Baker these days. He'd like his mind to let her go, but you can't order those things, visceral things, he thinks. At the sight of her the old familiar rhythm in his heart has kicked in, a dull sort of pulling. He doesn't want to feel it, it's unsettling, will take him down a dead end, he knows that for sure. He can't fool himself, though, the cut has been made, and she has somehow been wired into his emotions. He smells the clean scent of her, notes her hands shaking a little. It has taken courage for her to come, but she has overcome her fear. She makes him feel old beyond his years, already on the downward slope.

"Can I ask you something, Mr. Beck?" She hadn't known that she was going to, or that she cared about his answer.

He pauses, putting his head to one side as though considering.

"I guess," he says hesitantly.

"I've always wanted to know where you placed me in your class."

"Placed you?"

"Yes, was I white or Japanese to you?"

"Oh, I don't know. Know that I favored you, though."

"Wrong answer, Mr. Beck."

"What's the right one?"

"Wish I knew."

Some way along the road home she hears him calling and turns, squinting into the sun, waiting for him to catch up with her.

"You should read *Little Women*," he says breathlessly when he does. "My present to you, no need to return it." He hands over the book. "If you do read it, though, the answer to your question might be that I think of you as half Jo, half Meg."

She takes the book and laughs. "Half and half, of course, that's just perfect. Thanks, Mr. Beck."

Much as it goes against its citizens' idea that the United States is the most powerful nation on earth, there is no disguising the fact that the Japanese have come out on top. The attack, lit by the rising sun, planned down to the last detail, had been exquisitely efficient. People can't sleep easy in their beds anymore. To be American, it seems, doesn't mean you can't get your ass whipped.

"They won't catch us sleeping again," they brag in Angelina.

"Yeah, chose their time, all right, the sneaky bastards."

"Can't call what they did a fair fight."

But however much they puff themselves up, the realists among them know that it is going to take more than bravado to send those *cocky bastards* to hell. Angelina along with the rest of America is already paying in blood, Aaron's included.

"Not one condolence letter from anyone in town," Tamura says. "Not one word of regret for our loss."

The harsh realization that Aaron's death is to count for nothing in the judging of them brings with it an anger that Satomi nurtures. Anger feels better than the grief that comes when she is off guard.

At first Tamura refuses to write to Aaron's parents.

"They didn't love your father. They chose to lose him years ago."

"Maybe, Mother, but it's your duty to let them know. It's only fair."

Unable to resist the idea of duty, Tamura writes a single page telling them of Aaron's death. She says that she feels for them in their loss, but that she will never return to Hawaii herself. Perhaps one day Aaron's daughter Satomi might.

A few lines come in return. Aaron, they say, has been dead to them from the moment he chose to marry her and disgrace them. They are old now and have no wish to know his Japanese family. They ask Tamura to leave them in peace.

"That's the end of it," Tamura says. "It's what I expected."

"It doesn't matter, Mother. You did your duty, that's what counts."

They greet Christmas without enthusiasm. Tamura catches a bad case of flu and stops eating again.

"I've seen blood on the moon," she says. "It means that there is worse to come."

"Well, if there is, we'll face it together. We still have each other, Mother."

"Satomi, you do not understand that without a husband a woman has no purpose. There is no dignity in being a widow."

"There's dignity in being a mother, surely?"

When Tamura takes a turn for the worse, complaining that she is freezing one minute, burning up the next, Satomi runs to town in a panic and asks for Dr. Wood to call.

"He's not here," his wife says. "Babies still get born, Christmas or not. They call him out at all hours."

"Be sure to tell him when he gets back," Satomi insists. "My mother is very ill. Tell him it's urgent."

"Sure thing," the woman says, and closes the door on her.

It comes to her later as darkness falls, as her mother's temperature rises so high that she imagines insects crawling on her blanket, that Dr. Wood isn't coming.

"Don't worry, I'll make you better, Mama. I promise I'll make you better."

It's a week before Tamura rallies and takes a cup of soup, and the last of the sweet dark beans that she likes.

"Sleep and food is what you need," Satomi says. "Everything will be fine, you'll see."

While Tamura sleeps, she walks the mile into town stoking her anger to keep her courage up and raps twice on Dr. Wood's door.

"You didn't come. You knew my mother was ill and you didn't come." She faces him with a racing heart.

"Listen, girl, 'bout time you knew your place," he snarls. "Strutting around our town as if you own it. If you want a doctor, get a Japanese one."

"There isn't a Japanese doctor in Angelina, you should know that, Dr. Wood."

"Nothing much I can do about that."

"No, but you took an oath, didn't you, a promise to care for the sick?"

"I don't have to answer to you, girl. Best thing you can do is to get yourself home, learn some manners."

"You broke your word, Dr. Wood. My mother has never broken a promise in her life. Doesn't make you much of a doctor, does it?"

She walks home, hardly noticing the slanting drizzle that soaks through her jacket, and slicks her hair to the color of her mother's. Stopping at the roadside to wretch up a thin colorless bile, she thinks that it is one fight after another, will she ever get used to it? Maybe Mr. Beck had been right, maybe she and Tamura should leave Angelina. It feels to her as though it has already let them go anyway.

Next morning at dawn she takes the feed to the chickens and finds a bag of groceries propped against the wire of their run. Two bags of rice, a small sack of flour, two lemons, and a paper twist of tea.

I'll fetch more when I can, is faintly written in pencil on the bag.

Elena had come in the night as Hal slept. Satomi sits on the ground and howls.

"I'm sorry to have missed Christmas," Tamura says. "I know that you like it."

"I don't care about it, Mama. I never have, you know that."

It isn't true; despite Aaron's scoffing, Christmas has always seemed to her a magical time. Lily used to give her a little gift of candy and a homemade card, and Mr. Beck buys the class a big bag of peanuts in their shells to share. The general store dresses its window with cotton wool snow, and sets a SEASON'S GREETINGS sign fringed with tinsel above its door. She thinks it enchanting.

"When I was a girl," Tamura says, "even though we weren't Christians, I always loved the lights they put up along Nuuana Avenue. Do you think they have put them up this year, despite everything?"

"We could go and see. We could visit Father's grave and maybe even see your mother too. We have money in the bank. Let's use it, Mother. Let's go."

"No, that would not be right. I will never return to Hawaii. Your father would not like me to break our agreement. I don't need a grave to find him. He is in the fields, in the candlelight, and in you. In any case I couldn't bear to see his name there among the dead."

"I know, I know. I understand," Satomi says, although she doesn't. Why would her mother not wish to visit her husband's grave? Why would she not wish to break the cycle of their confinement?

"Should I get the Buddhist priest to visit you, Mother? I'm sure that he will come if we ask, and it might help you."

Tamura shakes her head. "I do not know him, Satomi. In any case, I have no religion left in me, it would be pointless."

THE ROUNDUP

THREE MONTHS AFTER Aaron's death, the order to vacate their home is delivered to them by Mr. Stedall, the man they now can't help but associate with bad news.

"It's not my doing," he says, his forehead creased in concern. "Don't shoot the messenger."

"What is it now, Mr. Stedall?" Satomi asks.

"It's not good, not good at all, I'm afraid."

"When was it ever?"

"November '41, I guess."

The notice of *Instructions to all persons of Japanese ancestry, both alien and non-alien*, is issued by something called the Civil Control Administration.

"Never heard of it, myself," Mr. Stedall says.

He has brought the leaflet on his own initiative, knowing that the Baker women don't go to town these days, where the notices are tacked on poles and shop fronts and are hard to miss. Better they should know and have time to prepare. Mrs. Baker has suffered enough shock for one small woman, surely.

They have four days to quit their home, four days to leave their farm and their lives. No wonder Mr. Stedall feels bad at being the bearer of such news. No wonder he rocks on his bicycle as he peddles away from them.

Along with their Japanese neighbors, they are to be sent to a detention camp and must present themselves on the due day at the Angelina assembly area, which turns out to be the hastily renamed bus station, out by the peach-canning factory on the road heading west.

By Executive Order 9066, Franklin Roosevelt demands that all those of Japanese ancestry, those with any Japanese blood at all, are to be excluded from the entire Pacific coast. That means all of California and most of Oregon and Washington too. It means the Japanese residents of Angelina, and it means Tamura and Satomi.

Satomi reads the notice to Tamura, the paper trembling in her hand so that the writing blurs and she has to keep starting over. Tamura sits upright and very still in her chair, the formality of the phrasing confusing her. Surely it can't be true; Satomi has put the emphasis in the wrong place, or she herself has misheard. What is a *non-alien* other than an American citizen?

"Are you sure it says that? Can it be possible that it says that?"

"It does say that, but I'll read it again slowly, to be certain."

When she has finished, Tamura rises from her chair and says quietly, "Yes, that is what it says, then."

"How can this man remove us from our home, Mother? Surely he doesn't have the right, it's un-American."

"He is the president of the United States. We are nothing to him."

"Father voted for him didn't he? He must have trusted him."

The shocking news seems too much to be absorbed in one go, but the awful certainty that there is no way out brings them to the edge of hysteria. Something hideous is about to happen to them, something without reason, a horrible thing that they are powerless to stop.

The questions come, each one prompting another that has no answer.

"Where will they send us?"

"What will they do with us?"

"How will we live?"

"What will happen to the farm?"

"We must stay together, whatever happens," Satomi says. "We mustn't let them separate us."

"No, we must not be separated," Tamura repeats, while harboring an unspoken terror that even their lives might be in danger.

In the raw panic that overtakes them, tending the crop seems pointless; even cooking is beyond them. They walk about in circles, the shock the news has brought dragging at their insides. Satomi, as though watching through others' eyes, sees their pacing as spinning, it's the nearest thing to spinning, she thinks. By dusk they are tired out. Sliding into static mode, they wait as though on alert for the ice to crack, the sea to swallow them up.

Sleep is out of the question. Satomi takes herself to her mother's bed, where they talk and hold each other until dawn breaks and they feel the need for coffee.

"How will we make coffee at this 'detention center'?" Tamura asks.

"I don't know, Mama, I don't know the answer to anything. Maybe they will make coffee for us."

She watches Tamura walk the tidy house, watches her touch every bit of furniture as though taking leave of old friends. She watches her stroke the curtains, and lock the linen box, and take down the china from the big pine dresser that Aaron had made for her.

Seeing her mother's pain, she determines never to love too much the place she lives in, never to allow any building to hold part of her in its fabric. Yet under the eviction threat she can't help feeling a new love for the place herself.

After a couple of days the fog in her head clears and memories come flooding as she paces around their property. Memories of Artie kissing her at the side of the log shack, putting his tongue in her mouth so that she could taste the lemonade he had been drinking, sweet and sour at the same time. She recalls his voice as clearly, as though he is standing next to her saying it over again: "Don't be a tease. Nobody likes a tease."

In the packing shed she stands in a shaft of light remembering a day when through her fingers she had watched, with dread in her heart, her father tenderly, one by one, drown five perfect little kittens that had been born in the dark behind the box stack.

"Two cats are all the farm needs," he had said, as though speaking of spades or pitchforks. Her father's certainty seems like something wonderful now, something safe and protecting.

And how old had she been that long hot summer when she had spied on her parents? Thirteen, she'd been thirteen, and all grown up, she had thought then. The memory of the girlish arc of her mother's back, her father's rough work hands, the glowing room, is still crystal clear. Tamura had been happy then. Would she ever be again?

It comes to her that wherever life is to take her, the Baker place is the only home she has ever known, and that all her memories of her childhood on the farm will come now with a serving of pain. Order 9066 will in her future mark her past, and make it hard for her to call herself an American.

They shakily go over the list of orders that came with the notice. They are to take with them only those possessions that they can carry themselves. They should include enamel plates, eating utensils, and some bedding. They are not to pack food or cameras. Radios are forbidden, as is alcohol. They must report at ten A.M. They must be on time.

Tamura begins packing the one small suitcase they own, while Satomi uses the old duffel bag that usually hangs behind the kitchen door, housing potatoes.

Apart from a few clothes and the Indian blanket from her bed, there is nothing much Satomi wants to take, so Tamura fills the rest of the duffel with things that remind her of Aaron. Mania possesses her as she packs his clothes and shoes, a bar of his shaving soap, an old tobacco pouch. She is not to be dissuaded.

"I need to breathe him in, I want to breathe him in," she says, weeping. "And what will happen to them if I don't?"

"What will happen to everything here? Just take your own things, Mama, just the stuff you will need."

Sick at heart, she watches as Tamura fills the bag, hiding their last small sack of rice in the bottom. The sight of it fills her with shame. They are refugees now, to be herded to God knows where in their own country.

Elena comes sneaking across the field, hugging the woods' perimeter so as not to be seen by her husband.

"I've heard they may search your place," she says. "You should burn anything incriminating. Things will be bad enough for you, no need to bring extra trouble to your door."

"We have nothing incriminating, Elena. What could we have?"

"Oh, I don't know, Tamura. Anything that could tie you to Japan, I suppose. Photographs, that sort of thing."

"Photographs? Oh, yes, photographs," Tamura says, confused.

She takes Elena's hand, her eyes stinging with tears. "You are a good friend," she says. "We will not forget you."

"Life's hard enough on the land." Elena is weeping too. "You'd think they could leave us in peace to get on with it. You don't deserve this, Tamura. Look after your mother, Sati."

They watch her until she is halfway up the field, watch her dart in and out of the trees, skimming the margin between field and wood. They watch her go, willing her on. If Hal catches her, this time they won't be around to see bruises.

Tamura goes to the yard and starts a little fire with sticks and grass. She takes the book of Japanese fairy tales that Satomi had loved as a child, the photograph of her mother standing outside her father's shop that she had kept hidden from Aaron, and lets the flames eat them.

"They would prefer us to burn ourselves, I suppose," she says.

The day before they are due to leave, they summon up the courage to go to the bank to withdraw the money from the farm account, only to find that it has been frozen. The clerk, polite but juiced up with the power to say no, says that it is the same for all the Japanese.

"Rules are rules, Mrs. Baker, but you needn't worry none. I guess it will only be a temporary measure."

"Ha! And whose rules are they?" Satomi sneers.

"Government rules, Mrs. Baker," he says, ignoring Satomi. "We all have to obey the government."

When they are back in the truck, numb with shock, a weary resignation overtakes them. It is becoming a habit to accept. Even so, Tamura is too upset to drive safely. She tries, but her steering is erratic, so that she veers toward the middle of the road, alarming the oncoming traffic.

"We need gas, Satomi." Her voice is thin, shaky, she's on the verge of tears. "Just enough to get us home, no point in getting too much. I'll pull in and you can drive back. Who cares if we break the rules now?"

At the gas station, the JAP TRADE NOT WANTED sign brings Satomi back to herself with a jolt.

"We have always bought our gas here," Tamura says, shaking her head in disbelief. "I remember when they started up and were glad of our business. How can they do this to us now?"

"Because they are idiots, Mother. Small-brained idiots, that's why."

"Let's go, Satomi, it doesn't matter. We're the same people; it's them who have changed."

"It does matter, and they should know it."

Tamura parks up by the pump with a sinking heart. Satomi holds her hand on the horn, rousing the chained dog to barking.

"We ain't serving gas to Japs no more," the red-faced youth she knows from school tells her. "You'd best try elsewhere."

"Who are you to tell me that, Kenny Buchan?" she shouts, getting out of the truck, walking around it to face him. She's so fired up it's an effort not to hit him. Tamura slides over to the passenger side, calling to her to let it go.

"My father died defending this country, defending you." Satomi pokes him in the chest so that he staggers a bit. "You weren't worth it."

The boy shrugs, takes a step backward. He knows Satomi Baker isn't above landing a punch, but you can't hit girls, not even Jap ones, not even the ones who hit you.

"Don't make no difference what you say, we don't serve gas to Japs." He is on his guard, just waiting for her to make a move.

Something about the set of his stupid face, the lank hair cut straight above his ears, the hillbilly overalls, makes her want to laugh.

"Relax, Kenny," she says. "You're not worth bothering with."

Getting behind the wheel, she winds down the window and calls to his retreating back, "Just a kid doing his mama's bidding."

Five hundred yards or so from the farm, they run out of gas and leave the truck on the single-track road, walking home in silence.

That afternoon Tom Myers, a greasy sort of man with small eyes and a brain to match, calls at the farm in the bigger of his two trucks.

"Saw your vehicle a way back," he says. "We had to shove it into the bank to get past."

"We ran out of gas, Mr. Myers," Tamura explains. "I'm sorry to have held you up."

"Sure, no problem. I've come to help you out, Mrs. Baker. I'll give you twenty dollars for everything in the house, and thirty for the truck. You won't do better anywhere."

"I don't think so, Mr. Myers, we are not about to sell anything."

"It's cash, Mrs. Baker, and I'm betting you could do with cash. In any case, none of it's any use to you now. Who knows if you'll ever get back?"

"I can't tell you that, Mr. Myers, I don't even know where we are going. I do know, though, that I'm not selling."

"Well, that's your choice, of course—not a good one, but yours. At least let me take that old truck off your hands. Left there, it'll just rust up, and you ain't getting gas around here anytime soon."

"As I said, Mr. Myers, we aren't selling anything."

"More fool you, then, Mrs. Baker. Let me know if you change your mind." He cracks a mean, broken-toothed smile and swaggers back to his truck. "It'll all get stolen, you know. You can bet on it."

"Only by thieves, Mr. Myers, only by no-good thieves." A small muscle tightens in Tamura's forehead; she keeps her shoulders straight. It seems important not to cry in front of Tom Myers.

Satomi puts her arm around Tamura's thin shoulders and hugs her. She has never loved her mother more.

"Your father always said that Tom Myers was so greedy that he would eat the world if he could."

It occurs to Satomi that it is a wonderful truth that, no matter who has the upper hand, people like Tom Myers will always make a poor showing against people like her mother.

The day arrives relentlessly as any other. A while before dawn there's a spattering of rain, then in the rising sun a rainbow arcs over the house.

"I used to think that was a blessing, a time for spells," Tamura says. "What a foolish woman I am."

It seems that hardly any time has elapsed in the space between Mr. Stedall bringing the leaflet and this morning. The four days have merged into one so that Satomi hardly knows what they have done with the time in between. Shouldn't they have already closed the shutters, locked the sheds, checked the rattraps? They need more time, much more time.

In an act more of possession than of habit, Tamura makes her bed, tucking in the sheets tightly, smoothing the cover.

"Check that you have left your room tidy," she calls along the hall in a thin, breaking-up voice.

"What's the point? Who is there to care?"

"Only us, I suppose. Still, we have our pride."

To please Tamura Satomi plumps her pillow, straightens the sheets, and leaves it at that. The bed looks bare now without the lively colors of her Indian blanket, which is rolled around Aaron's tools in the duffel bag. She has put her seashell mirror, along with her schoolbooks, Mr. Beck's gift of *Little Women*, and the necklace that Lily made her from melon seeds, in an apple box under the bed, and shoved it tight to the wall. It has made her feel better, as though she will be coming back.

"These are going for sure," she insists, bunching up the flour-sack smocks into a ball and throwing them into the trash. A chalky powder rises up and catches at the back of her throat. The smell is worse than mothballs, worse than anything. There are some things she won't miss.

Tamura doesn't like the waste of it. "Don't get rid of too much," she advises. "Once they discover you are only half Japanese, you may be allowed to come home."

"Remember what they said, Mama?"

"No, there's too much going on to remember everything."

"They said one drop of Japanese blood justifies profiling—one drop, Mama!"

"My drop," Tamura says quietly.

"Father would have said the best drop, and I agree with him. In any case, it doesn't matter what they say, I don't care if it's one drop or a hundred, I'll never leave you."

To save Tamura from seeing it, she had thrown out the last copy of the *Los Angeles Times*. It had been jubilant at the announcement of the detention order, referring to the Japanese community as the enemy within and stating that "*a viper is nonetheless a viper wherever the egg is hatched.*"

They attempt to make the most of their last breakfast in the house. Who knows when they will eat again? An omelet for Tamura, and two eggs sunny-side up for Satomi. Neither of them have much of an appetite, though.

"Can you believe it, Mama, five eggs this morning?"

"A farewell gift." Tamura manages a smile.

She had gone that morning barefoot on the damp earth to the chicken coop and collected the warm eggs from under her sitting hens.

"How lovely," she told them. "Your eggs are beautiful."

She would have lain down with her cackling chickens if she could. Buried herself in their warm straw, let the world go its brutal way.

Taking a quarter sack of grain that the rats had been at, she made a trail of it halfway up to the Kaplans' place.

"Shush, go." She set them on it. "I won't be stealing your eggs anymore."

"They'll follow it soon enough," she tells Satomi. "Elena might as well have the benefit of them. The cats will have to see to themselves. It is unkind, but what can we do?"

"Cats are survivors, Mama. They will adopt a new family, I'm sure."

"Are we survivors, do you think, Satomi?"

Mindful that her answer might collapse what is left of Tamura's optimism, she answers, "You bet we are."

Knowing it is a drink Tamura always turns to in difficult times, she makes a pot of her mother's green tea and pours them both a cup. As they are sipping it, two dark-suited men walk into the house without knocking. They leave the front door swinging open so that the breeze bangs the back one shut.

"Federal investigators, Mrs. Baker," the bald one says.

"Aren't you supposed to knock, or show a badge or something?" Satomi asks, shaken.

"It's just an inspection, nothing to worry about. Everything legal and aboveboard."

The men set about a search, emptying drawers onto the floor, rifling through the closets, pulling the linen off the made beds to look under the mattresses.

"What's this?" the unsympathetic one says, holding out the pathetic little box Satomi had thought to squirrel away.

"It's trash, have it if you want it," she says, hot with shame.

"If you tell us what you are looking for, perhaps we can find it for you," Tamura says from the floor, where she is picking up the debris from the drawers.

"Any guns in the place, ma'am?"

"One." She nods toward where Aaron's rifle is propped in the corner.

"Hunting man, was he, your husband?"

"Just to keep the crows off the crops, the fox from the hens."

"It's confiscated for the duration."

Tamura watches him pick up the gun, run his hand slowly along the gleaming barrel of it admiringly. It's Aaron's gun and it hurts her to see the man handle it.

"We need to see the farm accounts and the will," he says, laying the gun on the table. Guess your husband left a will?"

"He didn't, he wasn't expecting to die so young, you see," Tamura says in the same voice she had used to refuse Tom Myers the truck.

"Where do you keep your knives, Mrs. Baker?"

She points to a drawer set in the kitchen table, and the bald one, who has been staring at Satomi, opens it and takes out a long carving knife.

"Show me where you keep seed, sacks of feed, and the like, honey." He guides Satomi toward the door.

"Don't push." Satomi shakes him off.

In the barn, with the knife he splits open every sack in the place. Fertilizer and chicken feed spill across the floor.

"Nope, nothing in them. I didn't think there would be, but you never know, girlie, you never know."

"I guess you're gonna sweep up all this mess." Satomi raises her eyebrows and tucks a strand of hair behind her ear.

"Not me, honey, not my job. You got a pitchfork in here?"

He takes Aaron's long-handled pitchfork from the rack, beckoning her to follow him outside.

"Best to be thorough," he says, raking through the compost heap, disturbing the worms.

Back in the house, she stands by the chair that Tamura has slumped in.

"It's okay, Mama," she says in an effort to comfort. "Everything will be fine."

"Sorry, Mrs. Baker, but we'll have to confiscate the radio and these binoculars. You'll get them back after the war, though. Everything done within the law eh?"

"So you keep saying," Satomi says.

"She's pretty, the girl, real pretty, ain't she?" the bald one announces to the room in general. "Don't you worry none, honey. Nothing to worry about, you're in America."

"Yeah, we're in America, all right," Satomi agrees.

"No need to be snappy, girlie. It wasn't us who bombed Japan, now, was it?"

"Can we go now?" she asks. "You don't need us here for this, do you?"

The fear has brought on a need to pee, but nothing would induce her to ask the men if she might use her own bathroom.

At the road's edge they turn to look back at the house and see the one who didn't smile pinning a FOR RENT sign on their door. A last check of the mailbox reveals an unsigned note written in pencil on the back of a feed label. *Good Luck.*

For a brief moment Satomi imagines it came from Lily and instantly feels foolish. Of course it isn't from Lily. How could she have thought it even for a second? Lily has let her go for good. Most likely Lily has a new rule to add to her list by now. No such thing as an American Jap.

"It's from Elena," Tamura says. "I guess she didn't want to sign it in case of trouble. They only tenant the berry farm. It's not a good time to take sides, is it?"

As though she is going somewhere nice, Tamura has dressed in her finest. She has chosen her blue-flowered dress to impress, a little felt pillbox of a hat to comfort. She slips the feed label into her mock-leather handbag, snapping the clasp shut with a sigh.

"There are still good people in the world, Satomi," she says. "Good people like Elena."

Every so often along the road Tamura has to stop and put the heavy suitcase down. Each time she does, something holds Satomi there long after Tamura has caught her breath. It is as though she has never seen the road before, never noticed the sweet scent of the pine trees, the little pockets of cattails, or the wild allium shoots springing up everywhere. She wonders briefly if there will be pine trees where they are going. She squats to pee behind some brambles and it occurs to her that like a dog she is marking her territory.

"Give me your case, Mother. I can carry both."

Like Tamura, she is wearing her best too. Her white for-Sundays-only dress, and over it a wool plaid jacket that had been Tamura's. Her shoes, a present for her fifteenth birthday, have inch-high heels that slim her calves and lend her the stance of a young woman. Tamura looks short beside her. She picks up Tamura's case, anxious not to show her mother how scared she is. Along with the farm, along with Lily and Artie, along with everything, she is leaving her childhood behind her.

Tamura is not yet recovered from her Christmas flu, which seems to have permanently stolen her appetite. She is pale still, and too thin. Her once-black hair has strands of gray showing through; her lips, too, have lost color. Despite her mother's rallying moments, Satomi knows that Tamura is crushed, and she fears for her sanity. She has read of such things, of women going mad with grief.

They hadn't been expecting anything good—how could it have been anything good?—but they aren't prepared for what meets them at the relocation point.

"Why are there soldiers with guns?" Tamura says nervously, not really expecting an answer, but needing to give voice to her fear.

The bus station is heaving with Japanese families, dressed, like them, in their best. Old men sit on their suitcases, looking bewildered. A huddle of elderly women surround the Buddhist priest, who is clutching his beads to his chest. He looks ancient and tired, too confused himself to be of any help to them. Children are playing in the dust at their mother's feet; they are subdued, silent in their play, as if they know instinctively that it's not a time to be troublesome. A lost child pulls at the hem of Satomi's dress. The little girl has a label big as her hand pinned to her coat, with a number scrawled in black ink across it.

"Where's your mother?" Satomi asks her in Japanese, smiling so that the girl won't be afraid.

The child starts to wail, twisting the fabric of Satomi's dress in her tiny hand, stamping her feet in the dust.

Dropping the case and bag to the ground, Satomi picks her up, cradling her in the crook of her arm. With her free hand she clasps Tamura's trembling one.

"It's all right, Mama, we're together, it's going to be all right."

The desire to take to her heels has never been stronger in her. She wants to run as fast as she has ever run—run to the deep woods, where the sweet whispering of the ghost pines will comfort her, lead her back to what she knows.

A frantic mother comes to claim the lost child, relief and fury mixed in equal measure on her face. Tamura thinks she recognizes her but can't remember from where. She says a polite hello. The woman hurries off without a word.

"I am glad that you are not a baby anymore," Tamura says softly, looking around her with horror. "How are these mothers to care for their babies without homes?"

Neither of them mentions it to the other, but they realize at about the same time that fear has a scent, a faint odor that conjures up sweat and piss and stagnant water.

"Join that line over there," a civilian with an armband directs them.

"No talking," orders a soldier young enough to be Tamura's son.

"Why do they have guns?" Tamura repeats, wanting an answer now.

"In case we try to escape, I guess."

A man in a civilian suit pulls them from the line and tells them to stand by the back of an open Army truck.

"Who are you? What is your family name?" he barks.

"Our family name is Baker," Satomi barks back.

"Point out your family."

"It is just the two of us, we are mother and daughter," Tamura says.

"You don't look Japanese." He looks at Satomi, his tone a touch less harsh than before.

"Maybe not, but I am Japanese. Japanese enough for this place, anyway."

"Where is your father?"

"He's dead." She stares him down. "He died in the attack at Pearl Harbor."

He pauses for a bit as though trying to work it out, but doesn't comment.

"Put your luggage up here on the tailgate. Open it up."

There is an air of refined brutality about him, something chilling in his pale eyes. Without knowing him, they can tell he is enjoying himself.

"What's all this stuff?" he protests, pulling out one of Aaron's tools from the Indian blanket, scattering his shirts around. "If it is just the two of you, why have you brought a man's things?"

He doesn't seem like the sort of person who would understand that Tamura needed to "breathe my husband in," so Satomi doesn't attempt an explanation.

He finds the rice, and a mean grin spreads across his face as he throws it into the back of the truck. The sack splits open and a shower of grains patter onto the metal floor of the tailgate. Tamura's eyes fill with tears; her hand flutters to her neck.

"I'm sorry," she says. "We didn't know, you see—"

"You were told what to bring, it was clear enough." He sighs and rolls his eyes. "It's all confiscated. You people never learn. Go and join that line over there, you need to be fingerprinted and tagged."

By the time their bit of the line has reached the bus station's washrooms, the men have been separated off. While the woman watch, they are strip-searched for contraband, for razors, for knives, and for the liquor it is held would drive them to mutiny.

The once-familiar bus station, a place where Satomi and Lily had often sneaked cups of ice from the cooler by the soda machine, has become a place she hardly recognizes. There is no one behind the kiosk bar, no Coke or candy on sale, no familiar drivers to joke with them about being truant from school. A mile or so from home, and they have become *non-aliens* on American soil. They are beginning to understand what the previously inexplicable words mean. They are politicians' words, sneaky, self-serving, hiding-from-the-truth words.

Quite a little crowd of townsfolk have come to see them off, a few name-calling, but most looking sympathetic. Mr. Beck is there, his face clown-white, his eyes seeking out Satomi in the crowd. When he sees her, his lips tighten and his eyes narrow as though he is in pain. She half expects him to do something dramatic, pull her away from the others, perhaps, and declaim that he must have his pupil back. But he doesn't move a limb, not even to wipe his watering eyes, which he can't blame on an absent wind.

Satomi looks for Artie and finds instead his father, Mr. Goodwin, holding up a hand-painted sign that reads REMEMBER PEARL HARBOR. The slogan has become ubiquitous. It is on stamps, on luggage tags, on belt buckles and lapel pins, it's hard-baked into ice-cream cones. How could the Japanese-Americans, of all people, ever forget Pearl Harbor?

It is past four o'clock by the time they are given numbers and their internees' records, which, to add insult to injury, have printed on them the advice that they should *Keep Freedom in Your Future with U.S. Savings Bonds.*

Satomi scrunches hers and gives it to Tamura to put in her bag.

"Stupid people," she says, too loudly for Tamura's comfort. "How can we buy saving bonds when they have stolen our money?"

Hand in hand, they join the line for the buses. Tamura's hand is warm despite the fact that she is shivering. Everyone is speaking Japanese, too quickly for Satomi to make much sense of. She is used to the plainsong of Tamura's slower intonations. With a burning rage that she has no idea what to do with, she bites her lip and moves forward in the line.

Inside the crowded bus the women and children are packed together without their men. They set to wailing when they are told to pull the window blinds down.

"They are going to kill our husbands," one woman shouts. "They don't want us to see."

"Oh, my son," another wails pitifully.

The children, terrified at their mothers' fear, join in, so that the driver has to shout over the racket to be heard.

"Settle down. The men will join you at the other end. The blinds are to keep the sun off you. You don't want to fry, do you?"

Some are still weeping a half hour later when the convoy of buses pulls slowly out of the station to start on the three-hundred-mile journey to a place that everyone fears reaching.

In the gloom of the shuttered bus, Tamura occupies herself with helping an elderly blind lady to settle on the narrow seat in front of her. She places the woman's tiny suitcase under her feet to make her more comfortable.

"I am Mrs. Inada," the old woman says. "I am sorry if my cough disturbs you. My chest is bad, but I will do my best to be quiet."

"I am pleased to know you, Mrs. Inada. My name is Tamura Baker."

"Ah, Tamura is a good name. Do you have a husband, a son, left out there?"

"My daughter Satomi is here with me. My husband is dead."

"Ah, then we are both widows. But at least you have a child. Mine, like his father, is dead also."

"There's no shame, only sadness in it," Tamura says, propping the old woman's jacket behind her shoulders in place of a pillow, touching her hand lightly.

It is the first time Satomi has heard her mother confess Aaron's death out loud. That she said there's no shame in it is reassuring.

"You should try and sleep, Mrs. Inada. You will feel better after a sleep," Tamura says.

The old woman grabs her arm. "You won't forget I'm here?"

"No, I will look out for you."

Satomi releases her window blind and the hazy afternoon sun pools into her lap. She watches the familiar landscape slip slowly away, the pea and strawberry fields, and the sign that reads CROMER'S UNBEATABLE PEAS.

Pressed up against the dusty window, she says a silent goodbye to the cemetery and to the rusty water tower where she had often sought shade. She says goodbye to the clump of self-set blueberries at the edge of the swimming hole, where she and Artie had dipped into the cool water on long careless summer days; days that were full of heat and desire and ignorance. She says goodbye to everything that feels familiar and suddenly unbearably loved.

TEMPORARY ACCOMMODATION

J UMPING THE STEPS of the bus in one go, Satomi turns at
the bottom to help Mrs. Inada down.

"My case," the old woman cries. "I've left my case."

"I have it," Tamura assures her. "I am right behind you."

There is joy at being reunited with the men; husbands console
wives, and mothers hug sons. Everyone, though, is dismayed at
the sight of the long-abandoned racetrack, at the reek of decay, and
at the cold officialdom that meets them at their destination. How
are they expected to live in such a desolate place?

"It's horrible, nothing but a freezing half stable. How can this
place be meant for humans?" Satomi gazes around in disbelief.

A single bulb hangs from the ceiling of their allotted stall, cast-
ing a dismal low-watt glimmer. Two Army cots stand against the
wall, a thin blanket folded neatly at the end of each, nothing else.
No furniture, no means of cooking.

They are told to line up to be issued canvas bags and a measure
of straw to make their mattresses.

"I will collect ours, Mother, and Mrs. Inada's."

As the daylight fades to dark, Tamura guides Mrs. Inada into
the stall with her.

"You must stay with us," she says. "We will look after you."

She is full of pity for the old blind woman, and everyone has to share. Better her than a total stranger.

An hour or so later, Satomi returns with the make-do mattresses. She has seen unimaginable things in the lines to collect the narrow sacks, grown men crying, women staring as though in a trance, adults obeying orders like children.

Mrs. Inada perches uncomfortably on the iron rim of her cot while Satomi arranges the mattress for her. Through the thin walls an old man's complaints come to them in Japanese, his voice shaking with rage. They guess it is his daughter they can hear attempting to quiet him in English.

"America makes much of freedom," he shouts scornfully. "But it has never truly understood what freedom means. They will not have it that it includes the right to be different."

"It's best not to be political, Doctor," a male voice calls from a neighboring stall. "We are in enough trouble as it is."

"Let him speak, it's only the truth," Satomi shouts, and Tamura *tsks* and puts a finger to her lips.

Satomi wonders if the old man is a medical doctor. It would be a relief to her if he was; Tamura does not look well, her eyes are dark-rimmed and sunken, and there is something febrile in her color. She hasn't taken even the smallest bite of the bread they were given as they left the bus.

"Take just a little, just a taste, Mama," she coaxes, attempting to keep her eyes from the walls that have been so hastily painted that bits of straw and spiders on their run to freedom have been caught up in the wash. What looks to be a mouse tail coils in a ball of fluff in the corner of the room; the floor is beaded with mouse droppings and splatters of whitewash.

With her back to Tamura, Satomi makes a fist of her hand and pushes it hard into her mouth to stop herself from moaning. Her knuckles bruise under the pressure of her teeth, a smear of blood salts her tongue.

It smells as though something has died in the hovel, something bigger than a mouse—a rat, perhaps. She must hold on to herself, try not to be afraid; she has Tamura to think of, after all. But for the moment, at least, Tamura seems to be doing better than her. She is talking softly to Mrs. Inada, covering her tenderly with the Army blanket.

"You will be fine, Mrs. Inada," she says kindly. "You can sit in the sun tomorrow. Everything feels better in the sun."

Satomi thinks that Mrs. Inada is lucky to be blind. She can't see the grim hovel, be disgusted by its filth.

"We should lay head to foot, Mama." She eyes the narrow cot. "It will work better that way."

They take off their shoes and lay down in their clothes. Satomi covers them with her Indian blanket that still has the scent of home on it. She watches Tamura drift into sleep. How has this horrible thing happened to them? This is America, they are Americans.

Unable in her exhaustion to sleep, she lies listening to the noises of the camp, to Mrs. Inada's crusty cough, to the calls of strangers, and to the crying of babies. Misery moves in her, solid and heavy as a brick.

That night, as in the nights that follow, they wake cold from their troubled dreams to a mottled light sieving through the perforated wood of their stable. Tamura's dreams return her to the burning ones she suffered in the month after Aaron's death. They find her falling, pitching into a murky sea, black flames consuming her. Satomi's are of running on hard ground while being pursued by some dark predator.

Tired and defeated, they stand around during the days trying to find a way to be, which seems impossible without even the simplest of utensils, not even a stove to make coffee, a chair to sit on. There is no housework to do, no land to work, only lines to join: lines for meals, for latrines, for showers.

"You could spend your whole day just lining up for things," Tamura says. "Thank God your father is not here. He was a stranger to patience."

"I'm going to move you up to the front, Mother," Satomi says on their third day waiting in line for their turn in the bad-smelling latrines. "It's only fair. You are too ill to stand for hours on end."

But Tamura won't hear of it. She says there are those who are worse off than her, and claims that she is feeling a little better every day.

Their neighbor in the next stall, Dr. Chiba—not a medical doctor after all, but a geologist with a political turn of mind—has taken to spending time with Satomi. He likes that she is as angry as him.

"We must learn a new language now, it seems," he snorts. "'mess hall,' 'barrack,' 'issue,' 'latrine.'"

"Don't forget 'halt,' Doctor," Satomi adds.

They are told that they will be moving on. This place that even the guards seem ashamed of is only temporary.

"Where you are going will be better," they say. "Of a much higher standard."

In a welcome turn of events, Tamura, in caring for Mrs. Inada, has recovered the mother in herself. She fusses around the old woman, collecting her food from the mess hall so that she won't have to stand in line, washing her gently, brushing her hair, and spoon-feeding her the unpleasant soup that tastes of stale potatoes.

"How can we complain at our situation, Satomi? This old mother is blind, her husband and her only child are dead. She is ill—tuberculosis, I think. We at least have our health."

"Mrs. Inada is lucky to have you," Satomi says, feeling sorry for herself. "You are like a mother to her."

"I am sorry to have neglected you, Satomi," Tamura apologizes. "But I have found myself again, so you are not to worry about me. I will take care of you now."

"We will take care of each other, Mama."

Four weeks in, and things are going downhill fast for Mrs. Inada.

"It's worse than bad," Tamura tells Satomi on their walk to the mess hall. "She needs more than I can give her in this dirty place."

Her efforts, she knows, are merely a plaster on the deep wound of the old woman's disease. Mrs. Inada needs stronger medicine than kindness and thin soup.

"The old lady is very ill," she reports to the most sympathetic of the guards. "She coughs blood and cannot get up from her mattress. You must get her to a hospital or she will die."

And they do, taking Mrs. Inada off on a stretcher, telling Tamura not to worry. "She'll be taken good care of, nursed in an American hospital," they say, as though there were another, less desirable, kind.

"Her home is lost to her forever now," Tamura says, thinking Mrs. Inada close to death. "I wish that I could have done more for her."

"You did your best. It was more than anyone else did for her, Mama."

The few days that they had expected to be here roll through the weeks into the summer months. New inmates arrive daily, bewildered, unbelieving. People begin to get ill, diarrhea, vomiting, and a strange, never-before-seen rash.

"It's most likely the germs from the animal feces we smell about the place," Dr. Chiba hazards. "Couldn't be bothered to disinfect, I suppose. We are only Japanese, after all."

Tamura thinks it might be scabies. She saw an outbreak of it once among the sugarcane cutters in Hawaii.

"It's a disease of poor sanitation," she says. "We must keep ourselves clean, no matter how long we have to stand in line for the showers."

Among those without the rash, Satomi hardly has the space to feel sympathy. Her emotions are personal, her distress reserved for her own and Tamura's condition. Ashamed of their situation as she is, she feels herself an alien among the Japanese. Her mother may be Japanese, but these people are not her people. There are moments when she is all infant again, all gooseflesh fear, so that if she could find a place to be alone she would howl to the moon. There are other times, though, when her anger consumes her so that she shouts her feelings to whoever will listen, usually Dr. Chiba.

A couple of the men, brought low by their wives' longing for home, had challenged the guards, insisting on being set free. It comes as a shock to everyone when they are instantly put into solitary confinement until their cases can come to court.

Some consider making a break for it, but there is no way to get past the armed guards or over the barbed-wire fences. No way to make a run for home without risking life.

"They can call it what they like. They can call it impoundment, or enclosure, they can call it relocation as if it was our choice, but it is what it is," Satomi rages. "However they try to clean it up with crafty words, we are prisoners."

"Shush, Satomi," Tamura advises. "It's your rages that put people off you, not your white blood, as you would have it. We have hope, at least. The next place will be better, I'm sure."

"I'm not so sure. I wouldn't put it past them to herd us in even tighter, to build the fences even higher."

"I wasn't talking of fences. I was thinking that perhaps it will be warmer and maybe we will have more space. I would like it to have trees."

Dr. Chiba tells them that he has heard of some Japanese who refused to attend what is now being called with black humor "the roundup."

"They left the coast as soon as the notices to quit their homes arrived," he says. "They headed to the interior towns to seek work."

"Good for them," Satomi says.

"Yes, but it didn't work out. They were turned back by local peace officers, or herded out of town by armed posses."

"We might as well live in the Wild West, Doctor."

"I agree. It makes you feel for the Indians, doesn't it?"

"You spend too much time with that old man," Tamura says. "He is fixed in the past, you can't expect him to be optimistic."

"I like the doctor's company. No matter what they do to us, his spirit will never be broken. He is old, but he is not weak."

When the evacuation notices are finally posted around the camp, Satomi reads them with mixed feelings. She wants to go but resents being told where she must live. And then there is the unspoken fear shared by all the inmates since the shooting-dead of the old man who in his dotage walked beyond the barbed wire and failed to halt at the guards' command. Perhaps they are simply being rounded up to be shot.

"We are being sent to Manzanar, Mama. Wherever that is."

"I like the name, Satomi. It has a pleasant sound to it."

"It's Spanish for orchard," Dr. Chiba tells them. "It's mountain country, the Sierra Nevada."

"How lovely," Tamura says with a sigh, flashing Satomi a smile.

Having discovered in herself the ability not to think too much of home and all she has lost, Tamura departs the temporary camp with her heart lifted. Surely nothing could be worse than the terrible place they are leaving. Perhaps in this Manzanar they will have finer lodgings, a place to make tea, a table to sit around.

They might be free of the disgusting black beetles that thrive in their present quarters. "Stinky bugs," the children call them, making a game of stamping on them, their faces gleeful at the gratifying crunch, at the prize of the occasional ooze of eggs that squirm from the broken bodies like toothpaste from the tube.

Dr. Chiba and his stoic daughter are being sent to the Tule Lake camp, which he thinks might be of more geological interest than their present confinement.

"Your daughter is a girl with backbone, Mrs. Baker," he tells Tamura as they part. "You should be proud of her. She is of this century, not cast in the old mold."

"She came wrapped in her father's caul, Dr. Chiba. I cannot claim credit."

"Half her blood is yours, Mrs. Baker."

"Yes, more than one drop."

The old man spits on the ground. "Ah, yes, the one-drop profile. How they love that old southern standby."

"Don't tell me to make the best of it," Satomi says when Tamura advises as much. "If we make the best of it, we accept it. I will never accept it."

"Oh, Satomi, you are under the same sky as at home wherever you go. It is the same sun that sets and rises wherever you are."

MANZANAR

THE MAN-MADE GEOGRAPHY of Manzanar seems at first to place it firmly among the more ugly sights on earth. Tamura, reaching for optimism, points out to Satomi the beauty of the mountains in the distance, the sound of the water from the stream that margins the perimeter of the camp.

"Keep looking to the east," she says. "It is beautiful in the distance."

But even as she encourages Satomi, her own heart drops at the sight of the dusty acreage, at the ranks of squalid quarters, narrow and dark as coffins. Her disappointment is almost unbearable.

"We've been sent to hell!" Satomi exclaims. "Some orchard, huh?"

As they stand getting their bearings, the children of the camp are already at their favorite play.

"Kill the Nazis."

"Kill the Japs."

Their tinny shrieks shred what's left of Satomi's courage. How can they play in this desperate place, how can they be happy? All she wants to do is sleep a dreamless sleep until the devil has had his day, until he has grown tired of tormenting them.

"Damn it, we can't live here." she drops Tamura's case to the ground and covers her face with her hands. They are both shivering with the cold, their thin jackets little protection against the glacial mountain air.

"We have no choice," Tamura says. She picks up her case and heads toward the lines to be allocated a barrack number.

Situated between Independence and Lone Pine in Inyo County, Manzanar's ground had been a fruit orchard once, pretty then, perhaps, but rutty now, dirty-looking, with clumps of sagebrush hogging the land. A few gnarled half-dead pear trees are dotted about, black as witches' hats, their branches twisted as though in torture.

"Not the sort of trees you dreamed of, Mama."

It's almost autumn in Angelina, but winter comes early and hard in mountain country. The day is colder than any they have ever experienced, the sky dark, almost black. Satomi looks around for a splash of color in the camp but finds none.

"I'm sorry, my girl," Tamura says softly, as though she is to blame for their troubles. "You don't deserve this."

"You less than me, Mama."

Retreating to the horizon, the airless rows of barracks stretch beyond their vision. They have been constructed from planks harvested from old stables in such haste that no pride could be taken in the work. Wasted with age, the wood has splintered where it has been nailed unevenly to the studs that are already working themselves free. All sixteen of the barracks in the Bakers' allotted row are green with mold and warped where the tarpaper has rotted and peeled away.

"At least we have a stove," Tamura falters, almost in tears.

"But I don't see any wood, Mama."

"The beds are better here." Tamura pokes the hard Army cotton mattress. "They won't be so prickly."

At the end of each barracks block, three low buildings hunker down. The first, a laundry room, echoes with the dismal sound of dripping water. There are four deep sinks and some worn scrub boards. Cockroaches cling to the damp walls in the twilight gloom. The second building houses the foul-smelling latrines, where, with only an inch or two of space between the cracked pans, Manzanar's inmates must squat cheek by jowl with their neighbors, looking straight ahead so as not to offend. Only the last stall has a partition, a partition but no door, giving rise to the view that the intention was there but foiled, they suppose, by a dearth of wood.

"That will be the worst one to have, I should think," Tamura says as they inspect the facilities.

"Why, Mother? It looks like the best to me."

"Well, I imagine that people will check it first to see if it is empty. Whoever sits on that throne will be facing a receiving line."

The smell from the latrines makes Satomi wretch. She doesn't believe Tamura when she says they will get used to it. She never wants to get used to it.

Completing the squalid triad, a bleak shower house with a rough cement floor, its walls gloopy with soap scum, seems to Satomi to have been designed more for animals than for humans.

It isn't only the old who look at those buildings with horror. The young too feel the shame of having to share with the opposite sex, of being thought so little of. Of all that is hateful at Manzanar, the latrines are the things that seem to Satomi to diminish humanity the most. Never mind that fate has chosen them to be unlucky, or that they have lost their names and become government numbers: those terrible latrines speak more potently of their lost future as Americans than any of the other humiliations that are heaped on them.

Tamura and Satomi's barrack, indistinguishable from their

neighbors,' is placed two from the end of their row. The door doesn't fit, so that it has to be kicked shut, and there is a crack in the back wall as wide as a man's arm.

"Look, I can put my fist through this. Your chicken coop was a palace compared to this place, Mama."

"Oh, my sweet chickens," Tamura says in a shaky voice.

With her head up, glaring at the guards, Satomi goes about the camp collecting cardboard from the empty food boxes behind the mess halls. She ducks under the barracks, gathering up splinters of wood and rusting nails from the rubbish-strewn ground.

A guard passing her turns as she goes by and gives a low appreciative whistle. She stifles the urge to catch up with him, to spit in his face. She wants him to challenge her, to tell her collecting wood is against the rules. She wants a reason to kick his shins, to scream at him. She wants to scream herself hoarse, have a showdown.

"You will always have that problem," Tamura says pragmatically when Satomi tells her about the guard. "It's about men, nothing to do with being in Manzanar."

Stuffing the hole as tight as she can, Satomi spends hours compressing the cardboard, fixing the wood in a rough patchwork to the thin wall with bent and rusty nails, a rock for a hammer.

Tamura can't help thinking how useful Aaron's tools would be here. It had hurt to leave them with the pale-eyed man at the bus station. Perhaps he is using them himself; Aaron's big pliers, his pack of assorted screwdrivers, the little tool that she has forgotten the name of that he said he wouldn't want to be without, it was so useful.

"You have made a good job of it," she says, admiring Satomi's work. "Nothing will get through that."

But when their first dust storm comes, dirt and grit explode through the wall, sending the cardboard flying, crumpling the wood as though it is no more than paper. The force of the storm shocks them. It's like nothing Angelina had ever thrown at them.

"Like the winds of Neptune," Tamura says in amazement. They gasp and draw in their breath, laughing with relief when it's over.

"Oh, Mama." Satomi hugs Tamura. "You are the bravest person I know," and suddenly she is crying along with the laughter.

America is punishing them, the weather is punishing them. There is no forgiveness here, nothing gentle, only Tamura to hold on to.

She comes to know that flattened-out tin cans would have worked better on the hole. They are patched on most of the barracks, tacked around with nails that have bent in the gales but somehow managed to hold on.

"I expect your father would have known that," Tamura says.

The same unspoken rules of the inmates that had applied in the relocation center apply in Manzanar. Manners are all, and everyone must feign deafness, learn to look the other way, attempt politeness.

"Best not to comment on our neighbors' conversations," Tamura advises. "Not to be too loud in our own."

The partition walls are so thin that it is impossible to have a private conversation without being overheard. The sounds and smells that the human body is subject to come rudely through their walls, sighs and groans, spitting and farting.

But whatever the difficulties, the semblance of privacy must be maintained or neighbor could not look neighbor in the face. The children of the camp are beaten if they are caught spying through the knotholes of the barrack walls. They can't stop, though, as all the barracks look the same to them. It's easy to get lost, to think that they will never find their way home.

"I was looking for my mother," they wail when caught out.

"It would have been better to have arrived in summer," Tamura says, stating the obvious as she attempts to light a few sticks of wood in their stove. "It takes time to become accustomed to the mountain weather."

They are not prepared for the icy air, for the ground set hard as a hammer. The cold thickens the blood, makes movement sluggish. Even the birds hardly sing in Manzanar. They perch rather than fly, in case their wings should freeze and they should fall frozen to the ground.

"We don't have the clothes for it," Satomi despairs. "You must use my blanket as a shawl, Mama. Stay inside, your cough is getting worse."

As the relentless storms rock them, a leftover hoard of Navy World War I peacoats arrive and are issued to every household.

"One for everyone," they are told. "You see, America cares for you, we have your interest at heart."

The coats are large, all one size. They are too big for the children, and on the women they trail to the floor and hang over their hands. Made of felt, they sop up the rain, making them too heavy to wear on wet days. It takes a week to dry them out, and the scent of mold never leaves them.

"They're better used as blankets, I suppose," Tamura says. "They're so heavy in the wearing they make my shoulders ache anyway."

If they didn't know it already, Manzanar during their first winter confirms to them that nature is boss. The wind howls at them, sucking its breath in, shrieking it out furiously, a mad creature intent on blowing them to kingdom come. It slams at the electricity poles so that the light goes and they have to take to their beds as soon as darkness falls.

It's bad enough faced straight-on, but they prefer it that way, even when it blows hard enough to move stones as if they are nothing but bits of cinder. When it charges them from behind, the barracks shake and tilt alarmingly.

"It's about to go," is the shout, setting neighbors to help knock in the loose nails, hammer the wood back together. On such occasions something of the atmosphere of a barn-build overtakes the detainees, a barn-build where your fingers freeze and your eyes burn in the whipping wind. A barn-build with no picnic to look forward to.

Satomi, bundled up in her peacoat, which flaps unpleasantly against her calves, wanders the camp, not knowing what to do with herself. People hardly acknowledge her, they are shy to speak to the tall, angry-looking white girl. They have heard that her father died at Pearl Harbor, an American hero, it's said. So why is she incarcerated here with them? Surely she must hate the very look of them, her father's murderers. But if that's the case, then what of her mother, the pretty Mrs. Baker, as Japanese as any of them?

"There's bound to be trouble when you marry out of your race," they say. "Bound to be complications."

On her walks around the camp she lingers by the groups of old Issei men, those born in Japan, who cluster together rubbing their hands and stamping their feet against the cold. They hardly know how to be either, or what to do with their days. They would like to huddle inside but, unable to tolerate the beaten look of their wives, the sense of loss in their families, they prefer to face the deathly cold. Their breath freezes on the air as they crowd around the fires they light in discarded tin cans. They speak of the war in hushed tones, wonder how it's going, how Japan is faring. Perhaps they never should have left the old country, never should have sired American children. Old loyalties stir in them, they are children of the Emperor, after all. They play *go*, an ancient game with mysterious rules involving black and white stones. The game attracts a rapt audience of their peers, who squat on the ground watching the stones intently. One old man sketches them as they play, with a piece of charcoal on cardboard, making swift flowing strokes, stopping every so often to blow some heat into his bony fingers. Satomi likes his work, thinks him a genius of the understated.

The veins on the back of the old men's hands rise thick, dark as bark, to join the burn marks they suffer from getting too close to the red-hot cans.

At first she had watched the matches and, like the old men, she had stood too close to the braziers and burned her hands. But after a while she lost interest. The game moves too slowly to hold her attention for long, and something about the players' patience seems too accepting to her. The fight has gone out of the old men. It's worrying.

"Playing games as though everything is normal," she says to Tamura. "And they hardly seem to notice the cold even though their lips are blue."

"They notice it, all right, Satomi, but what else can they do to forget their shame? It will be better for them in summer. The air will be sweet, they won't need their fires. Just think of it, we will be able to leave our door open, to breathe outside without burning our lungs."

"Some of them might die of the cold before then."

"Perhaps that is what they hope for."

DOG DAYS

SUMMER, WHEN IT comes, is not without its own trials. Rains flood the latrines, so that excrement runs down the alley and bubbles up beneath the barracks, where it settles in thick slimy pools. Drawn to the toxic smell, flies swarm, causing the residents in the Bakers' row of barracks to name their road "Sewer Alley."

The children make a game of the infestations, seeing how many flies they can collect. They stack them up in old gallon jugs and empty bottles, any container they can lay their hands on. One boy proudly claims to have collected two thousand of the dirty, dark-bodied things.

With the winter behind them, Sewer Alley is always crowded now with inmates who prefer to live their summer lives outside. Used now to Satomi's aloof manner, and charmed by Tamura, their neighbors greet them with bows and good-mornings.

Satomi talks sometimes with the girls of her own age in the alley, but she hasn't made a special friend of any of them, doesn't want to. Lily's fickleness has made her cautious. There's a boy named Ralph a couple of barracks away, whom she often talks with. Ralph's a freethinker with an irrepressible desire to right wrongs. She likes to listen to him, likes his knockout smile. She's more interested in his friend, though, her neighbor's son Haru, whom she can hardly look at, he's so dazzling, so bright.

Unlike her, Ralph and Haru have chosen to attend the new high school, which is being held in the open on the ground by the mess hall. Books have to be shared, pencils too, and sometimes it's just too hot to sit on the earth with the sun scalding your head till you feel as though it will split open like an overcooked squash.

"It's worth it just to learn, though," Ralph says.

Volunteers are hurrying to finish building the wood and tar-paper block intended to house the students, to keep them from the extremes of the Owens Valley seasons.

"It will be better once we are inside," Ralph says. "You should come, Satomi. Don't let them steal your education too."

"I'll think about it." She knows, though, that she won't. School holds no attraction for her. It would be like returning to childhood, and in the vein of her father she doesn't care to be told what to do.

She had thought Ralph to be like her at first, half and half, but he turned out to be a different sort of half-and-half altogether.

"I am like you," he told her. "Only I'm half Mexican, half Irish."

He doesn't even have the one required drop of Japanese blood to explain his presence in the camp. It had been his strong feelings of kinship and outrage that had brought him to, and keeps him, in Manzanar.

"I grew up in the Temple-Beaudry neighborhood in Los Angeles," he tells her. "We were a mixed bunch, Basques, Jews, Koreans, Negroes. It didn't matter to us, we liked who we liked."

When Ralph talks it's like being in the light, Satomi thinks. He's a special person, sixteen but a man already, not afraid to say what he thinks. He had been a high school student when the order for the Japanese to vacate their homes had come.

"They were my friends," he says. "They'd done nothing to deserve it. It was unfair and cruel. We were taught the Constitution at school and we were proud of it. Now it seems like it was all just words."

Ralph's mother is dead, and his father, thinking him to be at summer school, didn't miss him at first. It came as a shock to learn that he had joined the Japanese students, his fellows from Belmont High, as they had boarded the buses to Manzanar.

His sister wrote often after they discovered where he was, pleading with him to come home. Ralph, though, insisted that he wanted to stay with his buddies. Eventually his father gave him permission to remain in Manzanar.

"They must be proud of you, Ralph," Satomi had said when he'd first told her his story. He had given one of his smiles and shrugged.

Word of his act was hot news for a while in the camp. It's no wonder, Satomi thinks, that he is so popular, or that he has become a Manzanar celebrity.

"How wonderful that he should do this for us," it's said.

"Ralph Lazo will be spoken of long after we are all dead."

Despite that it's summer, the dust storms are as promiscuous as ever. There are mornings when they wake in a shroud of grime covering them from head to toe.

"We will make this place ours," Tamura determines, doing her daily sweep. "If we care for it, we need not feel shame."

Satomi raises her eyes to heaven, wonders if her mother has gone quite mad.

Their neighbor to the left of them, Eriko Okihiro, Haru's mother, is of the same frame of mind as Tamura.

"My mother lives with us," she told Tamura with a wry smile at their first meeting. "I don't want her to feel ashamed of my housekeeping."

The Okihiros, all four of them, jostle for space in their barrack, which they have divided in two with a piece of sacking.

"We are two widows, a boy, and a girl," Eriko explained with pride. "We are used to better, of course."

Eriko, along with her old mother Naomi and her sulky daughter Yumi, sleep on one side of the sacking divide, her only son Haru, head of the household since his father's death, on the other.

Haru strides about the camp and the girls sneak sideways glances at him, blushing when he looks at them. Satomi is no exception, although she affects disinterest. He has to duck his head when going through doors, which embarrasses him and delights the girls. He is dark-skinned, dark-haired, too serious for his age.

"There's a bloom about him," Tamura says. "A pleasing sort of energy."

At seventeen years and one week old, Haru likes to remind people that he is in his eighteenth year.

"He's at that halfway stage," Eriko muses. "More man than boy, and proud, you know?"

It seems to Satomi that when she stands near Haru all she can hear is the sound of her blood rushing to her head, swishing around in her brain like weir water churning. It's mortifying. The first time he spoke to her it was as if he had stood on her heart, stopped its beating. She loses herself when she's close to him, finds it impossible to think straight. She can't stop the heat that rises in her face, the dreadful feeling that she is on the boil. The side effects of being near Haru feel at once horrible and delightful. She admires his reserve, which has nothing of humility in it. If she has a criticism at all, it is that there is little give in him.

She looks for failings in him like those she had seen in Artie but can find none. He is nothing like Artie. He isn't a show-off, for one thing, and somehow his bossiness is reassuring.

"You should listen to Ralph," he says to her. "School would do you good."

She puzzles over the fact that there is something familiar about him, as though in some unexplained way she already knows him. He is interested in her, that's for sure, but she senses his disapproval too, his irritation with her. He is always quick to criticize.

"You should work on those manners," he says. "It costs nothing to be polite."

It feels preachy to her, but it could be his way of flirting. He's hard to read.

The Okihiros came direct to Manzanar from Los Angeles. In their previous lives they had run a fabric shop in Little Tokyo, and there is something of the city in the way they talk, in their quick step. They seem to shine brighter than those that came from California's farmlands.

"You would have loved our cottons," Eriko tells Tamura. "We had striped and gingham—and silk too—well, special orders of silk—so beautiful—so . . ." Her voice trembles with the memory of it.

After a while she stops speaking of her old life. It is too painful to go on boasting about what you have lost, what you may never get back. And just thinking of the fabrics, their vibrant colors, the clean glazed crispness of them, tops up the hurt in her.

The Okihiros spend a lot of time sitting on the steps of their barrack, beside which they have made a miniature rock garden. Its elegant simplicity has inspired others to do the same, and now in Sewer Alley stone gardens are quite the thing. Such refinements, though, are not for the Sanos, who live on the other side of the Bakers—they think the effort a pointless exercise.

"Might as well put a dress on a monkey," Mr. Sano says.

Mr. Sano, a wizened little man, is in the habit of touching his wife in public, pulling her caveman-style into their barrack in the afternoons so that everyone knows what they are up to. Never mind their daughter-in-law, or their grandchildren, who are billeted with them.

Mrs. Sano finds it hard to look people in the eye in case she should meet with a disapproving stare. She feels too old to be the object of her husband's copious passion; besides, his behavior is not the Japanese way. But then, her husband has always taken his own path, lived in ignorance of others' sensitivities. There is nothing to be done about it.

"A monkey in a dress could be cute," Satomi says to Tamura, causing them a fit of the giggles, which turns for Tamura into a bout of coughing.

Despite that Tamura and Satomi are treated by their fellow inmates with a measure of reserve, Eriko is pleased to have them as neighbors. She has befriended them enthusiastically, thinking Tamura delightful, a kind and modest woman in need of a friend.

"She is shy, I know, but charming, don't you think, Mother? I liked her from the first."

"She's too thin," old Naomi says pragmatically. "Ill, I think."

All the Okihiros glow with health, notwithstanding the unappetizing diet at Manzanar: canned wieners and beans and watery corn that tastes only of sugar. The women agree, though, that it is getting better. Sometimes now there is miso, and even on occasions pickled vegetables.

Eriko's hair grows thick, her teeth are long and white, and her face has a rosy flush even when she isn't exerting herself. Her five-foot-three frame is built so squarely that she appears to have no waist at all. She is energetic for a woman of her weight, and strong too. She can pick Tamura up without effort.

"You're hardly an armful," she tells her.

In comparison to Eriko's bulk, Tamura's slight frame appears sweetly girlish.

"She's so pretty," Eriko remarks to her mother.

"Hmm," Naomi grunts, thinking that unless things improve with Tamura, her pallor will soon be a match for the mold that is inching its way up their walls.

"We are lucky to have Eriko and her family as neighbors," Tamura says. Some would have turned their back on us."

"Plenty did, Mama, some still do."

Those who came to Manzanar without family, the old and the bereaved, the paralyzed, even, have to bear the indignity of sharing with strangers. One poor woman, for reasons no one can understand, was separated from her husband and billeted with strangers. Now her husband shares with six men, and she is told that nothing can be done about it.

All of them, though, had resisted being housed with the Japanese woman and her half-caste daughter. Things are bad enough without the shame of that. Just by looking at the girl you could tell she'd be trouble.

Every time it seemed likely that one or the other of them were about to be paired with the Bakers, they had stepped aside and joined another line, leaving Tamura and Satomi standing on their own. The guards got the message eventually and didn't push it. You had to choose your battles.

"I'd share with you any day," one of them wisecracked to Satomi. "Just let me know when you get lonely, sugar."

"You've been lucky," Haru says. "Most likely you and Tamura would have had an old woman forced on you. You would have had nothing but complaints. And if it had been an old man you would have ended up doing everything for him. And just think of it, you have a room all to yourselves."

"I guess. Mother is a very private person, so she appreciates the space." She is thinking of Tamura's shame at her cough, her night cries.

"Yes, she is a fine lady," Haru says.

"She's a bit like you, Haru. She looks for the good in things."

"And you look for trouble where there is none. Anyway, I was thinking of asking your mother if she would let me use your room to study. Only when you are out, of course. My grandmother thinks that I can read and talk to her at the same time. I find myself going over the same paragraph again and again."

"Ask her. I guess she won't mind. I'm surprised you were allowed to bring books in, though."

"I only have a few, not enough for what I need. It bothered my mother more than the guards. She thought I should have used the space for more practical things. But if you think about it, books are more practical than dishes and bedding. Dishes and bedding can't promise a future, can't make you forget that you are not free."

"Would I like your books, Haru?"

"You? Well, maybe you would, I don't know. Did you enjoy reading at school? The classroom books, I mean."

"I guess I did."

"Well, it's good to read. We won't always be in this place. We should use the time here to make our future better, not let it slip through our hands like sand."

"Perhaps I'll borrow your books sometime. Okay?"

"Maybe. But are you sure you want to?"

"I do, I really do."

"You would have to be careful with them."

She can tell that he's unwilling, that he doesn't trust her with his precious books.

"It doesn't matter. It's fine with me if you don't want to share them." She can't keep the irritation from her voice. "I hear there's to be a library here soon, anyway. You're not the only one who wants to read, you know?"

"I know that." His voice is full of apology. Look, I've just finished *This Side of Paradise*, you can borrow it if you like.

"Oh, Fitzgerald, I've read it," she lies.

"Really! You've read the whole thing?"

He sounds just like Mr. Beck.

Taking her lead from Eriko, Tamura divides their barrack using the silk butterfly robe that Aaron had loved her to wear. She threads a stick through the arms, balancing each end on a rusty nail so that it hangs suspended, a pink quivering scarecrow.

"Oh, Tamura," Eriko enthuses. "It's beautiful, not real silk, of course, but beautiful just the same."

Tamura looks at the garment with disbelief—it is a design from ancient times, a piece of history that surely belonged to a different woman than the one she is now. What had induced her to pack such a thing? At the sight of its brilliance in dusty Manzanar, her thoughts turn to images of geishas, of obedience, of Aaron. Why had she allowed him to keep her in the last century? Why had she attempted to fix Satomi there with her?

"I would never wear such a thing here!" she exclaims to Satomi. "It would look ridiculous. I will never wear it again. You need some privacy, I can't think of a better use for it."

Fingering the robe, Satomi has to swallow hard to keep the tears at bay. Her saliva seems to have dried to sand. The silly, pretty thing is the very trinity of Aaron, Tamura, and her childhood self.

It isn't much privacy, a roughly hung gown that moves in the drafts as though alive, but she is grateful for it. She rests behind it stretched out on her iron cot, one of Haru's books in hand, imagining him doing the same on the other side of the thin divide between them. Her hand goes to the wall, where she holds it as though she can feel his warmth heating her palm. Sometimes late into the night she hears him turning the pages of his book, sighing.

Behind her pink screen she can deal discreetly with her monthly bleeds, while on the other side of it, Tamura, hawking up the muck from her lungs, indulges the idea of privacy too.

Tamura has quickly let go the expectations she had of Manzanar, and has settled to making the best of it. Satomi, though, along with half of the camp, is on alert, waiting. Waiting for news that their confinement has been a mistake, waiting to hear that the war has ended, waiting perhaps for something more terrible. Wherever people gather at Manzanar, hope and fear are the text of their chatter.

"Have you heard anything?"

"There seem to be more guards, don't you think?"

"Did I imagine a shot in the night?"

The slightest change in routine takes on meaning, unsettles everyone. And the rumors, like the dust storms, appear to arrive out of nowhere.

"We are all to be shot."

"I heard only the men."

"A guard told me we are to be shipped to Japan."

Being sent to Japan, for the Nisei generation, seems almost as bad as being shot. They are native-born Americans, after all, pumped with the notion of sadistic yellow bastards and murdering Japs. Why would they fare better in Japan? Japanese-Americans are a different breed than their ancestors. They are democrats, modern citizens, proud of the American way.

But some of the young men have begun to challenge this view. They call themselves the "Kibei" and welcome the idea of returning to Japan. It's their homeland, they tell each other, the land of their fathers, after all, they would not be imprisoned there. They go around in gangs, not listening to their elders, causing everyone problems. They challenge the guards by hanging around the fencing, and running through the alleys at night, calling out wildly to each other.

"They are nothing but trouble," Haru says. "They make things worse for everyone.

"At least they have spirit," Satomi argues. "You have to give them that."

"Ha, spirit, is that what you call it? Their spirit tars us all with the traitor's brush."

To help counteract their influence and show his loyalty to America, Haru has joined the American Citizens League. League members have asked to join the American forces. Haru, for one, can't wait to fight for his country, to go to war in its name.

But even his loyalty is challenged when a hundred and one orphans are rounded up and brought to Manzanar. The all-to-be-shot rumors gain momentum for a while. Why else would they imprison babies, what harm are they capable of?

Manzanar's director, Mr. Merrit, has been ordered by the Army's evacuation architect, Colonel Bendetsen, to confine the children to the camp.

Bendetsen has ignored the frantic pleas of the adopted families and the Catholic missions who have been caring for them to let the children remain in their care.

"They are our family."

"Only children, after all."

"How can it harm, for them to stay with us?"

Deaf to their pleas, he insists against reason that the children might be a threat to national security.

Some come to Manzanar from the white families who adopted them, grieving a second time at the loss of yet another set of parents. There are babies as young as six months old, the children, it's said, of schoolgirl-mothers from the other camps; there are toddlers taking their first precarious steps, and confused six-year-olds.

The babies, sensing change, cry for attention. The older ones gather together in silence, frightened at the deep pitch of the guards' voices, the dull metal gleam of their guns.

Manzanar's inmates are disturbed by the sight of the children. Seeing such innocence lined up feeds the sense they have that the madness has no limits.

"Why else would they be taken out of white homes, if not to kill us all?" they say.

"This must be the big, the final, roundup."

Racially the children are a mixed bunch, some with as little as one-eighth Japanese ancestry. The blond ones stand out among their fellows, reminders that even the tiniest trace of Japanese blood, no matter how far back in your family, condemns you. Watching those little souls arrive, it's hard for Satomi too not to feel so hated that genocide seems unlikely.

"How can those kids possibly be a threat to anybody?" she fumes, while Haru despairs. He wants to keep faith with his country, but at the sound of the children singing "God Bless America" he has to agree with Satomi that it makes no sense.

As the children settle into the Children's Village, the three large tar-papered barracks hastily erected to house them, fears of mass murder recede and other rumors get a look in. Hope floats around the one that says they are to be allowed home. But after a while hope itself makes them feel foolish. The more you hope for home, the farther away it seems to get.

Resignation is taking over so that even the horror stories of rats in the babies' cots fail to impress. Rats are no strangers in Manzanar, they have outnumbered the human residents from day one. In the company of cockroaches the ubiquitous creatures scuttle under the barracks, run across the beds at night. They have to be chased from the dripping water spigots, pulled each morning from the glue traps set on the many mess hall floors.

"Check my bed for me, pleeease," Satomi begs Haru every evening.

"They won't be there now," he says. "They come when it's dark, when you are sleeping." His voice takes on a ghostly moan. He likes to hear her squeal.

The scraps of good news that come, however small, are welcome and made much of. A post office is to be set up, an occasional movie is to be allowed, and there is an extra sugar ration on its way.

The bad news, though, is always major, always dramatic. Tamura and Eriko fly into a panic when they hear that a congressman, noting the high birth rate in the camps, has proposed that all Japanese women of child-bearing age should be sterilized.

"It would ruin our girls' lives." Tamura can't stop the tears.

"He must be a wicked man," Eriko wails, her arms tight around the squirming Yumi, who has only just started menstruating.

"No one's taking him seriously," John Harper, the popular camp doctor, says to Ralph and Satomi as they sit on the ground outside his office. "Congress is not completely mad."

"They'll have to shoot me before they try, the bastards," Satomi says, and Dr. Harper, not for the first time, is shocked at her language, impressed by her passion. Since they first met when she came to him with a splinter in her hand that had festered, he has felt a connection with her.

"This will hurt," he had warned. "I'm going to have to dig a bit."

He had laughed when she had cursed at the pain.

"Damn!"

"Never heard a Japanese female swear before," he said.

Since that time, she and Dr. Harper have shared what Haru

thinks of as an unsuitable friendship. Along with Ralph, they debate politics, discuss how the war is going, have conversations that
sometimes turn argumentative. They agree that America will win
the war and wonder together what life will be like when it is over.

Despite that he represents authority, it is hard, Satomi thinks,
not to like Dr. Harper. There's no doubt that he is a good man.
He may be ungainly, always dropping things, losing his papers,
searching for his spectacles, but none of that counts for anything.
Dr. Harper is a man filled with goodness and grace.

"There's a glow in him, don't you think?" she says to Ralph.

"Yes, that's it exactly, Satomi. He's the hail-fellow-well-met
sort."

Now and then, breaking the camp's rules with pleasure in his
heart, Dr. Harper gives Satomi his old newspapers. It staves his
guilt for a while, and what harm can it do? He never, before Manzanar, thought of himself as a rule breaker, but stupid rules don't
deserve to be followed. Rules that say people must be kept in the
dark, no papers, no radio, stay ignorant, beg to be broken.

"If you won't go to school, then it's time you went to work,"
Haru insists. You should stop bothering the doctor, Satomi."

"We're friends, Haru. We think alike. He agrees that America
has betrayed its Japanese citizens. Unlike Dr. Harper, I didn't hear
you complaining when they spoke of sterilizing us."

"There are fools in every government," he says, more to console himself than to placate her. "It was never going to happen."

Their neighbor Mr. Sano, with his usual lack of tact, has an
unpopular take on the sterilization threat.

"I can see the sense in it. Just look at the Hamadas," he declares, referring to the family of nine from the row behind Sewer
Alley. "Mrs. Hamada is pregnant again. The children run wild,
disturbing everyone. If they can't control themselves, it should be
done for them."

Tamura and Eriko look at him with mouths open.

"He is blind to his own faults," Tamura says.

"A disgrace," says Naomi.

Along with Eriko, Tamura takes a camp job sewing camouflage for the Army. She is paid six dollars a month, which, added to the prisoners' clothing allowance of three dollars and sixty cents, allows her to order little things from the Sears and Roebuck catalogue.

"You shouldn't be working in that drafty old hangar, Mama. It's not good for you. The dust from the cotton isn't giving your cough a chance."

"But I enjoy it, Satomi. I like the company, and it's fun. And anyway, what would I do all day otherwise? Besides, we need the money. You must have cotton for your dresses, thread and needles for me to sew them with."

At quiet times they go together to the mess hall and pore over the wonderful things the catalogue has to offer. Flower-printed head scarves, the prettiest shoes, silky nylons with straight dark seams, and pink suspender belts with rubber clasps that look like the teats from babies' bottles. The most popular items are the short white socks that are fashionable among the older girls, who think they look neat with their black oxfords. Satomi, though, prefers in summer to wear her oxfords without socks, and she likes simple skirts, the plain white T-shirts from the boys' section.

"No wonder the girls think you're odd," Tamura despairs.

Yumi, sparing no one her sulks, refuses to speak to Eriko until she agrees that she can give up the gray socks of the younger children and buy two pairs of the white ones.

"What can I do?" Eriko says. "She won't even listen to Haru."

"It's just a phase," Tamura says.

"Did Satomi go through it?"

"Sometimes, Eriko, it seems like she was born going through it. I can't say that she has ever been an easy child."

"She's not a child anymore, Tamura. I'd give up hoping, if I were you."

Eriko is used to hard work and enjoys the company too. She could have taken more pleasure in it if it hadn't been for having to kneel on the cement floor all day, which makes her knees ache.

"You are the only one not working," Tamura complains to Satomi. "All you do is read Haru's books and talk to Dr. Harper. No wonder you are bored. Work would console you."

"I won't do anything here that helps them, Mama. Nobody should. In any case, I am not bored, I love reading."

"You could help Haru with his volunteer work," Tamura persists. "Anyone can see how much pride he takes in it."

Haru has found his vocation and is teaching reading to the third-grade children. He coaches the softball team and helps distribute the care packages that come from the Quakers. Tin toys for the children, comics and pencils, and sometimes soft blanket-stitched scarves and hats.

Yumi was hoping for bobby pins, a watch, perhaps; instead she receives a fan made from cedar wood, which she hangs on the wall by her bed. She pretends that it is a silly thing of no use to anyone, but she keeps it free from dust so that it won't lose its scent, and no one but her is allowed to touch it.

Haru, a little embarrassed at the Quakers' charity, takes pleasure at least in the children's joy at receiving the toys. He could have earned eight dollars a month if he had wanted, laying drainage pipes around the camp, but he has his pride.

"It's insulting. Eight dollars! What other Americans would work for that kind of money? They would be paid ten times more." He may be loyal to America, but like Aaron he is not to be predicted.

"I'd have thought you would be happy to help, since you love America so much," Satomi teases.

"You don't know what you're talking about, Sati. Loving America and working for less than a citizen is not the same thing at all."

Yumi is at the camp school, and old Naomi Okihiro knits when she can get the wool, or sleeps her days away, dreaming of sunlit rooms and the plum tree she sat under as a child in Japan. Her English is not good, her nature suspicious, and, apart from Tamura and Satomi, she rarely speaks to anyone outside of her family.

Satomi won't admit it, but Tamura is right, the days are long and she is bored. They would be longer, though, if it hadn't been for Haru's books, for Dr. Harper's company.

Dr. Harper is taking up more and more of her time. He encourages her to call at his office, is debating with himself whether to take her on his rounds. The thing about Satomi is that she's not hampered by the cultural manners that keep his other patients from challenging him, from having the intimacy with them that he would like. And she must have somewhere useful to place her outrage, after all, some outlet for the kindness she smothers.

He questions her about the minutia of things that go on in the camp that he would otherwise have no way of finding out, listing them in his journal meticulously. *Liver served for five days on the trot,* he writes. *On the whole the Japanese don't eat liver.*

"My little archive," he says. "A gateway to memory for me, when Manzanar is over and you are all allowed to go home."

He is attached to his collection, to the grim photos he has taken of the sparsely furnished, poorly lit barracks, the portraits of the inmates, who smile for the camera and manage to look hopeful. He has blurry pictures of rats on the run in the latrines, bugs in the children's beds. He has drawings that the children at school have drawn in the dust; strange shapes, and trees without leaves, and guards with guns, stick men smaller than their weapons. He treasures the little carvings people give him in gratitude for his skills, naïve ironwood netsuke, hares and rabbits, rats with serpent tails, infants tumbling together with stones for eyes. It's a strange archive, but so potent that sometimes when he goes through it he imagines he can smell the camp, sweat and disease, dust and blood, and the burning reek of carbolic.

In his determination to let nothing of Manzanar be lost, he sees purpose in his job, and is able to keep faith with his country. There will be others like him, he thinks, Americans who witness the unfairness, the damage done. Others who, when the time is right, will work for recompense, for justice. He believes that Satomi will be one of them.

"You never stop writing in that thing," his wife complains. "I think you find that place more interesting than real life."

He doesn't challenge her on the "real life" thing, prefers to keep Manzanar, the revulsion it holds for him, from her. "Someone has to keep a record," he says. "I don't want to forget the truth of it."

MEDICAL ROUNDS

I SUSPECTED THAT SHE wouldn't go full term," Dr. Harper says to Satomi on their way to Mrs. Takei's barrack. "The lining of her womb might as well be paper, it's so thin with childbearing. If it's what I suspect, it won't be a pretty sight, Satomi. You don't have to come in."

"I'll come in," she says nervously.

He's burdening her, he knows, putting her to the test, but then we are all put to the test and he doesn't want to allow her the getout clause of ignorance. It's right that she should see things for what they are, right that she should be good and mad about it, and she's strong enough for the truth.

He's strong enough too, yet still he would like himself to be saved from the horrors that he sees, the ones that rob him of the free will to live a conventional, untroubled life.

Satomi hasn't visited this part of the camp before. It's the outer circle of the site, the periphery line of barracks that are the border between civilization and the rude acres of sagebrush. The barracks here take the full force of the winds, of all the extreme forms of weather their desert-floor home throws at them

"The badlands," Dr. Harper calls them. "Home to the stragglers, latecomers too shocked at the sight of Manzanar to push their way to the front of the lines."

Mrs. Takei's barrack is fourth from the end. Her husband is sitting on the steps with their children, seven boys who look to Satomi to be about the same age, although that can't be so. Their mother must have popped them out with hardly a space in between.

Mr. Takei stands when he sees them, stepping aside to allow them to climb the steps, bowing to them as though they are royalty. Dr. Harper puts his hand on the man's shoulder and sighs. The men look at each other with what Satomi takes to be resignation.

Inside, it takes a second or two for their eyes to adjust in the stygian light. Mrs. Takei is perched on the edge of the bed with her knees drawn up to her chin. Her face, Satomi thinks, as green as Palmolive soap. A dark stain pumps its way up the thin brown fabric of her dress, there's a puddle of blood on the floor, streaks of it across her face where she has pushed her hair back with bloodied hands.

Satomi shuts her mouth and holds her nose, a brief protection against the offal smell that comes hot to her nostrils. An acid sharpness of vomit clots at the back of her throat and she swallows hard and prays not to be sick. The stench and the blood are shocking.

Even though Dr. Harper had been expecting it, he shakes his head at the sight of Mrs. Takei in such a poor state. It has always seemed a little miracle to him that the body's odors are contained inside something as thin, as porous, as skin.

"When did the bleeding start?" he asks, easing Mrs. Takei gently down on the bed, straightening her legs.

"Last night." She lowers her eyes from his.

"*Tshh*, and you've waited this long to send for me," he says, not unkindly.

"The baby came quickly," she says, looking to the corner of the room, where a bloody towel-wrapped bundle lays lifeless. "I thought the bleeding would stop, but it just keeps coming."

"Water, please, Satomi. Lots of it, if you can manage, and the cloths from my bag." His movements are sure, his voice calm, his heart sinking.

Outside at the spigot, Satomi fills a thin tin bucket up to the worn part where holes pepper the sides, and gulps down the fresh air as if it were a long cool drink. She hesitates, not wanting to go back in, only moving when Dr. Harper calls her name urgently as though it is a question.

Inside, as the doctor is examining the dead baby, Satomi takes Mrs. Takei's hand. "I'm sorry, Mrs. Takei," she says. "About the baby, I mean." She meant to sound sympathetic, warm, but her voice comes out small, useless.

Mrs. Takei takes two days to die. The blood transfusions Dr. Harper administers seem to pump in and flow out in equal measure. Mrs. Takei can't hold on, either to the blood or to life.

She's buried with her baby in her arms, leaving her husband and her seven boys to fend for themselves.

Satomi carries the vision of that desperate day, the blood and the brutal sight of the parceled infant, around with her for weeks. Forever after, the smell of blood makes her queasy, sets her heart racing.

On her rounds with Dr. Harper, one crisis runs into another so that faces blur, names are forgotten. There are cases of adult measles, strange fevers, and plenty of the geriatric pneumonia that Dr. Harper calls "the old man's friend."

"Speeds them along the path to meet their maker," he says.

Mrs. Takei, though, stays in her mind with frightening clarity, as does the man with septicemia, who left untreated the cut he received from a broken pan in the latrines. By the time Dr. Harper got to him, you could feel the heat coming off his leg from a foot away. Thick pus oozed from the wound, and a long red line snaked up his skin from thigh to waist. In his spiking fever there was no sense to be had from him. He was hallucinating, thrashing about, shouting warnings to the wall.

Dr. Harper got him into the camp hospital and set up twenty-four-hour nursing, but he couldn't save him. The man's blood was poisoned, his organs failed, and he died in agony.

"Just from a cut," Satomi said to Dr. Harper in amazement.

"An easy route into the body for bacteria, Satomi."

"Yes, but just from a cut."

She wondered if the camp was the cause of the disasters, or whether such things happened in the world outside too. Perhaps she had just been unaware of them.

"It's the same the world over," Dr. Harper says. "It's just that here the lack of facilities, the poor hygiene, turns sickness to tragedy more often."

One case she knew that she could blame on the camp for sure was that of a boy a year or so younger than Haru. He had fallen into a depression and in his lowest moment had drunk industrial-strength chlorine, stolen from the mess hall while his mother was at work.

She had found him in agony, blisters the size of cookies around his mouth, his throat scorched from first swallowing the chlorine and then vomiting it up, so that he could hardly speak.

"He was always a happy boy before we came to this place," his mother said bitterly. "He wanted to be a doctor like you, Dr. Harper. He likes helping people."

"He still can be," Dr. Harper assured her. "You must help him to look on the world as promising. Keep him from attempting anything like this again."

"But he has spoiled his beautiful face. He will be scarred forever."

Dr. Harper, usually good with words, could find none. It

would be more than a bit of scarring the boy would suffer. What was inside, what his mother couldn't see, would be more of a problem.

"It's this place," Satomi hissed to Dr. Harper on their way out of the barrack. "This disgusting, filthy place."

There have been days since that time when she can't bring herself to accompany Dr. Harper on his rounds. Days when she just wants to forget other people's troubles. Sometimes it's more than she can manage to stay mad. She waits for Haru to return from work, losing herself in stories until he does. Books take her away from Manzanar, allow her to live other lives in her head for a while. And books are available to her now since the library has finally opened.

"We have a lot to thank the Quakers for," she tells Dr. Harper in a rare moment of gratitude. "That people who have never met us care for us, well, it's . . ."

He has never heard her so pleased, so fulsome about anything before. It's a good sign, he thinks, there must be balance in life after all.

Tamura, though, is not of the same mind.

"You need more than books, more than the company of an old man to fill your days," she says. She has never met Dr. Harper, and, like Haru but for a mother's reasons, she disapproves of the friendship. It's odd, for a start, and she worries that Dr. Harper is exposing Satomi to things best left to her elders. And there's the nuisance of Satomi pleading with her to let Dr. Harper examine her.

"Please, Mother. Just let him give you something for your cough, examine your chest."

"Soon, maybe," she says reluctantly.

"Keep out of the medics' hands for as long as you can," Aaron used to say. "Once they get their hands on you, it's all downhill."

———

Satomi loves the way Haru flirts with her now, even though he keeps up the pretense that she is still a kid. He plays at being irked that he has to put up with her, the annoying girl from next door, shaking his head when she teases him, letting the smile slip from him, frowning a little. He is on the point of kissing her, she knows, and just the anticipation of it warms her up.

Sometimes in the afternoons, to stop herself thinking of him, to keep her heart from flipping at the thought of them touching, she helps Mrs. Hamada out with her brood, washing the little ones' shining faces, taking their pudgy little hands in her own as she makes up games and tells them stories. She enjoys being with the children and it gives Mrs. Hamada an hour or two of peace, time to take a shower, to catch up with the washing.

"You had better be careful," Eriko says, smothering a smile. "Before you know it you'll be popular."

"Oh, it's just something to do," Satomi says.

"You don't have to apologize for it, Satomi," Naomi says, woken from her afternoon sleep by their chatter. "It's good to fill your days, to help others."

Unlike Naomi, Satomi is filled with restless energy and can't sleep in the day. At night her dreams are of a different sort than the old woman's.

"Mine are always about home, and food," Naomi says. "Sweet fried fish, red beans, rice soup."

In Satomi's, memories work themselves through her mind so that the past becomes whole again. She sees the fox, haughty by the porcelainberry bush, hears Mr. Beck's voice, "Know what 'exotic' means, Satomi?"

Sometimes she dreams of Tamura disappearing from her view like smoke dissolving as she reaches out for her. She wakes from those dreams to the form of the robe hovering over her like some Oriental specter.

"It's the same for me," Haru says. "I dream of losing my family. This place does that to you. It changes everything. Yumi no longer eats with us. She goes to a different mess hall with her friends, as though she is ashamed to be one of us. My grandmother's bones ache and her memory is going, she is losing the present, living more and more in the past. It makes me wonder how I am to take care of them here."

Confessing their fears, they find themselves one evening under a waxing moon, kissing for the first time. She has longed for it, imagined how it would be, but when it comes, when Haru leans in to her, she feels like running. Should she open her mouth and taste him, let him taste her, as she had with Artie? She wants to reach up and put her arms around him, pull him to her, but something stops her, some reserve in him, the uncomfortable idea that she wants it more than he does.

He is unflatteringly measured in his approach, in the small pause he takes as though he is debating it, fighting it.

When he does kiss her, there is nothing of the fumbling boy in him, he isn't carried away as she is. His kiss is an accomplished kiss, not hungry as Artie's had been. Not as wholehearted either, she thinks.

It would have hurt her to know that after, when they had walked in silence back to Sewer Alley, he was already regretting it, wishing that they had never gotten started. She is just a kid, after all, not that much older than Yumi. He doesn't want things to get complicated, messed up, doesn't want his mother and Tamura on his case, having expectations.

As the days pass, though, he can't deny that the scent of her, clean as a bolt of new cotton, the warm spread of her breasts pushed up against his chest, have stirred him up so that he can hardly think of anything else. A girl like her, offering herself, seems at once both shameful and irresistible.

"What's the matter with you these days, Haru?" Eriko asks. "You are off somewhere in your head all the time. Tamura is still waiting for you to fix the split in her floor."

"I'll get to it, Mother, just as soon as . . ."

And he will. He will stop wasting time thinking of Satomi, keep it light with her. He has his plans, has held them too long to let a pretty face hold him back. It makes him uncomfortable that he thinks of her a hundred times a day, that she takes his mind off more important things.

"I know that you like Satomi," Eriko says. "I have seen you looking at her, but I don't think that she is for you. And even if she is, that is more reason for you to treat her with respect."

"I'm not interested," he insists. "We're friends, that's all. We have things in common."

"What things?"

"Well, this place, for a start, and she's intelligent, you know, interested in books and ideas. I can talk to her."

The world as Haru had known it has slipped from his grasp, but he is determined to get it back. If he has to fight to be an American, then so be it. His family has worked hard to build the American dream. He believes in it still. Despite Manzanar, the stupid awful things that go on in the camp, he can't let the beautiful idea of the American dream go.

"I'm going to sign up just as soon as they'll let me. I'm going to sign up and fight for my country," he warns Satomi.

"Some country," she scoffs. "It isn't our country anymore. We're the enemy"

"No, we're not, and that's the point. Why can't you see that?"

"It's not me that's blind, Haru."

"Look, Sati, sometimes the things you love don't live up to your expectations. But you can't just give up on them, can you? Whatever you feel now, this is your country as much as anyone's."

"I don't see how you can think that in this place. You'd have to be mad to think that."

"I think it because all Americans are immigrants of one sort or another. Being white doesn't make you more American than if you're black or any color in between."

"Hard to believe that when you're locked up for it, though."

"No country in the world beats America, Sati. It's our home. We'll get over this."

"Well, I'm going to get out of it just as soon as I can. I'm going to travel the world and never come back here."

"What nationality will you put on your passport?"

"Oh, I don't know. I don't have a choice, do I? It would have to be American, I guess."

"Exactly, you don't have a choice. You are as American as the rest of us."

PIONEERS

HARU SAYS THAT they are pioneers at Manzanar, frontiers-people who must invent ways of coping with the little at hand they have to see them through.

"The Japanese are an ingenious people," he says. "We find answers to problems."

But even he runs for cover when the dust storms come. Everyone does. Ingenious or not, no one has found an answer to them. Sucking up dirt on their way into camp, they rain it back down on Manzanar's inmates on their stampede out. The gales are impervious to whatever Manzanar puts up against them. When they blow, there is nothing to be done but to huddle inside and wait them out, to bear the gritty winds that banshee-howl through the cracks in their walls.

Satomi and Tamura, with their knees up to their chins and their heads down, squat together beside their stove under the cover of a blanket.

"We are so often buried alive in the dirt," Eriko says, "that death, when it comes, won't seem much different."

"It's hell's mouth opening," Tamura says. "Spewing out its rage."

She has learned how to spot when the storms are on the horizon long before the distant moan of them can be heard.

"It's on its way," she warns with resignation. "The clouds are sitting right on top of the mountain, all bunched up and ready to pounce."

"Have you got your cotton strips ready, Mama?"

Tamura saves the camouflage off-cuts from the factory floor to cover her mouth with on her way to and from work.

"There is a use for everything," she says with satisfaction.

But Satomi can't accept as Tamura accepts. The storms might be an act of nature, but she rails against them as though they are man-made, as though they are prescribed punishment from the government.

"It makes me mad," she tells Haru. "Those damn storms are like living things, with a will to spoil. Each one makes Mother a bit worse."

But Haru's commiseration only makes her feel more helpless; his sympathy is passive, when what she wants is action.

"I don't know what you expect me to do about them, Satomi. We all have to bear them, even the guards."

"You could get angry, maybe."

"You are a silly girl. Everything makes you mad. I don't know why I bother with you."

For days after the storms blow out, Tamura and Satomi's eyes burn, it hurts their mouths to eat. The dust creeps into their bedding so that their skin is sore from their grit-beds. No amount of shaking will get rid of it. There are times when Satomi fancies that the dust is stacking up inside her, slowly turning her into the fabric of Manzanar.

Lone Pine, their nearest town, has a sprinkler wagon that settles the dust, and there is talk of the camp sharing it.

"It ain't that effective anyway," the guard called Lawson, who talks with her sometimes, tells her. "It just damps down the sidewalk for a bit, that's all."

"Still, it must be better than nothing, Lawson," she says, enjoying how easily he is made to feel guilty.

"You'll get used to it, girl, we all do. Inyo weather is a law unto itself."

"You'd think the mountains would give some protection, but they don't, do they?"

"Nope, where you get mountains, you get extremes. But they're pretty, ain't they? Cigarette?" he always offers. She usually accepts.

"I wouldn't say pretty, exactly."

She can't bring herself to admit it to him, but she is often moved, her heart filled to bursting, by the austere beauty of Manzanar. If she narrows her eyes and dismisses the clutter of the camp, she sees only the vast plains of the sky, the mountain peaks stabbing the clouds, inking them with indigo and purple and the kind of orange that Eriko calls *burnt*. In their jagged summits she conjures up church spires, and the roofscape of a city etched against the sky, a far-off Shangri-la.

But there's no escaping to that Shangri-la, there is no easy place to set her mind in Manzanar, there are no kind seasons to look forward to. It is a habitat of extremes that is always one thing or the other, too cold, too hot, too humid, it is never just right.

"Change is good," Lawson says. "Just when you think you can't bear the cold anymore, it gets hot. Things move fast in earthquake country."

On a day in a hundred-degree summer, when the tar paper on their roof is melting, turning their barrack into a furnace that near enough cooks them, she takes her complaints to Dr. Harper.

"My mother fainted clean away today, Dr. Harper. You could boil hot dogs on those barrack roofs."

"They faint in the mess hall lines too. We have always suffered hot summers here," he says sympathetically.

He thinks guiltily of the fans in his own house that his wife sets near bowls of ice to cool the air. There are no fans, there is no ice to be had in Manzanar.

"It's worse for my mother, she is so ill," Satomi says. "Her chest never gets better and she is too thin. It is very hard on her."

"Why don't you bring her to see me, Satomi? I would be happy to examine her, and I would like to meet her."

"You wouldn't believe how stubborn she is, Dr. Harper. No one would. People love her sweetness; they can't imagine how when she sets her will to something she can't be moved."

"And she doesn't want to come?"

"No, she says she is getting better, but she isn't. She isn't one little bit better."

"Well, if she would allow me, I could visit your barrack. I would like to see what sort of mother grows a daughter like you."

Naomi Okihiro refuses to see Dr. Harper too, even though a strange pain overtakes her heart every now and then and her arthritis aches worse than a toothache as it sets her bones to stone. Sometimes it throbs in her so fiercely that she can't get out of her chair, let alone make it to the spigot at the end of their alley.

"Do you need water?" Satomi checks with her every afternoon.

"No, I have plenty," she lies, wanting only her daughter Eriko, to see to her needs.

It is not uncommon for Eriko to return from work to find her mother so dehydrated that she can hardly speak. She must be wrapped in a wet sheet, made to sip water slowly until she returns to herself.

"Things are getting worse with her," Eriko says. "But she will not see a male doctor. She has her own way of doing things."

"Which is no way at all," Satomi says. "I prefer more modern methods, myself."

She nags at Tamura until, running out of will, her mother agrees to go with her to the camp hospital.

"It's a fuss about nothing," Tamura apologizes to Dr. Harper, making light, in her shyness, of her cough, the pain in her chest. "Satomi worries about me, but there are worse here. I can manage."

Dr. Harper is a little shy himself, taken aback by the feelings that the sight of Tamura has stirred in him. She is ill, that much is obvious, but it is more than a doctor's concern he is feeling. No sound has ever touched him quite as viscerally as Tamura's voice touches him. She is, he thinks, a woman of delightful beauty. Despite her pallor, he sees the rosy girl in her, the sweetness Satomi spoke of. The heat in him rises to match that of the day. It has been a long time since he has felt such a tugging, fluttering thing, such a soft explosion inside. He feels foolish. It is unseemly for a married man who won't see sixty again, a doctor, to feel so arrested by a patient.

"She won't complain, but this place is killing her," Satomi says, breaking into his thoughts.

"I can see you are not well, Mrs. Baker," he says, listening through his stethoscope to the thick thud of Tamura's chest as she responds to his direction to cough. "Perhaps a few days' rest will help."

"I have tried that, Dr. Harper. It only makes me more restless. I like to keep occupied. It is better to work, don't you think?"

He prescribes a tonic to build her strength, knowing it might as well be sugar water. He has no medicine to cure what she has, no magic. He is overcome with a profound sadness.

"I've seen that stuff before," Eriko says. "It's nothing more than treacle laced with cheap alcohol. Hot tea would do more good."

"I'll take it back and ask for something better," Satomi says, knowing that Dr. Harper will indulge her. He is a man with a conscience and likes to find answers to her challenges.

She longs for Tamura to be returned to her old self, wants her Angelina mother back. She has a picture in her head of Tamura sitting on their porch shelling peas, the glossy loop of her hair shining, her profile silhouetted in the soft light; she pictures her straining rice, stirring clothes in the copper boiler at the back of the house. There are no chores that can diminish Tamura's dignity. Her every movement has a refinement about it.

At night just before sleep she summons up a picture of the old Tamura in her head, hoping to dream of her in better times, of Aaron, of the farm.

Sleep, though, is a hard thing to sustain in the camp. Something is always on the boil with one or another of Manzanar's ten thousand inhabitants. Women give birth at all hours, and the ill and the old die, not always quietly, even though some of them welcome death. Crying babies and the moans of nightmares are the order of the confined nights. Worst of all for Satomi, though, are the noises that come from closer to home.

"I can't bear it," she whispers to Tamura through their silk partition, despairing at the embarrassing sounds of lovemaking that nightly beat through the half-inch division wall from Mr. and Mrs. Sano's room. Their enthusiasm seems quite horrible, considering they share their quarters with their daughter-in-law and their two grandchildren. Their son is confined to a citizens' isolation center in Catalina, for making too many complaints of a political nature.

"My son is a fine man," Mrs. Sano says. "He takes after his father."

Hardly a sound emanates from the Okihiros' side, but the Sanos live their life regardless and have no consideration at all.

Mr. Sano at sixty-five is a bent man, his back stooped from years of picking strawberries for a living, his skin like buffalo hide, but he is surprisingly energetic when he wants to be.

"He looks like a wrinkled old turtle." Satomi shudders. "More like eighty-five than sixty-five—ninety, even."

"It gives them comfort," Tamura says, mortified herself at Mr. Sano's grunts, his wife's high-pitched mews. "It's worse for their daughter-in-law, poor girl. She has a lot to put up with."

"But they are so old, Mother. It's disgusting."

"It is better not to whisper," Tamura advises, coughing out her words. "Whispering only makes our neighbors more interested in our conversation. I wouldn't like them to hear us talking about them."

Satomi is surprised at the strength Tamura has found to cope with everything that has been thrown at her since she lost husband and home. Her mother has a knack for friendship. People may still be suspicious of her strange daughter, a girl who thinks herself equal to her superiors, but their hearts are open to Tamura. They like her honest approach, her modesty.

" 'Honor' is the word for Tamura," Eriko says. "There's nothing false about her."

"Your mother is the sweetest lady," Ralph teases her. "Guess you must take after your father, huh?"

Tamura, the woman now that she would never have become if Aaron had lived, goes to work cheerfully and sings "God Bless America" every morning alongside the Stars and Stripes with her fellow workers in the breakfast line. When all they get is canned wieners and spinach cooked to slime, her complaints are merely for form. Yet there are times when she longs to hold one perfect just-laid egg in her hand, to touch it to her lips and feel its gentle warmth, times when she remembers the pleasure in being a wife, the joy of a good harvest. Recalling those things, it is a small embarrassment to her that she is happy at Manzanar.

"How can you sing, Mother? What is there to sing about here? And 'God Bless America,' of all songs!"

"You should try it yourself, Satomi. You can't be unhappy while you are singing."

However hard it is for Satomi to understand, the truth is that Tamura isn't afraid of anything anymore. Even the idea of death, close as she suspects it is, has found its place and settled. She has found friendship and laughter at Manzanar, and in the companionship of the Okihiros she has been returned to the camaraderie of family, albeit not one of blood.

Her love of country, of America, is strong in her. She caught that germ from her parents long ago and will never be cured of it. Japan for her is simply a place in her imagination, a legendary land where the fables of her mother's childhood are set. It is not to be confused with the Japan that drops bombs on America, the Japan that killed Aaron. She trusts in an American future.

"You have to let your anger go," she tells Satomi. "The only person it is having an effect on is you."

When Tamura gets food poisoning from a mess hall stew that had been reheated once too often, the residents of Sewer Alley are surprised to see Dr. Harper come calling twice daily until she is recovered.

"White men seem to like her," they gossip without spite.

Few in the camp escape the infections that stalk the place. Dirty water brings dysentery, proximity spreads whooping cough and the pitiless episodes of measles that are rife among the children.

"It seems the orphanage is always quarantined," Satomi observes to Dr. Harper.

"Yes, from fleas to flu," he agrees. "There's no end to it."

"Poor little things, without mothers to comfort them."

"I've noticed you talking to the children, Satomi. I've seen them run to you. They like you. You should help out there. Too many of your fellows speak of being an orphan as something shameful."

"Some do, I know. The Japanese word for it is *burakamin*, it means untouchable. But it's not a common view, Dr. Harper, we are not savages, you know?"

Apart from the diseases, people die of other natural causes too, of heart attacks and old age. Some, it's said, of shame and broken hearts, and there have been suicides. One man was so distressed at being separated from his family that he attempted to bite off his tongue; when that didn't work, he climbed the camp fence and was shot by a guard. Murder or suicide, it was hard to tell.

"Murder, of course," Satomi said.

"Perhaps," Haru dithered.

The hastily cleared ground of the once-tiny cemetery is constantly having its boundaries widened. The dead are quickly laid to rest, their families marking their graves with a simple ring of rocks. A small obelisk fashioned from stone has been placed in the heart of the graveyard as a monument to the dead.

"A consoling tower," Naomi says.

Tamura weeps for the dead whether she knew them or not. "They died wondering what it has all been for," she says. "They never found their way home."

One afternoon in the camouflage shed, suffering from lack of breath and cutting pains in her chest, she is carted off to the hospital barrack, where, serving as a ward, three iron beds are arranged in the open air alongside the hospital's latrines. There are two more beds inside and the part-time nurse tells Tamura to sit on one while she waits for Dr. Harper.

"It's written on your notes that Dr. Harper wishes to deal with you himself," she says, giving Tamura a suspicious look. "You'll have to wait while we find him."

Eriko, fearing for Tamura's life, rushes to find Satomi, who is in the showers, where she goes at quiet times to wash her hair with the scented soap that Lawson gives her. When she can't be found in her usual hangouts it's a fair bet that Satomi will be in the showers, lost in the sweet reward of floral foam.

"Your mother is stable," Dr. Harper says. "She has a weak constitution, of course, and the food poisoning didn't help, but . . ."

"How can she be stable? Look how she fights for breath."

"Don't pester Dr. Harper, Satomi." Tamura pants, struggling for air. "He is doing his best. It is not his fault. There is nothing to be done."

"Is that true, Dr. Harper? There is nothing to be done?"

"There are things you can do to help, Satomi. Keep your mother warm, see that she eats regularly. I would suggest that she gives up work on the camouflage nets, but I guess she'll fight you on that one. The dust there is full of fibers. It's a problem there's no answer to."

"Letting her go home would keep her from the dust, Dr. Harper."

"If it was up to me, Satomi, then . . . of course . . ."

If he had the power to order it, he would free all of Manzanar's inmates. He wishes with all his heart that he could save Tamura. It hurts him that he can't cure her. The thought that, like his wife, she might be disappointed in him too, adds to his feelings of impotence. Without reason he has taken on himself the blame for him and his wife being childless, it is the least he can do for the wife he had long ago lost interest in.

"Isn't there proper medicine for her cough, at least?"

"Well, nothing that will do much good. I'll see that she gets an extra blanket, though, that should help."

How can he tell Satomi what Tamura knows and has chosen not to tell her? The girl is bright enough to see others in the camp with the same condition. She just isn't ready to see it in her mother.

The tuberculosis has advanced beyond medicine. Tamura is already coughing up blood, having to sit upright through the night just to keep breathing. One foot in front of the other is the only way to go now. And Satomi looks scared enough already, no point in telling her there is worse to come.

"Have you thought about helping at the Children's Village, Satomi?" he says, to distract her. "I have spoken to them about you. They can do with all the help they can get, you know."

"If they'll have me, I will. Mother wants me to, and I guess that I do too."

"Good, it will suit you, I think."

"Just the thought of you helping there makes me feel better." Tamura smiles. "You are a good girl at heart."

"And there's other good news," Dr. Harper says. "You'll be pleased to hear that work starts on the new hospital this week. There will be more doctors coming to join us, Japanese ones among them. Things here are looking up."

"We won't be holding our breath," Satomi says under hers, but loud enough to be heard.

"No, no, it's for real. And there are to be more latrines too. We're gonna get on top of these infections for sure. You can count on it." He hopes that he is right. It seems to him that one way or another the whole camp is diseased.

"I'll keep my fingers crossed for new latrines, at least, Dr. Harper. Guess you've never had to wait in line for them yourself?"

"Well—" he manages before she interrupts him.

"We try not to notice the sour air, or see the sewage bubbling up through our feet. We put up with the paper always running out and the flies everywhere."

"I'm sorry they are so bad. It will help when there are more, I'm sure."

"You can't imagine how humiliating it is for the women in those lines, or how vulgar the men can be."

"No, I can't say that . . ."

Tamura joins in to help him out. "They only joke to ease their embarrassment," she says, frowning at Satomi.

"I will mention it to the superintendent in charge," Dr. Harper says. "You are right, something must be done."

Later, as Tamura sits chatting to Eriko, she protests Satomi's behavior. "I felt sorry for Dr. Harper, Eriko. Honestly, Satomi gives him such a hard time. They seem to be friends, yet still I am shocked at her lack of respect."

"She is too outspoken," Eriko agrees. "But there is nothing to be done about it, she is already made. In any case, I think that Dr. Harper likes her enough to forgive her. Did he give you anything for your cough?"

"Yes, a blanket." Tamura giggles. "What else can he do? Oh, and good news. He says that new latrines are to be built soon."

"Really? My mother will be pleased, if that's true. It's the old who suffer most. Mother will only go at the quietest time of day, and even then it's torture for her. It's the same for all the old women. They have to go in pairs, one always on guard for the other."

"Mmm, they were formed in Japan's clay. They are modest. We have become used to it, but they never will."

"Well, neither will I," Satomi's voice comes rudely through their dividing wall, against which she is propped with *Wuthering Heights* in hand. "I can't bear those filthy latrines."

"Oh, Satomi, it's not the same thing at all. And I notice you have no such inhibitions when it comes to the showers."

"It's no wonder people take against you," Eriko joins in crossly. "You never know when to be still, when to stay quiet. You are forever in the line for the showers, keeping people waiting."

If there is one thing that makes Eriko irritable, it's talking through the wall, it seems to her to be the height of bad manners.

But she instantly regrets her irritation, even though she is only speaking the truth.

Sometimes Satomi will finish one shower and straight off join the end of the line to take another. Her reputation suffers and people find relief in grumbling about her.

"Her manners are bad."

"It's to be expected, I suppose."

"But Tamura is so kind, so polite."

"She is a cuckoo in Tamura's nest."

"I hear she takes soap from the guards."

Tamura is gently critical too. "You must learn to manage. I do not like you taking things from Lawson, it will make you unpopular."

"Oh, Mama, I've never been popular here, now, have I?"

"Well, it's your own fault, you never try to please. And what does he want in return for the soap that only you receive?"

She doesn't like the question. It is her business, after all.

"He never asks me for anything. Ralph says that Lawson is kind to everyone, that he's a people person and likes to talk."

"Well, you won't have time to talk when you are working at the orphanage. You'll be too busy with the little ones."

"I'm looking forward to it, Mama. Don't be cross."

"And you are good with children," Tamura says, softening. "People will see that and like you better for it."

REMEDIES

T HE ORPHANAGE BARRACKS have their own running water and a small block of toilets for their own use. That in itself is enough to recommend them to Satomi, without the warmth
that opened her heart to the children on her first day there.

"They're sweet and naughty," she tells Haru. "And they smell
like kittens."

The babies, in their ignorance of desertion, cry as babies will,
but they are more easily comforted than the older ones—a clean
diaper, a bottle of warm milk soothes quickly enough. The others, though, suffer the feral instinct of wariness and hold themselves back from consolation.

"Oh, Mama, you should see them. So frightened of everything
that they wet the bed and think they will be beaten for it. Some
are like me, of mixed blood, you know. There's a red-haired
child, and two or three with golden hair. There's a little boy who
says he's Mexican. He speaks Spanish and only knows a word or
two of English."

"Perhaps you will find who you are among them," Tamura says
mysteriously.

Arriving at Manzanar with their tiny carrying cases, the children
have everything taken off them. Clothes are sorted into piles by
age rather than ownership. There are dungarees, little felt jackets,

knitted hats and shoes set in a line by size. It's easier to store their possessions together, to jumble them up, so that no one knows who came with what. Some came with nothing anyway, not even identity papers. Too young to speak their names, not knowing where they came from, no information can be coaxed from them. Satomi gives them names, guesses at their ages.

The few who have toys are made to share them, to watch, heartbroken, as a loved grubby doll, a tin car, is taken off by another child. One little boy has started a collection of empty bean cans, no one but him wants them, they are his alone. Another holds on tight to a small handkerchief, sniffing at it, rubbing it against his cheeks.

"It's not right," Satomi tells Dr. Harper. "They need families, people of their own." She is thinking of Mrs. Hamada's brood, their easy smiles, their confident fights, the love that bolsters them.

There are days in the orphanage when, despite the strict rules, chaos takes over, when it is hard to make yourself heard above the children's howling. The naughtier boys who misbehave have to run the "swat line." They dodge and dive between the legs of the children who need no encouragement to whack their fellows' hides. Whackers and whacked make a game of it, minding more the cross word than any physical punishment.

"They get bored," Satomi tells Haru. "There are hardly any books or toys. They can't think of anything to do but fight."

"You must be firmer, Sati. Bring order."

"They have so little, Haru. I can't bear to punish them."

"They have you, Satomi. They have food and a roof over their head. It's not a family, but nothing in life is equal. They cannot be allowed to run wild."

She hears his words as a reproach, hears his disappointment in her. If only he would stop lecturing and take her side for once. If only he would kiss her more often, hold her, tell her whatever she does is all right with him. She has competition for Haru, she knows. There are plenty of girls trying to catch his eye, girls who play better to his wanting-to-be-in-charge nature. She feels more challenged, though, by his view of the world, the formality in him, the way he thinks a woman should be.

"You have forgotten what it is like to be a child, Haru."

"You are right, I suppose. I think more like a father these days."

Soothed by the act of giving, the guard Lawson begins to bring gifts for the orphanage children, marbles, and crayons, his old baseball and glove, his daughter's discarded dolls. He is a man full of guilt for what he has to guard. His left-the-nest daughter is only a few years older than Satomi and according to him not unlike her in looks.

"She married a no-gooder," he says. "Lives five miles away, but we never see her."

Lawson's wife has Indian blood. "A quarter Shoshone," he says. "Although she is fierce enough for it to be Apache."

"He can hardly be accused of bigotry," Satomi defends him to Haru.

No matter what anyone says, it's fine by her if Lawson finds relief in giving the children presents, in giving her soap.

"You take it, honey, I know you girls like to smell good."

She doesn't like upsetting Tamura, getting on the wrong side of Haru, but where should she take her friends from in this place? The girls of her own age are wary of her, and so much duller than Lily ever was, for all her sneakiness.

"You don't give them a chance, Satomi. You don't give anyone but Dr. Harper and Ralph a chance. If you're unpopular it's your own fault," Tamura says.

If only Tamura knew the truth of it, how it is the other way around. How she is ogled by the men in the camp in a way the full

Japanese girls are not. How the one who is always offering her mother his place in the noontime lunch line had, in the alley that is the shortcut to the mess hall, exposed himself to her daughter. The sight of the sallow thing hanging there hadn't shocked her in the least, but she had kept the information to herself, not wanting Haru to know and feel obliged to do something about it.

"Oh, put it away, you fool," she had said dismissively.

"Sorry," the old man faltered, scrutinizing her face. "It was an accident. Everyone has accidents."

It had struck her as a pointless thing for the old man to do, like showing someone your snot.

And he isn't the only one to pester her. Without the inhibitions they would have been subject to at home, a few of the old men in their humiliation look around with their faded eyes and see her, the girl who is not really one of them, but lush and full of sap, with that American cocksureness about her. It's a mind-easing sport, tormenting the *movie star.*

"Hey baby, hey baby," they call in exaggerated jazz-speak. "You wanna help us out?"

She brushes aside their stares, the sight of their open mouths and their odd, quite terrible smiles. She tells herself they are beneath noticing. Quick to take offense, they feel insulted to be so ignored.

It would have surprised her to know that Haru sees it all and is angry with her for attracting the attention. He despises the old men. If they had been young he could have fought them, but the young men who pursue Satomi seem in better control of themselves, they have their pride, and their pursuit is only natural, after all. As it is, he has to content himself with the fact that his elders are not always his betters. When his world is made whole again, he hopes to forget the many disturbing ways in which Manzanar has altered it.

He should act honorably himself, he thinks, give Satomi up. It's only fair, but the feel of her as she melts into him in the dark places they find together, the scent of her skin, their long kisses, keep him wanting, keep him unsure. He tells himself that if he is certain of one thing, it is that he fears the life he would have with her more than he fears losing her. She will always try to pull him her way, refuse to be led, and she is a stranger to humility. She is too much for him, all heat and desire, lacking the rod of reserve he expects in a woman.

"Are we or are we not going steady, Haru?"

"There's no going steady here, Sati. Things are too unsettled to commit ourselves. We don't have to give our friendship a name, do we?"

"I was going steady with Artie before I was fourteen."

"That was just kids' stuff."

She wants to slap him at the same time as kiss him. "So this is nothing special, then?" she says, as though it hardly matters to her.

"We can't let it be. It isn't going to last."

Consequences hang over him, will trap him if he isn't careful. With luck he will be drafted soon, he can't wait to go, but it gnaws at him that Sati will have no one then to rein her in.

"You're too independent for your own good," he says.

"That's the American in me," she taunts. "Thought you liked everything American."

"Why doesn't she make friends among the girls?" he asks Eriko. "It's not natural, surely, to always be in the company of old men and boys."

"The girls bore her," Eriko says. "She's a swan among ducks, I suppose. Satomi goes her own way, you know that. Don't think that you can change her, Haru, you never will."

"It's unsuitable," he persists. "Dr. Harper is far above her in position, yet she challenges him at every turn. Things are bad enough with Yumi, without Satomi's example of do-as-you-like next door."

He complains, but the pull of her is getting stronger, he can't hold out for much longer, no matter his mother, no matter Tamura. She is at the root of his sudden awakenings in the night, the selfish need in him. His head says no, his stirred-up body doesn't want to hear. Sometimes when he looks at her, at her radiant skin, the waves of her dark hair breaking over her shoulders, he marvels at her interest in him. When she gives him that white smile, he sees her all bright and shell-clean and falters in his resolve. He desires her, but he doesn't love her, not enough to compromise his plans for, anyway. He takes refuge in criticism.

"You are upsetting your mother, you know, taking cigarettes and soap from Lawson. Your ration would last if you didn't spend so long in the showers."

"I'm just washing away Manzanar, Haru. In any case, the soap issue doesn't lather, you know that. It smells of disinfectant. What's wrong with wanting to be clean, to smell nice?"

She is prepared to take his disapproval. It is worth it if only to smell good for him, she so loves to smell good for him. And those few minutes when she stands under the water soaping her hair, rinsing it until it is squeaky clean, are heaven. Water alone doesn't cut it, it's the soap that satisfies.

"I will buy you scented soap," Tamura says. "What do I work for, if not to care for you?"

"Buy yourself things, Mama. Don't fret about me."

In summer the shower block, pleasantly warm for a change, presents her with a new problem. A colony of black horseflies have set up camp in the dank building, hovering over the scummy water that pools in the cracked floor, landing on her as she dries herself. She hates their popping eyes, their swollen blood-filled bellies. Everyone is disgusted by them. The ugly things refuse to be swatted away until they have drunk their fill of blood. Their bites leave great red swellings that take a week to subside.

The throbbing bite that Satomi suffered on her eyelid encouraged Tamura to find a remedy that would soothe it. It occurred to her that an infusion of tea and nettle might calm things down. When it did, she set about making other remedies.

Just as once she had sent Satomi to the woods in Angelina for mushrooms, now she sends her to pick the coarse mountain mint that grows at the west perimeter, to rummage in the mess hall trash for sprouting potatoes that she can plant around her barrack's steps.

People marvel at what Tamura gets out of the dry soil. She grows drills of radish to remedy sluggish circulation, makes onion poultices for flu, and in the summer months lettuce juice to clear the blood of infection. She has even found a use for the hated sagebrush that grows everywhere, poking itself rudely through the holes in the latrine walls, reminding them that they have left civilization behind.

"Mrs. Sano says that she makes a tea from it to cool fever," Tamura tells Eriko.

"Doesn't seem to be doing much for her husband's," Eriko says dryly.

"It would be hard to cure him of his burden, Eriko. It seems to work on others, though."

There is no science to it. Tamura goes on instinct, on childhood memories of her mother's concoctions. Some things work, most don't, but the word spreads, and often in the evening she has a line of patients at her door in Sewer Alley. There is comfort to be had in feeling that at least you are being treated, that you don't have to stand silent in the doctor's line. How can a doctor understand as Mrs. Baker understands? Her smile alone can cure.

Satomi complains that now she has no privacy at all. But it is a good excuse for her to spend more time with Haru, walking and kissing, and dodging the sweeping searchlights that at night hone in on their slightest movement.

Nothing that Tamura makes, though, touches her own cough or stops the hateful night sweats that soak her bedding, chilling her to the bone. Satomi lies feigning sleep, hearing her fighting for breath. It upsets Tamura to disturb her daughter's sleep.

"Go back to sleep," she says, when Satomi pulls aside the robe. "There is nothing you can do. It will be better in the morning."

And it always is a little better when the light comes, although she is fooling no one. Her ashen face mirrors her illness for the world to see, her breath has taken on the peculiar sweet-damp smell of blood and mucus.

"I feel better standing," Tamura says, relieved, when dawn comes. "I breathe better when I'm active."

"It's amazing that she keeps on working," Satomi tells Haru. Let alone that she stays up half the night mashing and blending, thinking up new remedies."

"You should learn from her," he says, unaware of how stern he sounds.

Tamura never fails to tend her little garden, or clean the barrack, even though Satomi has assumed the task to save her the effort.

"You do not even see the dust in front of your eyes," Tamura says. "In any case, I like to do it."

Eriko says that her friend's determination to keep going is something wonderful.

"Your mother is a most remarkable woman, Satomi. How proud of her your father must have been."

With her kind nature and generosity in sharing her concoctions, Tamura, as ever, draws people to her. Her warmth lends forgiveness to Satomi's offhandedness.

"It hardly seems possible the girl is Tamura's daughter," most say.

"She grows on you," a few reply.

There is a softening toward her, but Satomi will never be one of them and they judge her for it, ignorant of the fact that they too have their prejudices.

In return for Tamura's medications, presents come that it would be bad manners to refuse. No one wishes to be in debt, after all. A three-legged stool made from scrap lumber, flowers fashioned from paper, a vase formed from a discarded corn tin, and best of all a saucepan with a well-fitting lid.

"The water won't evaporate when we boil it now," Tamura says, thanking the giver delightedly. Water rarely reaches more than a low simmer on their lukewarm stove.

"Hmm, if you can get the wood for it," he says.

In gratitude for Tamura treating his children's boils with her soot-and-spider's-web paste, Mr. Hamada, who works clearing the land for the new farm project, brings a selection of the little wooden birds he carves in his spare time, for her to choose from.

"He is a true artist," Eriko remarks at the sight of them. "They may not have blood or organs, but there is life in those little creatures."

Tamura takes a long time choosing.

"They are all so beautiful, Mr. Hamada. How can I decide?"

In the end she opts for the smallest unpainted one, it seems to beckon her.

"It's a titmouse," Mr. Hamada says. "In life they are gray, with an eager expression."

The little bird sits in the cup of Tamura's hand, its wings half open, bringing to mind billowing clouds, wind in the grass, memories of birdsong.

"I love it more than anything," she says gratefully.

With these gifts, their room, like many others in the camp, has taken on a character of its own so that the word "home" has re-gained its meaning.

"Even in Sewer Alley people have pride," Haru says. "Pride in how you live is an ancient Japanese virtue."

The proof of the pride he speaks of is to be seen all around them. There are hobby gardens where flowers grown from seed bloom in splashes of welcome color, furniture made from scraps of wood, jewelry from chicken bones and the newfangled dental floss that sometimes comes free with toothpaste. Brushes hang neatly in line on exterior walls, and small rough-hewn benches are placed by scrubbed steps. Someone has positioned the splayed limb of a dead pear tree as a sculpture by their door.

"It's very pleasing," Naomi says.

"Fine now, maybe," Mr. Sano sneers. "Come winter it'll be better burned for firewood."

Everyone, it seems, is busy with some sort of crafting. Haru has made his mother a set of drawers from discarded cardboard boxes. And Naomi, with her failing sight, her arthritic hands, knits mittens for the orphans. She likes to feel useful.

"When I was young," she boasts, "my needles went so fast the wool crackled."

"Sparks flew," Eriko confirms.

Eriko has fashioned curtains for their one small window from a flowered skirt that the ever-expanding Yumi has grown out of.

"They look so pretty," Tamura says.

"Playing at doll's houses, I see," Mr. Sano remarks on his way past.

Longing to indulge her dressmaker's love of frills and bows, Tamura makes aprons for the orphans out of the factory off-cuts. She wishes she could have afforded better, pink and white ging-ham, perhaps, plaids with red in them. She would like to treat the girls, indulge herself in lovely things.

With Naomi's mittens, Tamura's aprons, and Lawson's toys, Satomi rarely goes empty-handed to the orphanage, where she spends the best part of her days caring for the babies, reading to the older children, letting them, to the superintendent's disapproval, clamber all over her. She tries to be even-handed with them but can't help favoring the serious little four-year-old, Cora, who is always at her side. The child, who she thinks resembles Tamura a little, has worked her way into her heart so that she can hardly wait to see her each morning, to pick her up, kiss the smooth cheek, the rosebud lips.

"Oh, Mama, you can't help loving Cora. She just melts your heart."

Cora has blue-black hair cut short, with bangs that frame her doll-pretty face. She is quick and bright, a frightened, brave little girl who knows how to please.

Satomi wonders what experiences have given Cora the extraordinary ability to sense what adults require of her. She is quiet when they want her to be, always helpful, and a little mother to the babies, quite capable of changing diapers and warming bottles.

As far as anyone can make out, and judging from the way she crosses herself at prayer, she must have come from a Catholic orphanage. Her papers have been mislaid, and when questioned she says she lived in a big house with other children. They guess her age to be about four, they would have said five, six even, if she hadn't been so small. She is certain, though, that her name is Cora. The superintendent says that it's not a Japanese name, unless Cora herself has mixed it up with *Kora*, the Japanese demand for, *Listen, you.*

"She is a sweet child," she says. "If only they were all like her."

Joining in with the remaking of Manzanar, the orphanage has planted a lawn, and built a wraparound porch to unite its three barracks. They plan flower borders, a swing for the children if they can find someone to make it.

There are no curbs or sidewalks in the camp, no stores, but if the barbed wire and the gun towers were suddenly to disappear, Manzanar these days might look, through forgiving eyes, much the same as any small American town. The American dream of hearth and home, although battered, seems to be recovering. Yet somehow Manzanar looking more like home only serves to highlight the fact that they are not free.

Frustration boils away under the surface. There is always the sense of waiting in the air, humor is more often than not dark, and irony has replaced optimism. The tension between the Citizens League and the Kibei is a constant, and to add to it, gangs of youths loyal to neither strut about the camp, less willing to please than their older siblings. The feeling that Manzanar's internees have that they are being unfairly, even cruelly treated, that they have lost something precious that can never be regained, refuses to fade.

RIOT

In the freezing air of December when no one is warm
enough and everyone is hungry for the food of home, a riot
erupts in the camp seemingly out of nowhere.

Settling down for the evening, and far from the heart of it, the
residents of Sewer Alley are among the last to open their doors, to
listen and try to make out what the distant rumble of feet, the
shouting, are all about.

Dr. Harper comes to advise Tamura to stay in their barrack.

"The military police have arrested three men for beating up an
informer," he tells her. "They took him from his bed and almost
killed him. We have him in the hospital. Everyone is angry at the
arrest, and there is a crowd demanding their release. I don't think
they are going to settle anytime soon. Please stay home, Tamura,
keep out of it. And put your light out, no point in attracting attention."

"It was kind of you to come," Tamura says, blushing at being
singled out by him. "We are all grateful, Dr. Harper."

"No need for gratitude, Tamura. I am concerned for you, that's
all." He fights the urge he has to stay, to keep by her side, to protect her. "Well, remember the light," he says, hovering at the
door. "I'll be in the hospital all night if you need me."

Hearing Dr. Harper's advice through the wall, Naomi asks

Eriko to leave their light on. "The moon's on the wane and I can't bear to sit in the dark. It makes the cold seem worse somehow." Her voice is wispy, shaking a little.

Naomi has had enough of the cold. Her hand is still bandaged from where it stuck to the barrack's frozen doorknob, pulling the skin from her palm as she tugged her hand free.

"It's stubborn to heal," she complains. "Old age makes the body stubborn."

She can hardly move these days, and knitting now is out of the question. The bones in her fingers are stiff, frozen into immobility.

Haru, on his way to Sewer Alley, stops Dr. Harper on his own way to the hospital. "It's nothing much, is it, Doctor? It'll all blow over soon, won't it?"

"Hard to say, could go either way, boy." He puts a hand on Haru's shoulder. "Look after them," he says, thinking in the moment only of Tamura.

Haru paces the alley, not knowing what he is looking for, his eyes tracking every movement. He guesses that the informer is a member of his own American Citizens League.

"Japanese Uncle Toms," the Kibei accuse league members.

"Traitors to America," the league members retort to the Kibei.

Haru thinks the Kibei mad, troublemakers, out to spoil.

As he paces, the news spreads. Mothers begin appearing at doors, calling their children in from play, worrying about where the older ones might be.

"Have you seen Toru?"

"Where is Yukio? He should be home by now."

Lights go out, people stop calling to each other. Sewer Alley, lit only by a thin portion of moon, looks dim and ghostly.

Eriko pleads for Haru to come inside, but he doesn't want to hide indoors like a coward.

"What could this informer have told them that would create all this trouble?" Tamura asks him on her way to Eriko's. "They already know there is gambling and liquor, they have always looked the other way."

"It's more likely to be that he has given them the names of those Kibei who call themselves Japan's underground. You must have heard their talk, Tamura, seen the way they stir up trouble."

"Yes, but they are only boys trying to be men."

"Maybe, but they are not harmless."

Tamura joins the Okihiros in their room, where Satomi finds her on her return from the orphanage. She has been running and is out of breath.

"I was worried about you. You are very late, Satomi."

"I came the long way around to avoid the fights. That show-off boy who works with Haru at the school asked me if I was with them or against them. I didn't know what he was talking about."

"Is the crowd dispersing?" Haru calls through the open door.

"I don't think so. I heard them shouting and chanting. I tried to find Lawson to ask him what was going on, but I couldn't see him anywhere." She is more excited than afraid, thrilled by the drama, the change of pace in the day.

"We must stay together," Eriko says. "There is safety in numbers."

"Yes, and at least only one stove will need feeding," Tamura says, looking on the bright side as usual.

For once Satomi approves of her mother's optimism. It's good to be near Haru, who at his mother's pleading has reluctantly come inside.

"Just for a moment, just to get warm," he says.

As they sit close, she attempts nonchalance, as though the salty scent of him, the warmth of his body against hers, isn't sending a run of pleasure through her. It hurts to love him so much, to be

the one who loves more. If only he would lose the desire to re-
form her she might in turn try harder to please him.

"I wish I could bring Cora here," she says. "Keep her safe with
us. She was so sweet today, clinging to me, not wanting me to
leave."

"She is safer where she is," Haru says. "No one is going to
bother with the orphanage."

They hear the rioters trawling the camp, seeking out the *inu*, a
word that Satomi has never heard before.

"It's a special word," Eriko says. "It means both dog and traitor."

"Oh, yes, I had forgotten it," Tamura says. "I have forgotten so
much."

There are bangs and shouts and the sound of running feet, and
Mr. Sano comes to tell them that the rioters are smashing up property and beating up those they have named as traitors to their race.

"We are herded here like animals," he says. "Our administrators
have been black-marketing our meat and sugar, and still there are
informers, traitors. Damn stoolies, no wonder people are mad."

"Are they traitors or just good Americans?" Haru is getting
more agitated by the minute. "It's not enough just to say that we
are loyal, Mr. Sano. We must prove it."

Mr. Sano stares at him scornfully. "It's the young who will be
the death of us," he exclaims, raising his hands in exasperation.
"Their blood is always hot, their passions ridiculous."

Eriko and Tamura can't meet each other's eyes for fear they
may laugh.

Shortly after Mr. Sano leaves, two wild-eyed young men with
baseball bats burst through their door, shouting something about
freedom before running off toward the new drainage works by
the cemetery.

"We should have listened to Dr. Harper and put the light out,"
Yumi says reclaiming her child's voice. She is shaking with fright.

The shock of the intrusion, along with the rush of cold air entering their barrack, has brought them to their feet. Eriko puts out their light.

"What's happening now?" Haru shouts after the men. "What's the latest?"

"We're taking control, you bonehead," one of them shouts back. "We're going to smash up the waterworks. Come with us."

"I'm frightened," Eriko tells Haru. "Your sister and grandmother are frightened. You must stay with us, Haru, please don't go out."

She thinks that Mr. Sano is right about the young. They want to be warriors, and Haru is no different. If he leaves their barrack, she fears that she might never see him alive again.

But he has had enough of being among the women, and when a burst of gunfire brings a few seconds' silence in its wake he makes for the door.

"I'm going to find out what is happening. I'll be back soon." He pulls his arm away from Eriko's hold on it. "Let me be a man, Mother," he insists, and she releases him.

"I'm coming with you, Haru."

"No, Satomi, stay with your mother. Your place is with her."

"Don't tell me what to do. I want to see for myself." She is out of the door before Tamura can say anything.

He begins to run, long strides that put a distance between them, making it hard for her to keep up. He wants to be with his friends from the league, he wants to find Ralph and talk it over with him. It's too shameful having a girl tagging along. But when she falls behind he gets worried and stops, looking back to see if she has turned for home.

"You shouldn't have come if you can't keep up," he shouts, catching sight of her. "Why must you insist on acting like a man?"

"Why must you insist on acting like my father?" she screams back.

As they near the mess hall, a gang of youths wearing white headbands scrawled with *toukon*, the Japanese symbol for fighting spirit, come toward them, chanting.

"Long Live His Majesty the Emperor."

They are wielding weapons, kendo fighting sticks, knives, some roughly made hatchets, anything they have been able to lay their hands on.

Satomi stops running, mesmerized by the sight of their brutal arsenal.

"Haru, Haru," she calls breathlessly, but her voice is thin, lost in the air. Without intent, the chanting youths knock her about in their charge.

The searchlights are tracking the boys and a wide cone of light has them in its sights, catching her in its beam too, blinding her so that it's impossible to see anything but the glaring white light.

The youths pass, leaving her in the dark as the quaking sound of the guards' oncoming feet running to catch up with the trouble-makers adds to her confusion. She stumbles down the nearest alley, pressing herself against the side of a barrack wall as they pass, kicking up a flurry of dust with their heavy boots.

Her hand goes to her heart as though to stop it from leaping from her chest, her lungs are burning from the effort of trying to keep up with Haru, she can feel her blood pulsing. Haru has disappeared, deserted her. She is alone and frightened in the moments before she hears his shout, hoarse and panicky.

"Sati, where the hell are you?"

"I'm here, over here," she yells from the shadows, as a man reeking of sweat and potato vodka grabs her arm, ripping the sleeve of her jacket.

"I'll save you," he slurs. "Stay with me."

As she struggles, Haru appears at her side, pulls the man off her, takes her hand roughly, and forces her to run with him.

In front of the jailhouse in the crammed square the searchlights dazzle. Ranks of soldiers have drawn a line three deep in the sand. The thought crosses her mind that next door to the jailhouse Dr. Harper is inside the hospital. He will be soothing his patients, who will be as scared as her, maybe. She would like to join him, but it would take a tank to make a path through the mob.

Corralled in front of the soldiers, who are attempting to hold their ground, the crowd moves like the sea, a huge tide of bodies surging forward. A truck is pushed through the soldiers' ranks into the jailhouse. Glass shatters, there is a crunching sound, a cheer goes up.

Haru is mouthing something to her that she can't hear—she thinks he is telling her to stay close, but in the throng's pitching they are forced apart, so that her hand is torn from his just as a guard takes aim and shoots into the crowd.

In the alarm the gunfire causes she is knocked to the ground, where, among the feet and the dust, things seem to go into slow motion.

In case another round should come and split the air as horribly as the first, she covers her ears with her hands and curls her body tight, knees up, head down.

Through the tangle of legs she can see a boy crouched on the ground like her, but somehow not like her. His body is still, his head twisted unnaturally to the side, his hand open as though it has frozen in the act of waving. As she looks, a spurt of blood wells up through his pale T-shirt, spreading across his chest, a red flower opening its petals. He slumps forward, and drops of blood plop slowly to the ground and mix with the dirt. And suddenly she is screaming, struggling to move, scanning the forest of legs for a space to crawl through. A booted foot treads on her ankle and the searing pain draws a yelp from her. She thinks she sees Ralph's legs through the stirred-up dust, cotton trousers, the sneakers that have lost their laces. He is too far away to get to.

"I told you not to come," Haru roars above her head, pulling her to her feet. "Did you really want to see that?"

"No. Did you?" Her body is shuddering, her legs weak, she is covered in dirt, bruises already blooming on her forehead, a dark graze on her ankle.

Acrid smoke fills the air as people begin to cough and splutter and hastily withdraw from the square. Something is happening to Haru, he can't seem to speak, and just as she begins to choke herself she sees that the whites of his eyes have become bloodshot.

"It's gas," he croaks.

Satomi takes his hand and they stagger away from the crowd, hoping to find some good air to breathe.

Three hours later they emerge from under the barrack where they took shelter. Shaken and silent, with each other, they return home red-eyed with the news that things are finally quieting down.

"There was no order to fire," Haru says angrily. "But they did anyway. There are two dead, and ten more wounded." He absent-mindedly picks up the sleeping Naomi's blanket, which has slipped to the floor, and covers her lap with it.

"Two boys dead," he repeats, as though he can't take it in himself.

"They used tear gas to calm things down," Satomi adds in a rush. "It was horrible, it made our eyes burn, and Haru was sick."

Haru looks embarrassed. "Nothing to make a fuss about," he says irritably, as Eriko forces him to sit. He is ashamed that he was the one to be sick. Satomi could have kept quiet about it, but she has no sense about such things. She allows him no pride.

"People were dizzy and stumbling all over the place, but angry too, really angry." She can't seem to stop talking, the words tumbling out of her as she moves restlessly about. Haru, sitting now, has gone quiet.

The bruises on Satomi's face have deepened to a livid puce, her clothes are torn and filthy. Pictures of the fallen boy, of his bloody T-shirt, flash horribly at intervals in her mind.

At the sight of Satomi bruised but alive, Tamura suffers the flash of anger that comes after child-lost, child-found, is over.

"You shouldn't have gone," she says disapprovingly. "You should have listened to Haru."

Yumi is picking at her skirt, hopping from one foot to the other. She needs to pee but is scared to go to the latrines on her own.

"You're sure it's all over?" she keeps asking Haru.

"Yes, go," he says. "It's all quiet now."

It is past dawn already and none of them, apart from Naomi, has slept.

Tamura goes to their barrack for her toothbrush, for the sliver of soap she is making last.

"I'll wash at the spigot this morning," she calls to Eriko.

When she returns she is in a better mood. She never sleeps much anyway, and what can she do about Satomi? The truth is the girl is a copy of her father, another Aaron. She won't be ruled.

"Should we go to work, do you think?" Eriko asks Haru.

"I think you should. We must help get things back to normal. I will walk my class to school. You come with me, Yumi. I'll see you into yours." He is finding relief in taking charge.

"I'll walk with you and Eriko, Mother," Satomi says. "Give me a moment to change. I guess they won't be opening the mess halls for a while, so breakfast will be late."

She holds Tamura's hand as they walk. It feels thin, more bone than flesh, as though she is holding a tiny newborn mouse. Eriko *tsks* at the mess the camp is in, shaking her head at the madness in the world.

There's a handwritten sign on their mess hall door: BREAKFAST IN ONE HOUR.

"We are fine, you know," Eriko says to Satomi. "You don't have to walk us like children. You're the one who is limping."

"I want to. I won't settle until I see Mother through the door. Then I'll backtrack and take the shortcut to the orphanage."

"Eriko's right, there's no need," Tamura agrees. "Who would want to hurt me? You go back, I know you want to check on Cora."

"No point, we're nearly there, Mama."

Across the way from the factory two white fire officers from Lone Pine stand beside a fire engine, looking around as though on alert for a predator.

Tamura and Eriko's supervisor is at the door ushering the workers in.

"It's on loan from the Forest Service, just in case," he says archly, nodding toward the fire engine. He has a cut above his lip repaired with four catgut stitches. Like a half mustache, Satomi thinks. It gives him a jaunty air, but no one mentions it. They have passed similar on their way here, closed eyes, cuts, swellings. Already it is bad form to ask what side you are on.

"Hey, little darlin'," one of the officers calls, giving a long low whistle. "Are you looking for a fight too?"

Tamura lets go of Satomi's hand and marches up to him. "Do you want to cause more trouble?" she asks as though talking to a child. "Is my daughter never to be left in peace?"

The soldier gives a nasty laugh and turns his back on her. A truck comes toward them slowly, two guards at its side gathering the wood from the smashed-up laundry tubs, throwing it into the back of the pickup as they go.

"Tricky customers, these Nips, go off like fireworks at the slightest thing. Better not to get too familiar," they advise the Lone Pine officers.

"I was going to wash my mother's clothes today," Eriko says placidly to Tamura. "Now what will we do?"

"They can't all be broken, Eriko. We will just have to share."

The mess hall bells are ringing in memory of the two dead boys. A strangely playful sound, betraying the sadness in the air.

"One was seventeen, the other twenty-one," the supervisor says. "Ten more wounded in the hospital."

On hearing who the dead boys are, Eriko says that she had known one of them.

"I can't believe it's him," she says, sighing. "He was a gentle boy, very polite to his elders. A good boy."

On her way to the orphanage, Satomi comes across Lawson overseeing a gang of Japanese who are sweeping the debris of the battle into piles in readiness for the truck to pick up.

"There'll be questions to answer," he says sorrowfully. "You can't just fire without an order, not in America anyway."

"Then why did they, Lawson?"

"The military got nervous, I guess. Things got out of hand, but still we have laws, don't we. You can't go around shooting people."

"Seems you have, though, doesn't it?"

"Not me, Satomi, not me. In any case, you'll get justice, you'll see."

"It's a bit late for that, isn't it?"

"I guess, maybe. Anyway, I'm pleased to see that you are all right, at least. How are you doing for soap?"

"Nothing against you, Lawson, but I won't be taking soap anymore."

The dissent in the camp has been revealed. Bones have been broken, blood spilled, to say the least. She doesn't know on which side to stand, but it would be wrong now to accept gifts from Lawson. Things will never go back to how they were. No doubt the dead will be buried, the wreckage of the battle cleared, but the riot has already left something less tangible than bodies and debris in its wake, a postscript provoked by outrage. The Japanese inmates are no longer sheep to be herded.

By the time she reaches the alleyway that is the cut-through to the orphanage, the bells have stopped ringing. A short tolling for two short lives, she thinks, surprised that death comes so unexpectedly to some.

And then the picture flashes into her mind again, the twisted head, that pathetic hand, the black blood in the dust. She pauses for a moment, looking back, trembling a little. It is very cold, the air quite still, for once. Apart from two old men sitting around a tin-can fire at its far end, the alleyway is empty. People are at work or behind the safety of their closed doors. Better to keep your head down on such a day. They should have known that, since Pearl Harbor, December is a dangerous month.

How can she go to work as though nothing has happened, resume her routine as easily as Tamura and Eriko seem to have done? She is so tired that if it wasn't for Cora she would return to Sewer Alley and sleep the day away. But Cora will be anxious, looking toward the door for her, and she wants to see the little girl, hold her close. Tears come streaming, she is suddenly filled with sympathy for the world, for the dead boys, for the look now in Yumi's once-innocent eyes, for the hurt that is Cora.

The desire for a cigarette comes as it often does, but she has none. She pictures herself setting the match, drawing deep, the familiar catch in her throat as the smoke snakes through her. Why had she let Haru talk her into giving them up?

"You don't have the money for them anyway, Sati."

"I could share yours."

"No, it's horrible to see a girl smoking. I can't bear the smell on you."

Halfway down the alley, as she stops to knot her scarf against the cold, her eyes are drawn to movement at an open doorway. Two boys of around Haru's age are joined together kissing. She stands stock-still, staring, her mouth open, her bottom lip pendulous. In the middle of the kiss one begins to unbuckle the other's belt, laughing as their lips part. They move in a secret primitive language, boy against boy, slim on slim, no curves, equal strengths.

It seems to her a nonsensical scene, like something out of those dreams that you feel shame for when you wake, as though you had conjured them out of the dark bit inside you that nobody knows about. The riot must have created a mad sort of electricity in the air, turned things on their head.

The one whose buckle has been undone catches sight of her staring, but she can't look away, she might as well be rooted in the frozen mud beneath her feet. His body stills for a moment, but then he returns her stare, exaggerating the incline of his head, raising his eyebrows in a sort of challenge that she has no idea how to meet. With a half smile on his face, he shrugs and kicks the door shut.

She doesn't mention what she has seen to Haru. Will never, she thinks, mention it to anyone. She feels sure that she wouldn't be believed.

After that day, whenever she thinks about those boys, their lean embrace, it seems to her that she has witnessed a wonderfully rebellious, entirely independent act. It's all wrong, of course, surely not what nature intended, but it pleases her to know that she isn't the only outsider at Manzanar.

She scans the newspapers that Dr. Harper gives her for reports of the riot and finds none. It's as though America has forgotten their incarcerated fellows. There is news of German U-boats harassing shipping on the East Coast; news of the movie actress Carol Lombard who has died in a plane crash, on her way back from a tour to promote the sale of war bonds. A radio station called the Voice of America has begun broadcasting, and the British have asked their citizens to bathe in five inches of water to help the war effort. There's a new drink called *instant coffee* and Glenn Miller has sold a million copies of "Chattanooga Choo Choo." Gas has gone up to fifteen cents a gallon, and Joe Louis has taken the heavyweight title in one. The world outside of Manzanar is in those pages, the world that interests America.

"What has happened to the American conscience?" Ralph asks Dr. Harper. "It's shaming that under pressure we have forgotten that we are a democracy."

"They may have reasons for censoring it," Dr. Harper suggests.

"Not so much censored as ignored, I bet," Satomi says. "I guess as far as news is concerned we're not worth the print."

The three of them sit in silence for a while musing on it.

The riot's fallout takes its effect. Everyone is on edge, captors and caught alike. The guards aren't so ready anymore with their smiles, and they don't call greetings from the gun towers as they used to. The known leaders of the Kibei are being segregated, ready to be sent off to the Tule Lake camp in northern California, where, droved together, it will be easier to control them. The meaner guards have their fun with them, telling them they are being rounded up for the firing squad.

"You creeps are gonna pay the price now," they taunt.

Haru is ordered to join a line to sign the new loyalty oath that will distinguish loyal Japanese from potential enemies. Signing your name on the *yes* form confirms that you are loyal to America, and if you are a male of the right age, you will be drafted into the Army.

"I'm happy to do it," he boasts to his friends in the line behind him as he signs with a flourish.

Ralph Lazo is not required to sign the loyalty oath, but he walks the eight miles into Lone Pine to register with the local draft board.

"We'll see those Germans off, eh, Ralph?" Haru says when Ralph returns.

"Sure thing." Ralph smiles. "Only hope I can stay with my buddies."

Those who refuse to sign are nicknamed the No No Boys. They are full of bravado, singing "Kimigayo," the Japanese national anthem, at the top of their voices. Not sure if they are to be deported or culled, they stand up straight, waiting.

The elderly Issei, who were born in Japan, have the toughest decision to make in the signings. If they autograph the *yes* paper, they automatically abjure their allegiance to the emperor of Japan.

"What are we meant to do?" Mr. Sano says in despair. "We are not allowed American citizenship. It will render us stateless."

It is the same for Naomi, who is more sanguine about it than Mr. Sano. "What difference does it make?" she says. "They do what they like with us whether we are citizens or not."

JOINING UP

ARE YOU SAD?" Cora asks Satomi.

"Yes, I am, Cora." It seems that little can be kept from the child. "I will lose a friend soon, you see."

"Not me?"

"No, not you. You're my special girl," she comforts.

She doesn't want to think about losing Cora, it's enough that Haru will be gone soon, that Tamura is fading by the day. Her love for the little girl has grown until it seems to her like a mother's love. She's touched by everything about the child, the feel of her hand in her own, her sweet silvery voice, and her eyes so clear, so honest that it hurts sometimes to look at them.

"You won't ever lose me, will you, Satomi?" Cora asks, subject herself to the fear of yet more loss.

"I will try not to, Cora."

It would be wrong, she thinks, to make promises. Lately Cora's nerves are getting the better of her. She has taken to sleeping under her bed with only her thin Army blanket for cover. Since security has tightened up, she is frightened by the guards patrolling past the windows, by the searchlights sweeping the dormitories at night.

"There are ghosts," she tells Satomi. "They want to take me away."

She keeps her few possessions with her, while she sleeps, in a small string-tied bundle so that in an emergency she can grab it and run.

"It's a responsibility," Tamura says when hearing of it. "You are like a sister to her."

The Bakers and the Okihiros in their evening routine sit bunched together on the wooden steps of their barracks. They drink tea and chat companionably. Not, as Naomi frequently remarks, that it can be called tea, really. Tea tastes quite different than the twice-used dregs that if you are quick enough can be had from the mess hall's kitchen.

"Hardly better than dust," she complains. "Still, it satisfies the habit."

Long after Naomi and Yumi have gone to bed, Tamura and Eriko stay talking in the dark, reminiscing about their child-hoods. They won't admit it, but they can't settle until Haru and Satomi return from their walk. Since the riot it's foolhardy to be out in the dark, but the young won't listen. They worry that their children don't have sense enough to stay out of trouble. They worry that since the riot the guards have become trigger-happy, they worry now about everything.

"Haru is a man now," Eriko says. "Yet I fret about him as though he were still a boy."

"It's hard to let them go," Tamura says. "I expect our mothers felt the same."

"I have never spent a day of my life without my mother in it," Eriko says. "You must miss yours, Tamura."

"I try not to think about her too much. Although I long some-times for the flavor of her food, a spoonful of her plum oil. You should have tasted it, Eriko." Tamura adds to her tea a shot of the potato spirit she brewed with a cure for chest complaints in mind. "Just the scent of it made my mouth water with anticipation."

"My mother is a poor cook," Eriko whispers out of earshot of Naomi. "Her rice is too sticky."

"Still, you are lucky to have her."

"This is your best medicine yet," Eriko compliments her, topping up her cup until it becomes more alcohol than tea. "It never fails to make me feel better."

By choice, Haru and Satomi on their evening strolls would have walked by the stream that tracks the north boundary of the camp, but the searchlights pick them out there as though for the guards' sport. They have been lit up more than once for everyone to see and know their business. Lately, though, they have found a place to be together in one of the Buddhist workshops that is never locked.

The priest, a trusting man, blind to the new order taking place around him, thinks more of the soul than of practical matters. He believes that filial duty is still the order of the day in Manzanar. What point would there be in going to the bother of replacing the lost key? There is little to steal, and not, he believes, even one thief among his congregation.

They dart into the hut separately, dodging the searchlights, bending their bodies low to the ground to cast a short shadow. Other couples use the workshop too, but it's first come, first served. No one wants to share.

If it wasn't for the reserve in Haru's nature that reminds her not to show herself reckless, Satomi would give her all and not care for the consequences. Haru must be the one in charge, it seems. While she might go against him in other things, she finds herself cautious in this. They are inching forward, but stubbornness and pride in his strength of will tortures them both.

"Nobody likes a tease," she mimics Artie, not understanding herself why since the riot she feels the urge to be the pursuer, to break the pattern of stop and start.

"Don't speak like a whore, Sati. You sound like the worst kind of white girl."

The touch of her tongue on his lips, her dress half open in invitation, is causing him problems. He wishes that she had been a whore, that she wasn't Tamura's daughter.

It's odd, he thinks, that she is not the one. He guesses that when the time comes he wants a daisy, not an orchid, for a wife. Satomi has been urging him on since he signed the loyalty paper. Her nature is sensual and he has only to go there, to take without asking. It's getting so that he can't trust himself. He's ready to run.

He longs more than anything now to have the chance to prove himself, to show America that he is made of the right stuff. He's determined to go to war, to be out in the world free of Manzanar and of Satomi's expectations.

For Satomi the thought that she is about to lose him translates into the strangest pains. She feels them in her lungs when he is near, a coiling twisting thing, and in the bowl of her spine, which aches when he touches her, and in her head, which throbs dully in her absent moments when his image lopes across her mind.

"So it's certain you'll be drafted now." She can't look at Haru, doesn't want him to see her pain.

"Looks that way," he says. "They won't take our loyalty for granted, so we have to prove it. I'm glad of the chance."

"Can't wait to go, can you?" The words are out before she can stop herself. They sound so self-pitying she would take them back if she could, swallow them whole.

"I haven't lied," he says defensively. "You knew I was going to join up first chance I got."

"So that's it, then, you're off?"

"Yes, it'll be soon, I think. Don't try to make me feel bad about it, Sati."

He has never promised her anything, after all. Why should he feel guilty?

"Things will be better here for everyone once we men are in uniform," he says.

"Ah, yes, men in uniform," she says sagely. "My father said the same when he went to fight for America."

All their conversations now are unsatisfactory and usually end on a quarrelsome note. It's hard for her to claim a calm moment in her day, one when the thought of losing Haru is not niggling there in the background, sucking the pleasure out of everything.

Tamura has noticed her distraction, the anxiety in her, the way her fingers drum on the covers of the books that Haru has listed for her as required reading.

The titles taunt Satomi. *The Last of the Mohicans. The Touchstone.* She is fed up with romance, with made-up lives. She is thinking of giving up reading altogether. These days happy endings seem just another thing designed to wound her.

"My heart hurts for her," Tamura tells Eriko. "But she has her pride still, I hope."

Eriko sighs. "We must trust Haru not to be foolish."

"We can't," Haru insists. "You're too young, I'm leaving. You don't know what you would be giving up."

"I'll be eighteen in a month. It's old enough."

"Stop it, Sati. Remember whose daughter you are."

He can't claim to have been a saint himself, but it's different for men, after all. He started young with white girls, real pretty ones who went all the way, girls who would eat you up if you let them. With Japanese girls, though, he has always felt a reserve, the need to respect, to think of their families. It is hard to know where to stand

with Satomi. She's neither one thing nor the other. He guesses that
if it hadn't been for Tamura, he would have taken her long ago.

"I know exactly what I would be giving, Haru. Don't treat me
as a child, I'm not Yumi."

"No, you are more daring than Yumi, more willing to take
risks. Your nature is a dangerous one."

It thrills her that he thinks her dangerous, hurts her too.

"Why can't you trust me? I'm not who you think."

"You have no idea who you are, Sati. I know you better than
you know yourself."

"I can be who you want me to be, Haru. I can change."

"Then I would have killed who you are."

When it's too painful to kiss, to hold each other, they lie on the
floor of the little workshop mute and motionless, a ruler's width
between their bodies, each feeling the other's heat, the other's
regret.

If ever they talk of the future, it is always about Haru's. In his
company she lets go of herself, it is him that matters, he is everything. Only the smallest part of her asks, *But what of me?*

She tells herself that if she could have Haru she would let go of
ambition, the desires she once harbored for her own life. She
would meld herself to his shape, conform to his manners, and
consider being a dutiful wife. She fears the loss of him more than
the loss of herself.

Haru stretches out on the workshop floor, eyes closed, listening
to the drone of the traffic beyond the wire fences. The fences they
had been made to put up to imprison themselves. Eight hundred
Japanese volunteers built Manzanar, the barracks, the latrines, the
hated mocking fences. Somehow the thought of it adds insult to
the injury of the place.

"They're there to protect you," Lawson says.

"Then why do they turn inwards at the top?"

"I don't know, Satomi, just the way they're made, I guess."

It's the same with the guns. It bugs her that they are trained into the camp, since no matter what Lawson says everyone knows they are there to keep internees in, not free men out.

"For me it's not so much the fencing and the guns that make it hard to be here," Haru says. "It's the waste of time. I want to get on with my life, join the Army. I want to go to college, to be a teacher. I want to do something I can feel good about."

His long silences irritate her, but against her nature she has learned when to be still, learned when not to speak. She takes her pleasure in lying next to him, hearing his breathing, imagining the life she might have with him. With surprise she thinks that she must be more like her mother than she had thought. She too is capable of sacrifice for the man she loves.

Sometimes, when the grind of a truck takes the rise of the road, Haru will jump up and pace the room.

"Listen to that, people coming and going as they please, living their lives free as birds just yards away."

He had seen a dog once sauntering by on the outside of the wire, tail up, wandering at will. *Even the dogs*, he had thought, *even the dogs*.

Satomi is impressed by the urgency in him, the barely contained animal energy that at Manzanar he has little outlet for. Despite wanting to hold on to him, she longs sometimes to pull apart the barbed wire, set him free, see him run toward the life that he is so certain waits for him.

Despite that Haru is on alert, the months pass without news of a draft date. She allows herself to relax into the idea that the Japanese boys will never be called to war. Never mind that they had answered *yes*. It's all talk, talk to keep them on hold, talk to keep at bay another riot. It isn't in the government's nature, she thinks, to trust its Japanese countrymen.

But then on an afternoon when the air is tender, the spumy clouds shot through with gold, a rosy day when work is finished and there is nothing to do but sit in the sinking sunlight watching Cora running with the Sewer Alley girls, Haru is summoned to the camp director's office.

"Time you took Cora back," he says, not looking at her, already looking toward the battlefield.

All down their alley the *yes* boys are pouring out of their doors, linking arms, talking excitedly. Haru joins them. His shoulders are back, his body taut and straight, he might already be a soldier. He is almost free.

She is late returning Cora, so that the child is hurried in to eat the meal that has gone cold on her plate.

"You shouldn't take her out if you can't get her back on time," one of the kinder supervisors complains.

"You won't report it, will you?" Satomi pleads. "She was so happy playing, I forgot the time."

"Favoring Cora hasn't gone unnoticed, Satomi. Don't push them to ban you from taking her out at all."

On the way back to Sewer Alley she comes across Haru sitting on the ground with Ralph and some of his Citizens League friends. They are smoking and talking animatedly, so primed up that Haru doesn't notice her at first. When he does, he signals with a brief nod of his head toward Sewer Alley. It's an order for her to move on, a dismissal.

"My papers have come. I'll be drafted in a week or so," he tells her later.

He turns from her as he says it, pushing his hands through his thick hair. He can't look at her, won't be trapped by her hurt.

"It's an all-Nisei combat regiment. Boys are joining from all over. We're getting our chance at last."

The delight in his voice cuts her so that she is too angry to feel sad. "You needn't look so pleased about it. You are leaving your family, after all." *Leaving me*, she wants to sob, *leaving me*.

"Look, I'm sorry about it, Sati. You're not going to cry, are you? It's bad enough for my mother and Yumi; if they see you crying, then . . ." His voice is hard, unkind. Kindness might encourage tears, he might make promises, risk the clean break that if he is strong is only days away.

"I'm not crying. I won't cry, you needn't worry. I guess I'll just go and get your books. You'll want your books back."

"You keep them. I won't have much time for reading for a while."

"I don't want them. I've finished them anyway."

"Okay, I get it that you're angry. Sure, I'm leaving now, but everyone will be out of this place soon. It's all going to work out, Sati, you'll see. Once Manzanar is behind you, you'll find what you want to do in life."

"I know what I want. You know what I want, Haru."

"What you think you want. Look, forget us for a bit, your mother needs you now. She's much worse, isn't she? Give her the best of yourself while you can, you will never regret it."

His words sting her. How can he think that she needs reminding of how much Tamura needs her? Death is loitering outside their barrack now, waiting for her mother to welcome it in. Tamura can hardly stand, these days; she has given up making her medicines, given up going to work.

"Just for the time being," she says. "Just for now."

Every inch of Tamura's body aches, she can hardly raise her arms, and she is subject to swellings in her legs and feet, to strange pains in her organs.

"It will pass," she insists to Satomi. "Don't make a fuss."

On Haru's last night in the camp, their last together, Satomi walks to the Buddhist workshop early, to be sure of it. The air is damp, speckled with squads of clustered flies, and dark is falling fast. In the noises off in the distance she can hear the crackling of an illicit radio, the ubiquitous low hum of conversation that is a constant in the camp.

There are always shadows in Manzanar, quick glimpsed movements, whispering in the alleyways. Rumor has it that the camp is haunted, that the ghosts of old inmates wander around trying to find their way home. It's nonsense, she knows, but still she is pleased when the stars come fast and the moon waxes full.

In the cupboard under the altar she finds a cloth and a small broom, and suddenly she is tidying and dusting like a housewife.

When Haru comes he is sulky with her, fed up with women's sad faces. He has heard Eriko crying in the night, and Naomi looks at him now as if each glance might be her last. He is borne down by the weight of women, the need they have of him.

"Take your clothes off, Satomi," he orders, his words as much a surprise to him as to her. "I want to see you naked, to remember you naked."

She hardly hesitates. First her dress, then her slip spilling down, then the Sears and Roebuck peach bras and panties saved and longed for, flung now to the floor. She can't help feeling pleased she had swept away the dust earlier. Shivering a little, she watches him watching her. If he wants her enough to take her now, she won't be bargaining for their future. She won't deny him, even if he is already lost to her.

He comes close, runs his hands from her breasts to her waist, drawing his breath in sharply when he reaches the soft measure of skin on the inside of her thighs. She is perfect and he yearns to be inside her, to take what he wants.

Dreading a last rejection, she puts her hands around his neck and links her fingers as though to chain him there, keep him close. His hair is damp from the shower, the scent of him sweet and familiar. She buries her face in his neck, the painful rise and fall of hope sinking her.

Something in Haru tightens and then breaks. It comes to him suddenly that he wants to hurt her, to make her see that want isn't the same as love. He has had enough of the struggle, enough of wanting, enough of everything at Manzanar. Shoving his hand between her legs, he lets his fingers enter her, pushing hard.

"Don't, Haru, it hurts," she blurts out, pushing him away so that he stumbles against a chair, knocking it over.

"See, you don't want it, you never did. It's good I didn't take you seriously, Satomi Baker."

"Is it?"

He doesn't answer; what is there to say? She's got the message. He is saved.

"What more could you want, Haru?" she says quietly before he reaches the door. "I'm asking nothing of you. Do you want me to feel ugly for the rest of my life?" Her words sound like blackmail to her; still, she can't help herself. "I know you want to, just as much as I do."

"Put your dress on, Sati. It's time to go home."

"No. You put it on for me."

What he had thought of as honor, so long harbored, falls from him in the putting on of the dress. It slips away unnoticed in the pretense, in the dance of him buttoning while she unbuttons.

Only later, when she looks back on it, can she give it words; hug to herself how it had been, the good and the bad of it, the bloody bit that hurt and the bit that felt like swimming deep, so that when she surfaced, everything shimmered in a beaded light. She had longed for it, thinking it would change everything, knows now that it will not. Haru is the same Haru, unbending as always, while she hurts more than ever.

Tamura says her goodbyes to Haru from her bed. She would like to have waved him away outside with the others, but her legs have swollen in the night and are too painful to stand on.

"You are a good son to your mother, Haru," she says. "And a good friend to us too. Don't get yourself killed out there, it is easily done."

She is thinking of Aaron, his last wave, that final faraway smile. Men, it seems, are always longing to be gone.

"Death is not the worst thing, Tamura." He kisses her forehead. "Even so, best not to look towards it, best to live in the day."

Tamura knows that he isn't talking about himself. She is near the end, although no one will speak of it for fear of attracting death a moment before its time.

Outside, Cora is with the others, holding Eriko's hand. She knows all the women are sad, but she is used to sadness, used to seeing people leave, having to leave herself.

"I'm staying," she says, letting go of Eriko's hand, moving to Satomi's side. "I'm staying, aren't I?"

"Yes, you are staying." Satomi picks her up, holds her tight. "You are staying, little one."

Seeing Haru vault onto the truck crowded with his friends, she is the first of the little group in Sewer Alley to turn away. He looks so handsome, so happy to be leaving. She takes a mental snapshot in case she should forget the look of him, his strong square hands, the soft blush of his eyelids, and the grace that Tamura speaks of. He will always be the one to pattern by now, she thinks. It will take that same reserve, the same taking charge, to stir desire in her. She is not pleased about it.

"If you don't count the women, it's just the old and the young left now," Mr. Sano observes.

"I must go to Mother," Satomi calls to Haru, putting Cora down. "Good luck, Haru."

"I'll write, Sati," he calls as the truck's engine starts up.

The words feel like an empty promise to both of them.

Eriko and Naomi are weeping. It's hard to watch their boy leave. He is going to war, after all, and to make matters worse, they know that Tamura won't rise from her bed again.

"It's not a good day," Naomi says, her old face crumpling as she swallows hard.

Yumi looks sullen. She can't bring herself to wave. Who will stick up for her now?

"Be an obedient girl, Yumi," Haru calls as the truck speeds up. "Promise?"

The day is a rare one, cold but bright, so bright and clear that the mountains appear to be hard up against the camp, so that you might reach out and touch them. Sunlight pours through the four tiny windowpanes of the Bakers' barrack, tracing a pattern of squares on Tamura's sheet. From outside, Satomi can hear the crows squawking overhead, she can hear Eriko fussing over Cora. It should be raining, she thinks. It should be as gray and cold outside as she feels inside. She could bear it better if the sun wasn't shining.

"He is not for you." Tamura takes her hand and puts it to her lips. "Give your affection to Cora now. That sweet child deserves someone of her own."

The advice that comes daily from everyone is constant. "Care for your mother." "Care for Cora."

It's good advice, but it's no cure for what she's feeling. And apart from the ache for Haru, so sharp sometimes that it's like the stitch in her side she gets from running, she is scared for Tamura, so scared that she can't deny any longer the truth that her mother will not magically recover.

Her talks with Dr. Harper are no longer about external events, about her complaints, about how the war is going. They are about practicalities, about helping Tamura, who refuses to leave their barrack, despite that the narrow dusty room is quite unsuitable for someone as ill as her.

"I won't finish my days in the camp hospital," she insists. "I don't want to be with sick people. I want to be with you, Satomi, and with Eriko."

Things have become worse faster than Satomi could have imagined, and now there seems little else in life but sleepless nights and days of listening to Tamura chasing her breath.

Eriko comes to sit with her friend while Satomi visits with Cora at the orphanage.

"It is only fair I have Tamura to myself for a bit," she says. "We have to catch up with our gossip."

At the orphanage, Cora, standing alone, twisting her hair in a new habit, runs to her.

"Will your mother die, like mine did?" she asks.

Satomi doesn't answer. She can't say the words that will give truth to her fears. Cora can't remember her own mother but knows that she is dead, knows she has lost what is precious.

"Shall we have a story, Cora? Would you like that?"

Cora devours stories, lives in them long after the telling of them is over. All the children like the stories Satomi tells, especially the ones she makes up, in which she likes to weave their names, their little habits. She is a good storyteller, and how should they know that they have become characters in such classics as *Huckleberry Finn* and *Treasure Island*? There is only so much she can invent, after all.

"You must be proud of who you are," she says, looking at the mix of them. "Your mothers and fathers were beautiful Americans. And you are all brave little Americans because you are like them."

In the telling to them of who they are, she is flooded with

gratitude for who she is herself. It is a wonderful thing to be the daughter of Tamura Baker, to have Aaron Baker's determined blood in her veins. How could she have ever thought otherwise?

"You teach me as much as I do you," she tells the children.

Cora hates sharing Satomi. She sets up camp next to her in the storytelling sessions, and has been known to shove away the children who get too close to Satomi.

"She is mine," she says, as though speaking of her little string-tied bundle of possessions.

"You mustn't mind that I talk to the others, Cora. It doesn't change the fact that you are special to me, you silly girl."

"Can I live with you when your mother dies, Satomi?"

"I will ask, Cora. But don't get your hopes up, they don't say yes to much, do they? But you can still visit, and I am here every day, after all."

She worries that Cora seems agitated these days, more needy than before. The orphanage can be a lonely place despite that it is full of children and loud with the crying of babies. There is too little for the children to do, and they are all suffering from loss of the familiar. Perhaps she shouldn't have allowed herself to get so close, but it is done now, she can't desert Cora, she loves her.

Dr. Harper agrees to ask permission from the orphanage for Cora to live with her, but not, as he puts it delicately, while Tamura is so ill. It wouldn't be fair for any of them.

"I can't imagine they will allow it anyway, Sati. It would hardly be a conventional arrangement."

He longs to get Tamura into his hospital, to see her cocooned in clean white sheets where she will be available to him the whole day long. He wants to care for her in her last days, be on hand to ease her pain.

"She should be in the new hospital," he tells Satomi. "You can't look after her properly in the barracks."

There is a morgue attached to the hospital, but he doesn't say that would be more convenient too. Taking the dead from the barracks is bad for morale, it unsettles the inmates. Since the riot and the No No Boys looking for trouble, tearing down the American flag, being insolent to the guards, they hardly need more to unsettle them.

"She wants to stay at home," Satomi says, quoting Tamura.

The absurdity of Manzanar being spoken of as home by her mother is not lost on her. Yet even in the face of the horror of the place she has come to understand that Tamura has experienced something rather wonderful in the camp, something that has restored her to herself.

Since she insists on staying where she is, there isn't much that Dr. Harper can do for his favorite patient, except to visit her daily, a pleasure, he thinks, more for himself than for her. He shouldn't favor patients, he knows, but who could not love Tamura, after all?

More like a nurse than a doctor, he plumps her pillow, places pans of steaming water nearby, futilely hoping to create a space in her lungs so that she might catch a few easier breaths. The science is not good; the hope, though, is a comfort. He has rigged up a line of oxygen, but Tamura doesn't want it, doesn't want to prolong things. In any case, it's hardly more than a placebo at this stage of her disease. Occasionally he takes the unearned liberty of a lover and strokes her hair, caresses her hand.

"You are pale yourself," she tells him teasingly. "I recommend lettuce juice twice a day."

They laugh together. He wonders if it will be the last time Tamura laughs, he wonders if everything she does will be for the last time. The thought of never seeing her smile again, or push her hair back in the delicate way she does, hurts too much to dwell on.

"It won't be long," she says, as though in apology for putting him to the trouble.

"I'm not listening," he replies. "I'm not listening, Tamura."

It seems to Satomi that Tamura must be shared with everyone, so that only a small part of her mother is hers alone. The days are taken up with Dr. Harper's visits, with Eriko's nursing, and with Naomi, who comes to sit with Tamura, talking to her all the time in Japanese, her shaky old voice full of tenderness.

Cora comes to visit too, eyes wide with curiosity at the sight of Tamura propped on her pillow. She is not sure what death is, except she thinks perhaps an angel might come to take Tamura away, like in the story she heard long ago but can't remember where. She has set up her daytime camp at Eriko's, where she can hear Tamura's labors through the wall. Eriko and Naomi are kind, but it is Satomi she wants, Satomi she waits for, as she takes Yumi's fan from the wall despite the fact that she knows that Yumi has forbidden it. She wafts it in front of her face to smell the sweet clean scent of cedar.

Only at night does Satomi have her mother to herself, lying next to her on the mattress that she has pushed up against Tamura's bed. She talks quietly until Tamura dozes off, hardly sleeping herself, terrified that she will wake to her mother gone.

"I know that you will be surprised to hear it," Tamura says softly, "but I have enjoyed my life here with you."

"You have enjoyed Manzanar, Mama?"

"Well, it is strange, but I have. After your father died, I couldn't imagine making a life of my own, having friends. Now our friends will help you after I have gone. Eriko is like a mother to you already."

"Nobody but you will ever be like a mother to me."

Eriko has stopped going to work. Every morning she boils water and gently washes Tamura's wasted body, she brushes her hair tenderly and brings her sweet pears and miso from their favorite mess hall, which Tamura has no appetite for. Her heart seems to shatter over and over at the sight of Tamura's smile, at the effort her dear neighbor still puts into their friendship.

"Try a little sip, Tamura," she encourages. "Just one little sip, for me."

Over time their neighborliness has turned to friendship, their friendship to love. They have become like loving sisters. Eriko is already grieving for the loss that is to come.

Tamura is not afraid. She thinks of Aaron and hopes that she will see him soon. He would be at odds with her for thinking it, but there is nothing to be done about that, she can't make herself believe in oblivion. And Satomi will rally, what else can the young do? She is strong and full of life. And even though Haru will not come for her, something tells her that her daughter will prosper. She is ready to go, worn out with the fight against the inch-by-inch drowning. She is longing not to come up for air.

"You have the choice of burial or cremation," Dr. Harper says, the words ringing brutally in his ears, sickening as the cracking of bones, so that he shudders and shakes his head as though to dismiss them. He should feel embarrassed for loving Tamura, he thinks, but he can't regret it. He has loved her in a way his wife would have thought of as betrayal, although no word of his had ever communicated that love, which he is certain Tamura did not return.

"It's up to you, Satomi," Eriko says. "It's you who must decide."

"Yes, of course we will do as you want, Satomi. I was her doctor, but we never spoke of it. Of such arrangements, I mean."

"She would have thought it bad manners to burden you, Dr. Harper. You are not an easy man to talk to about such intimate things."

It's not the truth, but in the moment she wants to hurt where she can, to off-load the terrible pain she is feeling.

"I did my best, Satomi, and you know, whatever small things we spoke about, your mother and I found pleasure in those conversations."

"I'm sorry, so sorry, Dr. Harper." She is ashamed. "I know that you did. My mother always said that you do your job honorably."

"Did she? Did she say that?"

He hopes that it's the truth, that he has been honorable with all of his imprisoned patients. His job, which started out as something patriotic he could do for his country, has become a burden to him. He is amazed now that he ever could have thought it would be anything else. Manzanar has knocked that idealism, and much more, out of him. It's a pointless place, a place to feel shame for. Thousands of people incarcerated in a monument to stupidity. And the time, money, and effort spent on things that don't work, that never have from the start. He feels only disgust at the cruelty of crushing people together as though they are livestock, not to mention the ridiculous business of guarding people who don't attempt escape. Food in, trash out, diseased sewers, schools without desks, orphans being guarded at play, lines to be able to eat, to wash, to shit, it is all a horrible, inhuman nonsense.

If there are such things as Japanese spies in his country, then it is the camps that have made them. Dissent has germinated behind the barbed wire and under the guns. And what is it that America is fighting for anyway, if not for liberty, and the freedom of its citizens? Along with that of its inmates, Manzanar has stolen a portion of his life too, robbed him of his pride in being an American.

"Here, Satomi." He sighs. "Your mother's death certificate is ready. You must sign in two places, there and there. Her ashes can be sent home, if that is what you want."

As though to soothe him, to steady his trembling hand, Satomi touches it lightly as she takes the pen from him.

"We will bury my mother here, Dr. Harper, at Manzanar,

close to her friends and neighbors. Angelina is not our home anymore. I have heard that there are strangers in our house, that our land has been given to them."

"I'm sure that you will get it back. War is tough on everyone, but every war has its end, and this one will be no different. We are getting on top of it."

"I don't care anymore. I wanted my mother to live to see it. I wanted to walk arm in arm with her from Manzanar, although she would have been sad to leave you all."

"At least you had the good fortune to have Tamura as your mother. What a stroke of luck, Satomi. What a start in life."

The past tense hurts. She has already overtaken Tamura, left her behind. She couldn't keep Tamura in the world, although on the night of her death she had held her in her arms in an attempt to transfer her own warmth, the life in her, to her mother.

"Don't leave me, Mama. Please don't go."

Tamura had lifted her hand to Satomi's cheek. Satomi, kissing it, had taken up the other one, kissing that too. Her mother's hands, rough from sewing the camouflage nets, from pulling sagebrush up by the roots, were nothing like the ones that she remembered from her childhood. She liked them better now somehow. The calluses and torn skin mapped Tamura's more independent existence, showed even in her failing that she had lived a muscular life.

"Listen to me, Satomi. Obey me this one last time."

She had to bend close to hear Tamura's words.

"Once you leave Manzanar, don't ever come back. Whatever they do with my body, I will not be here. I will be with your father somewhere, perhaps. And never think of the life you might have had if we had never come here. Make a better one."

Hearing more the cadence, the familiar rhythm, rather than the reason the words conveyed, Satomi was all pain. She was lost to everything except the idea of drawing into herself the sound of Tamura's voice, which had accompanied her her whole life. She feared the time was coming when it would be lost to her, when she might forget it.

"Take my little bird, Satomi," Tamura said. "Keep the little titmouse for luck. It is such a pretty thing, the most precious object I have. And, my sweet daughter, don't feed your anger anymore, you only nourish your own enemy."

The weight of Eriko Okihiro's hefty arm across Satomi's shoulders is causing an ache, but there is comfort to be had in her solidity, in the heat that emanates from her ample body.

So this is what being without Tamura is like. It's being homeless despite having a bed to sleep in, it's not caring if the sun shines, it's feeling nothing when the mountains turn from blue to mauve in the blink of an eye, it's being orphaned.

"You mustn't sleep alone tonight, Satomi. Stay with us, we would be happy to have you."

"I'm not afraid, Eriko, and there are things I must do."

She will clean their barrack, take down the silk robe and wash it with the rose bath crystals that Lawson has brought at her request. Surely Tamura will forgive her that. Rose oil would have been better, but it wasn't to be had.

"No such thing in Lone Pine," Lawson told her, shaking his head. "Nearest thing I could get to it was this."

It takes three washes to reveal the colors of the robe, to bring back to life the butterflies and the dark little moths. Only in the final rinse does the cheap scent of the bath crystals waft up the merest trace of rose. Still, it is the scent of Tamura. It catches at the back of her throat and suddenly she is doubled up on the floor moaning, her head buried deep in the wet folds.

"Oh, Mama, I can't bear it."

Naomi hears her cries and, breaking her daughter's rules, she calls through the wall.

"I am coming, Satomi."

"No, don't, Naomi. I am fine, and I must finish here."

A picture of Tamura wearing the robe comes to her; she is sitting on the floor by Aaron's chair, teaching her the words for the tea ceremony.

"*Wa*, for harmony; *kei*, for respect; *sei*, for purity; *jaku*, for tranquillity.

"It's a good day, Satomi, when you can feel all of these things and know that you have spent the hours well."

Tamura had been torn between the centuries, just as she has been torn between her two races. Satomi Baker, the very name says it all.

"Who am I?" she sobs. "Who am I without you, Mother?"

When the robe is dry she folds it carefully and takes it with her to relieve Eriko, who is sitting by Tamura's coffin in the morgue so that her friend will not be alone in such a place.

In death's stillness Tamura is wearing the dress she had worn on the day that they had left their farm. A modern American dress, as she would have wanted. With the robe folded neatly at her feet, her hands crossed, the paper money that Eriko has placed by her side so that she might pay the toll to cross the River of the Three Hells, she is returned to something of her old beauty. Satomi bends to kiss her, she must take her leave, but she is afraid to feel Tamura's cold lips on her own and can't move.

"We have to close the lid now, honey." says Dr. Harper's nurse with a pitying smile. She pushes Satomi toward Eriko, who is crying.

"Oh, Tamura," Eriko sobs as the lid goes down. "My dear, dear friend."

Dr. Harper wrote to Ralph to tell him of Tamura's death, and a letter comes to Satomi by return from him. It is a sweet letter, full of Ralph's humanity, his optimism for her.

Haru has written too, a formal letter of condolence. He can't get leave to be at Tamura's funeral. He wants her to know that he had admired and loved her mother.

She is grateful that she is not able to differentiate the pain of losing him from her grief for Tamura, which leaves no space to distinguish one ache from another. The loss of Haru, which had cut so deeply, seems such a tiny thing now in comparison to the loss of Tamura.

"Did he say anything else?" Eriko asks.

"I think that he may have, but a page is missing and the censor's pen has been at it."

"The contraband check is getting worse," Eriko says. "I've had pages of other people's letters mixed up with mine more than once lately."

Satomi doesn't tell Eriko that Haru had written that they were lucky to be safe in Manzanar; that the inmates of the camp have no idea of what people on the outside are suffering. Europe is being destroyed and we are lucky to be American, he says.

Well, she doesn't feel lucky. She and Haru will never agree on what being an American means.

"It is very annoying," Naomi says, tutting. "Perhaps what they blacked out was important. It's too bad."

"He sent you all his love, of course, and his good wishes to me."

"Oh, Satomi," Eriko says with a sigh.

"Would he have wanted me if I were entirely Japanese, do you think, Eriko?"

"Perhaps, but it isn't about being Japanese, is it? It's about love, and you can't summon that at will no matter what your race."

"I think it's about not being what people want you to be, Eriko.

I was never the person that Haru wanted me to be. Even the Japanese part of me is not compliant enough for him!"

The wind is getting up as Tamura is put in the ground. Strings of origami brought to honor her blow about like ribbons at a carnival, getting caught in tree limbs and in the mourners' hair.

Tamura's allotted plot is just a few yards from the little consoling tower.

"It's a good spot," Naomi says. "You couldn't ask for better."

"It's very dry," the Buddhist priest remarks. "You must remember to bring water in your offerings."

A rusty blackbird sits on the branch of a dead pear tree, shrugging in the damp air as though it is pulling up the collar of a feathery coat. It looks as miserable as the mourners.

"It's so cold," Naomi complains, and Satomi takes off her scarf and wraps it around Naomi's head, tying it in a knot under her chin.

"Just like Tamura. Just like your mother," Naomi says.

The wind is in wicked flight now, whisking the dirt from the ground, covering their shoes, worming grit into their mouths. It hums through the cluster of stunted apple trees at the margin of the burial ground, creating a lament on the air.

"We must be quick," the priest says. "The storm is almost here."

Satomi looks toward the mountains and gauges by the way clouds have not yet settled on the peaks that it won't hit full force until nightfall.

"At least this is one 'dust devil' that she won't have to suffer," Eriko whispers to Satomi. "She hated them, didn't she?"

"Yes, but I think I hated them more for her. I don't care when they come now. I can't even be bothered to fight them anymore."

Later that day, outside the Buddhist workshop as the storm moves closer, people file past her the grieving daughter, bowing, not smiling.

"So many have come to say goodbye to her," Dr. Harper says. "I'm not surprised, Tamura was easy to love."

Cora is at her side despite Eriko's opinion that it is a bad idea.

"She is too young to understand, Satomi. She will only be confused."

Perhaps it is all too much for Cora, the solemnity of it, the distraction of the grown-ups. But she had wanted to come, would have felt excluded if she had not been allowed to share the day. And, since beginning her work at the orphanage, Satomi has realized that children understand so much more than adults give them credit for. From the age of four she thinks they have a hold on pretty much everything.

It disturbs her that she knows so few in the line. How have so many of the inmates come to know Tamura? They all seem to be claiming her as their own someone special.

"I worked with your mother. Did she never speak of me?"

"She had a fine singing voice."

"She had no enemies."

"Tamura Baker will be missed."

Satomi recognizes the white-haired woman who is crying. She is usually to be seen walking around the camp carrying a shabby cardboard suitcase as though she has just arrived. There had been speculation in the first year or two as to what she might have in the case. Money or medicine, had been a popular guess, until it had split open in the mess hall one day, and was shown to contain nothing more than a child's rattle and a pair of baby shoes.

"She must have lost her child," Tamura had guessed. "That's a grief there's no recovery from. Make sure you give her a greeting when you pass her, Satomi."

At least the old woman could cry for a lost friend, whereas she herself, the beloved child, seems incapable of it. What is wrong with her? Her eyes are as dry as her mouth, her blood is slow, her heart dull and cold.

She calmly acknowledges the mourners one by one, unaware of the trail of blood that is seeping from her clenched hands, tinting her dress brick-red, as her nails bite into her palms.

"Who is the man with the bloated face, Eriko?"

"I'm not sure. I've seen him around, though. Probably someone Tamura was kind to, someone who used her salves. Plenty of that sort here today, I should think."

Mr. and Mrs. Sano come. He's holding his wife's arm firmly in case she should wander off. Lately Mrs. Sano has taken to muttering out loud, flicking her hands around as though she is beset by bees. She goes missing for hours on end, so that strangers bring her home from her wanderings, from her setting up home in their barracks. She doesn't brush her hair anymore, and where once she wouldn't look you in the eye, now she stares at people with a child's unswerving gaze. Her mind may be wandering so that she hardly knows who she is, but Mr. Sano still takes his pleasure of her. These days, though, his is the only moaning to be heard through the wall.

"We have come to sign," he says. "We have no complaints of your mother as a neighbor, at least."

"He is well practiced in rudeness," Naomi says, not bothering to whisper.

A condolence book has been placed on a table at the entrance to the workshop. It has fifty signatures in it by noon and a line of people waiting to sign.

"We are like Pavlov's dogs," the old man who had exposed himself to her says. "Trained by habit to wait in line for everything."

Yumi is playing jacks with a group of girls in the grime at the old man's feet. They are wearing freshly laundered dresses under their jackets, the hems already covered in dirt. Despite a coating of dust, their dark hair gleams, and their olive black eyes shine.

Hearing their chatter, Satomi is reminded of the schoolyard in Angelina, and memories of Lily are stirred. Haru's little sister has grown up while Satomi had been preoccupied with him. Under the stretched fabric of Yumi's dress her breasts are full, her hips rounding. She has already made out with at least two of the boys from the camp's softball team, and with her provocative stance she is the star of the baton-twirling troop. Haru, when he returns, will have his hands full keeping her in check.

"Go and play somewhere else," Eriko scolds, frowning at Yumi. "Have some respect."

"They only know how to live in the moment," Satomi says. "They are lucky; we lose the art of it as we grow."

But she feels herself that she can only live in the moment too. It's too hard to think of the future without Tamura in it. Grief has sapped her energy and she can't be bothered to wonder what she will do when freedom comes, except that she must somehow keep Cora in her future.

Like Aaron, Tamura now will only come to her in memory. There is no one left to share the recollections of her childhood with. Life is changed forever.

She has already been ordered to vacate their barrack, to leave the place that Tamura had made home. It has been allotted to Mr. and Mrs. Hamada. They have added a baby to their family of nine since coming to Manzanar, and are so overcrowded that in summer the older children prefer to sleep in the open underneath their barrack, despite that the rats run there. In winter, their human huddle keeps the warmth in, at least.

Mr. Hamada has turned their present barrack into a little palace with his carvings. Their door has a tree carved in relief on it, and lifelike birds perch on its branches. There is no doubt that he is a true artist.

The Sanos too have been told to move. They are to have the

Hamadas' barrack so that the bigger family can occupy both theirs and Satomi's old homes. Mr. Sano is full of complaints. He goes about with his old tortoise face screwed up with anger, his eyes dark and hooded.

"They have no consideration at all. I will have to move everything myself, my wife is incapable of anything these days. My daughter-in-law might as well not exist, she is so unreliable, always off somewhere."

Mrs. Hamada avoids Mr. Sano, but she apologizes to Satomi. "I am so sorry, but what can we do? And the older children are so excited at having some space to themselves. If it hadn't been us, someone else would have taken it from you."

"Don't worry about it, Mrs. Hamada, you are welcome. It can't be helped. It's only fair, after all."

"It is easy to tell that your mother lives in you, Satomi," Mrs. Hamada says, relieved that there isn't to be a fuss.

"You must stay with us or you'll be housed with strangers," Eriko insists. "You can have Haru's bed."

She can smell him on the blanket: soap and salt and something in the dry down that she couldn't have described but would have recognized anywhere. It's the tormenting essence of him.

She thinks of Aaron, who said that everything had its own peculiar smell, that he could tell what month it was simply by sniffing the air, it was the same for the time of day. He could smell fog before you could see it, smell the rare frosts that iced his fields before they arrived.

"What does fog smell like, Father?"

"It smells like the sea after a storm."

She hugs Haru's blanket to her, runs her fingers down the length of sacking that Eriko has left hanging. His books are piled neatly on the floor, a pencil as a bookmark in his yellowing copy of *The Grapes of Wrath*. She picks it up and starts to read where Haru has left off. He has underlined in pencil, <u>*migratory family, California.*</u>

When the time comes to leave the camp she will abandon Haru, let him go. For now, though, she burrows down with his books, his scent and his family nearby.

Since the superintendent has refused her permission to have Cora live with her, she spends most of her time at the orphanage.

"I can't blame them," she says to Eriko. "It's enough to take care of myself, let alone be responsible for a child. And I am a guest in your home, after all. But I so long to keep Cora with me."

She worries about what will happen to Cora when the war ends. There is talk that the children will be evacuated to places as far away as Alaska, to any orphanage, any family prepared to take them. They are little nomads who must make their homes over and over.

Dr. Harper has spirited away a letter he saw on the superintendent's desk as he was writing a report on a child with diphtheria. It was a request from a farmer in Oregon: "*I'll take any boy strong enough to work on the land.*"

"Shameless!" he exclaimed to Satomi. "Well, at least I can save one boy from the horror of that."

The letter will add to his archive, which grows daily. He squirrels away papers, takes his forbidden photographs, lists a daily count of the rats that he sees in broad daylight, in the mess hall kitchens, the latrines, on the roofs of the barracks nibbling away at the peeling tar paper so that the rain gets through. He has a collection of objects that have touched him and will be a better aid to memory than facts and figures, he thinks. There is a necklace made from bark strung with string that an inmate left in the hospital, it's strangely sophisticated, he thinks. He keeps a discarded wooden geta shoe, a split tin plate. He has made sketches of the new hospital, and one of the library. They look impressive, and after all there must in any archive be balance.

As time passes in Manzanar the seasons continue in much the same way they have done since Satomi first arrived. The camp's inmates suffer the same bitter winters, the same heat-logged summers, and the ever-present dust, always the dust. But the weather aside, even Satomi has to agree with Eriko, that over the last couple years conditions in the camp have improved.

Dr. Harper had been right. New latrines have been built, there are Japanese doctors in the hospital, and the inmates' health has stepped up a notch, as drug treatments are easier to come by. And now there's a barber shop, art classes, a camp newspaper; there's tofu and soy sauce to be had in the mess halls.

A shallow sort of settling has taken over from the restlessness that was, in the first year of their confinement, the more usual mindset. There's still talk of freedom, but an end to the war seems a distant prospect, and the question of who will win it, not yet to be predicted.

Satomi and Cora are closer than ever.

"Like you and Tamura," Eriko says sentimentally to Satomi.

Cora has turned out to be a good pupil in her classes, she's quick to pick up on things, and her skill at math calls Lily to Satomi's mind. But she is a fragile child, slow to trust, clinging to Satomi, jealous of sharing with her peers.

Haru has had leave only once, and then only for two days. He came to the camp, handsome in his uniform, bringing little gifts: violet scent for Satomi and Yumi, a sewing box for Eriko, and fleece-lined gloves for Naomi. He didn't walk out with Satomi, and she was never alone with him.

"He treats me like he does Yumi," she said to Eriko. "As though I am his sister."

"It's for the best, Satomi," Eriko said, not wanting to give Satomi false hope.

Haru had slept in his old bed while Satomi lay next to Yumi under her Indian blanket, unable to sleep at all. He is somewhere in Europe now, which distresses Eriko.

"Europe," she says, all concern. "What is there in Europe but war and the killing of our sons?"

"Will you take me to the new cinema?" Cora asks Satomi. "It cost ten cents and I don't even have one."

Since Cora first asked, they have never missed a show. They go together hand in hand, Haru's blanket under Satomi's arm for them to sit on in the damp sagebrush field where the screen is put up once a month. Cora's favorite is Flash Gordon. She loves the all-American boy, his unbelievably golden hair, the light that seems to shine out of him. The Emperor Ming is a popular hate figure. Along with the other children, and brave in their company, Cora shouts at him scornfully. At night, though, curled under her bed, she dreams of him in her restless sleep; dreams of his cruel eyes, his long clawlike nails.

"Is he real?" she asks Satomi.

"No, he is a person made up to frighten us. Just make-believe."

Satomi marvels at how the children lose themselves in make-believe. Their imaginings seem more real to them than their actual lives.

The boys are American heroes, playing capture the flag, fighting to keep the enemy from the Stars and Stripes. The girls play house, feeding pretend meat loaf and ketchup to the cotton stuffed dolls, knitted for them by fine women like Naomi.

In the late afternoons Satomi walks from the orphanage with Cora to Eriko's, where the child spends an hour or so being spoiled. She plays with the girls in Sewer Alley, hopscotch and kick the can. It's favoring her, and against the rules, but the supervisors look the other way. Cora is a special child, after all, a little angel. Who would deny her Satomi's attention, some time of her own?

"You are only making it harder on yourself," Eriko says, fussing around the child, pinching her cheeks, pulling her socks up. "Your heart will break when the parting comes."

"I will write to her, Eriko. And I will visit when I can."

"It won't be as easy as you think, Satomi. They have no idea where the children will end up. And even if they did, I'd bet a dollar that there will be a rule prohibiting you from knowing."

LITTLE BOY. FAT MAN.

S UCH NAMES," ERIKO says, tears streaming down her face
as she bites her lips until they bleed. "To give bombs pet
names as though they are family members."

Satomi shakes her head in disbelief. "Was America ever what
we thought it to be?"

"It is the bully of the world," Naomi says regretfully.

They didn't need to hear the reports of the atomic bombings
on Hiroshima and Nagasaki from the guards—the illegal radios
in Manzanar spread the news quicker. But those who heard it by
word of mouth thought it so exaggerated as to be more rumor
than fact.

How could such a weapon exist? A weapon that could kill a
hundred thousand in one go. How could a plane named *Enola Gay*,
in honor of the pilot's mother, house a bomb so big that it could
suck up and digest the earth till nothing remained but cinders?
What mother would consider such a namesake an honor?

But when Emperor Hirohito's capitulation speech is put out
over the Tannoy, they are convinced. They may never have heard
his voice before, but there is no room for doubt.

"It could only be him," they say.

"Yes. It is a samurai's voice. Ancient, from the old world. Like
your grandfather's grandfather might sound."

At first, not knowing the difference between atomic and normal destruction, people liken the devastation to that of Pearl Harbor.

"So the debt is paid," they say. "The score settled, honor restored."

Soon, though, the tales of a burning the like of which has never been seen, and of the annihilation of those sad islands where some of Manzanar's inmates have relatives, takes hold, and the reports become the stuff of Greek tragedy.

"They say it has cracked the earth's crust and will get us all in the end."

"There isn't a soul left, I hear."

"Even the children have gone."

"Even the ghosts."

In the privacy of their barracks some of those who have relatives on the burned up islands quietly sing the Japanese national anthem.

"Only out of respect," they assure each other. "In memory of Uncle Toru, of cousin Sakamoto."

Pearl Harbor has been revenged at last. The enemy has been crushed and there is talk of Manzanar closing. Two months pass before the official notice comes—the camp will close in November. Soon they will all be free.

"We need time to work out what it means to us," Naomi says with a quavering voice. "Just when we are settled, everything must change again."

"She is afraid to leave," Eriko says. "We are all a bit afraid, I guess. We don't even know if we will get our homes and businesses back. It's going to be a struggle."

"You are going home, then?" Satomi asks.

"Yes, we are going home." Eriko pauses, the words seem so strange. "Going home!"

"Haru will be pleased," Satomi says.

"Yes, he wrote as soon as he heard. He says that we mustn't let them relocate us away from the West Coast. He's keen on our rights to choose where we settle."

"Haru is right," Naomi says. "Who knows where they will send us this time if we let them? Another Manzanar, perhaps! We have heard the word 'relocate' before, I think."

"You must come with us," Eriko offers. "I don't know if we can get our shop back, we only rented it in the first place, but we must try. We left our furniture, even rice in the cupboard, we left everything. It's possible it's all still there, I suppose, but I hardly dare hope for it."

"Oh, Eriko, thank you, but I have to go to Angelina. We owned our farm outright and we left money in the bank, crops in our fields. My father would expect me to see that his life's work has not been stolen away."

"Then you'll come? After, when you have done what you have to, then you will come?"

"I can't, you know that. It would be wrong for me to live in the same house as Haru. He wouldn't want it, and neither do I."

"But what will you do, Satomi? Who will look after you?"

"I am near nineteen, Eriko, a woman. I will look after myself."

The words sound false even to her. What will she do? How will she live? A job somewhere, she supposes, a room of her own. She has longed for a room of her own, for privacy. The thought of it now, though, seems too strange to contemplate.

Tamura had advised her to go east if she had the chance.

"It will be better in the East," she had said. "The West will never forgive us for the Harbor."

The order has come from the War Department to demolish Manzanar. In its upheaval it begins to look again as dismal as it did when they had first arrived. Those who opt for relocation are already being shipped out to government housing projects, their barracks razed the instant they leave. The rats run for cover, the cockroaches scatter as the empty barracks are reduced to piles of lumber. Before the authorities have a chance to gather it up, the wood is snatched. With such a wealth of fuel, stoves blaze in defense against the bitter November air.

Outside the director's office, piles of papers are stacked high, waiting to be loaded onto trucks and sent off to the War Department.

"So many of them," Satomi says to Dr. Harper as they walk past on their way to the orphanage. "What are they, do you think?"

"Records of you all, I guess," he says, retracing his steps and scooping up a bundle, stuffing them into his bag.

"What will happen to them?"

"If I had to bet, I'd say they were on their way to the furnace."

The hospital wards, save for a bed or two left for emergencies, have closed. Tables and chairs are removed from the mess halls, the new school barracks are dismantled as the children are sent home to help their parents prepare for evacuation.

At the orphanage the children's things are being packed up too. When Satomi asks where the children are to be sent, one of the wardens shrugs her shoulders.

"Who knows?" she says. "We will be lucky to find places for them anywhere. Nobody wants Japanese children these days."

"I'm willing to take Cora with me. She will be happy with me."

"Oh, Satomi, you couldn't look after her. It will be enough to manage yourself."

"If I have my parents' money we could manage, I'm sure."

"I don't think the superintendent will just give Cora to you simply because you ask. It's a foolish idea and probably against the law."

"No harm in asking, though."

"Don't get your hopes up, you're bound to be disappointed."

She must have hope, though. It's too hard to think about letting Cora go without a fight. She conjures up a family who might treat her badly, an orphanage where love has to be shared out so that no child ever gets enough. Just the thought of it sickens her.

Knocking on the superintendent's door, she tells herself that she mustn't lose her temper. If she can just keep calm, smother her desire to insist, things will go better. Nothing much, she knows, works out when she loses her temper.

"Surely Cora would be better off with me than in an orphanage?" she says reasonably.

"It can't be done, Satomi. Simple as that," the superintendent says. "But you needn't worry about Cora. She will be the first to find a family. Such a sweet, obedient child."

"But she already knows me. We are like sisters."

"But not sisters. And there is no guarantee that you will get this money you speak of. How would you manage then?"

"I'll get a job, of course. We all have to work."

"Look, Satomi, it's kind of you, but it is a foolish idea. You will have problems enough of your own. We all will."

"Cora should be with me, we should be together." She can't keep the fury out of her voice.

"Don't blame me, Satomi. I'm Japanese. I have no authority in this place."

"Then I'll go to the director, he won't refuse me."

"If you must. Who knows, you may catch him on a good day."

The director, though, is too busy overseeing the dismantling of the camp to take time to see her. He smiles at her weakly on his way out of the office and directs her to one of his assistants.

"You'll need to write it all down." The assistant, busy with writing something himself, hardly looks at her. "Here are paper and pencil. Bring them back when you've finished."

The words are hard to find. The director doesn't know her, doesn't know Cora; how can she make him understand? She writes of the love they have for each other, of her hope for her parents' inheritance. *We are like sisters,* she assures him. *Surely whatever the circumstances it is better that sisters should be together.*

Her letter is put with others on a desk crowded with papers.

"It's very important," she says, noting the piled-high papers, the ones that have carelessly been allowed to slip to the floor. "Make sure that he gets it."

"Of course. I hardly need you to tell me how to do my job." He feels she has ordered rather than asked. "I can't guarantee that the director will have time to answer you."

But an answer comes a day later in the form of a brief note left for her at the orphanage.

What you request is not possible. It would be against American law for this office to grant you a child that is in the care of the state. You can rest assured that Cora is in good hands. Everything will be done to find all of the children suitable placements.

John Holmes
Assistant to Director Merrit

Eriko says that she shouldn't blame the director. It takes a special kind of person to break the rules, a hero like Ralph Lazo. Courage is needed, she says, to go against the regulations, to take the human decision.

"Don't expect humanity to triumph in Manzanar, Satomi. It never has before."

In Satomi's distress, old dreams of Tamura disappearing return to plague her sleep.

"You call your mother's name out in your sleep," Eriko says. "It is natural, I suppose."

"I think that Mama and Cora have become one in my dreams."

"It's cruel, I know, Satomi, but you must not think of Cora so much. You are an orphan yourself, remember."

But it's impossible not to think of Cora, of the child's dark eyes, her sweet mouth, and her dented innocence. Only she truly understands Cora, no one else will take the time to note her little ways, calm her fears, learn the things that make her laugh. Such a rare little laugh, but so joyful when it spills out of her. Who now will make up stories just for her, tell her that she is pretty, that she is their special girl?

"I will keep in touch with Dr. Harper," she tells the orphanage superintendent. Will you at least let him know where Cora is? I must be able to keep in touch with her."

"I'll do my best, Satomi, but I can't promise anything. We must hope that she stays in California, at least."

"That would be better than Alaska, I suppose."

"Yes, Alaska seems like another country, doesn't it? I know it's hard to hear, but you'll forget her, you know. We all have to think of ourselves in the end."

Cora isn't in the general playroom when Satomi calls at the orphanage the next day. She is sitting on her cot bed swinging her legs, her little black shoes polished, her dress starched, a knitted wool bow in her dark hair.

"I'm coming with you," she tells Satomi, her eyes welling with tears. "When you leave, I'm coming with you."

"I would take you if I could, Cora, but they won't allow it. I will find you, though, wherever you go. We will see each other again."

"You won't come for me. Nobody comes for me."

"I will come. When I am settled, Cora, I will come and visit

you. You may have your own family by then, a mother and father
to love you."

Cora's cries are pitiful, little mewls, muffled sobs.

"We have almost a week left together, Cora. Perhaps they will
show a movie, and school is finished, so you can come to Eriko's
and play with your friends in the alley all day, if you like."

Just a week, she thinks. Seven days left to console Cora, to
calm the little girl's fears, to gather herself.

Only the young are excited. For the rest, the fear of leaving the
known is mixed with apprehension for what lies ahead of them.
Some of the older ones would choose to stay in Manazar if they
could. They have established it out of nothing and want it to live
on. Once the majority have left, space will not be a hard thing to
come by, and they have had enough of the sadness of looking
back, they want the world to forget them now.

"They must go," Lawson says. "The Supreme Court has ruled
the camps illegal. In any case, how would they live? The mess
halls won't be working, or much else, I imagine."

"So now this place is illegal." Satomi can't keep the sneer out of
her voice. "Does it ever occur to you, Lawson, that to be American is to be governed by fools?"

"Well, you can vote them out now. That's progress, ain't it?"

Dr. Harper tells her that he is relieved beyond imagination that
the camp is finally to close.

"You may not believe it, Sati, but you have been my conscience
in Manzanar."

"I think that honor should go to my mother, Doctor, don't
you?"

"No, your mother's sweetness was a gift to me, but it was your
anger that stirred my own."

She visits Tamura's grave for the last time. *She's here beneath my feet*, she thinks, summoning to mind her last view of Tamura in her freshly laundered dress, blocking from it how her mother's body must look now. She thinks of the weather to come at Manzanar, of the sweeping winds and the deep snowdrifts, of the cold moon that will for always now shine down on Tamura's little plot. She won't ever be able to think of the seasons at Manzanar without picturing Tamura's grave suffering them. She hardly knows anymore the little girl in her who whispers with a sob, "Goodbye Mama."

Out of the blue Dr. Harper has offered to drive her to Angelina, to help her with her claim to the farm, and to whatever monies remain in the Baker bank account.

"You will need someone on your side, Satomi. They won't take a girl of your age seriously. When it comes to money, such people don't take justice into account."

His wife is furious with him. She has seen the girl, a pretty enough one for a wife to be suspicious of a husband's motives. But when she thinks about it, Satomi is not pretty, exactly, she is beautiful, and, strangely, beauty is less of a concern to her than pretty.

Still, he is too old for the long drive. She knows it even if he doesn't. And he will be gone for days, and for what? To appease some ache in him, some need to feel he is paying an overdue debt to humankind.

"Don't ask me to go with you," she says. "It's a ridiculous idea."

"It will do me good to see a bit of this country," he says, hoping she isn't playing for an invitation. "And the girl needs help."

"There are plenty of others who need help. Why her?"

"I couldn't save her mother," he says, knowing that it's not a good enough explanation.

"No doctor can save everyone."

"No, but I would like to save her."

———————

In the unaccustomed warmth of Eriko's barrack, Satomi takes her leave of the Okihiros. It is hard to believe that Manzanar is over, that she will never sleep in the barrack again. Despite the heat from the stove, roaring now with its belly full of unrationed wood, she can smell the familiar scent of mold, feel the damp. She squints to keep back the tears.

"It's painful to part," Eriko says.

"It's not too late to change your mind and come with us," Naomi offers.

Suddenly the offer is tempting, the idea of merging herself into the Okihiro family a comforting one.

"Thank you, Naomi, but I must go to Angelina. I'm determined to get some justice for my parents. They have to pay me the value of my father's land, allow me the savings he sweated for. They think that giving us twenty-five dollars and a few ration coupons will keep us quiet—it's an insult."

"They would like to wipe out our memories of this place," Eriko says. "Forget that we have been judged, imprisoned without trial."

"It doesn't matter what they would like, only the gods can take away our memories," Naomi reminds them.

Yumi is excited. "We are going home," she sings.

"I don't want to think of home," Eriko says nervously. "Not until we know for sure that we still have one."

Driving with Dr. Harper in his old Plymouth past the lines of people waiting for the same buses that brought them into Manzanar to take them out of it, Satomi turns her head for a last view of the mountains. Their summits are hidden in the mist, rocks in the wheeling clouds. At their foot the rubble of Manzanar is already being swept away by the winds, buried in the dust, their human stain scoured. The camp has been a grubby aberration on the map of the twentieth century, but soon it will be as though it never was.

Nausea stirs in her stomach, rises through her body, fills her mouth with a metallic wash. She is all emotion, frazzled, hurt, outraged. And she is leaving Tamura behind and is afraid now of what is ahead of her.

Reminiscent of that first roundup in Angelina, people mill around, sitting on their cases, looking agitated. Children with their family names now, rather than the old hated numbers pinned to their clothes, cling to their parents; old people wait to be told where to go by the soldiers, who have put their guns aside.

As they head toward the gate, they come across the orphanage children being shepherded onto buses. There's no room for them to pass and Dr. Harper slows the car to a stop and cuts the engine.

Satomi shivers, her skin prickles as she scans the line for Cora, but she is nowhere to be seen. Their leave-taking had been hard on both of them, unsatisfactory. Satomi had expected Cora to sob, but she hadn't been prepared for her own rising panic. She had attempted calm, hadn't wanted to frighten Cora with her own fears, but it hadn't worked.

"I kissed her, hugged her," she told the Okihiros. "But she isn't reassured. She thinks that I will forget her."

She reaches across to the old duffel bag on the backseat of the Plymouth, fumbling around for something.

"I have it," she says, opening the door and leaping out. "I won't be long, Dr. Harper."

The first bus is passing through the gate before she reaches the second already on the move. Cora could be gone, on the road, lost to her. Without hope she bangs on the bus door, holding on to the handle doggedly so that the driver has to stop his vehicle and open up. To her relief, Cora is seated up front behind the driver.

The child's face is expressionless. She is on the edge of her seat, sitting upright as though ready to take flight. The metal buttons on her felt coat are done up to the neck, she is wearing the yellow mittens that Naomi knitted for her, her arms straining tight around her little bundle of possessions.

"Oh, Cora, you're here. I thought I'd missed you."

Cora doesn't smile, doesn't say anything as Satomi bends down in front of her.

"Be quick," the driver says crabbily. "You're holding everyone up."

"Look, Cora, see this little bird?" Satomi opens her hand to show Tamura's carved titmouse sitting in her palm.

Cora nods and touches the little beak.

"He is called a titmouse, Cora. He is sweet, isn't he?"

"Is it for me?"

"Well, I'm giving him to you for a little while. He was my mother's gift to me and it hurts me to part with him, so I will want him back when we next meet. Keep him safe, Cora, and I will come for him. It won't be soon, but I will come."

She imagines for a moment hauling Cora off the bus, the two of them making a run for it. But she knows that they wouldn't get far, and what then?

"You getting off or staying for the ride?" the driver says, putting the bus into gear. "Either way, I'm leaving now."

"Okay. Okay. What difference will a few seconds make?"

She kisses Cora's cheeks, her tiny lips, touches the collar of her coat. Everything about the child is diminutive, fragile. She is filled with shame. She has failed to keep Cora with her.

"Where are you heading to?" she demands of the driver.

"Back to the relocation camp, we hand them over there."

"And then? Where are they taken then?"

"How the hell should I know?"

Waving the bus away, she attempts a smile, but her lips tremble, her eyes spike with the tears that come instead. Cora presses her nose to the window, gives a hesitant half wave as her face crumples in distress.

In a futile effort to comfort herself, Satomi sobs, "She'll be fine. Who could not choose Cora?" Then Dr. Harper is at her side, his arm around her shoulders, guiding her back to the car.

"It's not fair, Satomi," he says. "But you will make it right one day. I truly believe that you will. For the time being, though, you must find a way that allows you to remember what is past without spoiling the present."

He hands her his handkerchief, starts up the engine, and swallows hard. They are all counting what is lost, he thinks.

"It's so odd to just be driving out, no one to stop us," she says, drying her eyes with his handkerchief, which smells, like his shirt, of laundry powder.

"Well, then, we'll play a fanfare to mark the day." Easing the old sedan into a leisurely roll, he hits the horn in three short playful toots. A guard looks up and tips his hat to him. He feels almost festive.

Near the gate, Mrs. Hamada steps out of a bus line and waves them down.

"I am sorry that you had to leave your home for us, Satomi. Good luck with your life."

"You needed the space more than me, Mrs. Hamada. Did the children enjoy it?"

"They did. My little Ava said that she could smell roses there. '*It smells of roses, Mama,*' she would say."

RETURNING

THINGS LOOK PRETTY much the same in Angelina, the same stores, the same church, the same crumbling plaster walls on the post office building. Even Mr. Stedall's dog, gray in the muzzle now, is lying in its usual place by the post office door, waiting for him to finish work.

But it's not her Angelina anymore. It's a weird and disorientating place, at one and the same time both strange and familiar. Like a still from some old movie, where she remembers the scene but has forgotten the plot.

Dr. Harper has parked up by the general store and they are sitting in the car gathering themselves after the long drive.

"So, first thoughts?" he asks.

"It's so much smaller than I remember," she says.

"Well, that's the way it is when you visit old haunts."

"Yes, I've read that. Didn't believe it until now, though."

It isn't only about things being smaller, although the schoolyard, immeasurable to her childhood eye, she sees now is merely a yard or two of asphalt, the main street no longer than Sewer Alley. It's more that she feels herself to be a stranger in the town, a town that she knows fears strangers. Yet the sight of Angelina quiet in the afternoon sun fills her with longing, a longing that she knows it can never satisfy.

"We all experience it at some time," Dr. Harper says sympathetically. "A yearning to go back to how things were. It's not so much the place we miss, I think, but our childhoods."

Out of the car she stands in front of the school, unable for a moment to move. She hasn't thought of Lily for a while, but now, closing her eyes, her old friend appears in absolute clarity, the scattering of freckles on Lily's low cheekbones, the wary look in her eyes. A tingle runs the length of her body, makes the hairs on her arms stand to attention. For a second she wishes those old skipping days back. Oh, Lily, Lily.

The wind, the wind, the wind blows high
Blowing Lily through the sky.
She is handsome, she is pretty,
She is the girl from the golden city.
She has a boyfriend, one, two, three.
Won't you tell me who is he?

"Don't go so fast, Sati, I can't jump in," Lily's voice echoes through her mind.

Mr. Beck is in her head too, staring, ogling her as she skips. He's a thin, insubstantial figure, hovering with bell in hand. Playtime over.

"I feel sick," she says, opening her eyes, swaying a little.

Dr. Harper puts his hand to her forehead. "No fever," he says. "I diagnose time-travel sickness."

"You're so smart." She smiles at him.

He sighs. "Just old."

As though he hasn't moved since she last saw him, Mr. Taylor is in his usual place behind the counter of his drugstore, mixing sodas, bagging up candies. He licks his fingers to open the paper bags one by one, lick—flick—open—fill, never missing a beat.

How Tamura had loved those candies, how they had satisfied the sweet tooth that she had been ashamed to indulge in front of Aaron.

She wonders if while they have been incarcerated Mr. Taylor has given a thought to his old customers. Has anyone in Angelina thought about the Baker women?

Dr. Harper orders them coffee at the counter; it comes in thick white mugs that her lips have trouble getting around. She's used to thin tin, hasn't drunk from china since that last breakfast with Tamura in the farm's kitchen.

Why had she and Tamura never ordered coffee? It was too ordinary, she supposes something that could be had at home. Bubble-gum soda had been the thing. She had loved the sweet marshmallow taste of it, but had Tamura really liked the childish drink too? Perhaps she had only ordered it to please her daughter, to share in the fun.

"You're the Baker kid, aren't you?" Mr. Taylor says. "You've grown a bit."

Across the street the bank sits shiny in its glossy slick of brown paint. Housed between the general store and the haberdasher's, it makes its neighboring storefronts look drab. The sidewalk in front of it has been scrubbed, bleached to white, its cleaned-daily windows gleam. If a bank can't show a good front, then things must be on the slide.

Back in the street, she gets an acrid whiff of smoke from Cromer's Cannery, it takes her a while to place it. When she does, she thinks of Lily's cousin Dorothy, of Davey Cromer not wanting to marry beneath him, denying responsibility for the baby. She thinks of Angelina's unforgiving hierarchy.

Dr. Harper pats her back, gives her a smile, and pushes open the bank's door confidently. She can tell that he is nervous too. The clerk is smoking behind the polished grille. He's just like any store clerk, she tells herself, taking a deep breath. Selling a different kind of stock, is all.

"We'd like to see the manager," Dr. Harper says.

"Sure, I'll ask. Want me to tell him what it's about?"

"It's private business," Satomi says.

He looks at her quizzically, puckering up his brow. "You're Sati Baker, aren't you? I'm Greg, Artie's big brother."

"Oh, sure, I recognize you. How have you been?"

"Got shot up in the war, right leg not much use, but I manage."

"How's Artie?"

"Haven't heard from him in six months. Working at a fifty-cent dance hall in San Fran, last time he wrote. Always fancied the big city, didn't he?"

"Couldn't wait to get away." She doesn't ask about Lily.

"Guess you know your farm's been sold? Guess that's why you're here. What name shall I say?"

"Satomi Baker, of course. And this is Dr. Harper."

In his airless office at the rear of the bank the manager stands to greet them. He's a fleshy-looking man with a tobacco-stained mustache, a sham smile, a stranger to her. A sour man, she decides on the spot.

The room is small, stuffy, its faded green blinds drawn against the sun, giving a false impression of coolness. Used to mountain weather, she had forgotten how humid it can get in Angelina in November. A fan rattles the air around and she stands in front of it, closing her eyes for a moment.

"Bill Port. Pleased to meet you, Doctor." He offers his hand from across the desk, ignoring Satomi.

"John Harper. Likewise."

It comes as a surprise to her, his name, John; she hadn't known it before. Why had she never thought to ask? "Dr. Harper" has defined him well enough, she supposes.

"And this"—Dr. Harper turns to Satomi—"is your client, Miss Satomi Baker."

"So, all the way from Manzanar, Doc! I've heard tell of the place." He allows his eyes to settle on Satomi for a moment. "Good of you, very good of you to help the girl." His voice has a gloopy mucus gurgle to it, like the sound stirred-up river mud makes.

"Emphysema," Dr. Harper tells her later. "Strange disease for a bank manager."

"Sit, sit. How can I help?"

"Your clerk told us that you have sold my farm," Satomi says quietly. "I don't recall giving you permission to do that."

He is taken aback by the way she has launched straight into things.

"We didn't need your permission, Miss Baker. Associated Farmers bought up a lot of the land around here with the government's permission. They plan to grow on a big scale. Best thing for Angelina."

"Why didn't you need my permission? I own the farm."

"Well, that's debatable. No papers to show that you or your mother had a legal stake in anything."

He didn't like her tone, she was pretty uppity for a girl, too sure of herself. He guessed that was a fault with lookers, they expected you to dance to their tune. Her father was the same, he hears, chip on the shoulder, looking for trouble, thinking himself better than the whole town put together.

"So you sold my farm from under me. What did I get for it, Mr. Port?"

"Well, offhand without looking at the papers, I seem to recall something near three hundred dollars. Land isn't bringing much these days, less than a quarter of its prewar value, I'd say." His eyes slide from Dr. Harper's. "We've all had to make sacrifices for America, no doubt of that."

"I don't believe you had the right to accept an offer on my mother's behalf, Mr. Port. Mine, either."

"Well, let's get things straight here, young lady. It isn't exactly your farm, now, is it? It was your father's, and he didn't leave a will, so I reckon you should be grateful to be getting anything, considering." He flips open a pack of Chesterfields and offers Dr. Harper one. "I go through three packs of these a day, Doc," he confides as though they are old friends. "You won't find a smoother smoke anywhere."

"Considering what, exactly, Mr. Port?" Dr. Harper asks, declining the cigarette.

"Well, considering the war and what took us into it." He sneaks a look at Satomi, confirming to himself the Jap in her. "It changed everything, Doc, you gotta know that. Angelina isn't as trusting as it used to be, we rely on ourselves these days, don't want foreigners owning our land. And I guess you don't need telling how people in these parts feel about Pearl Harbor? You won't find Japs working the land around here anymore."

He's easy to despise, Satomi thinks, disgusting, full of bigotry. But she holds her anger back, she isn't here about Bill Port. She's here about Aaron and Tamura, she's here about the farm that they had loved and had worked together. They had picked and packed their crop with care, sheltered their little family in the house that Aaron had built. It's about Aaron's pride in his land, the way he had resented every cent spent on living, thinking land the only thing worth shelling out his dollars for. If she doesn't fight for it, it will be like forgetting who her father was. It will be like saying her parents' life counted for nothing.

"Did you take a commission on the sale, Mr. Port?"

"Just the usual."

"Seems like everyone did well out of my father except his family. I could fight you on this, Mr. Port. The law's still the law, isn't it? Our farm wasn't yours to sell, let alone for three hundred dollars."

"Sure, you could go ahead with that, but I'd advise you to take the money, Miss Baker. We can string the process out, if that's what you want. I'm simply showing goodwill on the bank's part." He purses his lips so hard that for a moment they disappear altogether and he seems fishlike.

"Goodwill! You've stolen my father's farm. Is that goodwill?"

"No need for that kind of talk in here, miss." The worm of his mustache hair quivers delicately as though in tune with his shaking voice.

"Nobody's stolen anything. There's been a war, and the government had to take over deserted land. It would have gone to ruin otherwise."

"We didn't desert it voluntarily, Mr. Port. We were shipped out against our will."

"Well, that's nothing to do with me, nothing to do with the bank. Guess if you don't want to take what's on offer you could write to our head office, although I hear they're pretty snowed under, what with all the claims folk are making. Could be years before they clear the backlog. Even then there'd be no guarantees you would get more, no guarantees you'd get anything. As I said, it's all a question of goodwill."

He's sure of himself, has the law on his side, and the mother being dead makes things easier. And everything has been stamped by the government, after all. Not to mention that it's his duty to do right by his employers, by his American customers.

"However you care to describe it," he scoffs. "Twelve acres is hardly a farm."

"Plenty of farms the same around here," Satomi says. "And

there's our house, what about our house?" She is thinking of how her father had transformed the small cabin that he and Tamura had first bought into a home fit for a family. She is thinking of the cool apple light in Tamura's comforting kitchen, the lean-to laundry with its copper boiler and wooden hanging rails, the familiar scent of rice and miso.

"Not much more than a shack now, I'm sorry to say. It's due for demolition any day soon."

"Seems like sharp dealing on the part of the bank to me," Dr. Harper says. "Whatever shape the house is in, surely combined with the land it must be worth more than three hundred dollars."

"Well, you have to take into account that the place had a tenant for a while, Doc. Yugoslavian fellow, turned out he was a drinking man, he let the land run to ruin. They had a fire a couple of years back and half the house burned down. Knocked the value out of it. You're a doctor, a man of the world. I guess you've seen it all in your time. A drinking man can run things into the ground quicker than you or I can blink."

Dr. Harper is disappointed in himself; he's finding out that when it comes to matters of finance he's no match for the likes of Bill Port.

"I guess it would help if you paid interest on the money, and added your commission to it," he says. "You should do that, at least. United Farmers is a big company, they got the land at an unreasonably low price."

"Can't do it, I don't have the authority. I might wish it different, but that's the way it is. What I'm offering is the only deal to be had in Angelina today."

"Well, I guess you know the deal stinks." Dr. Harper shakes his head and turns to Satomi. "A bird-in-the-hand, Sati?"

Bill Port opens the desk drawer and withdraws a checkbook in anticipation.

"You intend on staying around Angelina, Miss Baker?"

"What do you think, Mr. Port?"

"Girl like you, I guess not. I reckon not many of the Japs will come back. Being resettled elsewhere, I hear."

A girl like you, a girl like you. How many times has she heard that? What did he mean by a girl like her? He didn't know her, not like she knew him, anyway. *A man like you, Mr. Port,* she thought, *at home in Angelina, small town big fish, big fish small mind.*

"And my parents' account with you. That had money in it. My mother told me there should be around a hundred dollars in that."

"Maybe there was, I seem to recall more like seventy. We closed a lot of accounts around that time. They were small feed, mostly, cost more to manage than made sense. They weren't being used, you see."

"We could hardly use it while we were interned, now, could we?"

"You'll have to take that up with the head office too."

"I guess there's going to be a long line at the head office."

"I guess."

"I'll have to let it go, then. I've given up waiting in line."

"You make sure you don't go spending it all at once, now." he hands the check to Dr. Harper.

"A young girl with all that cash, eh, John?" He winks at Dr. Harper. "Pretty dresses, makeup, gone in a flash if she's not careful, eh?"

"You've made it out for two hundred and sixty dollars," Dr. Harper says, confused.

"Tax." Bill Port moves toward the door.

Satomi takes the check that Dr. Harper hands her and waves it in the air. "What would you do with the money, Bill?" she says, experiencing a moment of pleasure as his body stiffens at the use of his first name.

"Well, Satomi, I . . . guess . . ."

"Oh, better if you call me Miss Baker, Bill. More professional, don't you think? Me being your valued customer after all."

The color rises in Bill Port's face. His hand trembles as he lights a fresh cigarette from the stub of his old one. *Damn Japs, who the hell does the girl think she is?*

"You'll cash the draft for her here, today?" Dr. Harper makes it sound like a demand.

"Sure, Doc, we're here to help."

"I guess you know the girl's been cheated, Port? But then, that's the business you're in, it seems."

"Look here, Doc, no need for that kinda talk. I've never cheated anyone. It's the way things are, that's all."

"Do you like your job, Bill?"

"I sure do, Doc. I like to help the folks in Angelina get along. How about you?"

"More than I thought before I met you, Bill. I can see now that there are worse things than being a small-town doctor."

Back on the sidewalk, Dr. Harper takes her hand as they cross the road, although there is no traffic in sight.

"Nothing seems respectable anymore," he says as they settle themselves in the car. "The man was shameless. Time was when bank managers could be trusted, when fairness counted."

"I didn't really expect anything different, Dr. Harper. Felt I had to make a stand, though."

"What now?"

"Well, maybe it's not such a good idea, but I guess I'd like to take a last look at the farm."

"You sure that's what you want, Satomi? If there's been a fire, it may, you know . . ."

"I'm not sure, but let's go anyway. I know I'll regret it if I don't."

"And after that?"

"I'm thinking of heading East, New York. My old teacher, Mr. Beck, advised it once, my mother too. I think they were right. I've money now for the fare, and a bit besides. Things around here aren't going to change anytime soon."

"I can help you there, Satomi. My cousin Edward and his wife Betty live in New York. Maybe they could put you up until you find your feet."

"Are you sure, Dr. Harper? You've already done enough for me."

"I'm sure, and why not call me John?"

"I like calling you Dr. Harper. Calling you John would make you seem like a stranger to me. Besides, my mother wouldn't have approved. It's only proper to give you the title you've worked for."

They smile at each other, sharing the memory of Tamura.

"I imagine New York won't be easy, you know?" he says. You're a country girl, after all. It's a pretty hard place to make your way in."

"Well, I'm not expecting easy, and it feels as right as anywhere, I suppose. There's nothing left for me in Angelina. I guess I'd rather be Japanese in New York than in California."

"I envy you," he says. "It's the American way to up sticks, start over."

"Well, I'm going to give it a try."

"And you won't be alone. I'll call my cousin before you get there, so you'll be expected. Maybe he can help find you work, and you'll have a place to stay until you can sort something out for yourself. His wife is kind, and he's a warm person."

"It must run in your family."

"You sound surprised."

"No, not at all. My mother was a good judge of character."

They stop for gas on the way. The JAP TRADE NOT WANTED sign

is still there, but it's a stranger who comes to serve them. He fills
the tank without looking at her.

"Time to take that sign down, don't you think?" Dr. Harper
says, with a flick of his head toward it.

"I'll think about it." The man grins at him.

"It's sickening, makes me ashamed, Sati."

"Oh, Dr. Harper, you have nothing in this world to feel ashamed
about."

Along the road out of town she asks him to stop the car. He
waits with the window down, watching her pace the road, feeling
her panic. It won't be light for much longer, they should hurry.

She squats down and picks up a handful of earth, letting it run
through her fingers, testing its friability in the way that Aaron
used to do.

"It's good earth here," she calls to him. "You can grow anything in it."

"You don't have to go, you know," he says. "Maybe it's better
to remember it as it was."

"It's only a few hundred yards or so down the road," she says.
"We've come this far, how can I not go?"

She half expects to see their old truck still stalled at the roadside, but it is gone.

"You can tell it was a good building once," he says, noticing
the set of her shoulders as the house comes into view. She's pale,
attempting to rally herself. He wants to comfort but can't think of
how—words, he knows, won't help.

The spectacle of the ailing house is hard to look at. Her chest
tightens with the memory of how it used to be. A sudden desperate longing for Tamura overtakes her.

There are cracks like lightning hits in the whitewashed windowpanes. All the frames are rotting away, and Aaron's tough old
enemy bindweed races up the smoke-blackened walls to the roof.

KEEP OUT. PRIVATE PROPERTY is splashed across the padlocked door
in red paint.

"I could break the lock easy if you want, Sati."

"Oh, Dr. Harper, I didn't have you down as a housebreaker."
She gives him a tense smile. "I can get in through my bedroom
window if I want. I've done it often enough before."

"Sure?"

"Sure."

"There's no hurry, Sati." He doesn't care about the dark coming now. "Take your time"

"Okay."

At the back of the house she hunkers down by the kitchen door
and smothers a wail. She doesn't want to upset Dr. Harper. She
thinks of what she has lost, what she can never get back. Her
mother, she knows, would say different, she would say that she had
a happy childhood and that can never be taken from her.

The kitchen door is padlocked like the front one, but no KEEP
OUT warning. She doesn't want to go inside; just standing in the
yard is pain enough.

It's a surprise to find Tamura's henhouse still standing. No hens,
the straw swept out, a few molding seeds set in the mud floor. A
child's basket stands rotting in one corner with peppercress growing through it, she doesn't recognize it. How Tamura had loved
her hens, those homely little things that she had thought beautiful. How she had cared for them.

Their packing sheds have been knocked down and replaced
with long aluminum buildings. Neat piles of boxes stand around
stamped with the United Farmers logo. A chemical smell hangs in
the air; the place feels dead. The years of her father's attention
have been swallowed up, gone. Aaron's passage through his land
forgotten. There's nothing left of him for her to see or touch or
smell. Home is nowhere to be found on the ground here.

On her way back to the car she flips open the mailbox; it's empty. A moment of disappointment connects her with her younger self, as though the place isn't dead to her yet. How she had loved to find things there, seed catalogues, Aaron's paper. She remembers the penciled note from Elena that had brought comfort to Tamura.

"I need to go back into Angelina. One more thing to do."

"Sure, we should find a place to stay for the night anyway. It's getting late."

She looks at the white orb of the sun low in the sky, a rising slice of moon already visible. She remembers how the sun takes its time here, dunking its way down into the woods before dropping out of sight. They have twenty minutes at least before dark, she guesses.

"I doubt anyone would give me a room in Angelina, Doctor."

"Then we'll drive to somewhere that has a better class of people." He is angry on her behalf.

At the side door of the post office, Mr. Stedall, with his dog at his feet, is oiling the chain on his bike. It's the same old bike, with its straight handlebars, the big bell that looks like a shiny hamburger. In his post office uniform Mr. Stedall looks the same too, a handsome man, she notices now, if you like thin. He smiles at her, anxious, bracing himself against life.

"Hello, Mr. Stedall. Remember me?"

"Satomi, isn't it? How's your mother?"

"She's dead, Mr. Stedall. She died in Manzanar."

"That's too bad." He looks crestfallen. "Nice woman, your mother."

"Are the Kaplans still at their place? I'd like to send Elena a note."

"He is. She died around the time you left."

"Elena died?"

"Yep, one of those freak-type accidents. She fell and hit her head against their tractor. Never woke up."

"I can't believe it, Elena dead."

"News to you, maybe; it's an old sore to Hal, though. He grieved something terrible. I reckon he'll never get over the shock of it."

"Do you know, Mr. Stedall, I can't help wondering sometimes if the devil lives in Angelina."

"Can't blame you for thinking it, Satomi."

THE GREAT PORT

Southport Street
New York

Dearest Eriko,

Dr. Harper forwarded your letter and it has found me at last. He's been such a good friend to me in so many ways that I wonder now why I was so hard on him in the camp. His letters come to me as if from home, just as yours did. I guess for me now home is not so much a place as the people I love.

I should have answered sooner but as you can see by the address I have left the West Coast behind me. Honestly, Eriko, it takes so much time to settle in this city, it's a crazy place and it's so big, I could never have imagined how big.

I was sorry to hear that Little Tokyo has changed so much and that the Negroes have taken it over. I know you hoped for familiar faces but I guess most inmates opted for relocation hoping for better things. You'll make friends, though, I'm sure. We learned the lesson of getting along with each other well at Manzanar, didn't we? If you can live alongside Mr. Sano you can live alongside anyone.

I can see you smiling as you read this thinking that most learned that lesson better than me. I guess I'll never walk in my mother's shoes, that's too much to hope for, but I'm trying.

The camps are never spoken of here. As far as New York is concerned they may never have happened. We Japanese are as much to blame for that as the government, there seems to be a conspiracy of silence among us. Why should we be ashamed, though?

It must be good to have your business back, even if as you say people only buy cheap cotton these days.

When I thanked Dr. Harper for helping me, for taking me back to Angelina, he said that it was the least he could do for Tamura's daughter. He had tears in his eyes, Eriko, and his voice trembled. He said that he had been very fond of Tamura. I think that he loved her. I think that Dr. Harper is a romantic. He saw the girl in my mother from the start, the very thing I think my father loved in her too. Perhaps men are more romantic than women altogether.

It seems to me you have to be lucky to do well in New York, lucky to get a job, lucky to make friends, lucky not to be taken in by the "con men" that hover on every street corner. Dr. Harper's cousin Edward warned me about them. He said to be careful or they would empty my purse before I knew it.

People here are infected with the "New York" bug. Everyone wants to get rich. I guess that dream makes New York what it is. People see what it has to offer and are ambitious for it. Edward says that there are more victims of hope here than in any other city in the world.

I don't stand out here at all. Everyone seems to be a refugee of one sort or another. There are Japanese around, and lots of Chinese, and honestly I don't think most people can tell the difference. I'm always being taken for Italian anyway. Still, I cherish my Japanese half, the half that makes me part of you.

I know now, though, that I will never be just right for every-one, none of us will. There's nothing to be done about that.

I'm not sorry that I came here, although I can't get used to the thin light or the small sky, and there's too much concrete and not enough green. And you will find it strange that I miss the mountains. A part of me is forever spinning, not knowing quite how to settle. The contrast between here and the camp is extreme. It rocks me sometimes, but I'm not afraid. I know you can never be free of the past but I'm determined not to live off it, to make it an excuse for every bad thing that happens.

Today is a good day, but they are not all good. It's odd to be lonely in a city teeming with people. For all the awful things about Manzanar, I don't remember ever feeling lonely there. The other night from the harbor I heard the Queen Mary blow. It sounded marooned, just like me.

When I first arrived I stayed with Dr. Harper's cousin and his wife. They have a tiny apartment and I had to sleep on an "Easy" bed in their sitting room, which was fine for me but not so nice for them I imagine. Being childless they weren't used to sharing their small space. They tried not to show it but I think that they were uneasy with me there. I moved a couple of weeks ago into a small room of my own—I have a gas ring and a sink and a bed that drops down from a cup-board. Luxury.

There's no rationing here, you can even get steak if you have the money. I long sometimes though for miso and, oddly, for mess-hall rice.

My room has a window looking onto a brick wall. It's dark but it's better I suppose than peering into someone else's apartment. My neighbor in the room next door, Mrs. Cope-land, is very old, eighty perhaps. She has a sharp tongue but manages to be charming. She won't take a shower until I return from work. "Listen out for me, darling," she says. "I'll die in that shower one day."

She has no family here but is well known in the neighborhood. I only see old people in this building. I'm pretty sure I must be its youngest resident.

Dr. Harper's cousin got me a job in their local library unpacking and putting out the new books. The good thing about that job was all the books I got to read without it costing me a cent.

I have taken a job now in the cloakroom of the Clare House Museum. It's known for its collection of Flemish paintings, and it has two galleries full of French porcelain. Are you used to using china again now?

This job pays more than the library one, but I'm not sure that it's a step up. I take in hats and hang up coats all day long. Sometimes it feels like I am hiding in my cubicle, keeping myself from the world. See, I am not as brave as I would like you to believe. But I get to see the art, and the director, a man who goes around straightening pictures and looking for dust, although I guess he has more important things to do, says that he likes my look and my manner, and that he is sure my fluency in Japanese can be put to good use. "But Japanese," he says, screwing up his face. "Are we ready to hear it?"

Are you wondering about Cora? I think of her all the time. I'm still angry that they wouldn't let me have her. It would have been hard but I think we could have managed. What should I do, Eriko? What can I do about that? I don't suppose you have heard anything? Dr. Harper is trying to find out where she is so that I can write to her. You would think that he was asking them to disclose a state secret, but as he says, the likelihood is that they don't know where she is and can't be bothered to find out. I long to know how she is doing, and

I watch for the mail and hope. Please look out for her. You never know, it's possible she could turn up somewhere in Little Tokyo.

It made me smile to hear that Yumi is getting hard to handle. I miss her naughtiness, the way she laughs that cheeky laugh and you have to forgive her everything. Children of the camp are bound to be unruly, I think.

I'm not at all surprised that Haru has become a hero. He always gives the best of himself. I read that his combat unit was among the bravest, the most decorated of them all. And Ralph too, so brave that they gave him the Bronze Star for bravery in combat. Was it Manzanar that made them so strong, do you think?

Please give my love to your mother, and to Yumi, and my best wishes to Haru.

I miss you all, Eriko.

Satomi

The air in her apartment building smells bad, a stale, ever-present, meaty sort of odor. It's the first thing to assail the senses on entering the building, before the crumbling walls and scuffed floors meet the eye.

"It's the stench of poverty," Mrs. Copeland says. "I've lived here for twenty years and I'll never get used to it."

"I know of worse, Mrs Copeland. But it sure is unpleasant."

"Well, be like me, darling, plan to get yourself a rich man and move on." Her laugh is not without bitterness.

Mrs. Copeland calls herself "a woman of independent means." It's her way of describing how she struggles to live off the diminishing capital from the sale of her small dress shop that she retired from seven years before the war.

She is curious about Satomi, about the American internment camps, horrified at the idea of them. She couldn't believe what went on in them at first, but now she is angry on Satomi's behalf, appalled that it's not only Germany to be condemned.

"A black mark against us," she says. "Such a tragedy, for you to have lost your mother there."

She is mourning herself, for her German cousins, the last of her known family, whom she hasn't heard from in years.

"They must be lost, like all those others," she says. "I'll probably never know what happened to them."

As old as she is, Mrs. Copeland volunteers at the local refugee center twice a week, helping in the kitchen, handing out second-hand clothes, pinning up the lists of people looking for their relatives. You never know, someone might turn up there who knows of her cousins, and what else is she to do with her time anyway?

"And your Cora," she says to Satomi. "Your hope is realistic. Keep your spirits up, there's a chance you'll find her."

To counteract the smell in her building, Satomi scents her room with the cheap bleach she buys at the big Woolworth's store a block from her building. She cleans like a demon these days in a way that would amaze and please Tamura. Her room has become her refuge from the city, a place where she doesn't have to be on alert. In its shabby confines she can let go of the confident show she puts on at work and in the subway, when the panic of being underground rattles her.

Like a true city girl, she jostles for space in the coffee shops with the best of them, shouting her order over the counters, where the help hardly ever return a smile. She is learning to be a New Yorker by pretending to be one. Life in the city is tricky, people move fast, have no patience, and she is always running to catch up, to wise up.

"Keep your foot hard down on the gas, it's the only way," Mrs. Copeland advises.

Her wages run out by Friday, so that she lives during the weekends on her last bit of bread, a smear of butter. And she has lost weight, so that she notices that she is skinnier than the better-fed New Yorkers she sees around her.

Apart from her fare to New York, she has twice broken into the money she got for the farm. Once to buy a child's charm bracelet for Cora, which she couldn't resist. It has a little bell hanging on it and a tiny bucket, and space for plenty more. She keeps it in a chocolate box that was left in the trash at the library. The box is well made, a three-layer deep one, shiny brown edged with gold, she can only imagine the kind of chocolates it housed. It's surprising to her the things that New Yorkers throw away. She has put a dollar in the box along with a little peg doll Mrs. Copeland saved for her from the refuge. It helps her to collect things for Cora, to keep the child in mind.

And for herself she needed clothes for work, two dark skirts, two shirts, one white, one striped, and a jacket for colder days. She is reinventing herself, creating a new style. Haru would not approve of the short hemlines, the high-wedged heels of her shoes. Oxfords don't cut it in New York. She tells herself that she must stop judging things by what Haru would think. She can please herself now.

There's plenty more she'd like to buy, a dress or two, ankle-strap shoes in the softest leather like nothing she ever saw in the Sears and Roebuck catalogue. She's tempted but can't bring herself to be so extravagant. The money put aside is her safety net, the last bit of Aaron and Tamura to make her feel cared for. It's hard to be without kin.

She sees families together and feels intensely lonely, aches to be among the Japanese again. But when she speaks to them in Japanese they don't hang around.

"They think I'm a strange white girl," she tells Mrs. Copeland. "Guess I look like trouble to them."

Her neighborhood teems with every sort, Germans, Polish, Chinese, Romanians, Italians, and Jews like Mrs. Copeland. She wonders if there's such thing as a pure New Yorker. It should make her feel included, but she has never felt so alone.

"Don't let New York gobble you up," Mrs. Copeland says. "Take the first bite yourself."

On a Sunday afternoon when her building is hushed with the slumbering old, she takes the advice and walks the streets to the park to sit on the grass and watch the passersby. A Japanese family is doing the same nearby, father, mother, three well-behaved children. Just the sight of them lifts her heart, the familiar dark hair, the lyrical sound of Japanese catching her by her heels.

"It's a lovely day, isn't it?" she says in Japanese. "Such a lovely day." –

And there it is, that confused, suspicious look. How is it that a white girl speaks Japanese so well?

"My mother was Japanese," she tries to explain as they gather their things and hurry off. "We were in Manzanar," she calls after them. They half turn, bowing their heads, smiling to be polite.

Since Pearl Harbor, since Hiroshima and Nagasaki, since the camps, they are afraid. They've done nothing wrong, but it's best to stick to your own. They fear being singled out, being noticed.

She remembers Dr. Harper's parting words to her. "Find a way to be that allows you to remember the past without spoiling the present." Well, she's trying.

She's still grieving for Tamura, still longing for Cora, and there's a low fever, a desire in her that it's hard to admit to. She has a longing to make love again, to be lost again in the intimacy she had that one time with Haru. It bothers her that she may be the loose kind, just as Lily had suspected. Are women meant to have such thoughts?

Men approach her and she isn't sure how to judge their natures. They are not of the kind she knew in Angelina or in the camp.

"Everyone's on the make, darling," Mrs. Copeland warns. "Watch yourself."

And she does, although she hadn't been prepared in those early days working in the library for her first date in the city to end so badly.

"Randal Daly, pure Irish," he had introduced himself to her as she was stacking books on the crime section shelves.

A nice enough guy, she thought, a library regular who devoured detective novels. He ran an oyster stall at the Fulton Fish Market and smelled of the lemons he cleaned himself off with at night. He was big and comfortable-looking, not handsome, but a good face, she thought. She hadn't minded his brashness; she was getting used to brashness, it was a New York thing.

She had dressed with care, folding her hair into a soft chignon, smudging her lips with a rose-colored lipstick. She bought fifteen-denier nylons, not caring that they were impractical. She wet her hands and ran them from ankle to thigh, setting the seams straight. It was good to feel pretty.

"My God, is it you?" Mrs. Copeland said appreciatively. "Be careful, now. You're still on the wrong side of green for New York, you know."

He had taken her to Sloppy Louie's restaurant near his work, a favorite with the fishmongers.

"I eat breakfast here every day," he said. "I like to be near the river."

The restaurant was spacious; they were early, but it was already more than half full. Randal thought it a bad idea to eat late.

"Better to give things time to go down," he said.

On their way to the table he greeted people at theirs, exchanging pleasantries, slapping the men on the back, complimenting the women.

"It'll be jam-packed in an hour," he said proudly, as though it were his own place doing so well.

The barnlike eatery was decorated with things of the sea, model sailing ships marooned in rye bottles, giant lobster claws hooking the air, hulking oyster shells glued randomly on the walls. It was hard to hear over the din of people chatting, calling to the waiters, clattering the cutlery—it reminded her of the mess halls in Manzanar. A brothy scent of fish, rich and steamy, made the room feel warm and living. It was good to be out, to be part of the world.

Randal's cheeks had turned red in the heat of the room; she wondered if her own had done the same. He ordered for her.

"I know what's good," he said.

"That's fine." She was glad, nervous at the thought of having to make a choice.

"You'll like the chowder," he said, proffering the pepper. "It's good with pepper."

He had advised against the eels. "Dirty things," he said. "Bottom of the harbor trash, night scavengers. Only fish I never touch."

He did most of the talking, telling her that he liked his job, it gave him a good living, and there was more to oysters than people thought.

"Got to know the good from the bad, the sweet from the sour," he said. "Trade secret how it's done."

He had never dated anyone who worked in a library, he said with a laugh. "Guess you're pretty smart, but nothing wrong with that."

"Oh, not so smart. I'm only the shelf-stacker."

He had an odd way of not responding, as though he hardly

heard her, as though he were working out what he was going to say next himself. Perhaps, though, it was only that he was lonely too, eager to talk.

By the time dessert came she knew his age, the kind of movies he liked, "westerns and detectives." She knew that his mother was dead and that he lived with his father, who worked with him in the fish market.

"This place is the best, isn't it? Louie's Italian like you," he said over coffee, waving to the proprietor. "Married to an Irish-American. It's a good combination, like you and me."

She laughed, used to the mistake. "Oh, I'm not Italian, Randal. I'm half Japanese."

The moment she said it she saw the effect it had on him. He couldn't have been more surprised if she had reached across the table and punched him in the face for no good reason. He stared at her, confused, his eyes screwing up as though he were trying to work out some difficult math problem.

"What?" His face darkened. His voice was suddenly harder, mean.

"You're a Jap? A Jap?"

"Yes, I'm Japanese. I'm Japanese and you're Irish. So?"

He stood up without looking at her, kicked the chair aside, and threw a few dollars on the table.

"Warn a guy next time," he flung at her, heading to the door.

The room went quiet, people began to stare. She watched him clumsily navigating the tables, heard his "Jesus" addressed to no one in particular. She put a napkin to her lips, swallowed hard, fighting nausea.

"You okay, honey?" the woman at the next table asked. "You don't look so good."

Outside the restaurant, she felt disoriented, out of place on the sidewalk in the dark. It was raining, the drops falling like snow, thick and slow. The insistent whisper of the river came to her. She thought of the eels Randal had spoken of curling in the deep dirty depths of the harbor, comfortable down there in the dark, knowing their place.

She wasn't sure where the subway was, hadn't wanted to ask a stranger, so for the first time in her life she took a cab.

Angry at herself for being such a bad judge of character, she couldn't wait to get to her room, to bolt the door and be alone. It was hard to admit to being hurt—that would be giving Randal and his kind the upper hand—but she couldn't sleep that night, something horrible scratched in her.

Next morning as Satomi picked her mail up, Mrs. Copeland called to her over the banister.

"How did it go, honey? Is it love?"

"Let's put it this way, Mrs. Copeland: the man was hardly a prince."

"I told you, darling, it's a hard-hearted city."

The letter in her mail was from Eriko. The news was sad. Naomi had died. Her heart had given out in her sleep.

I'm grateful that she didn't suffer, but I miss her so much, Satomi. My only comfort is that she is with Tamura. Now we are both orphans.

Another link gone. She didn't have to cry about Randal now, she could cry for Naomi, beloved Naomi, contrary but kind Naomi, Naomi who with her arthritic hands had knitted mittens for orphans.

After the incident with Randal, New York didn't seem so scary to her; she had survived her baptism and hadn't drowned. If anything, it had become more like Angelina. Not everyone was on your side.

It went against her nature to take advice from someone like Randal Daly, but she determined in the future to make it clear from the start to anyone who was interested, who she is.

There had been other dates that had gone better, but none of them had stirred her much. She had no idea what she was looking for, someone like Haru, perhaps. None of them, though, fit that bill. Not the guy who was all over her in the first hour, or the one who thought himself funny but wasn't, or the nice one who got on her nerves. Sometimes she thought it would be better just to stay at home, where nothing was required of her.

Now she takes refuge in books, in the conversations that she has with Mrs. Copeland about relatives finding each other, about the joy of being found. Nothing interests her more than those stories of reunion.

"It happens," Mrs. Copeland says. "Not that often, but when it does, it's wonderful. You should see their faces when they discover a brother, a cousin, when a loved one is found alive and longing to hear from them."

Satomi can't help picturing a scene where she and Cora are reunited. She imagines them walking together holding hands, eating in the diner three blocks down that serves ten different flavors of ice cream, sitting in the movies thrilling to Flash Gordon.

"You're haunted by that child," Mrs. Copeland observes. "But you must make a life for yourself before you can make one for her."

It's good advice, not that Mrs Copeland seems interested much in her own life. She is looking toward death with the sort of practicality that Satomi thinks must come with age.

"I thought my time was up the other night, could see myself lying in that shower clear as day. But it was just a dream."

"How horrible for you."

"No, honey, I don't mind those dreams so much. No one lives forever, and they sort of prepare you for what's coming."

AT CLARE HOUSE

Y OU'RE NEW." JOSEPH Rodman takes his time handing
Satomi his coat. The party at the museum is almost over, but
he is not sorry to be late, he is more often late than not for most
things. His expectations of the show, of his fellow guests, are low.

Satomi nods her head slightly, doesn't answer. Her hand is out,
ready to take his coat, but he is fiddling in the pocket searching in
a disinterested way.

"You've lost something?"

"No, not really, just playing for time."

"Playing for time?" she turns from him, takes a hanger from
the rail, wonders why she feels embarrassed.

He can't quite place the accent. She's definitely not a New
Yorker, more West Coast than East, he thinks. The low pitch of her
voice, and her unhurried way of speaking is measured in comparison to the city's gabble. He likes the cool look of her. It's strange
that he should be so instantly charmed, especially as she has nothing
of the boy about her, except maybe a linear sort of elegance.

"I'd rather look at you than what's on show here tonight," he
says. He isn't flirting, it's the truth.

She's used now to New York flattery, but his compliment
doesn't feel like flattery—not the standard kind, at least. She senses
that the usual banter doesn't apply here. She sees sympathy in his

stare and is irritated. Has he worked out that she's hiding in the cloakroom? Does he feel sorry for her? He is making her uncomfortable, and she wishes he would hand over his coat and go away.

"My name's Joseph. Yours?"

"It's Satomi. Satomi Baker."

"Satomi?"

"It's Japanese."

"But you aren't . . ."

"I'm half Japanese."

"Perfect. Quite perfect."

Time is running out for Joseph, and if a woman must be courted, if he must keep his promise, then perhaps she is different enough to be the one.

On her way home that evening Satomi wonders whether she was right to refuse his dinner invitation. She's bad at jumping in these days, less willing than she used to be at taking chances. New York makes you cautious. And Joseph Rodman is like no one she has ever known, although there is something of the museum's director about him. She wouldn't know how to be with a man like him.

Two weeks later and on his third request she agrees to dinner, providing that it's somewhere not too smart.

"I don't have the clothes for anywhere smart."

The moment she accepts the invitation she regrets it. It seems to her that Joseph Rodman is a man who expects perfection. He is so well groomed as to be intimidating, he smells of cologne, and he is obviously rich, coming from a world she can only guess at. Her father would not have approved, would hardly think him the kind of man for his daughter. And Tamura, who judged men by Aaron and found most of them wanting, would she have approved? Satomi's mother would have been kinder than her father, of course, less willing to judge.

"Go," Mrs. Copeland has encouraged, feeling herself *in paren-tis*. "Plenty of time to lie low when you're old."

"Remember, nowhere fancy," Satomi warns, hoping it might put him off.

But he is stirred by the idea of it, of finding somewhere "not too smart," of being out with the hat-check girl on an ordinary date.

You could start from scratch with a girl like her. He has found a Vermeer languishing in a cupboard, a delight of color and com-position. All she needs is the right frame. Relief floods him. Things might work out after all.

It seems to Satomi that Joseph under his smartness has a good character, although he doesn't give much of himself away. A frank smile and impeccable manners are hardly enough to go on. He's conceited, that much is obvious in his head-to-toe neatness, the sleek cut of his hair, the perfect ovals of his nails. But are such things flaws? Perhaps that sort of perfection is natural for the rich, how would she know? She has noticed that in art, though, his eye is taken by the simple—a costly sort of simple, but still a taste she shares.

Joseph, despite his exacting style, has honed his taste to be the opposite of that of his widowed mother, Dulcibele, who revels in what he considers to be a vulgar sort of fondness for the overdone. His infrequent visits to her glittering white mansion on the shores of the Hudson are uncomfortable, the times they come across each other in town unwelcome to them both.

He blames his mother's selfishness for not caring for his father, for the broken thing in himself that he's finding hard to fix. She can't be blamed, though, for the promise his father had extracted from him. A deathbed promise, he thinks dramatically, although it was given months before the old man died.

"You must marry, Joseph. It's the right thing for you."

"I don't think I'm made for marriage, Father."

"But it will make you happy, Joseph. I know it. Promise me. Promise me that you will."

His son must make an heir to the Rodmans' great fortune, just as he had done himself. It's a duty not to be dodged. A man of Joseph's tastes could too easily lose the way. At the very least, a wife on his son's arm would put paid to the gossip. A pretty one might even switch Joseph's taste to the more conventional.

With the promise given, the old man when the time came had let go of life with a deep sigh and a pleasurable sense of relief. Joseph, along with the Rodman fortune, was left with the pledge, and the novel feeling of being committed.

Unused to courtship, he fumbles through his now-regular outings with Satomi, pleased when she finds his jokes funny, flattered when he has her attention. He is already fond of her, charmed by how different she is from those smart uptown girls his mother has her eye on for him. Having a girl on his arm is odd, but not as unpleasant a sensation as he had feared.

Satomi feels more the Angelina girl than ever when she is with Joseph. Before him, she hadn't thought herself to be so ignorant. But she's learning, and she likes it. She knows now that wine is not for her, but she enjoys the bookish flavor of whiskey and the taste of a New York strip steak. It's amazing to discover that she likes opera, amazing that she should even go to the opera. The linking of Satomi Baker with Joseph Rodman is so extraordinary a thing that she is tempted herself sometimes to repeat in her head, *a girl like you*. She loves the plays Joseph takes her to on Broadway, even though he often thinks them poor. It's shocking to her how little impresses Joseph.

"What's he like, darling?" Mrs. Copeland asks Satomi as they stand in their hallway together, looking down through the window at Joseph's waiting cab in the street below.

"Um, he's sort of fine, I guess. He makes me laugh quite a lot, and he's rich, I think, but he's not for me, really."

"Are you sure, darling? The words 'lucky girl' come to mind."

But Satomi doesn't so much feel lucky as false. Despite herself she can't help judging. Joseph is far too extravagant, too wasteful. To see him leave food on his plate, wine in his glass, is painful to her. He buys things just to try them, a new brand of cigarettes that he throws away after one drag, books that he likes the cover of but will never read, and so much cologne that it makes her dizzy.

Yet the sense that Joseph, like her, is dislocated in some way draws her to him. And there is something of Dr. Harper's warmth and wit about him that she likes. She wonders what it's like to be him, to never have to worry if there will be enough money at the end of the week for food, to never question your good fortune or deny yourself anything.

Oh, money, she can hear her mother say. *It isn't a child of your own, or even a fresh-laid egg.*

I wish I could be like you, Mama, she replies in this conversation in her head. *You always knew the path to take.*

In Joseph's efforts to charm Satomi, he tells himself that art is the thing. If he can't seduce with his manliness, he will do it with art. So they stroll the long arcades in the hushed atmosphere of New York's galleries, gazing at the glorious paintings of battles, of lush naked women, and of misty landscapes. She can recognize now the pure light of a Raphael, the sweeping brushstrokes of a Gauguin.

It pleases the teacher in Joseph. He hopes the passion on the canvases will satisfy enough to deflect for a while what he imagines must be Satomi's expectations of him.

He takes her to those restaurants that have an intimate atmosphere, but where he doesn't have to be alone with her. He is saving himself from those moments when a different man would take the opportunity to make his move, those moments that could lose him the game. In its own way it is a romantic sort of wooing, he thinks.

Satomi, though, is confused as to what she and Joseph are, exactly. It seems to her that he is more teacher than boyfriend. There's something about him that she can't get a hold of. Perhaps it's the sense she has that Joseph is in hiding, she wishes she knew from what. Whatever it is, though, it doesn't feel like a regular boy-girl thing. She's relieved that he hasn't made a move, but she can't help thinking it strange, asking herself questions. *Why doesn't he kiss me? Why is taking my arm to cross the road the nearest he gets to touching?*

Aware that he is not pulling off the boyfriend thing, he steps up what he thinks of as treats for her. He takes her on a tour of his New York. They pound the streets, and visit the grand buildings of Lower Manhattan. He points out ornate ceilings and reels off dates.

"This is New York classical," he says, trawling her to the Cunard Building to marvel at its great hall. "Nothing much left of New Amsterdam these days, but the American Renaissance style compares with Paris, with Rome, even. It's marvelous, don't you think?"

It's a step too far, but she can't help laughing.

"Oh, for goodness' sake, Joseph, no more, please. Let's get some coffee. I can't face another museum, another bank, another set of Corinthian columns."

Buildings are not her thing and she is bored, reminded of those times in Mr. Beck's class when her mind had wandered, when she and Lily had caught each other's eyes and raised them to heaven.

"It's the worst thing, to be bored," Joseph says. "Sorry, Sati, I'm a fool. What would you like to do?"

He is glad that she speaks up for herself, that she is not in his thrall. It would feel more like cheating to him if she was.

"I'd really like to visit the Statue of Liberty, and I want to ride the elevator to the top of the Empire State Building."

"Really! You know it's twelve hundred and fifty feet above the ground up there?"

"Are you scared of heights, Joseph?"

"No, only of tourists." They both laugh.

If only they could agree to be nothing more than friends, she would be able to enjoy his company better. Joseph makes the best of friends; he is good at listening when she needs to talk, easy with her silences when she doesn't. But though it seems to her that they are playacting the man woman thing, though nothing of what they are to each other is spoken about, she senses that he is aiming for something different than friendship. So, as though she is cheating, she feels guilty when she goes with someone else on a date without telling him.

"Only to save his feelings," she says to Mrs. Copeland.

"Really?" Mrs. Copeland shrugs her shoulders, raises one eyebrow.

Knowing nothing about Joseph, Dr. Harper's cousin Edward, in a matchmaking move, had set it up.

"Pete Elderkin. A nice guy," he said. "I think you'll hit it off."

And he is a nice guy, sort of. Fresh out of the Army, with a crew-cut bullishness about him, Satomi can tell he is the sort of man who takes life on the run. He had grabbed himself a job in a big cross-state delivery business, in the same week of his demobilize from the Army. Competition doesn't bother him, only standing still bothers him, he says.

"I'll make it up to transport manager in no time," he tells her. "I pretty much run the place on my own now. Wouldn't surprise me if I end up owning the whole damn thing."

It wouldn't surprise her either, since he has that bounce-back thing about him. Nothing is going to keep him down.

They walk in the park and she feels small beside the bulk of him, she was used these days to walking with Joseph, who is slim and only a couple of inches taller than her.

Pete tells her about his time in the Army, about the war, about the German concentration camps he has seen. He believes that America has single-handedly set the world to rights.

"God, those German bastards," he says. "Europe's had it. It's the most decadent place on earth. Thank God for America."

America this, America that, he is in love with his country; nothing bad about that, she supposes, it reminds her of Haru. But he takes it too far, until she wishes he would stop crowing about the US of A, as he calls it. It feels to her like preaching, like one of Haru's lectures.

"We live in the most decent country on earth," he says. "You'd know that if you'd seen what I've seen."

"I was in a camp too. An American one," she ventures. "I wasn't thanking God for America then."

He looks away from her, gives an embarrassed laugh as though she has made an inappropriate joke.

"Sure, Edward told me. But hell, it's not the same thing at all."

"No, maybe not. Still, it was a camp. It was imprisonment."

It wasn't the same thing, she knew that. She had read about those concentration camps, the inhuman things that went on in them. Mrs. Copeland often spoke of it, had periods of depression about it, cried for her lost relatives, and thought herself lucky as a Jew that she was also an American. You couldn't compare Manzanar to those malignant places, yet still she thought it wrong to judge the camps against each other. It occurs to her that there is a ranking of what it was okay to talk about in these postwar times. Germany's treatment of the Jews, fine; America's of the Japanese, not.

"Things happen," he says. "Long as they work out well in the end, I guess."

"You can't just dismiss innocent people losing their homes, being caged, Pete. What if it had been you?"

"Yeah, I kinda see your point, but . . ."

"Really?" she senses that he hasn't seen her point at all. "I don't think you can bear to think about America being in the wrong about anything." She wants him to know that just because things had been worse in Germany, she wouldn't be silenced about the camps in America.

"Well, I'm not sure that's—"

"There were deaths, some would say murders, in Manzanar. Boys shot, an old man killed for refusing to halt at the guards' command. And plenty who didn't survive the conditions. Did you know that orphaned babies were imprisoned there?"

"Look." He is in a conciliatory mood. "I guess I didn't think it out. Let's not talk about it, huh. The war's over, after all. We'll make a proper night of it next time, shall we? Start over."

It was unforgiving of her, she knew, but she couldn't help herself. "No next time," she said lightly. "I don't think we're going to work out."

Pete Elderkin was never going to think it out. His blind love of country, what seemed to her to be his denial of what went on in the American camps, played on her mind for a few days until a letter from Dr. Harper arrived, which put things back in perspective. She hadn't been making too much of it. It was cheating yourself to love in ignorance, to love what you didn't know, and wherever it took place injustice was injustice.

I hadn't realized I had collected quite so much. It's a bigger archive than I had at first thought. When you are ready I want you to have it. I'm not expecting you to do anything with it, but I'm shocked by the silence of our leaders, the lack of an apology. Perhaps the time's not right yet, but someday you might be pleased to have it, if only to show your children.

She isn't sure that she does want it. His reports on sick inmates, the personal things he has collected, the photographs and the journals that will surely include Tamura's life, her death, might be too much for her. He might as well be handing over the earth of Manzanar, her mother's grave, the dead riot boys, the skin and blood of the camp's inmates. She is afraid of Dr. Harper's archive, of the pain it will cause her to go through it.

I'm still trying to trace Cora, he assures her.

I've written to various orphanages. They take their time replying, but none so far know of Cora. I think it means that she must have found a family, which would be the best news if only we could be sure of it.

Her own efforts to find Cora are not nearly enough, she thinks. She feels powerless, hardly up to the task, so far away from wherever Cora might be. And none of the letters she has written to government offices have met with any success. The chocolate box is filling up with trinkets for the child, satin ribbons, a necklace, a child's hairbrush, things she is beginning to fear Cora will never see.

But along with Eriko's less frequent letters, Dr. Harper's serve to anchor her, keep her linked to her past. Manzanar is always with her, Cora too, but New York is an intrusive city and won't be ignored.

With her feelings of home stirred, she writes to Haru care of

Eriko, a short exploratory letter to ask if he thinks of her as she does him. Even if he doesn't, she asks him to make inquiries in his locality about Cora, to visit the orphanages on her behalf.

My feelings haven't changed, and I feel brave enough to ask if yours have. I could return to California, but I would only come if you wanted it.

His answering letter is brief, lecturing in tone:

You must let Cora go, make your own life now, Satomi. It would be a mistake to return here. Stick to what you have chosen.

It hurts to read his disinterest on the page, the truth of his feelings written so bluntly. It's obvious to her now that Haru had only found her beautiful on the outside. The thing between them, so large a part in her life, had after all only played out in a minor key in his. She must shed the hope she harbored that one day they would be reunited. The truth is bleak, but at least she won't miss the preaching.

Joseph has kept her from what he terms *society*, from any introduction that might go wrong, that might offend her. You never know how uptown will react to outsiders, and he doesn't want to see her hurt. He introduces her to his best friend Hunter, though. Not much of a risk, he thinks, as Hunter isn't cursed with snobbery or, amazingly, with bitterness. Wheelchair-bound for life since being wounded at Pearl Harbor, Hunter has a lighthearted take on even the most serious things in life.

"Satomi's father was killed at Pearl Harbor," Joseph tells him straight off, wanting them to have something in common, even something so horrible. "It's extraordinary that you were both there, don't you think?"

"So he and I were colleagues-in-arms, then," Hunter says, taking her hand, smiling at her.

"I guess."

"I was luckier than your father. Just the legs," he says, as though they were the smallest of concerns.

She thinks it ridiculous that this boyish man, dressed like an Ivy League frat boy, still sporting a childlike smile, would have ranked over her father. But she instantly likes him, can see why Joseph is so fond of him, why even in a wheelchair he is, if Joseph is to be believed, able to play the field with one cute girl after another.

"Don't know what you've done to my boy," Hunter says. "I've never seen him so happy. It's a surprise."

On their dates now Joseph greets her with a brief kiss on the cheek. He never kisses her good night, though, suspecting something more will be expected of him if he does. He picks her up from her building in a cab, returns her in a cab. He can't bear the subway, can't bear being crushed up against the masses. It's surprising to Satomi he has never learned to drive.

"I was a chauffeur-driven city boy," he excuses himself. "You're a country girl; I bet you had old trucks and tractors to practice on."

"You guess right." She laughs, thinking with a pang of their old truck, of her mother facing up to mean old Tom Myers.

They eat early and unless he takes her to the theater he has her home by ten, as though he is expecting an anxious parent to confront him. She is beginning to think that he has other places to go. It doesn't bother her, she is forgiving of him. As unlikely as it seems, she believes that Joseph needs her friendship more than she needs his.

On a damp evening when the thought of another rich meal in an uptown restaurant fills her with gloom, she suggests that they go to the movies.

"Can't bear being in a crowd in the dark," Joseph says. "You never know who you will be sitting next to in a movie house."

"You mean ordinary people, Joseph?"

"Well, perhaps."

"I'm ordinary."

"Rubbish, dear girl. You are extraordinary."

She likes to believe that her reasons for being with Joseph are because he is entertaining, because they are both lonely, because they have developed an intimacy outside of the physical. There is truth in this, she knows, but she isn't sure these days that she doesn't enjoy the money thing a bit too much, the presents of clothes and jewelry that Joseph has begun buying her. She fights with herself about it, but she is seduced by the beauty that money buys, the fineness of the life it offers. She appreciates the luxury of decent food, the balanced weight of silver cutlery, and the crisp white linen of restaurant tablecloths. It's hard to resist the treat of fresh flowers and the expensive perfumes that Joseph sends on such a regular basis that she is on first-name terms with the delivery boys who bring them to her door.

"You mustn't," she had said at first as the presents began arriving. Even to her the words had sounded hollow, halfhearted. Would Tamura be disappointed in her? Is she disappointed in herself? Is this who *a girl like her* truly is?

Joseph takes no notice of her protests. He enjoys buying her presents, enriching her life, he thinks.

"We'll need to buy you a dress, something wonderful. I've tickets for *Petrushka*." He waves them at her. "You're going to love it."

And she does love it, is reliving it in her head in the cab on the way home, so that she is shocked out of her reverie when they reach her building to see an ambulance parked outside with its doors open, the neighbors gathered on the sidewalk.

"It's Mrs. Copeland," a gray-haired man in his dressing gown calls to her. "They're bringing her body out now."

Her hand flies to her mouth, she shakes her head, begins to tremble.

"Are you sure it's her?"

"Yeah, I'm sure. 'Less she's got a twin. I'm the one who found her."

She hasn't seen her friend for a couple of days and feels guilty now, responsible somehow. Had Mrs. Copeland been feeling ill in those two days, had she called out for help and found none?

"Did she slip in the shower?" she asks.

"No, she had a weak heart, you know?"

She hadn't known, Mrs. Copeland had never mentioned an unreliable heart to her.

"I found her in the hallway," the old man boasts. "She had her key in her hand, couldn't tell if she was on her way in or out."

It's hard news to take. She will never see Mrs. Copeland again. She will never talk with her, or laugh at her jokes, never again buy her little treats. Mrs. Copeland, like Tamura, had loved candy.

She is stunned, the joy of the evening, her delight in *Petrushka* evaporated. She had forgotten how easy it is to lose people, how separation comes so swiftly.

Seeing how upset she is, Joseph touches her shaking shoulder.

"Come home with me, Satomi," he offers. "You don't want to be on your own tonight. It's obviously been a shock."

"No, but will you come inside with me, Joseph? Just for a little while."

He is repelled by the room's dimensions, its shabbiness, and the rooming-house smell of the place. But he sets to making her tea, pained at her empty cupboards, the dime-fed gas fire.

He thinks of his spacious Art Deco duplex on Fifth Avenue, of the stylish straight-limbed furniture, the pale rugs, and the discreet lighting. The walls there are hung with the clean lines of Cocteau drawings and naïve paintings. There's nothing on Satomi's dingy walls, except a small mirror in a chipped frame. While he can walk through his apartment unimpeded by clutter, go from room to room forgetting even how many he has, she hardly has space to breathe in the doll's-house scale of hers. He has glimpsed her poverty, and it's meaner than he'd thought.

"It's very beautiful," Satomi says on her first visit to Joseph's home. "It's the perfect apartment."

She is seeing it at its best, on one of those flushed Manhattan evenings when the zodiacal light lends beauty to the skyline of the metropolis, when the palaces of Ninety-first Street, as Joseph calls them, seem washed with gold.

"It is, isn't it?" he says, satisfied. "It's the most beautiful apartment in New York, I think."

She is good at seeing his melancholia off, a thing he suffers from on and off. He loves that she approves of the understated style of the place, that she matches that style, looks right in it. He has no idea that she doesn't feel right in it, doesn't feel at ease in its lofty space. Her emotions are still informed by Manzanar, her eyes still measure on its scale.

On later visits, though, when she is used to it, comparisons with the camp fade. She looks forward to being there, to being with Joseph, and now that she knows that there's no criticism in it, she even finds his teachy side charming. The contrasts in her life are great between what was and what is, but then, as they are always saying in New York, *Only in America.*

As for Joseph, he marvels that her single company is often

enough for him. It's a first. He is popular among his set, but apart from Hunter, he has never sought particular friendships. They are too intrusive, too exposing.

He likes to watch Satomi reading, her slim legs tucked beneath her on his low sofas, unconsciously graceful as he might have arranged her there himself, just so. If he has to, he could live with a girl like her. And he does have to. What kind of man, after all, would break a promise to a dying father?

On the night he decides to propose, he catches sight of himself in a mirror, eyes gleaming, lips dry, and recognizes the expression. He has glimpsed it before and knows it appears when he gambles against the odds. It's the look that lets him down in poker. Satomi will be astonished, taken off guard, his timing may be wrong, but there's danger too in waiting. How much longer will she continue to cruise along with him before some stranger, some more appealing man, comes along and takes them both by surprise?

"Well, I have to say this place certainly suits you, Sati." The words sound rehearsed, as they have been. "You look at home here."

"Do I?"

"Mmm, just as we are with each other, wouldn't you say?"

"Sure, I would, Joseph."

He pops the cork of what he hopes will be a celebratory bottle of Dom Pérignon. He would prefer his usual evening martini, crushed ice and more vermouth than gin so that it is extra dry, no olive, but a lemon twist, and leave the bitters out. And she might enjoy a whiskey more, but he wants to do things by the book, so champagne it has to be.

"Champagne, dear girl," he says, clinking their glasses.

"Are we celebrating something?"

She senses his excitement, his unaccustomed nervousness, and sits up straight, unsettled now herself. As he hovers with the glasses, she is suddenly filled with affection for him. Joseph is not as cool as he would like her to think. In those times when he spares her his sophistication, he is more like a little boy, sweet and naughty, entirely unpredictable.

"We may be," he says hopefully. "Celebrating something, I mean."

He hates that he can't be honest with her, but he can't risk the truth of it. Learning that he doesn't want to bed her or any other woman might scare her off. He consoles himself with the truth that he cares for her, loves her in his way. And if she accepts him she will benefit from the arrangement too. She is alone in the world, vulnerable. He will take care of her, share his wealth, save her from that squalid little room with its mean gas ring, the sink with the black crack running its length, harboring goodness knows what germs. He was meant to find her, she was meant for better things.

He thinks briefly of the boy he slept with the night before. He had been less than honest with him too. He hardly remembers his name, any of their names. It's a long list, after all. He takes a guess at Chuck. Chuck had it in spades, all right, the look that gets him every time, full lips, snake hips, the walk. The look he likes, the character not so much.

Joseph had long ago given up the battle of fighting his nature, but still he is torn between the sensual and the intellectual, and the boy had been quite stupid, had spoiled the pleasure of the act by talking too much.

"I can come again. Tonight, if you like. Shall I come tonight?" He had made a joke about the coming bit, but it had sounded too much like pleading, for Joseph to agree.

"No, I am going abroad," he lied. "I'll find you when I return."

It's remarkable to him how quickly the joy disappears the moment the coupling is over, a switch flicked. He never hangs around for long. All he wants is to hoof it to the familiar surrounds of Li's hangout, where, since he was eighteen years old, opium dreams have guaranteed oblivion.

"Joseph? Are we celebrating something?" she prompts.

"I hope so."

"You're being mysterious. Come on, tell me what it is."

"It's just this, Sati, and I don't want to make a big deal of it . . . but here goes. I want you to know that I won't ever be careless with you. Whatever happens between us, I'll make sure that nothing like Manzanar ever touches you again. If you let me, I'll be your protector, your best friend."

"Oh, Joseph, there's no need. I—"

"Let me finish, Sati." He runs his hand through his hair, finding himself more nervous than he could have imagined. "More champagne, let me fill your glass."

"Are you trying to get me drunk?" She's on edge now, guesses what's coming, hopes she's wrong.

"I'm trying to ask you to marry me. I want you to marry me, dear girl."

He hadn't planned on blurting it out so bluntly. He can see that she is stunned.

"But why, Joseph?"

"Why does anyone ask a girl to marry them?"

"You tell me."

"Well, it would annoy my mother, and that's never a bad thing." He instantly regrets his flippancy.

"My parents married because they loved each other so much that there was no other option," she says.

It's not that Joseph is unattractive to her, but when she thinks of how it had been with Haru that one time, how it had completed something in her, the idea of accepting Joseph's proposal seems ridiculous.

"I love you in my way Sati," he says. "But if I'm honest about the reason for wanting to marry, well, the truth is that I made a promise to my father to marry. You're the only girl I have ever met that I can imagine sharing my life with."

"Is that the truth?"

"Yes."

"The whole truth?"

"Who ever tells the whole truth?"

"Joseph!" Her face widens in surprise.

"I know, a shocking thing to say."

"In any case, Joseph, I can't say yes. Love is supposed to be the thing, isn't it? The thing that goes with marriage."

"It's not the law, is it, Sati? And it needn't be our rule, we can make our own. And to be blunt, that kind of marriage was never in the cards for me. You have to trust me on that."

"Well, I don't. Love is like luck, it comes when you least expect it." She wishes they weren't having this conversation. She feels put on the spot, unkind. She gulps the last of her champagne and coughs as it goes down the wrong way.

"You're a romantic," Joseph says, patting her back. "I didn't have you down for one."

"Is that so bad?"

"No, a bit unrealistic, though."

"It's a crazy idea, Joseph. Honestly, can you see us together for life in that way? We like each other, but . . ."

"Well, how many married people can say that?"

"Plenty, I guess. You're such a cynic."

"You can't lose out, you know. You'll never have to worry about money again. Never have to want for anything."

"I don't think money keeps you from wanting."

"Maybe not, but I can give you the sort of life you deserve. I'll never be cruel to you, and I'll be your best friend. You have had enough of struggle, surely?"

"Yes, but my struggles don't have much to do with money."

"Don't tell me you're a secret heiress."

"Not unless you count ninety dollars or so as the definition of heiress."

He can't stop the pity he feels from reaching his eyes. She has ninety dollars to face the rest of her life with, small change to him. It would scare him witless to have so little, yet she seems unafraid.

"In any case, Joseph, what you see, what you think you know, is only the smallest part of who I am."

"Who are you, then? Tell me the worst of it."

"Well, for one thing, I'm not as nice as you think."

"Did I ever say that I thought you were nice?"

"No, but anyway, apart from that you would find me very hard to live with. There are days when I don't want company, when nothing much pleases me, when you would find me horrible to be with."

"I know that already, Sati, I'm the same. We will leave each other to our own devices on those days."

"I'm argumentative, you know? I wouldn't give you an easy ride."

"I know that too."

"Oh, it doesn't stop there." She is irritated by his refusal to let her off the hook. "I take long showers that use up all the hot water and I refuse now to wait in line for anything. And however you might want to change me, in the way that men do, it won't work. If my father couldn't do it no, one can. Would you want to be saddled with such a person for a wife?"

"I would," he says, joining her on the sofa. "There are six

bathrooms in this place and the hot water never runs out. Shower to your heart's content. I'll see to it that you never have to wait in line for anything. And the last thing I want to do is change you."

"I'm not a virgin, you know." She hopes to shock, to stop the marriage talk.

In the pause as he thinks about it, he realizes that he knew that she wasn't. She is too complete to be a virgin. That guy Haru she told him about, he supposes. It hardly makes a difference, except that she is being honest with him, whereas he can't find trust enough to be the same with her.

He puts his arm around her, feeling the womanly slope of her shoulder, the swell of her breast against his chest. Because it is Sati and her body is slim, pared down, it isn't unpleasant, but it is disturbing. It's hard for him not to shy away from the way women are made, from the heat that comes off them. They are designed to drip milk and blood, and there is something animallike at their core, something deep and murky. He has felt a faint disgust at it since infancy, since first being aware of the smothering sensation he suffered as a baby at his mother's fulsome breasts.

He feels himself drawing away and rallies. He must marry, that's that. He wants her, just doesn't *want* her. They are the answer to each other's problems, they are synchronicity.

"Well, I'm not a virgin either." He smiles. "So we are equal, dear girl."

"Stop, Joseph. Please let's stop talking about it."

"Take a chance on me, Sati. Don't be like those dreamers waiting for fortune to shine on them. They always die disappointed, you know."

She moves on the sofa, creating a space between them, wishing she were somewhere else. Joseph isn't giving up.

"Just imagine for a moment all those dull little rooms in New York, filled with people growing old, hoping to win life's lottery.

To be chosen!" he says. You know that *Only in America* thing? It works for one in a million, maybe. You could be the one."

"They may have love, Joseph. You always dismiss love."

"Because that's the biggest con of all, don't you think? Put up with all the dross and wait for the great romance, the one true love that will surely transform everything."

"Perhaps when it comes, it does. Perhaps it's worth waiting for."

"I thought that you had already been burned by that fire."

"Mmm, maybe."

"You have to make things happen yourself, Sati. Take the opportunities when they come."

"And you're my opportunity, Joseph?"

"Why shouldn't I be? Look, it can get pretty cold out there on your own, you know. You have so little to lose just now, so much to gain if you say yes."

On her third glass of champagne, and caught up in the force of Joseph's words, she is relaxing into the idea. Being married to Joseph would be an adventure, would be extraordinary. And what if she waits for true love, what guarantee is there that it will ever come? Maybe it has already left for good, left with Haru. Maybe its very nature is to be one-sided, to wound the one who loves most. She's had enough of being the one who loves most.

Joseph feels the give in her, the leap to the finish line in himself. It would be too hard to lose now; he will never find anyone who fits the bill as well as Satomi Baker. She is offbeat, unexpected, and off the New York society radar. She is his last chance to save himself from those uptown girls with their long teeth and above-reproach credentials.

"There is no reason, Joseph," his mother insists, "why you shouldn't marry a Whitney, or a Cameron. The Rodmans have earned their place in society by now, I should think."

"God forbid it, Mother. The boredom would kill me."

He can't imagine ever being bored with Satomi. She is open to the world, to ideas, and surprisingly sure of herself, given her background. He likes the idea of being a teacher in their relationship even though she is not always in the mood to listen to him. It is something he can offer her that has nothing to do with money. These days the thought of being married to her seems like something he wants rather than something imposed on him.

"Say yes, Satomi. Don't sleepwalk your life away waiting for things to happen to you. Decide that they will."

And in the moment, in the picture he has drawn so vividly of the kind of life that he can offer her, but mostly in the terrible idea that it is possible to sleepwalk your life away, she hears herself asking for time.

"Of course, of course. Take as much time as you need." It's in the bag, he thinks. "Absolutely no hurry."

A memory of the honest intimacies of love, of Aaron lightly touching Tamura's hand as he passed her, of Tamura lighting his cigarette with sweet concentration, comes to her with a pang. She dismisses it. The thought of making things happen, of not waiting around for luck to choose her, is suddenly appealing. Luck hasn't done such a great job for her in the past, after all.

"I should have gone down on one knee, shouldn't I?"

He kisses her lightly on the lips, the lime-sharp cologne scent of him overpowering. She leans into him, returning the kiss, feeling his mouth close against her half-open one, feeling herself a fraud. Could she love him, make love with him? He is almost handsome, certainly glamorous. It's not enough, she knows.

If she turns him down, will she ever get out of her dismal room, with its brick wall view, the memory of Mrs. Copeland an ever-present ghost in the hallway? There are times when that room seems to her to be the loneliest place on earth. How long had

Mrs. Copeland been fading in hers before her death? Perhaps Joseph is right. You have to seize your opportunities.

"Your family, Joseph? Can't imagine they'd be happy about you choosing me, somehow."

"There's only my mother, some odd upstate cousins. They hardly matter. I never see them if I can help it."

"How sad for you."

"Not really. My father's opinion is the only one I ever cared for, and he would have loved you."

UPTOWN

Y OU CAN'T STAY in that awful place. You don't have to decide the marriage thing now, just come and stay as a guest." Joseph's insistence, her own fear of stasis, had driven the decision.

"I can't bear the thought of you in that nasty little room. Look at all the space here. Have your own rooms, as many as you want." A nervous tick had fluttered at the corner of Joseph's right eye. If she turned him down it would probably mean that marriage was off the table too.

"I won't bother you. I'll just be your landlord for the time being. Only a nicer one than you have at present."

"But what will people think?"

"What people?"

"Oh, you know."

"It's nobody's business but ours."

"Still no pressure?"

"I told you, no hurry."

"Well, maybe for a while."

"Or forever, if you like."

She is shaky about it. It feels risky, the choice a loose woman might make, certainly one Tamura would have advised against. Is this the rashness in her that Haru saw when he called her dangerous?

Her regular kind of life has collided with Joseph's extraordinary one and she feels like a child grasping at something too big for tiny hands to hold on to. But since Mrs. Copeland died she can hardly bear to be in her building anymore. Things have changed there, and not for the better.

A woman in her early sixties has moved into Mrs. Copeland's room. She has a tight unfriendly smile, a buttoned-up way of walking, and the smell of cheap rye and perspiration wafts from her as she passes. She hadn't been there a week when she began banging on the wall when Satomi played the radio, although her own plays on high volume all through the night.

Satomi, glad to go, has packed up her things and moved in with Joseph. But strangely, while living with him has dispelled her loneliness, it has only added to her sense of displacement. Questions come to her mind so that she can't settle; is she grabbing at the chance to forget the past, is she excusing herself from the promise she made to Cora? Is she letting Dr. Harper down, failing to live up to Ralph Lazo's example?

Be honest, she tells herself, *you wanted to be saved*. But from what? From the effort of making her own way, perhaps, from collecting dimes to feed the gas meter in her insistently cold room, or from the shower water running cold before she's had time to rinse the soap from her hair. But it's mostly, she thinks, from the dreadful fear she suffers of nothing changing. *I wanted to be saved from real life*, she thinks. Perhaps, after years of want, it is simply greed for a bigger slice of the cake.

Joseph finds himself completely satisfied in the waiting for her answer. He has done his part. He isn't breaking his promise, it's just on hold. For the moment nothing needs to change and he is at peace.

But in his splendid apartment the girl she knew has been replaced with another, less certain one. Who is this person wandering the huge rooms, gazing at paintings worth thousands of dollars, trailing her fingers on sculptures of the kind she would normally only see in museums? Nothing in her past life had hinted at the one she lives now with Joseph. She's in alien territory, attempting to merge. In her daydreaming moments she imagines herself becoming part of the art, alive only when looked at.

Sometimes to steady herself she has to close her eyes, to hold life at bay for a moment or two. She summons pictures of Angelina's woods, wraps herself in its greenery, smells the wild mint that she imagines still grows around the sitting stone, and sees the fox, wild and clean. She breathes deeply, gathering herself like an actress waiting for the camera to roll so that she can play her part. It has all happened too quickly, she has hardly had time to adjust to city living, and life with Joseph may be luxurious, but it's big and scary too.

What more could you possibly want? she asks herself, and knows the answer.

What she wants is Tamura making tea on their little stove, dented metal mugs, a radish or two in the right season. Oh, to sit with Tamura on the barrack steps, the mountains dark as forests in the distance, the sound of Yumi arguing with Eriko, and Cora's little arms around her neck, the sweet child smell of her. That was real life, this one the fantasy.

It's so strange to miss Manzanar, isn't it? Eriko writes in her latest letter.

I can't quite remember how to be out in the world. An alarm triggers in me at noon, shouldn't I be going to the mess hall? My eyes still hold the ground looking for wood for the stove. Three years out of a lifetime is hardly much, yet it seems like the bigger part of it.

Satomi is herself still held by Manzanar, by a horrible longing for it. Dr. Harper says he understands. He thinks she is missing it in the way a soldier might miss the war. You don't want to go back, but nothing in the so-called real world engages you quite as much.

Joseph says he understands too. Perhaps he does. He has offered help with finding Cora, but she can tell that he's not eager to back his offer up with action.

"Perhaps the time is not right yet," he says, thinking this extra dimension of Cora will move them further apart.

Neither of them mentions what they know now, that love is the key, after all; that they are missing that mysterious transformer that turns like to love. They are both pretending.

She finds herself longing for Haru, not so much emotionally, that hunger is fading, but for the physicality of him, for the man scent of him. Joseph smells of soap and cologne, of minty toothpaste and hair cream. There's no balance, it seems to her, between them, they are too compatible.

At night in her lofty room, sleep holds out stubbornly against the ache in her, an ache that she knows Joseph can't cure. She tells herself it's just a primitive urge, the animal part that isn't subject to reason. She's embarrassed by it, but the sensation won't go away. It's like defrosting, she thinks, that painful, burning itch when you hold frozen hands to the fire.

Disturbed by the daily compulsion she feels to run, to scuttle back to a life dictated by her own circumstances, she overrides her fears with a determination to hold on to the Satomi Baker that Tamura would recognize.

"I'm a kept woman," she jokes with Joseph. "It's got to stop."

"You insist on paying rent, so you're not kept in the true sense," he says. He hardly knows what to do with the cash she hands him every week. He tips hotel doormen more for whistling down a cab.

"You're sort of my protégée." He likes the sound of it better than the kept woman thing.

"Well, at least stop buying me presents all the time. You know I can't return the favor."

"You must have the right clothes. How can I take you anywhere without the right clothes?"

He escorts her to Dior, enjoying as much as her the parade of evening gowns cut from fabrics so fine they feel like gossamer.

"You'll need a fur to go with that, shoes for that bag, earrings if your hair is to be swept up."

There are twelve negligees in her dressing room drawers. A glut, she thinks. Their colors blush reproachfully through sheets of thin tissue, peach and primrose, lilac and eau de nil. No such thing as mend and make do in Joseph's world. She can't deny, though, that she loves the feel of silk, the slope of the high-heeled shoes. It's all a sham, she thinks, but the thrill of dressing up is a childlike pleasure. Will she ever be able to settle now for less?

"Who needs twelve nightgowns?" she had groaned at the sight of them.

"Just a start, dear girl," Joseph had said, the bit between his teeth now.

He has found a new and distracting occupation. He hasn't enjoyed himself so much since what he thinks of now in retrospect as his good war. He was playing a part in that too, playing the straight guy, a guy just like the rest of them.

"I wanted to be like them, not the spoiled rich guy."

She feels pity for him, can't imagine that he pulled that one off.

"It's hard to have secrets," she says.

Joseph had turned down his mother's bought offer to work in the White House as some sort of an assistant to an assistant, choosing to spend his war years in the Army instead.

"I don't want to cower at home while the rest of you go to war," he had told Hunter, who was already in uniform.

"What were you doing while I was in Manzanar?" Satomi asks.

"I was in the thick of it in Italy. A bit of a shaky start, I suppose, but I got used to it."

She's surprised. It's hard to picture Joseph in uniform, hard to picture him fighting. When she says as much, he looks hurt.

She couldn't know it, wouldn't guess at it now, but he had been determined not to whine about things; he may have been afraid, but he couldn't bear the idea of being a coward too. Along with his fellows he had experienced the minor and major miseries of war with stoicism and a black sort of humor that his comrades came to rely on; sleeping in wet clothes, the lack of tobacco, stinking mud in their boots were better borne with humor.

The physical difficulties he suffered are forgotten; the memories of dead bodies, bloated silhouettes floating downriver, blood and limbs and the carnal stink, are not so easily let go.

"You're not the only one with unwanted snapshots in your head," he tells Satomi. "Still, I don't regret it. I enjoyed the friendships. It was good being with guys who had your back."

"You still have friends, Joseph."

"Yes, you and Hunter. The rest are hardly what you would call friends."

"Why don't you have a get-together with your Army buddies?"

"Because it could never be the same again. Money distances you in civilian life, sets you apart."

Joseph's fortune is over thirty million dollars. Less than the Woolworth heiress, which irritates his mother, but he's getting there. In addition, he owns a sixteen-story apartment building on Fifth Avenue, a spacious house on Fishers Island above a long white Connecticut beach, and now his father's beloved yacht *Windward*.

All this, and he doesn't even have to run the family business, which rolls on, an unstoppable juggernaut, adding to his wealth by the minute. He's the major shareholder in the Rodman group of companies, but it's a relief to the board that he won't be joining them. He may be a Rodman, but they know what he is, and besides, he has no head for business.

"You hardly need to work, Sati," he says, floating the idea of enrolling her in an art appreciation class. "You deserve to be educated."

"No, I must work." Her tone leaves no room for argument.

The longer she is with Joseph, the stronger her doubts become, the more she questions her reasons for being with him. As much as it feels safe, it doesn't feel right. If it's a means to an end, she doesn't know what that end might be. She doesn't like the feeling that she's being anesthetized or that she's using Joseph.

At Clare House she can tell by the way her fellow workers have begun to treat her that they know about her changed circumstances. Some are overly friendly, others almost hostile.

She hasn't told Edward about Joseph; he would be certain to write to Dr. Harper about it. She can't bear the idea of Dr. Harper being disappointed in her.

So a new address, Dr. Harper writes.

Is your room better than the last? No shared shower, I hope. The address suggests that you have had a promotion at work. It's uptown, isn't it? Let me know how life is treating you.

In her reply she is vague. Her uptown address implies more than a small promotion, but it's true that she's no longer the hatcheck girl. The director, on Joseph's insistence, has put her on the front desk, where she gives out information, guides people to the exhibits, looks too exquisitely turned out to be there at all.

Returning each evening to the apartment, to its air of serenity, she is always pleased to find Joseph there. He waits with her whiskey and his martini ready: "First drink of the day," he lies. Joseph, she knows, likes her company in the little ritual, and although she often would have preferred tea, she doesn't want him to be the only one giving.

Her life is more comfortable than it has ever been, but nothing dispels her dark days, those times when she wakes with a snake squirming in her stomach, the sensation of panic that there is still something left to be done for her mother. The pain at the loss of Tamura, the fear that she will never see Cora again, are always there waiting to surface. She feels spoiled, imprisoned by luxury, lost.

In the museum she studies the families who come with more than a little interest. Mothers with their children, little hands held fast, and the secret smiles between them. Once, watching a father clumsily attempting to button his child's coat, she was transported back to the time on the bus that took Cora away, Cora in her little buttoned-up felt coat.

"It's cold outside," the father said, patting the little girl's head as she struggled against his efforts. "Gotta keep you warm, honey."

She's anxious that Cora might not be in such a family. The picture of that happy little group, the father on bended knee, the mother smiling, often returns to alarm her.

"I know that you can never forget Manzanar." Joseph is good at picking up on her mood. "But I'm going to show you a different world, Sati. Take you to wonderful places. We'll travel and I'll teach you to ski and to sail. Wait till you see the yacht. She's a beauty, and there's nothing as great as being out there on the water. You'll love it."

The months roll on, six of them gone before she realizes that she can't go on working at Clare House. Photographs of her and Joseph are appearing in the society pages. People approach her in the museum, smiling, making a fuss.

"It is you, isn't it?"

She and Joseph are caught at the opera, at the white gloved fund-raisers, at the sort of lush parties she had never before suspected existed.

> Mr. Joseph Rodman and his companion Miss Baker at the Plaza Hotel Review. Miss Baker is wearing a stunning full-length Balenciaga dress with emerald earrings from Tiffany's.

She blames herself for the hollow feeling that she can't get rid of, the sense she has that she is an impostor. It seems ungrateful not to appreciate what she has been given, but it's all too much and she wants to start again at the beginning. She's swimming in Joseph's slipstream, not making her own life, and this particular American dream, as indulgent as it is, is not her dream. It's more like Lily's or Artie's dream, she thinks. Joseph's life is like cotton candy, tempting at first, then so sickly sweet that your teeth begin to ache.

Dr. Harper's postcard comes as it did the year before on the date of Tamura's death:

> Things change, memories fade, but I will always remember Tamura Baker with gratitude.

The same two lines as last year, a tradition now she knows he won't break while he lives. She holds the card close to her heart, picturing her mother's face, hearing again the sound of her voice. It's time to live up to Tamura, to act for herself.

———

On the morning she hands her notice in at the museum, the city looks shabby, uncared-for. It has rained in the night and the steaming sky suggests there's more to come. A chemical sort of green streaks the clouds, gobbling up the light. The buildings and sidewalks have morphed to gray, litter flaps around in the gutter. She passes two down-and-outs sleeping in the hard bed of a doorway, their heads beneath old newspapers, their feet slippered in paper bags.

Inside Clare House the glow of the overhead lighting lifts her mood. The air is warm, centrally heated, so that people loosen their scarves and take off hats as soon as they are through the door. She loves the place, doesn't want to leave, but her colleagues there have become as ill at ease with her as she is with herself. And it's not fair to the director, who forgives her lateness, forgives the Mondays she can't make it in because Joseph wants to stay on Fishers Island, go sailing with her and Hunter, and lunch at the Yacht Club.

Joseph's generosity to the museum assures indulgence, a looking the other way at lateness, at absence. The director thinks it a small price to pay, a little lateness, a day or two missed. Strange that she should be there at all, but the museum has the best of the deal.

It's not the way it was meant to be, she thinks, as she apologizes to him. Things were meant to be normal, a job, meeting someone, marriage and children. Oddly, those things seem harder now to attain than the lifestyle of the Manhattan rich.

"Of course I understand," the director says. "Your life has changed since you started here. I could tell you were meant for better things. When will you go?"

She hadn't thought of when. She will need time to tell Joseph, for him to get used to it. The director will need time to replace her, and she will need time to find another job, a place to live. She is suddenly nervous about what lies ahead.

The director, noticing her hesitation, feels a stab of sympathy. She seems unsure, a little afraid. He can't help thinking the girl is out of her depth, pitched in the middle, in the tug-of-war between ordinary and extraordinary.

"Take the rest of the day off and think about it," he says kindly. "Weeks, months, if you would prefer. Whatever you decide is fine with me."

She walks around the city at a loss as to what she might do to fill the day. Joseph will be out, but the housekeepers from the service he employs will still be cleaning the apartment. He can't bear being there while they're working.

She had laughed at him when he told her how uneasy he is with them, but she can't face the cleaners herself today.

In a half-smart café she idles time away nursing a coffee that's weak and tastes of chicory. From her window seat she watches a bunch of girls coming out of a bakery, biting into giant pretzels and laughing; there's a woman in a phone booth wearing a red shallow-bowl hat, a match for the velvet collar of her coat. She is shaking her head, gesticulating with her hand as she speaks; a man flags down a cab, but it doesn't stop. She can't hear his shout, but guesses it's a curse, recognizes his crude finger gesture.

Nothing out here is perfect, the weather's bad, people don't smile much, everyone seems in hurry, but it's real life and she wants to join in.

By the time she gets back, the apartment, dim in late afternoon shadow, smells of polish, and the freesias that are Joseph's favorite flower. She turns the lights on and a Charlie Parker record for company, and makes herself a cup of tea to drink while she bathes.

It still feels strange to be in Joseph's apartment without him there. His afternoons are spent at the country club drinking with Hunter or at the Racquet or Union Club being smart with the Madison Avenue tribe. He whiles away his days waiting for the

evening, when he will take her out, show her off in uptown restaurants and the smart functions that have melded into one in her
mind now.

Tonight they are going to a hospital benefit. Just the thought of
it brings on a sigh. She knows she will feel as nothing against Joseph's people, their sureness, their smart show of boredom.

When Joseph has had enough of it he will send her home in a
cab, go on to indulge in the life he keeps secret. She doesn't mind,
she tires long before him and would prefer to read anyway. He is
always there when she wakes, though, making—without vodka,
he says—his morning Bloody Mary, her tea.

"You're a man for the moon hours," she tells him, and he
laughs.

Before he showers she can smell the night on him, kerosene,
she thinks, and something sharp, it's not unpleasant.

"Why kerosene?" she asks.

"You imagine it," he says, not wanting to tell her it's the lamp
oil from Li's place, where he buys his share of bliss.

He wants her approval, can't imagine that he would get it if he
were to tell her the truth of his life. Never mind his need of opium,
what would she make of his lovers, those uptown boys who claim
to be the sons of Russian princes, and the less salubrious breed
who strut between Seventh and Hudson dressed up in boots and
Stetsons?

But she has guessed Joseph's secret. He is living a lie, and the
damage of it is always there between them. It's not so much that
he looks at men when he is out with her, more that he never notices women, unless to observe how badly they are dressed, how
overperfumed.

"Just spray in front of you, dear girl," he advises. "Then walk
into the mist. It's vulgar to overscent."

Whenever she thinks of the time after the riot at Manzanar,

those boys kissing at their barrack door, she knows that Joseph is like them. She had thought that what she had seen was the result of some strange after-riot electricity in the air. But of course it hadn't been that, it's something more, something she can't get a handle on. It makes her feel ignorant, let down by her years of reading. Where had she missed it in those novels that seemed to leave out nothing of life? Had she failed to see a coded message in those lyrical sentences that more worldly people would have been aware of? She is irritated with Joseph. Why didn't he tell her? She didn't have him down for a cheat. She doesn't know if she approves or not, but Joseph is still Joseph, after all, whatever his needs.

Alone in her marbled bathroom, she spies the shockingly expensive bottle of Patou's Joy perfume on the beveled-glass shelf. Its luscious tones call to mind a grown-up sophistication that is not hers. The scent, which she doesn't like, which doesn't suit her, is the real thing—she's the phony.

"You're going to love this perfume," Joseph had said, handing her the exquisite crystal bottle. "It will be your signature fragrance. It's very you."

"Very me?"

"Mmm, smoky and not too sweet. It doesn't smell like makeup as most of them do. You know that powdery Max Factor scent."

She didn't know. Often doesn't know what Joseph is talking about.

She catches a glimpse of herself in the bathroom's mirrored wall and pauses, sponge in midair. With her hair wet, and makeup-free, she might still be the girl from Angelina. She throws the sponge at her reflection and watches a soapy trail sneak down the mirror.

"Where have you been?" she asks quietly, and answers herself: "In a coma, perhaps."

It's hard to hurt a friend, but he must be told that she can't marry him. If she marries at all, she knows now that it must be for love.

And she will tell him that she doesn't mind about that thing he wants to keep from her, the thing she doesn't have a name for. She is glad not to be ignorant about it anymore. And after when she leaves the soft bed of his life they can still be friends. More equal friends. She can't take from him anymore. She must start again, do better.

She will be forgotten soon enough, she imagines, even though she and Joseph have become quite the beautiful couple. Her picture appears so often in *Harper's Bazaar* that she can't anymore walk Fifth Avenue without being recognized.

"You never take a bad photograph," Joseph tells her when they relive their social life through the magazine's society pages.

And there in the pictures is the polished woman who is her but not her, a manicured, gleaming woman with the light capturing her just so. The girl from the camp is lost, the angry girl in her mother's hand-me-down jacket and twice-heeled shoes. Where's the sense in her life now? It's a film, a play, an ongoing dream.

The articles never mention the Japanese in her. Well, who could tell? Who could be sure? Those eyes, the elegantly long neck, the fine skin, all surely good enough indications of breeding. And nobody wants to stir up the bitterness, after all. This is New York, the victorious capital of the world, where nothing shocks, where its "*pulled-up-stakes*" minorities must go on believing in its endless possibilities. There should be no horizons, no barriers to anything in this earthly paradise.

She can't help wondering if Lily, trawling through her hand-me-down magazines, sees and recognizes her. She hopes so, not so much for revenge, more that she doesn't want Lily remembering her as a victim. If Lily is capable of it, she doesn't want her pity.

She has stayed too long in the bath; the water has cooled to the wrong side of comfort, and the skin on her fingers has wrinkled. Shivering a little, she examines herself in the mirror, looking to find in her face, her body, what men might see. All she sees, though, is a girl watching. She looks at her nakedness and it is nothing to her, as it is to Joseph, as it was in the end to Haru.

In her wardrobe, shimmering like jewels, hang the evening dresses from Molyneux and Coco Chanel, lavender silk, gold satin, and her favorite, the Dior midnight-blue velvet that she will wear tonight to the hospital benefit.

There are gloves and little beaded evening bags, lace handkerchiefs, nylons so fine they would seem invisible when held to the light if it hadn't been for their seams. It's odd, but she's looking forward to living without such luxuries; such beautiful things are a responsibility. She can't remember, though, where the clothes she brought with her have gone. It's unsettling.

You will be fine, my girl, Tamura's voice comes to her, as though it is there still in the ether. She will always be able to hear Tamura's voice.

She thinks of Cora's little knitting-wool hair bow and everything in her hurts.

DAUGHTER OF HAPPINESS

THERE'S SOMETHING VERY sweet about Joseph when he gets home. He has brought her flowers, a cloud of dark anemones with the white ones taken out so that their garnet colors put her in mind of old tapestries.

"Don't know why they put those white ones in," he says. "White flowers only go with white flowers."

She is amused by him caring about such things, and touched that he takes such care when choosing her something as simple as a bunch of flowers. For a moment she wavers, wondering if she is doing the right thing in leaving Joseph. Being rich doesn't make his need of her any less, and will she ever do better than him, ever be safer than she is with him? Maybe he is right to question whether true love exists. Tamura had despaired of her never taking the sensible path. Perhaps for the first time she should take it now?

Two hours later, as the band at the hospital benefit plays "Rum and Coca-Cola," she is in a different frame of mind. Among Joseph's smart friends, those sure-of-themselves bankers and their urbane wives, the familiar feeling of loneliness has overtaken her. It's not so much that Joseph's friends exclude her, more that they judge her on the superficial level of her Japaneseness. She is

Joseph's exotic girlfriend, not one of them but someone who adds color to their numbers. She will never be an intimate among them, never be at ease with them. She suspects that Joseph has chosen her for the same reason. That exotic thing always in the mix. It comes to her that the so-called safe path is not for her; that it is quite likely a life with Joseph may be neither safe nor sensible.

And Joseph tonight is adding to her disenchantment. There's something wrong with him, she can tell. His movements have speeded up and he seems distracted, not quite connected to what's going on around him. He has left her twice at their table, heading off somewhere with mumbled excuses as if he is late for an urgent appointment. She is used to his mood shifts, but it is uncomfortable being left at the table to charm in his place.

"Come and dance with me," she says, catching sight of him lurking behind a pillar.

"Sure," he says, slurring the word a little. "Sure."

He is clumsy on the floor, not like Joseph at all, who is usually precise in his steps, easy to follow. Exposed out there under the bouncing light of the revolving mirror ball, she wishes she hadn't asked him to dance with her, wishes that she hadn't come this evening, pretending that this is her life, that she is at home here among this other tribe.

And suddenly Joseph is spinning her and she is falling, twisting her ankle, breaking the heel of her shoe, and Joseph is on the floor beside her, smiling a lopsided smile, his eyes looking at but not seeing her. What is the matter with him?

"Let me help." The voice is deep, not quite baritone. "Give me your arm, lean on me. It will hurt to put weight on that foot."

She lets him take her weight as she limps back to their table.

"I'm Abe Robinson, by the way. I'm a doctor."

"I won't be long, dear girl," Joseph mumbles, and rolls his way to the bathroom.

Abe Robinson has her foot in his hands, putting pressure where it hurts, wincing when she does at the pain of it.

"Not broken," he assures her. "But a sprain can hurt worse, I know."

"Thank you." A familiar feeling runs through her, the same one she experienced when she first caught sight of Haru.

"No more dancing for a while." He says with a smile.

"Shame," she says, returning the smile, attempting lightness. "Will you have a drink with us?" It's foolish, but she doesn't want him to go.

"Thank you, but I'm with someone." He points across the room to where a girl, a frowning girl in a shiny dress, is looking toward them.

"Oh, of course, you must go."

"It would be better not to drink anymore, you're going to need a hefty dose of painkillers for a couple of days." He fumbles in his pocket for a pen, picks up a napkin, and hands both to her. "I can call on you tomorrow, if you like. Check your ankle."

She writes the address down, hands it to him, and feels a pang as he walks back toward the waiting girl. Stupid, she tells herself. A few minutes in his presence and she hardly knows herself. It must be the champagne, it always puts her in a silly mood.

Joseph returns just as Abe Robinson turns and says, "Ice, lots of it. And keep the leg up."

"How high?"

"Oh, above your heart if you can."

Four months on, and Joseph is still blaming himself. If he hadn't been so high that night at the hospital benefit, Satomi never would have met Abe Robinson, and she wouldn't be leaving him now. He thinks of it as leaving him, as though he is the lover in this threesome, although she has been dating Abe from the first moment they met.

"So I'm going to lose out to Mr. America," he says.

"Oh, Joseph, you and I, we're better off as friends," she says consolingly.

"Ouch." He slaps his hand to his chest as though she has cracked open his heart.

"It's true, Joseph, you know it is." She's sad for him, but there's nothing to be done about it.

"Damn that dance," Joseph says brightly. "That damn dance."

He can hardly remember the dance that brought Abe Robinson into her life, except that it had a rumba sort of beat about it. But whatever the stupid rhythm had been, he should have caught her. Would have, if it hadn't been for the snort he'd taken discreetly behind a pillar in the moment before Satomi found him and pulled him onto the dance floor.

"All my stupid fault," he says now. "That's the trouble with the good stuff, you never know if it will take you mellow or hard."

"I'm glad of it, Joseph."

She is more than glad, despite the fact that she has wavered over the months, that she still has her doubts about her and Abe. The love between them feels equal and she can't get used to it. Strange, she thinks, that it should be so hard to trust in love. She had imagined when love came it would drown doubt, but perhaps doubt is the ingredient in the mix between men and women that keeps the love alive. Where there is light there must be shadows too.

But doubts aside, she feels blessed, blessed to have slipped, to have broken the heel of her beautiful shoe, to have turned her ankle.

Abe had felt the current between them on that first night too. Such a beautiful patient, flushed cheeks, strands of dark hair escaping from their burnished knot, the grace of her. He took it all in and knew he was setting his sights high.

Earlier that evening he had watched her from across the floor until something in him had faltered so that he had to look away to steady himself. He had been struck by the odd couple that she and Joseph made. The man appeared obsessively neat, hair tamed, his smooth skin so closely shaved as to make you wonder if he had a beard at all. And the tux so perfectly cut it might have been carved on him. Not the sort, he thought with distaste, to have gone for girls.

"She's in all the magazines," his girlfriend Corrine said sharply, following his gaze. "She's got it all, the looks and the money."

"His money?"

"I guess. He's the Rodman heir."

"They're married?"

"Engaged, perhaps. Not sure."

She didn't project socialite, he thought. Rather she looked lost, out of place. He wanted to know her, to save her, he thought, at the same time as telling himself that was a ridiculous idea. He couldn't shake the thought, though. Not for the first time he felt false being with Corrine. Something must be done about that. To think that he nearly hadn't come. That he had dreaded it. Corrine had been stupidly excited at him winning the tickets in the hospital raffle, wouldn't hear of him giving them away.

"It'll be stiff, formal. I hate that kinda thing," he had said, trying to talk her out of it. "We won't know anyone."

"It'll be great," she had insisted. "Just what the doctor ordered."

Her medical jokes had been wearing thin for months, but he gave in, hired the ridiculous suit, and polished his shoes to a patent shine. And now he and Satomi are together and it's how it should be, or at least it will be when he gets her away from Joseph. It makes him uneasy that she lives with the man, even though he believes her explanation as to why.

"We're friends, Abe," she says. "Nothing more."

"But it's odd, Sati. You have to give me that."

"Why not think of us as landlord and tenant, then?"

"It's the 'us' about it that I don't like, honey."

Satomi hates that Abe doesn't want to know Joseph, that he avoids him whenever possible. She understands it, though, they are poles apart in everything, and despite the fact that Abe has chosen her, he is in most ways a conventional man.

At their first meeting Abe's smile had made her want to run and to draw closer at the same time. Everything about him connected with her at what later she would remember with fondness as being her heart. At the time, though, it had felt more visceral, stomach-dropping, throat-constricting.

Nothing about him had jarred, still doesn't. His physicality touches her more than anything, his brown unwary eyes, his dark curly hair, and the scent of him that brings the earth to mind. There is symmetry in his weather-worn face, an open-aired look that sets him apart from the more usual pale-faced New Yorkers.

She had liked immediately the authoritative pitch of his voice, the way he had loosened his bow tie, which he was obviously ill at ease in, the way without being asked people had cleared a space for him.

But she questions now if there is such a thing as love at first sight. All that drowning, heart-pounding, mouth-drying thing that night may simply have been lust, the girlish longing for a man as masculine as Abe to carry her off. But it's love now, all right, the sweet and the bitter of it, the open and the guarded heart, the full-blown flower of it. Being with Abe is like being taken by a river: there's nothing you can do about it except let the water have you.

A regular caller now, Abe never comes up in the elevator. He gets the doorman to call the apartment while he waits downstairs in the lofty atrium.

It has set a pattern, Joseph thinks. Abe summoning, Sati running.

"He doesn't like me," he tells her flatly.

"He doesn't know you," she says. "He will like you when he gets to know you."

Abe's dislike, which Joseph senses is more like distaste, feels familiar to him. He has experienced it before. Abe's kind of man judges his kind harshly. It's to be expected. He has no doubt that Abe will ride off into the sunset with Satomi. His kind, the tall, tieless kind, always get the girl. Money, he knows, isn't going to get him out of this one.

"He's too conventional for you," he attempts. "He'll always be a doctor, nothing more. You won't have travel, or new people, adventures."

Satomi is living the life now that has always been a mystery to him: walks, and the movies, and meals in diners that he has never heard of. And bike rides in the park. Bikes when there are cabs. It makes no sense. And what's worse, every weekend in Freeport with Abe Robinson's mother, Frances, a woman who Satomi says is reserved with her.

"She has a good heart, though," she assures him. "It's just that Freeport's a pretty tight community, friendly enough but wary of strangers, I guess."

"Just as you told me Angelina was."

"I never said friendly, did I?"

He has shown her the best of New York, given her a cultured life, and she is settling for Freeport.

He can't fake being pleased for her, he is too sorry for himself. But there is time, he thinks, time for them to fall out of love. They have only known each other a few months, after all, less than half a year. Flash fires burn out quickly. In his less optimistic moments, though, he's resigned to her leaving; the pair are hopelessly attracted, it's just a question of when, he knows.

When comes on an evening when a buttery sky, pinkish to the west, leaks its color into the apartment as Joseph is mixing their drinks.

"Abe has asked me to marry him," she ventures, accepting the whiskey he is offering.

"And?"

"And I've said yes, of course."

"Are you sure, really certain? It's all a bit whirlwind, isn't it?"

"Maybe, but it doesn't feel like that. And we both want it."

"Well, marriage, it's a big step. You might live to regret it."

"What else can we do? Abe hates me living here with you. That's natural, isn't it? And we want to be together."

"Have an affair. Get it out of your system."

"I don't want an affair, and neither does Abe. We're sure about each other and we're going to marry. Be happy for me, Joseph."

"So when will it be, this marriage?"

"As soon as we can arrange it. A couple of months or so."

"I'm used to you, Sati. I'll never find anyone like you. You're abandoning me to those uptown mustangs with their long teeth—it's cruel, you know. I'll get eaten."

"Joseph, you shouldn't marry at all." She is firm. "Your father loved you; if he had known how hard the promise would make your life, he would never have let you make it."

"But I did make it, and broken promises breach the dam."

"So do lies, Joseph."

"Yes, I'm sorry about that."

"I don't mind, it's only that you didn't . . ."

"Tell you, I know. I should have been honest. I've always been devious when I want my way."

"Well, I know now."

"I guess you think I'm all out of sync?"

"I can't say I understand it. It seems strange to me, I've never heard or read a word that describes it."

"Oh, there are plenty. 'Homosexual,' 'queer,' 'ponce,' 'nancy boy,' take your pick."

"I don't like any of them. It doesn't matter anyway, we'll always be friends."

"Mmm, if it's to be allowed."

"I'll allow it. Don't worry about that."

"I'm going to miss you."

"I'll still be in New York."

"But not my New York. I mean, a doctor, dear girl! You'll end up spewing out babies, living in Queens or somewhere just as awful. Where do doctors live anyway?"

"Queens, actually! Jackson Heights, to be precise. And I don't think that I'll be spewing babies out, as you so charmingly put it, but I want them. Abe wants them too."

"And what about Cora? You're not going to ditch her too, are you?" It's a cheap shot, he knows.

"Oh, Joseph."

"Sorry, Sati. It's the wound speaking."

She feels guilty, found out. She has hardly given Cora a thought since meeting Abe. Of course she will never give up on finding Cora, but she has finally found something that holds its own against Manzanar. There is a sweet sort of mathematics in the balance now between good and bad luck.

"All's well that ends well, eh?" Joseph says when she tells him as much.

She packs a small suitcase, skirts and tops, a warm jacket, and the chocolate box wrapped against damage in a nightdress. She takes a last look at the jewelry, the evening gowns, the furs that have always made her think of the fox in Angelina's woods. She's sure now that she won't miss any of the fancy dress that never truly belonged to her.

"For God's sake, Sati, it's your jewelry, what would I do with it?"

"Sell it, I suppose."

"You should sell it. It will give you more than enough to see those babies through college."

"Abe doesn't want me to take anything. He says that he wants to be the one to buy me things."

"Very caveman, very masterful, but pretty stupid. Can you really see yourself managing on a doctor's pay?"

"I've managed on less, much less. In any case, why do you imagine that everyone who doesn't have a fortune is poor? Abe isn't poor."

"Let me open an account for you. I want you to have your own money."

"Look, Joseph, I can't take your money. Abe won't stand for it. I can't go against him. Put me in your will, and then live to be a hundred, please."

"Okay, sweet girl, if I must."

They kiss awkwardly, and she feels a stab of guilt for leaving him hurt. Joseph has joined those she thinks of as her family, him and Dr. Harper and Eriko, a small band but true, she believes.

"How will I manage without you, Sati?"

"Just as you did before you met me."

"Oh, yes, that way, I remember now."

The room has darkened as they speak. She puts the suitcase down, and from habit begins switching on the table lamps. Joseph draws the curtains against the dismal evening.

"See what a happy domestic scene we make?" he says.

Outside the window, gray clouds fold in on themselves, a southerly wind pelts rain at the pedestrians. It's the kind of rain Joseph hates, the kind that uses up the cabs, and soaks you through as though your clothes were made of blotting paper.

In the lobby Abe is waiting for her impatiently. Waiting for his girl. He is feeling out of place in the company of the deferential doorman, among the Jackson Pollocks and the huge showy arrangements of silk flowers. He is too outdoorsy to appreciate such man-made displays of wealth. He likes walking, and eating in homely restaurants; he likes the humanity of his patients, his mother's warm house in Freeport, and the little sailing boat that was his father's, his now. He loves his dog, Wilson, loves the friends he would go the whole mile for, and now he loves Satomi, the girl who makes him feel as though luck loves him.

"I have to go, Joseph." She is eager to be with Abe, to have the goodbyes behind her.

"Yes, you must."

"See you soon, then." She settles for the prosaic.

"Yes, on Saturday at your wedding. Ridiculous, isn't it?"

"Not to me."

"It's not too late to change your mind. It's a woman's prerogative, after all."

"Joseph!"

"Sorry, Sati. Go claim your life."

The elevator doors open to Abe's back as he paces the lobby. She pauses, watching his long stride, feeling the heat rising in her. Little beads of rain are quivering on Abe's dark coat like tiny balls of mercury. As he turns toward her, she smiles, imagining a hundred little stars shining in his hair too.

It's not to be a big-deal wedding. No St. James' Church, no big fat reception at the Plaza, as it would have been with Joseph. She's relieved.

"A New York justice of the peace will do us, honey?" Abe had said. "Simple. Our way."

Dr. Harper has sent his best wishes:

I'm relieved to see that I haven't put you off marrying a doctor.

Eriko has splurged on a wire: her words are formal, the usual congratulations. Satomi had hoped for more, but wires are expensive, and formalities on such occasions are the Japanese way, she knows.

Abe's mother, Frances, stands at his side in front of the big mahogany table in City Hall. She's almost as tall as Abe, conscious of it, so that she stoops a little. She is puffy under the same brown eyes as her son's, hoping that no one thinks that she has been crying. The little bags are annoyingly hereditary, what can she do?

She would have preferred a church wedding for Abe in Freeport, the minister she knows, the sea as the backdrop. Her son and this girl have only known each other a few months. Why couldn't they wait a decent amount of time? He had been going out with Corrine for longer, after all. She doesn't know yet whether she likes Satomi or not. The girl is challenging and not at all the sort of daughter-in-law she has pictured for her son. She would have liked the known, not Corrine, if the choice was hers, but still a local girl, someone like herself, she supposes, a more familiar kind of girl. She wants to be happy for him, and Abe, by her side, is grinning at her, brimming over with happiness, so what has she got to complain about? She tells herself it's not so much to do with Satomi, it's just that she's suffering the jealousy of a mother losing her son to another woman.

As Satomi walks the length of the room to stand by Abe's side, she is a little unsteady on her feet. It's the aspirins she took earlier, she supposes. She shouldn't have washed them down with champagne, but the headache had been bad and Joseph had said they would work quicker that way. And they did, accounting now, she suspects, for her dreamlike state.

"It's your wedding day," Joseph said. "You must drink champagne, it's the law."

"Whose law?"

"Mine, of course."

He had booked the suite at the Carlyle for her. Somewhere for her to stay in the few days before the marriage.

"A time of grace, dear girl. A good place to think things over."

"It's lovely, Joseph, but a whole suite . . ."

"My wedding present," he had insisted. "The bone doctor can't object to that, can he?"

Surprisingly, Abe hadn't.

"Enjoy it while you can," he had warned lightheartedly. "Our finances aren't quite up to the Carlyle."

Our finances, us, we—the words fit, not strange at all, she is finally home.

But bathing in the spacious bathroom with the hotel's scented soap, she had experienced a wobble. Would this feeling of euphoria burn out somewhere soon along the line? Does true love really exist? Is Joseph right, has it all happened too quickly? It won't work if, like her father, like Haru, Abe wants to change her. She has looked for signs of that but has found none. All she has seen is his approval.

Wrapping herself in a huge white towel, she returned to the glamorous bedroom to dress. If only Tamura could have been with her, if she could have known Abe, reassured her.

He's the one, isn't he, Mama?

She is struggling to leave the life of Tamura and Cora and Manzanar behind her, to make this new one with Abe.

Hunter had joined them in the suite for the wedding breakfast, eggs and hash browns, and sharp out-of-season strawberries with butter cake. He sat upright in his wheelchair, looking anxiously at Joseph as though his friend might crumble to nothing at any moment.

But Joseph, in full actor's mode, was playing the good loser. Besides, he was considering Satomi's advice about not honoring the promise. If he reneged on it, his life would be restored to the one that suited him best. But to break a promise to a dying father is a sickening thing.

Living with a woman other than Satomi held only terror for him. It was a dilemma. He'd go to Europe after the wedding. Think about it as he walked the streets of Paris, consider the way to go in the beauty of Rome. He needed a break, needed to put the promise on hold for a while.

"You look wonderful," he told her, admiring the simple blue shift, the fresh camellias fixed in the loop of her hair. "It's down to my influence, of course."

After the ceremony she and Abe run through the stinging storm of rice thrown enthusiastically by the small wedding party, Abe's laugh bursting from him, big and genuine. The ache in her has gone, and it's nothing to do with the aspirin, she knows.

Abe's best man Don, his old school friend from Freeport, poses them on the steps of City Hall and clicks away with his camera until his film is used up. The day is cold, bright, and dry, a good day for walking, but they pile into cabs and make their way to Lutèce for lunch, Frances's treat. More champagne, and toasts to their happiness, and Hunter loud in his drunkenness, weeping a little, nobody is sure for what. Joseph leaves before dessert to take him home.

HEAT WAVE

ABE'S LIFE, THE normality of it, she supposes, takes a bit of getting used to, but she isn't the only one acclimatizing. His hometown friends are hesitant with her, suspicious of her past. What is she doing with Abe, a girl like her, the uptown queen of the society pages? Has she really given up a fortune to be with their friend? Is she playing games?

"They'll come around," Abe comforts. "In any case, who cares what they think? You're my girl, not theirs."

They had expected him to marry Corrine, the one Satomi has eclipsed. She is a local girl, after all, known since childhood, highly strung and needy, it's true, but familiar, one of them. Still, Satomi isn't putting on any airs. They'll make the effort for Abe's sake.

Frances, who hadn't cared much for Corrine, is settling to the idea of Satomi, so when Satomi asks her about Corrine she doesn't hold back.

"'Pretty' and 'prissy' are the words I'd choose." She laughs. "I guess she knew she would have a hard job hanging on to him."

"How come?"

"Oh, well, it's just my opinion, of course, but it never seemed right to me. Abe always wanted his friends around when he was with her, never seemed at ease when it was just the two of them. And Corrine couldn't bear being on the water, couldn't swim, was scared of drowning, I think. You couldn't blame her for that, but Abe loves the water, you can't keep him off it. It caused problems. It wasn't like it is with you. He can't wait to get you alone. Even I feel in the way sometimes."

"Oh, Frances, you shouldn't. Abe adores you." She is embarrassed, not yet comfortable enough with Frances to be talking about Abe and the love thing.

"I guess," Frances says. "I understand, though. His father and I were a love match too. No matter how long it lasts, you can't beat that, can you?"

"You can't. Its good luck, isn't it?"

"Mmm, better than winning the lottery. And you deserve some luck, Satomi, after what you've been through, losing your father and mother so young."

Satomi feels protective of Tamura, at a loss as to how to describe to Frances the loveliness that was her mother. Abe understands, though, he speaks of Tamura softly, with a tactfulness that leans toward affection, as though he might have known and loved her too.

"Does Abe ever talk about his father to you?" Frances hurries to fill the silence between them. She thinks that she will never feel entirely at ease with Satomi, silences must be filled, eye contact kept to the minimum. Abe chose not to pattern by his mother when choosing his wife, so they have little other than him in common.

"He says that he has fragments of memory of him, pictures that come to him sometimes. He remembers being picked up and thrown in the air, having his hair stroked as he fell asleep."

"I'm glad he remembers anything at all," Frances says. "He was only three when Ben had his heart attack."

"Oh, my poor Abe," Satomi says. "And you too, Frances."

"I can't tell you what it did to me. Ben had never shown any

signs of being ill at all, you see. Well, nothing that I noticed, anyway. He'd been sailing all that day, and I should have been with
him, only I wanted to stay home and cozy up. I'll never forgive
myself for that."

"You couldn't have known."

"No, but I just wish that I'd been with him. I guess it wouldn't
have changed anything, though. But he was so close to home, to
me, when it happened, you see. I saw his boat come into port from
the kitchen window, saw him on deck, and I waved, but he didn't
wave back. Didn't see me, I guess." She is surprised to find herself
confiding in Satomi, but can't seem to stop. "I was in the middle
of making an egg cream, his favorite. I laid the table and waited,
but he didn't come. I remember being angry that he was puttering
around without a thought for me—that is, until it got dark and he
didn't come, and didn't come. I found him in the cabin lying on
the bunk, peaceful as could be. I knew straight off that he wasn't
sleeping."

"And then it was just you and Abe."

"Yes, but I was hardly a mother to him that year. I did my best,
all the practical things, you know. My heart wasn't with Abe,
though, it was with Ben."

Tears spring to Satomi's eyes at the thought of it. She remembers the time after Aaron had died, the way Tamura in her misery
had forgotten that she was a mother too.

"Did you never consider marrying again, Frances?"

"Only once, much later, but it wouldn't have worked. I was
always measuring the guy against Ben. It sounds crazy, but just
the fact that the socks were different, the choice of newspaper, it
switched me off somehow. You know how it is when you love
someone. You can't stop comparing. And it wasn't just that Ben
was a catch, the handsome local doctor that everyone liked, although I guess all that helped. It was more how he made me feel

about myself, about us as a couple. I wanted to have that feeling again. It just never came with anyone else."

Frances is surprised at how easy it is to confide in Satomi, but she's still anxious. It's her own kind of snobbery, she thinks, but the high-living thing feels dangerous to her. Maybe Satomi will miss it when married life settles down. She can't imagine what it does to you to have such a fortune at your disposal. And the beauty thing is startling, exotic, and she isn't used to startling or exotic. But she can see why Satomi has given up a fortune to be with Abe. It is Abe, after all, and the girl has steel.

"I guess you are finding it quite cramped in Abe's little apartment, huh?"

"It's pretty small, but I have lived in smaller and it's very comfortable, and besides, we are here almost every weekend. And oh, my goodness, Abe's shower is wonderful, so much water, like Niagara Falls."

"Oh, don't tell me you're that easy to please." Frances is genuinely surprised. The girl had lived in a fourteen-room duplex in Manhattan, but she raves about a shower that works in a two-room apartment in Jackson Heights.

"There's nothing as precious as water, Frances. Nothing in the world."

"Well, while we're on the subject of water, you might want to please Abe and learn to sail. Sailing's a big thing around here and Abe has loved it since he was a little boy."

"Oh, I've sailed with Joseph. He always says that it's the best thing . . ." It occurs to her that she is always bringing Joseph into the conversation.

"Do you mind me talking about him?"

"It takes time to let people go. And I guess that you loved him once."

"I still do. Not in a way that is anything like the way I love

Abe. I'll tell you all about it if you want. You won't like it, though."

"Whenever you're ready, honey, I don't need to know."

"I don't want you to think badly of Joseph. Abe doesn't like him, and that's natural, I guess, but he's my best friend in New York. He's a good person."

Frances, with memories of Ben stirred, has trouble imagining what sort of affair Satomi and Joseph had. It was a one-in-a-million chance that Satomi should even have met a man like Joseph, let alone move in with him without being married. But then, who is she to criticize? She couldn't claim to have been the virgin bride when she married Ben. They may not have lived together, but they had the boat with its cozy cabin, and times have changed, after all.

Everything is upside down since the war. People don't trust that they have time anymore. And Satomi must have been lonely in New York, straight out of her years of confinement in the camp. Were there really those places in America? It doesn't bear thinking about.

Abe, usually so considerate of her feelings, doesn't want to hear about Joseph. No matter what Satomi wants, he can't imagine ever having the man as a friend. Joseph's kind unsettles him, he doesn't understand such desires, doesn't want to know about them. If there's anything that disturbs him about Satomi, it's that bit of sophistication that Joseph has exposed her to, the experiences he wishes she'd never had.

And if he's honest, the Cora thing bothers him too. He feels bad about it, but it's hard to understand the connection Satomi feels with the child. He's doing his best, though, fighting off the thought that there's nothing like your own flesh and blood. If Satomi wants Cora, then he can live with it. Whatever happens, whatever compromises they have to make, they're strong enough to weather them.

"We'll want to start a family of our own one day," he says.

"I want that too, Abe. It would be wonderful if Cora is with a family, and happy. That would be fine with me. I just need to see her, to know that she's okay."

But what, he thinks, if she never finds her? Will it come between them, that bit of her that will always be longing, the bit he can do nothing to make better?

New York drips in a heat wave that reminds her of the one in Angelina.

Fresh out of the shower, Abe leaves for work in the mornings, his shirt sticking to his back before he is out the door.

"I've never known it quite this bad," he says. "What I'd give to be on the water."

The temperature is hitting triple digits, blistering the paint on their windowsills, creating asphalt heat islands that bubble up between the trees on the sidewalk. The apartment sweats its way through August with them, no air-conditioning, but the fan going furiously.

"It seems to affect me more than you," Abe says. "How do you manage to look so cool?"

"Years of mountain weather," she says.

The electric feeder cables fail intermittently, so that more often than not their evenings are spent in the dark. In the blackouts they eat dinner by candlelight and read in the greenish glow of a shared flashlight, balanced precariously above their heads in the ironwork of the bedstead. The cold water runs warm, so to save money they switch the water heater off.

"With that and the cuts, we'll halve the energy cost," Abe says.

On investigation Abe discovers the puzzling hum in the bathroom to be a wasp's nest inside the extractor fan. He pours a poisonous powder down through the blades and the wasps go mad, darkening the room as they emerge heading for the light, covering the windowpanes in a thick humming curtain. For days after Satomi comes across dead ones on the floor and the window ledges, two floating in the milk jug.

On his day off, when the sweet cooing of their neighbors' pigeons stops, Abe goes to the roof to investigate and comes back with the news that their drinking water has evaporated in the heat.

"Dead," he says. "Never seen the like. I know for a fact they top that water up every morning before they leave for work."

When they can't sleep, they sit outside on the fire escape and Abe reads the night sky to her, pointing out the stars and the constellations. He loves naming them, as though the words conjure up something magical for him, Ursa Major, and Minor too, Lupus the wolf, and Orion the hunter.

"You get to know the stars at sea," he tells her. "Nothing like a clear night at sea."

It doesn't matter that the butter melts in their ailing icebox, that the milk goes sour in a day—nothing outside of the two of them matters. So what if they can't sleep in the heat? The hot nights are made for love anyway, for talking, for planning their future.

There is nothing like making love with Abe, nothing like the scent of him, fresh and green like ferns. And no feeling compares to the exquisite sense she has that they belong to each other, that they are complete. If the world went away and they were alone, it would be enough.

When Abe covers her, something in her breaks, a break he fills so completely that she forgets the camp, forgets Cora, forgets everything. And after, returned to herself in those quiet moments meant for expressing truths, there is only a small sense of remorse that she hasn't yet told him of Haru. He is hardly resigned to the idea of Joseph in her life, without testing him with a past lover. And he would mind, she believes. He is a predictable man, true to the morals of his time. Abe knowing about Haru wouldn't break them, but she can't bear the thought of hurting him.

While Abe works, she plays housewife, cleaning the apartment, washing and ironing, shopping for their food. The chores are not enough to fill the day, and time stalls in the waiting-for-Abe hours. Long before she needs to, she takes the streetcar across the Queensboro Bridge to meet him from work. She sits on their special bench reading the same page of her book over and over, not able to concentrate on anything but the idea that he is somewhere close, that she will see him soon. Sometimes she changes benches so that he will have to look for her, so that she can watch him looking for her.

They talk of getting a bigger apartment, of how it will be when they have children. "Not yet, but soon," Abe says. They have the names all ready, Aaron for the boy, Iris, after Abe's beloved long-dead grandmother, for the girl. She considers bringing Cora into the conversation but can't seem to get the words out.

"It must be Aaron for the boy," Abe says generously. "He must know he was named for a hero."

Of course they will have a boy and a girl, and in that order. They have found each other and will have everything they want. They are blessed, aren't they?

On Abe's summer break, they go to Freeport. The heat is not so bad on the coast, there is always a breeze and the nights are cooler than in the city. Abe is happy there. So she is happy there.

They sail every day. He's surprised how good she is at it.

"Captain and mate," he says. "Not sure which of us is captain, though."

She watches him raise the sail, admires the muscles in his tanned arms, the creases around his eyes as he squints in the sunlight. Love and lust collide and meld softly in her.

Anchored in port, he takes her on the cabin's impossibly small bunk, still surprised that she is as eager for it as he is for her. They always end up in a heap on the floor, tangled in the cover.

"We'll be black and blue all over if we don't stop this." She laughs. "Then what will Frances think?"

"Let's never stop this, Sati, never, never."

And after, beer straight from the bottle, hauled up from its net in the sea where Abe keeps it cooling. They play cards on deck with Wilson bunched up at their feet, snoring in his doggy sleep. They stay till dark, not wanting to share their time with anyone, not even Frances.

Abe introduces her to *his* Freeport, to the shopkeepers and the people who hunker down in the place after the tourists have gone. They are overly polite with her, cautious.

"Don't let it worry you," Abe says. "They don't matter."

Satomi is reminded of how hard it is to break into the circle. There have been so many circles in her life that she has skimmed around the edge of, never quite making it to the inside. Abe is the only one who sees her for who she is, who loves her because she is Satomi. Artie saw too much Japanese in her, Haru not enough. With Abe, though, she's just right. Even if she never quite fits in with those others he loves, she's inside the circle with him.

"It's a different world in winter," he tells her. "The sailing's not so easy, but I like it better. You'll see, you'll love it in winter."

They walk the canals and on through the fields of pure white salt marshes that open out to the clean Atlantic Ocean.

"It's beautiful, isn't it? Have you ever seen anywhere so beautiful?"

She thinks of Fishers Island, of Joseph's sleek yacht *Windward* cutting through the gray-green ocean. Her first sight of it had taken her breath away.

"No, never, it's just perfect," she says.

He takes her to the Kissing Bridge over the Millburn but refuses to kiss her.

"I've kissed too many girls here," he says seriously. "You're not a bridge-kissing sort of girl, you're for keeps."

"Did you kiss Corrine here?"

"Oh, sure I did, her and a few others besides."

They stroll along the Nautical Mile, where in the Crab Shack Abe's friends, home for the summer, join them. Abe's order is always the same, steamed clams and his favorite light beer, brought to the table in glass pitchers, the liquid trembling gold in the sunlight.

"Nothing like Freeport steamers," he says.

It's a pleasure he savors, dipping each one first into the clam broth, then into the little tin pot of melted butter that comes on the side.

Sitting next to him, with the sound of the gulls bullying, the warmth of his thigh against hers as he helps himself to her fries, Manzanar it seems to her was a time in the life of a different girl. Finding Cora is not so much forgotten as put on hold. It's a honeymoon period for her and Abe. She is slipping into place, no longer defined by her experiences in the camp.

"I can't believe that I have found you," she says. "Just when I wasn't looking."

"It was meant," he says simply.

Back in New York, the heat in mid-July is still fierce. Abe, after having her to himself in Freeport, is reluctant for her to contact Joseph.

"We have our life, honey. It just doesn't fit with his."

"I have to keep in touch with him, Abe. Asking me not to see Joseph is like me asking you not to see your mother. It's cruel."

Their first real argument, though, comes not over Joseph but about Satomi wanting to work.

"You didn't mind living off Joseph's money." He would take the words back if he could. They are unfair and he knows the truth of it.

"I worked for most of the time I was with him," she defends herself, hurt by Abe's tone. "In any case, Abe, it's not the same thing at all. I'm lonely here with you gone all day."

"I don't want you working, Sati," he says flatly. "I can support my wife, I should think."

When she greets him with the news that she's taken a job, as a receptionist at the Bridge Hotel, near his hospital, a frown flits briefly across his brow before he raises his hands to heaven and gives in. She won't be ordered, and he loves that about her. She can't be anyone other than who she is.

"I don't like you working, honey, but if it's what you want . . ."

"You'll hardly notice it, Abe. And it's not forever. Just until we settle, start a family."

The words "settle," "start a family" wrap themselves around her. They're imbued with warmth, with normality. She likes that the language of her world has changed to that of the all-American girl.

Joseph comes to the hotel, winces at the sight of her behind the desk, at the cheap plastic name badge on her dress. His face is a little drawn. He is a few pounds lighter than when she last saw him. He has had trouble finding the hotel, since the cab dropped him on the wrong street. He walked three blocks out of his way before discovering the mistake.

She has no name for the sweet feeling that floods her at the sight of him. Perhaps it's what a sister would feel after not seeing a loved brother for a while.

"God, you look healthy," he says. "But I can't say those clothes do much for you. You look like a schoolteacher."

"I like this dress, its Abe's favorite."

"Now, why doesn't that surprise me?"

Out of the Manhattan village, he's a tree unearthed, too elegant for the sullied midtown territory that she now inhabits. His imported Savile Row suit is fine worsted wool, his soft brogues of obvious quality. He's tanned from his European tour and it gives him a slightly racy look. She remembers the first time that she saw him and had thought him vain. She knows better now: his extreme neatness is his shield, the meniscus he puts between himself and the world.

"I'm getting used to life without you, I suppose." He sighs. "But New York is not the same. I need pastures new, feel the urge to be off again."

Since her wedding he has been working on the Cora thing. No news yet, but he gives her his latest report, all neatly typed up. Families who have adopted Japanese children have been contacted, there are letters from the governor's office with assurances that they will search records but can promise nothing. It's suggested that they should look farther afield, out of the state if need be.

"Anything from Dr. Harper?" he asks.

"Nothing, only that he thinks her name might have been changed, as he can't find a record anywhere of any Cora. It's as though she has disappeared from the world."

"She'll turn up, dear girl." He touches her cheek lightly. "Oh, and believe it or not, Hunter is getting married. A Connecticut family, one of the Harrison girls, Laura. You met her on Fishers Island, remember? She's been sweet on him since they were kids. His family is pleased."

"I'm pleased too. Lucky girl, to have Hunter."

"You'll come to the wedding, of course?"

"Well, it's not Abe's sort of thing, and he doesn't like me going places without him." She can feel herself blushing.

"And what Abe says, goes?"

"Do you really think I've changed that much?"

"Well, I live in hope that you haven't. You look the same, although rather like a rare orchid in a tin can behind that desk. It's quite upsetting. Let me take you to lunch."

"Okay, I'd like that, but nowhere too smart. One of us has to look out of place, so it might as well be you. Somewhere that would suit a schoolteacher would be best, don't you think?"

The offer of a job with the Long Island hospital group comes out of the blue and Abe jumps at the chance.

"We can live in Freeport, buy a house, have our babies. What do you say?"

He hadn't needed to ask, they both knew the answer to that.

He would take up the position in December—time enough to pack up and give notice at the apartment, to honor his contract at the hospital, and for them to find a home of their own in Freeport.

"You can start looking for a house right away," he says. "Give up your job and stay with Frances. She'll love helping us find the right thing. I'll come every spare moment I get." He will miss her, but he will be sending her home, putting her somewhere safe, somewhere away from Joseph. The light of their future is beckoning, and he can't wait to be done with the city.

"It's a wonderful piece of luck, Sati."

"So wonderful," she agrees, even though she doesn't want to leave. Joseph is hardly a threat, and she would rather stay with Abe in Queens until they are ready to move.

There is something confirming, though, in the idea of being in Abe's childhood home, of finding a house of their own, waiting with his mother for him to return to them. Tamura had told her once that women must get used to waiting.

"Work and wars, Satomi," she had said. "It's the women who wait."

In Abe's childhood bed she wakes periodically through the night, gauging the time by the depth of darkness, the quality of the light seeping through the curtains from the sea. Will she ever be able to sleep comfortably on her own again?

In his boyhood room, full of boyish things that Frances can't bear to get rid of, her clothes are squashed up tight against Abe's outgrown ones in the small wardrobe. There are pictures of sailboats on the walls, balsa-wood planes hanging on strings from the ceiling, a baseball nestled in its glove on a shelf, as though waiting for Abe to pick up the game where he left it off.

Among the debris of his childhood there hardly seems room for her. A photograph of Wilson as a puppy, jumping for a ball, ears flying, jostles for space on the small bedside table alongside a picture book on sailing, and two huge pebbles with the faint tracery of fossils inking their surface. She puts the book and the stones in a box under his bed, and the well of her memory is taken to that other bed she put a box under all those years ago. Shoving aside his puzzles, the miniature tool set, and a browning pile of comics, she swallows hard and attempts to banish the memory of that day, of that Angelina girl.

"Move anything you like," Frances had said lightly, but didn't tell her where she might move it to.

When Abe comes on his precious time off, the bed is too narrow for the both of them. They lie knotted together, close and uncomfortable. He pretends not to mind, she does too.

"It's cozy," he says.

"Mmm."

It's nothing against Frances, but she feels stifled being in such close quarters with someone she hardly knows. There is something of camp living in it that unsettles her. And she has noticed how Abe becomes more of a son than a husband in his mother's house. She misses having him to herself, misses the apartment. The need to find a place of their own is urgent in her.

"I'll go with whatever you choose," Abe says. "Long as it doesn't break the bank."

When she finds it on the fifth house viewed, it's obvious to her that it's the one. The day is dazzlingly bright, the noon sun high, the late summer day hot, yet the salt marshes on which the house sits appear to her like fields of pure untrodden snow.

"It looks solid enough," Frances says, seeing Satomi's delight.

It will blow their budget, so they will have to decorate it themselves, make do on the furnishings, but it's perfect.

"Square-built. Nineteen twenties, I guess," Frances says.

Satomi loves the unadorned frontage that belies the charm of its spacious interior. There isn't much of a garden, but you can see the ocean from all sides, and the rooms are filled with light.

"It's beautiful," she says.

"A lot of upkeep," Frances says. "And nothing much will take in the ground here. The salt, you see."

When Abe comes home on the weekends their time is spent decorating, sanding down the woodwork, peeling off the dark wallpaper, painting the rooms in soft grays and blues, the colors of the ocean.

They make love on a blanket on the floor, the smell of paint and ozone mingling in the air. The urge, frequent and overwhelming, can't be resisted.

"We'll move in as soon as the bed comes," Abe says. "What more do we need?"

"So many things." She laughs, picturing them sleeping in a big comfortable bed with cotton covers, a crib by the side of it.

"We'll be in by the end of the month," he says, and kisses her. "Wish we could have Wilson with us here, but it wouldn't be fair to take him."

"A puppy of our own, then?" she suggests.

"I guess."

The windows of the salt marsh house are open in the day to the tang of the marshes. There are drapes now at the windows, a sparse assortment of furniture in the rooms, and Frances has donated two rag rugs. The house has become a home.

There's no picket fence around her salty garden, and she refuses to wear an apron, but she is assuming the identity of the suburban, middle-class American wife, loving it so much that Manzanar has retreated to the less conscious part of her mind. She is hit by the certainty of love, by the contrast of her life with Abe to the unreal time she had spent with Joseph.

She gets a card for the local library, does her marketing at the store that Frances shops in, even has a laundry day. Frances is teaching her to cook Abe's favorite dishes, pickled beets and creamed codfish, broiled chicken and cornbread. People seeing her with Frances include her in their greeting, begin to recognize her when she is on her own. She sees the reserve in them still, but doesn't mind so much. She believes Abe when he tells her it's the same for all newcomers in Freeport. It takes time, that's all.

"Before you know it," Frances says, "you'll be a local."

They have Abe's best friend, Don, and his girlfriend over for dinner, and Abe helps her roast a chicken and she attempts a pear pie. She's a wife like any other. She's happy.

Abe sees and loves the difference in her. She's all his now, apart from those irritating times when she comes to stay overnight with him in the city, and hooks up with Joseph while he's at work. He doesn't mind so much anymore the idea of Cora. That unreachable bit of Satomi, the times when she seems remote from him, has to do with Cora, he thinks. He would like to find Cora too now, to see Satomi at peace.

In their city bed his passion spills over so that he is not always tender. She doesn't know, as Abe himself doesn't know, that it's payback for Joseph. But she's as eager, as demanding as him for it. When he falls asleep across her, she revels in the intimacy of his trust, his sharp after-sex scent. She bears without complaint the weight of him until he chooses to roll away from her.

She is determined not to let the camp impinge on their life, or allow the odd socialite life she had led with Joseph damage them. To make a balance sheet of what is gained, what lost, would be mad. She will be grateful, ignore that contradictory thing that stirs in her heart when memories of Cora are evoked. The girl who was Satomi Baker is lying low under the identity of Mrs. Abe Robinson.

At Abe's request she goes to the city to bring back the last of their things from the apartment. He has to work and the new tenants are eager to take possession. She packs their linen, her books, and the toaster they bought because the grill on the old cooker had stopped working. There's the tin tray illustrated with the New York skyline, and some cream china cups with gold rims that they found together in a bric-a-brac store. There's the silver-framed photograph of their wedding, Abe's binoculars, the alarm clock.

Abe has a week on nights and will sleep in one of the on-call rooms in the hospital.

"It's torture being apart," he says, kissing her.

"Worse than torture," she groans.

They sleep in the apartment for the last time, picnicking on sweet rolls and potato chips, making love in the creaky bed with its cheap mattress.

"We won't miss it," Abe says.

But she can't let go of the ache of leaving. She will never get used to endings.

Abe puts her on the train to Freeport, hauling the packed suitcases onto the rack above her seat in the empty compartment.

"You'll need someone to help you down with those at the other end."

"I'm stronger than you think, Abe."

"I know it, honey. You are strong and I love you. Still, find someone to help you with them anyway. Promise?"

"Promise."

His kiss is firm, without passion, she's disappointed. She can tell he is distracted, wants to be on his way.

"Only a few days before I'll be home for the holiday," he says. "I'll get the earliest Hempstead train I can, and be with you before you know it."

"Time to wish away," she says.

"Frances makes such a big deal of Thanksgiving you're not going to believe it. She'll love having you to show off to."

"I've had enough of missing you, Abe."

"I'll be home before you know it."

She hangs her head out of the window, holding on to the sight of him as he pauses, waving briefly, before striding to the exit. He hates goodbyes, she knows. There's pleasure in knowing what he hates, goodbyes and new shirts, ginger chocolate, milk in his coffee, surprises.

She knows him as he knows her, and everything is as it should be. But as he disappears from her view a feeling of melancholy invades her, and for a moment she debates leaving the train, catching up with him, the pair of them laughing at her silliness. But the train is already moving. It's love, she supposes; with love comes the feeling that every minute apart you are risking something.

"Just till Thanksgiving," she comforts herself. "Just till Thanksgiving."

PENN STATION TO BABYLON

ON THANKSGIVING EVE Frances is in the thick of it. She hasn't been able to keep the smile from her face all day. The oven's heat at full blast is fierce; a fresh-baked chocolate cake is cooling on the table, pumpkins are on the boil, steaming up the windows so that she has to open the door to let the cool air in. It reminds her of last year and all the years before, when she has done the same. Only this year it feels different, nicer, she has to admit. She has Satomi with her, Abe's Satomi, and now she needn't worry about him anymore, he has found his girl.

"Give those cranberries a stir, will you, Sati? I think they're beginning to stick."

The candied smell of the simmering berries, of the sweet pumpkins that she will mash to velvet for her special pie, spice the air.

"I want to get all this out of the way before Abe gets home. We always have hamburgers with my tomato relish on the night before Thanksgiving, and I haven't even started on them yet."

"I can't imagine ever being able to cook like you, Frances."

"Oh, you're learning. And I bet you already have a few of your own traditions."

"I don't know, maybe. We always have a drink on deck after we have put the boat to bed." She flushes at the thought of what else they do, but that is hardly for Frances's ears. "And we never go to sleep on an argument, if you mean that sort of thing. But nothing to do with food, Abe is still a better cook than me. He often cooks for himself in the city."

"Good heavens, does he? I've only ever known him to heat beans."

Both women fall silent as they picture him in their minds. Frances summons her big broad boy waving to her as he comes into harbor, a bitter-sweet reminder of his father. Satomi feels rather than sees his presence, the bulk of him, firm lips, strong hands, that odd contrast of feelings he induces in her, safe and risky at the same time.

"Oh, my God, the turkey." Frances's face is flushed, she is hot, excited. There's nothing like getting ready for Thanksgiving to gin things up.

"We have to cover it with bacon, give it a coat of maple syrup to sit in overnight."

"This Thanksgiving stuff is a real workout, isn't it?"

"Didn't your mother do it?"

"Not really, my father didn't care for turkey. He preferred my mother's Japanese dishes. The mess hall in the camp made an effort, but it was hard to be thankful there, even for the patriotic ones."

"And you didn't feel patriotic?"

"No, not the slightest bit. I spent my whole time at Manzanar angry or afraid. I never felt like celebrating."

"And now?"

"Oh, now everything is different. I want to celebrate with you and Abe, be thankful."

"Where were you last Thanksgiving?"

"We were at the Yacht Club at Fishers Island, Joseph and me, and his best friend, Hunter. He loves it there in the winter and it's smart to be at Fishers for the holiday." She wishes she hadn't said it. The words have a show-off, brittle feel to them.

"Did you enjoy it?"

"Yes, Joseph was in good form, he always is when Hunter is around."

"I guess you miss him, huh?"

"Well, I can still see him in the city when I go."

"You could have asked him here, you know. It would have been a bit odd, but he is your friend, and we will have to get used to that, I guess."

"I thought about it, but honestly, I don't think Abe is ready for that yet, and Joseph wouldn't know what to do with himself in a normal family."

Frances laughs. "I'm glad you think we're normal."

Satomi doesn't want to think about Joseph tonight. Thinking about him induces feelings of guilt, the idea that she is not entitled to her happiness. She has attempted in small ways to make Joseph a part of her and Abe's life, but neither man seems willing to give friendship a try. Inch by inch and without intention it feels as though she is letting Joseph go.

Perhaps, though, her feelings of guilt are really about Cora, about the child she has promised to reclaim. Now that Abe is willing, she must put more effort into finding Cora; she will never be completely happy, she knows, while what happened to that little one remains a mystery. She is due a letter from Dr. Harper anytime soon. Perhaps he has found a trail for them to follow.

Frances, noticing that Satomi has fallen into one of her reveries, puts aside the cooking and suggests they go outside. "We could do with some fresh air," she says, guiding Satomi to the door.

Unhooking Abe's waterproof from the stand on the porch, Satomi hangs it around her shoulders. It flaps against her calves, reminding her of the peacoat issue at Manzanar. She can feel the curve of Wilson's ball in the pocket against her thigh.

The day has been cold, mostly overcast, but as they look up at the night sky the clouds part, allowing a slice of moon to light the sea. It plays on the tips of the waves as they roll into the harbor. All along the coast where sea strikes shore the coves shift in an undulating silver seam.

"Just look at that," Frances marvels. "The moon and the black sea. Now, that sure is a sight."

Satomi slips her arms into the sleeves of Abe's jacket as the moon dusts up behind a cloud. It's Thanksgiving eve and Abe will already be on his way home. It's time to shower, to loosen her hair and put on the blue cardigan and the narrow Capri pants that she brought from home to change into, because Abe says she looks sexy in them.

"You make everything you wear look a million dollars, honey."

"It's an odd time of day," Frances says, turning back toward the house. "Too early for a drink, too late for a nap."

Out on the Richmond Hill track, stalled in the dark, the Hempstead train, with its air brakes jammed, sent its flagman with flag and lamp to slow down the oncoming Babylon train, only four minutes behind it.

Press accounts in the aftermath of the collision made much of the fact that the Babylon train had been barreling down the line close to sixty-five miles an hour when it slammed into the rear of the stationary Penn-to-Hempstead with a boom some likened to the sound of an atomic bomb.

The truth of it was, though, that the motorman of the Babylon, too late to do much about it, had made out in the gloom the stilled train, the panicked flagman at the side of the track frantically waving his flag. In the last seconds of his life he had applied his emergency brakes, slowing his speed to more like thirty than sixty. Still, thirty was speed enough to shunt the Hempstead train seventy-five feet along the track, to toss its last car higher than a house, and send the onrushing train slicing down the middle of the Hempstead, causing "overcoating." Such a word, such an ugly addition to the human vocabulary.

They hear the news of it on the radio as Frances is cutting a lemon for their gin and tonics. It doesn't seem real at first, a story told to frighten, so that you might laugh at it after, might think what a fool you were to have been taken in. It's a Halloween story, not a Thanksgiving one.

"It won't be Abe, not Abe," Satomi cries. But Frances doesn't hear her; her head is full of, *Not again, please, God, not again.* Her knees have buckled under her so that she has to hold on to the sink to keep upright. And Satomi, seeing her distress, can't go to her. If what she sees in Frances is a mother's intuition, then it is a horrible thing. A thing she can't bear the sight of.

The news is coming at them unrelentingly, the voice on the radio almost hysterical. Satomi is shaking, Frances whimpering. On and on it goes, the reporter's voice rising at each new discovery. They listen, sucking the words in, finding it hard to breathe them out.

Neighbors from across the track are the first on the scene. They had been deafened by the sound of the crash, sickened by the sight of it. The train cars are high above the bank, too high for them to reach at first. They had rushed for ladders, blankets, first aid. They are eager now to give witness.

"The ground shuddered. You felt the noise as much as heard it."

"We had to jimmy those doors open to get them out. People were screaming in pain, beating at the windows."

"There were limbs everywhere, arms and legs on the floor, hanging from the windows."

"They were packed like sardines in their own blood."

In Frances's sweet-smelling kitchen they hear on the airwaves fire engines and ambulances ferrying the wounded to the hospital. For some there isn't time even for that, so surgeons have converted the kitchen of a nearby house into a crude operating theater. They work under a bare bulb on the family's kitchen table covered with a sheet.

"People are giving their all," the reporter shrieks.

"Abe will be helping them," Frances says in a moment of hope, her voice hard and emotionless. "He'll be needed there tonight."

"But Abe always goes in the first car," Satomi wails. "He says it makes him feel that he is getting home quicker." She is on the floor now, rocking herself back and forward, banging her head against Frances's leg.

And suddenly Frances too has crumpled to the floor, torrents of hot tears streaming from her eyes, although she doesn't feel as though she is crying. She is merely comforting Satomi, who has gotten everything out of proportion.

Satomi doesn't want to go to the funeral. She doesn't want to see Abe lowered into the wintry ground, see the casket that Frances had chosen on her own, because Satomi is a coward, because she couldn't bear to even look at one.

"Satin-lined oak. Their best line," Frances had reported back in a papery voice.

Satomi had put her hands over her ears. The words were disgusting to her. "Satin-lined," "coffin." What had those things to do with Abe?

If she goes, how will she be able to leave his beautiful broken body there alone in the hard clay? How will she ever be able to say goodbye?

She thinks of Abe's face, the firm set of his mouth, the tiny chip on his third tooth in, the stubble of his beard when he doesn't shave. He can't be dead. In her grief she is more like her mother than ever. Like Tamura, she wants to retreat under the covers of her bed, to never come out.

A magical sort of thinking has taken over her mind. She looks to find him in the stars, in the tiny pearl-eyed bird puffed up with rancor that this morning as she woke in Abe's childhood bed had pecked at the window as though it were trying to get in. Tap, tap, the hammer of its beak shaking the glass.

"Where are you, Abe? Come back to me," she had shouted at the bird, frightening it away.

She had told Frances about it, as if Frances knew about such things, might translate some mysterious Morse code message for her.

"They dig in the putty for insects when the ground's too hard to mine," Frances said pragmatically. "It's the same every year."

Every bone in Abe's body had been crushed, every organ bruised, but it is the tear in his heart leaking blood that is given as the cause of death. A small tear no bigger than a dime, no bigger than a dime. The thought of that little leaking hole breaks her own heart.

"I can't go, Frances," she had sobbed. "Don't make me."

Frances had pleaded with her at first and then insisted.

"You must go. It's Abe's funeral. It's the right thing to do. The only thing left you can do for him. You will regret it always if you don't."

Weak with grief, she had given in.

Frances buttons up Satomi's coat for her, advises gloves, and hugs her briefly. Satomi wonders how Frances can bear to worry about her, how she can think of anyone else but herself. Her mother-in-law's shoulders are hunched, her mouth pinched; she seems smaller somehow, as though she is shriveling by the minute.

"It's cold in that church, even worse in the cemetery," Frances says.

A stony misery creeps through Satomi's body. Time has run out, and she can't remember when she last told Abe that she loved him, and she hadn't yet told him of Haru. She will never, now, be able to tell him anything ever again.

The minister in his church is comfortable in his role. He enjoys the onstage part of his ministry, the sweetness of christenings, the joy of weddings, even the somber air of funerals. He performs well in front of his audience, as he sometimes guiltily thinks of his congregation.

"We think with great sympathy," he says, "of Abe's new bride, widowed after such a brief marriage."

It was to be his only reference to her. He speaks of Abe's history in Freeport, of the town's love of Frances, their love of her boy. It seems to Satomi that he is saying their long knowing of Abe has the bigger claim to grief at his loss.

But she's being unfair, she thinks, small-minded, possessive. Abe had been popular everywhere, always. No one knew better than her how easy he had been to love.

Abe's friends, some holding hands, some with their arms around each other, make a space for her at the graveside. Without the glue of Abe to bind them, they seem already to be separating from her. Their parents, who have known Abe since childhood, stand around the grave too, ashen-faced, their eyes slipping to Abe's father's headstone nearby. They are touched by their children's grief, secretly thankful that it is not one of their own, who might so easily have caught the Penn-to-Babylon that night.

The rain has come on, so that people begin opening umbrellas. Red and blue canopies, a yellow one with blue raindrops dancing on it, carnival colors, she thinks, as Abe's best friend, Don, moves to her side, sheltering her under the shade of his black one.

It takes a while for the exaggerated moan of the fair-haired girl she hadn't noticed before to reach her. Satomi has held herself back from giving vent to the animal part of herself and looks toward her with curiosity. People are embarrassed by the awful sound, they shuffle their feet, cough politely as though to cover it.

It's Corrine, clutching a spray of snowberries to her chest, swaying uncontrollably. Nothing to be done, she has always been a bit of a drama queen.

"Shush, Corrine. Be brave for Frances's sake." A man Satomi doesn't know puts his arm around Corrine's shoulders, a bit too firmly for it to be thought comfort.

Abe's colleagues from the hospital cluster together uncomfortably, their medical skills of no use here. The neighbors from Jackson Heights who had hardly spoken to her, but had thought him a fine neighbor, have come. They have all known and liked Abe. It is odd how she feels an outsider.

Joseph had phoned in distress, concerned for her.

"Oh, my dear girl, I'm coming. You will need me."

"No, don't come. It wouldn't be right. I don't want you to come."

He had been hurt at her dismissal, but she couldn't picture Joseph among Abe's people. He would have been a distraction, would have highlighted the fact that she is cut from a different cloth too.

At the sight of Abe's coffin she is reminded of Tamura's. Were they together now, Abe and Tamura, forever linked by their love for her? She shakes the thought away. She is already feeling the burden of ghosts.

On the walk back, Frances takes her hand as though she is a child. People arrive at the house. Women fuss in Frances's kitchen, food appears as if from nowhere. It is as though a party has broken out. She goes upstairs, and Frances follows.

"You need sleep," Frances says, undressing her.

"I'll come down soon, Frances. I just need a little time."

Sleep is the only thing that holds attraction for either of them. Satomi would sleep forever if she could, but as though an alarm is set in her she can only manage an hour or two at a time. She lies on the bed and buries her head in Abe's pillow. Even the scent of him is fading, she thinks.

"I'm sorry, Frances, it should be me helping you."

"We'll help each other, Satomi. Abe would want that."

"I can't say his name, Frances. It feels like my heart is ripping too when I try."

"Day by day, inch by inch," Frances says, without belief herself.

"Yes, day by day," Satomi repeats mechanically.

"You will stay with me here for a while, won't you, Sati, just for a while? I want to be with someone who loved Abe, someone he loved," Frances says.

"Come back to the apartment," Joseph says. "Let me take care of you, just until you put the pieces back together."

She considers briefly living on her own in their house by the salt marshes. But the thought of occupying their bed without Abe, of taking down a book from the shelves that he had made for their living room, is too painful. She will never live there now, not without Abe. Hope has been eaten up there, sent packing.

She stays with Frances, holed up in Abe's room, breathing him in as her mother had breathed her father in all those years ago. She will look after Frances, make her eat, make her go for walks, act like a daughter-in-law is meant to.

She finds herself either full of a terrible nervous energy or so tired that she can't lift herself from the bed. Sometimes she shuts her eyes and prays that when she opens them she will find herself ten years into the future, ten years away from the misery that runs through her blood, contaminating everything. She can't pray, as some do, for it all to have been no more than a horrible dream. To close her eyes and imagine Abe returned to her wouldn't save her from the pain of opening them to the knowledge that he never would be.

Frances's friends come to comfort.

"Be grateful for the wonderful summer you had here together, for the precious time you shared," they say. "It will get better."

Like Frances, they are the best of women, the best of American mothers. Unlike Frances, though, they rarely say the right thing.

Her days are filled with what is needed next, as though Abe is directing her in some way. Sleep when you must, eat when you remember, sit with Frances, look at the photographs with her, cry with her, make her laugh, and lie with her so that she can sleep a little. And Frances does the same for her in return.

She dreads the nightmares that come in her troubled sleep, black featureless landscapes where she can't find who she's looking for. She doesn't dream in color anymore.

Frances lets her fuss, acquiesces in the game while looking herself for a reference point back to the routine of her old life, which seems to have escaped her.

They find comfort in focusing on Abe's dog, it is the only thing they can do for him now. Wilson won't eat, not even the delicious stews of marrow bone that Frances cooks for him. He lies across the door to Abe's room, head on paws, his body curled around one of Abe's old shoes that he found on the porch, as though he is made for misery.

"Come on, old fella," they imitate Abe. "You can't go on like this, now, can you?"

They go through Christmas in a daze, no decorations, no tree, but "merry Christmas" slips from Frances's lips as Satomi appears at breakfast. Some atavistic memory has triggered the words without her consent.

"I don't think that I will ever be able to cook a turkey again."

"It doesn't matter, Frances, I couldn't eat it anyway."

They walk the two-mile strip alongside a distant canal without seeing anyone, returning home to soup and cornbread. In bed by nine, they have survived their first Christmas without Abe. They are both glad to see the back of it.

Frances rallies first. Perhaps because she knows what her life will be like now, knows what to expect from it. There are no decisions for her to make, the cycles of grief are familiar to her, there will be bad and better times, times so completely terrible that she will look back on them and wonder how she has not been made mad. And even when she thinks that she is better, she knows that the pain will come slicing out of nowhere, catching her off guard. The thought of it exhausts her, but she must start the living of those times, or walk into the sea and be done with it. She tells herself that she doesn't have the courage for that. She isn't made for Greek tragedy.

And Wilson has perked up, pleading for walks, dropping his ball at their feet, hanging around the kitchen before his mealtimes, his big begging eyes full of expectation. He has a better sense of timing than them, knows instinctively when to let go.

Letters have come from Dr. Harper and Eriko. They are worried about her, shocked at what has happened.

It is too cruel, Dr. Harper writes. *A terrible thing.*

It must be borne, Satomi. You don't deserve it, Eriko says.

Her answering letters are brief. *I'm fine, getting better,* she lies. *Don't worry about me.*

She has refused to see Joseph. It's ridiculous, she tells herself, but seeing him would feel like she was betraying Abe.

"Not yet," she says when he phones, his voice all hurt. "I'm not ready to see anyone yet."

By spring she has taken to spending her days on the boat. She doesn't sail, never releases it from its moorings, but in its narrow confines her grief feels contained. She lies on the bunk and reads all day, books from the Freeport library, novels and biographies, books about fishing and the care of dogs, anything that her eyes settle on. She knows now a little about fly fishing, about trees and plants, and Emma Bovary, and Tiny Tim.

She hides in the boat's cabin, unseen, but hearing, outside, the lapping of the water, the voices of Freeport's sailing community.

"Shh," she hears, when someone remarks on the permanently anchored boat. Freeport knows she is there.

When Satomi's tears are no longer a release, when sleep overtakes reading as her choice of escape, Cora inches her way into her grief. She goes through the box of trinkets, touches the little hairbrush, the charm bracelet, the ribbons. And suddenly self-pity is replaced by shame. She is ashamed of herself. It's obvious to her now that if anything good is to come out of Abe's death, she must find Cora. She must give her all to the search, go to California herself. She can't hide from it or begin again until she does. But she's so horribly tired, and how can she leave Frances? It's hardly fair.

Frances, noticing the change in Satomi, the worrying way the girl has now of watching her, takes it to be a turn for the worse in her daughter-in-law.

"Satomi, honey, you can't go on like this," she appeals to her. "Asking me all the time if I am better, when it's obvious to me that you are not. You are too young to let your life just drift. You have to think about what you want to do with it."

"I'm fine. Don't worry about me."

But she does worry. It is time for Satomi to go, but she will have to be the one to move her on, Satomi isn't able.

"This isn't what Abe would have wanted for you. It isn't respecting his memory to just fade away, you know?"

"Well, Abe isn't here, is he? He left us, didn't he?" Her voice is shaking, she is furious. It surprises her, she had no idea she was so angry.

In the silence that follows her outburst, they realize they are both angry with Abe, that they have been simmering for months.

"How could he leave us, Frances? How could he do this to us?"

"He didn't do this, honey, it was an accident, we can't help accidents." Frances tries to regain some equilibrium, it's horrible to find herself angry with Abe.

"I know. It was a stupid thing to say. I'm sorry, Frances. I'm going to bed now. I didn't mean that about Abe, of course I didn't."

"Honey, this is what I mean. It's six o'clock. You're sleeping your life away."

Next morning, with her decision made, Frances watches Satomi make a poor breakfast of coffee and a single slice of toast. She watches her absentmindedly push her toast around the plate, leave the coffee to go cold. The look of the girl never fails to surprise her, she is gloriously striking even though she has lost weight and isn't taking care of herself. It's a waste.

She would like to keep Satomi with her, a companion in grief. It would be wicked, though. Satomi has years ahead of her to find someone else to love, to love her. She has held herself back from saying as much for too long. And if she's honest, between them they keep the pot of grief for Abe constantly on the boil, neither willing for the other to heal.

Dear Mr. Rodman,

I believe that Satomi has asked you not to come to Freeport, but I think that she needs you now and I would like you to come.

I don't seem to be able to help her and I don't think that we are good for each other at present. Grief is always stronger in one or the other of us at any given time, so that there are few lighthearted times in this house anymore.

She is sadly lacking family and as far as I can make out you are her only friend in New York. Can you think of what to do for her?

I should warn you that it won't be easy trying to talk her into anything. She can be very stubborn, but I guess you know that.

I feel strongly that you are the one to help her now. I hope that you will understand that I am not trying to get rid of her. I want to do my best for her. I'm convinced that the best is not to be found here in Freeport.

She will be angry that I have contacted you and I feel bad not taking her into my confidence about it, she is not a child, after all. But she would only arrange to be off somewhere if she knew that you were coming, so I must risk her wrath.

I hope that you will come soon.

With warmest wishes,
Frances Robinson

GATHERING

B EING BACK IN Joseph's apartment doesn't bother her. It's nothing more than a staging post to her now. And it's not for long, just time enough to find a home to bring Cora to if that's what's needed.

Frances has offered to deal with the sale of the salt marsh house. There's no point in hanging on to it, and if she is to make a home elsewhere she will need the money.

"It's temporary," Satomi tells Joseph. "So, ground rules: no presents, no outings, no talk of marriage, just friendship."

"Agreed. What's better for us two than friendship?"

"Oh, other fish to fry, Joseph?"

"Possibly."

Joseph has never known her so full of determination, so sure of her agenda. She has made herself known to the Japanese community in her old New York neighborhood, and won't be ignored this time. She has persisted, and some of them on her behalf are looking for Cora too now, writing to their relatives on the West Coast requesting information. And she has joined the Japanese American Citizens League, who are fighting to put right the injustices the Japanese internees have suffered. It's amazing to her that she didn't know they existed outside of the camp before. They had fought for the right of Japanese-Americans to join the military then, and given Haru back his pride. She hopes with their help she can do the same for herself now.

She is entitled to a fairer settlement of her farm, they say. They will help her fight for it. It will be her purpose now to find Cora and be part of that fight.

Frances phones. The salt marsh house has sold.

"So soon, Frances."

"Well, it's a good enough house, Satomi."

She thinks of the airy rooms, the unsullied light, the way it sits so solidly on its patch of earth. She wonders if the washy colors that she and Abe loved are to the new owners' taste. Perhaps it is already returned to the more conventional browns and creams that she and Abe had thought dull. Who, though, could not love the view of those bleach-white marshes, the way the streams braid through them on their way to the ocean? She would have stayed there if she could, if Abe hadn't lingered in every room. One Robinson widow will have to do for Freeport.

"They look like a happy family," Frances says. "Four children, little sweethearts. Oh, and a puppy. That house needs a dog, don't you think?"

"Yes, it's a house meant for joy." She breathes deeply.

"Oh, Sati, I'm sorry. Damn my practicality. I didn't think."

CAPE COD

T HERE HAS BEEN a letter from Dr. Harper. His search has come up with news of a child called Mary who might be their Cora.

Only the tiniest clue, Satomi, so I'm warning about having high hopes. I wait for months for replies to my inquiries, and when I get one there is hardly any information at all. The child is in a Catholic orphanage in Los Angeles, she is of the right age and came to them without papers, and that's about it. It's by no means confirmed to be Cora. I've twice followed this kind of information up without success. It's unlikely, but I'm hoping for third-time lucky. And how many Japanese Marys do you know? It's likely her name was changed to Mary. It's that Catholic thing, claiming people for the Church, naming them after saints. Still, Mary, hardly the most original, is it? No one can verify anything because the child came via another orphanage and no one thought to ask how she ended up there in the first place. I'm waiting for them to send a photograph. I'll be in touch if and when they do.

The news, brief as it is, has astonished her, as though finding Cora had been a fantasy, something she longed for but couldn't quite believe in. She has to agree with Dr. Harper, the chance that it could be Cora is slim, but the thought of it has made her anxious to find a home, to make it ready.

"You can bring her here if you want," Frances had offered.

Satomi knows that she won't. If the child is Cora, she wants to take her to somewhere permanent, somewhere that is forever.

Joseph is unsettled by the news. He thinks of Satomi caring for the child, making a life out of it, giving up her own. Her hopes are up, though, and he can't bear the thought of her being disappointed.

"What are the chances this Mary could be Cora? It's a long shot at best," he warns. "It might not be her, dear girl. You do know that, don't you? We have no idea whether this Mary was even in Manzanar."

"She's an orphan, a Californian Japanese, so she must have been there." She doesn't want Joseph's doubt, she has enough of her own.

"It's possible she's a recent orphan, don't you think?"

"Possible, but if she's not, then she must have been in Manzanar. It was the only camp with an orphanage. Every orphaned West Coast baby, toddler, and child ended up there."

"Extraordinary." Joseph scowls.

"Well, just the threat of those babies," she says. "Who knew what they were capable of?" She had meant to sound sarcastic, but her voice shook as a surge of the old anger surfaced.

She thinks of the children, their dear faces, their names fresh on her tongue. She remembers their characters, the half-feral little boy who was always in trouble for fighting, and the two-year-old slow to speak, whose first word when it came was, *Wait*.

"God, that whole thing, the camps, Cora, it's awful, Sati," Joseph says. "Unfair."

Suddenly she is weeping, haunted by the images in her head. She sees Cora's questioning eyes, Tamura's eyes, she has always thought. She pictures her shy smile, hears her sweet voice. She has let Cora down, not worked hard enough to find her. All through her time with Abe she had let Cora slip. She had indulged herself in happiness, thought it her time, her due. She had played at being an all-American wife, reinventing herself as someone who hardly remembered the suffering in the camp, the people who had meant so much to her. Why had it taken Abe's death to show her how badly she had lost her way?

"I'm going as soon as I hear back from Dr. Harper, Joseph. I'll find us a home, Cora and me, and then I'm going to California."

"What can I do to help?"

"You could send a car to bring Dr. Harper from Lone Pine to Los Angeles."

"I thought a plane, dear girl. A small plane, you know."

"I think he'd like that."

"If it must be by the sea, must be out of the city," Joseph says as they set out from uptown, "Martha's Vineyard is the place." He has a house in mind. A house perfect for Satomi, he thinks, fingering the details in his pocket.

"Why there in particular?"

"Well, you'll like it, that's for sure. And I know people there who will look out for you."

"I don't need people to look out for me."

"Everyone needs people looking out for them, Sati. I don't know why you have to go at all. What's so bad about the city anyway?"

"Oh, apartment buildings, sirens in the night." She is thinking more, though, of where she wants to be rather than where she does not. It's still the East for her, but not the city, not farmland either, somewhere new to make her own.

"I hardly know you these days," Joseph says.

She isn't hiding anymore, doesn't need him to save her from

anything. There is an air of impatience about her, she is on the move. He is the one running to keep up.

He hopes she'll settle for Martha's Vineyard, it's familiar territory, and he can visit her there whenever he wants. He hasn't told her, but he has found a new love, a Russian who claims to be a count, although he hardly believes that. Suddenly he is ready for monogamy, ready to let go of the promise to his father. *I'm like a boy again*, he thinks, *all mouthwatering desire, viewing the world as though it has just been made, thinking everything in life good enough to bottle. Satomi was right. Love is the thing.*

On the Vineyard, Satomi's expectations of it and the house are not met. "I thought this house was made for you." Joseph can't hide his disappointment.

"Well, for one thing, Joseph, I can't afford it."

"Don't let that be a problem, Sati. I can help, you know that."

"You do enough already."

She wants it to be the money from the Freeport house that buys her new home. A gift to her and Cora from Abe.

"It's not for me, far too big," she says, thinking of the atrium that mimics a hotel lobby. The house is full of such pretensions, the atrium, the Cinderella staircase, the high ceilings decorated with overblown plasterwork. And the air in it is stale, sour, lifeless somehow.

"Who lived here before, Joseph?"

"Oh, some old aunt, I expect. It's always some old aunt. These houses don't come up too often. Dead aunt's shoes, you might say."

Outside, the dark waters of Nantucket Sound seem to isolate the island, imprisoning its inhabitants. She had hoped for color, reflection, but the sea looks cinereous, black in parts, as though pools of oil swim just below its surface.

"Might as well be barbed wire," she says as they board the ferry back to the Cape. "Sorry, Joseph, but I can't live here."

"But the Vineyard is charming, everyone says so."

"It's not for me."

A half a mile or so from the small town of Eastham, with a relaxed realtor and details in hand, they view a cedar-shingled cottage that sits on the bay, looking east toward the Atlantic Ocean.

"It's ready to move into," the realtor says. "The owners have moved on."

Satomi smiles. "I can breathe here," she says.

"It's too small," Joseph insists. "A doll's house."

"It's perfect, Joseph. Just the right size for Cora and me, and a spare bedroom for you when you come."

He imagines himself with Leo, his Russian, in the attic bedroom, and smothers a smile. The details promised three spacious bedrooms.

"If you don't mind the ceiling touching your head," he says. "And you would have to shoehorn wardrobes into them."

The cottage is a child's drawing of a house, a broad-framed building with end gables and a chimney right in the center of the steeply pitched roof. It has been built low to withstand the Cape's storms in winter, and to be cool in summer.

There are chalky blue shutters on all but the attic windows, and there's a wooden porch with steps down to the shore. Clumps of beach rose not yet in bloom streak across the sand for as far as the eye can see.

"*Rosa rugosa*," the realtor says. "Grows like a weed around here. Miles of red, in its season."

"Miles of red," Satomi repeats dreamily.

Long ribbons of memory are stirred in her. The plant had grown in Angelina at the roadsides, on bits of scrubland, anywhere that the earth was dry. Tamura had thought it pretty. Aaron had dismissed it as a weed.

She had conjured up a place like this in her imagination moons ago, so that now it feels like coming home. She and the house suit each other.

"Everything could do with a coat of paint," Joseph says, trying not to let his exasperation show.

She nods, although she finds the shabbiness of it rather charming. The house is more than a shelter. You can feel the life in it. Hardy people have lived here, fishing folk, perhaps.

"Whalers, at one time," the realtor says, as if reading her thoughts. "Trawling for right whales."

"How do you spell that?" Joseph's interest is roused.

"Just as it sounds. They were called that because they were right in every way. Big creatures full of baleen, their blubber so thick you could float them in dead. Easier to bring ashore, you see."

Satomi wanders off, leaving Joseph and the realtor talking.

"Leviathans," she hears him say. "Enormous heads. You occasionally see their tail flukes from here. Getting to be a rare sight, though."

Over the sound of the sea, the gulls can be heard impudent in the air. The soft *phut* of an outboard motor churns in the distance. Behind her and farther along the beach, other cottages are scattered about, and behind them an acre or so of woodland, where stringy stands of pitch pine are set among bayberry and beach plum. It's a bare-boned landscape, a monochrome wash. Japanese calligraphy comes to mind, and she adds an imaginary skein of geese, a dark arrow of them in the pale sky.

Promise, she thinks, is thick in the air here, in the vinegar-sharp trace of bramble, the vibrant tang of ozone. Even with the dipping sun hot on her face she can imagine winter here, snow and the spindly trees with their roots gripping the earth as they bend in the wind toward the ocean. It's the edge of the land, the tipping point, where everything holds on tight to its bit of America. The late afternoon light is too pure to be called dusk, it's a moment in time that no one has bothered to name.

Something taut in her is unwinding itself, settling. If home is to be found anywhere, she feels that it is here. Cora, she thinks, will have the bedroom with the faded wallpaper, shells on a flowing seaweed tracery. The light in the room comes from the sea, soft slate with touches of violet. An old paddle fan fixed to the ceiling has a string pull hanging from it, low enough, she thinks, for a child to reach. She will take the room opposite for herself, which, like Cora's, looks out over First Encounter Beach.

"The Indians named it," the realtor says in answer to Joseph's question. "They had their first sighting of the pilgrims on this beach, apparently. Nothing much has changed here since then." He laughs. "Only joking, we're pretty much up to scratch and you hardly see Indians around here anymore." He is thinking movie Indians, the bow-and-arrow kind.

"Well, Cora and I will be like the pilgrims. We will make our home here from scratch. The natives will get used to us."

This perfect house has decided her, she won't wait for a photograph of the child now. She will write to Eriko and Dr. Harper to let them know she is coming. She is counting on Mary being Cora. She must be Cora.

Shivering with the weariness of the insomniac she has become since hearing that Cora might be found, she yields for a moment to a feeling of panic. If it is Cora, how will the child feel about being claimed by her? Chances are she feels let down, double-crossed, even. Maybe Satomi is keeping her promise too late to do either of them any good. If they had guessed Cora's age right in the camp, she will be eight, nearly nine now. She will be different, just as Satomi herself is different. They have made separate journeys, after all.

"Fascinating," she hears Joseph say to the realtor. "Don't you think so, Sati?"

"Mmm." She has no idea what they have been talking about.

"One last look," she says, and turns from them.

Inside the house a more settled feeling overtakes her. It's as though she has already taken possession of it, and it of her. She sits on the box seat in the hall below a row of wooden coat pegs, and listens to the dull crush of the ocean as it runs through the eelgrass and stirs up the shingle at the shore break. Framed by the open door, her view of the water is contained, so that the ocean seems barely wider than a lake. She hadn't known there were so many shades of gray. In the distance the horizon shimmers, a pearly line of pewter tinged with mauve. Such tender colors that her heart begins to ache.

Joseph calls that it's time to go. He is hungry, and wants to try the Nellie's Inn oysters that are famous in these parts. And then they must get back to the city. He will introduce her to Leo, tell her she was right about the promise.

"No need to fret, dear girl," he says. "You have found your home."

PROVIDENCE

In ERIKO'S SMALL but immaculate apartment above her shop, Satomi wonders how it is possible for them to have become so shy with each other. Manzanar had been their territory, of course, the familiar ground they had stood on, yet she had lived seminal years with Eriko, shared Tamura with her, shared too much to ever feel unknown by Eriko.

"I had forgotten how beautiful you are," Eriko says.

Satomi looks out of place in Eriko's family room, a polished not-of-her-world sort of woman. The kind of glamorous woman, Eriko thinks, that you read about rather than know. She even smells expensive. There is nothing visible of the camp girl left in her, not even that look that marks out inmates, the wariness that says it could happen again. The look she notices in her own mirrored reflection each morning.

"You don't sell fabric anymore, Eriko?"

"There's no call for it. People don't dress-make much around here these days."

She is in the work-clothes business now; cheap checkered shirts, thick cotton overalls, and her special line, the felt fedoras ubiquitous among men from the worker up.

"And Naomi's gone." Satomi hardly dares say it. "It's hard to believe. I'm so sorry, Eriko. Dear Naomi, it hurt not to be with you when I heard. I know how hard it is to lose a mother." She puts her arms around Eriko and can't let go. In Eriko's familiar scent, her comforting bulk, she is a child of the camp again.

"It's just me, Eriko. Whatever you see, it's just me," she sobs.

"I know, Satomi. Of course it's you." Eriko is relieved. She touches her hair affectionately. "It was just in the moment, you know. I had you in my mind as you were in Manzanar."

"And Yumi, and Haru?" she asks, finding it hard to swallow.

"Yumi is married. Can you believe it? She is far too young, but she is happy, even though they have no money and there's a baby on the way. Haru teaches in a Japanese school near San Diego. He wants me to join him there, but I can't leave Yumi."

"And he's married?"

"Yes, he is married, Sati."

"Happy?"

"I think so. He works too much for the future, though, to enjoy the present."

"I'm glad for him, Eriko."

"Really, Sati?"

"Yes, really. I can see now that it would never have worked for us. We were children then."

"Well, it seems to me that there's no boy left in him now. He is all duty."

Eriko makes tea, "real tea," she says, and they share a look. They are waiting for Dr. Harper to arrive from the airport, and the thought of seeing him again excites them.

"What will you do if it isn't Cora?" Eriko asks.

"Keep looking until I find her."

"Good girl."

Satomi feels sixteen again, happy to have Eriko's approval.

"And your home, Sati? What is your home like?"

"It's simple, clean, not enough furniture yet. The breeze from the ocean blows through it, front door to back, just like the house I shared with Abe. You would like it, I think. It won't be a home, though, until I have Cora. I need to see her grow up, see her happy to be an American."

"And are you happy with being an American now?"

"You know, I guess I am. But then, it's easier on the East Coast, so many nationalities that I hardly stand out at all. And they seem to have won a different war than the one we fought. People there hardly know about the camps."

"How is that possible?"

"It's unbelievable, isn't it? Quite wrong that they are never spoken of."

"I'm as much to blame as anyone for that, I suppose," Eriko says. "None of the Japanese left around here speak of them much. We are ashamed, I think. Yumi says that she won't tell her children, that there's no point in making them afraid. She wants them to grow up fearless, like Haru."

"But the shame is not ours, Eriko. We must never let it be ours. You should tell Yumi as much."

They pause for a moment in their talk, both thinking of Yumi as the child she was in the camp, plump and naughty, one of the new breed of disobedient daughters.

"I miss your mother still," Eriko says. "She is the one I miss most in life."

She leads Satomi downstairs to the shop, which has a CLOSED sign on its door. The air there smells of felt and disinfectant.

"Roaches everywhere," Eriko says. "Just like Manzanar."

"We should keep a lookout for Dr. Harper." Satomi goes to the window. "He is a stranger to this district."

"It was brave of you to come alone," Eriko says. "And flying too"

She hadn't wanted Joseph to come with her. Cora doesn't

know him, after all, it will be enough that Satomi is there with
Eriko and Dr. Harper.

In any case, Joseph is caught up with Leo, and hates, these days,
to be parted from him for long. It turns out that Leo is a count
after all, the genuine article. He is new to the city but has found
old friends among his fellow émigrés in New York, and has been
embraced by the Russian Nobility Association. According to Joseph, new blue blood is rare, and is to be feted among his fellow
exiles.

"We are a novelty," he says. "The latest distraction."

She has never seen him less cynical, or so openly happy.

"We are always at some ball or other," he says. "There are at
least a hundred dates that must be celebrated with the most extravagant parties that you can imagine. Anything and everything
demands a celebration, Peter the Great's victory at Poltava, Go-
gol's birth, Romanovs visiting from Spain, things I never knew
about before Leo. It's quite extraordinary."

Russian nobility, it seems, has the good manners not to pry
into their friendship, their particular arrangement.

"We dance with the girls for form's sake," Joseph says. "But the
truth is that I'm the nearest thing that Leo is going to get to an
heiress.

She is relieved not to feel responsible for Joseph's happiness
anymore. Leo is a good match for him, an artist at heart, and the
most perfect of traveling companions. Maybe among the disposed
Russians Joseph will at last find a place where he can settle.

"And you, Sati," Eriko breaks into her thoughts. "You have
been married and widowed since I last saw you. It seems astonishing to me."

"Oh, Eriko, I wish you could have known Abe."

"So many gone." Eriko sighs. "To lose your man so young."
She reaches out and pulls Satomi to her.

The tears that come are nothing like those she had shed in the months after Abe's death. They fall warm and soft, without the accompanying urge to howl.

"I took a strange journey after Manzanar, Eriko. My mother would have loved Abe, but she wouldn't have approved of my choices before he came along."

"Maybe, but I never heard her judge anyone. Tamura understood how life can overtake you."

Dr. Harper has been counting the days since the letter from Satomi came. And now the time is here, he is on his way and will see for himself the circle completed. He is hopeful now that the child is Cora. The photo that came is grainy, blurred at the edges, showing a shy-looking girl, older than the Cora he remembers, of course, but something in her stance seems familiar to him. He is ashamed to discover that in their dark-eyed, soft-featured prettiness, all Japanese children's faces look alike to him. He imagines that all white, gray-haired old men look the same to them too. It's no comfort.

His records of Manzanar are packed in boxes, piled up in his garage, ready to send to Satomi when she is finally settled. His heart has been rocking a bit lately, giving him a warning or two. He suspects that if he hoards his little archive for much longer, it will end up as kindling for his wife's fire when he is gone.

It's an unconventional documentation, he knows, a strange collection, but telling all the same. The time is surely coming when the Japanese will fight for compensation, when they will insist on the longed-for apology. He is convinced that Satomi's spirit, her strong open heart, will make her part of that fight.

He asks the cabdriver to stop across the street from Eriko's shop. He needs a minute or two to compose himself. The journey from Lone Pine in the single-engine plane had been something he had looked forward to as eagerly as a boy, but the excitement of it has stirred old ambitions, present regrets. Looking down on the landscape as the little craft battled the wind, seeing woods and rivers, a tiny dot of a boat on the ocean, he was filled with self-reproach. He should have done more with his life, had adventures, been braver.

He watches the women behind the window talking animatedly, waiting for him to come, two where there should be three. It's strangely hurtful. He feels like sitting down on the sidewalk and weeping. Oh, why couldn't Tamura be there waiting too? He shakes his head, takes out a handkerchief to dab at his moist eyes. His recently acquired varicose veins thump uncomfortably in his legs. He hates the look of the raised blue tracks that run along his white liver-spotted skin. He can't remember when he last looked at himself with any satisfaction. His wife is right, he is vain for his age.

To his old man's eyes Satomi looks the same. Eriko is only a little fuller, her dark hair streaked with gray now, that's to be expected, after all. It's good to see them in the real world, good to have Manzanar behind them. Since they left, the place has reverted to wasteland, a picked-over plot he averts his eyes from when driving past.

It had been awful seeing off the last of Manzanar's inhabitants, the old ones who had to be forced out. Painful to observe the women watching their homes demolished, and the old men wondering how they were meant to provide now, how they could feel proud of anything. He thinks that there are too many kinds of impotency to wound men.

And to add insult, those awful lectures, compulsory, so that it was hard to feel like the free men they were told they were now. Inmates, it was insisted, must learn how to behave in the outside world, how to get along with their fellow Americans. The sermons had done little to ease their bewilderment. Having suffered the loss of everything that had been theirs before incarceration, they had wept at their separation from the known. Those old boys were a lost tribe he couldn't feel optimistic for, no matter how much he tried.

It was astounding to him to read that some in the House of Representatives were still angling for their repatriation to Japan. It made him sick with shame. He wrote as much to them, but they never replied.

It's a joyful reunion, a hug for Satomi, a clasping of hands with Eriko.

"It's been too long," Dr. Harper says. "And so much has happened, especially to you, Satomi."

She smiles at him, registering the tremble in his hands, noting that his eyes are a little paler than she remembers, his step slower. She wonders how many times she will see him again, and it comes to her that she loves John Harper. That he means too much to her to let his work be forgotten. She puts her arms around him, lays her head on his shoulder for a moment.

"I'm ready for it now. Send me your archive," she says softly. "I won't let it go to waste. I promise."

Of course, she and Tamura and their kind were not the only victims of the war. There are victims of all kinds all over the world, she knows. Yet still she feels there is a need for justice, for someone to admit that at worst the incarceration had been a wicked betrayal, at best senseless. She doesn't want to see the Japanese inmates' story cleaned up, rewritten, as she and Tamura had rewritten Aaron's story. She wants to be part of the reconciliation, to be around for the longed-for apology. She may never escape her ghosts, but her memories are lighter now and she is healing, she knows.

"We should go," Dr. Harper says. "Put an end to Cora's waiting."

———

The Sisters of Charity are housed in a three-story red-brick building. There are bars at the windows, no curtains, smudges on the glass. The place looks shabby, halfhearted, uninviting.

The three of them pause in front of the rusty playground gates as if by order, and Satomi pushes the bell, which immediately creates a hissing of white noise.

"Yes?"

"It's Dr. Harper and Mrs. Robinson," Dr. Harper says in the strongest voice he can muster. Since his school days he has felt uneasy around the religious. When he was young it had to do with guilt for his boyhood sins, he supposes. Now he thinks it's most likely the fear of a day of reckoning.

"Come through the yard and ring the visitors' bell on the front door. Someone will come for you."

Satomi is the first to enter the bitumen quadrangle. She takes a deep breath and sends Eriko an anxious smile. In place of flowers, litter is caught up in the tufts of needlegrass that grow at the base of the high wire fencing enclosing the playground.

"To keep the children from the road," Eriko says quickly, as if to reassure Satomi. "At least it doesn't turn in at the top."

They are all thinking of the fencing at Manzanar, and look around nervously as though seeking gun towers, guards. A chalked map of hopscotch on the ground is fading under the sun. Garbage cans are lined up against the building, spilling over with refuse.

"It's horrible, horrible," Satomi says, feeling the sweat pooling under her arms and in the palms of her hands. The awful realization that Cora may be here feeling, herself forgotten, panics her.

"It's not so bad, is it, Eriko?" Dr. Harper says. "The street is nice enough."

"No, it's not bad at all," Eriko says. "Not bad at all."

"She's as fenced in here as she was at Manzanar," Satomi says, not willing to be comforted.

Whenever she had thought of finding Cora, her imaginings had been kinder than the sight of this place. They had included lawns and flowers, trees to shade the child from the sun. She realizes now with shame that they were nothing but pretty pictures, good only for soothing herself.

There is a choice of bells on the black-painted door, a foot-high polished brass crucifix nailed to it. Satomi pushes the VISITORS bell and hears a faint ringing from deep in the house's interior. It reminds her of the one in Mr. Beck's lodgings.

Inside, on the checkered linoleum that runs the length of a narrow hall, so narrow that they have to walk in a line one behind the other, they file behind a nun, who has not spoken, only indicated that they should follow her. Something soapy sticks to the soles of their shoes as they walk, making them squeak. There's a sickly scent of cheap beeswax, the trace of past meals in the air.

"It smells like the mess halls," Eriko whispers.

"Institutional," Dr. Harper says. "Mess halls, hospitals, they all smell the same."

In the Mother Superior's large and comfortable office, Sister Amata, a fluttery sort of woman in a brown habit, who coos somewhat like a pigeon, is sent to find Mary.

"She doesn't know you are coming," she says excitedly as she leaves the room.

The Reverend Mother too is a pale bird of a woman, hawk-nosed, with small brown eyes that Satomi fancies are seeking out quarry. But when she speaks, her voice is soft, her stance kind.

"She has no idea that you have been in touch," she tells them. "She may not be the right one, your one. She came without papers from an orphanage that was being demolished. They called her Coral there, but she could have been Cora, I suppose. Coral did not seem to us a suitable name, and we wished to spare her teasing, so we named her Mary. On the whole she is a helpful child, but she doesn't speak much, and is subject to temper tantrums at times."

Satomi wants to yell, *Of course she is. How could she not be?* The cost to Cora of being left, unloved, she is sure has been a terrible one. But a sudden dread stops her from speaking. Her chest feels heavy, her mouth dry as ash.

"Was she originally at Manzanar?" Dr. Harper asks, anxious now that he has projected Cora into the blurry photo, glad that he had decided against showing it to Satomi.

"I have no idea. I've never heard her speak of it."

"So you have never asked her about the camp? Never wanted to know about her life before she came here?" Satomi, finding her voice, can't keep the criticism out of it.

"No, we have been advised not to talk to the children about the camps. The Japanese children here are in the minority, it would set them apart from their fellows. In any case, all that's better forgotten, don't you think? The important thing here is that we are all Catholics, children of God."

The Reverend Mother finds herself hoping that her Mary is not their Cora. If she is, she will not, she thinks, be brought up in the faith. And after all, it's not as if they have a blood claim on the child. But the promise of Joseph Rodman's astonishingly generous check if she is the child they are looking for is surely a gift from God, a benediction. They could expand, take more children, build a schoolhouse, the possibilities are endless.

And the Mother House, their spiritual home is expecting to receive a good portion of the money. It is only through donations, after all, that the order survives, that it can fulfill its calling in the world, where there is so much human misery to alleviate. One small child in exchange for so much, how can she say no? Mary's soul is not in the balance, after all. Their bishop, on hearing that the child may have found a home, had hurried to confirm her in the faith so that her soul is already saved. And the Blessed Virgin Mary, the child's namesake, has her in her sights.

"We have given the children extra playtime in honor of your visit," Sister Amata trills on her return. You will be able to see Mary at play, make your decision without the child knowing."

In the yard the children dart about. Their cries are distracting and it takes time for Satomi to start singling out the girls one from another. Some of them are at hopscotch, some skipping, but Satomi hardly looks at them. She thinks that Cora will be standing alone, indulging in the lonely child's habit of watching, but she is nowhere to be seen.

"She's there, right there." Eriko grasps Satomi's hand and points out Cora, who is next up to play hopscotch.

Dr. Harper and Eriko are smiling, there's no mistaking that it's Cora. She hasn't grown that much, legs a little longer, and her hair too, but she is still a narrow child, small for her age, pretty as ever.

At the sight of her, Satomi draws in her breath, her hand flies to her mouth, tears stab in her eyes. There's no mistaking that it's Cora, and she can't quite believe it. She finds herself yearning for Tamura. That blue-black hair, the girlishness, the bow perched as precariously on her head as one of Tamura's hats.

"Oh, Cora, little Cora."

After all her imaginings of running to the child, their joyful reunion, she is suddenly afraid, can't seem to move. Sister Amata puts her hand on Satomi's shoulder and propels her forward.

"It's her, isn't it?" she says, and Satomi nods.

Slowly, as one by one the children stop to watch the visitors, Satomi moves toward Cora.

"It's Satomi, Cora. Do you remember me?" She is trembling, her voice not her own.

Cora takes a step backward, hangs her head, and looks at the ground.

"No," she says quietly.

"From Manzanar, Cora. I'm Tamura's daughter. Your friend. You know me, Cora."

Cora has pictures in her head of the camp, of Tamura and Eriko, and especially of Satomi. They are, she thinks, the people of her dreams, the people she suspects she has made up. It's scary to see them now in the flesh, not knowing what they have come for.

"You will have to forgive me for taking so long to come," Satomi says. "I'm sorry, Cora, so very sorry."

She longs to kiss the child's sweet tilting lips, hug her to herself, but she doesn't want to frighten her.

"I want to take you home with me, Cora. We have a lovely house to share. We will be like sisters. Will you come with me?"

Cora doesn't answer; she just stands staring at Satomi, her body swaying a little, her hands clasped tightly together.

"Speak up, Mary," Sister Amata says. "You must answer the lady."

"Don't hurry her," Satomi snaps. "Give her time."

Cora narrows her eyes, she is thinking, figuring things out. She recalls now her time on a bus, the way she had watched Satomi standing in the dust, waving and crying. And now Satomi is crying again, it's strange to see a grown-up crying. Satomi's not her mother, but she knows now she belongs to her in some way, some good way.

"Do you remember me?" Eriko can't resist.

Cora looks at her and nods. Splashes of memory are filling her head. She does know Eriko somehow. Even the man with the white hair is familiar. She remembers rooms made from wood, she remembers playing in the dust and the glimmer of kindling burning in a stove. It's all connected with the things that she keeps in a bundle under her bed. She gives a faint smile, then turns suddenly and runs back into the house.

"I'll go," Sister Amata says, raising her hand in a gesture for them to stay where they are. "She is frightened, I think."

But before she reaches the house, Cora comes flying out the door, rushing past her. Her face is flushed, she is excited.

"I have it," she says to Satomi. "I have it here."

The little wooden titmouse sits in the middle of her open palm, rocking as though it is breathing. Silence gathers as they all stare down at it. Dr. Harper is the first to move; he reaches out, gently touching its wing, connecting himself for a moment to Tamura.

"You have it, Cora," Satomi whispers. "You have our sweet bird."

Cora puts her hand into Satomi's. "You're real," she says. "I thought that you were from a story."

Satomi takes Cora's hand and turns toward the gate. She is thinking of their white-shingled home, where there is fresh linen on the beds and there are puzzles and dolls waiting for Cora, cookies in big glass jars, and the shiny brown chocolate box with its trinkets of hope.

Tamura would have approved of the dresses hung behind the door in Cora's bedroom. Against her own taste, she has bought the prettiest she could find. And best of all there are books, *Gulliver's Travels*, *Anne of Green Gables*, *Heidi*, stories to nourish the child's soul.

Cora will play at the edge of the ocean in the clean air, with the water licking her feet. She will collect shells and ammonite pebbles, make sand castles. And she will run shrieking from the scuttling crabs, hear the whales sounding out in the bay. There is still enough of childhood left to turn the tide.

And for herself, whiskey in the kitchen cupboard, fresh-ground coffee, the big-bellied stove that works like a dream, and no shortage of wood. If happiness can be willed, she will set herself to the task, make it hers and Cora's.

She will open Dr. Harper's archive boxes and go through them with Cora. They will relive their life at Manzanar together, so that Cora will know her own life's journey.

She will make an index of the archive, write her own story of the camp, and, when the time is right, show it to the world. And surely the time will be right soon. So much depends on good timing.

She thinks of the sea at the Cape, the way it laces itself around the caterpillar of land at Eastham, turning at its end in the shape of a question mark. And the East, she thinks, is the place, the place where Pilgrims landed, where seasons have their time, where the sun rises.

ACKNOWLEDGMENTS

It is such a pleasure to thank all the friends and colleagues who have helped me with the writing of *A Girl Like You*.

My heartfelt thanks go to my editor, Alexandra Pringle, for thinking me worth the risk, and for sticking with me through the difficult times. And thank you to Erica Jarnes at Bloomsbury UK, for her insightful suggestions and calming presence. I am grateful to Nikki Baldauf, Lea Beresford, and Dave Cole from Bloomsbury USA for a great job in overseeing the American production of the book.

So many thanks to the talented Gillian Stern for her outstanding guidance. Gillian gives 100 percent at all times, as well as a master class in "less is more." I'm grateful to my agent, Robert Caskie, who saw the potential of the story in the brief outline I presented him with, and enthusiastically took it to Bloomsbury. May he always be so successful. As always my thanks go to Clive Lindley, for his invaluable advice, his knowledge, and his generous help. I would like to thank Roy Kakuda from the Japanese American National Museum in Los Angeles, a child of the camps, who shared his time and memories with me. I am indebted to Richard Gregson for his invaluable help with the first draft. Thank you to Jenny Clifford for Oahu cemetery. Those others who helped with read-throughs, with research and in so many helpful ways, were Lucy Dundas, Isabel Evans, and the ever encouraging "shedettes." I would also like to thank Trina Middlecote for keeping the technology working.

A NOTE ON THE AUTHOR

MAUREEN LINDLEY was born in Berkshire and grew up in Scotland. Having worked as a photographer, antique dealer and dress designer, she eventually trained as a psychotherapist. Her first novel, *The Private Papers of Eastern Jewel*, was published in 2009. She lives in the Wye Valley on the Welsh borders with her husband.

Accounting Theory
Integrating behaviour and measurement

Accounting Theory

Integrating behaviour and measurement

Sven-Erik Johansson
Lars Östman

Stockholm School of Economics

PITMAN PUBLISHING
128 Long Acre, London WC2E 9AN

A Division of Pearson Professional Limited

First published in Great Britain in 1995

© Sven-Erik Johansson and Lars Östman 1995

British Library Cataloguing in Publication Data
A CIP catalogue record for this book can be obtained from the British Library

ISBN 0 273 60512 7

10 9 8 7 6 5 4 3 2 1

Typeset by Avocet Typeset, 19 Church St., Brill, Aylesbury, Bucks.
Printed and bound by Clays Ltd, St Ives Plc.

The Publishers' policy is to use paper manufactured from sustainable forests.

CONTENTS

PREFACE

This book has its origins in a long collaboration between the authors. For many years we have shared the responsibility for research and tuition in the field of accounting and managerial finance at the Stockholm School of Economics. We have also shared an interest in the integration of external (financial) accounting and internal (management) accounting, focusing on the use of accounting information and its effects on the behaviour of the user. Accounting measures are used to a large extent as a basis for judgements and decisions on the financing and the financial planning of an enterprise. The players of the financial markets make extensive use of such information. Thus, the areas of accounting and managerial finance are by their very nature closely related.

In our view empirically based knowledge and experience of accounting systems and of the use and the users of accounting reports are very important. Our own research and the research we have initiated have had an empirical orientation to a large extent. We have both had the great privilege of many insights into the practical side of accounting. In Sweden shareholders may appoint a lay auditor to supplement the professional auditor (auditing firm) of their company, and we have acted as lay auditors for many years in companies from many different industries. This has given us a ring-side seat for observing management behaviour. We have also a long experience of teaching on executive courses and seminars where informal discussions with the participants have been very rewarding in terms of insights into the use and users of accounting information. In addition we have both been appointed Swedish accounting standards setters and have worked with a Swedish credit rating agency. Our common background in terms of practical experience has contributed to the development of a shared view on the use and usefulness of accounting measures.

Our areas of research differ with regard to emphasis on certain subject areas. Lars Östman's research has been focused mainly on behavioural accounting while Sven-Erik Johansson has been more oriented towards the basic theories of valuation and the measurement problems related to rate of return on capital, consolidated statements and inflation accounting. As a consequence Lars Östman has the main responsibility for Part One and Part Three and Sven-Erik Johansson for Part Two. We share the responsibility for the book as a whole.

This book will be of interest to researchers, to producers and users of accounting information and to graduate students of accounting. The book is not presented as a formal research report, although it is based on research findings to a considerable extent. We have also utilized our own – sometimes rather unsystematic – observations to achieve the main goal, i.e. to present a broad view on accounting and an approach integrating financial and management accounting as well as measurement and behavioural analysis. As the reader will find, this approach means that we cover most aspects of accounting. It would not be possible, therefore, to report and make references

analytical rigour is at risk, at least in the long term. This may affect how resources are allocated and used. Firms' endeavours to achieve economic efficiency and the way economic efficiency is measured are fundamental forces in a society. At the same time, the effects of accounting and economic information are not necessarily favourable, at least not to everybody and in all respects.

In an attempt to throw light on the problem, there are good reasons for going back to the basic questions. What are the essential functions and real effects of accounting information, in a firm and in a society? What factors affect the actual content of the information? What conclusions ought to be drawn, when systems are designed or individual values interpreted? Are any measures concerning a firm and its components of general relevance, regardless of the specific effects those parties and individuals are aiming at? If so, what are the measures? Does a greater emphasis on the potential effects mean that analytical rigour is lost, causing negative repercussions on firms and society? If so, how can this be avoided?[1]

Whether there will ever be *one* single and fairly complete theory covering the use, effects and design of accounting information, and what practical guidance such a theory might give is debatable. However, broad perspectives are needed to design, interpret and evaluate accounting information. In addition, a theoretical approach is required, where effects in a broad sense are considered, together with fundamental measurement principles of a traditional type. Our aim is to take one step in this direction. There is little point, in this context, in regarding the internal and external uses of accounting information as two separate phenomena.

In order to analyse the relevant measures, our starting point has been to examine the functions of such measures, the probable behaviour of information users and the probable effects. We have tried to focus on behaviour that has been observed, rather than on rationalistic assumptions. Paradoxes about the role of information are easily found, at least at a superficial level. For example, whilst, it is argued that traditional accounting measures are not particularly important in financial markets due to legal conventions, senior management apparently pay considerable attention to what figures are actually reported to the public. Further, whilst players within a firm are very keen to achieve what are regarded as satisfactory levels for the measure used (a strong driving force for profit centre managers, for example), they are not always particularly aware of how these measures are constructed.

This book starts, therefore, with the idea that accounting information, above all, should be instrumental in meeting demands for economic efficiency, in the broadest sense, both in firms and in society. It analyses how the claims of owners and lenders can be formulated, how public information can be drawn up and interpreted with this in mind, and how internal systems can affect the efficiency of the firm in a broad sense so that external claims can also be satisfied. Demands on the firm derived from the owners' claims represent a minimum threshold requirement for the firm – often, the inability to meet such claims poses a financial threat to the firm and its employees. We must deal with how measures and targets for various objects (e.g. business units, functions and products) relate to one another, as well as the aggregate effects of all economic and accounting information about the firm. The relations between external claims and internal intentions are one important area. How, for instance, could purely financial measures be imposed on the production of services, which are themselves almost impossible to measure, without any undesirable, damaging effect on the quality of those services?

Thus the main aims of the book are the following:

1 *To treat all kinds of information related to the economic efficiency of the firm within one coherent totality.* Financial accounting, management accounting, product costing and capital budgeting are instruments for solving the same general efficiency and resource allocation problems. There is much to be said for deeper analysis of the similarities and dissimilarities between these various instruments and of the total effect of these instruments, all of which in fact serve similar purposes. In theoretical literature, the various fields – financial accounting, management accounting, capital budgeting, traditional corporate finance and recent finance theory based on economic theory – have had their own separate development, albeit with some overlap. The interdependencies are apparent; an analysis of information and control issues within a single coherent framework could be an important supplement to development within each separate field.

2 *To point out the similarities between internal and public information systems more clearly than has commonly been the case in the past.* In the authors' experience many of the fundamental measurement problems are similar, irrespective of specific use. Therefore, we do not make a basic distinction between 'financial' and 'management' accounting, nor between 'external' and 'internal'. Some information is internal in the sense that it is available to players within the firm. Part of this information will become public. The emphasis which is to be attached to information that becomes public is an open question in internal control systems. The interdependencies between what could be labelled 'internal' and 'external' systems are often strong; in the authors' experience increasingly strong. Objectives of achieving publicly published goals naturally determine what is emphasized internally; what is meaningful information internally, on the other hand, is often relevant to an external user. The borderline between what is external and internal use has also become less clear: employees at various levels acquire shares and options in the firms in which they work, sometimes because senior management want to create incentives for employees.

3 *To base our discussion of measurement principles upon a well-founded concept of organizational roles and effects of accounting measures.* Behavioural approaches and analyses of measurement problems are not normally considered together. Traditional accounting literature mostly builds on rationalistic and fairly general assumptions about firms'

objectives and individuals' behaviour. It has proved difficult to arrive at solutions to specific design issues on such a general basis; the Financial Accounting Standards Board's 'general frameworks' project may serve as an example. On the other hand, as a research field, 'behavioural accounting' has produced valuable research findings on the functions and effects of accounting measures in firms and society; behaviourally oriented and process-oriented studies on accounting are no longer uncommon. Links with measurement problems have mostly been weak, however.

4 *To give weight both to the firm as a organizational unit and to the owners/lenders.* Microeconomics-based financial theory has often given a very strong ownership perspective, or at least a market perspective, to the activities of firms and has given an inadequate picture of organizational life. Conversely, literature on management control has often had such a strong emphasis on an internal organizational perspective, that external claims from owners and lenders are hardly visible at all. A realistic and more complete analysis of accounting information requires that all these perspectives are considered simultaneously.

5 *To emphasize the rates of return required by owners and lenders but, at the same time, to consider the effects of firms' activities from a broader perspective* (which partly follows from the points above). The objective functions of financial theory models often mean that share values should be maximized as a step towards rational resource allocation in society. Conclusions founded on this basis have also proved to be of some direct practical value. However, in general, they represent a limited perspective, which must be combined with other perspectives if problems of average complexity are to be solved. The stumbling block in many complex information and control problems may often lie in the merging and balancing of different perspectives just as much as in the analysis of each individual problem within a particular isolated and narrow framework. Theorectical models existing within narrow frameworks are seldom sufficient to explain actual choice of information or to develop information systems.

Throughout the book, description of the use and the effects of accounting take precedence over analysis of design. As mentioned above, we try to represent 'observed behaviour'. One essential aspect of this is traditional empirical description both of our own observations and those of others. The book is based on observations over many years in processes in which we have participated, for instance, as consultants or standard setters. Scientifically based description is insufficient and incomplete for the general framework provided here. With regard to the nature of descriptions, a relatively limited number of very important sources has been preferred to an extensive list of references.

Of course, this book must be read with this background in mind. The descriptions of the use of accounting may, to a large extent, be regarded as soundly based hypotheses. As a whole, priority has been given to breadth rather than depth; many areas are covered very broadly. Certain aspects are included more in the interests of presenting a total picture rather than as a result of their intrinsic value. One example is the chapter on financial markets (Chapter 4).

The book consists of three parts.

- *Part One, Accounting information – its use and design*, opens with a general description of the use of accounting information, both publicly and internally (Chapter 2), followed by a general analysis of the basic criteria of good measures and a further presentation of the book's approach (Chapter 3). One of the main ideas of the book is that accounting measures and their required levels should be integrated with the valuation models applied in the financial markets, and so the rates of return required from the owners' and lenders' point of view are described in Chapter 4. The functions and the content of public accounting information systems (Chapter 5) and of internal accounting information systems (Chapter 6) are also discussed. Part One concludes that traditional accounting measures have important advantages from a control point of view after all, not least as regards return on capital. The ability to make comparisons between accounting numbers and reference levels is perhaps the most important element in the use of accounting information. Thus, comparability is a major problem when accounting systems are designed or individual data are interpreted, both externally and internally.

- *Part Two, Traditional return on capital – its importance and limitations for comparative purposes.* The main theme of Part Two follows on rather naturally from the conclusions drawn in Part One. After introducing some principal ideas (Chapter 7), we discuss the use and limitations of traditional periodic measures, first under non-inflationary conditions and then under inflationary conditions (Chapters 8 and 9 respectively). We especially analyse the information value of adjustments for changes in general price levels and specific prices. The substance of such adjustments is more a background for the interpretation of traditional accounting information, than for the design of measures. We then use inflation accounting concepts to analyse relationships between required rate of return levels, product pricing and alternative concepts of income and return on capital (Chapter 10). The final area covered by Part Two concerns control problems due to difficulties in co-ordinating accounting information for a group and its subsidiaries (Chapter 11).

- *Part Three, The information needs of a firm and its components*, describes a coherent system of measures and their required levels for the following important business entities and components: the self-sustained firm, business units, functional units, products and capital investment projects. When information systems are specified, or given data are interpreted in a professional manner, there is a need for some idea about what the characteristics of good information are and how the different methods relate to each other. The system described in Part Three can play this role as regards information needs shared by many parties interested in a firm and its components. Measures and their required levels are described in a general way for each type of business entity and component with emphasis on how various forms of requirements relate to each other. After an introduction to the principal ideas (Chapter 12), we discuss business units (Chapter 13), independent firms (Chapter 14), functional units (Chapter 15), products (Chapter 17) and capital investment projects (Chapter 18). Chapter 16 provides an extended analysis of the profit responsibility concept.

Broad perspectives are needed to interpret and evaluate accounting numbers and financial information. This book tries to present *one* such view, and aims at least to draw attention to the need for such overall pictures to supplement analysis of individual problems.

NOTE

[1] There has been some interest in fundamental questions of a related kind in recent years. Important examples are the Financial Accounting Standards Board's work on 'conceptual framework' in the financial accounting field and Johnson, H. T. and Kaplan, R. S., *Relevance Lost: The Rise and Fall of Management Accounting* (1987), which is about internal systems.

PART I

Accounting information – its use and design

CHAPTER 2

The use of accounting information

Financial measures are a fundamental part of information about firms and their components. Some are based on various accounting conventions, such as historical cost and the convention of prudence. Others are computed in accordance with economic theory and the opportunity cost concept. All financial measures fulfil important functions in governance processes at different levels in a society. Realistic insights into what these functions are and how they work in practice are essential for the design of measures and interpretation of their values. In this chapter we try to provide such a basis for a discussion about public and internal information.[1]

OVERVIEW

Economic efficiency in some sense is essential for all societies and organizations, i.e. utility of output must be reasonable in relation to the sacrifice involved in the resources expended. To support this, therefore, the effects and usefulness of output have to be identified and evaluated, and this judgement should in turn affect resource allocation, which determines the scale-setting and orientation of various activities. An aid to operational efficiency is also needed, i.e. a study of how output and sacrifices relate to each other within the frameworks chosen. The information is functional from the perspective of a certain economic system if it is instrumental to the economic efficiency of that system. In the reverse case, it is dysfunctional.

Corporate governance in a market-oriented society mostly takes the form of financial control through markets. This means that those who are able to satisfy payment claims can survive; a long-term condition is competitive products that provide revenue. Central planning, in a society or in a firm, means that a central power has the right to make corresponding decisions. Most in-dividuals aim at some kind of economic efficiency even without the aid of any formal control system, i.e. their intention is that their own acts and those of others should lead to some degree and some form of economic efficiency. Information may strengthen and direct this behaviour. In a firm, information may support internal intentions as well as external demands. We define economic governance processes as actions related to the design and use of information concerning economic efficiency. Important factors when information is used in this context are:

- the interrelationships between analysis and action,
- the handling of uncertainty,
- the importance of reference levels, and
- the processes of faith and loyalty.

Information is not only used as an analytical tool for decision-making.

oriented society takes the form of financial control through markets: those who are able to satisfy payment claims are able to survive; a long-term condition for this is competitive product lines that produce revenues.

There is also a central body in a market economy – the state – but its ability to exercise control is debatable. The instruments of that body are administrative systems such as laws and other rules, and financial systems, including taxes, fees and transfers of funds. In this way, representatives of the state set the rules for processes in both vertical and horizontal directions.

A market economy may induce formal sub-optimization from the point of view of society, for example because the cost to a firm is not necessarily identical to the cost to society. Costs that are important and controllable at society level may not affect the individual firm at all. On the other hand, costs that are fixed at society level may, in the short run, correspond to variable costs for a firm The risks of sub-optimization must be balanced against the advantages of a market system; in particular, with respect to the following:

- *The possibility of surveying the situation.* Very complex decision problems are divided into more manageable sub-problems.
- *The customer orientation.* Production is directed towards what customers are expected to pay for and hence for which they express preferences.
- *The incentive structures.* Income from previous periods directly conditions the financial future of the unit, which is important; this also often applies to economic incentives for individuals.

The fundamental choice between the two allocation mechanisms – market system or central planning – and analyses of the characteristics, have proved relevant not only for a society's economic system, but also for management control within firms. In recent decades, it has been very common for firms to be divided into profit centres, i.e. areas of responsibility for which requirements are formulated in terms of accounting measures such as income and return on capital. This is an internal form of financial control; cash flows and measures in financial terms are guiding devices.

The main idea behind profit responsibility is that profit centre managers should be given relatively wide authority. Their position should in many ways be similar to that of managers of self-sustained firms, especially as regards current operations. The delegation of authority is intended to have several positive effects. First, it is difficult for senior management to be knowledgeable enough about all the issues, especially in large firms; delegation means that each profit centre manager can handle a more manageable area. Second, delegation means that at least managers just below senior management level have greater scope for action and presumably more motivating tasks than they would otherwise have. This facilitates the recruitment of competent, qualified staff.

To what extent, therefore, can pseudo-market rules be applied as a part of internal management control? In principle, the relevant pros and cons are the same at both society and corporate levels. Their relative importance, however, is affected by level, since an individual, coherent firm is more controllable than a national social system. At the level of the firm, senior management is a central power with clear responsibility for a limited whole; the prospect for reasonable overview and for intervention are relatively good. In a society, however, there are an enormous number of active units and individuals; furthermore, the more complex trade-offs between different goals are not connected to an organizational whole in the same way.

2.1.2 External demands on organizations

As separate units, all organizations are dependent on the financial resources they can access, either through their earning capacity or grants. They are separated from their principals in different ways. As a result of that, the kinds of sources which are accessible to them also vary. In reality, an economy contains organizations with varying needs to comply with pure market requirements. For example:

Firms registered on a stock exchange

With these firms in principle, all transactions occur under market conditions. For this type of firm, self-generated earnings determine survival. Besides being a source of finance in themselves, self-generated funds are also a basis for shareholder expectations about future returns on the stock and hence for the availability of funds from this market. They are also the basis for creditworthiness. Working under the constraints of self-generated earnings, the board and the senior management of a firm can decide the business orientation and the level of financial risk at their own discretion. In this sense, the firm has its autonomy in the business areas as well as the financial sphere.

Many owners of such registered firms hold their shares for purely financial reasons. In principle, they act according to financial logic; they aim for the optimum combination of risk and return. The basis of such return is the cash flow from the firm from which they benefit.

These firms have two external governance mechanisms affecting their activity:

● market mechanisms: the need to comply with the demands made by financial markets and product and resource markets, and
● instruments of the central authority, the government.

In practice, market-oriented solutions thus deviate from the conditions of a pure market model. For a market economy to function, firms must generate sufficient equity on market terms to be able to bear the risks associated with their activity. For systems in actual use, one of the most essential questions is whether society and market conditions really allow this to happen.

State and
municipal
organizations

These are, typically, dependent on allowances, e.g. through budgeting processes. Representatives of the owners' interest judge the quality of output and resources spent, as well as the need for resources for the future. Individual decisions about activity orientation are thus, to a large extent, directly connected to financing decisions which determine scale-setting.

The prime interest of the ultimate 'owners' is that certain socially motivated services are carried out in an efficient way. Elected and employed representatives look after this interest. Essentially, they act according to a political logic with regard to decision processes and priorities. They judge the urgency of various tasks and allow funds to be utilized for relatively restricted purposes.

Family-owned
firms

Certain organizations have neither access to the equity market nor do they have access to periodic resources through a budgeting process. Family firms are one major group in which the owners' intentions and capacities determine how financial resources are supplied and withdrawn. Owners of such companies in particular, but also major shareholders in listed companies, may have decisive non-financial motives which go back to their views on the role of the firm and the family in society.

Co-operative
firms

These organizations supply goods and services to their owners, for whom these products are of direct use in a professional activity or their private lives. They lack important external sources of finance. The goals of the owners as a group and how the firm as such develops may be of little concern to an individual owner compared with his use of goods and services. Owners' primary concern is quality of goods and services and trading conditions. At least from a short-term perspective, this interest may be in conflict with the aim of giving the firm as such a strong financial position. From a firm's point of view, these two interests may either be regarded as two constraints or, alternatively, one interest may be regarded as an optimizing goal, while the other is regarded as a constraint. Whether a co-operative firm has financial autonomy or not in the sense mentioned above depends, amongst other things, on whether pricing is on market terms or not.

In this book we concentrate on firms registered on stock exchanges. The entire book is relevant for these firms, while for other kinds of organizations only certain parts of the book are of direct interest. For example, the discussion of financial markets will have only indirect relevance for organizations funded through grants in a budget process, and only to the extent that such a discussion can give a perspective on the mechanisms in these organizations. On the other hand, the analysis regarding functional units involves issues that are of direct relevance, because management control is fundamentally similar for a state-owned or municipal organization and the functional units of a financially self-sustained firm. We will also tend to discuss governance in a vertical direction rather than governance in a horizontal direction.

2.1.3 Role of information in economic efficiency

Most individuals at any level in an organization aim at some kind of economic efficiency, even if there is no formal control system. Economic efficiency, in some shape or form, is an impelling force. Certainly the degree and orientation may vary, but the social make-up and background of individuals encourage them to apply some economic criteria to their behaviour. The individual's own intentions are not the only motive forces – reactions to external demands are also a relevant factor.

Basically, the possibility of reinforcing and directing efforts to achieve economic efficiency is the reason for using accounting measures. Internal intentions and external demands are highlighted by such measures and the likelihood of realization may therefore increase. Besides, the operationalization in terms of accounting measures may in itself produce further, more precise intentions and demands. The measures as such may play an important role when output is evaluated, resources are allocated and operational efficiency is stimulated. The measures are functional with regard to a certain economic system if they are instrumental to the economic efficiency of that system. If the reverse is the case, they are dysfunctional.

The role of external demands varies. Some units are in a good financial position and have an excellent reputation and therefore also a freedom of choice that other units lack. The attitude to external demands varies between managers. Sometimes the external demands and expectations are imposed very loosely; some unit managers even seem to develop an ability to keep those who represent external demands at a distance. In some cases, these representatives deliberately refrain from imposing strong demands. In all these cases, intentions and expectations within the unit express ideas which are generated internally

External demands and expectations, strong and weak, exist at all levels, however. The unit must satify some of them in order to access financial resources. Customers must find the products attractive. Owners/lenders have payment claims. Business unit managers require single functional units to contribute to their total operation. Demands from those who provide direct access to essential financial resources are especially powerful, of course. Group management making direct demands on business unit managers or banks claiming interest and instalments may serve as examples. Sometimes the external demands and expectations determine the boundaries for the activities of an individual unit. This is especially evident at the corporate level in a market economy. A firm must meet claims for payment in order to survive.

Those who have some kind of responsibility for a firm must look at economic efficiency with regard to that specific firm and its ability to meet unconditional external demands, e.g. the ability to generate sufficient cash. Directly or indirectly, these basic external demands affect units and individuals at all organizational levels:

● *The entire firm*, represented by the board and senior management.

- *Business units*, represented by divisional managers, subsidiary managers or other managers with similar responsibilities.
- *Functional units*, represented by functional managers.
- *Individuals within functional units*.

Demands and expectations at one level are related to the necessary intentions at the level below. In this sense, there is a chain of requirements. Choice and definition of measures and required values of measures, must to some extent relate to each other at different organizational levels, at least conceptually. Our approach has similarities with that of Cyert and March (1963):

> ... organizational goals are a series of independent aspiration-level constraints imposed on the organization by the members of the organization coalition. (p.117)

For a society, this chain of requirements is crucial to the ultimate effects of measures and the overall efficiency of the economic system. The link between external claims and internal management control is particularly important. Control procedures and measures affect the conditions of life for human beings in many respects, inside and outside the firm. What goods and services are supplied and on what terms? What will the income of individuals be? What kind of working assignments will they have? What kind of collective interests will be satisfied, notwithstanding the difficulty of defining this for all individuals in a society?

2.2 REAL FUNCTIONS OF ACCOUNTING INFORMATION

It is usual these days – especially in academic textbooks in the North American tradition – to give greater emphasis to the 'decision-making' function. There are very good reasons for this. In the processes mentioned above, however, accounting information does not always function only as an analytical tool for decision-making. Other functions, sometimes rather more diffuse, both inside or outside the company, are also very important in practice and need to be described.

2.2.1 Accounting information as any aid to individual decision-makers

Individuals may use accounting information for their own decisions and viewpoints in several ways:

Own decisions   The measures give direct guidance to users in their work. For this purpose, it is important that total accounting information gives early warning about revenue and cost tendencies. This is an important function for players within the company, for shareholders and lenders and for workers' unions in wage negotiations.

Self-confirmation   Accounting measures can be conceived as measures of personal success and they can be related to the individual's own intentions. A manager may consider changes in share prices or in income from this point of view just as a functional manager may regard the cost level of a function and process in the same manner. The need for such professional satisfaction can be just as important as the need to satisfy the demands of principals or other external expectations.

Learning   Accounting measures contribute to the building up of knowledge in the long term. They stimulate a learning process about an individual's own efficiency and ways in which efficiency can be improved. In particular, accounting measures stimulate enquiry: formulating questions, investigating and finding answers provide knowledge about the company and its surroundings.

2.2.2 Accounting information as a means of vertical communication

The reporting of management to owners represents one of the most fundamental and classic functions of accounting, i.e. 'stewardship'. Similar roles exist at different organizational levels: owner/senior management, senior management/business unit managers and business unit managers/ functional managers. Superiors and subordinates need information from their own particular points of view.

1 *The superior makes demands on the subordinate* and information is a tool to express these *ex ante* and to conduct the corresponding reviews. Internally, a principal exercises this influence, first by expressing expectations regarding the actual choice of measures, and then through the possibility of intervention concerning values of the measures. This facilitates delegation, which is important. In the case of public information, the situation is similar. In particular those who represent large shareholdings may strongly influence the work of the board and the selection of senior management; in practice, they can often act virtually in the same way as internal principals. Shareholders with minor holdings, acting alone, have hardly any influence on management; but they can still use given information in the corresponding manner, partly by buying and selling shares, and partly through elected representatives who achieve sufficient power.

2 *The subordinate requires dialogue about demands.* Certainly the need to clarify demands from principals varies from individual to individual. Managers often emphasize their independence and fail to mention the direct importance of contacts with their principals for the decisions they make. They rarely consider excessive intervention a problem, but many experience the difficulties of developing a constructive and living dialogue. (It is perhaps not astonishing that, in their own role as superiors, they often have a different view of relations between principal and agent.) In any event, accounting measures may be important bases for internal discussions with principals in hierarchic organizations.

The main owners – normally represented on the board – are a special case. First of all, they are the most visible principals for management. They are also to some extent agents in relation to the other shareholders. How they regard accounting measures can be traced back to a mix of these two roles.

As indicated, corporate governance has similar elements at all organizational levels. At the same time, the differences are also important, in particular the relationship between shareholder and senior management in comparison with purely internal relations inside the firm:

- A relatively strict financial logic often typifies shareholders. Cash flows and their resulting measures are crucial. Internal players perhaps tend to follow a slightly different logic, with a focus on the unit as such, or the employees, or even consumers.
- Financial arguments, related to required cash flows and required rate of return, are more absolute and dominant than many other arguments within the company where trade-offs can be achieved to a higher degree.
- The availability of accounting information is different, including background knowledge. For ordinary shareholders the insight into the company extends as far as public information allows; in addition interpretation is more difficult for an information user who is at a distance from ongoing activities.
- In the public process, there are clearly less opportunities to communicate precise expectations from one level to another, and to conduct thorough reviews in accordance with this principle.
- Dissatisfied principals outside the firm have different options to those inside the firm. Shareholders may sell their shares. In rare cases they can make speeches at the annual general meeting. In quite extraordinary cases, they may pursue legal claims. A superior in the internal context can make direct interventions within the boundaries of what is feasible in accordance with internal, often implicit, rules of the game.

2.2.3 Accounting information as a means of horizontal communication

The members of a certain unit have various contacts with units that provide input and units and individuals which are receivers of output, i.e. goods and services. Information in general and accounting information also may be a very important element in this horizontal process. For example, in the internal co-ordination between production and selling units it may be essential for product costs to be analysed at different stages of an integrated chain. Product costs may also attract considerable interest from the public. Customers often have viewpoints about what 'the real costs' are for certain products. They may react to what is said to be a cost-based price.

Accounting values may be the basis for negotiations with external parties such as workers' unions, customers, suppliers and banks. The measures may be an important instrument by which the company can convince these parties of its arguments. At the same time, accounting values may give these external groups a basis for their own actions. The workers' union may obtain information to support its arguments. A bank can refer to actual figures, not merely to general arguments, to defend its actions.

2.2.4 Accounting information as an element in the business activity *per se*

Accounting measures and values of such measures may be an integral part of business activity. First, actual accounting numbers may have an immediate effect on cash flows, wealth, companies and individuals. We refer to this as a 'post-contracting role'.[2] The terms of many agreements are related to accounting measures and their values, e.g. at acquisition agreements. What dividends are legally permissible may be defined with regard to accounting measures. Banks must satisfy certain capital requirements, i.e. some form of debt/equity requirement. The financial worth of companies or individuals is directly affected when accounting values determine tax payments made by a company or bonuses for individuals. Business activities *per se* may thus be affected by how measures have been defined and what the outcome in accounting terms is. The actual content of agreements and laws will therefore be partly determined by how accounting measures are defined.

Accounting data may also have a more indirect but nonetheless important effect on cash flows and financial worth for companies and individuals. The effect on share prices is one obvious example. A special group in this context are shareholders who are also involved in company activities, as board members, employed managers or other employees. Another example is economic information which affects public ratings and hence the level of interest costs for a company.

2.3 GOVERNANCE PROCESSES

We define economic governance processes as behaviour related to the design and use of information regarding economic efficiency. We are interested here in the role of accounting information in such a process, given the real functions described above. The following central elements in such a governance process are discussed below:

- the mixture of analysis and actions,
- the treatment of uncertainty,
- comparisons with reference levels, and
- trust/loyalty processes.

These four factors are basically interdependent and to some extent reinforce each other.

2.3.1 The mixture of analysis and action

Economic efficiency is achieved through both analysis and action: performance and final results, particularly with regard to accounting information, are ultimately the crucial factors. An analysis based on accounting measures is only one part of a total control process, albeit a very important part. The attitude towards analysis as compared with action/execution varies between individuals. Some are very keen to have a sound intellectual basis for their actions, including analysis of accounting measures; their strength may actually be the very analysis itself. Some are active searchers for information, others are receivers of the information that systems provide on a regular basis. For instance, many well-educated and knowledgeable shareholders actively search for information about registered companies through various channels, including information from the company. Those who feel less in need of an analytical basis may have their strength in execution. Some of the non-analytical users will not give risks too much thought, and in addition have a strong conviction that their own acts will decide the final outcome.

It is common to find that individuals who use accounting information do not attach too much importance to accuracy, in the sense of precision of measurement values, reliability of measuring methods and perhaps not even the relevance of the measures. Users also often interpret values in the way they are accustomed to, regardless of the more exact meaning (so-called functional fixation).

Knowledge about the measures as such varies considerably. The prerequisites of shareholders for the interpretation of accounting information also vary. Empirical studies of internal use also show that knowledge about content, measuring techniques, etc. varies greatly both within and between different categories of players. For example, we have found that knowledge about applied rate of return measures was not very good among some of the leading players at divisional level, while others were more knowledgeable. We have also found that many supervisors at lower levels lacked knowledge about reporting systems that concerned them.

Even knowledge about activities that are reflected in the measures may vary to a high degree, which in turn affects the interpretation of available data. This applies both for internal and external uses. The possibilities of investors examining the company's choice of measurement rules is a much debated question. On the one hand, empirical studies in the sphere of capital market theory indicate that stock market prices are not affected by accounting valuations, e.g. if inventory is valued according to first-in-first-out or last-in-first-out. The very acts of managers, however, often indicate an alternative experience and conviction. For instance, managers pay a great deal of attention to the effects of different valuation principles on the well-being of the firm. Certain decisions may even be dependent upon the accounting method used. This illustrates the weight senior management may attach to book solidity, despite the fact that actual financial strength of a company naturally is independent of the accounting method. The view is apparently that external judgement of a company will depend on which accounting rule is applied for a given business transaction. In such a world the choice of accounting rules certainly becomes more important than it really should be.

The distance from analysis to final outcome, and the importance of the role of an accounting analysis, may vary from one field of activity to another. The following areas will each have special characteristics with regard to accounting analysis.

- *Execution of individual financial transactions*, such as trading of shares or other securities, acquisitions/sales of equipment or taking up loans.
- *Physical production/selling/development in a continuous operation*, the physical activity as such, including support activities such as marketing, administration, etc.
- *Managing and supervising*, by those who carry out the purely physical activities in the second category.

These areas vary in certain aspects: the relative importance of financial information; what sets the boundaries for available courses of action; how close the user is to the operational tasks that ultimately affect economic outcome; the need to convince other people; the role of long-term financial factors.

The pure investment decision on the stock market, that is, the purchase or sale of shares, is an extreme case. Financial information will be an important part of the basis for the decision and many courses of action are available. Analysis may provide the immediate impulse for a decision with a direct effect on the economic outcome, but the direct, visible consequences for a wider circle of people are few. In particular, public information is used for such transactions with these prerequisites.

Often, however, the relationship between analysis, action and outcome is quite different. The internal use of accounting will be one element in an organizational process. Product and resource structure and the character of the product and resources influence the feasibility of actions in the short and long term. The position of a unit and its players in the corporate organization is also of the greatest importance. First, there is a more or less explicit organizational structure. There are also rules governing what decisions certain individuals actually have the authority to make.[3]

The lower the individual's position in the organizational hierarchy, the more operational in nature are the actions taken. In many cases, for example in process industries, information will be produced very close to the originating activity, and often in non-financial terms. This kind of information provides opportunities for immediate reactions. The degrees of freedom for such actions will be determined by the structure of the production system. One important question is what can be done by those who operate an automated process, for instance. Those who have managerial and supervisory functions at different levels, and thus work at a distance from the purely operational activities, must influence the physical process by influencing other people. This situation requires a different pattern of behaviour *vis-à-vis* accounting information than financial investments or purely operational activities.

For senior management, the main task is to give structure to the activi-

seldom have an important effect on action. Therefore, reference levels may often be described as an interval, rather than a single value. Effects of deteriorated values can be discussed with this as a background. Corrective action tends to be provoked only when the accounting numbers deteriorate appreciably in relation to a given interval of reference. Change 2 and change 4 in Fig. 2.1 illustrate this:

M2 As a result of the change, the number drops to the interval.
M4 The number of the measure is below the interval after the change but not before.

When the position in relation to the reference interval does not change to a substantial degree, the inclination for action is weaker. Changes 1, 3 and 5 in figure 2.1 illustrate this:

M1 Even after the change, the number is clearly above the reference interval.
M3 The number is within the interval before as well as after the change.
M5 The number is already below the interval before the change.

Reference values change over time, as a result of experience. New levels emerge for old dimensions; in an extreme case the reference level may be based entirely on the outcome of the previous period. What seemed unrealistic the previous year, may be regarded as achievable in the following period. New dimensions to compare with may also be added: for example, those who have made only comparisons with previous years may be asked

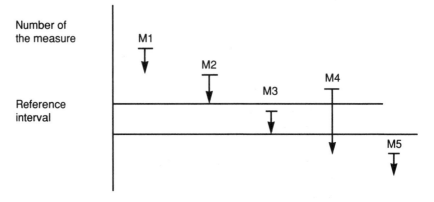

Fig. 2.1 Relation between accounting numbers and reference levels

to compare figures with values for competitors for future periods. At the same time, it is important to point out that users do not adjust their reference levels to changed conditions regularly enough. A level that has been considered acceptable tends to continue to be a reference point, irrespective of how measurement methods and the surrounding environment change (one form of so-called functional fixation).

An important issue is thus how reference levels are set both publicly and internally. In the case of public information, the procedures for establishing share prices, including reporting in the media, is of central importance. For internal information, one key issue is the extent to which very precisely stated levels of corporate requirements affect actual reference levels for isolated individuals and in turn their behaviour. Part of this internal problem has been dealt with in a vast fund of empiricial and theoretical literature, with particular regard to the effects of budgets. We confine ourselves to a few statements.

● Required levels for accounting measures of profit centres may have an important impact on behaviour. This has been shown, for example, in our own empirical studies.
● Required levels perceived as unachievable usually do not have any positive effect on behaviour. Required levels will not matter if they are too remote from the present numbers.
● Many explicit required levels in companies cannot be changed on an ongoing basis, in line with changing conditions. This is not feasible, or at any rate not meaningful, in an organizational process. Required levels and reference levels cannot therefore be modified without some amount of friction.

2.3.4 Processes of faith and loyalty

Agency theory has had a very dominant role in accounting literature descriptions of control processes in recent years. Obviously, these theories represent an important structure for accounting use: there is a superior and a subordinate. Everybody has a tendency to look after his or her own interests in a rather narrow sense. Information is unevenly distributed. On the basis of this self-interest, there is a need to monitor the behaviour and outcome of subordinate units. Naturally, there is empirical evidence supporting this structure.

However, this is only one side of the coin. From our empirical observations over the years, we draw the conclusion that some alternative ideas and concepts seem to be just as important, especially the concept of trust.

Trust is a very important element in every economic system: trust between the members of a certain organization at different levels internally, between lenders and borrowers, between shareholders and management, between buyers and sellers. Without trust, there is a need for control mechanisms and regulations, which in turn may influence the function of the economic system in a negative way. As long as there is trust between different parties, an economic system may function relatively well; otherwise some processes that are time-consuming and require mental energy will have to be implemented.

For those who have put resources into a unit or have given someone an assignment, the question of trust is important in several ways. Above all, as

managers. Principals should support and co-operate with agents to achieve common goals but at the same time they should be prepared to question, for example, on the basis of accounting numbers. When important decisions are made about persons and capital investments, the choice is often the result of careful consideration, and it is essential for the principal to radiate confidence. After the decision, however, continuous review cannot be so thorough. The measures will be less important initially as an instrument for questioning. After a while, however, the question of whether the confidence in the agent was really justified will arise.

2.4 EFFECTS OF ACCOUNTING INFORMATION

The importance of accounting information for decisions and outcomes is often indirect. There is not necessarily a direct relationship at a given point in time between the value of a measure and certain decisions. Many important effects only become evident in the long term. There are gradual effects on frames of reference, attitudes and knowledge. In many cases the important effects will occur indirectly, through the advantages of organizational forms made possible by accounting systems.

2.4.1 Effects on frames of reference, attitudes and organizational design

It is a common empirical observation that accounting information is used in processes where individual values of measures and individual documents play a role which is difficult to identify. One important form of influence, which is not exactly visible, is the effect on perspectives and incentives.

It is important to identify some categories of incentives in this context:

- *Economic incentives related to the individual:* based on the development of stock prices; based on the performance of the company or a sub-unit; a fixed predetermined fee, normally an ordinary salary.
- *Incentives related to the satisfactory financial condition of the company.*
- *Intraprofessional incentives.* Many professionals find satisfaction in exercising a certain activity in a professional manner. Capital investors may enjoy the business process as such. Employees may be stimulated by a high degree of independence and the possibility of professional development. Representatives, e.g. of employee unions, are satisfied to participate in a process they regard as meaningful for their members.
- *External incentives.* Players may be devoted to the idea that their activity should be useful for customers and play a positive role in society as a whole, or in a global context.

Although there are mutual relationships between these types of incentives, they nevertheless indicate different motives and interests. They also indicate the relatively complicated prerequisites for the use of accounting measures in a company.

For some players within a company, measures affect wealth, directly or through share prices (if internal information is a basis for public information). To the extent that they see their personal efforts influencing their salaries, this may stimulate their efforts. The way in which outcome is measured in accounting terms will directly or indirectly affect their personal financial situation.

Other internal players lack individual interests of this kind. The weight individuals attach to economic efficiency for a particular unit is a part of their general professional ambitions in the widest sense, including the desire to have a strong position in relation to other players within or outside the company. This ambition is one of many driving forces, and its relative importance may change for an individual over the years. The issue here is how accounting measures may affect this ambition.

For owners with the view that shares should give a good return, the interest of economic efficiency in a traditional sense is obvious; their use of public information has been investigated in a considerable number of empirical studies. It is less well known how accounting information affects frames of reference and attitudes among those who represent the logic of political organizations and employee unions. No doubt, debates on excessive profits or increases in wealth on a bullish stock or real-estate market affect the prerequisites for political decisions.

Meaningful information requires both that something essential is captured and that reliability is perceived to be sufficiently good. A user tends to be attracted to the information that confirms and reinforces views he or she already has. Given the pattern of incentives described above, the question is what role accounting information may have on frames of reference and attitudes, especially the fundamental attitude to economic efficiency:

● To what extent will economic information systems affect attitudes regarding economic efficiency among groups that do not have economic efficiency as their dominating, natural logic, e.g. groups with a strong emphasis on intraprofessional values. Will they observe economic factors to a greater extent, and be inclined to act on such a basis?

● Will such systems reinforce existing frames of reference among those who have economic efficiency as their dominating natural logic, e.g. many shareholders and managers? Will their field of vision be narrowed and even more constrained to those factors which have an effect on (measured) economic efficiency? Will they therefore place less emphasis on non-financial conditions, and be less inclined to act on a non-financially oriented basis?

● Will conceptions about economic efficiency be affected by the choice of measure? To what extent? Will different groups of players have different perceptions?

Several of the more important effects of economic information in a company are indirect in relation to decisions and economic outcomes. They are often not even visible, at least not in the short run:

- Measures make reviews possible and thus also delegation and organizational forms that would otherwise not be possible.
- Measures, conceived as signals of requested behaviour, can be powerful pedagogical instruments to clarify areas of responsibility for different players and management expectations.
- Measures stimulate players to improve their knowledge of their sphere of activity and its economic structure.
- Measures may have a significant impact on the players' attitude to their activities. The actual role of the measures is often to affect attitudes to economic efficiency – what we term economic orientation. This in turn plays an important part in the behaviour and decision-making of the players. Economic orientation is an attitude to economic efficiency for an individual's entire activity or a part of it. Economic orientation can be vague and unspecified and may appear, to varying degrees, as a general cost-consciousness or profit-consciousness. Economic orientation may also be very well confined to certain types of economic consequences.

Economic orientation in a unit may change. It is well known, for example, that an atmosphere of economic crisis and the threat of a plant closing down often influence attitudes to economic efficiency. The perspective of efficiency will be more important under such external pressure.

2.4.2 Effects on individual decisions

To some extent, measures may be directly linked to individual decisions. This may be the case in situations such as the following:

Discussion about certain issues is initiated

In many cases, measures have no significant effect on action, for example, because the problem is of a non-financial nature or because players have no strong economic orientation. In other cases, the player has a strong economic orientation but the numbers do not play a very important role; despite the numbers, people do 'the best possible' or 'as well as they can' in each situation to achieve a satisfactory economic outcome.

In many cases, however, measures indicate the need for action, i.e. they stimulate considerations about, e.g. the acquisition of a share in a company or increased sales promotion. To many players and on many occasions, measures play this role, particularly internally. Values of measures in budgets, reports, predictions and so on give the impression that the situation and development is unsatisfactory in terms of some critical factors, thus giving rise to some consideration. Our empirical studies contain numerous examples. At the same time it may be noted that accounting measures, especially those of an aggregated nature (for example, income), often attract insufficient attention as they are weak signals. One reason is the character of the control process described in the previous section.

If a player is remote from what is shown in the accounting numbers, his ability to interpret numbers will be impaired, and he may have an additional need for supplementary information to clarify a situation. The distances may be of organizational, cognitive or geographical nature. A shareholder or even a board member who lives at a great distance from the daily life of a company, has a cognitive disadvantage in relation to senior management. At the same time, a supervisor with close experience of a production process has an advantage in relation to senior management.

Alternatives can be evaluated before execution

First, certain economic calculation techniques are used: for example, methods to evaluate investments in shares or production facilities. Then, players consider how alternative courses of action affect values of measures for an organizational unit. Again, the question is how the measures are used: as an analytical tool for decision-making, as a confirmation of ideas that already exist, or to argue for standpoints that have been taken for other less powerful reasons?

Decisions can be evaluated after implementation

This can be done in more or less unsystematic forms. A particularly striking example is the diligence with which players will look for arguments – for themselves and/or others – that justify a choice they made in the past.

NOTES

[1] We regard all financial measures as part of 'accounting information'.

[2] Compare Beaver, W. H., *Financial Reporting: An Accounting Revolution* (1989), p. 6.

[3] Product and resource structure is a term for the types of products the unit delivers and the types of resources that are available for this.

The fact that information may have effects is in a way the very reason for its internal use. Senior management may choose systems designed for their own purposes. It is, however, not always self-evident what effects should be aimed at in individual cases. Some effects are difficult to observe, but nevertheless fundamental, for instance, in a case when the choice of measures conditions the choice of a certain organizational structure. Periodic reviews in terms of income and return on capital may, for example, facilitate desirable organizational forms that would be difficult to introduce without such reviews. Other not so easily observed effects of accounting information are more limited, but nevertheless important.

The effect dimension is also a very obvious basis for evaluation of public information, both when systems are designed and information is given. The following are a few important examples:

1 Effects at the overall systems level. A legal accounting system is designed to protect creditors, and therefore rules for valuation and dividends are determined accordingly.
2 Attitudes towards measures among players are influenced by views on significant direct effects, for a company or individuals: for example, changes in accounting rules may affect tax payments of a company, the level of official income of a company may influence employee benefits.
3 Those who report often take into consideration the impression made on the public. Such aspects are natural for managers who perceive that accounting methods affect external analysts' picture of a company, and therefore, for example, share prices, loan conditions and the stock market's opinions about the senior management.
4 Senior management may believe that certain aspects of a public report will have unfavourable effects internally. In a bank or a construction company the value of a loan or a construction project will not be written down due to the fear that this may result in less forceful action on the part of internal managers. In another company, senior management may believe the value of fixed assets should not be depreciated because it would be too easy for subordinate managers to achieve the internal financial goals.

Many views on (existing or planned) systems or information to be provided thus fall back on ideas about what it is important to achieve/avoid and how accounting numbers contribute to this. The strength of such views and the perceived degree of freedom may vary; both will influence the intensity of actions and reactions. One player may promote an alternative that gives favourable, or at least mostly favourable, effects from his or her point of view. Another may accept an alternative, where the possible effects are at least not strongly opposed to his or her interests.

3.1.2 Representational criteria

Representational criteria refer to how well a measure captures individual events or units in a striking manner. According to these criteria, there should be a congruence between a measure and the economic character of a transaction or an activity. 'Economic character' refers to the economic consequences of alternatives, for example, in selecting the product line, or capital investment or pricing decisions. It may also refer to the actual organizational role of a unit. The controllability criterion is a classic and important representational criterion of this kind; we discuss this in more detail in Part Three.

Sometimes, achieving congruence between units and measures is an almost insoluble problem. This is especially true for corporate groups. Accounting for a group should be undertaken as if the parent company owned the assets and had the debts directly, which is obviously not the case. Accounting for a subsidiary/division should be carried out as if the unit were operationally and perhaps also financially independent of the group, which normally is not the case either. The choice of accounting measures then means a choice of analogies and the evaluation of their effects.

A common demand is that good business deals should be positively reflected in the accounting. According to this view, for example, the success of a currency position during a certain period should produce a corresponding positive effect in the accounting numbers for the same period. Congruence between measures and the business significance of events captured is consequently the evaluation criterion. It is also a common experience that those who exercise control and those who are controlled have a different emphasis on measurement systems criteria in relation to representational criteria. Those who exercise control have a tendency to support an overview and therefore comparability, i.e. measurement systems criteria. Those who are controlled want fair judgement in relation to each other on the one hand, but, on the other hand, they have an even stronger wish to see measures that are relevant for evaluation in their specific case, i.e. measures that include everything for which they deserve to be given credit.

3.1.3 Measurement systems criteria

Measurement systems criteria refer to the entire measurement process in which accounting numbers are produced and used, not the content of a single measure in itself. Such criteria thus concern the quality of how the data are captured, transformed and used. Public information requirements have often involved aspects of this kind.

1 Measures may be evaluated with regard to the extent data are verifiable, have a reasonable degree of certainty and lack personal bias. These are important qualities both publicly and internally. A special quality, particularly for data in annual reports, is the fact that these data are subject to reviews and statements by auditors. This, in turn, requires that the accounting should be verifiable, and reasonably free from personal bias.

2 Measures may be evaluated with regard to comparability criteria.

Comparability may concern comparisons between companies, with special types of reference factors such as the rate of return required on the stock market and comparisons over time. Comparability may be good in one respect and bad in another. It is particularly important that measure-ment systems should permit comparisons between companies within a country and between companies in different countries. Another quality is that components of a measure are consistent with each other and with the overall purpose of the total accounting system. Consistency gives measures a clear meaning which in itself facilitates different forms of comparison.

One type of measurement systems criteria can be entitled resource criteria. Administrative problems experienced by companies and society in pro-ducing and using economic information need to be considered: for instance, the effect on the measures of possible changes in the way in which data is captured and registered. This is true both for public and internal information. For public accounting, costs mainly fall on one party, a company, and utility essentially falls on another party, players in the environment.

3.1.4 User criteria

User criteria refer to how information and measures are adapted to the attributes and prerequisites of users. There are several kinds of such criteria. Acceptance criteria and simplicity criteria are especially important. Good measures should be accepted and be understandable to users. Simplicity requirements are often mentioned, both with regard to income and balance statements in large companies and individual units. Negative views on reports with regard to this aspect are common, not least with public infor-mation. Acceptance has a central role for internal information systems. For public systems, company acceptance is an important issue. The views of company managers responsible for the provision of information largely depend on their judgements of effects, particularly if their company might appear in an (undeservedly) less than satisfactory light.

3.1.5 The relationship between criteria

Explicit or implicit perceptions about effects on individuals' activities, financial markets, etc. are in practice often the ultimate criterion when choosing accounting measures. Sometimes, the relationship between measures and effects is not very immediate; for example, an accounting method is assumed to increase confidence in public accounting, which in turn is assumed to affect the functioning of financial markets.

Criteria other than effects may often be regarded as a step in an evalu-ation of effects. If accounting information is to have desirable effects, a reliable and reasonably well-accepted measure of good representation is usually necessary. The intentions for these other criteria must be chosen with regard to possible effects. The less immediate the effects are, the more importance the other criteria may have. They may even almost represent a goal in themselves as illustrated by the following fictional statements:

'It is important to have consistency between and within accounting measures.'
'The strict controllability principle should be applied.'
'It has a value in itself that the members of an organization appreciate the system they work with.'

There are interrelations between dimensions that representational, measurement systems and user criteria reflect. The user's perceptions about measures are probably dependent on how striking the representation is considered to be in an individual case. If measurement systems criteria are fulfilled, this will affect how striking the information is in a given case, etc. Nevertheless, the aspects are basically different. The criteria may very well be in conflict with each other. For instance, it has become more and more common to compare representational and consistency criteria. One example is transactions with securities that are quoted on a market. From a representational point of view, it could be argued that traditional accounting is not preferable in individual cases. At the same time, consistency between components of a total income concept decreases if traditional accounting principles are not used in a particular case.

A discussion of accounting measures will often involve a number of arguments; both principles and consequences will be mentioned and their relative importance will vary. It may be argued, for example, that principles should be more important in public rather than in internal information. The intended effects with traditional public accounting have often been of a very general character, such as protection of investors and especially lenders. The relative importance of the four types of criteria varies over time and from country to country.[1]

3.2 FUNDAMENTALS OF THE APPROACH

The general approach described below is based on one fundamental criterion: that the collective interest of economic efficiency in the broadest sense will be promoted (see Chapter 2). Ideally, the information should have favourable effects on how resources are allocated and used in a social economic system. The link between external and internal processes is crucial – these two governance processes must not be regarded as independent of each other.

3.2.1 The need to judge cash flows in a market economy

A company in a market economy must satisfy requirements with regard to market-based payments and competitive products. In a legal sense, a company has its own identity: it has formal legal rights and obligations. It must meet demands for payments for different forms of resources and risks. Its cash flows must be sufficient for all demands on payments which result from activities with different time scales: for example, for resources in operations, for obligations to lenders and for market-based dividends to shareholders.

Future cash flows set the absolute boundaries for the survival and development of a company. They determine future capability to fulfil contractual obligations towards lenders and other parties. They are also the basis for the value of shares. Hence, senior management and all those who have or may have demands on payments from the company, have a common interest in judging future cash flows. All those who have an interest in the survival of a company have reason to clarify the company's capability to satisfy external unconditional demands. Besides these common interests, everybody has a need to judge whether a particular interest can be satisfied under certain time constraints. Everybody needs to know how plans and outcomes of the company relate to his or her own specific demands.

A primary concern in our discussion is that companies, if possible, should be able to develop and survive. From this point of view, it is a necessary condition to fulfil the demands of financial markets, i.e. to generate cash flows that are sufficient in relation to these demands. Ultimately, there are reasons to look at every part of the company from this point of view. In a market economy, all sections of the company need to be analysed with regard to the cash flows involved, directly or indirectly: divisions, functional areas, products, customers, investment projects, etc. Some of the objects will cause direct inflows as well as outflows; some have more indirect effects on inflows, while others also have indirect effects on many outflows. It is important to judge these effects as far as possible for each object.

3.2.2 Role of traditional accounting in a system based on cash flows

From the background indicated above, the natural main accounting procedure may appear to be to monitor actual, and possibly even expected, cash flows. This is problematic, however, for several reasons:

1 Periodic cash flows are not a good base for many of the comparisons that accounting measures should be used for. The description of the use of information (in Chapter 2) serves to emphasize the importance of comparability and of meaningful, easily established, reference levels.

2 With regard to the actual character of governance processes, particularly the risk of bias and rhetoric, continuous reviews should be based on events that have occurred and been documented rather than on pure expectations. It is difficult to make a distinction between expectations that are constantly put forward (and yet are perhaps unjustified) and expectations that are well founded. An income concept with a dominating position in practice must thus be based on something else.

3 Some of the objects, e.g. functional units, have only limited direct effects on cash flows on their own. Many indirect effects arise in interaction with other objects.

In a complex, uncertain world of continuous events, it is not convenient to build accounting information, not even the major areas of it, on expectations and outcome for cash flows. Another kind of information is needed: information that can be produced period by period, permits verifiability, relates back to what has been previously reported and should be relevant for future cash flows from different time perspectives. Some users will even use it as a basis for prediction of cash flows. Different forms of numbers, measures, but also qualitative data, will be important in the information system.

1 *Conventional measures*, i.e. financial numbers according to some form of accounting convention. We summarize measures based on the same general valuation principles under the heading 'type of measure'. There are many types – the traditional income concept based on historical cost is dominant in 'traditional accounting', especially in the public field.
2 *Economic measures*, i.e. measures that relate to the economic value and the opportunity cost, e.g. a discounting model. The purpose of all economic measures is to capture the economic character of defined alternatives as far as is necessary in each individual case. The borderline between conventional measures and economic measures is not clear-cut.
3 *Quantitative measures in physical terms*, especially volumes and time measures of different kinds. For our classification, it is more important that a measure's use has implications for economic efficiency, rather than whether financial terms are applied or not. Measures in physical terms are appropriate for many production and selling processes.
4 *Qualitative information,* when it is a part of a governing process. It may give direct guidance or a more varied picture of a situation captured by a measure. One example is qualitative criteria for the evaluation of capital investment projects. Another example is data from interviews or questionnaires in market research or employee surveys.

Traditional periodic measures for areas of responsibility are the core information in economic systems at both society and corporate levels. Clear responsibilities with meaningful and understandable requirements are an important basis for governance at all levels. Defining responsibilities in financial terms may clarify role expectations and responsibilities that would otherwise have been less clear. Accounting measures for well-specified organizational units make demands very clear and easy to understand and therefore the possibilities of enforcement increase. Organization and governance processes may be regarded from this point of view. It may be advantageous to divide up major projects into sub-areas for which certain cost levels can be required, based on experience. Companies in the financial markets may be treated in a similar manner; if group structures are reasonably straightforward and senior management have a clear role, it is easier to identify responsibilities and formulate demands.

Traditional accounting measures (as well as economic measures) fulfil an important logical function from a governance perspective. They make complex economic systems work. Delegation is often necessary and requires periodic measures that are reasonably robust, as we have stated above. Accounting measures satisfy this need. Delegation assumes that those who are responsible for different units pay close attention to ongoing performance in the terms used to formulate their responsibility. Such measures must be related to the organizational role of local units rather than to the information need at the central level if the decision had not been delegated.

If, for example, a company is organized into profit centres, the measures must be primarily designed with the object of facilitating review of profit responsibility. Marginal cost from the overall point of view will not necessarily, and perhaps seldom, be the most significant piece of information. It would have been the most important piece of information if representatives at the central level had been responsible for deciding individual cases, if this were in any way possible. Those who have local responsibility defined in accounting terms may thus very well make decisions which differ from those made by people who, hypothetically, have the opportunity to overview the whole system. This result may of course seem unfavourable with regard to systems logic, but it should be weighted against the fact that accounting measures make an (often necessary) delegation of day-to-day work possible.

Analyses of capital investments, products and other similar objects have traditionally been based on economic measures in the sense mentioned above, i.e. measures based on the economic value concept and the idea of opportunity costs. There are good reasons for this, but this is not always satisfactory from a governance process point of view. Marginal effects on more robust periodic measures, i.e. traditional accounting measures, may have to be judged as a supplement. This might perhaps be seen only as necessary and regrettable compliance with legal regulations, but it is often rational from a governance point of view. With expectations, which are difficult to quantify, used as the basis in accordance with strict economic logic, there is an ongoing need for feedback on previous expectations, and therefore an ongoing need for verifiable outcome measures.

Qualitative information is important, particularly because financial measures often provide relatively late indications as to what is happening in a business process. The reason is not only, and perhaps not even primarily, that the accounting process takes time and that therefore the measures will be of less importance. The basic reason is the time lag before problems regarding employees, product development, marketing, etc. show any indication at all in conventional accounting measures. Measures at an aggregate level may be especially difficult to interpret, or even misleading, because they summarize many different individual processes. This problem is, of course, most noticeable at the higher level in a major organization.

3.2.3 Rate of return on capital as an important indicator

As stated above, periodic accounting measures for companies and parts of companies are important for the economic system of society. The following factors are important:

- Measures should have relevance for future cash flows in the company.
- Measures should facilitate comparability between objects; reference levels have great importance and it is especially important that accounting values for a company can be related to external demands which are critical for survival and development.
- Measures for companies should be comparable with the measures of separate business units within the company (e.g. traditional divisions) so that internal control is facilitated.
- Measures for separate business units should be at least conceptually comparable to measures for objects at the lower levels, so that internal control is also facilitated in this respect.

Information systems based on rate of return on capital perform well in these respects. Plans and outcomes for rate of return, period by period, are an important element in assessing cash flows from different perspectives. Rate of return measures also generally permit meaningful and simple comparisons between companies over time. Important reference levels for rate of return values are generally relatively easy to find for external and internal users.

In particular, comparisons may be made with the long-term external demands on a company. The price of equity capital in the stock market is an important benchmark for rate of return, both for an entire corporation and separate business units. From a company point of view, the level of profitability in relation to this benchmark is critically important for survival and development. From the shareholder's point of view, this gives a good basis for judging future cash flows and rate of return on shares. Therefore, it is meaningful for the company itself and for the stock market to follow the company and separate business units using required rate of return on the market as a benchmark. Even if such a comparison does not have the same immediate interest for parties with contractual conditions, it will nevertheless also give them important information. It indicates both how the company/business units meet survival requirements and what scope there is from a profitability point of view to satisfy residual demands.

The significance of the rate of return concept, although not the technical details, is relatively simple and easy to understand for the ultimate users in the financial markets and for the players in a company. The concept permits relatively stable reference values over time, which is often not the case with pure cash flows. The main idea is simple. The measure shows the interest the owner of capital receives; this can be related to generally known phenomena such as interest on bank savings or other expressions of the market price of capital.

In our experience, rate of return measures for internal use have in many cases proved to have excellent qualities in relation to the important attributes of financial goals:

- They have motivated the players.
- They have been accepted.
- They have been easy to understand.
- They have been effective as a result of their quantification.
- They have been consistent with delegation throughout the whole company – and this also applies to parts of the company for which measures in non-financial terms have been employed.
- They have been shown to provide sufficiently stable goals.

Thus, rate of return measures as a basis for management control have often been effective. It is normally easy to get acceptance for the idea that a company and its units should survive and develop; goals related to this are perceived as meaningful. In particular, income and rate of return measures facilitate organizational forms that would be difficult to carry out without a review in such terms. Perceived as demands on the unit, rate of return measures may involve a powerful pedagogical instrument to clarify the responsibility of specific managers, especially at higher levels. Furthermore, they can be related to various other types of accounting measures at lower levels. At such levels, economic efficiency can be expressed in terms that are internally relevant with regard to the nature of activities at each level and at the same time are conceptually related to the overall return on capital goals for the entire corporation.

3.2.4 Design and use of accounting information

Those who use information for a certain purpose, or decide what kind of information a system should contain, have a varying degree of freedom regarding choice.

- Some will decide, without preconditions, what measures and supplementary information to use.
- Some will decide about the measures, but with certain restrictions (e.g. that conventional accounting principles should be applied); further information in addition to these measures can also be chosen.
- Some will have certain measures as a given starting point but still have the possibility of adding further information; these are the conditions, for example, for the internal reporting of a local unit or when a company provides public information.
- Others will use a given set of data without any supplementary information, to interpret the content and to realize the deficiencies and advantages; that is to say the prerequisites for an external reader of an annual report, for example.

In all of these cases, some guidelines about what information is appropriate are necessary. Such a model would be useful both for system designers and information providers in specific cases, even if there are restrictions as to how close it is possible to approach the ideal. Experienced, competent information users confronted with certain data also need to evaluate the advantages and disadvantages of the information provided for financial control purposes: what is the significance of the measures and what supplementary information should be sought. The need for such consideration in specific cases has become increasingly important.

Considerations regarding existing and new systems involve asking the following questions:

- *Existing systems*. What forces affect the content of an existing system? How appropriate will that content be for the most urgent information need? To what extent should and could measures be adjusted to be more appropriate, e.g. an income measure? What supplementary information is required?
- *New systems*. How should a new system be designed? What are the most important measurements and comparisons to focus on with regard to internal objectives about business activities and external claims on the activities? What information is needed, apart from the measures?

With a broad view of the role of accounting, return on capital measures will be a core component in models for appropriate information, giving guidance to information providers, system designers and information users. Return on capital measures are an important instrument:

- for judging long-term survival for an individual company,
- for judging the company in relation to the specific claims of various parties, and
- for resource allocation in a society.

The limitations and deficiencies are, however, also important in all these respects, and these must be reflected in how data is interpreted, adjusted and supplemented.

The main points of our discussion are:

1 Rate of return measures are an important tool for judging future cash flows in the long term. An efficient internal and external information system should therefore have the following features:

- Prerequisites for measuring rate of return should be as good as possible.
- Rate of return measures should play a dominant role when companies and separate business units are assessed.
- Measures should be designed so that comparisons with cost of equity capital in the long run on the stock market are facilitated.
- The reference levels emerging for rate of return measures should be congruent with cost of equity capital in the stock market, at least in the long term.

However, rate of return measures inevitably provide only a partial picture of future cash flows from any perspective. Further information is thus needed for a more complete picture. A strong desire to achieve favourable

in internal management control. It is an alternative or a supplement to other ways in which expectations can be communicated: for example, statements about desirable actions and conduct by management in a particular situation indicating what senior management considers urgent.

Demands, implicit or explicit, with a strong influence on society and companies, are a major force. Accounting measures reflect these demands. This power also depends on the governance process as such, including whether and how required/expected levels are communicated. Those who can affect this process thus have an important governance tool at their disposal.

3.3.2 Bases for required levels

Levels must refer to a particular object and period. Certain levels, but not all, are strongly associated with the content of formal reporting systems, e.g. budgetary values and the values for preceding periods. Fundamental distinctions can be made with regard to the time and object considerations.

- *Running permanent targets* are not limited to single periods or object units, e.g. discount rates that operate on a continuous basis, rates of return on capital stated for a company without time constraints or standard costs for mass or process-oriented production.
- *Period targets* are expressed for a certain period, e.g. budgetary values or predictions for a year.
- *Object targets* are expressed for single object units, for example, predicted cost for a certain construction object.

Targets with different ranges can affect each other in a planning and review process. For instance, moving targets for business units may influence annual budgetary values which, in turn, may affect predictions in the course of a certain year.

Targets in an information system focusing on future cash flows should ultimately be based on the demands of the financial market. This is not only true for an entire company but also for corporate units: demands and targets at one organizational level must be related to demands and targets at lower levels. This does not mean that the implicit or explicit levels of the financial community should automatically be transferred to a single part of the company, especially not in a continuous control process. Quite the contrary, there are a number of alternatives to be considered in principle in individual control processes:

Targets based on potential refer to what is possible for the company or some corporate unit to achieve with regard to conditions which are more or less specified.

- What rate of return on capital can be expected for a company with the requirements which the financial community finds realistic?
- What rate of return on capital can be achieved for business units with a given structure in terms of production, technology and markets?

- What rate of return on capital can be achieved for business units if the technical structure or the product market structure, or both, change?
- What cost level is feasible for a functional unit with a given structure?

Targets based on needs refer to a required minimum level with regard to some critical condition for a unit, regardless of the possibility of achieving it. This is a threshold requirement with regard to some decisive external demand on a company. Attaining an adequate level to achieve a competitive position in different markets is an obvious example – primarily in financial and product markets. These targets relate to the demands in the vertical and horizontal governance processes of a society: to satisfy the market based minimum demands of shareholders, to generate a rate of return sufficient to finance a development activity necessary for a competitive position in a product market, and to be able to maintain a competitive level as regards to product costs. These needs are so essential that executives of an entire company or a certain business unit must react if they do not appear to be satisfied. Deviations from such targets are an important indication that action is required.

Targets based on historical experience refer to levels attained in previous periods.

Targets based on external comparisons refer to levels attained in units with similar conditions. This kind of target can often be regarded as one form of target based on potential.

Demands and targets for economic measures are principally based on opportunity cost, e.g. a discount rate or a minimum level for the internal rate of return for a capital investment. Such demands and targets may express the cost of acquiring alternative resources or of using available resources in an alternative manner. They represent needs and potentials, respectively.

In the long run, all companies need to fulfil demands in the vertical and horizontal governance process. Demands from the owners, and other demands derived from this source are critical. Targets based on needs are, in this sense, more fundamental than targets based on potentials in lower organizational units. Defining and attaining targets in the short and long term for corporate units may subsequently be regarded as a part of the process of achieving these more fundamental demands. The inability to achieve targets based on needs may be seen as a strong threat to long-term development/survival of an activity.

NOTE

[1] The popularity of these criteria in academic literature has varied over time. Traditionally, literature within the 'financial accounting' area has had a strong orientation towards measurement systems issues, but the effect dimension, in particular, has attracted increased attention in recent years. Hendriksen, E. S. and van Breda, M. F., *Accounting Theory* (1992) is one example of a work with a broader orientation in which all types of criteria are clearly represented. Literature on management accounting has traditionally emphasized relevance and effects.

CHAPTER 4

Cost of capital in financial markets versus rate of return on book capital

In Chapter 3 we discussed how measures and targets for a company and its component parts should ultimately be based on the demands of the financial markets. For a further analysis of information systems, we thus need a more thorough discussion of these demands and their relationship to the company's rate of return on capital and cash flows.

OVERVIEW

A company has contractual obligations to most of its interest groups. A residual payment arises only when all contractual compensations have been made; usually the residual risk is associated with owner capital. Corporate residuals are the source of a series of payments to which shareholdings provide entitlement; shareholders have the right to this series of payments which is unlimited in temporal terms. They receive their return in the form of dividends and share price changes. The risks of shareholders will be expressed in terms of unpredicted variations in this return and will to an essential extent be based on the residual risks of the company.

On a well-functioning stock market, there will be states of equilibrium, where the expected rate of return on the shares is at the same level as the rate required by the market, i.e. the cost of equity capital. The individual investor in shares who acts according to financial logic considers justified share prices as well as probable market reactions, including share price movements caused by phenomena other than the dividend capacity of the company. He or she is looking constantly for alternatives with a better combination of return and risk than the present portfolio. For the stock market as a system for resource allocation, it would be desirable for long-term company prospects to have a considerable impact on share prices.

Loans from a market are (almost always) limited in time. The series of payments that is associated with a loan, i.e. interest and instalments, often involve predetermined amounts and time schedules. This also applies to rate of return. The perspective of those analysing creditworthiness will therefore be different to the perspective of those analysing stock prices. Credit risk is crucial. Creditors receive no bonus when the company income is better than normal. Therefore, in the first place, it is necessary for them to evaluate the possibility that due payments will not be made and they will try to adjust the predetermined risk premium to the risk level perceived. Costs of capital in the stock market and the loan market provide the critical financial prerequisites for the survival and development of a company.

4.1 RATE OF RETURN IN FINANCIAL MARKETS

Securities in the markets for shares, long-term loans and commercial papers represent standardized rights. They have a market value[1] that is primarily based on expectations about the series of payments to which the holder is entitled. Shareholders and creditors can utilize the values of such rights either through selling at the market price or through payments (periodic and non-periodic) from the company. Their fundamental demand is to get their invested capital back and expected return beyond that.

4.1.1 Financial flows of firms

Different parties make different kinds of contributions to the activities of a company. The size of compensation will depend on varying supply and demand conditions in various markets. Because the future cannot be foreseen with certainty, there are risks: the possibility that the outcome of an act is favourable or unfavourable in relation to expectations.[2] Therefore not everybody can have a predetermined contractual amount. Inevitably, decisions about investments for the production of goods and services mean financial risk taking, because the future consequences of different actions cannot be predicted with certainty. This is especially true in a market economy, where citizens have options to choose between alternative products.

The ways in which different parties bear the financial risks through the kind of compensation they receive for their engagement in company activities, are an important issue. In the simplest case, compensations for all parties except one, are stated in predetermined amounts, while the remaining party can claim whatever remains thereafter, i.e. a residual – which may even be negative. The size of compensation for residual risk taking is conditional upon outcome.

If investment and production are to be accomplished in a world of uncertainty, somebody must be willing to take the residual risk. An expected compensation for residual risk taking is a prerequisite for willingness to take such a risk and for accomplishing such plans. In principle anybody could bear this risk: creditors, suppliers, employees and customers can in principle choose between an agreement with a fixed predetermined amount for their planned involvement or a compensation that is conditional upon outcome and residual payment. In the latter case, compensation must normally be greater than a predetermined (risk-free) compensation.

A company has contractual obligations to most of its interested parties. Obvious examples are payment of predetermined wages and payment of predetermined interest costs to a bank or purchasing prices to a supplier. Contractual obligations are associated with some contract-related risk for the receiver. Compensation is conditional in the sense that a company will not be able and willing to fulfil conditions under all circumstances; access to cash is, for example, a necessary condition for payments in accordance with the contract. In certain cases, the formula for compensation is pre-determined through an agreement, while the amount is conditional upon outcome. For salaries, bonuses, etc. compensation is often related to outcome for the part of the company where the employee is active. Compensation may also be related to the outcome of the entire company, which is especially common for senior management, but may sometimes also be the case for a larger group of employees (profit-sharing schemes).

The compensation mentioned above is thus contractual, if not always predetermined in terms of amount. A residual, on the other hand, arises only when all contractual compensations have been taken into account; this makes the residual risk special. When the contractual compensations are made under market conditions, we refer to the residual income of the company as its profit. Residual risk is commonly related to owner capital. Residuals of the company are the source of a series of payments that shareholders are entitled to. This source, in turn, originates in flows from all activities in a firm: current business operations, financial operations, sale of subsidiaries or separable resources. Dividends from the company are decided within the legal framework for owner rights, as regards both rules for decision-making and restrictions on capital distribution.

4.1.2 Securities

Owners and lenders are paid because they contribute financial resources and take risks. The cost of capital in the stock markets and loan markets is principally determined by the opportunity cost to the investor of funds and the level of risk: for shareholders risks mainly based on the residual risk of the firm, and for creditors the more limited risks related to contractual obligations on the part of the company. The rate of return required by the creditors is affected by the risks of bankruptcy or other payment disturbances.

Shares

A share entitles its owner first to some influence over company activities through legal arenas such as the annual general meeting. The owner is also entitled to a series of payments from the company which is not limited by time. This series of payments (normally) consists of dividends, the growth of which is based on how a company's specific residual develops. Annual income for a shareholder can be measured as the sum of dividends received and the change in the market value of the shares. Annual rate of return can be defined as annual income in relation to market value at the beginning of the year.

EXAMPLE

Assume that the price of a share is 200 at the beginning of a year and 220 at the year-end. Assume also that 10 has been received as a dividend at the year-end. Annual income is then 20 + 10 = 30 and the rate of return is 15 per cent, i.e. 30:200.

Under ideal conditions, shareholders are indifferent to the form of return as long as total return is sufficiently high. In practice, however, form does matter, for example, because income tax is levied at a higher rate for dividends than for capital gains, or because an owner wants to access cash without selling some of his or her holdings.

Risks of shareholders can be expressed in terms of unpredicted variations in the rate of return for shares; to an essential extent these risks are based on the residual risks of the company. The unpredicted variations in rate of return for the share, however, do not directly follow unpredicted changes in income for the company, at least not in the short term.

Loans

Loans from a market are (almost always) limited in terms of time. The series of payments on a loan, for interest and instalments, is often predetermined regarding amount and time; thus a rate of return *ex ante* is also determined. In a pure case, the series of payments is not related to how any company-specific residual performs. Return on interest-bearing investments can take the form either of a coupon payment or a holding gain, depending on the market-interest situation and the coupon interest conditions of the loan; however, there is no growth as a consequence of a company-specific residual. The coupon rate varies in its significance to the total return.

4.2 REQUIREMENTS OF OWNERS

The most fundamental motive for a stock market is that it creates a governance process, where companies are stimulated towards more customer-oriented and resource-efficient production. The major driving force is the vertical governance process.

4.2.1 The relationship between cost of equity capital, expected dividends and share prices

Cost of equity capital and expectations about the firm's rate of return on equity are central variables when the value of a series of dividends from a continuous business activity is to be determined. This can be illustrated by a common model for valuation of shares, according to which the value is determined as the discounted value of future dividends for eternity. Expected dividend at the end of Year 1 is labelled D_1. Dividend is expected to grow at a constant rate, g. Shareholders' required rate of return k, – the cost of equity capital – is constant over time. Then a value of a share at the beginning of Year 1, P_0, can be determined according to the following formula:

$$P_0 = \frac{D_1}{k - g}$$

According to the model, dividends will increase from D_1 to $D_2 = D_1(1 + g)$ from Year 1 to Year 2, etc. The value of the share will then also increase, $P_1 = P_0(1 + g)$. According to the model, growth of dividends is the determining variable, controllable by the company. Growth of possible dividends in the long-run is conditional upon the long-term rate of return of equity and the proportion of annual income retained in the company. The relations are basically the following. Expected dividend is dependent on expected profit and expected pay-out ratio (the ratio of dividend to income). Future income, in turn, is affected, however, by what proportion of income is retained in the company and what future return these funds provide, that is:

- Expected income depends on expected return on equity after tax.
- Expected equity depends on expected income and the expected pay-out ratio.

In addition, equity is affected by share issues. For the time being, we will disregard increases of visible value due to accounting methods that can affect the size of book equity.

A permanent growth of dividends can only be attained through a combination of increasing income and increasing equity, i.e. not through an increase in the pay-out ratio or successively increasing return on equity above a certain level. Generally, the mathematical relations are as follows:

1 *At constant income*, dividends can increase successively only through a successively increasing pay-out ratio.
2 *At increasing income*, dividends can increase successively even without a higher pay-out ratio.

Furthermore,

a *When equity is constant*, income can increase successively only when return on equity increases.
b *When equity increases*, income can increase successively without any increase in return on equity.
c *Equity will be constant*, only if total income is distributed as dividends.
d *Income will be constant*, either if return on equity and equity are constant or if equity increases and return on equity decreases.

The combination of 2 and b gives the best empirical explanation of permanent growth in dividends and is also the most realistic basis for expectations of such growth. Few companies might be able to raise dividends through ever-increasing pay-out ratios and at the same time show a constant income and decreasing return on equity (1 and d). It is also very rare that a company can increase return on equity year after year for a long period of time (2 and a).

Predictions about dividend growth may be based on the analysis above. Given a particular equity at the starting point (E_0) predicted income in the following year (I_1) can be computed as predicted return on equity after tax multiplied by initial equity, E_0, i.e. $I_1 = R_E \times E_0$. Let the ratio of dividend (assumed to be paid out at the end of the year) to income be denoted as d. Given a certain assumption about d, dividends can be predicted as $d \times R_E \times E_0$. Equity at the end of the year will then be

$$E_0 + (1 - d) \times R_E \times E_0 = E_0 [1 + (1 - d)R_E].$$

Growth of equity will then be

$$E_0 \times (1 - d) \times R_E$$

If R_E and d are assumed to be constant over time, growth for equity will be the same as for income and dividends, i.e. $(1 - d)R_E$. We ignore, as before, growth in equity due to share issues or appreciation of asset value and other capital changes that are not related to income.

The relationship between expected return on equity (R_E) and the cost of equity capital (k) is crucial to the relationship between the value of the series of payments for a share and the equity of the company. If R_E is equal to k, the value of a share will also coincide with the equity per share, irrespective of the pay-out ratio. Long-term rate of return for the company is thus the essential factor, not how dividends are distributed from year to year.

EXAMPLE

Assume that equity at the beginning of Year 1 is 200, income in this year is 30 and the corresponding dividend is 10 (to be paid out at the end of the year). Dividends and income may be expected to increase by 10 per cent a year. This is accomplished because the return on equity is 15 per cent. A third of the profit will then be paid out as dividends and two-thirds will remain in the company for growth of equity, and will thus also grow by 10 per cent yearly. The pay-out ratio of 1/3 corresponds to a dividend to equity ratio of 1/3 x 15% = 5%. A continuous growth in accordance with this pattern justifies a share price of 200, identical with the equity of the company, provided that the cost of equity capital (k) is 15 per cent, identical with expected rate of return on equity:

$$P_0 = \frac{10}{0.15 - 2/3 \times 0.15}$$

If the company does not attain a rate of return on equity at the same level as the cost of equity capital, the value of shares will be lower than equity per share. This is also true irrespective of what proportion of income is paid out in dividends. Assume that the company mentioned above is expected to achieve only a 7.5 per cent rate of return. Then, income in the first year will be 15 and with the same pay-out ratio as in the preceding case, dividend will be 5 and equity will grow by 5 per cent. A continuous growth in accordance with this pattern justifies a price of 50, which is 25 per cent of the initial equity:

$$P_0 = \frac{5}{0.15 - 2/3 \times 0.075}$$

The above model complies with a classical picture of a company. A combination of resources is utilized year after year in an operation that requires capital and provides a continuous return and cash flows that make dividends possible. However, cash flows which can be distributed may also be raised by selling off separable resources. This has become more common. Companies thus take advantage of the value of a future stream of payments in its entirety on one single occasion, rather than in parts over a longer period for a continuous activity. When selling off a resource, the company will undoubtedly receive one relatively large amount immediately. For obvious reasons, this is particularly common in the case of assets that are bought and sold on reasonably well-established markets and are relatively separate in relation to other company activities, i.e. they can be sold without any negative repercussions on the remaining part of the firm.

For separable assets, nominal market value has often, but certainly not always, increased during the holding period. So-called holding gains have arisen (we will return to the corresponding measurement problems). Assets are then sold at a higher price than book values according to traditional accounting rules. At the same time, cash is free to be used for growth in other assets or for amortizing debts. There are many examples of separable assets: water power facilities, forests, real estate and shares – both the whole stock in a wholly owned subsidiary or minority items.

In many companies there are dedicated activities aimed at acquiring and selling separable resources. In many cases the element of 'holding gains' can be an essential element of the income and cash flow streams of a company. For certain companies and certain industries, this element has sometimes become part of a total strategy. For instance, during periods of a weak construction market but a strong real estate market, construction companies have systematically built up a portfolio of real estate that may be sold in due course. Some industrial groups have developed competence in acquiring companies, restructuring them and subsequently selling them off.

4.2.2 Principal functioning of the market

For rational investors to be willing to make an investment in shares, they must expect the sum of the dividend and the value increase to produce an annual rate of return that is sufficiently high to justify the increased risk of a share in comparison with other investment alternatives.

It is worth considering at this point some of the main concepts of financial theory.

● A first element in shareholder compensation corresponds to the possible return for a so-called risk-free investment, i.e. an investment at a fixed interest rate and without credit risk. Investments in government bonds are an example.

● A second form of compensation is a risk premium for investments in shares:

a There is a general risk premium for shares. Imagine a 'market portfolio' including all the shares on a certain stock exchange. The risk that is associated with such a portfolio is called the systematic or unavoidable risk of the portfolio. The rate of return required on the market for such a portfolio is the sum of the 'riskfree rate' and a risk premium for this unavoidable risk, the risk that cannot be eliminated through diversification.

b There are specific risk premiums. The risk premium associated with shares of a certain company may be higher or lower than the general premium, depending on how it is judged that the future rate of return for the specific share will correlate with the rate of return for a market portfolio.

Inflation complicates the use of the above approach to determine the required rate of return for share investments. The traditional risk-free rate is risk-free only in nominal terms. As future inflation cannot be predicted with certainty, a certain nominal interest rate corresponds to an uncertain real interest rate defined (approximately) as the difference between a nominal annual rate and expected annual inflation. A risk-free real rate of interest assumes the existence of index-based loans. The required rate of return for investment in shares can be said to consist of the following three components:

risk-free real rate of interest + expected inflation + risk premium.

The risk premium, in itself, may depend on expected inflation.

It is difficult to measure, and therefore to observe, the rates of return required on the stock market for an individual company. One reason is that owners change over time and are to some extent anonymous to the executives of a listed company. A further complication is that tax rules vary for different categories of investors, which may cause them to require different rates of return before tax. Historical data for very long periods are sometimes used as a basis for estimating the cost of equity capital. The assumption then is that the rate achieved historically for long periods is an acceptable approximation to the required rate.

On a well-functioning stock market, states of equilibrium will emerge where the expected rate of return for a share is at the same level as the required rate. If the expected rate is higher than the required level, new buyers will tend to appear and cause prices to increase until balance is achieved. In the corresponding manner, owners will supply shares and cause decreases in the price if the expected rate is lower.

If the market expects the rate of return on equity for a company to be at the same level as the cost of equity capital, the share price will coincide with the equity per share in a state of equilibrium, according to the model discussion above.

EXAMPLE

Let us now build on the previous example. Suppose that the expected rate of return on equity and the cost of equity capital are 15 per cent. Suppose, furthermore, that a third of income is distributed as dividends, i.e. equity is growing by 10 per cent in the course of a year. The required rate, 15 per cent, is thus met by dividends, 5 per cent, and growth of the share value, 10 per cent (with these assumptions the stock price will increase in the first year by 10 per cent, up to 220).

If the company is expected to attain a lower rate of return on equity than the cost of equity capital, the stock price will be lower than equity per share. If the company is expected to produce only 7.5 per cent, income will be 15; if a third of income is paid out as dividend, the same as in the previous case, dividend will be 5, i.e. 2.5 per cent of equity, and growth 7.5 – 2.5, i.e. 5 per cent. In a state of equilibrium, the stock price is then 50. Then rate of return required by the owners, 15 per cent, is thus also met in this case; besides the dividend, 5, the value of the share is expected to rise by 2.50. (At the coming year-end, price can be expected to be 52.50, based on the assumption that dividend is 5.25 and the growth g is still 0.05.)

A company with an expected R_E below the cost of equity capital will not have access to new capital. A necessary condition for a stock market to allocate more capital to a company, at the very start or in a later share issue, is that the expected rate of return in the form of dividends and share price increases will achieve at least the rate required in the market. In turn, expected return on equity must be at least in line with the cost of equity capital.

Return on equity in a company below the cost of equity capital can provoke reactions in the market. When the actions taken make it more probable that the company rate of return on capital will approach the cost of equity capital, players in the market will revise their expectations about income and dividends. Then, in turn, share prices will increase towards the value of equity. Active investors in the market are always looking for shares and companies with such potential. The opportunities for value increases conditioned by this kind of development are one of the most fundamental driving forces in the system.

Shareholders who act according to strict financial logic are constantly considering whether expected rate of return – including consideration of risk – could be increased by changing the portfolio. Subsequently, they will always be chasing shares for which improved prospects have not yet had a full impact on share prices; their conviction or hope of improvement may be valuable before it is shared with too many others. For the corresponding reason, they are prepared to sell shares in companies that are reasonably profitable: even if the rate of return is higher than an acceptable minimum level, an alternative investment might be even better. With a company that has reached a high rate of return and with a share price that has been adjusted to such a rate of return, negative changes in expectations are perhaps just as probable as further positive changes.

Increases and declines in share prices are caused by changes in the required rate of return or expectations about the company. We use our previous example to illustrate how an increase in the market price can be interpreted as revised expectations about the future rate of return on equity at a given pay-out ratio.

EXAMPLE

We assume that the price of the shares increases at the beginning of Year 1 from 200 to 300, exceeding the equity per share by 50 per cent. One reason may be that, from now on, the rate of return on equity is expected to exceed the rate required by the market; therefore income and dividends are expected to develop more favourably than previously expected. If the market expects a new higher constant rate of return on equity for Year 1 and coming years, and an unchanged pay-out ratio, a share price of 300 would correspond to an expected constant rate of return on equity (R_E) of nearly 17 per cent:

$$P_0 = \frac{200 \times 0.169 \times 1/3}{0.15 - 2/3 \times 0.169} = 300$$

It may be unrealistic to expect R_E to permanently exceed the cost of equity capital. Assuming that such a gap is closed after five years the price of 300 corresponds to an expected rate of return on equity in the company of about 26 per cent during the next five-year period and a rate of return on equity of 15 per cent thereafter in accordance with the statement shown in Table 4.1:

Table 4.1 R_E higher than the cost of equity capital for five years

Year	1	2	3	4	5	6
Equity at beginning of year	200	234.7	275.3	323.0	379.0	444.7
Income R_E = 0.26)	52.0	61.0	71.6	84.0	98.5	
Dividend (1/3)	17.3	20.3	23.9	28.0	32.8	
Share price at beginning of year	300 (200)	328	356	386	415	445
Value increase during the year	28 (+100)	28	30	29	30	
Rate or return on shares, per cent (without initial value increase)	15	15	15	15	15	

In both these cases, those who hold shares when expectations change benefit from a value increase (100), as part of their total return for Year 1; thereafter, the yearly rate of return returns to 15 per cent in the form of dividend and value increases as long as the expectations are unchanged.

The corresponding mechanism naturally works in the opposite manner when expectations change in a negative direction. Assume that the market at the beginning of Year 1 is reducing its expectations about the rate of return on equity for the coming five-year period, from a level of 15 per cent to a level of 10 per cent (see Table 4.2):

Table 4.2 R_E lower than the cost of equity capital for five years

Year	1	2	3	4	5	6
Equity at beginning of year	200	213.3	227.6	242.7	258.9	276.2
Income ($R_E = 0.10$)	20.0	21.3	22.8	24.3	25.9	
Dividend (1/3)	6.7	7.1	7.6	8.1	8.6	
Share price at beginning of year	163 (200)	180	200	223	248	276
Value increase during the year	17 (—37)	20	23	25	28	
Rate of return on shares, per cent (without initial value increase)	15	15	15	15	15	

At revaluation at the beginning of Year 1, there is a decrease that does not favour those who are shareholders at that moment; new prices are set so that the annual expected rate of return for the shares is to be 15 per cent on a continuous basis. Such a drop can evidently occur as soon as lower return on equity is expected, even if the rate on equity for the company is above the cost of equity capital.

4.2.3 Valuation of shares in practice

The conditions for measurement are in reality obviously more complicated than in our model. It is not easy to compare the cost of equity capital with the rate of return on equity for the company. Assumptions about behaviour of stock market players are also idealistic. To what extent are these players really prepared to react? What do they react to? To what extent are well-founded expectations about the long-term development of a firm really decisive for their actions? Systematic knowledge is limited about many such issues of great importance for systems logic, despite a great amount of research about stock markets during recent years.

One question is how inclined different groups are to act and react. What principle determines whether they retain, sell or buy shares? Are strong economic incentives needed for direct acts? Do evaluations occur at long intervals and without a thorough detailed analysis? Are relatively small potential economic benefits sufficient for a shareholder to consider a transaction?

A group of owners can be assumed to have a basically long-term relationship to particular shares. Even when only powerful reasons would force them to sell, they may from time to time consider their position from a strategic or financial viewpoint. Reactions are especially probable when the long-term return on the shares is low and income and, at the same time, dividends do not seem to develop satisfactorily. Well-organized groups among long-standing owners may react; the annual general meeting and work on the board then become legal arenas. Groups of potential owners with the intention of making a turnaround may appear, with different repercussions for the company and senior management. For sellers, it has surprisingly often been financially advantageous to sell and thus contribute to new business combinations. Buyers have often proved to have strong optimistic views as to what new combinations may mean in terms of increased economic power and higher levels of dividends and income.

For many investors, shares can be regarded purely as an investment, i.e. without the strategic intentions that some conglomerates may have, for example. For a company listed on the stock exchange, owners and their representatives are to some extent a relatively anonymous and changeable group:

- institutions/companies making investments on their own account;
- individuals making investments on their own account;
- intermediaries, acting on behalf of others, especially other individuals.

Certain differences may be expected between professional and non-professional investors, but also within each group, with regard to:

1 how frequent new appraisals are made;
2 how information from companies is interpreted and perceived;
3 how ideas about justified and probable share prices are formed; and
4 what investment alternatives constitute the basic comparisons.

To some extent these differences are reduced because professional advisers/ intermediaries play an important role and may have similar views. Nevertheless, differences in several respects will remain.

1 Everybody has his or her own basis for evaluation, with varying degrees of sophistication, and varying levels of similarity with normative theoretical models for share valuation. Certainly, not all shareholders have well defined views about what rate of return they should require.
2 Investors vary in the amount of time and knowledge they have available, and hence their prerequisites for making independent analyses based on original information from companies also vary. For many investors, intermediaries are key players.
3 Views about alternative investments and their availability vary. Many investors are more or less passive; others search actively for alternatives on the domestic capital markets; others search actively on markets based

2 There is some form of risk premium, specific for individual loans, and basically encompassing the risk that obligations will not be fulfilled.

The sum of risk-free interest and risk premium is the rate of return required by the creditor.

The value of a loan can be determined through an ordinary discount model. At a certain point of time, value is the sum of two components:

● *the interest payments*, discounted at the present market interest rate for a given risk and maturity;
● *the instalments of the capital amount*, discounted at the market interest rate.

The value of a loan on a certain occasion may deviate from the nominal value if the coupon interest rate deviates from the market interest rate. Furthermore, the value of an outstanding loan at a fixed rate of interest can increase and decrease if the market interest rate decreases or increases, respectively. Those who invest at a specific time can obtain the present market rate of return, which can be attained through different combinations of coupon rate and value changes.

EXAMPLE   Assume that somebody invests an amount of 100 in a five-year, newly issued loan that offers a 10 per cent coupon rate at the end of each year. Assume also that the market rate is 10 per cent when the loan is issued and for the following two years. At the beginning of Year 3, the market interest rate increases to 11 per cent. The value of the loan then drops to 97.4, i.e. the discounted value at the 11 per cent discount rate for the three remaining interest payments (10 each) and the capital amount (100). One alternative for the investor is to keep the loan, which will give him three interest payments of 10 and the capital amount 100 in three years. In that case, he or she will get a return of 10 per cent on the original investment. A second alternative, however, is making funds available (97.4) for a new three-year investment that will provide 11 per cent each year until the loan is due. This will give him three interest payments of approximately 10.7 (0.11 x 97.4) and the capital amount of 97.4 after three years. For this second alternative, the five-year period has also provided a 10 per cent rate of return on the original 100. The combination of coupon rate and value increase is different, however.

4.3.2 Valuation of loans in practice

For a creditor, interest development over time is often the predominant issue. Expectations about inflation and interest rates in different time periods play an important part in determining what interest rates and maturity periods the investor is willing to accept. The main preoccupation of his or her judgements – and often professionalism – is how to manoeuvre continuously with regard to the possible changes in the market interest rates. These considerations are based essentially on knowledge about loan markets and the general economy, at the national and international level.

The evaluation of individual issuing companies concerns the capacity to fulfil the predetermined payments, not possible residuals as such. The purpose of credit rating is to judge the probability that a creditor will receive payments for interest and instalments on a loan of a certain maturity. Thorough knowledge about companies and methods of analysis for credit rating are required, rather than knowledge about interest rate relationships. That is one reason for the existence of special rating agencies. Their function is to provide statements only to the extent that credit risk is concerned. For those who buy and sell interest-bearing papers in the commercial paper market and the long-term market, rating analyses are one basis for decision along with other considerations, e.g. about the general development of interest rates.

Rating essentially means a publicly available risk evaluation of a large number of issued loans. On that basis, a contractual compensation can be determined as the sum of risk-free interest and a risk premium, differentiated with regard to the rating. In a well-developed capital market, a rating is almost a necessity if the market is to be available for a certain loan. In less developed markets, credit rating will increase availability, especially for issuers who are not so well known.

When credit ratings are made, the ability of a company to pay is naturally in focus. Contractual compensation will not increase if the company develops more favourably than predicted. A creditor benefits from better safety margins for the payments (and improved opportunities for further profitable deals). But beyond that, there is no real advantage. Unfavourable events, however, may be detrimental to the creditor. The absolutely predominant purpose of a credit rating is thus to achieve as reliable a prediction as possible for the probability of friction in payment flows. The difference in analytical approach compared with the valuation of shares is obvious; in a stock market a high risk may be compensated by the possibility of a rate of return above the normal level. For credit rating, a high rate of return for a company is not an unambiguous advantage. It may even indicate a high risk level which may be unfavourable with regard to the ability to make the contractual payments.

It is natural that ability to pay and financial strength in different forms receive special attention when a credit rating is made. Factors that promote ability to pay are positive, e.g. stable payment surpluses in different business segments, a satisfactory relationship between operating income and interest costs, a relatively large amount of cash and a relatively high proportion of separable assets with a realizable market value. The basis for evaluation is the analysis of key financial ratios for the company, followed by the analysis of the elements of risk that might mean strains for the company in different time scales and the resources which are available to handle those strains. Particular characteristics of each business in these respects, and the individual company's position, are examined thoroughly. The qualitative element in these analyses is often particularly stiking in comparison with what outsiders seem to expect.

Rating decisions mean an evaluation of probabilities. It is therefore unavoidable that outcomes may differ from what is indicated. Events may also occur for which the probability is so low that rating in advance will not be visibly affected. It is not satisfactory, or possible, to base predictions of probable outcomes entirely on analyses of business activities as such. Prediction of player behaviour, and expected patterns of action, will sometimes be a necessary, if incalculable, element. Historically, however, the leading rating institutes have proved to have good predictional ability, which has been the basis for their considerable importance and reputation in the loan markets.

NOTES

[1] The concept 'market value' refers to the fact that the price is settled in a process between separate parties which perform according to business logic and have a degree of freedom normal in a commercial process. The price of a share settled through the stock exchange is often an example of such a price.

[2] In common language, 'risk' usually refers to the possibility of unfavourable outcome, while in economic literature it also includes 'opportunities' of favourable outcomes.

CHAPTER 5

Public accounting information

Some information about a company and its component units which is produced for internal purposes will also become available to the public.[1] It then plays a part in several processes outside the company. No single individual user of public information has the clear privilege of defining its aims and content. Ultimately, this is what makes necessary the whole complicated process of setting standards. What are the possible and desirable changes in the content of the system, given the many forces affecting company information in specific cases? What guidance for assessing economic effiency and long-term cash flows does public information give? What supplementary information is needed, if any? These points of concern are just as useful for analysing public information from the financial market perspective as are attempts to derive appropriate content without constraints.

OVERVIEW

Public information about companies is used in many external processes, each of which has its own logic. When no single user has the privilege to define the purpose and content of the system, all public information, regarded as a system, grows in a rather complicated way in which different players have their own professional focus:

1 leading players in the company which provides the information,
2 standard setters at the national level, and
3 standard setters at the international level.

An independent company (normally in the form of a group) and its main business units are natural objects for public accounting information. Traditional accounting owes its essential importance to financial control in society partly as a result of its orientation towards historical data and short periods.

The prerequisites for measuring rate of return on capital and using such a measure are important for resource allocation and control of efficiency in a national and international economic system. Comparability with the cost of equity capital is especially important. Public levels of reference for profitability of a company, as they appear in the media and in stock markets, often have short-term perspectives in relation to industrial processes.

Standard setting is necessary for comparability between companies, i.e. similar transactions, and those only, should be reported in the same way by different companies. When there is compliance with a law or a standard, companies account for the same transactions in a similar way at least in a formal sense, and this is important. Real general comparability, however,

Employees

One important group is the employees at different levels and their local and central representatives. The majority in this group have to use publicly available information as regards the entire business group or major segments of it, either in the form of the annual reports or through employee magazines, specially produced videos, special speeches by management or through the media. This ongoing information does not, however, focus on the financial well-being and possible development of a particular place of work, which would probably be what employees are most interested in.

For employees and their representatives, many views on companies and general economic conditions are often based on original corporate accounting information and affected by how it is presented. They form a partial basis for decisions about wage demands and negotiation arguments, at the local and central level. This is illustrated, in particular, in public debate about wages and the many references in such debates to profitability measures reported by the media. Public information will also contain information about special aspects that workers' unions may pay particular attention to: for example, capital expenditures for plants, research and development. For representatives at the central level, interested in some specific issue, data about an individual company primarily contributes to the picture for an entire category.

Customers, suppliers and competitors

These groups may also be interested in public accounting information. Annual reports, in particular, may contain a great deal of valuable information. Monitoring competitors and formal information systems covering competitors have become increasingly common – annual reports are one important source of information in this context. Customers/suppliers may obtain a view of the financial position of a business partner they are dependent on, but also an idea about the scope for price negotiations, when profitability levels for the business units concerned are presented. Both joint activities and special interests may thus be in focus when customers or suppliers look for information about a business partner.

Official bodies, the general public and their representatives

A further group for which public information is important represents the general interests of society and the political world. The most obvious example, essential in many countries, is that taxable income is based on public data, especially when the published financial statements are, more or less in their entirety, the basis for taxation. There is one fundamental argument for such a relationship: income measures considered to give the best picture of the activities in public statements should at the same time be the most accurate basis for fair taxation. Other arguments concern technical aspects: it is efficient for the stability of both public accounting and taxation that the two functions are intertwined. In some countries, taxation is, in principle, independent of public accounting. Even in such systems, however, the valuation is to a large extent identical for tax and financial reporting purposes.

Public information may also be used by social authorities in other ways.

At a concrete level, accounting is often important in individual lawsuits, both in civil and criminal cases. At a more general level, the real meaning of a legal rule may in fact be determined by what accounting measures are used and how they are defined; tax rules and capital adequacy requirements for banks may serve as examples. Decisions on legal frameworks and economic control tools at a society level may be influenced by the picture public accounting information provides to groups of citizens and their political representatives. This function is explicit in countries, where accounting data are included in statistics about society and therefore in turn may be the basis for action in that society.

5.1.2 Systems designers

With no single individual user empowered to determine purpose and content, public accounting systems emerge from a rather complicated process. Groups of players with various professional interests participate. Basically, the content of the system will be determined by players at three levels:

- the company that provides information;
- standard setters at national level;
- standard setters at international level.

At a national level there are not only law makers, but also private and government institutions, whose standards are complied with to a varying degree. In a few countries court practice plays an essential role for the detailed design of the system. At an international level, standards are set first by professional organizations such as the International Accounting Standards Committee and second by organizations with primary duties other than accounting standards, such as the European Union (EU), the Overseas Economic Co-operation and Development Agency (OECD) and the United Nations (UN). Internationally important standards may also include standards mandatory at some stock exchanges, but not necessarily developed there: for example the stock exchanges of New York, London and Tokyo.

Through their impact on legislation, politically elected representatives are a primary group influencing the content of the accounting system: parliament, government and senior ministry officials. Issues that attract political attention are in their focus. Their views on standard setting issues reflect this, naturally. In recent years there are some examples of political issues with relation to accounting: co-operation over national boundaries, privatization of industry, relations between government and industry, the influence of employee organizations, crises in the financial sector, the battle against financial crimes and policies to support economically weak regions.

In a few cases, accounting rules are really an instrument to tackle problems which have attracted political attention. More often, however, certain aspects on development and content are important for the main political issue, while central accounting problems as such are of a more peripheral interest. If a government has a certain view on how national rules should be adapted to conditions within the European Union, the treatment of accounting issues must not deviate. If relations between government and industry evoke strong feelings, general aspects in this sphere may play a more important role for standard-setting procedures than an interest in accounting development. Such factors determine how interested elected representatives are, and what they are interested in. Like other players, they have their special and legitimate interests; public accounting systems as such are rarely a primary priority in their world.

Accounting standards in existing legislation have usually been based on some fundamental idea about the desirable effects. Some general and important effects on the economic system at society level have often been the goal: for example, creditor protection or improvement of the stock market functions. When the law was made, there was hardly any reason to consider effects in more detail. In many cases, the explicit intention has been not to regulate details.

Standard-setting bodies have either been created with one professional group and its perspective as a base, or have had more mixed compositions and purposes. The perspective of the groups involved and their representatives will consequently be especially important for the development of public accounting systems.

Representatives of shareholders, employees and financial analysts

Certain groups have a role for which access to corporate public accounting information is required. Representatives of such interests are keen that they personally and/or their principals should function in such a role. Stock analysts and their representatives are examples, as are shareholder or employee representatives. These players, perhaps more so than others, request extensive information; the effects on the company itself, if any, may not be a primary aspect. While individual shareholders or employees can seldom get what they want in terms of information from the company, representatives who share their perspective may influence the information provided, both at a general level and in the case of individual companies. Such representatives try to arrange for the satisfaction of the needs of individual users within their group, or at least what they believe these needs are. They may also be expected to attach considerable importance to the attributes and reactions of users, i.e. user criteria.

Auditors

The accounting system as such is under the professional auspices of auditors. This is very important in the present context. It would be astonishing if auditors and their organizations did not safeguard the accounting process as such. More than most other groups, they may be expected to emphasize measurement systems criteria. Standards may give a certain protection against consequences such as litigation and prosecution. Uncertainty in legal respects is reduced if the auditor's role is to safeguard the application of clear and legally defined accounting standards, 'good accounting practice', 'US GAAP', etc., i.e. clear rules as to what makes special remarks in an auditor's report necessary. As a group, auditors can be expected to aim at an essentially neutral view on the effects of measures on company activities. Individual auditors, however, do not need to be quite unaffected by their experience of the effects on their clients.

Company representatives

Senior management and representatives of companies providing information are particularly interested in the operations of their own companies and what can be done to improve them. The attitude of management to accounting rules is characterized, among other things, by if and how company activities are affected. A sceptical view or objections may arise above all when the rules are considered to give an excessively unfavourable picture of desirable actions, which may make them even more difficult to carry out, e.g. aqcuisitions that are under consideration. Senior management thus have a tendency to apply a form of effect criteria when they evaluate accounting methods.

Conflicts of interest are inevitable within the standard-setting bodies and/ or between standard-setting institutions and the companies which provide information. The multiplicity of professional perspectives, with associated criteria, are reason enough. The requirement of maintaining a consistent system within a country with its own tradition is basically in conflict with the idea of facilitating comparability with leading companies in other countries. The requirement that all transactions should be handled consistently in accordance with the traditional view and at the same time in accordance with their economic significance represents another fundamental conflict of interests. The problem of satisfying both these demands at the same time has increased during recent years. High inflation rates and unstable currencies make interpretation more difficult and restrict the information value of traditional accounting. Long-term capital investments, financed by loans, may initially affect traditional accounting income negatively. Economically sound actions designed to balance inflows and outflows in a certain foreign currency against each other may be reflected as a currency loss in traditional accounting. This is often regarded as a deficiency of existing accounting systems. Discussions on the need for new methods, in conflict with previous practice, will often follow as a consequence.

The state of public accounting systems sometimes causes concern; the failure to comply with standards has been regarded as a serious problem. This has been an urgent issue, particularly in professional accounting circles. It is hardly astonishing that senior management, and their representatives, perhaps do not look at development in the same light. An information system which provides an overview is seldom as important for those who are controlled, as it is for those who exercise control or at least are responsible for the information system. The compliance issue has received a great deal of attention in many countries. New standard setting institutions with a broad representation have been created. In particular, it has been regarded as increasingly important that representatives of information providers shall be included in those organizations.

circumstance perhaps constitutes the most decisive, and sometimes forgotten, role of accounting in capital markets. Verifiability is an important quality from a control point of view.

Whatever valuation bases individual investors may have, most of them will shape and successively revise expectations about companies. Continuous links between expectations and outcome, facilitated through periodic accounting measures and other public information, are fundamental to financial control. Companies provide data that is at least partially the basis of investor expectations, and they are also very much aware of the fact that subsequent outcome could be compared with data provided in the past. Successively reported outcome can then be related to previous data and be a partial basis for new expectations, and so on.

Such a feedback process in individual cases, company by company, is essentially possible with all information systems that satisfy a minimum level of comparability over time. This function is fundamental and extremely important. Intentions beyond that – for a more refined resource allocation and efficiency control in a (national and international) economic system – drastically increase demands on public accounting systems.

With the latter type of aims, there is reason to consider the prerequisites for measuring rate of return and the use of such measures. Most models of share valuation based on company development contain critical prediction variables that are in some way related to expected and/or actual return on equity. Outcome values indicate to the shareholder what resources have been generated for dividends or growth, and furthermore provide a basis for expectations about the future rate of return. The level of the figure, and changes in it, may also indicate potential external pressure against the company, possible share price movements and ability to survive in the present form. The latest rate of return level compared to the cost of equity capital may provide guidance as to predicted and actual changes in rate of return over time. Rate of return measures thus provide basic data of interest to the majority of owners, irrespective of their individual ideas about growth in dividends and share price setting. For lenders, who must assess the probability that interest payments and instalments cannot be managed, various indicators of the risk in operations and financial structure are of primary interest. The ability to actually achieve a certain rate of return is one such indication.

The measurement systems of international groups will inevitably be particularly complicated and difficult to understand. The basic reason is the complexity of the situations, events and transactions to be described. Of course, simplicity of measures should be given high priority. For an ultimate user – receiving information from intermediaries – it is, however, perhaps most urgent to provide simple and understandable financial ratios. Sufficient knowledge to understand and interpret the particulars of income statements and balance sheets may be more important for intermediaries than for the ultimate users. In this case, it is critical that the ultimate user has reason to trust accounting information provided by the company and the intermediaries. There are two considerations:

1 Is the main essence of the measures reasonably straightforward to understand for an ultimate user who lacks the capacity to investigate details?
2 How likely is it that intermediaries will pass on meaningful numbers?

An individual user should be able to make direct, reliable comparisons in different forms without going into definitions in detail. If direct comparability is not possible, the usefulness of the measures for resource allocation and efficiency control decreases. The efficiency of markets deteriorates, because transaction costs increase due to the need to interpret and the risk of misinterpretation. Comparability is not unambiguous, however. From the perspective of the financial investors alone, several forms of comparison are valuable and cause conflicting requirements to some extent on the measurement systems:

- It is essential to aim at comparability over time for a given company.
- It is essential to aim at comparability between companies. Differences between the measures of various companies should exist only if there are important differences between the activities of the companies.
- Consistency between income and capital measures is an advantage in measuring return on capital, and so is consistency within each component. Various components built up in accordance with a central concept basically represent an indivisible entirety. Deficiencies in this respect make the interpretation of numbers more difficult, which in turn makes a great many important comparisons more difficult, for example between cost of equity capital and accounting numbers of the company.
- The measurement system in each country should be consistent with the fundamental purposes of the standards of that country. If, for example, a national system is primarily devoted to creditor protection, adaptation to international standards or stock market needs, item by item, may cause the content of the measurement system to become increasingly difficult to interpret.
- It is a basic advantage if income and capital values are congruent over time, i.e. appreciations and depreciations of assets and debts should be treated as income items.

Different forms of comparisons compete with each other to some extent. The form of consistency which is preferable depends on the form of comparability regarded as most urgent – consistency is a means of attaining a certain form of comparability. The question is what comparability should have priority from the viewpoint of financial control. Furthermore, what level of direct comparability is reasonable? How much comparability can and should be built into the measures and how much can and should be taken into account on a supplementary basis?

In our view, in the first place continuous information should indicate the ability of various units to survive in terms that are general, easily accessible and reliable. We therefore emphasize comparability for units in relation to the rate of return required by the financial markets, especially cost of equity capital. Traditional accounting based on historical costs also has its strengths

allocation in a society. In addition, there is a basic need, common to many interested parties, to assess the possibility of companies and sub-units attaining market-based targets. For us, it is natural to emphasize rate of return measures in this context. As we described in Section 3.2, such measures not only give guidance to investors but also to most interested parties in and around a company, both with regard to the financial stability of the company and its sub-units, and also for the special demands of various parties. Those whose compensations are related to the outcome of the total company can judge the size of their compensation. Everybody can receive signals as to whether their payments from the company are threatened or not.

Irrespective of its underlying purpose, a continuous, public accounting system should support comparability between companies: similar transactions should be treated similarly by all companies, despite the multiplicity of those who provide information independently. To what extent then can comparability be improved through standard setting and more standardized information from companies? Many players attach considerable importance to accounting data, which in itself means that the scope for setting well-specified, unambiguous standards is limited. The problem is particularly visible when conflicts of interest are built into the standard-setting bodies, i.e. when many perspectives are represented in the institutions at the same time. The Swedish example may serve as an illustration. Evolutionary endeavours encounter many obstacles in a small nation, where public accounting is the basis for taxation, has a fundamental focus on creditor protection and also needs to be adapted to international standards and practice. The Swedish experience can perhaps be summarized in the following way:

1 It is difficult to introduce standards which produce accounting numbers that make the activities seem more unfavourable for any major group of companies. It is especially difficult if the representatives of these companies think that there is some doubt about the fundamental basis of the method.

2 It is difficult to deviate from standards that are internationally established. At the same time, it may be difficult to decide what standards to adapt to, when the important international recommendations do not coincide.

3 It is difficult to deviate from the structure of traditional accounting, i.e. to deviate from the convention of prudence and accounting at historical cost.

4 It is difficult to reduce the freedom of companies to choose between accounting methods in areas where companies have been used to such freedom.

5 It is difficult to carry out changes which mean that corporate tax payments increase.

6 It is difficult to modify disclosure drastically in corporate accounting.

7 It is difficult to carry out a change that requires more administrative resources in the important corporate sector which is affected.

When restrictions of this kind are piled on top of each other, there is an obvious risk that there is no real solution to some accounting issues. Either changes will be very time consuming, will not occur at all or there will be compromises; most parties can agree to such a compromise, if necessary, but no one will be entirely satisfied. The forms, *per se,* for making decisions in a standard-setting institution may be an important feature of the rules. The greater the demand for uniform solutions, the more abstract the standards will be. Players who have an important position in 'negotiations' may have a strong influence on standards; they often argue for the best solution in individual cases without giving much consideration to the measurement system in its entirety. Even leading standard-setting institutions, such as the Financial Accounting Standards Board (FASB) in the USA, sometimes seem to have responded to interests that are strongly argued and lobbied: for example, the translation differences in group accounting, valuation of inventory and goodwill valuation. In these cases and others, the effect-oriented views of information providers have been just as important as the demands of users and more purely theoretical ideas.

Co-ordination between international and national standards is especially problematic – the so-called harmonization issue. Harmonization involves both measurement and disclosure. Unanimous opinions about basic definitions of financial statements are fundamentally difficult to achieve; most countries have built their national structures on more or less specific main concepts. Some national systems, as in the USA, have a strong emphasis on the demands of financial markets, illustrated by the fact that the leading standard-setting institution, the FASB, works on behalf of the SEC, the Security and Exchange Commission. It is also often said that annual reports in the USA should be seen first and foremost as 'reports of stewardship', i.e. descriptions of how executives have put funds contributed to profitable use. In other countries – in northern Europe, including Germany – the starting point has been creditor protection. Shareholders, for example, should be prevented from taking out excessive dividends and thus putting payments on loans at risk. In other countries again, the emphasis on accounting data as a part of social planning may be an important starting point. Examples are not confined to the old communist regimes. Differences between the various national systems thus appear: detailed regulation versus the idea that a 'true and fair' view should govern in each case, and the matching concept versus valuation on a conservative basis.

For many years, international standards were relatively vague. They expressed some kind of acceptable lowest common denominator for the countries involved. Some changes have occurred, however, due to stronger pressure as a result of increased listing on leading stock exchanges and increased efforts on the part of several international organizations. As at the national level, the question is what effects standard-setting procedures will have on the rules. Representatives of most countries would like to see a common solution to accounting problems but preferably in line with their own views. In some cases, the decision-making procedures of international bodies have been adjusted to take this into account. What internal consistency can be achieved in international standards, if they prove to be possible at all? A further key issue is to what extent the national standards of leading countries will really be affected by such international standards. Inertia in the real harmonization of fundamental questions is inevitable; besides, as mentioned above, international forces may cause a lack of internal consistency in each country.

National development in small countries often aims at achieving some degree of harmonization between local rules and international standards. To some extent, this is like shooting at moving targets, both in terms of time and space. It may, for example, be noticed that international standards for the valuation of assets and debts in foreign currency have meant different views on one of the most important issues – how currency losses should be treated period by period.

Standards of international importance have normally evolved in an environment with some specific accounting tradition. They may then become a model for certain rules in a nation which, in fact, has a different tradition. Influences from a foreign environment may thus affect internally consistent national standards, which may have repercussions on the possibility of simple interpretation of the essence of accounting numbers and on the description of the main principles of a national system. When forces are not strong enough to defend uniformity in the measurement system, this may mean a long-term threat to possibilities of interpreting accounting data. On the other hand, national standards cannot be developed without taking international models into account. These aspects represent an important and difficult problem of balance when national standards are set.

5.3.2 Effects of standards on corporate information

The problem of ensuring that standards are implemented in the information that companies provide – the compliance problem – has its background in the actual role of accounting numbers in the governance process of society. The advantages of general compliance appear mainly at the collective society level and hardly at all at the individual company level. From the point of view of a particular group of senior management, the immediate interests of their own company are more important than the quality of public information systems. There is no doubt that many managers attach considerable importance to the choice of measures and how their companies will appear in terms of accounting measures. It is also obvious that business deals sometimes – and perhaps increasingly often – are adapted to suit the formal conditions for some seemingly attractive accounting method. The perception appears to be that external assessments of the company will vary, depending on the accounting rules which are applied to given transactions.

These are fundamental forces that hardly any system of standard setting can be expected to handle, at least not completely. More detailed standards may be met by considerations about how the formal conditions should be fulfilled, rather than compliance with the underlying concept. It is not surprising that managers – like other groups – consider accounting from their own professional perspective; it would in a way be more astonishing if they saw quality of accounting as a goal in itself.

Standard-setting endeavours must thus be based on realistic assumptions about actual accounting applications. The following interactive variables are important:

1 how specific and uniform standards are,
2 the level of sanctions associated with inadequate compliance (i.e. the overall consequences for a company if a certain standard is not complied with), and,
3 the effects of standards on information provided by companies.

The following considerations must be taken into account.

● The more powerful the sanction system, the higher (formal) compliance will be.
● The more powerful the sanctions, the greater the need for detailed and unanimous standards will be.
● The more powerful the sanctions, the less parties will be willing to accept very specific and unanimous standards (at least in the case of certain influential parties).
● The more specific standards are and the more powerful sanctions are, the more difficult it is to develop accounting in the long run when prerequisites change.
● The more standards emphasize supplementary information rather than measurement, the more companies will consider it possible that they will be able to comply with standards.

In certain cases, implementation is simple, because the sanctions would be serious, for example to be excluded from a stock exchange or to be faced with a mandatory order issued by a government authority. In a vast number of cases, however, there are hardly any sanctions, apart from unfavourable comments in the media. With such vague sanctions, compliance will largely depend on how standards stand up to overall evaluation from the information provider's point of view. Are standards accepted or is compliance otherwise regarded as important enough in relation to other considerations? In order to increase the possibility of acceptance, the very process of developing standards has often been changed, especially as a result of a broader representation in the standard-setting bodies, in order to ensure that the content of standards will have a better chance of being accepted. In addition, the legitimacy of the very process should cause a higher degree of acceptance in individual companies. To what extent such effects really occur, *de facto*, is disputable. Trends based on experience in different countries do not seem particularly encouraging.

The sanction system, in a broad sense, may thus be vital to implementation. Sanctions vary in their severity. Obligations to provide supplementary information are a weak form – a statement by the auditors in their reports or a statement by the company board announcing that certain deviations have been made and the consequences of this in terms of amounts. According to this concept, compliance should be forthcoming if companies want to avoid negative publicity. This discussion naturally assumes that it is possible to define deviations in reasonably simple and uniform terms; as we shall discuss below, this is not always the case. One alternative is therefore that companies should describe apparent deviations and also important borderline cases. Such supplementary information should provide a better basis for individual cases, on the one hand, but, on the other hand, it is doubtful whether this would result in clearer standards.

An increasing problem in recent years, both for companies and users, is the formal obligation of international companies to satisfy several partially different information needs at the same time. A listing on several stock exchanges means that the company needs to meet mandatory standards at least both on the domestic stock exchange and abroad. Furthermore there may be local recommendations that are not mandatory. The differences are confined to a few areas – such as accounting for taxes, currencies and goodwill – but this is still enough for income and rate of return levels to be affected more than marginally.

5.3.3 Standard setting and comparability

Accounting measures have the quality of expressing extremely complicated processes in a few numbers; this quality is especially remarkable for the complicated activities of international groups. Detailed comparability may hardly be possible, even with very strict standard setting:

1 General, and therefore often abstract, accounting rules may only give limited guidance on how certain, future transactions of individual companies should be treated. If standards are not specified in detail, there will be scope for interpretation. In some individual cases, it may be discussed whether the actual conditions deviate from the conditions conceived when the general rule was written. In such cases, it is not always self-evident what constitutes a deviation from a standard. 'The periodic pressure' on executives will often characterize internal discussions about public accounting. The justification of methods with acceptable effects may be just as important as attempts to determine, without preconceived ideas, what measure could give the best picture.

2 Specifying standards in great detail is not necessarily a way to solve the problem. Certainly, companies sometimes tend to choose the formal conditions of a business deal, standardized or unstandardized, so that a certain accounting measure can be defended. They may thus deviate from the spirit of the rule in question, which may restrict genuine comparability between different companies.

3 The purpose of standard setting is that identical or similar transactions should be reported in the same way by all companies. However, it is a

very difficult task to produce relatively short standards and at the same time define which transactions should be regarded as sufficiently similar to justify the same accounting treatment. How differences in similar but not identical deals should affect accounting may be a matter for discussion. It is often said that the real content of a transaction should be the decisive factor, not formal conditions ('substance over form'). Boundaries are diffuse, however. Assume that a company has several reasons to take a loan in which interest payments are unevenly spread out over time. Should these interest costs be subject to the same accounting treatment as a traditional loan?

4 Some measurement issues are not covered by standards at all. At a detailed level, and also for some individual, more important issues, standards may fail to provide real guidance. In certain areas there may also be options which are explicitly mentioned; alternative methods are permitted. Companies tend to demonstrate greater differences in their accounting than the special features of their activities really justify – with this background, it is hardly surprising.

When standard setting has the intended effect, companies will treat certain transactions in a similar way in their accounting, at least formally. Apparently comparability in this context has increased, which is important and often critical if accounting is to be a basis for direct comparisons. However, it is not certain that real comparability, as a whole, has increased, even with regard to such transactions. Standard setting requires that a strict principle is formulated for a certain type of transaction. This is justified, in particular, by the risk of abuse from a (small) number of those who provide information although a principle of this kind may give an inferior picture in specific cases. A stricter and, in certain respects, less relevant rule, will thus reduce the quality of comparison between 'non-abusers' but will permit comparisons for a larger group of companies. For example, a general basic rule may state that non-monetary fixed assets should be depreciated over their economic life; this general rule is made more strict as regards goodwill as a result of an upper limit for the depreciation period in order to produce a higher degree of uniformity and to prevent abuse. Comparisons between loyal users of the general principle idea can be weakened as a result of this second specified rule; at the same time abuse of the general rule can to some extent be prevented.

Comparability between data from different companies may thus be limited, even if everybody complies with formal standards. A rather super-ficial look at income and capital figures, and stated valuation principles, may give an unsatisfactory picture of similarities and differences between companies. This is especially true when international comparisons are made. There is a risk of superficial rather than fundamental harmonization, for example due to friction mechanisms and differences in basic national ideas, as described above.

Comparisons at the international level may consequently cause problems, even where there are international standards and compliance. There are major difficulties in attaining real internal consistency in measures which can be used for international comparisons. However, when measures are employed for international comparisons, internal consistency is especially important because differences in inflationary rates and interest rates between countries may be crucial, creating a considerable impact on accounting numbers. There are good reasons for simple conversions between alternative income and rate of return concepts. In addition to these problems, the effects of business conditions and social systems (including tax systems) must be distinguished from the effects of differences in measurement systems.

The actual contribution standard-setting and increased standardization makes to greater real comparability is to some extent an open question, especially at the international level. One minimum objective is that direct comparisons between the most accessible corporate accounting data should be fruitful. Accounting methods should not prevent this. It should be possible to compare the main items in financial statements, and key ratios based on them, without thorough studies of footnotes and detailed assumptions. Standard setting should have this minimum target.

5.3.4. Interpretation and use of measures in public information systems

The form and degree of comparability that actually emerge in public accounting systems is a consequence of systems development. No central authority has the right to decide on systems development. As a result, systems evolve in an interaction between standard setters and those who provide information, at international and national levels. Those who use accounting for financial control purposes have reason to ask what accounting numbers really involve and what comparisons can be readily made without a more thorough analysis. Apart from interpreting numbers in this way, the qualified user must consider what supplementary information is desirable and accessible. Accounting numbers is a valuable, but only partial, basis for financial investors who are ultimately interested in short- and long-term cash flows. They show an incomplete picture of how factors of importance for future cash flows have performed over a certain (short) period. As a result, they must be supplemented by the user's general impressions and/or more formal information. It is important to keep the following considerations in mind. (A more thorough discussion follows in Part Two.)

1 Not all important differences between companies are captured by accounting measures. The need to stick to one measurement principle, based on historical cost, means that accounting for the entire company or certain sub-units *per se* will be incomplete and possibly even misleading with regard to the economic essence of certain phenomena. For instance, unrealized value changes on real estate and shares do not affect traditional accounting income. Accounting based on market values should no doubt reflect current conditions more accurately in this respect. For many purposes, fixed assets which are still in use after many years should

preferably be valued at replacement costs or through discounted cash flows, rather than at historical cost. If economic aspects of this kind are not reflected in accounting numbers, as they are not in traditional accounting, they must be taken into account in another way when comparisons are made between companies.

2 The conflict between measuring periodic income and financial position is a classic issue. The dominating guideline is often prudent valuation of capital; this is, of course, especially true in countries where standards have been designed with regard to creditor protection. Few mechanisms in traditional accounting and review processes counteract the possible undervaluation of assets and overvaluation of debts. For this reason, income figures must be interpreted with extra caution. Risk reservations may have been made and if the outcome becomes more favourable than anticipated, reserves decrease and affect periodic income.

EXAMPLE

Assume that a company has 50 in annual income for three consecutive years, before taking into account its involvement with Customer C. In Year 1, A fears that C will cause a loss of 20, which pulls down income for this year. From a conservative point of view this is without doubt a good method. During Year 3 however, it appears that the loss is only 5, not 20. Accounting income will be 30, 50, 65 for these three years, which provides good income growth in superficial terms. If income had been computed in accordance with the real loss on customer C, income numbers would instead have been 45, 50, 50, which gives quite a different impression of the growth.

A sophisticated user with expected cash flows as his or her main guideline needs to interpret accounting numbers with regard to the special characteristics of the individual company as a financial unit, i.e. the structure of the company in terms of cash flows. Strengths and weaknesses not captured by financial key ratios must be observed. Such an analysis also provides a basis for judging the need for supplementary information, both quantitative and qualitative.

To a large extent, accounting data are used for continuous or occasional judgements without any thorough analysis. But such uses involve a dilemma. On the one hand, there is a need for concrete, short-period data for a company. On the other hand, the system rarely permits particularly far-reaching conclusions for such short periods: income for one year, or even more tangibly for part of a year, will inevitably often be unreliable. Conclusions will not be reasonably uniform until a few years have passed. Those who base their decisions on short-term accounting numbers will in fact often make comparisons that are less reliable than what they may seem on the surface.

In Parts Two and Three, we discuss the design and use of accounting measures from the perspective indicated above.

NOTES

[1] We choose the terms publicly/internally instead of, for example, externally/internally. Thus we indicate that some information gets attention inside as well as outside the company and other information gets attention internally; purely external information in the sense of information observed only externally, seems to have minor and decreasing importance for the issues we discuss.

[2] This discussion is partly conditioned by how 'groups' are defined. We return to this issue in Chapter 14.

CHAPTER 6

Internal accounting information

In contrast with public information, internal information has a self-evident higher-level user whose intentions and aims determine systems design. Senior management have the privilege to determine the prerequisites for the content, use and intentions of internal systems. The systems design is on senior management's terms, with rules for public systems as an important prerequisite. Internal information concerns entire corporate groups and units within such groups, naturally with a relatively strong emphasis on the units.

OVERVIEW

Systems for the continuous production and distribution of accounting data are normally the most important source of economic information in a company. Efficiency measures in purely financial terms will not be so clearly meaningful lower down in an organization and closer to physical operations. At the same time, management in an independent company needs to judge possible corporate cash flows in relation to external financial demands and to evaluate different activities from this perspective. What is the earning power of the total company? What is the ability to pay on an ongoing basis? How do various parts of the company contribute in these two respects? There is thus – or should be at any rate – some integration between control processes in a company; in a way this is the ultimate sign of an independent company.

Accounting data systems, both central and local, and the ways in which they capture, process and store data, determine what information can be produced in a company. Senior management have the privilege of defining the guidelines for the content. From a control point of view, both a superior financial perspective and the more operational perspectives of various activities are necessary. Basic conditions for the company such as external demands, the need for cash flows and the cost of capital affect internal information requirements. Measures and targets for individual parts of the company, however, cannot be regarded as merely directly derived from conditions for financial markets. There is scope for tailoring individual information systems to different parts of a group. The degrees of freedom vary in accordance with the measures and targets senior management apply to the units, the reward structure related to this, the information sub-units must deliver upwards and the extent to which they need to integrate with company-wide systems. Sub-units have their independence on senior management's terms.

In internal systems, a focus on organizational responsibility is important, but revenues, costs and capital for market objects such as products and customers are also critical. Rate of return measures for an entire company and their larger business units often have a key role; they have a conceptual correlation with the cost of equity capital and can at the same time be related to measures for various sub-units. Relations must be clear between the following variables:

1 the cost of capital in financial markets,
2 the internal minimum threshold levels for a company and sub-units, and
3 levels chosen to affect a number of players in a continuous control process.

In internal systems, targets can be expressed explicitly and distributed throughout an organization and hence play a part in continuous review. Targets for an entire company, which is the basis for determining targets for business and functional units, may principally be deduced from:

- the cost of equity capital in the stock market,
- the expectations about companies implicitly made in share prices, or
- the need to generate internal financial resources to develop company competitiveness in product and resource markets.

6.1 INTERNAL CONTROL PROCESSES AND INFORMATION

Internal accounting information is a basis for management control in the company, i.e. it should be used directly or indirectly for control processes at different levels. In the case of a company in a market economy, it is necessary to analyse and affect cash flows and their determining factors.

6.1.1 Users

At each level in a company, accounting information is the basis for fundamental control issues: How should resources be used? Is operational efficiency sufficient? Continuous assessment of organizational units is of particular importance.

If efficiency measures are expressed in purely financial terms, these will not be clearly meaningful lower down in the organization and closer to physical operations. Other measures of efficiency may be more natural and considered more relevant for a specific activity. Measures for a production activity in physical terms often serve as an example. Economic efficiency from the company and owner's point of view, in whatever way it is measured, is hardly a primary concern for the personal goals at lower organizational levels. The emphasis placed on professional ambitions and what ambitions receive priority may differ from those at higher levels. Intraprofessional norms without a financial profile may be more important, as may the pleasure of helping a customer for its own sake, not just as a means to achieve the financial goals for a company.

At the same time, the senior management of an independent company must regularly judge possible cash flows of the company in relation to external financial demands and evaluate various activities from this perspective. Ongoing ability to fulfil contractual obligations is an immediate and necessary condition for survival. Capacity to achieve, in some sense, adequate levels of income and dividends sets a second determining limit, often just as decisive in the long run. The most fundamental information requirements of senior management can thus be stated as follows:

● What is the earning power of the entire company in comparison with external financial demands? Efficiency measures in overall financial terms are important in this respect for those who have management tasks at a high level, close to external demands.
● What is the ongoing payment ability of the entire company, in different time scales? The capacity to fulfil obligations when debts are due sets an initial constraint on any activity. Subsequently, assessing capacity and risk levels in this respect are of fundamental importance; a strategy for handling these kinds of situations is also needed.
● How do different parts of a company contribute in these two respects. Are these sub-units a burden from either perspective?. An internal information system should be a basis for decisions about scale-setting and orientation, and for evaluation of operational efficiency.

There is thus – or should be at least – some integration between control processes in a company; in a way this is the ultimate sign of an independent company. Different sub-units may be regarded as, and may actually even be, more or less independent in different respects. Their local control process does not have very evident relations with processes for the rest of the company. This may represent a value in itself and/or be efficient from the entirety point of view. Nevertheless, interdependences of activities mean that a local process is subordinated to the control process of the entire independent company, at least implicitly. There are always financial relationships and often operational relationships too.

The relationship between a superior and subordinates will always be asymmetric, i.e. in reality one can make decisions over the others. This is also the case when local units appear to be very independent in superficial terms. The degree of asymmetry may, however, vary considerably:

1 Detailed rules are prescribed.
2 Explicit demands are stated, but no detailed rules.
3 Demands are implicit and few.
4 There are no real demands, not even implicit ones.

It is common to define responsibility in accounting terms and sometimes targets are also explicit. Principals want to encourage people immediately below them and to have the possibility of review. This has often proved to be a powerful way of influencing attitudes, especially if it is combined with financial incentives. Senior management, in particular, use information systems in this way. They also communicate expectations and mainly professional values to major groups of employees; the possibility of attracting attention both internally and in the media provides a platform.

'In our group one financial ratio, and only one, is important.'

'When we compare ourselves with the Americans and the Japanese it is apparent that all of us in our company must try harder to improve stock turnover.'

Through accounting information, top executives aim at certain effects, which is not at all the same thing as evaluating alternative actions on a strictly analytical basis. In Sweden, this role for accounting was accentuated during the 1980s; high profile conferences and campaigns to spread management messages also became very common.

6.1.2 Providers

Accounting data systems, both central and local, determine what information is available within a company. Principles for collecting, registering and storing data can be discussed as follows:

Database organization

The overall structure for storing accounting information may vary very much from one company to another. Several bases often contain data of importance for economic evaluations in a wide sense. How do these bases relate to each other? Databases with externally oriented data have frequently been integrated with internal accounting, while others have relatively distinct systems for these two purposes. Departmentally oriented accounting and product costing can be handled in separate systems or together. Central and local databases may have different sizes relative to each other, and vary in their ability to link up with each other. Other databases and systems of importance for economic efficiency can likewise vary in their ability to interface with accounting information systems in a more narrow sense.

Registration principles

In terms of identification concepts, a company can aim at far-reaching uniformity or a balance between central and local considerations. The level of detail must be judged with regard to both its contribution to clarity and its cost.

Methods for collecting data

The main problem is how sufficiently detailed data can be captured with acceptable accuracy and costs. Important developments have taken place in this respect. Data of significance to economic analysis have become increasingly easy to collect in a direct link with actual business events and information flows which are necessary for the operations as such. This applies to many retailers, for example.

To some extent, accounting data systems represent a problem area in themselves. Capital investments and operational costs are often immense. It is not always easy to compare systems value to costs. Neither is it easy to analytically relate issues involving information needs and ideal accounting measures with knowledge about systems structure and processes required to develop and handle data systems as such. Consequently, it may be difficult to determine the extent to which differences between alternative accounting data systems in the market can really affect the availability of important information, which is ultimately the crucial factor in the business community.

6.1.3 Systems designers

The users with immediate responsibility for the activities to be controlled, at different levels, are key groups when internal systems are being designed. This also applies to the leading personnel in the accounting and control departments. A user in a superior position – in senior management – determines, directly or indirectly, the prerequisites for systems development based on his or her other views, ambitions and needs for information.

Over time, an important degree of competence and experience will have been gathered about accounting data systems as such, via the services of systems suppliers, or alternatively of consulting firms. Systems suppliers have developed networks, so-called user associations. Some players, inside or outside the company, will have computer and systems competence, but no business or accounting competence; they are also key groups when systems are designed. Given their competence and roles, they have naturally focused on data systems as such, rather than on management control in a wider sense. They represent a comprehensive and increasingly diversified field of competence requiring its own professional surveillance. In this field, as in so many others, attention attached to systems as such must be combined with ideas about how the system can help to solve the problems that ultimately need to be solved, in this case the very down-to-earth need to analyse and influence cash flows.

6.2 PERSPECTIVES OF SYSTEMS DESIGNERS

Senior management basically determine the character of the vertical control processes in a company. They also strongly influence rules for horizontal control processes, for example the relations between sub-units operationally related to each other. It is also their privilege to define guidelines for systems content. How can this privilege be used, and how should it be used? Control concepts, cost of information and forms for systems development set limits on the information needs which can be met within a company.

6.2.1 Overall financial demands v. local operational demands

Senior management need to influence and follow up the entire operation they manage on behalf of the owner. From their perspective, a group system for accounting measures and targets basically represents a tool for influencing people and outcomes. Such a system signals a need for action. It articulates strong expectations for the members of the organization; sometimes resulting actions can be taken very rapidly and produce relatively immediate effects. Defining targets or redefining financial responsibilities can be done without any real change in the underlying data systems. However, many effects are conditioned by changes in the existing data systems structure, which inhibits change in areas of responsibility and measures.

From a more analytical point of view, different forms of data should be easy for senior management to compare conceptually with each other in group systems: between the entire company and sub-units, between areas of responsibility and products, between cost of equity capital and the internal rate of return targets, etc. Each form of comparability makes its own demand on consistency in computations. Management (or any other internal systems developer at any level) need to clarify what types of comparability, and therefore consistency, are mandatory in continuous systems. Measures and targets at a certain point in time should ultimately be relatable to cost of equity capital. Clarity as well as knowledge about relations between alternative accounting methods will be important for the choice of continuous systems and for a qualified interpretation of data on a specific occasion. It is important that the following aspects should be considered:

● Various objects should be conceptually related to each other, e.g. it should be clear how values of products or capital investments relate to values of organizational units.
● Various measures should be conceptually related to each other, e.g. for organizational units at different levels.
● Targets for different objects should be conceptually related to each other and to rates in financial markets, e.g. rate of return on capital targets for business units and discounting rates for capital investments.

One perspective for developing internal accounting systems is thus based on overall financial demands: cash flows, the rates of return required and time scales of financial markets are determining factors in this context. Another perspective takes local activity as its starting point. The need for overall comparability in a group perspective may be in conflict with the need for locally relevant information. Measures and targets directly reflecting the demands of financial markets do not necessarily also reflect special conditions for individual sub-units. Information systems often need to be adjusted to encompass the core of the individual activity. Other variables than cash flow and financial measures must often be analysed; time perspectives and targets may also differ. Differences in approaches are perhaps most clearly indicated if an activity-oriented perspective – with company and sub-units in focus – is contrasted with one form of financially oriented perspective: microeconomic financial theory. According to this approach, the owner perspective is strongly emphasized; the decisive factor from society's point of view is the extent to which activity will have an effect on the expected rate of return and risk for the owner.

Differences between these two perspectives naturally involve some of the most fundamental questions about an economy. It is outside the terms of reference of this work to discuss these issues in detail. Our view is that both perspectives are needed in corporate governance. The internal systems should stimulate a continuous focus and dialogue on potentials for the company and sub-units to survive and develop under market conditions. Cash flows and the rate of return required by financial markets are determining factors. Measures and targets for individual sub-units in day-to-day control may, however, not only, or even primarily, be directly deduced from conditions in financial markets. They must also be chosen with regard to the operational character of local activities. What are the working conditions for those who ultimately have to execute purely physical activities?

At each organizational level, data are required for two forms of information needs. First, it must be possible to summarize and relate data with regard to financial demands from owners and creditors to the entire company. Second, the need for local information, specific for each activity, must be satisfied. Data should be stored close to the source of events and be quickly available to those who can affect events in the first instance. In many cases, it is not appropriate to collect detailed data locally, transfer it to a central level for some processing and overall analysis and subsequently take it back to the local level in a processed form for action. It is important that better systems approaches exist in this respect, following centralized solutions employed in previous decades.

6.2.2 Degree of freedom for sub-units

As mentioned above, relations between management and employees are not symmetrical. Most senior managements do not have the intention of making them symmetrical, even if they express far-reaching decentralizing intentions. Some factors determine actual degrees of freedom for the sub-units: what type of demands and targets do senior management attach to sub-units, what information must be communicated upwards from these units and to what extent are links with central data systems required.

Information technology nowadays makes many control philosophies feasible in practice. Are relatively autonomous units to have access to separate systems? Should central management make detailed functional decisions supported by systems which are closely integrated for the entire company? Data systems may be built for either situation. The choice between different systems structures therefore goes back to more fundamental issues about the degree of freedom for sub-units in business activities and systems decisions, for its own sake or for the benefit of a company as a whole. What are the desires of management at group level and subordinate levels if technical restrictions are no longer such a decisive factor? What is possible with regard to operational dependencies which are essentially determined by the nature of activities? One example of dependencies is the inevitably common use of a basic facility (such as a national communications network).

The degrees of freedom for individual sub-units' systems will vary in many respects:

1 *Measures*. To what extent are sub-units allowed to use different concepts and terms for (broadly) the same phenomena and different detailed definitions for the same concept? Originally, perhaps geographically dispersed punch-card systems could give disparate definitions, e.g. in the field of sales reports. Reports to a group central unit should obviously be as consistent as possible in these respects; still in practice this represents some restrictions for sub-units. What freedom should sub-units be allowed as to concepts, definitions and terms when all aspects are taken into consideration? A related issue is the extent to which consistency should be required in underlying registration concepts.

2 *Database organization*. What data should be stored in an organization, and where? Which systems should be related to each other so that usable data can be easily transferred? In the initial decades of computerization, the obvious solution often meant that central databases played a key role. New prerequisites have, however, appeared, not least the development towards relations databases. Questions about availability and distribution forms are closely connected. To whom should data in central and local databases be available? In what form should distribution take place? To what extent should this be co-ordinated in a company or left to individual sub-units to decide?

3 To what extent should *computer-aided activities* be co-ordinated within a company? Should, for example, sub-systems for production and storage be integrated with each other, even if they represent different organizational units and the idea is to give these units some autonomy. Should common systems for production planning be used for similar units in different regions, at the expense of autonomy for each business unit?

4 How should *computer power* be divided and co-ordinated between sub-units? To a large extent, this is related to many of the choices mentioned above in points 2 and 3.

5 How should *procedures and routines* be arranged for information routines at the planning and review stages? Should strict and detailed time schedules for a central unit in reality be one of the most important restrictions for sub-units, as may be the case in a group budgetary process? At what level should capacity for analysis of accounting data and subsequent actions be placed – this is the most common and important ingredient of control work.

6 How should responsibility for *developing and maintaining systems* be distributed between units if software and hardware are operated in different places in a company?

What does participation in common development work of this kind mean for the long-term degree of freedom for business units and other relatively independent units in the company?

A decentralized profile for systems solutions in these dimensions may be advantageous from different points of view, particularly with regard to motivation. When data systems are developed – and in professional literature – such an orientation is often described in very positive tones. The underlying fundamental perspective seems to be that companies and sub-units should be organized and controlled on their own terms, rather than as a reaction to signals from superior institutions in a hierarchical structure.

The structure of an accounting information system must be decided with regard to the philosophy for degree of freedom for sub-units. For instance, data systems may look different for a functional unit depending on whether it is a cost centre or a profit centre. Quite frequently, information systems have a longer lifetime than philosophies of organization and control in a company. Systems should therefore have organizational flexibility; existing structure should not in practice prevent changes in overall control philosophy. In order to achieve such flexibility, it is important to clarify when systems are designed what main forms of control are possible, i.e. what forms of economic responsibility are realistic. Hence, an analysis of responsibility and the roles of sub-units is an important starting point when systems are designed, even if existing control forms are not currently questioned.

6.3 CONTENTS

Accounting data attracts considerable continuous attention in internal work, either through paper-based reporting or, to an increasing degree, through electronic media. In the following, we will discuss the content of such systems employed in day-to-day operations: objects, measures and targets.

6.3.1 Objects

Internal systems must, of course, reflect both the entire company and the various sources of cash flows. What is the origin of inflows and outflows? What are the objects affected as a result? Some considerations, which may partially overlap with each other are:

● *Product flows.* Segmenting information in accordance with product flows produces objects that are relatively independent of each other: revenues for a certain object defined from a business point of view can be related to costs for the same object.
● *Organization.* Segmenting information in accordance with organizational units is a necessity. In certain cases, this dimension will overlap with the product flow dimension; this is often a favourable structure from the point of view of management control.

● *Capital investments.* The financial situation of a company or sub-unit will be strongly influenced by large capital investments; these effects must be assessed. This is therefore important both at the planning and the review stages.

● *Customer segments.* This object may be categorized by geographical criteria (countries, regions) or need characteristics. This dimension may, but need not be, reflected in the organization of a company.

An important aspect of choice of objects – and measures – is the importance of defining meaningful and influential targets. For what objects would such levels most easily be computed and play an essential role: entire responsibility areas, parts of responsibility areas, products or customers? For what measures will such targets be most easy to establish: rate of return on capital, income, costs or volume and quantities? This plays an important role for the effects of accounting measures on decisions.

It is important that financial responsibility is clearly stated, preferably in accounting terms; it may be necessary to adapt the organization to facilitate this. Measures and targets for entire responsibility areas will often provide important indications and significant results. Periodic measures are an important basis when judgements from a total perspective are made. This may be their strongest attribute; an unsatisfactory impression for an entire activity will often provoke action. This is especially true for entire companies or business units and to some extent also functional units. Similarly, each individual type of resource may be assessed, and this is perhaps more important in practice than judging the total use of resources for a function unit. Direct effects on certain items may thus also result.

From an organizational point of view, we classify objects with regard to the type of output, resources and capacities. Ultimately, our basis for partitioning is the activities cash flows can affect and how this occurs. Entire companies, consisting of several operations and a finance function are obviously one type of object; we are also interested in business units and functional units:

Business units   The most common category consists of divisions and subsidiaries with important degrees of freedom in continuous operations but which are dependent on superior management for financial resources. The total resources of a company are allocated by senior management with regard to the interests of the entire organization. In such cases, the generation of equity has ceased to be the decisive basis for its financial position. Sub-units are naturally dependent in the sense that they compete for common resources (financial and others), internal deliveries may occur, etc. Some business units may have a more autonomous position from a financial point of view; equity is generated and accumulated in ways more similar to those of an independent company.

Functional units   These include units for producing, selling and R&D. Managers of such units deal with only a functional sector of a company or a business unit.

Within this sector, they should utilize and process a given quantity of resources. They may also take some part in procuring these resources, perhaps also negotiate prices and wage levels. They receive funds for developing their units as a result of decisions by superior managers. Output from different functions must be co-ordinated. For these different reasons there is thus a very strong dependence between units. Consequently, organization and decision systems must mean more detailed regulation than at previous levels. We make a distinction between three different types of functional units:

- *Production units* produce or procure goods or services, to be sold by another unit within a company.
- *Sales units* sell goods and services, produced and procured by another unit in the company.
- *Support units* are to some extent programme units; costs are determined by periodic decisions about frameworks for activities. Typical examples are units for research and development, advertising and maintenance.

From a business point of view, there is an especially strong internal interest in objects for which external revenues and corresponding costs can be meaningfully compared. *Product costing* has therefore often had an important position in functional organizations. In divisionalized companies, which have been especially common in recent decades, the focus has often been on satisfactory profitability for entire divisional areas. Possibly, evaluation of single products has attracted somewhat less attention in these organizations, both when products belong to a single responsibility area or are shared between several such areas. Analyses from a product perspective might produce different conclusions compared to a responsibility area approach. Systematic information is very limited, however, as regards the significance of responsibility versus product concepts in management control. Moreover, new objects have become accepted fairly recently, or at least become more emphasized, e.g. the *customer concept*. It is beginning to become increasingly common for companies to define profitability targets for individual customers and groups of customers.

Product costing and customer costing are important steps in a chain of financial requirements ultimately originating in financial markets; costing methods should stimulate product and customer structures which permit financial demands to be satisfied in the short term as well as in the long term. Among other things, it is important that calculations affect the setting of the scale and orientation of the company. Capacity must not be built up on the basis of products – and customers – which do not satisfy long-term requirements.[1]

6.3.2 Measures

Measures, subject to continuous observation, are vital in management control, especially periodic measures for objects for which there is an explicit personal responsibility. Measures should be chosen with regard to

fulfil an important function. The essential question is what is a satisfactory level of output with regard to given prerequisites for an activity. In such a context it is often considered essential that players perceive requirements more or less as commitments; in other words, demands affect actions directly. In such cases targets based on potential are required, or at least targets related to potential.

There is organizational friction in demand processes. Targets can seldom be changed to keep pace with changing conditions (see Section 2.3). This friction has fundamental importance for demand processes and their effects. When targets are expressed explicitly in a company, it is important to consider how alternative measurement methods and targets may function under various possible conditions during their lifetime. In Part Two we discuss methods and targets from this point of view.

6.4 INTERNAL PERSPECTIVE OF REQUIRED RATE OF RETURN FOR A TOTAL FIRM

Targets for an entire company are an important basis for a demand process within a company. In principle, such targets can be deduced in one of the following ways:

- from rates of return required in the stock market;
- from expectations on company performance implicit in share prices;
- from the need to generate funds internally for company development in order to achieve a competitive position in product and resource markets.

The target for rate of return on equity after tax may in turn be converted into a corresponding target before tax. Given certain ideas about debt-to-equity ratio and interest cost level, certain targets for rate of return on capital employed before tax may also be computed.

6.4.1 Targets derived from rate of return required on the stock market

One possibility for identifying company targets for rate of return on equity, is to identify the rate of return required in the stock market, the cost of equity capital, k.

Assume that assets and debts of a company are entered at market values. For market value of shares to be identical with company equity, expected R_E should be at the same level as the rate required in the market, k (stated in Chapter 4). If expected rate of return on equity is below the cost of the equity capital market, and therefore the market value of shares is lower than company equity, this represents a problem for a company. The most obvious point is that share issues may not be possible. In a pure market, nobody is willing to invest an amount of money when market value will immediately drop. Of course, profitability may improve and new capital may contribute to income corresponding to the rate required for new capital. But experience shows that it has proved difficult to undertake share issues if historical and/or expected return on the entire equity is unsatisfactory in relation to market requirements.

Another force is more visible in the daily life of managers. Enforced changes for a company become more probable, either as a result of actions by powerful owners or due to acquisitions by new owners who foresee a potential for income improvements and share price increases. Experience indicates that companies with such a profitability and share price profile will often be candidates for acquisitions, and this is by no means surprising. Restructuring in connection with new business combinations naturally means a threat to the survival of a company in its existing form.

It is thus important for a company and its management to follow continuously how the rate of return on equity relates to the cost of equity capital and the future trends. Certainly, owners can take actions at various rate of return levels, when expectations are not realized or when alternative investments and combinations are expected to give an even higher return. However, the distance between the company rate of return on equity and the cost of equity capital is an important indication. The more positive this distance is, the more probable it is that the activities of a company may continue without any structural actions at owner level.

Some managers regard total return on outstanding shares as a primary goal, while others consider that this is more of a threat to the survival of the company. With the latter view, a company should define targets in terms of rate of return on equity after tax, a level corresponding to cost of equity capital should be regarded as a long-term minimum goal and the company's economic results should be continuously related to this level. With both views, however, it is important to identify the distance between company rate of return on equity and the rates required by the market – the cost of equity capital.

In our examples above, a rate of return level required by the market is very easily converted into a target level for company rate of return on equity. Under real conditions, relationships are more complicated. In particular, valuation of assets and debts in actual accounting is almost always based on historical cost and the realization principle. Book values of assets normally underestimate current market values, which reflects more accurately the capital on which a company should provide a yield. When rate of return targets are based on income and capital concepts in line with traditional accounting, such a level may consequently need to be adjusted. This problem area is discussed in more detail in Part Two.

6.4.2 Targets derived from expectations implied in share prices

Recurrent comparisons between expectations and outcome are no doubt important for share price movements. The phenomenon is important for those managers who want to avoid external actions due to unfavourable development. It is of some interest for them to notice the expectations implicit in share prices, and what outcome is required to defend a certain

separable resources operation are to be defined must be considered. Second, the contributions made by such operations, year by year, in traditional income and dividend terms and how this in turn affects current operations must also be considered.

For a separable resources operation, it is natural to follow up the development of market values on a continuous basis. If there are year-by-year income measures internally, measures in real terms are of particular importance, i.e. measures showing value changes on specific assets in relation to general purchasing power. Such measures are easy to interpret and understand, especially when there are well-developed markets for separable assets and such assets may be sold without important strategic repercussions to other company activities. It is natural to define targets for separable resources operations for a multiple-year period from this point of view.

Usually, it is also important for companies with a separable resources operation to consider income in conventional accounting terms. The question is therefore, what income contributions in these terms should such an operation give, year by year, mainly as a result of sales. The traditional rate of return on capital for an entire company may be computed as income for continuous operations and separable resources operations, in relation to booked capital. When a company with major separable resources formulates its target for continuous operations in traditional terms, it can hardly disregard how separable resources operations relate to the rest of the company. If there are operational links, e.g. when construction activities and real estate activities are combined within a single company, opportunities and threats for separable resources operations may affect targets for the rest of the company.

6.4.5 Some conclusions about targets[5]

The three methods mentioned above for deducing targets for rate of return on capital produce internal targets with varying degrees of stability. Targets adjusted to variations in share price expectations could be remarkably unstable. Targets deduced from rates required in the stock market should be changed, especially when there are major changes to inflation and interest rates. Targets based on internal financial needs are affected by changes in investment plans, with regard to volumes and prices.

Required rates linked to the stock market and variations in share prices would produce particularly unstable targets. Corporate management must weigh up two important factors against each other. First, they should observe how company actions affect the stock market and consider expected reactions as signals for actions. Capital market theory places a strong emphasis on this aspect. Second, internal prerequisites for the systematic and stable development of large organizations must be established, in which individuals have varying motives for action. Continuous adjustment to signals from the stock market is hardly desirable in view of the instability involved, even if it were feasible.

Particularly in the short term, these two perspectives may often be in conflict: corporate management may not be able to communicate the company's future prospects to the stock market sufficiently well. An owner's self-interest is not necessarily consistent with that of the company. Other variables, apart from fundamental corporate variables, may affect share prices. The two perspectives are more consistent with each other in the longer term, however. Therefore, we regard rates required in the market as an important benchmark for company earning power and as a long-term minimum target for a company competing in the stock market. A target based on needs, in the sense which we have used the term above, has sufficient stability to provide a basis for internal management control. Attaining this level, however, does not provide a guarantee against external financial threats. Nor are the intentions of a company, in practice, usually confined in this way, nor should they be. We shall not enter into a discussion of what is usual and desirable in this latter respect.

Targets for rate of return on capital, based on financial conditions for survival, are thus important control tools. When such levels are quantified, they are based on fundamental assumptions, such as estimates of rates required by the market or estimates of the necessary growth rate of a company. The degree of accuracy which can be achieved in this respect is not overwhelming, to say the least. Targets formulated cannot be more accurate than basic assumptions. When such levels are applied out of their financial context, they may often appear more accurate than they really are.

NOTES

[1] This does not imply any statement about costing methods. Either the full costing method is used and the cost of equity capital is included in total cost, or the cost is calculated according to the variable cost method (direct costing). In this case, targets for contributions must be chosen with regard to the fact that financial requirements are only partially covered by variable costs.

[2] Compare e.g. Johansson, S.-E. 'Growth of Capital, Capital Structure, and Rate of Return', in Brockhoff and Krelle (eds), *Unternehmensplanung* (1981).

[3] Under Miller and Modigliani's model assumptions, the value of a company will not be affected by the choice of debt-to-equity ratio. Debt-to-equity ratio, however, according to our empirical observations is an important variable in practice. We base our discussion on this experience. Compare Miller, M. H. and Modigliani, F. 'Dividend Policy and the Valuation of Shares', *Journal of Business*, 1961.

[4] Compare Donaldson, G. *Managing Corporate Wealth* (1984).

[5] The analysis of these issues is enlarged and developed further in Section 13.4.

PART 2

Traditional return on capital – its importance and limitations for comparative purposes

CHAPTER 7

Introduction to Part Two

In Part One, measures of rate of return on capital played a crucial role and for this reason we focused on analysing related measurement problems. In Part Two we analyse the usefulness and limitations of these measures for different types of comparison.

7.1 FRAME OF REFERENCE

There are several reasons for using the same methods of measurement in public (external) and management (internal) reporting. Thus legal rules and recommendations issued by standard-setting bodies for external purposes will also be applied internally and constitute the framework within which our main approach will be applied.

The realization convention and the money measurement convention are extremely important in external financial reporting. Reporting assets at historical cost represents a consistent application of these conventions. Prudence is also a fundamental principle, implying that losses are recognized when they become known, even if they have not yet been realized.

Accounting based on the conventions of realization, money measurement and prudence is referred to as 'traditional' accounting. Measures of rate of return, based on measures of income and capital in traditional accounting, are referred to as 'traditional' measures of rate of return.

In Part One, we emphasized the crucial role that rates of return on capital play in the process of financial control. Rate of return on book equity is the central measure in formulating the profitability goal of the company or group as an entity. In a considerably idealized and simplified form, our main approach to the co-ordination of the control of the business entity and its components can be described as follows.

- The rate of return after tax on book equity of the company should in the long run at least equal the return required by the investors in order for them to become or remain shareholders (the cost of equity capital). It is assumed to be a condition for the survival and development of the company that it can achieve the return required by investors on their investments. Survival is the company's fundamental objective.
- Another financial goal is that the company should achieve or maintain a certain debt-to-equity ratio.

- On the basis of a given debt-to-equity ratio and predictions of future borrowing rates and tax rates, the company derives the pre-tax rate of return on capital employed which is required to achieve the target rate of return on equity. The next step is for senior management to determine target rates of return for corporate divisions, subsidiaries or profit centres, to which the capital employed has been allocated, without delegating responsibility for financing.

- The dividend policy is defined in terms of dividend-to-profit ratio, which can be transformed into a dividend-to-equity ratio. Assuming a constant rate of return on equity and a constant dividend-to-equity ratio, equity, profits and dividends will have the same growth rate. If, in addition, the debt-to-equity ratio is constant, the capital employed and the debt will grow at the same rate as owners' equity. A basic assumption is that the growth of equity is only affected by retained earnings.

- Thus, profitability goals in terms of return on equity and capital employed, and targets for the debt-to-equity ratio, dividend policy and growth of capital, are integrated and mutually related.

- Assuming that the market value of equity is determined as the discounted value of future dividends and that investors expect that the company's target for rate of return on book equity (= the cost of equity capital) and dividend policy will be achieved, the market value and the book value of owners' equity will be the same.

Reference levels are another fundamental concept in our frame of reference. Rates of return and other accounting measures are used for:

1 comparisons between different periods (interperiod comparisons);
2 comparisons with the cost of capital;
3 comparisons between companies (intercompany comparisons);
4 comparisons between the company as a whole and its component parts, and between different parts of the company (intracompany comparisons).

Our tentative analysis of the usefulness and shortcomings of traditional measures of rate of return is based on the use of these measures for this kind of comparison. An integrated feature of such an analysis is comparison of measures based on traditional accounting with measures based on alternative accounting principles.

The shortcomings and limitations of traditional accounting have certainly been much discussed over the years in accounting literature. Special attention has been paid to the limitations related to the realization and money measurement conventions. To a large extent the discussion has had a theoretical orientation based on rational economic decision-making. Few systematic studies have addressed the question of how the use of traditional accounting for economic control is influenced by the shortcomings of measures under various measurement conditions. We do not intend to fill this knowledge gap entirely. One purpose of Part Two is to identify conditions which are very favourable or unfavourable for the comparative use of traditional measures of rate of return. Another purpose is to analyse alternative measures as a basis for the interpretation of traditional measures and the need to supplement them, in view of their limitations. Special attention is paid to various forms of reference levels since they are important components in the financial control process.

7.2 VALUATION ISSUES

We assume that the income for period t is a function of the valuation of assets and liabilities at the beginning and at the end of period t. The basic issues are as follows:

- How should products be valued? What costs are allocated to inventory at the beginning and the end of a period? In which period are revenues recognized?
- How should resources be valued? At what values are they stated at the beginning and the end of a period? What are the corresponding expenses for a period?
- How should financial obligations be valued? What are the beginning and ending values? What are the corresponding periodic expenses?

In dealing with problems of valuation, it is practical and advantageous to observe the distinction between non-monetary and monetary items. Valuation of non-monetary items is often more complicated.

7.2.1 Non-monetary resources and products

In the industrial cycle of acquisition of resources, production and sales, measurement problems can be characterized as follows:

a At which stage of the cycle may products be stated at a value exceeding the cost of acquiring the related resources? A profit is a function of all the activities during the total cycle but cannot be recognized on the way towards final completion until the critical activities stage has been passed and revenues and expenses can be measured with sufficient certainty. Normally, invoicing of complete products or services to a creditworthy customer is considered to be the critical stage.

b What production costs should be allocated to the products for which revenues have been recognized during a period? What resources are more related to the total production capacity than to individual products and how should these capacity costs be allocated between different periods? What costs should be allocated to products manufactured during a period and be recognized in the valuation of inventory and later on be included in costs of goods sold?

c What operating costs should be treated as expenses during the period in which they are incurred? The IASC defines product cost as 'cost incurred in bringing the inventories to their present location and condition'. This means, for example, that administrative support in the manufacturing stage is regarded as a product cost. Other administrative costs and sales costs are expensed as they are incurred. R & D and similar costs are usually treated in the same way, although they will affect future revenues.

d What costs of financing should be regarded as product costs and be included in the book value of inventory? This question results from the need for capital in order to manufacture products. Different countries have different standards. International Accounting Standard 2 represents a flexible but restrictive view with regard to borrowing costs:

> '... are usually considered not to relate to putting the inventories in their present location and condition'.

The Financial Accounting Standard Board in the US has taken the position that no borrowing costs should be included in the inventory value of goods which are produced routinely or repetitively in large quantities. Some national standards allow allocation to inventory of interest on borrowed capital but not on equity capital.

e Similar problems arise in deciding on the interperiod allocation of capital expenditures and related non-monetary resources. What should be capitalized and what should be treated as expense? What should be included in the capitalized cost of acquisition? How should this cost be allocated as expenses in future periods?

f Under what circumstances should inventories and other non-monetary assets be written down and be stated at values lower than the cost of acquisition? What are the guidelines? The intended use of the asset should be relevant. Market value can be a guideline with regard to assets which are held for subsequent sale. When the asset is successively and continuously utilized, the valuation may be based on an estimate of the future usefulness of the resource. In both cases, the main issue is what indications on a reduction in value should be observed and recognized as criteria for write-downs.

7.2.2 Monetary rights and obligations

Certain monetary contractual rights and obligations are directly associated with current operations and are, in consequence, more operational than financial in nature, for example accounts receivable, accounts payable, advances received from customers and liabilities to employees. As a rule, it is not difficult to value these types of items.

Other monetary contractual rights and obligations are more the direct result of purely financial decisions, made by financial officers and steered by the firm's financial policy. In many cases, there is conflict between the basic principles of traditional accounting and the criterion of representational ability, i.e. the ability to reflect the economic substance of the individual transaction. This refers mainly to the timing of income recognition and the netting of unrealized gains and losses. Accounting for financial instruments is an area in which there is, and has been, considerable development. We confine ourselves to certain fundamental issues.

In discussing monetary rights, there are reasons to consider whether they are traded on an active market, and whether the rights include fixed interest and have a maturity date or whether they are residual, with no maturity date.

Thus there are four cases to be considered.

1 *Non-marketable rights to time-limited cash flows, including contractual interest.* Examples are bank loans, promissory notes and accounts receivable. When should this type of asset be valued below its nominal value? One aspect of the problem concerns the payment ability of the debtor (the bankruptcy risk). What criteria should be met in order to write down a claim due to doubtful creditworthiness? It is probably not unusual in practice for companies to employ different guidelines for allowances for losses having regard to the degree of uncertainty. Sometimes it is argued that intentions and the efforts to make the debtor fulfil his total obligations are to some extent dependent upon whether allowances for losses have been made or not. This is used as an argument for not recognizing non-recoverable losses until they are known with certainty. Banks sometimes help customers with liquidity problems by reducing contractual interest payments (with or without agreements for subsequent compensation for these reductions). Should interest losses as a result of revised contracts be recognized when they are realized or in the period when the contract is revised, by using the present value of expected future cash flows as the basis of valuation? In the latter case the book value will gradually increase and the increase will be recognized as interest revenue.

Similar problems arise if the originally contracted rate of interest is zero or positive but obviously below the market rate and the reason is that the creditor obtains some form of 'hidden' interest as compensation. Accounts receivable is one example. Compensation for credit allowed is included in the price of the goods and is thus reported as sales revenues if no adjustment is made. In order to reveal the 'hidden' interest, the sales transaction should be booked and the initial amount of accounts receivable stated at the equivalent 'cash price', i.e. the discounted value of the amount to be paid at the date of maturity. The principle of materiality seems to be of great relevance in accounting standards for the recognition of 'hidden' interest.

If the contracted rate of interest represents a market rate and there are no doubts about the creditworthiness of the debtor, a claim is booked at its nominal value, even if the market rate increases after the date of the contract. The reason is that the claim is not marketable and the intention is to hold on to it until it matures.

2 *Marketable rights to time-limited cash flows including contractual interest.* Examples are placements in debt instruments on the money market or the bond market. The additional issue in relation to (a) is the question of how changes in the market rate should be recognized, when

the choice between holding or selling an asset at a known market price is a continuous and real process. Valuation at market price means that the income for a period will be the same whether holding gains or losses at the end of the period are realized or not. Valuation at the cost of acquisition means the income is influenced by a decision to realize such gains or losses. Thus, the choice between holding and selling may be influenced by this. If it is intended to hold an instrument until the date of maturity in order to secure a given return on the investment, then recognition of changes in the market value due to changes in market rates would be inconsistent with the original intention. Thus, the issue is whether the valuation of this type of financial instrument should reflect the investment intention. The problem of objectivity and verifiability is not related to market value but to intention.

When an instrument is acquired at a price less than the amount to be received at maturity (e.g. zero coupons instruments), recognition of changes in the market value not due to changes in the market rates is necessary in order to measure the correct interest rate for the investment.

3 *Non-marketable rights for residual cash flows without time limits.* Investments in unlisted companies is a typical example. How should the cost of acquisition be determined when the compensation does not consist of cash or interest-bearing claims on cash? When should a lower value than acquisition value be considered? The economic value to the owner is the discounted value of the cash flows the owner expects to receive during the future holding period.

4 *Marketable rights to residual cash flows without time limits.* When should increases in market values be treated as income? When should reductions in market value be recognized? How should the intention behind the investment be taken into consideration?

The basic issues regarding monetary obligations can be described as follows:

5 How should a line be drawn between obligations to be reported as liabilities in the balance sheet and other obligations. A liability is a monetary, quantifiable and unconditional obligation resulting from previous transactions or other past events. As a result of previous events, the enterprise has a present obligation to make future payments. Most obligations are contractual and unconditional. The contract specifies the amounts and timing of unconditional future payments, which can thus be determined with a high degree of certainty. In some cases there may be uncertainty with regard to the existence of an obligation and/or the amounts and timing of future payments. The probable outcome has to be estimated. How probable and measurable should future payments be in order for them to be recognized as a liability? Uncertainty about the existence of an obligation and about the amounts to be paid characterize situations in which disputes about the interpretation of a contract arise and where the outcome is pending decisions of a court or a negotiation process. Furthermore, tactical considerations may influence manage-

ment's willingness to report and quantify a liability under dispute. Thus, reported off-balance contingencies may include uncertain liabilities.

6 What basis of valuation should be used for obligations recognized as liabilities in the balance sheet:

- the nominal value of the received consideration;
- the nominal value of the capital to be paid;
- the discounted value of future payments.

The first two alternatives often give the same result; bank loans or trade credits received are stated at their nominal values. One issue is what role the contractual formal interest payment should play. Should only contractual interest be recognized as expense for the period when the interest is paid or accrued? Or should the recognition of interest expenses and the valuation of liabilities be influenced by other conditions:

- The amount to be repaid may be larger than the amount received, because the contractual interest rate is below the market rate. The discounted value as basis for valuation means that reported interest expenses reflect the market rate at the initial transaction date (providing this rate is used as discount rate).
- The contracted interest rate may not be constant, for example initially below and subsequently above the market rate, but may be equivalent to a constant market rate.
- Debts in foreign currency can result in currency gains or losses – in addition to contracted interest payments? These gains or losses can be regarded as part of interest expenses for debts in foreign currency.

As mentioned above, sometimes there is no contract which specifies the amounts to be paid to fulfil the contract. The conditions under which payments have to be made are fulfilled but the amounts to be paid are uncertain. The liability has to be estimated. A typical case is provisions for guarantees in construction contracts. Another example is provision for taxes, when there are doubts about the interpretation of the tax rules.

An additional problem is the existence of interdependent transactions, which is of particular relevance – although not unique – in dealing with monetary rights and obligations. This in turn raises the following questions:

7 How can financial transactions be delineated to enable measurements of the income effects of each individual transaction? The practical implication of this problem increases as new financial instruments are introduced. Many financial instruments are interrelated, particularly in terms of risk. Financial transactions are dependent on operational transactions. Foreign currency loans are raised to hedge investments in the same currency. Options are used to protect the value of an investment against a reduction in the market price. How independent is the option transaction considered to be in relation to the investment decison?

7.2.3 Two basic issues

The measurement of periodic income involves two main processes, as illustrated in the sections above:

● identification of resource/product relationships, i.e. relationships between the volume of utilized resources and the volume of products at various stages;
● determination of how these volumes of resources/products should be priced and valued.

The choice of measurement methods has to be based on analysis of these two processes. The second process includes the relationship between the periodic income and changes in specific prices and the general price level. The principles applied are of fundamental importance in measuring income and return on capital. The comparative analysis of alternative accounting methods in Part Two emphasizes these questions strongly and provides a basis for the continued analysis in Part Three, which addresses the resource/product relationships in greater detail.

7.3 THE PROBLEM OF COMPARING ACCOUNTING METHODS

A comparative analysis may have one of the following purposes:[1]

● to identify the measurement errors of a given method;
● to describe differences between the methods compared.

One condition for fulfilling the first purpose is that we define an ideal method of measurement as a basis for comparison. The traditional approach in accounting literature is to regard the classical theory of capital value as the ideal theoretical framework and to use the principles of measuring 'economic income' and 'economic value' as the ideal principles for measuring income and capital. According to this theory, developed, for example, by Fisher and Lindahl, the value of capital assets is measured by discounting the future cash flows that the use of the asset is expected to generate.[2] The income of a period is measured as the cash flow during the period minus the difference between the capital value at the beginning and at the end of the period. The rate of return on capital is identical to the discount rate applied, if future cash flows can be predicted with certainty.

By comparing measures of income and capital of, say, traditional accounting with the economic income and economic value respectively, we can identify measurement errors in traditional accounting. In a world of uncertainty, it is difficult, in practice, to measure economic income and economic value and in addition it is impossible to define the concepts precisely.[3] Nonetheless, they are considered to be an ideal starting point for evaluating a given method of accounting.[4] Expected future cash flows determine the value of a financial system. This point was emphasized in Part One.

In order to identify and quantify measurement errors accurately, the methods compared must be applied to identical transactions. As the errors can be a function of the transactions, considered comparisons should be made for various sets of transactions. An analysis of measurement errors related to traditional linear depreciation, for example, will be very complex if realistic conditions concerning the structure of plant and equipment are to be taken into account. A comparison will be extremely complicated if the intention is to identify all kinds of differences between traditional measurements of income and capital and measurements of economic income and capital under various assumptions concerning, for example, changes in specific prices and general price levels, uncertainty about future cash flows and changes in expectations.

Description and analysis of differences between various 'applied' methods of accounting is a more modest intention. The degree of complexity will vary with the methods compared. It is easier to analyse the difference between FIFO and LIFO with regard to rate of return on equity than to compare traditional accounting and current cost accounting.

Some transactions may be a function of the applied accounting method. Thus, a meaningful comparison by assuming identical sets of transactions may not be possible. This stumbling block for comparative studies is related to the following two roles of accounting:

● the post-contracting role[5];
● the role of motivating and influencing the behaviour of users.

The post-contracting role

There are many examples of the post-contracting accounting role. A contract with senior managers stipulates that they will get a bonus provided the reported net income (measured in accordance with US GAAP, for example) is higher than X. A contract with a bank provides that a loan is automatically due if the company's debt-to-equity ratio exceeds a certain level. The outcome of a contract is thus dependent upon a reported accounting number or ratio and the contract describes how the numbers or ratios should be measured. The agreed conditions for, say, a bonus must be dependent upon the accounting method to be applied. It seems very unlikely, however, that a contract could be adjusted to the choice of accounting method in such a way that the final consequences would be independent of the choice of accounting method. Thus the post-contracting accounting role distorts a comparative analysis to be based on identical transactions. In Sweden and some other countries, 'financial reports' and 'tax reports' are to a large extent identical. Taxes to be paid will be a function of the accounting method applied.

The motivational and influential role

The role of accounting to motivate and affect user behaviour was a central theme in Part One. Thus, it is important to consider this role in an analysis of methodological problems when comparing accounting methods. A comparative analysis of accounting methods based on the assumption of identical sets of transactions, ignores the fact that management behaviour and related transactions are not independent of the accounting method applied.

One very fundamental assumption in our study is that a target rate of return on equity should reflect the profitability required for the long-run survival and development of the enterprise. Obviously, this target rate is not independent of the method chosen for measuring net income and equity. It is not a reasonable hypothesis that a target rate based on traditional accounting and a target rate based on current cost accounting will have identical behavioural effects. One crucial question is how the setting of targets and the use of targets is affected by and adjusted to the shortcomings of traditional accounting.

7.4 THEOREMS OF COUNTERBALANCING ERRORS

Although one method of valuation, e.g. for inventories, results in a lower book value of inventories and equity than another method, the net income of the period may be the same. In elementary accounting textbooks we learn that this will be the case if the difference between the compared book values is the same at the beginning and at the end of the period. The difference at the end of the period counterbalances the difference at the beginning of the period.

Our comparative analysis focuses on rate of return on equity and the rate of equity growth. Therefore it is useful to specify the conditions under which two different accounting methods result in the same return on equity or the same growth rate. We use a numerical illustration to specify three elementary 'theorems of counterbalancing errors'.

EXAMPLE

In Table 7.1, we compare a theoretically correct measurement (C) of equity (E) and a measurement (W) which deviates from C. The deviation is referred to as a measurement error. Net income (I), rate of return on equity (R_E) and the rate of growth of equity (E') are compared in the two alternatives. The difference between the equity at the beginning of the year (E_b) and the equity at the end of the year (E_e) corresponds to retained earnings, and the dividends (D) are paid at the end of the year. There are no new issues or other capital contributions from the owner.

The example illustrates the following three theorems of counterbalancing errors, which from a mathematical point of view are truisms, and the relationships between the measures studied.

Table 7.1 Illustrations of counterbalancing errors

	Case 1 C	W	(W - C)	Case 2 C	W	(W – C)	Case 3 C	W	(W – C)
E_e	1100	900	−200	1100	876	−224	1100	880	−220
− E_b	−1000	−800	+200	−1000	−800	+200	−1000	−800	+200
= ΔE	100	100	0	100	76	−24	100	80	−20
+ Div.(D)	20	20		20	20		20	20	
= I	120	120	0	120	96	−24	120	100	−20
R_E (I/E_b)	12%	15%	+3%	12%	12%	0%	12%	12.5%	+0.5%
$E\,' = (\Delta E/E_b)$	10%	12.5%	−2.5%	10%	9.5%	−0.5%	10%	10%	0%

Theorem 1

If the absolute error in measuring equity is the same at the beginning and at the end of the year, the net income will be the same in alternatives W and C, i.e.

if
$$E_b(C) - E_b(W) = E_e(C) - E_e(W)$$

then
$$I(W) = I(C) \qquad [7.1a]$$

Further
$$R_E(W) = R_E(C) \times E_b(C)/E_b(W) \qquad [7.1b]$$

and
$$E\,'(W) = E\,'(C) \times E_b(C)/E_b(W) \qquad [7.1c]$$

Theorem 2

If the error in measuring equity grows at a rate equal to the rate of return on equity, the rate of return on equity will be the same in alternatives W and C, i.e.

if
$$\frac{E_e(C) - E_e(W)}{E_b(C) - E_b(W)} - 1 = R_E(W)$$

then
$$R_E(W) = R_E(C) \qquad [7.2a]$$

Further
$$I(W) = I(C) \times E_b(W)/E_b(C) \qquad [7.2b)$$

and
$$E\,'(W) = E\,'(C) + (D/E_b(C) - D/E_b(W)) \qquad [7.2c]$$

Theorem 3

If the error in measuring equity grows at the same rate as equity, then the rate of growth of equity will be the same in alternatives W and C, i.e. if

$$\frac{E_e(C) - E_e(W)}{E_b(C) - E_b(W)} - 1 = E'(W)$$

then

$$E'(W) = E'(C) \qquad\qquad [7.3a]$$

Further

$$I(W) = I(C) \times \frac{E_b(W)}{E_b(C)} + D \times \frac{E_b(C) - E_b(W)}{E_b(C)} \qquad [7.3b]$$

and

$$R_E(W) = R_E(C) + (D/E_b(W) - D/E_b(C)) \qquad\qquad [7.3c]$$

A similar analysis can be made with regard to capital employed and related measures of income, rate of return and growth of capital. If the error in measuring capital employed grows at a rate equal to the rate of return on capital employed, the rate of return will be the same in alternatives C and W. (It is assumed that income before interest expenses and tax is related to capital employed at the beginning of the year.)

The methods of measurement which are compared only provide the same rate of return on capital employed under very specific conditions. If these conditions are fulfilled for the company as a whole, it is very unlikely that they would also be fulfilled for each division (or other sub-unit) of a company with different fields of operations and different asset structures.

In the example above, we have chosen to compare a correct method of measurement with an incorrect method. Thus we can use the term measurement 'error', Of course, the theorems are valid in any comparative analysis of two different accounting methods, both of which are incorrect in relation to a theoretically ideal method. In such a case, it would be more appropriate to use the term 'difference' rather than 'error'. In subsequent chapters, the third theorem will be of particular interest.

NOTES

[1] *See* Beaver, W. H. *Financial Reporting: An Accounting Revolution* (1989), p. 67.
[2] Fisher, J. *The Nature of Capital and Income* (1906).
Lindahl, E. *Studies in the Theory of Money and Capital* (1939).
[3] Beaver (1989), p. 88.
[4] Beaver (1989), p. 4.
[5] Beaver (1989), p. 6.

CHAPTER 8

Traditional periodic measures with stable prices

Interperiod comparisons are of fundamental importance to business analysis. In this chapter the relevance of traditional measures for interperiod comparisons are analysed on the basis of the views expressed in Chapter 7 and particularly the perception of economic income and economic value as ideal for comparative purposes. General price level changes are disregarded in this chapter.

OVERVIEW   Linear depreciation has such widespread use that it can be regarded as a characteristic of traditional accounting. As a rule, linear depreciation deviates from economic depreciation and causes errors in measurements of the rate of return. Economic depreciation is a function of the time pattern of expected future cash flows generated by the use of the object under valuation. Gradually diminishing cash flows will usually imply gradually diminishing (degressive) economic depreciation. Thus, economic depreciation is higher than linear depreciation during the initial phase of the economic life of the object under valuation, and lower later in its economic life. The annuity method of depreciation is sometimes used instead of linear depreciation. The former method will be equal to economic depreciation if the cash flows are expected to be constant during the total economic life. The market value is a measure of the economic value of assets, which are separable from the current operation. The economic income of these kinds of asset is the change in the market value during the period plus the cash flow generated by the use of the assets.

Economic income and value include unrealized capital gains, in contrast to traditional accounting. We emphasize that both economic income and value are ideal for measuring the rate of return and that verifiability, objectivity and a reasonable degree of certainty are important criteria for income recognition. It is desirable that negative income components match revenues with which they are related. The realization convention and the convention of prudence can often imply a poor matching of revenues and expenses and of income and capital in measuring rate of return.

8.1 ECONOMIC INCOME AND TRADITIONAL INCOME

We make a distinction between economic value, generated in current operations by periodic cash flows, and economic value generated in separable resources operations by selling resources and thus sacrificing future cash flows. The comparison of economic income with traditional measures of income will to some extent have different characteristics in the two cases. Although it may be hard to draw a clear-cut borderline between the alternatives in a given company, we will discuss them separately in the following section.

8.1.1 Cash flows from current operations

A common approach in accounting research has been to study a single asset. e.g. a machine, on the assumption that the future cash flows generated by the use of the asset and thus the economic value and changes in it (depreciation) can be determined with certainty.[1] Furthermore, it has been assumed that linear depreciation is a characteristic of traditional accounting. The difference between economic and linear depreciation and its effects on income and on rate of return on invested capital are analysed. To illustrate this approach we use the following example.

EXAMPLE   A company has been established to pursue a single project with a useful life of five years and no uncertainty about future cash flows in Year 1, Year 2, ... Year 5. They are: 1000, 800, 600, 400 and 200 respectively (all cash transactions are made at the end of the year). The cost of acquisition is 2418 and the expected scrap value after five years is expected to be zero. Under these assumptions, the expected internal rate of return on the total investment is 10%. At the time of acquisition, the present value of expected future cash flows is 2418 (provided that the discount rate equals the expected internal rate of return). This is the value of the investment at the beginning of the first year. At the end of the first year, just before the inflow of the first receipts, the value of the investment has increased by 10% to 2660. Immediately after having received the first cash flow of 1000, the value of the asset has dropped to 1660. This amount is the present value at the beginning of the second year of the remaining cash flows (800, 600, 400 and 200). The economic depreciation during the first year is 2418 − 1660 = 758 and the economic income is 1000 − 758 = 242. The economic value, depreciation and income is presented for each of the years in Table 8.1.

Table 8.1 Economic value, depreciation and income of an investment with certain cash flows

Year	Cash flow	Economic depreciation	Economic income	Economic value (1/1)
1	1000	758	242	2418
2	800	634	166	1660
3	600	497	103	1026
4	400	347	53	529
5	200	182	18	82

The rate of return, calculated by relating the economic income to the economic value at the beginning of the year, is 10% each year (the amounts are rounded off and so the rate is not exactly 10%).

In textbooks on capital budgeting, we learn how to calculate the internal rate of return of a project with given annual cash flows and a given cost of acquisition. In accounting textbooks we learn how annual measurements of economic value, economic depreciation and economic income can be made *ex ante* and as a result obtain a constant annual rate of return equal to the internal rate of return on the total investment.

In Table 8.1, economic depreciation is diminishing year by year. We refer to this pattern of depreciation as degressive depreciation. This pattern is a consequence of gradually diminishing cash flows. Linear depreciation in traditional accounting will first be lower and will then become higher than degressive depreciation. Linear depreciation, applied in our example, would be 482 (rounded off) per year, resulting in a reported income of 516 in Year 1, 316 in Year 2 and so on. The rate of return on book value would be 21.3% in Year 1, 16.3% in Year 2, 8% in Year 3 and negative thereafter. Thus, the application of linear depreciation instead of economic depreciation would mean major measurement errors.

Economic depreciation is a function of the pattern of expected cash flows and the internal rate of return. The measurement error of linear depreciation will vary with the cash flow pattern. Constant or gradually increasing cash flows mean progressive economic depreciation. Thus, linear depreciation will first be higher and then lower than economic depreciation and the rate of return on the book value will gradually increase. The measurement error can be very substantial if the cash flows during the initial years and thus economic depreciation are negative. In some industries the annuity method of depreciation is used. This method is consistent with economic depreciation only if cash flows are expected to be constant. With uncertainty, economic value will change at the point of time when expectations about future cash flows change. Thus, the measurement error related to the combination of linear depreciation and traditional accounting may be caused by this type of change in the economic value.

If the analysis model is extended to consider a set of several machines with identical economic lives and patterns of cash flows but of different ages, previous research has shown that the measurement errors of the depreciation of an individual machine more or less offset each other. It is well known that the total sum of depreciation each year will be the same regardless of which method of depreciation is used, provided that it is used consistently and that the age structure of the machines is symmetrical (e.g. one machine is one year old, one is two years old, etc.). The book value, however, and the rate of return will be dependent upon the method of depreciation. As pointed out in Chapter 7, it is extremely difficult to analyse errors in measurements of rate of return under realistic conditions concerning the structure of plant and equipment with regard to age, patterns of cash flow, growth rate, etc. This will be illustrated further in Chapter 9.

8.1.2 Cash flows from separable resources

In principle, market prices are the best starting point for estimating the economic value of separable resources held for the purpose of disposal or sale. These prices are determined in a process of negotiations between independent players, both applying business logic and with normal freedom of action in the commercial process. The market prices reflect anticipations about future cash flows generated for the owner by the use of the resources.

In this connection, a period's economic income can be measured as the change in market values plus the cash flow obtained during the period. In contrast to traditional accounting, unrealized gains are included in the income and market prices are the basis for the valuation of capital. This type of measurement method will be discussed both in this and the following chapter.

8.1.3 Economic income and the need for verifiability

In Chapter 7, we described economic income as the ideal frame of reference in an analysis of the usefulness and limitations of measurements of rate of return on traditional book values. In Part One, we emphasized the importance of satisfying the need for verifiability, objectivity and a reasonable degree of certainty. Both are reasonable viewpoints; unfortunately, it is difficult to reconcile them. Economic value is based on expected cash flows. When new information becomes available and expectations change, the gains or losses due to these changes are recognized in the same period. In a world of uncertainty, however, income recognition must satisfy the criteria of verifiability and objectivity. The problem of income recognition has no ideal and well-defined solution, not even in principle.

There is a more or less continuous flow of new information with varying degrees of relevance to the expectations about future cash flows and cost of capital. The continuous price fluctuations on the stock market illustrate the probable consequences of a hypothetical implementation of economic theory in the valuation of balance sheet items.

To satisfy the need for a robust accounting system, it seems obvious that only significant and permanent changes of economic value, due to new information, can be recognized. Recognition of positive changes in the economic value of long-lived assets is in conflict with the realization convention if the carrying amount based on historical cost is less than the economic value. Revaluations to adjust for a significant and permanent gap are allowed in some legal systems and accounting standards.

Recognizing a negative gap between the economic value and the carrying amount of a long-lived asset is in accordance with the convention of prudence, but may be difficult to reconcile with the criteria of verifiability and objectivity. Expectations are subjective and hard to verify. However, it may be possible to verify new negative information, events, etc., which cause significant and permanent revisions to management's expectations about future cash flows and/or cost of capital.

It is interesting to notice that the FASB has chosen this approach in the *Exposure Draft on Accounting for the Impairment of Long-Lived Assets*[2]. The FASB believes that it would be appropriate in concept but not practical to evaluate each asset for impairment each year. Therefore it is proposed that long-lived assets should be reviewed for impairment only when events and changes of circumstances indicate that the carrying amount of an asset may not be recoverable. Most of the events and changes of circumstances that are presented as examples seem to be reasonably verifiable and objective. One example is a projection or forecast that demonstrates continuing losses associated with an asset. This means that a continuing positive but low return on the carrying amount is not considered to indicate that the recoverability of the carrying amount should be assessed. If there are indications that the carrying amount of an asset may not be recoverable, an estimate should be made about the future cash flows generated by the expected use and eventual disposal of the asset. If the sum of the expected future cash flows – undiscounted and without interest charges – is less than the carrying amount, an impairment loss has to be recognized, based on the fair value (economic value) of the asset. The cash flow test is regarded as a practical approach to implementing a permanence criterion to avoid recognition of write-downs, reflecting only temporary market fluctuations. The implication of the test is that an impairment loss is not to be recognized if the carrying amount is expected to be recovered, even though no cost of capital is recovered. Regardless of the issues of verifiability and objectivity there is an important theoretical and practical problem involved in the application of the economic concepts. One problem is well known: that of interdependency. The revenues of a firm are a function of the co-ordination of and collaboration between numerous separate factors of production. Assets generate joint cash flows, which can not be split up logically and allocated to each asset. The FASB exposure draft addresses this problem and proposes that assets should be grouped when they are used together and generate joint cash flows.

The matching of cash flows and groups of assets is certainly a complex process when expected sales is a function of the integration of R&D, manufacturing and marketing, and only capital expenditures for tangible assets have been capitalized.

We have presented a summary of FASB's exposure draft as it is an interesting attempt to handle the conflict between the economic criterion and the criteria of verifiability and objectivity.

From the viewpoint of financial control we will make the following comments on recognition of impairment losses. The choice between writing down or not writing down an asset is a choice between:

1 improving or not improving the future reported rate of return on the capital affected by the decision, and

2 increasing or not increasing the debt-to-equity ratio.

What are the effects on the setting of financial goals? What are the behavioural effects? How are interperiod and intracompany comparisons affected?

Questions of this kind are relevant from the viewpoint of management control. The answers may vary. In certain situations there is an empirically verified preference for the write-down alternative. This is the case when a new management is hired in order to restructure a company and improve a historically unsatisfactory profitability. The new management are very anxious that assets are not overstated, that provisions for restructuring costs are made, etc. The application of the convention of prudence becomes a critical issue. This convention, without being very well defined, has strong roots in some countries and the application may include a considerable degree of subjectivity.

When losses are reported and other events occur, indicating that the carrying amount of assets may not be recoverable, management usually takes actions in order to reduce cost and/or increase revenues, i.e. to increase the economic value of assets. In fact one of the purposes of a control system is to initiate such actions. Often restructuring decisions are taken, including reduction of the number of employees. Then there are three different components in estimating eventual impairment losses:

1 the future cash flows if no restructuring is made,
2 the future cash flows (excluding restructuring cost) if restructuring is made, and
3 restructuring costs (cash).

The difference between the present value of (2) and (1) must not be less than the present value of (3). The restructuring costs include the compensations to be paid to the employees who are dismissed or retire before the normal age of retirement. The present value of (2) represents the economic value of the group of relevant tangible assets plus the intangible asset in terms of restructuring investments (3). In practice restructuring costs are expensed without recognizing at the same time the benefits of the restructuring.

Expenditures for R&D, software systems, re-organizations, marketing and similar intangibles with expected positive effects on future cash flows, have in recent decades grown faster than capital expenditures for tangible assets. In some industries, e.g. the pharmaceutical industry, the investments in intangibles dominate. Therefore, capitalization and amortization of such expenditures in compliance with economic theory is an urgent issue for standard setters, guided by conceptual frameworks including the criteria of verifiability and objectivity. When these expenditures are booked as expenses, a very significant gap is created between the economic value and the book value of this kind of intangible assets. The implications of this gap are discussed further in Section 8.2.

8.2 TRADITIONAL ACCOUNTING PRINCIPLES AND MEASUREMENT OF RETURN ON CAPITAL

In traditional accounting, based on the conventions of realization and prudence, there is a tendency for income and capital to be poorly matched as a basis for measuring the rate of return on capital. This problem will be discussed in the following sections.

8.2.1 The matching principle and the return on capital

Traditional accounting of a continuous flow of events and transactions in a world of uncertainty is based on certain fundamental conventions and principles. One is the realization convention, which in its simplest form means that income should not be recognized until it is realized through a sales transaction. Another is the convention of prudence, i.e. that assets and liabilities should be stated at prudent values and that losses should be recognized as soon as they can be predicted.

There is a conflict between these conventions and the matching principle. Traditionally, this principle concerns the relationship between the revenues and expenses of a given period. The expenses should represent the sacrifices made to obtain the revenues for the same period. In measurements of return on capital, the focus is on the relationship between income and capital. In this context, the matching principle may be interpreted in the following way: capital should be a prerequisite for achieving the income reported and the income should be regarded as 'return' on capital.

As interperiod comparisons are of fundamental importance, the matching principle meets the criterion of representational ability. One aspect of this criterion is that income and capital are allocated to periods in such a way that the measure of rate of return on capital reflects the business intention of the actions during a particular period. Otherwise, there is a risk that the measure will not be accepted or that economically irrational decisions will be made in order to report a satisfactory return. Thus, there are good reasons to analyse the conventions of realization and prudence from the perspective of matching.

8.2.2 The convention of prudence: understatement of capital

The practical application of prudence – a prudent value of assets and liabilities – varies from country to country, due to differences in term of legislation, tradition, etc.

The convention of prudence may mean a poor matching of revenues and expenses and/or poor matching of income and capital. It is well known that the economic value of certain capital expenditures is not recognized in the balance sheet. The usual examples are investments in research and development. When expenditures for research and development for new products, new markets, etc. are recorded expenses, an obvious deviation is made from the principle of matching revenues and expenses. This kind of expenditure will generate future revenues and is poorly related to the revenues of the period in which these intangible investments are made. The revenues of the current period are to some extent the fruit of R&D in previous periods.

Although the booking of R&D as expenses is a deviation from the matching principle, the income reported for a given period may be the same as that which would have been reported if the matching principle had been applied and R&D had been capitalized and depreciated over the useful life of the investment. The reason is the mechanism of counterbalancing errors discussed in Chapter 7.

If the correct capitalization and valuation of R&D result in the same book value at the end of the year as at the beginning of the year, the income will be the same as reported without capitalization (Theorem 1).

Identical measures of income, however, would mean non-identical measures of return on capital. To obtain identical rates of return on equity, the book value of capitalized R&D must grow at a rate identical with the rate of return (Theorem 2). A prerequisite for the identical growth rate of equity is that the book value of capitalized R&D grows at the same rate as equity (Theorem 3). The book value of capitalized R&D will grow at the same rate as the R&D expenditures, if the same method of depreciation and assessment of useful life is applied to all investments.(*See* Section 7.4 for explanation of theorems.)

If the conditions for counterbalancing errors with regard to rate of return or growth of equity are not fulfilled and non-capitalized investments are substantial, a measure of rate of return may have an unsatisfactory representational ability and supplementary control mechanisms may be necessary in order to avoid the risk that R&D and similar expenditures will be reduced to improve profitability in the short term at the expense of long-term profitability.

In this section, we have used non-capitalized investments as an illustration of the consequences of the concention of prudence. Other consequences can be discussed in a similar way with a focus on the rate of return and growth of equity, and the theorems of counterbalancing errors.

8.2.3 The realization convention and historical cost as basis of valuation

In its simplest form, the realization convention means that income is not recognized until realized by a sales transaction. The principle of using historical cost as a basis of valuation of assets is derived from this convention. This traditional principle of valuation may result in a poor match between income and capital as regards measurements of rate of return on capital.

To illustrate this statement, we start by considering a major expansionary investment, involving the acquisition of land, plant and equipment, raw materials, etc. It takes two to three years until this investment generates revenues. During this period the investment has a negative effect on the rate of return on capital. Total assets increase. The income statement is charged with expenditures for planning, administration and other expenditures, which are caused by the investment but not capitalized in accordance with prevailing accounting standards or for tax reasons.

Investments which are strategically sound and profitable in the long term should be carried out regardless of their initial negative impact on the return on capital. These effects are well known to managers with experience of using rate of return on capital as a control instrument. Some companies handle this problem by a temporary reduction in the target rate. As major investment projects do not usually occur at regular intervals, the conditions for counterbalancing errors are not favourable.

Investment in inventories can also cause a poor matching of income and capital. Certain decisions regarding purchases or volumes of production are related to sales during subsequent periods. Increases in inventory do not affect the operating income of the same period but affect the volume of assets and thus the rate of return on capital.

Matching problems of this type are of particular importance where construction companies and other similar firms with capital-intensive and time-consuming projects apply the completed contract method of revenue recognition. In these companies, there may be considerable variations in the volume of orders obtained and thus variations in work-in-progress. The income recognized in one period refers to orders which to a large extent have already been produced and which have tied up capital during earlier periods. In addition, the following points should be observed in an analysis of the matching problem within the construction industry.

1 Usually the book value of work in progress does not include the costs of preparing and producing offers and other costs necessary to obtain an order. This prudent valuation reinforces the variations in operating income caused by varying relations between orders obtained and orders recognized as income.

2 To some extent, the agreed price is often dependent upon the volume and timing of advances from the buyer who receives interest on these payments in the form of a price reduction. This 'hidden' interest expense reduces the operating income of the period when the sales price is recognized as revenue. The interest is neither reported as a financial expense for the related liability, nor accrued in the correct manner. The relative size of advances varies and thus the capital employed (reduced by advance payments). There may be a poor correlation between:

  ● the 'hidden' interest, which reduces the operating income of a certain period and
  ● the payment of advances which reduces capital employed in the same period.

Poor matching of income and capital is also typical for financial investments stated at historical cost. As an illustration, we may take investments in shares, which are expected to generate dividends and capital gains.

During the holding period, when only dividends are reported as income, the reported rate of return on the investment will be low but will increase as the dividends grow. When the accumulated capital gains are realized the rate of return will be misleadingly high. Measurement errors with regard to rate of return on capital or growth of capital for a total portfolio may be counterbalanced if there is a continuous flow of purchasing and sales transactions.

In a company, say an insurance company, with a large portfolio of shares a decision by management to realize capital gains or losses can have a great impact on the reported rate of return on investments valued in accordance with the realization convention. For internal purposes, measurements of portfolio management are usually based on market values. Supplementary information about market values and unrealized capital gains is provided in annual reports in the Swedish insurance industry. There is also a tendency to report a net income figure including unrealized capital gains as supplementary information.

NOTES

[1] See e.g. Anton, H. R. 'Depreciation, Cost Allocation and Investment Decisions', *Quarterly Journal of Economics*, 1956 and Harcourt, G. C. 'The Accountant in a Golden Age', Oxford Economic Papers, 17, 1965, pp. 68–80.

[2] Financial Accounting Standard Board, Financial Accounting Series, No. 132–B, November 29, 1993.

CHAPTER 9

Traditional return on capital with price-level changes

The analysis in Chapter 8 was based on the assumption of stable price levels. In this chapter, we drop this assumption and try to analyse the limitations of traditional measures of rate of return on capital as a result of fluctuating general price levels. A key question is the comparability of rate of return on traditional book equity with the cost of equity capital. Intercompany, intracompany and interperiod comparisons are also considered, with special focus on the timing and pattern of capital expenditure at various stages of an inflationary cycle.

OVERVIEW

The traditional method of measuring, referred to as the T-method, is compared with the current cost method, referred to as the C-method, in which unrealized holding gains in nominal terms are recognized as income. It is assumed that the only difference between the two methods is the treatment of unrealized nominal holding gains on plant and equipment. If these gains grow at the same rate as the T-equity, the growth rate of the T-equity and of the C-equity will be identical, in accordance with the third theorem of counterbalancing errors. Under this condition, referred to as the 'ideal' condition for applying the T-method, we can determine exactly how the rate of return on T-equity should be adjusted in order to be comparable with the rate of return on C-equity and with the cost of equity capital. The growth rate of T- and C-equity will be the same if all the following conditions are fulfilled in a company whose only fixed assets are machines:

1 All the machines have the same economic life and the relation between the number of new machines and the number of scrapped machines is constant.
2 Historic inflation has been constant since the first of the existing machines was acquired and the cost of acquisition increases at the same rate as the general price level.
3 The rate of inflation during the current year is the same as the rate under 2.
4 The rate of growth for the machines' book value T is the same as the rate of growth for C-equity.

The consequences of variations in the rate of inflation are analysed. If the rate of inflation falls after periods of constant rate of inflation, T-equity will grow faster than C-equity and the difference between the rate of return on T-equity and that of C-equity will increase. The rate of return on T-equity will be misleadingly overstated, particularly during the initial periods following a significant fall in the rate of inflation, even if the age structure of the machines is constant. The consequences will be reversed if there is a significant increase in the rate of inflation. T-equity will grow more slowly than C-equity and the rate of return on T-equity will be understated. Obviously, it is difficult to adjust target return rates to take this type of limitation in the T-method into account.

The more irregular the capital expenditures are and the higher the rate of inflations is, the more obvious the limitations of the T-method will be. During periods of low investment activity, T-equity grows at a slower rate than C-equity and vice versa. The economic life of the machines is also relevant with regard to intracompany comparisons. It should be observed that the T and C book values of the machines may grow at approximately the same rate if we look at the company or the group as a whole, but not if we focus on various sub-units. This may limit the possibilities of meaningful comparisons between measures of capital return rates for the group as a whole and those for its sub-units.

The differences between the T-method and the C-method will be insignificant – even in inflationary periods – if a company's assets are dominated by monetary assets. Thus meaningful capital return comparisons can be made within and between banks and companies with non-monetary assets which are of no material importance in relative terms. The combination of:

1 considerable general price-level fluctuations,
2 considerable variations in capital expenditures and thus in the age structure of plant and equipment, and
3 balance sheets dominated by non-monetary fixed assets,

creates extremely unfavourable conditions for capital return comparisons when the T-method is applied. The very strong limitations of the T-method in these kinds of circumstances are reduced if comparisons are based on multiperiod average returns.

9.1 MEASUREMENT CONDITIONS UNDER INFLATION

The main objective is to analyse and identify the limitations of traditional accounting during inflationary periods. Traditional accounting is compared with current cost (value) accounting as developed by Edward and Bell.[1] We assume that current cost accounting is a useful approximation to the ideal basis of comparison, e.g. the principles of measuring economic value and economic income. In Chapter 10, we discuss how realistic this assumption is.

9.1.1 Current cost accounting and traditional accounting

The fundamental difference between current cost accounting (without adjustments for changes in the purchasing power of the measurement unit) (referred to as the C-method) and traditional accounting (referred to as the T-method) is that the latter method is based on the realization convention. Positive value changes of assets during the holding period (holding gains) are recognized in current cost accounting when they occur.

To simplify our analysis we assume that the only difference between equity (E) measured in accordance with method T and method C is due to unrealized holding gains on non-monetary assets and that all holding gains are due to increases in the general price level.[2] Unrealized holding gains at the point of time t are denoted by K_t. The difference between the net income of the C-method, $I(C)$, and the net income of the T-method, $I(T)$, is assumed to be identical with the difference between unrealized holding gains at the end and at the beginning of the period for income measurement. That is:

$$I(C) = I(T) + \Delta K_t \qquad [9.1]$$

$$\Delta K_t = K_t - K_{t-1}$$

$$E_t(C) = E_t(T) + K_t \qquad [9.2]$$

The rate of return on equity (R_E), is measured by relating net income to equity at the beginning of the period. That is:

$$R_{Et}(C) = \frac{I(C)}{E_{t-1}(C)} \qquad [9.3]$$

$$R_{Et}(T) = \frac{I(T)}{E_{t-1}(T)} = \frac{I_t(C) - \Delta K_t}{E_{t-1}(C) - K_{t-1}} = R_{Et}(C)$$

$$+ [R_{Et}(C) - \frac{\Delta K}{K_{t-1}}] \times \frac{K_{t-1}}{E_{t-1}(T)} \qquad [9.4]$$

Some important conclusions can be drawn from [9.4] (*See* Theorem 2 in Section 7.4.)

If

$$\frac{\Delta K_t}{K_{t-1}} = R_{Et}(T)$$

then

$$R_E(T) = R_{Et}(C)$$

If
$$\frac{\Delta K_t}{K_{t-1}} < R_{Et}(T)$$

then
$$R_{Et}(T) > R_{Et}(C)$$

Assuming that

$$\frac{\Delta K_t}{K_{t-1}} = i_t \qquad [9.5]$$

$$R_{Et}(C) = i_t + r \qquad [9.6]$$

where

i = rate of inflation
r = real rate of return on equity

then

$$R_{Et}(T) - R_{Et}(C) = r \times \frac{K_{t-1}}{E_{t-1}(T)} \qquad [9.7]$$

The assumption [9.5] means that nominal unrealized gains grow at the same rate as the general price level and are thus constant in real terms. Assumption [9.6] means that the rate of return on equity is constant in real terms and the nominal rate varies with the rate of inflation.

EXAMPLE   Let us assume that $E_0(C) = 150$. Further we assume that the expected constant rate of inflation is 10%, the target real rate of return is 5% and the target nominal rate is 15%, equal to the cost of equity capital. The expected constant pay-out ratio is 1/3 of I or 5% of $E_{t-1}(C)$ and thus the expected nominal rate of growth of equity, net income and dividends is 10%. Under this assumption, the market value (P_0) according to the Gordon model will be:

$$P_0 = \frac{0.05 \times 150}{0.15 - 0.10} = 150 = E_0(C)$$

Assuming that unrealized holdings gains (K) will grow at the same rate as inflation and the ratio of K_t to $E_t(T)$ will be constant and equal to 50%, then the target nominal rate of return on equity in traditional accounting, $R_E(T)$, will be

$$15\% + 5\% \times 0.5 = 17.5\%$$

The dividends (D) will correspond to 7.5% of $E_{t-1}(T)$. The market value (P_0) will be

$$P_o = \frac{0.75 \times 100}{0.15 - 0.10} = 150 = 1.5 \times E_o(T)$$

The difference between the target rate for $R_E(T)$, 17.5% and for $R_E(C)$, 15%, corresponds to the difference between $D/E_o(T)$, 7.5%, and $D/E_o(C)$, 5%, and is thus a function of the pay-out ratios (*see* Theorem 3, Section 7.4). The lower the pay-out ratio is, the less the difference is (all other things being equal). Assuming a constant ratio, 1.5, of $E(C)$ to $E(T)$, expected dividends of 3% of $E(C)$ and 4.5% of $E(T)$ and a target for $R_E(C)$ of 15%, this means that the equivalent target for $R_E(T)$ is 16.5% and that the expected growth rate of equity, income and dividends is 12% in both cases.

9.1.2 Traditional return on equity versus cost of equity capital under 'ideal' conditions

As a basis for the continued analysis, we make the following assumptions:

- The enterprise presents traditional accounting and supplementary information in terms of unrealized holding gains, allowing the market to estimate $I(C)$ and $E(C)$.
- One requirement for the long-term survival and development of the enterprise is that the average $R_E(C)$ corresponds to the cost (market price) of equity capital (k), i.e. the return the owners require on their investments in shares in the enterprise.
- The market value of the enterprise at a given date is equal to $E(C)$ at the same date, if the market expects a future constant $R_E(C) = k$, a constant pay-out ratio and the same growth rate for $E(C)$, $I(C)$ and dividends.

We assume that contracts with management, employees, banks and other stakeholders are based on traditional accounting. The motivational role of accounting is assumed to be related to traditional measures.

The state of unrealized gains growing at the same rate as $E(T)$ is referred to as the 'ideal' condition for comparing $R_E(T)$ with nominal cost of equity capital under inflation. It is ideal in the sense that we can specify how to adjust a target for $R_E(T)$ because of the limitation of traditional accounting, not recognizing unrealized holding gains. From Sections 7.4 and 9.1 we know that under ideal conditions $R_E(T)$ has to be higher than $R_E(C) = k$ and the difference corresponds to the difference between $D/E(T)$ and $D/E(C)$.

9.2 TRADITIONAL MEASURES OF RETURN ON EQUITY UNDER LESS THAN 'IDEAL' CONDITIONS

In this section, we analyse the relationship between the growth rate of unrealized holding gains, the age structure of plant and equipment and price level changes. We specify conditions under which $E'(T)$ would be equal to $E'(C)$ and analyse the consequences of deviations from these conditions. We limit the analysis to numerical illustrations regarding capital expenditures for machines with identical economic lives.

9.2.1 Constant age structure and rate of inflation

A necessary condition for $E(T)$ and $E(C)$ to grow at the same constant rate is that the assets valued in accordance with the T-method and the C-method, and thus the unrealized holding gains, grow at the same rate. Therefore, we analyse the conditions for identical rate of growth for book values according to the C-method (book value C) and book values according to the T-method (book value T).

EXAMPLE

As our instrument of analysis, we use a classical model of a set of machines with constant age structure and no growth in real terms (even age distribution). The current cost of acquisition is assumed to grow at the same rate as the general price level. Other assets and all the liabilities are assumed to have identical book values under the T-method and the C-method and to grow at the same rate as $E(T)$ and the general price level. Further, we assume that the rate of inflation (i) is constant, that $R_E(C) = i + 5\%$ equals the cost of equity capital, that there are no income taxes, and that the growth rate of $E(C) = i$.

The more specific assumptions are:

1   A set of machines consists of ten machines with an economic life of ten years and a rate of depreciation of 10% per year; at the beginning of each year an old machine is scrapped (salvage value = 0) and is replaced by a new machine.
2   The historical cost of acquisition of the oldest machine is 10 and the replacement (current) cost increases by 10% per year; after ten years the replacement cost for the oldest machine is 26.

Under these assumptions, the book values according to the T-method and the C-method will be as follows at the end of year 10:

C-method		**T-method**	
Replacement cost	260	Cost of acquisition	160
– Accum. depreciation	<u>–130</u>	– Accum. depreciation	<u>–76</u>
Book value	**130**	**Book value**	**84**
Unrealized holding gain (130 – 84)			**46**

In Year 11, the book values change as follows:

	C-method	**T-method**
Opening balance	130.0	84.0
+ Reinvestment	26.0	26.0
+ Holding gain	15.6	
– Depreciation	<u>-28.6</u>	<u>17.6</u>

= Closing balance	143.0	92.4
Increase in book value	13.0	8.4
Rate of growth	10 %	10%
Unrealized holding gain		
Opening		46.0
Closing		50.6
Increase (50.6 – 46.0)		4.6
Rate of growth		10 %

The replacement cost at the end of the year is 260 x 1.1 = 286. The C- depreciation 28.6, is equal to the reinvestment (26) plus the holding gain related to the reinvestment (2.6). The increase in the book value (13) is equal to the holding gain on the opening balance.

The historical cost of acquisition is 176 at the end of the year. The increase from 160 to 176 is equal to the difference between the reinvestment at the beginning of the year (26) and the historical cost of acquisition of the machine, scrapped at the beginning of the year (10). The cost of acquisition of the total set of machines will grow by 10%. The book value each year will be 52.5% of the total cost of acquisition and grow at the rate of 10%.

The opening unrealized holding gain is 46.0. The realized gain, defined as the difference between C-depreciation (28.6) and T-depreciation (17.6) is 11. The closing unrealized holding gain is 50.6. The total holding gain of 15.6 is thus the sum of the realized gain (11) and the increase in the unrealized gain (4.6).

The crucial point is that the book values compared have the same growth rate. The example illustrates that book value C and book value T will grow at the same rate, = to the rate of inflation, if all of the following three conditions are fulfilled concerning physical units of plant and equipment:

1 The units have uniform economic lives, uniform rates of depreciation, the same cost of acquisition in real terms and the same number of units replaced each year.
2 The historical rate of inflation has been constant since the first of the existing units was acquired.
3 The same rate of inflation will continue.

The first condition implies that the number of units is constant. This is a special case of a more general condition, namely, that there is a constant relationship between the number of new units which are acquired and the number of units which are scrapped each year and that thus the age structure is constant. The annual nominal amount invested in new units will grow at a constant rate due to the combined effect of a constant rate of price changes and a constant rate of growth of the number of units.

EXAMPLE   In our example, the unrealized holding gains grow at the same rate as $E(C)$. Thus $E(T)$ and $E(C)$ grow at the same rate. The difference between $R_E(T)$ and $R_E(C)$ is dependent upon the ratio of unrealized holding gains to $E(T)$. We assume this ratio to be 1/2 and thus $E(C)/E(T) = 3/2$. We have assumed that $R_E(C)$ is 15% and that the dividends are 5% of $E(C)$. Thus they are 7.5% of $E(T)$ and $R_E(T) = 15\%$ + 2.5% = 17.5%. In a market where investors expect $R_E(T)$ to be 17.5% and $E(T)$, $I(T)$ and dividends to grow at a constant rate of 10%, the market price will be equal to $E(C) = 1.5 \times E(T)$, provided that the cost of equity capital is 15 % and the Gordon model of valuation is applied.

It is obvious that $E(C)$ and $E(T)$ will grow at the same rate only under very specific conditions with regard to plant and equipment and related unrealized holding gains. In the following section we will illustrate the consequences of deviations from the conditions that the rate of inflation is constant and that the age structure is constant.

9.2.2 Variable inflation rate

The growth rate of book value C will vary with the rate of inflation if the number of machines in our model is constant. The growth rate during a given period, t, will be a function only of the rate of inflation during period t and is unaffected by inflation prior to period t. The growth rate of book value T will be a function both of the inflation before period t and during period t.

EXAMPLE   To illustrate these statements, we change our initial assumption about a constant rate of inflation and make certain alternative assumptions about the rate of inflation (see Table 9.1).

Table 9.1

	Year 11	Year 1-10
Case I	5%	10%
Case II	15%	10%
Case III	10%	0%

The accounts for Year 11 will be as follows in the three alternatives:

	I		II		III	
	C	*T*	*C*	*T*	*C*	*T*
Opening balance	130.0	84.0	130.0	84.0	50.0	50.0
+ Reinvestment	26.0	26.0	26.0	26.0	10.0	10.0
+ Holding gain	7.8		23.4		6.0	
– Depreciation	−27.3	−17.6	−29.9	−17.6	−11.0	−10.0

= Closing balance	136.5	92.4	149.5	92.4	55.0	50.0
Increase	6.5	8.4	19.5	8.4	5.0	0
Growth rate	5 %	10 %	15 %	10 %	10 %	0 %

Unrealized holding gain

Opening	46.0	46.0	0
Closing	44.1	57.1	5
Change	−1.9	11.1	5
Growth rate	−4.1%	24.1%	∞

In Case I, where the rate of inflation decreases, the book value T grows at a faster rate than book value C and the unrealized holding gain has a negative growth rate. In Case II, with an increasing rate of inflation, the consequences will be the reverse. In Case III, the rate of inflation increases after ten years without inflation. This increase has no effect on the book value T, as the reinvestment is made at the beginning of the year at the same price as previous replacements. Thus, there is a considerable deviation from the growth rate of book value C. However, if the future rate of inflation is 10%, the gap will gradually decrease and will be closed after ten years.

To illustrate differences between $R_E(C)$ and $R_E(T)$ and between $E'(C)$ and $E'(T)$ in the three cases, we make the assumption that the difference between $E(C)$ and $E(T)$ at the beginning of Year 11 is equal to the opening unrealized gain, that $E(C)$ is alternatively (a) 100 and (b) 200 and that $R_E(C) = i + 5\%$. Under these assumptions, $R_E(C)$ and $R_E(T)$ will be as in Table 9.2.

Table 9.2

	$R_E(C)$	$R_E(T)$	
		a	b
Case I	10%	22.0%	14.2%
Case II	20%	16.5%	18.8%
Case III	15%	10.0%	12.5%

If the dividend for Year 11 is 5% of the initial (beginning) $E(C)$ and thus $E(C)$ grows at the same rate as the inflation, $E'(C)$ and $E'(T)$ will be as in Table 9.3.

Table 9.3

	$E'(C)$	$E'(T)$	
		a	b
Case I	5%	12.8%	7.7%
Case II	15%	7.2%	12.3%
Case III	10%	5.0%	7.5%

In Case I, where the current rate of inflation is lower than the previous rate, the T-method overstates the return on equity and the growth rate of equity. In Cases II and III, where the current rate of inflation is higher than previously, the situation will be the reverse. The higher the ratio of unrealized holding gains to $E(C)$, the greater the difference between the measures compared.

The conclusion is that variations in the rate of inflation cause a considerable limitation to the usefulness of $R_E(T)$ as a basis for comparison with cost of equity capital and with previous periods. Comparisons based on, say, five years' average return should improve the comparability as a rule. In comparing actual outcome with a target rate it should be observed that targets cannot be continuously adjusted to inflationary changes in the cost of equity capital. A target rate has to be kept constant for a number of periods for administrative reasons. If a fall in the rate of inflation and the cost of equity capital is reflected in the target rate with a time lag, the reported $R_E(T)$ and the target for $R_E(T)$ will both be overstated during the lag-period. In other words, limitations of the T-method in comparisons between outcome and target may to some extent be counteracted by the inflexibility of the target for $R_E(T)$. This comment is made to illustrate that in an analysis of the limitations of traditional accounting, we also have to consider behavioural aspects and 'imperfections' in the target-setting procedure.

Our numerical analysis is based on very simplified assumptions. Obviously, it would be extremely complicated to consider more realistic assumptions concerning price changes, the structure of tangible fixed assets, etc. It is hoped that our analysis is sufficient to show that a significant fall or rise in the rate of inflation reduces the usefulness of $R_E(T)$ for comparative purposes. It should be observed that we have illustrated the initial effect of a fall or rise in the rate of inflation. The initial gap between $R_E(C)$ and $R_E(T)$ will be gradually reduced if the future rate of inflation is stable. In a situation in which a long period of high inflation is followed by a period of stable prices, $R_E(T)$ may be much higher than $R_E(C)$ during the first year of stable prices and, in our example, the gap will not be closed until all the machines have been acquired at the same price.

Finally, interest in inflation accounting seems to vary with the current rate of inflation. The limitations of traditional accounting, however, are very much related to the length and the strength of historical inflation and its impact on unrealized holding gains. There is a need to make adjustments for inflationary effects even under periods of stable prices.

9.2.3 Variable age structure

As the next step in our analysis, we consider variable age structure for the set of machines and real growth (increased capacity). First we analyse the consequences of increased capacity by making the following change in the previous assumptions.

EXAMPLE   At the beginning of year 11, the number of machines is increased from ten to eleven by acquiring one machine in addition to the replacement, thus affecting the age structure. The book values change as follows:

	C	T
Opening balance	130.0	84.0
+ Acquisitions	52.0	52.0
+ Holding gain	18.2	
− Depreciation	−31.5	−20.2
= Closing balance	168.7	115.8
Increase in book value	38.7	31.8
Rate of growth	29.8%	37.9%
Unrealized holding gain		
Opening		46.0
Closing		52.9
Increase		6.9
Rate of growth		15.0%

Book value T has a higher growth rate than book value C in the year when the expansion occurs. The unrealized holding grows at a lower rate than book value C. The situation will be the reverse in subsequent years, provided no additional increase in capacity occurs. The growth rate of the unrealized holding gain, 15%, is higher than the assumed growth rate of $E(C)$ (10%) but equal to the $R_E(C)$, which is assumed to be 15%. From [9.4] in Section 9.1, it follows that $R_E(T) = R_E(C)$ and that $E'(T) < E'(C)$ for Year 11. Without expansion during subsequent years the growth rate of unrealized holding gains will gradually be lower and $R_E(T)$ and $E'(T)$ will be higher than $R_E(C)$ and $E'(C)$ respectively. Obviously, the conditions for comparisons between $R_E(T)$ and cost of equity capital or previous years will be unsatisfactory.

Lack of continuity in capital expenditures causes changes in the age structure of plant and equipment and makes it difficult to achieve meaningful return comparisons under periods of inflation.

EXAMPLE   To illustrate this statement, we assume all the machines are acquired at the beginning of Year 1 and are replaced after ten years. The assumption regarding a constant rate of inflation of 10% is kept unchanged. The accounts for Year 1 and Year 2 will be as follows:

	Year 1		Year 2	
	C	T	C	T
Opening balance	100	100	99.0	90
+ Holding gain	10		9.9	
− Depreciation	−11	−10	−12.1	−10

= Closing balance	99	90	96.8	80
Rate of growth	– 1%	–10%	– 2.2%	–11.1%

Unrealized holding gain		
Opening	0	9.0
Closing	9	16.8
Increase	9	7.8
Rate of growth	∞	86.7%

The book value T will be reduced annually by 10 and the negative growth rate will gradually increase up to –100% in Year 10. The book value C will also be reduced because the depreciation will increase and the holding gain will decrease. After the first year, the growth rate of unrealized holdings will be gradually reduced. It will be negative when the difference between the depreciation C and the depreciation T is higher than the holding gain on the opening balance.

Assuming $R_E(C) = 15\%$, $E'(N) = 10\%$ and initial $E(N) = 100$, $R_E(T)$ will be 6% in Year 1, 16.3% in Year 5 and 27.2% in Year 10.

During the first four years the growth rate of unrealized holding gains is higher than $R_E(C)$ and thus $R_E(C)$ is higher than $R_E(T)$ with the largest difference in Year 1. During subsequent years, the situation is the reverse. There is hardly any need to comment on the limitations of $R_E(T)$ measures for comparative purposes under the conditions assumed.

The development described above is valid for each individual object of investment. Continuous investment is a prerequisite for growth of compared book values of the aggregate of investments at roughly the same rate under periods of inflation. After and during periods of inflation the usefulness of $R_E(T)$ for comparative purposes may be highly limited in enterprises characterized by significant non-monetary fixed assets with long economic lives and by considerable discontinuity in capital expenditures for replacements and expansion. Acquisition of a large company with a considerable portion of non-monetary fixed assets may cause similar limitations with regard to the consolidated $R_E(T)$. The age structure of plant and equipment may be fairly constant for a group as a whole but not for various sub-units. This will disturb return comparisons between the group and its sub-units, and between sub-units.

The greater the lack of continuity is and the higher the ratio of unrealized holding gains to $E(T)$, the more limited the usefulness of $R_E(T)$ will be for comparative purposes. In periods with low capital expenditures, $E'(T)$ will be lower than $E'(N)$ and vice versa. An extreme case is investment in power plants with long economic life and no expansion.

9.2.4 Favourable and unfavourable conditions

Earlier in this Chapter, we specified the 'ideal' conditions under inflation for the usefulness of $R_E(T)$ in comparisons with the cost of equity, with other enterprises or previous periods. The conditions have to be fulfilled for all the enterprises or periods compared. A stable rate of inflation and stable age structure of plant and equipment are the key conditions. Obviously there are favourable conditions for comparability when monetary items, valued in the same way in the C- and T-methods, dominate the balance sheet, as is the case in banks and other financial institutions. Favourable conditions exist also for a trading company in which working capital is the predominant balance sheet item and where there is a stable turnover of inventory. The combination of a high ratio of unrealized holding gains to $E(C)$ and considerable variations in the rate of inflation and in the growth rate of capital expenditures represent extremely unfavourable conditions. Under these conditions there are obvious difficulties in using $R_E(T)$ as an instrument of control. Alternative or supplementary measures are called for and such measures will be discussed further in Chapter 10.

NOTES

[1] Edwards, E. O. and Bell, P. W. *The Theory and Measurement of Business Income* (1961). Due to the comparative purpose of our analysis, some deviations from the Edwards and Bell model are made.
[2] To a large extent this analysis is valid even if holding gains represent relative price changes. Our assumption simplifies the analysis and is rather conventional in this context.

CHAPTER 10

Adjustments for changes in specific prices and the general price level

The limitations of traditional accounting measures under stable and variable general price levels were discussed in Chapters 8 and 9, respectively. Against this background, inflation accounting and current cost accounting are now considered as alternatives or supplements to traditional accounting. Such an analysis can be useful for the setting of financial goals, and the choice and interpretation of accounting measures, even if traditional measures dominate current reporting.

In Chapter 9 we made no distinction between specific and general price-level changes. The comparison between traditional and current cost accounting was made in nominal terms, without adjustments for changes in the purchasing power of money. In this chapter, these changes are considered, as well as the relationship between current cost accounting and the concept of economic income and economic value. We also address product costing and capital budgeting. We assume that the historical and expected rates of inflation are not neglible but are not extremely high. Various forms of comparisons are used:

1 the comparison between the cost of equity capital and internal targets for the rate of return on equity,
2 the comparison between the required return on capital employed, product costing and income measurement, and
3 interperiod comparisons.

OVERVIEW
Inflation accounting means that all measurements are made in monetary units of uniform purchasing power (referred to as constant dollar accounting in the US). A comparison between traditional accounting and current cost/constant dollar accounting has to be made in two steps:

1 a comparison between traditional accounting (the T-method) and current cost/nominal dollar accounting (the C_n-method), recognizing nominal unrealized holding gains on non-monetary assets, and
2 a comparison between the C_n-method and current cost/constant dollar accounting (the C_r-method), recognizing unrealized real holding gains.

The nominal rate of return on capital in accordance with the C_n-method can be translated into a real rate and vice versa when the rate of inflation is given. Thus the C_n- and the C_r-methods give equivalent information about the rate of return on capital.

Does inflation accounting give the user any useful additional information in relation to traditional accounting? This question has been studied mainly from the viewpoint of external users (investors and creditors). The answers have been negative on the whole. The research findings are hard to interpret and uncertain. Less attention has been paid to the usefulness of inflation accounting for internal users (management accounting). Our hypothesis is that an important advantage of management inflation accounting is that a goal for the rate of return on capital can be formulated as a real rate, which is more stable than a nominal rate when the general price level is fluctuating. Income taxes, however, create a problem, because they are based on nominal measures of income. Therefore a constant real rate of return *after* tax does not – under variable rates of inflation – correspond to an equivalent constant real rate of return *before* tax.

Requiring a certain real rate of return on capital investments means requiring recovery of the purchasing power of the invested capital plus the required interest. This concept of real return is the basis of the general purchasing power method for inflation accounting which deviates from the C_r-method in that unrealized real holding gains are not recognized until they are realized.

The operating income of the C-method is measured on the basis of the current cost at the date of delivery (the date of income recognition). This matching of revenues and expenses is only consistent with the principles of product costing (*ex ante*) on condition that the product cost also refers to the current cost at the date of delivery. This condition is often unrealistic, when the contract which specifies price, terms of payment, etc. is entered into long before the date of delivery. The estimates of product costs are based on the information available at the date of the contract and the expectations at this date about changes in specific prices and the general price level from the contract date to the dates of delivery and payment. The condition may also be unrealistic if, for administrative or other reasons, the enterprise cannot currently adjust its sale prices to changes in the prices of input factors and the cost of capital and thus has to apply fixed prices for a certain period of time.

The players' perceptions about the relevance of unrealized price changes of inventory vary with the conditions for estimating product costs and controlling these changes. Unrealized price changes are important and relevant components of income, if one of the aims of the purchasing policy is price speculation.

There are some possible limitations to the usefulness of current cost valuations of non-monetary fixed assets. As a rule these assets are valued at the current cost of acquisition for new assets less accumulated depreciation, based on the same rate of depreciation and the method of linear depreciation as applied in traditional accounting. In other words, the ratio of the book value C to the book value T will be the same as the ratio of the current cost of acquisition to the historical cost of acquisition. This valuation model is compared with a model derived from the theory of economic life of equipment, which is also used as a frame of reference for a discussion of a theory of historical cost depreciation under realistic conditions of unstable price levels. The growing operating inferiority of existing capital equipment in relation to new modern capital equipment is a crucial variable in determining economic life of equipment and the pattern of depreciation. It is a reasonable assumption that the operating inferiority is gradually increasing in such a way that the economic depreciation is gradually decreasing (degressive depreciation) and generates lower book values than linear depreciation. The overstatement of asset values resulting from the application of linear depreciation may be a stronger limitation in current cost accounting than in traditional accounting with respect to product costing and measurements of return on capital.

The development of the current cost of acquisition can be of direct commercial interest. The real (relative) changes in this cost are often a function of the business cycle and market demand. Acquisitions at 'old favourable prices' can be an important relative advantage in relation to competitors who invest at the current 'high' price level. The situation can also be the reverse. In this type of situation, unrealized holding gains may acquire a very concrete meaning and be perceived as an important component of income.

There is an old tradition in some Swedish industries to apply the C-method, at least partially, in product costing and management accounting, and to apply the T-method in public financial statements. Thus, the current cost of plant and equipment is used as a base for measuring what is called 'calculatory' interest. The latter item includes interest on both debt and equity capital, but the rate applied often represents a nominal borrowing rate. Obviously, it is inconsistent to combine a nominal rate of interest and current costs for non-monetary assets, if nominal unrealized holding gains do not counterbalance the 'calculatory' interest, which is not the case in practice. This inconsistency has been common in practice, and this is still the case. 'Calculatory' current cost is thus a partial application of the C-method for internal management reporting.

In these reports, the operating income is measured on a current cost basis and the operating margin is used as a measure of profitability instead of the rate of return on capital employed. This margin often has a important effect on the return on capital. Thus, it is an important indicator of the rate of return on capital employed. Various forms of profit margins and other ratios are often less sensitive to the limitations of the T-method than measures of return on capital and are used as substitute for, or supplementary information to these measures. It is important to understand the limitations of the usefulness of traditional measures of return on capital in order to explain the use of other ratios as 'return indicators'.

10.1 METHODS OF INFLATION ACCOUNTING

The characteristic of inflation accounting is that the balance sheet items at the beginning and at the end of a period are measured in monetary units of the same purchasing power (constant dollar accounting). The real (constant dollar) income is the change in equity measured in this way, plus dividends minus the capital contribution, which are also measured in monetary units of the same purchasing power (the same money value). The same principle is applied in the income statement.

10.1.1 The general purchasing power method and the current cost/constant dollar method

Two methods of inflation accounting predominate in the accounting literature:

1 the general purchasing power method, and
2 the current cost/constant dollar method.

The essential difference between Method 1 and Method 2 is the valuation of non-monetary assets and the interperiod allocation of real holding gains on these assets.

Method 1 means that non-monetary assets are stated at historical costs, adjusted for general price-level changes from the date of acquisition to the current closing date. Thus, real holding gains are recognized when they are realized. The realization convention is applied in real terms but not in nominal terms.

In current cost/constant dollar accounting, unrealized real holding gains are recognized as income in the period when the gains occur.[1] The valuation of non-monetary assets is based on the current cost of acquisition at the valuation date. In measuring real net income, expressed in the money value at the closing date, the balance sheet items at the beginning of the period are increased by the rate of inflation during the period and thus adjusted to the money value at the closing date. In principle, the same unit of measurement should be used in the income statement.

A common issue in the debate on inflation accounting is whether it is meaningful to use a consumer price index or a similar index in measurements of real income. An argument against this type of index is that it does not reflect the relevant price changes, namely, the price changes of the input and output factors of the individual enterprise. Our view on this issue is based on our basic frame of reference with regard to measures of return on capital. The rate of return on equity should be comparable with the cost of equity capital.

The nominal annual net income in current cost accounting is equal to the difference between the equity at the end of the year and the equity at the beginning of the year without adjustments for the rate of inflation during the year, provided no transactions between the enterprise and its owners take place during the year. The nominal rate of return is comparable with the nominal cost of equity capital. If we want to measure the real rate of return on equity to be compared with the real cost of equity capital, the critical question is what type of index the market uses in converting a nominal return, required on its investments, into a real return. According to our observations, a general price index (usually a consumer price index) is used both in financial contracts, including index clauses, and in financial journals and analyses, where nominal rates are translated into real rates. Our conclusion is that a nominal rate of return on equity should be converted into a real rate by using the same type of index that is used on the financial markets in converting nominal market rates to real rates. We assume that this index is a consumer price index.

10.1.2 Traditional accounting and current cost/constant dollar accounting

In an analysis of the differences between measures of traditional accounting and real (constant dollar) measures of current cost accounting, it is rational to divide the analysis into two steps:

1 the differences between the traditional measures and the nominal measures of current cost accounting, and
2 the differences between the nominal and the real measures of current cost accounting.

The former differences were discussed in Chapter 9. They refer to unrealized nominal holding gains in current cost accounting which are recognized as income in the period when they occur and which in traditional accounting, are not recognized until they are realized.

A numerical example will be used in the analysis to illustrate different income components in traditional accounting (T) and current cost accounting (C), both with and without adjustments for price level changes (C_n and C_r respectively). Furthermore, we illustrate the difference between C_r and the general purchasing power method, referred to as the P-method. As shown below, components of the P-method are required as a basis for measuring various income components under the C_r-method.

EXAMPLE

In this example, we only consider measures which are relevant in measuring rate of return on capital employed. The accounting year is 19X6. To simplify, we assume that all transactions occur at the end of the year. This means that all current transactions are stated in the same money value. The capital employed at the beginning of the year is the basis for measuring rate of return. The capital is reduced at the end of the year by an amount equal to the T-income. Thus the initial and final amount of capital employed in accordance with the T-method will be the same. Further assumptions are as follows.

1 The rate of inflation in 19X 6 is 10%.
2 The acquisition cost of the initial inventory is 200 and increases by 10% during the year. The volume of inventory is unchanged. The holding gain is 20 and is realized at the end of the year.
3 The fixed non-monetary assets consist of machines acquired at a cost of 600 and depreciated at a rate of 10% per year. The machines were acquired in 19X1 and their book value at the beginning of 19X6 is 300 in accordance with the T-method. The accumulated rate of inflation in the period 19X1–19x5 is

50%. The current cost of acquisition at the beginning of 19X6 is 1000 and increases during the year by 5%.

Under these assumptions, the book values, the amounts of depreciation and the holding gains are as follows:

	T-method		*C*-method		*P*-method	
	1 Jan	31 Dec	1 Jan	31 Dec	1 Jan	31 Dec
Book value	300	240	500	420	450	396
	(0.5 x 600)	(0.4 x 600)	(0.5 x 1000)	(0.4 x 1050)	(0.5 x 900)	(0.4 x 990)
Depreciation		60		105		99

Holding gains
Unrealized

		nominal	200	180
			(500 − 300)	(420 − 240)
			50	24
	real		(500 − 450)	(420 − 396)

Realized

	nominal	45
		(105 − 60)
	real	6
		(105 − 99)

Capital employed as per 1 January and 31 December 19x6 has the following components:

	T-method		*C*-method		*P*-method	
	1 Jan	31 Dec	1 Jan	31 Dec	1 Jan	31 Dec
Monetary net assets	100	140	100	140	100	140
Inventory	200	220	200	220	200	220
Machines	300	240	500	420	450	396
	600	600	800	780	750	756

The income statements for 19X6 and the rates of return on capital employed are reported as follows:

	T-method	*C*-method		*P*-method
		Nom.	Real	Real
Operating revenues	1100	1100	1100	1100
Operating expenses (excl. depreciation)	−930	−950	−950	−950
Operating income before depreciation	170	150	150	150
Depreciation	−60	−105	−105	−99
Operating income after depreciation	110	45	45	51

	I(T)	I(C_n)	I(C_r)	I(P)
Realized holding gains				
Inventory		20	0	
Machines		<u>45</u>	<u>6</u>	
Operating income plus realized holding gains		110	51	51
Unrealized holding gains (losses)[2]		−20	−31	
Operating income plus realized holding gains		90	20	51
Net interest revenues	<u>10</u>	<u>10</u>	<u>0</u>	<u>0</u>
Total income	<u>120</u>	<u>100</u>	<u>20</u>	<u>51</u>
	$I(T)$	$I(C_n)$	$I(C_r)$	$I(P)$
Rate of return on capital employed	20%	12.5%	2.3%[3]	6.2%
	$R(T)$	$R(C_n)$	$R(C_r)$	$R(P)$

The example illustrates

- that the difference between $I(C_n)$ and $I(T)$ is equal to the unrealized nominal loss (−20) (this type of difference was analysed in Chapter 9);
- that the difference between $I(C_n)$ and $I(C_r)$ is equal to the difference between nominal and real realized and unrealized holding gains (20 + 45 − 20 − 6 + 31 = 70) plus the difference between nominal and real interest revenues (10 − 0); the total difference (80) can also be explained as 0.1 x 800, i.e. the rate of inflation 10% (0.1) multiplied by the working capital;
- that the difference between $I(c_r)$ and $I(P)$ is equal to the unrealized real holding loss (−31).

From our earlier analysis, we know that the condition for $R(T) = R(C_n)$ is that the nominal unrealized holding gains grow at a rate = $R(T)$. In this example, this growth rate is negative and thus there is a substantial negative difference between $R(C_n)$ and $R(T)$, which can also be explained by the fact that $I(T)$ is higher than $I(C_n)$ and, in addition, the initial capital employed in accordance with the T-method is lower than the capital in accordance with the C_n-method.

The difference between $R(C_n)$ and $R(C_r)$ is a function of the rate of inflation and, more specifically, is equal to the rate of inflation, 10%, plus 0.1 x 2.3.

Theorem 2 can also be applied in comparing $R(C_r)$ and $R(P)$ (*see* Section 7.4). The condition for $R(C_r) = R(P)$ is that the unrealized real holding gains grow at a rate equal to $R(P)$. In our example this growth rate is negative and thus $R(P)$ is greater than $R(C_r)$. If we had assumed that the current cost of acquisition of machines had increased by 11.3% instead of 5%, the rate of growth of unrealized real holding gains would have been 6.2% and $R(C_r)$ = $R(P)$ = 6.2%.

The rate of growth of unrealized real holding gains can be analysed with the same model as that applied to nominal holding gains in Chapter 9 and is a function of the historical and current changes in real prices and the age structure of the machines. In the same way, we can analyse the relationship between the rate of growth of unrealized real holding gains and the difference between the rate of return on equity or the rate on growth of equity as measured by the C-method versus the P-method.

$R(C_n)$ and $R(C_r)$ contain the same information about return on working capital. Thus, if $R(T) = R(C_n)$ and, in addition, $R(P) = R(C_r)$, all the methods compared would be equally informative in terms of capital return but not in terms of growth of capital. Conditions for $R(T) = R(C_n)$ are a constant rate of historical and current nominal price changes and a constant age structure. Conditions for $R(P) = R(c_r)$ are a constant rate of historical and current real price changes and a constant age structure. The latter conditions may be less restrictive but still very unrealistic.

10.2 INFLATION ACCOUNTING AS EXTERNAL INFORMATION

Inflation accounting has mainly been discussed and analysed in the context of external reporting and external users of accounting information. We have insufficient knowledge to judge the potential of inflation accounting as an alternative or supplement to traditional accounting. Inflation accounting has rarely been applied in countries other than those with hyperinflation. (The most well-known exception is the Philips group in Holland.)

The primary purpose of inflation accounting is to make it possible to base multiperiod comparisons on measurement units of uniform purchasing power. Such measures have not been generally available for external users, although partial inflation accounting was recommended by the FASB as supplementary information over a relatively short period. It is debatable what the outcome of a comparative study of the information value of inflation accounting versus traditional accounting would have been if inflation accounting had been the primary information source and if real income, real rate of return, etc. had been published and had been as easily available as the corresponding traditional measures. We realize that this question is not interesting to readers who are convinced that the market is always rational, and gather and use the information which is considered to be most useful.

If real measures in accordance with the C-method do not contain useful additional information in relation to traditional measures, this may be for the following reasons:

1 that information about unrealized nominal holding gains is not useful (or is gathered in some other way); or
2 unrealized nominal holding gains grow at the same rate as traditional equity and therefore do not provide the user with a better basis for forecasting growth of income and dividends in nominal terms; or

3 C_r-measures do not provide any useful additional information in relation to the C_n-measures.

With regard to (C), it is obviously unimportant whether the rate of return on equity is compared with the cost of equity in nominal or real terms, provided the same deflator is used. The market can convert $C_n$measures to C_r-measures, even if this conversion is not made in financial statements. It is a reasonable hypothesis, however, that comparisons over several periods with varying rates of inflation are facilitated if, for example, income and rate of return are measured in real terms and all items in financial statements represent the same purchasing power.

A key issue in empirical research has been whether inflation-adjusted measures contain any additional information compared with traditional measures and therefore contribute to a better understanding of, or explanation of, the connection between accounting measures and share prices or the connection between accounting measures and the risk of bankruptcy. The conclusion has roughly been that inflation-adjusted measures do not contain any essential additional information.

However, the findings are hard to interpret for several reasons. Different forms of complete and partial inflation accounting have been used. The effects of inflation adjustments have not been isolated from the effects of differences between the nominal measures, converted to real measures, and traditional nominal measures. We have insufficient knowledge about the importance of lack of knowledge and experience of inflation accounting.[4] Inflation adjustments are common within certain sectors.

Wage negotiations in Sweden, for example, have been conducted increasingly in terms of real wages since the acceleration of the rate of inflation following the oil crises of 1973. In the financial market, the combination of accelerated inflation, high marginal tax rates and taxation of nominal returns has caused increased attention to, and more public information about, the concept of real interest, particularly real post-tax interest. Low, often negative, real borrowing rates after tax have encouraged high-leverage investment in shares and real estate, in the expectation that this would generate nominal holding gains which were not fully subject to taxation, and not until the gains were realized. The market has learned to think and calculate in real terms. Inflation-adjusted information has been available for comparative analysis of different financial investments and of different periods. This is not the case when it comes to information about real income and real rate of return within the industrial sector in countries who have not experienced hyperinflation.

Our experience, probably shared by most teachers of accounting, is that students regard the area of inflation accounting and its concepts of purchasing power changes, real income, etc. as rather difficult. They feel that inflation accounting is of insignificant practical importance, with the exception of countries and periods with very high rates of inflation. Thus the area has a low priority for students, which is in turn aggravated by the small number of classroom hours devoted to inflation accounting.

Knowledge is rapidly forgotten and not supported by any practical application other than the computation of real wages and real interest before and after taxes.

As indicated above, the main focus of research on inflation accounting has been its informative value to external users.[5] In a way, this is rather odd. It would be at least as reasonable to focus on the usefulness to internal users. If inflation accounting were the most rational tool for management's evaluation of the economic efficiency of the enterprise and its components, then it would be natural to use the same measures in financial reports to shareholders, creditors, etc. The absence of inflation accounting can be explained in a similar way. Are the benefits of inflation accounting to external users judged to be less than the costs, which explains why inflation accounting is not used as a management tool? Is the usefulness for management purposes perhaps too limited to justify financial reporting in real terms? Is the benefit to both external and internal users perhaps less than the cost of providing inflation-adjusted measures as supplementary information?

In the following sections, we will analyse the usefulness of the concepts and measures of inflation accounting for management control.

10.3 TARGETS FOR REAL RATES OF RETURN ON CAPITAL WITH RESPECT TO TAXATION AND INFLATION

Our hypothesis is that stable targets are desired in controlling the profitability of the unit and its components. Rate of return targets should be valid irrespective of price-level changes. It is a reasonable hypothesis that the real cost of capital is more stable than the nominal cost. Thus, real rates of return on capital should be preferred to nominal rates. This may be of particular importance in an international group operating in several countries with varying rates of inflation. Inflation accounting is a tool for controlling the ability of an enterprise to attain required real rates of return on capital.[6]

Taxation of nominal income creates a problem, however, which is illustrated by the following example.

EXAMPLE   Assume that a stable target is set for the real rate of (post-tax) return on the equity of the total enterprise (group). Divisions are controlled by real rates of pre-tax return on capital employed. Thus a required level of post-tax return on equity (R_E), assumed to be 10%, has to be converted into a required level of rate of pre-tax return on capital employed (R_{CE}). Further, we assume that nominal income is subject to taxation. To simplify our analysis, we assume that the nominal income of current cost accounting is subject to taxation at a rate of 40%. The additional assumptions are as follows: the debt-to-equity ratio (D/E) = 1 and the real borrowing rate (R_D) is 6% before taxes.

Table 10.1 illustrates how a given target of real post-tax rate of return on equity is converted into a target real pre-tax rate of return on capital employed under varying assumptions about a constant rate of inflation, and assuming the pre-tax borrowing rate to be 6%, the debt-to-equity ratio to be 1 and the tax rate to be 40%.

Table 10.1 Converting real post-tax rate of return on equity (R_E) into real pre-tax rate of return on capital employed (R_{CE}).

		Rate of inflation (i)			
		0%	5%	10%	15%
a	R_E real post-tax	10.0	10.0	10.0	10.0
b	R_E nom. post-tax $(a + i + i \times a)^7$	10.0	15.5	21.0	26.5
c	R_E nom. pre-tax $(b/0.6)$	16.7	25.8	35.0	44.2
d	R_E real pre-tax $(c-i)(1 + i)^7$	16.7	19.8	22.7	25.4
e	R_D real pre-tax	6.0	6.0	6.0	6.0
f	R_{CE} real, pre-tax $(d \times \frac{1}{2} + e \times \frac{1}{2})$	11.3	12.9	14.4	15.7

The example illustrates that real pre-tax R_{CE} increases with the rate of inflation. The reason is that real pre-tax R_E increases due to the assumed taxation of the nominal income in current cost accounting. If taxation were based on real income, the real pre-tax R_E would have been 16.7% (or more exactly 16 2/3%) and the real pre-tax R_{CE} 11.3% (or more exactly 11 1/3%) regardless of the rate of inflation. From the difference between real R_E before and after taxes, (d – a) in Table 10.1, we can conclude that nominal taxation means that the effective tax rate on real income before taxes increases from 40% to 49%, 56% and 61% as the rate of inflation increases from zero to 5%, 10% and 15% respectively.

The analysis will be still more complicated if we assume traditional accounting as the base of taxation. We then have to consider the difference between C_n-income and traditional income as illustrated in the example in Section 10.1, where unrealized nominal holding gains constituted this difference. If these gains are positive and positively related to the rate of inflation, taxes based on traditional income will be lower than those implicit in Table 10.1, given the same tax rate of 40%.

The above analysis should be sufficient to illustrate the complications of converting a required real post-tax rate of return on equity into a required real pre-tax rate of return on capital employed. It is rarely possible to combine a constant target for real post-tax R_E with a constant target for real pre-tax R_E under conditions of price level changes and a system of nominal taxation. The additional complications faced by an international group, operating in countries with different systems of taxation and different rates of inflation, are obvious. However, the conversion procedure is also complicated, if traditional accounting measures are applied. In addition to the limitations of traditional measures of capital return, different tax rates and rules of taxation within a group will cause considerable complications in converting required post-tax rates of return on equity into pre-tax rates of return on capital employed.

The following conclusions, which are of considerable importance, can be drawn from the analysis above. If taxable income is greater than real income before taxes and the gap is positively related to the rate of inflation, the effective tax on the income and thus the required real pre-tax rate of return on equity will be higher, the higher the rate of inflation is. To compensate for higher real taxes by price increases means that prices increase faster than general price levels. It is obviously not possible for all enterprises to apply this pricing policy. An increased tax burden in real terms may make it difficult to attain a real post-tax rate of return on equity equal to the real cost of equity capital. Inflation accounting as a tool of management control can contribute to better insight into this kind of problem.[8]

Inevitably, required rates of return on capital are imperfect instruments of management control regardless of the measurement system applied. This must be taken into account in practice. There is a need for other supplementary instruments. The complications involved in using real rates of return on capital as instruments are not decisive arguments against such measures.

10.4 TARGETS FOR REAL RATES OF RETURN ON CAPITAL, PRICING AND INCOME MEASUREMENT

If an investor requires a real rate of return on capital, this means that the purchasing power of the capital should be recovered plus the required real return. We assume that product costing for pricing purposes should provide information about the prices required to attain the required real return. Capital has to be allocated to individual products and groups of products. To simplify the analysis we start by discussing the pricing of goods acquired for sale.

10.4.1 Basic relationships for a trading activity

In this section, we disregard the impact of a system of nominal taxation on the real pre-tax rate of return on capital employed, which has been discussed in Section 10.3. We start with some viewpoints on capital budgeting in real terms, which are relevant to the following analysis.

The present value of an investment project is *ex ante* independent of expected future price-level changes if both the discount rate in real terms and the purchasing power of expected cash flows are independent of expected price level changes. In such a case, the nominal cash flows behave as though they were indexed. With a given expected rate of inflation, the present value will be the same if the following conditions are met:

- if future cash flows, transformed into the purchasing power of money at the date of investment, are discounted at a real rate of interest, or
- if the nominal cash flows are discounted at a nominal rate of interest.[9]

The reason is the following relationship between the nominal rate of interest (n), the real rate of interest (r) and the rate of inflation (i):

$$n = r + i + i\,r$$

The relationship is valid both *ex ante* and *ex post*. A required real rate of return on capital can always be transformed into a nominal rate with equivalent informative value, provided the rate of inflation is given.

A discount rate, representing a required real rate of return on the investment, implies a requirement of recovery of the purchasing power of the invested capital plus the required real return. The implication is not recovery of the real replacement cost, which is the frame of reference for the C_r-method with its matching of sales and current cost of goods sold. Thus, the P-method of inflation accounting is more consistent with capital budgeting in real terms.

Planning and review of outcome must be based primarily on nominal cash flows and nominal accounting measures. Planning has to be based on information about expected price-level changes and the development of the specific prices of different factors of production. Cost estimates for pricing purposes should give information about what prices customers should pay to cover all current product costs and recover the allocated capital plus the required interest.

As a basis for the following numerical analysis, we assume that the enterprise aims to price its products in a manner which is consistent with profitability goals in terms of real rates of return on capital employed and equity, and that reported income should be measured in a way consistent with the principles applied in cost estimates for pricing purposes. We first restrict our analysis to two capital components, namely, inventory and receivables in a trading enterprise, and consider only the following components:

- the historical and current costs of acquisition of goods,
- interest on inventory, and
- interest on receivables related to the sale of goods.

We need to make a distinction between 'cash price' and 'credit price'. The cash price is the hypothetical price to be paid for goods sold and goods purchased if no credit were granted by the enterprise and its suppliers. The difference between the credit price and the cash price represents the interest (including risk premium) for credits granted to customers and credits granted by suppliers respectively. The cash price for goods sold is the sum of the cash price for goods purchased and the interest on inventory. Under these assumptions, how should the 'cash price' and the 'credit price' be determined in order to achieve the required real rate of return on capital employed? How should operating income and the rate of return be measured?

EXAMPLE

We study a rather unrealistic case with a time lag of one year between the purchase and the sale of goods and a collection period of one year, both for accounts receivable and accounts payable.

We assume:

- that goods are purchased on 1 Jan 19X1 at a cash price of 10 000,
- that the suppliers are paid on 31 Dec 19X1,
- that the goods are sold on 31 Dec 19X1,
- that the goods sold are paid for on 31 Dec 19X2.

The general price level is first assumed to be stable during 19X1 and 19X2, both *ex ante* and *ex post*. The required real rate of return on capital employed is 5%, which is used as calculatory interest. To simplify calculations, the same interest is applied to inventory as is applied to receivables in spite of the different risks. After the date of sale the relevant risk is the bankruptcy risk; before this date there is also the risk that the goods cannot be sold at the calculated price.

Under these assumptions the calculation will be as follows.

Cash purchase price	10 000
Interest on inventory (0.05 x 10 000)	500
Cash sale price	10 500
Interest on receivables (0.05 x 10 500)	525
Credit sale price	11 025

The cash sale price is assumed to be 10 500, and equal to the present value of the receipts from the customers one year later.

In the next step, we assume a rate of inflation of 10% in both 19X1 and 19X2. The calculation will now be as follows if both a real interest rate of 5% and an equivalent nominal interest of 15.5% are applied.

	Real	**Nominal**
Cash purchase price	10 000	10 000
Price-level adjustment	1 000	
Interest on inventory		
r. 0.05 x 10 000 x 1.1	550	
n. 0.155 x 10 000		1 550
Cash sale price	11 550	11 550
Purchase-power loss	1 155	
Interest on receivables		
r. 0.05 x 11 550 x 1.1	635	
n. 0.155 x 11 550		1,790
Credit sale price	13 340	13 340

the increase in the real purchase price during the year. Obviously, it would be unreasonable to apply nominal interest for the capital tied up in inventory. This would imply compensation for the purchasing power change of invested capital (0.1 x 10 000) and, in addition, recovery of the current purchase price. The income statement in accordance with current cost accounting would be as follows:

	Real	Nominal
Revenues	12 050	12 050
Current cost of goods sold	11 500	11 500
Operating income, excl. holding gains	550	550
Realized holding gains	500	1 500
Operating income, incl. holding gains	1 050	2 050

The real operating income, 1050, represents a real rate of return of 9.5% on invested capital (1050/11 000) and the nominal operating income a nominal rate of return of 20.5%, i.e. in both cases a return of 4.5% in excess of the required return. The real operating income exclusive of holding gains represents a return of 5%.

The recognition of the real holding gains leads to a reported return in excess of the required return. The reason is the conflicting purposes implicit in the pricing model. The purpose of recovery of the current cost is to maintain the 'physical capacity' and to secure resources for financing the replacement of resources utilized. To require a real rate of return on invested capital means to require recovery of the purchasing power of invested capital plus return on this capital. To reconcile the two purposes, real holding gains have to be included in the pricing model as a reduction of the required interest on the holding of inventory.

10.4.2 Price risks, product costing and income measurement

In the last section no consideration was paid in product costing and pricing to the uncertainty and risk concerning expected inflation and current costs at the date of sale (delivery). This can be realistic when the date of contracting price and terms of credit is the same as the date of delivery and sales prices can be continuously adjusted to new information about current costs and price-level changes. These conditions may be valid for a very limited part of the real business world.

In this section, we consider the risks which result from a time gap between the date when price and credit terms are agreed and the date of delivery of goods sold. We limit the discussion to two typical cases:

1 manufacturing of products as per customers' specification, and
2 manufacturing of standard products, the prices of which are fixed for a certain period by price lists, contracts and similar agreements.

The analysis covers not only raw materials but also other cost components, although costs of plant and equipment are excluded and discussed in a later section.

Sale of products as per customers' specifications

As a rule, the contract date is prior to the date of starting the manufacturing of products as per customers' specifications. The contracted prices can be fixed or cost-related as a result of cost-plus agreements or index clauses. We discuss first the case of fixed prices, when the seller bears the risk of price-related deviations between actual and estimated costs (*ex ante*). This risk is present even under a stable general price level, which does not mean that all prices or costs of capital are constant. It is reasonable, however, to assume that this risk increases in inflationary periods but that at the same time greater efforts are made to hedge the price risks. Estimated product costs may be based on:

1 known or estimated prices of goods and services at the date of acquisition, or
2 estimated prices of goods and services at the date of delivery.

In Case 1 the prices can be known because goods and service have already been acquired or contracted at the date of contracting (or offering) an order. The price-risk exposure of a fixed-price sale contract may be partly hedged as a result of contracted fixed prices from the suppliers, contracted rents, insurance premiums, etc. Collective agreements with the employees concerning wages during the production period can also reduce the risk. However, cost estimates of wages may imply a rather unique risk factor during periods when very time-consuming renegotiations of old agreements take place. A unique order may occur with regard to the date of the agreement, the date of delivery of services and the date of payment. An agreement can be applied retrospectively with the consequence that the services are delivered before the date of agreement and partly paid for in a lump sum with a long time lag.

When the cost of manufacturing and related prices are unknown at the contracting date they have to be forecast and price-level changes from the contracting date to the date of delivery have to be taken into consideration. The time period may be very long for contracts including guaranteed performance or other performance or other similar guarantees.

The seller is exposed to a purchasing-power risk if the contract allows a term of credit and the contracted fixed price represents a credit price. The risk is that the actual price-level change from the date of delivery to the maturity date deviates from the expected change, reflected in the pricing model. In the construction industry, the seller often tries to eliminate or reduce this risk by agreements on advances from the customer, which influence the contracted price. A proportion of these advances is paid when the contract is signed, can be invested and increases interest revenue (before the project is started) as a direct consequence of the construction contract. It is not unusual that the cash flow is positive at some stages of a large project due to advances and accounts payable and that capital employed is

2 We have studied current cost accounting which measures the operating income by matching the sales revenues and the current cost of goods sold at the date of delivery (date of income recognition) and specifies realized nominal or real holding gains (on inventory) from the date of acquisition to the date of delivery of goods sold. This method is not quite consistent with pricing aimed at the recovery of the current cost at the date of delivery plus a required return on working capital. The return reported will deviate from the return required if the general price-level changes deviate from changes in current costs; i.e. if real holding gains are realized. The conclusion is the same if the measurements are made in nominal or in real terms.

3 Inflation accounting in accordance with the general purchasing power method is consistent with pricing aimed at the recovery of the purchasing power of invested capital plus a required real capital return.

4 We doubt the relevance and the representational ability of current cost accounting in industries where sales prices and credit terms are contracted long before the goods are delivered (or produced) and where the risks of contracted fixed sales prices may be partly hedged by contracted prices for input factors. The more unstable the price level is expected to be and the longer the time gap between the contracting date and the delivery date, the greater the need to hedge the price. The construction industry represents an extreme case. The sales price is often contracted before starting production and cost estimates are based on the information available under the process of preparing an offer. The timing of income recognition, however, is more important than the method of measuring costs. Income recognition in accordance with the percentage of completion method leads to a more meaningful matching of income and capital employed than the completed contract method. The size and timing of advances from customers, can affect the size and variations of working capital in such a way that it becomes a poor basis for measuring capital return.

5 Measurements and specifications of holding gains are consistent with a speculative purchasing policy aiming at holding gains as a means of achieving required rates of return on capital.

10.5 TARGETS FOR REAL RATES OF RETURN ON FIXED ASSETS

The traditional book values of fixed tangible assets are a poor basis for measuring return on capital if considerable accumulated price changes have occurred since the assets were acquired. One purpose of current cost accounting is to provide a more meaningful base. How well this purpose is fulfilled depends upon the method of valuation and the method of depreciation applied. In this section, we discuss these problems of valuation and particularly a model of valuation which is often applied in practice. Our theoretical frame of reference is the theory of economic life of equipment and the related theory of depreciation.

10.5.1 Pricing and income measurement

Simplicity seems to be an important criterion in management decisions on methods of measurement. Linear depreciation is the most common method of depreciation. The main explanation must be that this method is simple to apply.

When restating the book value of fixed assets on a current cost basis (the C-method) instead of on a historical cost basis (the T-method), the usual presumption seems to be that the ratio of the book value T to the book value C should be the same as the ratio of the historical cost of acquisition to the current cost of acquisition. Thus, if the historical cost of acquisition is 200 and the current cost of acquisition is 300 and if the book value T is 50% of 200, then the book value C will be 50% of 300. If historical cost depreciation is 10% of 200, then current cost depreciation will be 10% of 300. We will utilize this relationship between historical costs and current costs in this section on pricing and income measurement.

Further assumptions are added to illustrate the relationship between product costing and income measurement.

EXAMPLE

As in our previous analysis, we assume that cost estimates are made to show the sales prices required to reach target rates of return on capital. We limit the calculation to the portion of the price which is to cover depreciation and interest (derived from the target rate). The opening book value C for 19X1 is 50% of the current cost of acquisition 300. This cost is expected to increase in 19X1 by 10%, which is equal to the expected rate of inflation. The depreciation and the real rate of interest, assumed to be 5%, which should be recovered by the sales price at the end of 19X1, are as follows:

Depreciation (0.1 x 300 x 1.1)	33.00
Interest (0.05 x 150 x 1.1)	8.25
	41.25

The income statement for 19X1 in accordance with the C_i-method, limited to the relevant components, is presented below. The historical cost of acquisition, adjusted for accumulated price-level changes between the beginning and the end of 19X1 are 320 and 352, respectively.

Revenues	4..25
Depreciation	−33.00
Operating income	8.25
Real holding gains	
Realized (33 − 0.1 x 352)	−2.20
Unrealized [0.4(330 − 352) − 0.5(300 − 320) x 1.1]	+ 2.20
Income (incl. real holding gains)	8.25

Income, including real holding gains, is equal to the calculated interest and represents a real rate of return of 5% on the initial book value C, adjusted for the change in the power of money in 19X1. The reason is that the nominal current cost of acquisition changes at the same rate as the general price level and therefore the net of realized and unrealized real holding gains is zero.

To illustrate the effect of different rates of price changes, we assume that the current cost of acquisition increases by 5% instead of 10% in 19X1. The price calculation will be as follows:

Depreciation (0.1 x 300 x 1.05)	31.50
Interest (0.05 x 150 x 1.1)	8.25
	39.75

The corresponding income statement is presented below.

Revenues	39.75
Depreciation	−31.50
Operating income	8.25
Real holding gains	
Realized (31.50 − 0.1 x 352)	−3.70
Unrealized [0.4(315 − 352) − 0.5(300 − 320) x 1.1]	−3.80
Income incl. real holding gains	0.75

The total real holding gains (losses) are −7.5, equal to a decrease of 5% in the real current cost of acquisition, times the initial book value (150). The real holding losses have to be included in the price calculation and the revenues increased by 7.50 in order to obtain an income including real holding gains, representing a real rate of return of 5%.

Real holding gains (positive or negative) are not usually included in cost-related models of pricing, either in textbooks or in practice. However, depreciation on a current cost basis is often considered to be an appropriate calculatory cost. It is consistent to combine such measures of depreciation with a calculatory real interest. In principle, the operating income (excluding real holding gains) of the C_r-method is consistent with these calculations (if we disregarded the time gap between the date of contracting sales and the date of delivery, discussed in Section 10.4). Reporting real holding gains is not consistent with these principles. How is information about real holding gains on fixed assets used in management control? We do not know the answer to this question for rather obvious reasons: the lack of practical application of inflation accounting and the lack of empirical research. Hypothetically, we would expect concepts such as responsibility, the possibility of exercising control, and confidence in the precision of the measures to be of considerable relevance in a study of the use of information on holding gains.

In the following sections we address the issue of precision by relating the method of linear depreciation, applied in the previous numerical examples, to the theory of economic life of equipment and the related theory of depreciation. In this theory a distinction is made between capital equipment which is not expected to be replaced and capital equipment which is expected to be replaced.[11] We also address the issue of generating a theoretical background for the choice of historical cost depreciation method in a world of unstable price levels.

10.5.2 Capital equipment not to be replaced

The value of capital equipment which is not to be replaced is measured by discounting the cash flows expected to be generated during the remaining economic life. There is a relationship between expected inflation and expected nominal cash flows. The purchasing power of expected cash flows is not independent of expected inflation. The reason is – disregarding the general economic effects of inflation – that specific price changes which affect the cash flows may deviate from the general price-level changes and these deviations may vary with the rate of inflation. The real discount rate may also be dependent on the expected rate of inflation. Thus, a valuation has to made on the basis of explicit expectations about inflation and specific prices.

EXAMPLE

We assume that a ship is acquired at the beginning of 19X1 at a price of 100 000 and is immediately chartered for a period of five years. The contract provides that annual rents will be paid at the end of the year in accordance with Table 10.2. The freight market is expected to be weaker during the latter part of the period. The contract also provides that the party chartering the ship will acquire it at the end of 19X5 at a price which is equivalent to a purchasing power at the beginning of 19X1 of 59 000. The expected rate of inflation is 10% per year.

Table 10.2

Year	Rent
19x1	20 000
19x2	23 000
19x3	25 000
19x4	20 000
19x5	20 000

The discount rate applied (equal to the internal rate of return) is 10% in real terms, corresponding to 21% in nominal terms at the expected rate of inflation.

Based on the expectations at the date of acquisition, the present value (the economic value *ex ante*) at the end of 19X1 can be calculated by discounting the real cash flow expected during 19X2–19X5. The *ex ante* economic value at the end of 19X2, 19X3, etc. can be measured in the same way. The concept of 'real cash flows', however, has to be defined (i.e. the purchasing power of the monetary unit used in measuring real cash flows has to be defined). The nominal cash flows can be transformed into the purchasing power of the monetary unit at the date to which the valuation refers (the closing date), i.e. the end of 19X1, the end of 19X2, etc. This means, however, that the economic value at the end of 19X1 is not measured in a unit with the same purchasing power as the unit used in measuring the economic value at the end of 19X2.

We refer to this valuation as *PPC valuation* (purchasing power at the closing date or current purchasing power).

The nominal cash flows can also be converted into the purchasing power of the monetary unit at the date of acquisition. We refer to this valuation as *PPA valuation.*

EXAMPLE

The economic values at the end of 19X1, 19X2 and 19X3 are stated in Table 10.3.

Table 10.3

	PPC	*PPA*
19x1	101 000	91 818
19x2	99 210	81 992
19x3	95 045	71 409

We can also make *ex ante* annual measurements of the real economic depreciation, the real economic income and the real rate of return, as illustrated below.

PPC statements

Changes in the economic value

	19x1	**19x2**	**19x3**
Economic value as per 31 Dec	101 000	99 210	95 045
Economic value as per 1 Jan	100 000	101 000	99 210
Nominal change	+1 000	−1 790	−4 165
Inflation adjustment[12]	−10 000	−10 100	−9 921
Real change (depreciation)	−9 000	−11 890	−14 086

Real economic income

Rents	20 000	23 000	25 000
Economic depreciation	−9 000	−11 890	−14 086
Real economic income	11 000	11 110	10 914
Real rate of return[13]	**10%**	**10%**	**10%**

The nominal economic income for 19X1 is 21 000 (20 000 + 1 000) and the nominal rate of return 21%.

PPA statements
Changes in the economic value

	19x1	19x2	19x3
Economic value as per 31 Dec	91 818	81 992	71 409
Economic value as per 1 Jan	100 000	91 818	81 992
Change (depreciation)	– 8 182	–9 826	–10 583

Income statement

	19x1	19x2	19x3
Rents	18 182	19 008	18 782
Economic depreciation	–8 182	–9 826	–10 583
Real economic income	10 000	9 182	8 199
Real rate of return	**10 %**	**10%**	**10%**

The sum of the annual economic depreciations in the period 19X1–19X5 is 41 000 and the final residual value of the ship is 59 000, equal to the real selling price.

How to decide historical cost depreciation	Assuming a comparison is to be made with traditional accounting, prepared *ex ante* on the basis of expected cash flows, we would have to decide on the pattern of depreciation of the historical cost of acquisition. Do we have, or can we establish, any theoretical basis for this decision?

The money measurement convention is one of the foundations of traditional accounting. This convention implies that traditional accounting is based on the assumption of a stable purchasing power of money or that changes in the purchasing power of money are ignored.[14] Allocating the cost of acquisition of a fixed asset over the expected economic (useful) life of the asset by means of annual depreciations means that the depreciation amounts represent the same purchasing power of money as the historical cost of acquisition. But what should be the theoretical basis for the choice of a pattern of historical cost depreciation in a real world, where changes in specific prices and general price levels occur and are expected to occur? This question is of fundamental importance but rarely addressed in accounting textbooks.

One interpretation of the implications of the money measurement convention is that the economic life of assets and depreciation should be estimated under the assumption of price-level stability, despite the fact that the actual investment decisions and cash flow expectations are based on and influenced by anticipated price-level changes. Hardly any information is available on hypothetical behaviour under the assumption of price-level stability if the price level in reality is expected to change. The investment decision, the economic life and the real value of expected cash flows are not |

independent of expected price-level changes. Our conclusion is to reject this approach to establishing theoretical foundations for the choice of the pattern of historical cost depreciation in a world of unstable price levels.

An alternative approach is to consider actual investment decisions, actual estimates of economic lives and of future nominal cash flows, in order to transform the nominal cash flows into the purchasing power of money at the date of acquisition and to calculate the capital values and the annual depreciations in the same manner as in the PPA statements. This approach leads to the paradoxical conclusion that inflation economic accounting is required as a basis for estimates of historical cost depreciations. What are the alternative approaches? Historical cost depreciation in terms of the nominal change of value in the PPC statements is in conflict with the realization convention, as the change is affected by unrealized inflationary holding gains.

Is it meaningful to search for a theory of historical cost depreciation in an inflationary world? It is important to raise this question. But which criteria would then guide the allocation of the cost of acquisition among the different sub-periods of the economic life of the asset? In the final analysis, the basic issue is the conflict between the monetary money measurement convention and the realization convention, and changes in specific prices and the purchasing power of money.[15]

There is one argument in favour of the PPA approach. This argument is of great relevance in a comparative study of various method of inflation accounting and traditional accounting and in discussing how to adjust traditional accounting with regard to changes in specific prices and the general price level.

We illustrate the argument by referring to the PPC and PPA-valuations. PPC values on the end of 19X1, 19X2 and 19X3 represent the economic value at the respective closing date. Assuming that the economic PPA values are applied in traditional accounting, it would be meaningful to adjust the book value for general price-level changes by multiplying the book value by the change in the price-level index from the date of acquisition to the closing date. The same applies to the measurement of depreciation. Any deviation from the economic PPA values would make an index adjustment of the traditional book value less meaningful. Thus, one criterion for the choice of the method of historical cost depreciation is that the method should generate book values which are meaningful as bases for price-level adjustments in order to approximate current economic values. It should be observed that a partial price-level adjustment is made in consolidated statements, when the book values of fixed assets in a foreign subsidiary are translated at the exchange rate at the closing date, provided that changes in exchange rates are in harmony with the purchasing power theorem. It is often stated that adjusting traditional book values of capital equipment for general price-level changes is economically less relevant than adjusting them for changes in the current cost of acquisition (the replacement cost). Our example illustrates that this statement is not valid when no replacements are considered. The replacement case will be discussed in the next section.

Our tentative conclusion so far is that a theory of historical cost depreciation can be derived from the economic theory of depreciation provided the measurements are made in monetary units which represent the purchasing power of money at the date of acquisition.

Economic theory tells us, however, that the economic value of capital equipment changes as expectations about future cash flows and the cost of capital change. If, in our example, the initial expectations about the annual rate of inflation are revised at the end of 19X2 and no inflation were expected after 19X2, then the economic value at the end of 19X2 would increase. Recognition of such an increase in traditional accounting would be in conflict with the realization convention or with legal accounting standards, although there is a tendency in the current standard setting process to recognize realizable market value and to allow restatements in order to recognize major unexpected changes in the value of capital equipment. This is one illustration of necessary reservations regarding our tentative conclusions. Each reservation, however, gives rise to the question of alternative approaches to generate a theory of historical cost depreciation (a question we shall not be addressing further).

Considering the complexity of the issue of historical cost depreciation and the need for simplicity in practice, it is not surprising that simple rules of thumb such as linear depreciation dominate both in practice and in traditional accounting textbooks. The theorems of counterbalancing errors may reduce the limitations of linear depreciation in measuring income, rate of return on capital or the rate of growth of capital.

These theorems are not very applicable in measuring the traditional income and rate of return of an individual investment project. The extent to which they are applicable is dependent on the rate of inflation. We conclude this section by illustrating differences between the economic rate of return and the traditional rate of return of an investment in capital equipment with a relatively long useful life under the assumption of rather moderate inflation. Interest in inflation accounting seems to vary with the current rate of inflation. The example illustrates that a relatively low rate of inflation over several years implies considerable limitations in the relevance of traditional measures of rate of return on projects with a long useful life.

EXAMPLE   The following assumptions are made:

- An investment in real estate is expected to generate a cash flow with a constant purchasing power during Years 1 to 10 and with a purchasing power which declines by 1% per year during Years 11 to 20.
- The expected market value after 20 years is, in real terms, 50% of the cost of acquisition.
- The required economic real rate of return on invested capital is 8%.
- The expected annual rate of inflation is either:
  A 0% during Years 1 to 20, or
  B 4% during Years 1 to 10, and thereafter 0%.

- The annual historical cost depreciation is 2.5% of the cost of acquisition.
- The traditional rate of return on capital is measured by relating the annual cash flow minus depreciation to the book value of the real estate.
- The rate of return measured by relating the economic income to the economic value is 8% in case A (both in nominal and real terms), and 12.3% in case B in nominal terms and 8% in real terms in Years 1 to 10, and thereafter 8% (in nominal and real terms).

The development of the traditional rate of return on invested capital in Case A and Case B is described in Fig. 10.1.

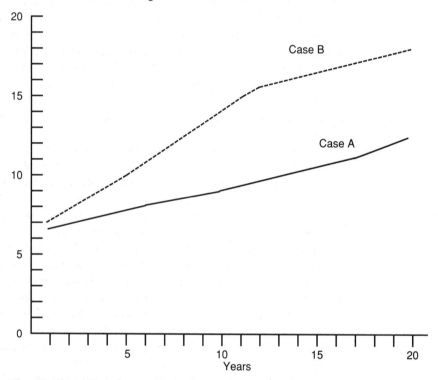

Fig. 10.1 Traditional rate of return on equity in Cases A and B

The following observations may be made.

In Case A (no inflation) the deviations from the economic rate of return (8%) are rather moderate. In Year 1, the linear depreciation is greater than the economic depreciation and therefore the traditional return (6.7%) is below the economic return. The traditional return increases by 0.2–0.3 per year, is approximately equal to the economic return after seven years and has its largest deviation from the economic return in the final year (4.2%).

In Case B, the traditional nominal rate of return is to be compared with the nominal economic rate of 12.3% during the first ten years when the annual rate of inflation is 4% and with the economic rate of 8% after Year 10, when the constant price level period starts. The deviations are somewhat larger in Years 1 to 10 than they are in Case A. The most interesting observation, however, is that the deviation increases dramatically in Year 11 (15% to 8%) and reaches its maximum in Year 20, when the traditional return is overstated by approximately 10%. The reason is that the current cash flows in Years 11 to 20 are almost 50% greater than in case A, due to the accumulated inflation in Years 1 to 10.

The analysis in Chapter 9 showed that changes in rates of inflation increase the limitations of traditional measures of rate of return on capital. The real estate example in this section illustrates additional limitations due to linear depreciation. The effect is obviously dependent upon the chosen assumptions about the time structure of expected cash flows and its effect on economic depreciation. If we had assumed that the real value of the annual cash flows and economic depreciation were gradually decreasing, the deviations from the economic rate of return in Case B would have been smaller. This is illustrated in the next section.

10.5.3 Capital equipment to be replaced

We follow the classical pattern and begin our analysis with the assumption of stationary conditions, which implies no technological development, no changes in specific prices and the general price level, and no uncertainty.

Under stationary conditions

Under these conditions, the rationale of replacing an old machine sooner or later with a new machine is explained by the gradual increase in the current operating costs of the old machine (maintenance costs included). The operating inferiority, defined as the difference between the current costs of operating an old machine and the operating cost of a new machine, gradually increases and finally reaches a level at which a replacement is estimated to be more profitable than continued use and replacement at a later date. Estimations of the economic life are, in principle, a process over time in which the alternative of immediate replacement is compared to the alternative of replacing the machine at a later date (usually the following year). The choice of replacement date for an existing machine is dependent upon the estimated economic life of a new machine. The theoretical models are usually constructed in such a way that all the machines in a perpetual chain of replacements have the same economic life.

The subjective value of an existing machine at date t is defined as the minimum price the owner would demand to be willing to sell the machine at date t and buy a new machine instead of retaining the machine and replacing it at the end of its economic life.[16] We use economic value as a synonym for subjective value. The economic depreciation is the difference between the economic value at the end and at the beginning of a period. The sum of a period's economic depreciation and the interest (target rate) on the economic value at the beginning of the period is referred to as 'the cost of capital utilization'.

The consequence of this model of valuation is that the sum of the cost of capital utilization and the current operating cost (or operating inferiority) will be the same in each year of the total economic life. This means that there is a 'state of competitive neutrality' between companies using machines of different ages (all other things being equal) as well as between intra-company use of machines of different ages. The operating inferiority of an old machine is offset by lower costs of capital utilization. The development of the operating inferiority during the economic life determines the course of economic depreciation.

With technological development

As a next step, we consider technological development but retain the assumption of general price-level stability. Technological development can affect the operating costs, revenues and the costs of acquisition, assuming a given volume of production. There is an interdependency between these variables. A typical case is that new machines are more automated and therefore more expensive, but require less input of labour and improve the quality of the products. More rational methods of manufacturing new machines reduce the price. Technological development can also imply improved efficiency of existing old machines. New techniques mean higher productivity and a basis for higher wages, which also have to paid by enterprises using older technology. These are only a few examples of the consequences of technological development.

We focus on the relationship between technological development and the course of economic depreciation, the economic value of an old machine and the price of future alternative machines. The estimate of the economic life of a new machine and its course of economic depreciation requires forecasts both about technological development and its effects on, for example, the price of future alternative machines and about the operating costs of these machines. As indicated earlier, there are considerable theoretical problems involved in determining the economic life of a newly acquired machine as it is a function of the economic life of future 'challengers'. Here, we can only point to the existence of these problems. Two important conclusions, however, may be drawn from the theoretical models.

1 The competitiveness of an existing machine (in relation to new challengers) can gradually become weaker for two reasons:

   ● The operating costs increase and/or the revenues decrease as the machine gets older.
   ● New models (challengers) have lower operating costs and/or generate higher revenues than the existing machine did, when it was new. This disadvantage may be offset by higher prices for new models.

2 Expected price changes for new challengers due to technological changes and their effect on operating costs have an impact on the economic life of an existing machine and its economic value. Thus, the economic value of an existing machine does not change when expected price changes for new challengers occur. Revisions in the price expectations, however, affect the economic life and the economic value of an existing machine.

It is a reasonable hypothesis that the operating competitiveness of an existing machine tends to decrease as it gets older and an existing machine cannot be charged with such high costs for capital utilization when it is old as it can when it is new. Operating costs and new technology will not develop at a steady rate. During an initial period of use, competitiveness can increase as the trimming and adjustment is completed, the skill of machine operators improves, initial unused capacity is reduced, etc. Age-related deficiencies and expected or unexpected competition from new technology will mainly have a strong impact at a later stage of the lifetime in an existing machine.

There are obvious difficulties in depicting a realistic course of depreciation in a simple and practical model. Theoretical models are usually based on the assumption of a continuous, often linear, increase in the operating inferiority, resulting in gradually decreasing annual economic depreciation.

There are few empirical studies of the course of economic depreciation. The studies made by Terborgh on various means of transportation (cars, trucks, etc.) are an interesting example.[17] The main conclusion is that the depreciation accumulated during the first third and the first half of the economic life is at least 50% and 66% respectively of the cost of acquisition. Linear depreciation is described as 'a gravely retarded method of depreciation for productive equipment'.[18] It may be suitable to formulate a verifiable hypothesis of the course of economic depreciation in terms of accumulated depreciation during various intervals of the economic life, such as the first third, the first half, etc. However, the formulation has to be qualified by taking into account important variables which affect the competitiveness of existing units of equipment, such as partial rebuilding, improved maintenance or planned initial overcapacity which is to be used up after a number of years.

With changing price levels

The relationships, discussed under point 2 above, between the economic value of an existing machine and the prices of future challengers are valid even under the assumption of changes in the purchasing power of money, provided the economic value is measured in the purchasing power of money at the date of acquisition. Estimates of economic life, value and depreciation have to be based on forecasts about general price-level changes, nominal or real prices of future challengers, and the operating cost for existing equipment and for future challengers. The economic value of an existing machine, measured in the purchasing power of money at the date of acquisition, is not affected when predicted changes in specific prices of the general price level occur. These changes are considered in the *ex ante* estimate of the economic life and the course of economic depreciation. This means that the ratio of the economic value of an existing machine to the historical cost of acquisition is not equal to the ratio of the economic value to the current cost of acquisition, which, in real terms, is higher than the historical cost if all measurements are made in the purchasing power of money at the date of acquisition. A real increase in the current cost of acquisition, due to increased automatization and the related reduction in

The total nominal T-cost of capital utilization decreases by a constant amount (262.5), equal to 21% of the annual depreciation. The total real cost declines by gradually decreasing amounts.[19] The relative error in measuring the T-cost of capital utilization is smaller in the case of a constant positive rate of inflation than in the case of no inflation. The error is a function of the rate of inflation and the related nominal rate of interest. At a rate of inflation of 5% and a nominal rate of 15.5%, the ratio of d to e is 88.9% in Year 1. It increases to 97.4% in Year 4 and to 105.8% in Year 5 and is subsequently higher than the ratios in the table above.

Finally we study the costs of capital utilization following from the application of the C-method and linear depreciation of the current cost of acquisition (referred to as the C-costs).

EXAMPLE

As the current cost is assumed to increase at the same rate as inflation, the real C-cost of acquisition, measured in the money value at the date of the acquisition, is constant and equal to 10 000. The real C-cost of depreciation will be identical with the T-cost of depreciation, i.e. 1250, and the real C-costs of capital utilization identical with the corresponding T-costs, under the assumption of no inflation. This means that the ratios of the annual C-costs of capital utilization to the annual economic costs of capital utilization will be same as the L/E-ratios presented above. The spread of these ratios is larger than the spread of the ratios of the T-costs of capital utilization to the corresponding economic costs, assuming a constant rate of inflation of 10% per year. This illustrates that the T-costs of capital utilization may be a better approximation to the economic costs of capital utilization than the C-costs, if

● linear depreciation is applied both in the T-method and the C-method;
● the real economic depreciation is degressive; and
● there is constant positive rate of inflation.

Thus, the limitations of the combination of linear depreciation and the T-method in measuring the costs of capital utilization can be reduced by inflation. The limitations of the combination of linear depreciation and the C-method are not reduced by inflation.

Conclusions

It is obvious that our numerical examples do not permit any generalizations. They are based on the assumption of linearly increasing operating inferiority, leading to gradually decreasing economic depreciation in real terms. Although the assumed operating inferiority function may be unrealistic, an assumption of linear real economic depreciation seems more unrealistic than an assumption that the real economic depreciation is lower in a later than in an earlier stage of the economic life of capital equipment. Based on this assumption, we draw the following conclusions.

It is uncertain if the intended effect of the application of the C-method – i.e. to obtain a more relevant capital base for measuring return on capital than the capital base of the T-method – is achieved in an inflationary economy, when linear depreciation is applied in both methods. Furthermore, due to technological changes it may be difficult to find a measure of the current cost of acquisition that allows a meaningful comparison with the historical cost of acquisition of an existing unit. One illustration is an increase in the real current cost of acquisition due to a higher degree of automation. The limitations of the applied C-method have to be compared to the limitations of the applied T-method.

The theoretical frame of reference for the valuation of capital equipment which is to be replaced may be useful in making qualitative tests of the measurement results of the applied C-method. Does the C-cost of capital utilization make the existing equipment competitive with new, modern equipment, taking into account differences in terms of operating costs, product quality, etc.?

Such a test may reveal the lack of realism of the approach of letting the ratio of the current cost of acquisition to the historical cost determine the ratio of the book value C to the book value T. More sophisticated approaches may be needed to improve the quality of book value C as an approximation of economic value.

Sometimes there is no logical basis for determining the economic value of an individual asset. The reason is that there may be a technological interdependence or interaction between various parts of an entity's collection of plant and equipment. Relationships may exist between the construction of the buildings and the machinery and between various machine units. In an extreme case, a change of technology may imply that a new factory has to be built and a few highly automated machines may replace a large number of old manually operated machines. In such a case, there are no meaningful measures of current costs for each individual component of the existing collection of plant and equipment.

Our description of theoretical and practical problems as regards the application of the C-method is certainly not complete. Our intention has been only to illustrate that this method may also have considerable limitations in measuring costs of capital utilization and return on capital for comparative purposes. The conclusion is that there are several situations in which there is reason to doubt whether the C-method will solve the problems related to the limitations of the T-method. Other alternatives should be considered, and this is the main theme of the following sections.

10.5.4 Leasing and revaluations of capital equipment

The limitations of the T-method as a capital base for measuring rate of return on capital for the entity or its components can be affected by various forms of revaluations and transactions, such as the following:

1 Plant or equipment is rented externally or internally, instead of being owned by the entity or being included in the capital base of a division or other sub-units.

and price-level changes in calculating depreciation than in calculating interest. How should the use of a nominal rate of interest be interpreted, regardless of the principles applied in measuring the capital base? A hypothetical interpretation is that simplicity is such an important criterion that it dominates over other criteria. It is easier to apply a uniform rate of interest than different rates. It is easier to understand the concept of nominal interest than the concept of real interest.

It is not unusual to exclude interest in product costing. A possible interpretation is that it is considered to be more simple to add a profit margin, based on experience or market conditions, than to include calculatory interest. When the rate of interest applied represents a borrowing rate, an additional margin is required to cover the risk premium on equity capital. Profit margins are a common basis for financial control and will be addressed in the following section.

10.7 OTHER FINANCIAL RATIOS AS INDICATORS OF CAPITAL RETURN

Rate of return on capital employed can be measured as the ratio of operating income to sales, referred to as the *profit margin ratio* (return on sales), multiplied by the ratio of sales to capital employed, referred to as *capital turnover*. A breakdown analysis of the profit margin can be made by relating, for example, profit before depreciation or contributions from groups of products to sales. In a similar way, a breakdown analysis of the capital turnover can be made by relating sales to accounts receivable, inventory, etc. as described in the well-known DuPont Chart, which is further discussed in Section 13.3.

The rate of return on capital employed can thus be regarded as a function of the ratios described above. There are, however, relationships between these ratios (e.g. an increase in sale prices improves both the profit margin ratio and the capital turnover), and some ratios can be proved empirically to be more stable than others. Changes in the rate of return on capital employed are more associated with ('explained by') changes in certain ratios (e.g. the profit margin ratio may vary much more than the capital turnover). Historical observations may form a basis for a consensus opinion within a certain industry as to which profit margin ratio is required to achieve a satisfactory level of capital return. A set of ratios can be used as indicators of capital return. Control is focused on these ratios. The choice of ratios may be guided by the following criteria, for example:

● impact on the rate of return;
● sensitivity to the limitations of the *T*-method;
● possibility of frequent and rapid follow-up.

The following comments on empirical data related to the impact on the rate of return are based on a study of 560 Swedish industrial companies in the period 1966–72.[22] There is strong correlation between changes in return on capital and changes in the profit margin ratio.[23] Changes in profit margin ratios are affected in different ways by different cost components. Changes in the ratio of labour costs to sales have more explanatory power than changes in the ratio of depreciation to sales because they are more correlated to changes in the rate of return on capital. The costs of depreciation tend to grow at a lower rate than sales. Changes in the ratio of operating income before depreciation to sales are often an important indicator of changes in the rate of return on capital employed. This ratio is unaffected by the limitations of linear depreciation of historical costs and may thus receive priority in accordance with the second criterion.

The *contribution margin ratio*, defined as the ratio of sales minus variable costs to sales, can usually be reported more frequently and rapidly than margin ratios, based on estimates of full costs and interperiod allocations of fixed costs. Reports on contribution margins for short periods are sometimes based on standard variable cost and may be regarded as reliable due to previous experience of small variances between actual and standard variable costs. Within the construction industry and other industries dealing with projects requiring considerable time and capital, estimates of the profitability of pending orders have high priority in management reports. The estimated profit margin ratio, based on the contracted prices and estimated order costs, is a traditional measure of profitability, which is also used in the current follow-up process. Management seems to have experience-based perceptions of which ratio level reflects satisfactory profitability, even though they are not related to explicit capital return targets.

Different ratios can be used simultaneously to control operational efficiency of profit centres or other units of responsibility. Thus targets can be set for the contribution margin ratio, receivables turnover and inventory turnover. Accounting measures can be combined with other kinds of measures, which are relevant for the efficient use of capital and are unaffected by the limitations of the *T*-method, although they can mainly be used for interperiod and intracompany comparisons.

We return to the issues discussed in this section in Part Three.

10.8 THE CHOICE OF LIMITATIONS

In this chapter, we have studied current cost accounting in nominal and real terms (the C_n-method and the C_r-method) and the general purchasing power method (the *P*-method) as alternatives or supplements to traditional accounting (the *T*-method). The background is the limitations of the *T*-measures of rate of return for comparative purposes, discussed in Chapters 8 and 9. Various limitations of the alternative or supplementary methods have been identified. Thus, there is a choice between different forms of limitations. We conclude and to some extent summarize this chapter by using some of the criteria, described in Chapter 3, to evaluate the alternative methods. We assume the following qualities of accounting control systems to be desirable.

1 Targets should be kept stable.
2 The system and its components should be easy to apply and to understand.
3 *Ex ante* data should be followed up with desired frequency and speed and the data required for this procedure should be available (data capturing).
4 The system of measurement should be uniform.
5 The capital base should be relevant for measuring rate of return on capital (with economic value as the criterion of relevance).

Points 1 and 2 regarding stability and simplicity can be classified as user criteria, and Points 3 and 4 as measurement system criteria, while Point 5 denotes criteria of representational ability. It is not possible, however, to make very strict classifications as the different criteria are interrelated (*see* Section 3.1).

10.8.1 The evaluation of the C_r-method and the P-method

1 Targets for real post-tax return on equity can be kept more stable than corresponding targets in nominal terms when the value of money is unstable. However, real pre-tax targets are affected by price-level changes, when nominal income is subject to taxation.
2 Measures in real terms are harder to understand, which may to some extent be due to lack of experience and educational training.
3 Problems of follow-up are similar to those facing a parent company in a country without inflation which wants to control a subsidiary in a foreign country with inflation and which wishes to use the currency of the parent company as the accounting unit for control. The subsidiary has to use two accounting units and prepare reports both in the local currency and the group currency. Budgets must be based on expectations about the local rate of inflation and changes in the exchange rate. In the follow-up procedure, information about the exchange rate is currently available but not about the rate of inflation. Information about the consumer price index or similar indices may only be available on a monthly basis and with a time lag. This restriction of data capturing would obviously be a problem in a system of control based on accounting measures in real terms. The more frequent the reports are, the more disruptive this restriction becomes. Lack of continuity in the process of price-level changes will also cause various types of problems in regular reporting.
4 Nominal accounting measures are required for legal reasons, for planning and control of cash flows, etc. Real measures are based on nominal measures which are transformed into monetary units of uniform purchasing power. Two sets of units of measurement are required. Measurement of real income requires that all the items in the balance sheet at the end and at the beginning of the period are measured in units of uniform purchasing power. In traditional accounting, items in the

balance sheet at a given date are not measured in units of uniform purchasing power, since non-monetary assets are stated at historical costs, thus representing a historical money value deviating from the money value at the closing date. The nominal change in T-equity during a period cannot be converted to a meaningful real change by adjusting for price-level changes during the same period. Historical cost as a basis of valuation has to be abandoned. If the public financial statements have to be prepared in accordance with the T-method and the system of management control is (partly) based on measures of real return, the measurement system is far from uniform. Management is faced with a trade-off between the disadvantages of the T-method and the disadvantages of a non-uniform measurement system.

5 The C_r-method – in contrast to the P-method – recognizes unrealized real holding gains as income. The choice between C_r-equity and P-equity as a basis for required real rate of return on equity is dependent upon the perception of the relevance of real holding gains (e.g. in planning, product costing and measurement of performance). In principle, the C_r-equity should be a better approximation of the economic value, although the P-equity can be measured more objectively.

10.8.2 The evaluation of the C_n-method

1 Frequent substantial changes in the nominal rate of interest generate a conflict between the objective of target stability and the objective that a target nominal return on equity should reflect the nominal cost of equity capital. This conflict exists under constant money value, but is aggravated by changes in the value of money and the use of nominal measures.

2 The concepts of realized and unrealized holding gains may be perceived as cumbersome. The reason may be that they are regarded as not very meaningful or relevant. However, holding gains, in certain situations and businesses, can be regarded as important measures in the planning and measurement of performance. This is primarily the case with separable resources but may also apply when the timing and size of purchases of goods and capital expenditures are affected by expected future price changes and speculative objectives.

3 In accounting theory, the operating C-income is measured by matching revenues and the current cost – at the date of sale (revenue recognition) – of goods sold. Strict adherence to this principle gives rise to obvious problems of data capturing when there are a large number of transactions, many products and frequent price changes. The current costs of plant and equipment are often estimated by means of index series, which are not available with the frequency and speed needed for short-term reports. The current costs of raw materials may not be available on a continuous basis. Simplifications/approximations have to be applied (e.g. by using standard costs, based on expected average current costs for one or several report periods). From Section 10.4, we know that the matching

of revenues and current cost at the date of income recognition can be inconsistent with the principles applied in product costing. This may be the case when sales prices and terms of credit are contracted before the goods are manufactured or when fixed prices are applied for a certain period.

4 If the public financial statements have to be prepared in accordance with the T-method and the system of management control (partly) is based on the C_n-method, the measurement system is not uniform. However, it is less complicated to reconcile T- and C_n-measures than T- and C_r-measures.

5 The capital base of the C_n-method should principally be a more useful and relevant base than the T-base for measuring rate of return on capital. This usefulness is reduced, however, if linear depreciation which deviates from economic depreciation is applied. Technological development makes it difficult to make meaningful comparisons between the historical cost of acquisition and the current cost of acquisition of capital equipment.

Our tentative evaluation of the P-method, and the C_r- and C_n-methods is obviously not complete. It is an illustration of an approach to evaluation. We have illustrated how the pros and cons of a method can be derived by utilizing a number of criteria related to both the behavioural and measurement aspects of accounting. Assuming that the T-method has to be applied in preparing public financial statements, it is easy to understand why inflation accounting is not applied internally as a tool of management control in spite of the potential limitations of the T-method under inflationary conditions. Other means of handling these limitations have to considered. We have pointed out that the limitations related to the historical cost basis for valuation of capital equipment are less for a group as a whole than for each of its components, as there is a greater chance of counterbalancing errors at the group level. This chance is particularly small at the product level. Therefore, it is not surprising that a current cost approach is applied in firms, using the full cost method in product costing for purposes of pricing and profitability control without taking into account unrealized holding gains. We have referred to the tradition in the Swedish engineering industry, where calculatory current cost depreciation and interest on a current cost basis are included in estimated product costs, although this practice is not uniform, and nominal rates of interest are used in an inconsistent way.

The limitations of the T-method in measuring return on capital can also be considered by the use of ratios, which are indicators of return on capital but are not sensitive to these limitations. The ratio of income before depreciation to sales, the turnover of accounts receivables and the turnover of inventory are examples of these ratios.

Our basic frame of reference is that no accounting measures are perfect. The application of the methods should be adapted to take this into account. Thus, knowledge of the imperfections is important.[24] More empirical research is needed to find out more about the relationship between the use of accounting data and the limitations of the data, particularly the limitations related to changes in specific prices and in the general price level.

NOTES

[1] Unrealized real holdings gains (losses) on debts and receivables due to changes in their real market values should also be recognized. The market price changes if the contracted rate of interest is fixed and the market rate of interest deviates from the fixed rate. We assume in our analysis that the contracted rate is equal to the market rate.

[2] The difference between closing and opening accumulated unrealized holding gains. In measuring real gains the accumulated real gains as per 1 Jan (50) are restated in the money value as per 31 Dec (50 x 1.10 = 55).

[3] The income is related to the opening capital emloyed restated in the money value as per 31 Dec (800 x 1.1 and 750 x 1.1 respectively).

[4] See Bell, P. W., *Current Cost/Constant Dollar Accounting and its Uses in the Managerial Decision Making Process*, University of Arkansas–Fayetteville McQueen Accounting Monograph Series (1986), p. 21.

[5] There are exceptions, e.g. Bell, P. W. (1986).

[6] Compare the following statement by Edwards, E. O. and Bell, P. W. (1961), concerning concepts of real income '. . . their principal function is a means of establishing real rates of return . . .' (p. 264).

[7] See Section 10.4 concerning the relationship between nominal and real rates of interest.

[8] See McCracken, P. W., 'Inflation Profits and the American Economy', in Griffin, P. A. (ed.) *Proceedings of the Financial Accounting Standards Board, Financial Reporting and Changing Prices* (1979).

[9] See Johansson, S.-E., *Taxes – Investments – Valuation* (1961), p. 162.

[10] See Accounting Principle Board (APB), Opinion No. 21, 'Interest on Receivables and Payables'.

[11] The following two sections are to a large extent based on Johansson, S.-E. (1961), in which the mathematical models for determining the economic life, the economic (subjective) value and the economic depreciation of capital equipment under conditions of unstable price levels are presented in an appendix.

[12] Adjustment to restate the value as per 1 Jan to the purchasing power of money as per 31 Dec. The adjustment can also be regarded as an elimination of the inflationary holding gain, included in the nominal change.

[13] Real income related to the economic value as per 1 Jan plus the inflation adjustment.

[14] See e.g. Paton, W. A. and Littleton, A. C., *An Introduction to Corporate Accounting Standards* (1946), p. 23 and American Institute of Accountants, *Changing Concepts of Business Income* (1952), p. 19.

[15] See e.g. Edwards, E. O. and Bell, P. W. (1961), Chapter 1.

[16] See Johansson, S.-E. (1961), p. 52 and Lindahl, E. (1939), p. 96.

[17] Terborgh, G., *Realistic Depreciation Policy* (1954), pp. 39–47.

[18] Ibid., p. 47.

[19] The mathematical model of the annual change is

$$i(1 + i)^{-t}[(r + i + r \times i)(1 - \frac{t - 1}{N} + \frac{1}{N}] + (r + i + r \times i)\frac{1}{N}x(1 + i)^{-t}$$

where i = the rate of inflation
r = the real rate of interest
N = the economic life.

[20] For a more complete description of this development, see Samuelson, L. A., *Models of Accounting Information Systems* (1990), Chapter 3.

[21] The practice, prevailing in the early 1990s within the engineering industry, has been studied at the Gothenburg School of Economics and Commercial Law by Ask, U. and Ax, C. in their not yet completed thesis 'Product Cost – New Conditions'. We have had the priviledge of previewing the results of a survey of 100 enterprises concerning calculatory depreciation and interest.

Thus, the co-ordination of financial goals for the entire group and for the separate legal entities can be difficult to handle due to the different valuations of assets (and liabilities) and the vague meaning of these differences. The management of a company, the ownership of which has just been changed, is not willing to accept increases in the required rate of return on capital, unless the change of ownership generates positive synergies for the company. It seems rational to relate the required return on new acquisitions to the purpose and the expected consequences of the acquisition for the entire group.

Foreign subsidiaries, parent-established or acquired, cause additional problems of co-ordination due to changes in currency rates and the different costs of capital in different countries. The control of a foreign subsidiary is usually based on local financial statements, prepared in the local currency, and on the local cost of capital. How should the required rate of return on the consolidated equity measured, say, in Swedish Kronor, (R_{SEK}) and the required rate of return on the equity of, say, a United States subsidiary (R_{USD}) be co-ordinated? The method of translating the financial statement of foreign subsidiaries is also a variable in technical co-ordination. The rate of return on equity measured by relating the translated US income to the translated US equity is equal to R_{SEK}, provided that

1 a positive (negative) difference between R_{SEK} and R_{USD} is equal to the annual appreciation (depreciation) of US dollars in relationship to Swedish Kronor, or
2 the closing (current) rate method of translation is applied, and
3 the exchange differences are recognized as income.

The third condition is in conflict with the prevailing accounting standard, which requires that exchange differences, due to the application of the closing rate method, are accounted for as adjustments to stockholders' equity. The first condition may be fulfilled *ex ante* but hardly on an annual basis *ex post*. Equity hedging is rational from a co-ordination perspective. It is a rather obvious conclusion that it must be extremely difficult to co-ordinate financial goals within a multinational group in such a way that the return required on the capital invested in each separate subsidiary is consistent with the required return on the consolidated capital of the entire group.

11.1 THE GENERAL MEASUREMENT PROBLEM

There are several ways of organizing intragroup financial control and various way of solving the problems of centralization versus decentralization in national and multinational groups.[1] We have to base our analysis on very simplified assumptions in order to illustrate some fundamental measurement problems facing all groups. We assume that each subsidiary is a wholly owned operating unit with a high degree of autonomy. Financial goals for the entire group are specified in terms of the post-tax rate of return on the consolidated equity, the pre-tax rate of return on the consolidated capital employed, the debt-to-equity ratio and the pay-out ratio. The subsidiaries should be controlled so that the group achieves its financial goals.

The general measurement problem in co-ordinating the financial goals for the group and the financial goals for separate legal entities of the group is a problem of comparability between the financial statements of the group and those of the legal entities, particularly the subsidiaries.[2] The main reasons are the following:

1 Some assets and liabilities of the legal entities are stated at values in the consolidated balance sheets which differ from those in the balance sheets of the legal entities. Intragroup receivables and liabilities are reported in the legal entities but eliminated in the consolidated balance sheet.
2 Foreign subsidiaries are usually controlled, on the basis of accounting measures, in local currencies, while the financial goals for the group are based on consolidated statements with the currency of the parent company as the accounting unit.
3 The capital structure of the group is not the weighted average of the capital structures of the legal entities, because the consolidated equity is not equal to the sum of the equity of each legal entity.

The usefulness of consolidated financial statement as an instrument for the setting of financial goals is also a function of the consolidation principles applied, for example the treatment of goodwill and the method of translating the financial statements of foreign subsidiaries. The type of comparison problem experienced and the level of complication are dependent upon whether a subsidiary has been established or acquired by a parent company and whether a subsidiary is domestic or located in a foreign country.

11.2 PARENT-ESTABLISHED DOMESTIC SUBSIDIARIES

We define a parent-established subsidiary as a subsidiary which is started and equity-financed by the parent company. In this case only intragroup profits give rise to deviations between the valuation of the subsidiary's asset in the consolidated balance sheet (referred to as valuation at group level) and in the balance sheet of the subsidiary (referred to as valuation at subsidiary (company) level). These profits may involve inventory or other assets, subject to intragroup transactions. The intragroup profits are eliminated in the process of consolidation. The profits have to be realized by means of sales to parties external to the group in order to be recognized as consolidated income. Intragroup profits related to inventory are probably normally only a minor disturbance factor in the co-ordination of required returns at group level and at subsidiary level. These are tolerated with regard to lack of precision in the use of measures (see Chapter 2).

Certain kinds of intragroup profits may be significant. One example is intragroup real estate transactions. Real estate within a group is transferred at market prices to a special real estate subsidiary, from which the other group members rent the real estate they previously owned. One purpose is that they should be charged market rents for the facilities used. Another purpose is to eliminate 'old' and low book values of real estate from the capital employed by the operative subsidiaries and thus make the capital base more meaningful for profitability control and comparisons between operative subsidiaries. However, the real estate is stated at the 'old' values in the consolidated balance sheet with the same limitations, that were eliminated at the company level. This valuation gap has to be handled in some way or another in the process of co-ordinating return targets at group level and at the subsidiary level.

The responsibility of a subsidiary can sometimes include the capital structure, subject to the restrictions decided by the senior management of the group. To simplify, we assume that the permitted debt-to-equity ratio of a subsidiary should be derived from the target debt-to-equity ratio of the group. This gives rise to some technical problems of co-ordination.

The reason is that the equity of the group does not correspond to the sum of the equity of the parent company and the equity of the subsidiaries, even if there are no inconsistent valuations and no intragroup transactions. The equity capital contributed by the parent company to the subsidiaries is eliminated in the process of consolidation. Therefore the debt-to-equity ratio of the group is higher than the weighted average of the corresponding ratios of the legal entities, as illustrated in the example below.

EXAMPLE

	P	S	Group
Shares in S	100	—	—
Other assets	<u>550</u>	<u>450</u>	<u>1000</u>
	<u>650</u>	<u>450</u>	<u>1000</u>
Debts (D)	450	300	750
Equity (E)	<u>200</u>	<u>150</u>	<u>250</u>
	<u>650</u>	<u>450</u>	<u>1000</u>
D/E	$2\frac{1}{4}$	2	3

The target debt-to-equity ratios for the individual group members must (on average) be lower than the group target. This may confuse a manager who is not familiar with the consolidation procedure. The relation between the capital structure at the subsidiary and at the group level can be described in this way.

A change in the (non-intragroup) debts of a subsidiary (ΔD_s), changes (all other things being equal) the debt-to-equity ratio of the subsidiary by

$\Delta D_s / E_s$ and the debt-to-equity ratio of the group by $\Delta D_s / E_g$ as $\Delta D_s = \Delta D_g$. Thus the ratio of the subsidiary's equity (E_s) to the group's equity (E_g) determines the effect of a change in a D_s / E_s-ratio on the D_g / E_g-ratio. The group effect of an increase of E_s due to a capital contribution from the parent company, is dependent upon how the contribution is funded by the parent company. If it is funded by debt the D_g / E_g-ratio increases, although the D_s / E_s-ratio decreases. If the goal is to maintain a given D_g / E_g-ratio, the co-ordination problem is limited to permitted changes in the debt-to-equity ratios of the group members.

11.3 ACQUIRED DOMESTIC SUBSIDIARIES

Additional problems of co-ordination appear when a parent company acquires a new subsidiary. The reason is that the price paid for the shares may deviate from the book value of the net assets of the subsidiary.

11.3.1 Valuation at group level and at subsidiary level

An acquisition of a new subsidiary can be regarded as an indirect acquisition of the net assets of the subsidiary. The price paid for the shares represents the indirect cost of acquisition of the net assets existing at the date of acquisition. The price has to be split up and allocated to the balance sheet items of the acquired subsidiary. The values allocated to the individual assets represent the group's costs of acquisition of these assets. These costs may deviate from corresponding book values in the subsidiary's balance sheet at the date of acquisition. Thus, a given asset may be stated at values in the consolidated balance sheet which differ from values in the balance sheets of the subsidiary. We refer to this as different valuation at group level and subsidiary (company) level, or as 'consolidation adjustments'. The problems of co-ordination are illustrated in the following simplified examples.

EXAMPLE

An existing group is enlarged by the acquisition of all shares in company S at a price of 100 million Swedish Kronor, SEK 100m. The acquisition is financed by a non-cash issue of 500 000 shares at an issue price of SEK 200 per share (the market price). The number of shares is increased from 2 to 2.5 million. The group is a conglomerate with the policy that the subsidiaries will have a high degree of autonomy. New acquisitions are mainly regarded as a financial investment without synergies for the group. The required rate of return on capital employed is 14% at the group level. The book equity of S at the date of acquisition is SEK 50m. The difference between the price paid for the shares, SEK 100m, and the book equity of S is allocated to a lot, stated at SEK 25m in S's balance sheet. In the statements below we calculate (in SEK million):

● the group's capital employed, capital structure, net income budgeted for the next year and some financial ratios on the assumption that S is not acquired,

- the corresponding data for S, and
- the corresponding data for the group on the assumption that S is acquired.

	Group without S	S	Group with S
Lot	—	25	75
Capital employed (excl. lot)	1000	175	1175
Total capital employed (CE)	1000	200	1250
Debt (D)	600	150	750
Equity (E)	400	50	500
	1000	200	1250
Operating income	140	35	175
Interest expenses	−60	−15	−75
Income before taxes	80	20	100
Taxes (25%)	−20	−5	−25
Net income	60	15	75
D/E	1.5	3.0	1.5
R_{CE} (pre-tax)	14.0%	17.5%	14.0%
R_E (post-tax)	15.0%	30.0%	15.0%
Income per share	SEK 30		SEK 30

The assumptions have been chosen so that the financial ratios of the group are unchanged by the acquisition of S.

Obviously it would be irrational to require a rate of return of 14% on the total capital employed, 200, in S. It would be rational, however, if S's book value of the lot were written up by 50 to 75, i.e. if push-down accounting (new basis accounting) were applied. In Sweden and many other countries, push-down accounting cannot be applied systematically due to legal restrictions or for tax reasons. Therefore our analysis is based on the assumption that push-down accounting is not applied.

The rational solution seems to be that the control of S is based on the expectations underlying the acquisition. If S is expected to achieve a sustainable rate of return of 17.5% on the book value of capital employed, this rate should be the obvious target rate.

However, the co-ordination of targets for the group and targets for acquired subsidiaries becomes increasingly difficult if this approach is systematically applied to all new acquisitions and the group structure is frequently changed by new acquisitions. This problem is addressed further in the following sections.

11.3.2 Valuations at group level

In the example above we assume:

1 that the difference between the price paid for the S shares and the book equity of S is allocated to an asset not subject to depreciation,
2 that the financial ratios of the group are unchanged by the acquisition, and
3 that there are no synergies.

In the following analysis, these assumptions are changed and special attention is paid to goodwill and related synergies.

The price a buyer is willing to pay for the shares of a company is theoretically determined as the discounted value of the cash flows the buyer expects to receive as a consequence of the acquisition. It is impossible to find a causal relationship between all the components of these cash flows and the separate assets and liabilities that are indirectly acquired. In spite of this, the price paid for the shares has to be split up and a 'price tag' applied to all assets and liabilities that are added to the consolidated balance sheet as a consequence of the acquisition of the shares. The buyer's costs of acquisition for the indirectly acquired assets have to be specified, as well as the compensation for taking over the obligations related to the liabilities of the company. The traditional approach is first to estimate the fair value (at the date of acquisition) of each separate balance sheet item. If the purchase price of the shares exceeds the fair value of the net asset, the excess amount is usually labelled goodwill. A negative difference is accounted for as badwill or as a deduction from the market value of fixed tangible assets.

The residual economic life and thus the future rates of depreciation are not the same for buildings, machines and goodwill. Thus the future consolidated income statements are affected by 'the choice of price tags' on the various items and the residual goodwill. It is rarely possible to measure the fair value of each balance sheet item in an objective and unambiguous way. Management may to some extent control the valuation process and choose from different alternatives. Our hypothesis is that the choice will be made with regard to expected short-term consequences on the group's P/E (price to earnings) ratio and other financial ratios which are considered to be relevant for investors. The option that minimizes consolidated annual depreciation is preferred. The choice is not primarily made with regard to management control and intragroup co-ordination of return targets.

Accounting for consolidated goodwill has been a contentious issue in Europe in recent years. One reason is the frequency of acquisitions resulting in considerable amounts of goodwill. Another reason is the lack of

It would certainly not be surprising if the senior management considered that the financial ratios of the group inadequately reflect the commercial effects of the acquisition and thus question the accounting standards applied. There are good reasons to argue that:

- goodwill should be depreciated with regard to the expected durability of the synergies;
- the period of depreciation should not start until the restructuring is completed; and
- provisions should be made in the consolidated balance sheet at the date of acquisition for the restructuring costs, which are a direct consequence of the acquisition and which have reduced the purchase price.

The first argument is in conflict with prevailing accounting standards if the synergies are expected to be permanent. The second argument also seems to be in conflict with prevailing standards. It is not surprising, however, that management argue that international groups competing for the same acquisition target should apply the same standards for accounting of business combinations, even though the application of the standards cannot wholly satisfy the criterion of representational ability.

11.3.3 The measurement problems from a control perspective

An acquisition of a subsidiary gives rise to an accounting process in which the purchase consideration for the shares is transformed into costs of acquisition of separate assets and 'negative costs of acquisition' of separate liabilities. The acquisition of the shares is accounted for as though the separate assets and liabilities were directly acquired with a 'price tag' on each balance sheet item. These 'price tags' are inevitably *ex post* constructions, as the total purchase consideration seldom represents an aggregate of separate 'price tags' *ex ante*. The transformation is made in accordance with certain norms and conventions, which can hardly be so specific and clear-cut that the scope for subjective judgements and tactical considerations is eliminated. Neither can the norms be equally suitable in each individual case. Deviations from the form or substance of a norm occur and 'creative accounting' takes place. The norms for goodwill depreciation are a good illustration as far as Sweden and some other countries are concerned. The consequences have been as follows:

- The consolidated statements become a more uncertain and imperfect basis for financial goals such as the rate of return on equity, the rate of return on capital employed and the debt-to-equity ratio. This statement is particularly valid when groups grow by means of frequent acquisitions.
- Large acquisitions at prices which deviate significantly from the book equities of acquired companies have often a considerable effect on financial ratios at group level. Major items of goodwill on consolidation often have a negative effect initially. To reduce the negative impact on income per share, group management is tempted to write off goodwill

without charging the income statement, which makes it more difficult to make meaningful interperiod comparisons, intercompany comparisons and other forms of comparisons.

● The co-ordination of returns targets at group level and at subsidiary level becomes difficult to manage due to valuations which are not comparable and to the unclear meaning of the valuation differences. The management of a newly acquired subsidiary is not willing to accept increases in the required rate of return on capital unless the change of ownership is expected to contribute positive synergies to the company. Restructuring of a group as a consequence of new acquisitions may have an impact on several group members and change the conditions for the setting of future targets. The expected consequences for all members have to be taken into consideration. Frequent acquisitions may make the co-ordination process extremely complicated.

11.4 FOREIGN SUBSIDIARIES

Foreign subsidiaries involve additional measurement and control problems. Our analysis of these problems is based on the following assumptions. Targets at the group level refer to consolidated statements with the currency of the parent company as the accounting unit. The financial control of foreign subsidiaries is based on accounting measures in local currencies.[7] The main issue is the rate of return required on the equity of a foreign subsidiary in order to achieve the target rate of the group.

11.4.1 The problem of co-ordination

A basic problem arises when the cost of equity capital is different in the parent country to that in the country of a subsidiary. To illustrate this problem we assume that the required rate of return on equity at group level is equal to the cost of equity capital of the parent country and that the required rate of return on the equity of a subsidiary is equal to the local cost of equity capital. We assume that changes in the relevant currency rates correspond to differences between both rates of interest and rates of expected inflation. We assume the reporting currency of the parent company to be SEK. Three different measures of the equity of a foreign subsidiary can be distinguished:

1 *The equity in local currency*, defined as the difference between the book values of assets and liabilities in the balance sheet of the subsidiary.
2 *The equity in the reporting currency of the parent company* (SEK in our example), defined as the book value in the consolidated balance sheet of the net assets of the subsidiary.

If intragroup transaction are disregarded, the difference between (2) and (1) has two components:

In the following sections, we study the consolidated balance sheet at the end of the first year with the assumption that the actual outcome corresponds to the expected outcome.

11.4.2 The closing-rate method of translation

In this section we apply the closing-rate method to our example.

EXAMPLE

We assume that the closing-rate method is applied in translating D's balance sheet from DEM to SEK. This means that the German subsidiary's total assets and liabilities at the end of the first year are translated at a rate of 3.15. The net income of DEM 10m is translated at the average rate of 3.075. The exchange (translation) gain can be calculated as the average amount of equity, DEM 105m, multiplied by the change of exchange rate, 0.15. The consolidated balance sheet at the end of the first year (without regard to dividends) is presented below.

	Q SEK m	D DEM m	Group SEK m
Shares in D	300	—	—
Other assets	—	310	967.50
	300	310	967.50
Liabilities	0	200	630.00
Equity 1/1	300	100	300.00
Exchange gain			15.75
Net income	0	10	30.75
	300	310	976.50

The net income of the group, SEK 30.75m, represents a rate of return of 10.25% on the initial equity, SEK 300m. The net income plus the exchange gain represent a rate of return of 15.5%, equal to the target rate for the group. Thus the exchange gain has to be included in the net income of the group in order to achieve parity between the required rate of return on equity at group level (15.5%) and the corresponding rate at subsidiary level (10%).

From this point of view, it is irrational to treat the exchange gain as an adjustment of equity in accordance with the prevailing accounting standard. It should be observed that the closing rate method implies a partial recognition of unrealized holding gains on non-monetary assets in conflict with the realization convention. If the increase in the exchange rate of 5% in our example is equal to the difference between the Swedish and German rates of inflation, the non-monetary assets of D are written up in the consolidated balance sheet with this difference, which can be interpreted as a partial price-level index adjustment.

Above, the rate of depreciation of the Swedish currency in relation to DEM has been assumed to be equal to the difference between the required rate of return at group level and at subsidiary level. If this is not the case, no parity is achieved between the target rates, even if the exchange gain is recognized as income. Parity can be achieved, however, by hedging the equity of D.

Consolidation adjustments, discussed in Section 11.3, complicate the co-ordination of required return on capital at group level and at subsidiary level. The existence of foreign subsidiaries means an additional complication if the consolidation adjustments are only reported in SEK and are not subject to translation, which has been the predominant accounting practice. To illustrate these problems, we change the previous assumptions in the following way.

EXAMPLE

The German company D, is a going concern acquired by the Swedish holding company, Q. The balance sheet of D at the date of acquisition is the same as the initial balance sheet in the previous example. D is expected to achieve a net income and dividends of DEM 20m per year. The theoretical market value at a cost of equity capital of 10% is DEM 200m, which is the price paid by Q and equal to SEK 600m. The difference between this price and D's equity in SEK, is allocated to assets not subject to depreciation. The consolidated balance sheet at the end of the first year is presented below.

	Q SEK m	D DEM m	D SEK m	Elim- inations	Group SEK
Shares in D	600	—	—	−600	—
Other assets	—	320	1008.00	+300	1308.00
	600	320	1008.00	−300	1308.00
Liabilities	0	200	630.00		630.00
Equity 1/1	600	100	300.00	−300	600.00
Exchange gain			16.50		16.50
Net income	0	20	61.50		61.50
	600	320	1008.00	−300	1308.00

The sum of the consolidated net income and the exchange gain represents a rate of return on equity of 13%, i.e. below the group's required rate. D's reported rate of return on equity is 20%. If push-down accounting were applied and D's assets at the date of acquisition were revalued from DEM 300m to DEM 400m, the exchange gain would increase by SEK 15m. The group's reported rate of return on equity would be 15.5% and D's corresponding rate 10%.

We conclude that the co-ordination of required return on capital at group level and foreign subsidiary level is facilitated if push-down accounting is applied and exchange gains and losses are reported as income and not as adjustments to equity.

11.4.3 The MNM-method of translation

The application of the MNM-method creates greater problems of co-ordination than the closing-rate method (provided exchange gains and losses are recognized as income in measuring rate of return on capital). To illustrate this statement, we return to our original example.

EXAMPLE

Assume that the MNM-method is applied in translating the balance sheet of D from DEM to SEK. Some additional assumptions have to be introduced:

- The balance sheet at the date of acquisition includes non-monetary assets with a carrying amount of DEM 100m at this date and of DEM 95m at the end of the first year; this amount is translated at the rate which applies on the date of acquisition (3).
- The depreciation of non-monetary assets is DEM 5m, translated at a rate of 3, and that the income before depreciation DEM 15m, translated at the average rate of 3.075.

The consolidated balance sheet at the end of the first year is presented below.

	Q SEK m	D DEM m	Group SEK m
Shares in D	300		—
Non-monetary assets	0	95	285.00
Monetary assets	0	215	677.25
	300	310	962.25
Liabilities	0	200	630.00
Equity 1/1	300	100	300.00
Exchange gain			1.12
Net income	0	10	31.13
	300	310	962.25

The group net income including the exchange gain is SEK 32.25m. The rate of return on equity is 10.75% (32.25/300), which is below the group target, although D has achieved its local target rate of 10%.

The reason is that non-monetary assets are translated at the exchange rate that existed at the date of acquisition. The MNM-method is consistent with the basic principle of historical cost as the basis of valuation. Thus, this method of translation has the same limitations as the *T*-method, not recognizing unrealized holding gains in measuring income and the rate of return on capital.

11.4.4 The measurement problems from a control perspective

Even though our numerical analysis is based on extremely simplified assumptions, it highlights the main problem in co-ordinating the required rates of return at group level and foreign subsidiary level. There are no specific problems if exchange rates are stable and no gap exists between the domestic and foreign rates of interest. Unstable exchange rates and interest gaps lead to problems.

The method used in translating a subsidiary's financial statements in the local currency into the group's reporting currency is of decisive importance. Our analysis shows that the closing-rate method is more appropriate than the MNM-method for the co-ordination of the required rate of return on the equity of the group and the required rate of return on a subsidiary's equity (measured in the local currency), provided the exchange differences are recognized as group net income in measuring the rate of return on equity. The exchange gains can be interpreted as unrealized partial holding gains.

Lack of parity between changes in exchange rates and interest gaps complicates the co-ordination, unless hedging of the subsidiary's equity is applied. Thus the hedging policy is crucial from the viewpoint of profitability control. The combination of the closing-rate method and equity hedging is consistent with a policy of (a) using local financial statements and local cost of capital as instruments in controlling foreign subsidiaries and (b) using the consolidated statements and the cost of capital of the parent company as instruments in controlling the total group. Once more, it should be emphasized that the hedging policy is only meaningful from a co-ordination perspective if the exchange differences are recognized as income, contrary to the prevailing accounting standard. In groups which apply the MNM-method, it would be advisable to combine hedging with a financing policy under which a subsidiary's equity should be equal to the net monetary assets. Consolidation adjustments which are only stated in the reporting currency of a group cause additional complications, which can be reduced by the application of push-down accounting. There are often, however, legal and other restrictions on the application of this method of accounting, although the accounts for consolidation purposes may differ from the statutory accounts.

Co-ordination of the required return at group and at subsidiary level is an extremely complex process in a multinational group. This process of co-ordination is one of many issues that should be studied in future research on accounting control systems in international groups.

11.5 CONDITIONS AFFECTING FINANCIAL CONTROL OF A GROUP

The assumption underlying the analysis in this chapter has been that the required rate of return on the equity of a subsidiary is derived from the required rate of return on the equity of a group, based on the parent company's cost of equity capital. Central control is based on the consolidated financial statements. Our summarizing conclusions are presented in terms of favourable and unfavourable conditions for the application of such a model of target returns.

The following conditions are favourable.

- Large share of domestic (non-foreign) parent-established (non-acquired) subsidiaries without considerable intragroup profits or changes in these profits.
- The following characteristics of acquisitions: small differences between the cost of acquisition and the equity of the subsidiary at the date of acquisition (small consolidation adjustments); no substantial goodwill on consolidation and/or consistency between the useful life and the total period of depreciation.
- The subsidiary has been owned for such a long time that no consolidation adjustments remain in the consolidated balance sheet.
- Stable relationships between the reporting currency (assumed here to be SEK) and the currencies of the countries in which foreign subsidiaries operate.
- Low frequency of acquisitions which appreciably change the capital structure of the group.

Very unfavourable conditions will exist if a group has been built up to a large extent by acquisitions with the following characteristics:

- Considerable differences between the valuation at group and subsidiary levels of indirectly acquired assets and liabilities (considerable consolidation adjustments); considerable goodwill on consolidation and substantial gaps between the useful life and the total period of depreciation.
- Large synergies and related restructuring costs, with financial consequences not only for the acquired company but also for other 'old' members of the group.
- Considerable acquisitions in countries with unstable exchange rates in relation to the reporting currency.
- Frequent acquisitions with immediate effects on the capital structure of the group.

It is a reasonable hypothesis that our assumed model of co-ordination is unrealistic under unfavourable conditions of the kind we have illustrated above. The profitability control of subsidiaries has to be based on levels of reference other than the cost of equity of the parent company: for example, comparisons with previous years, expected outcome of an acquisition, local cost of capital and local competitors. A bottom-up approach in budgeting is more probable than a top-down approach. The more difficult it is to construct measurement systems with satisfactory internal and external consistency, the greater the need for a wider range of supplementary measures and methods of control.

NOTES

[1] See e.g. Bursk, E. C., Dearden, J., Hawkins, D. F. and Longstreet, V. M. *Financial Control of Multinational Operations*, Financial Executives Research Foundation (1971) and Czechowicz, I. J., Choi, F. D. S. and Bavishi, V. B. *Assessing Foreign Subsidiary Performance: Systems and Practices of Leading Multinational Companies*, Business Corporation (1982).

[2] This problem has been studied in, for example, Engshagen, I. 'Financial ratios for groups versus legal entities' (only in Swedish) (mimeographed research report, Stockholm School of Economics) (1987).

[3] 600 + 150 + the additional loan of SEK 50m to finance one-third of the cost of acquisition.

[4] All these costs are not booked in S but divided between all companies involved in the restructuring process.

[5] 60 + 15 + 0.1 x 50.

[6] The goodwill depreciation is assumed to be not deductible for tax purposes; thus the taxable income is 80.

[7] This means that translation gains and losses are not part of the foreign subsidiary managers' responsibilities, which seems to be the most common approach in performance evaluation of foreign subsidiaries. See, e.g. Derimag, I. S. 'The Treatment of Exchange Rates in Internal Performance Evaluation', *Accounting and Business Research*, Spring 16, 1986, pp. 157–164.

PART 3

The information needs of a firm and its components

CHAPTER 12

Introduction to Part Three

Systems for continuous information will chiefly focus on traditional accounting measures for areas of responsibility. What measures and targets are appropriate in such systems – for an independent company, business units, functional units, products and capital investments? What are the pitfalls of the measures applied? What supplements are needed? How do measures and required levels for different objects relate to each other? These are questions of interest both for those who choose information with a relatively high degree of freedom and those who are given certain measurement values to evaluate in an existing system. They represent a meaningful approach to information needs for financial control in a market economy. This is the theme of Part Three, which builds on the foundations established in Parts One and Two.

12.1 BASES OF THE APPROACH

As we emphasized in Chapter 3, there are common interests and information needs for many parties within and around a company in a market economy. They have reasons to make a company able to satisfy all external demands in the long term and to evaluate the possibility of company success in this respect. Many players also need to evaluate future cash flows from a somewhat shorter perspective. These common information needs are discussed in this Part. In addition, each party may have its special interests and information needs related to these interests; there may even be conflict between such a specific interest and a more common interest. This aspect is discussed to a certain degree, e.g. the special interests of owners, lenders and employees, but the primary focus of Part Three is the information needs with regard to governance in a market economy.

We discuss appropriate information, object by object, for companies, business units, functional units, products and capital investments. Measures and targets are analysed for each type of object. In particular, we try to clarify how various forms of required levels relate to each other. Both when information is chosen and when given data are interpreted, some concept of what constitutes appropriate information and relations between alternative measures is required. In Part Three, we present a coherent structure for various objects, measures and targets with an emphasis on the characteristics of traditional accounting measures. Such a description can give guidance for design, interpretation and/or supplementation of information in individual cases (*see* Section 3.2). Of course, ideas about how appropriate information can be used vary: degrees of freedom for internal players are different to those for external players, and furthermore various internal sub-groups and players have different possibilities (*see* Chapters 5 and 6).

Consequently, the analysis in Part Three covers entire companies as well as component units and is relevant for both external and internal assessments. Earlier discussions about processes for the use and design of information (Part One) and about the usefulness and limitations of income and rate of return measures (Part Two) are the essential bases of the analysis. The underlying concepts are as follows:

1 Direct and indirect effects of activities on cash flows are the ultimate and essential evaluation basis for all objects in a market economy.
2 In an uncertain world, it does not follow that expected and actual numbers for cash flows will be the main measures for continuous control. Traditional accounting measures are important, partly because bias and rhetoric are natural elements in processes where information is used. Measures with a considerable element of expectation will probably not reflect the state of most units very accurately, despite the undoubted logical advantages from a theoretical point of view.
3 Comparisons with various forms of reference levels are a most crucial element when measures are used. Comparability in a broad sense is therefore a major problem both when information is selected with a considerable degree of freedom and when given information is analysed, both externally and internally.
4 Traditional rate of return measures are helpful in some respects for comparisons, but are obviously not perfect for this purpose. In particular, shortcomings concerning allocations between periods and matching are of considerable practical importance. Such shortcomings must be taken into consideration when accounting numbers are interpreted; other data for certain objects, often as a supplement, may be required.
5 It is very important to clarify relationships between objects, measures and targets:

● Measures of financial markets and measures within companies should be related to each other, at least conceptually, i.e. it should be clear how one measure relates to another.
● Consistency both between and within income and capital measures is an advantage.
● Measures for various objects, should be related to each other; for example, it should be clear how accounting numbers for products and capital investments relate to figures for organizational units.
● It should be possible to relate internal measures for objects at different aggregation levels to each other.
● It should be possible to relate various types of target to each other, e.g. rate of return required by the stock market, rate of return required for companies and business units and the internal discount rate for capital investments.

6 The cost of equity capital is a central benchmark – the rate of return required by the stock market. The position of a company in relation to this level gives important indications about the company's ability to survive. Therefore, the extent to which a rate of return measure is a good approximation to market rate of return measures is very important.

7 If possible, measurement components with shortcomings which cause reactions which are not functional for future cash flows should be avoided.

Comparability is an important means of achieving effective financial control in society and within companies – between companies, between a company and its component parts, and between the levels required externally and internally. Conflicts of interest will clearly occur with regard to current systems for continuous information. Each system for continuous information will inevitably be based on priorities regarding what should be compared and what forms of consistency are important. For reasons already mentioned in Chapter 3, systems for continuous information aimed at financial control should emphasize comparability especially with regard to the rate of return required by the market. A sophisticated user should at least be able to find out how measures should be adjusted in principle for comparisons with cost of equity capital. Similar considerations also apply for those who design a system. In both cases, a clear picture is needed about how possible accounting numbers for various objects relate to each other. What relationships are there between various measures, between various targets and between certain measures and certain targets?

12.2 A DESCRIPTION OF THE FINANCIAL SYSTEM

We begin with some concepts about how cash flows are related to different objects and how the cash flows for markets, companies and company components relate to each other The following considerations are important when describing objects with regard to cash flows:

- *Separability*. In what way are cash flows bound to a certain object and to what extent are they common to several objects?
- *Mechanisms for scale-setting*. In what way are resources made available?
- *Timing*. When do inflows of operating activities occur in relation to outflows?
- *Stability*. What predictable variations are there and what unpredictable variations are possible in operating activities?
- *Controllability*. To what extent and in what time scale may inflows and outflows of operating activities be affected?

A general description of markets, companies and business components is appropriate at this point.[1] In financial markets shares, bonds and commercial papers are traded and represent a series of payments which vary in terms of amount, time and risk. As has been shown in Chapter 4, the value of these rights is related in various ways to the (future) cash flows of an independent company. The cash flows of a company, in turn, are related first to flows of operating activities, and then to flows of acquisitions or sales of subsidiaries, major capital investments and external financing.

Cash flows for operating activities tend to vary, depending on how capacity is built up and used. Within each individual business, capacity is created, maintained and utilized in order to produce a certain volume of products and to execute various kinds of support for this activity. Size and character of capacity and conditions for utilization are important factors for an operating activity from a financial point of view:

- What is the physical of capacity in each particular case?
- What size is this capacity in relation to total resource input?
- To what extent and how quickly can capacity be increased?
- How long before inflows are received must capacity be built up?
- To what extent is capacity irreversible: what conditions are there for decreasing capacity in terms of amount and time scale?
- What opportunities exist for alternative use?
- Does a unit influence sales prices for products and to what extent can its cost structure affect these prices?
- What possibilities are there to affect the volume sold, in the short and long term, and thereby utilize full capacity?
- What would cause interruptions in operations and what would their consequences be?

We choose the following concepts to describe fundamental product and resource relationships from this starting point.

- Revenues and some of the costs are transaction-related, i.e. they result from the transactions in which products are produced and sold. Examples are costs for materials, components and provisions.
- Many operational costs, e.g. for personnel and equipment, occur when capacity is built up, and are not related to each transaction as such.
- Some of this capacity is product-related, i.e. closely associated with individual products and product units.
- Some other types of capacity are function-related, i.e. involve functions common to several product areas.

In practice, it is very difficult to draw a clear borderline between transaction-related costs and capacity costs, but nevertheless the idea is fundamental to financial control. To a large extent, the cost level of a company is determined by expectations regarding a more or less remote future. To some extent, this is true for most costs; the purchase of merchandise expected to be sold the following week also represents capacity building in a restricted sense of the word. For certain costs, however, the problem of irreversibility is particularly important. We use the term capacity costs for resources which are intended to have lasting use, often over several years.

With this frame of reference, we are able to analyse all types of operations. Similarities and differences which are important for cash flows can be identified. The structure of cash flows may be similar for operations in different industries. Compare, for example, a bulk-chemical unit with a pulp mill or a coffee-roasting establishment with a petroleum refinery. On the other hand, there may be considerable differences between operations in industries which are close to each other: the financial profiles of a travel agency and an airline company are quite different, despite the fact that both sell travel services. From a financial control point of view, the attributes of objects with regard to cash flows are the important factors. Even a superficial comparison is sufficient to reveal differences between the following types of activities:

- process production with heavy capital investment;
- research-based activities;
- service production based on professional knowledge;
- real-estate administration;
- trading in which personnel and inventory are two important ingredients.

Strategic decisions concerning operations to be undertaken and their main orientation and capacity are made at group level. As a result of these decisions about scale-setting and orientation, fundamental capacity risk is also given, i.e. the risk that the capacity chosen can prove more or less favourable. In the case of an individual business unit during a certain period, responsibility for capacity is more limited; it is certainly possible to modify capacity size to some extent, but the function of the business unit will not often extend much beyond loading and utilizing the capacity which is available. Such units are managing a volume risk in this respect. For each functional unit, tasks are even more limited: they should carry out their activities for a given capacity and achieve satisfactory operational efficiency for all the resources used. They have no independent role to play as regards all the associated inflows and outflows.

Expansion of the capacity of an operation assumes capital investments of a tangible or intangible nature, or decisions causing outflows more or less at the same time as (expected) inflows. The latter is the case, for example, in many service companies. After fundamental decisions about scale-setting are made, a company will have a capacity at its disposal which may or may not have an opportunity value. Individual products will require both transaction-related resources and product- and function-related capacity.

12.3 MEASURES AND TARGETS FOR A SYSTEM OF OBJECTS

In accordance with our approach, the appropriate information for a certain object is based on two factors: the activity structure in respects relevant to the cash flows and the character of the control process.

1 *Activity structure from cash flow point of view.* Which activities, output and resources belong together and which belong to a certain object? How

12.4 CONTROLLABILITY CONCEPT

Controllability is a fundamental criterion for evaluating the appropriateness of measures for organizational units. In general terms, the controllability principle means that outcome variables that can be affected should be attributed to each organizational unit. This is a principle relevant at all levels. Self-sustained companies in a market economy must have actual autonomy both for financial and operational activities. The real responsibility of internal units is related to what they can affect; responsibilities verbally stated by superiors should be in agreement with this. Because we emphasize accounting measures for organizational units, there are reasons for a fairly thorough discussion of this point.

Controllability with regard to a certain measure can in principle be determined by three factors, namely, freedom of action, impact and measurability (*see* Fig. 12.1).

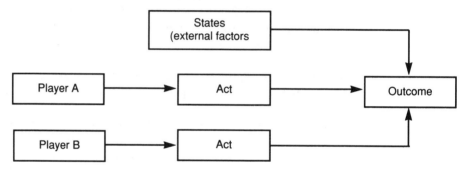

Fig. 12.1 Controllability

- *Freedom of action* of a unit indicates what courses a unit can follow within the framework of the organization.
- *Impact* is defined as the actual effects of steps taken by a unit. This variable indicates what role actions taken by a unit will play in relation to factors in the environment and what other internal units will do.
- Accounting numbers actually reported depend on *measurability*, i.e. to what extent numbers in fact reflect changes in a variable to be measured. Opportunities and costs of collecting, storing and transforming data set limits on the possibility of measuring the effects which individual players can exert on outcome, in addition to the basic problems of establishing a causal relationship.

The exact meaning of the controllability principle cannot be regarded as obvious. One possible interpretation would be: the activities that a player alone makes decisions about – and only these – should be reflected in a measure. Authority to make decisions regarding a certain activity is the decisive factor in this case; outcomes influenced in this manner are to be included. It is desirable to eliminate influences from other sources, but this may be very difficult. Strictly speaking, it is very seldom possible to separate influences from external factors from interaction with other internal units. The actual division of labour in accordance with an organizational chart is, however, a basis for what should be regarded as controllable, at least in a formal sense.

Another approach concerns the influence a player may exert on ultimate outcome, irrespective of the formal division of activities in an organization. With regard to effects, it can be argued that all such effects on behaviour and economic outcome should basically be considered. This approach is also in line with microeconomic agency theory. According to this view, it is appropriate to let the rewards of an agent depend on outcome data reflecting his or her own actions as well as variations due to external factors. This is not really consistent with an interpretation of the controllability concept strictly based on formal authority.

In principle there are two arguments for a wider controllability concept, both implied above. First, there are reasons for attributing effects mainly referable to other units, if this makes a unit more inclined to consider its interaction with other internal units. For example, a sales unit, burdened with some cost deviations originating in a production department, may be inclined to consider its influence on such deviations. A profit centre, burdened with interest costs of inventory, may perhaps try to affect the capital tied up, even if there is a centralized inventory system managed by another internal unit. The second reason is the need to encourage reactions against external factors that cannot be affected in themselves. A unit may devote attention to such circumstances, create flexibility with regard to change and take action to achieve adjustments. When units bear (part of) the consequences for changes in the external state of affairs, they may be more inclined to act in this direction.

A broader responsibility concept may make internal relationships particularly complicated and make them appear as such. Responsibilities will be less clear. This is important, because in practice a common control problem is precisely communication difficulties. Complicated responsibility patterns are difficult to communicate. A company will probably not be able to communicate a number of measures reflecting the essence of reasonably clear responsibilities.

Still, with our effect-oriented approach, a broader controllability concept is appropriate, and we define it in the following way. Controllability, is the possibility of a player (or unit) contributing to outcome. With regard to financial control, controllability may be described as participation in risks relevant to cash flow development. What role does a player play regarding the incidence of various risks and the way in which they are handled? Participation in company risks does not follow any simple organizational divisions: a production unit will indirectly affect risks in sales activities, just as a sales unit will affect risks in production activities.

What is regarded as controllable is thus extended beyond the strict, formal divisions of an organization. Effects of alternative measures must be evaluated from case to case according to the following. Assume that certain components are included in one alternative. If we now consider a second alternative, one further component will be less controllable than the others. What will the marginal effects of this be?

On the one hand, an incremental component may produce a desirable ultimate outcome in certain specific aspects. It could also result in different attitudes to assigned tasks. Possibly, such a shift could be traced to changed economic responsibility or at any rate responsibility perceived in a new way. Such changes have sometimes proved to be very stimulating. On the negative side, three possibilities should be considered:

1 Measures may include elements which are difficult to control; some of the previous effects may get lost.
2 A new component may not be observed, or is actively disregarded, and therefore nothing happens, which in itself reinforces a generally negative attitude towards control instruments.
3 Certain undesirable side-effects occur, e.g. because certain deficiencies in measures due to new components provoke unfavourable behaviour.

Many trade-off problems in this area can be largely formulated in the following way. An extension of a measure could produce some important advantages. However, it is far from certain that players will react, sometimes due to significant measurement difficulties. In the worst case, the most important role of measures may be jeopardized, i.e they lose their importance as an indication of the position of a total unit. Potentially, advantages may still be important. Before system changes have been implemented, it is often difficult to predict reactions in individual cases. Only practical implementation can prove if there are any positive effects, or if a point will be passed where additional measurement problems will make measures lose their fundamental importance. Of course, serious cases in which elements which are difficult to control are significant in size may be easily recognized in advance. These are also the cases which it is most important to avoid. We have seen such cases in practice. Neither the manager formally responsible, nor his superiors, then consider the wider responsibilities as something real. From a financial control point of view, this is a situation with the most negative effects, and can sometimes be disastrous.

NOTES

[1] A more detailed description of certain objects appears in the following chapters.
[2] We later use the term 'activity structure' in this sense.

CHAPTER 13

Business units

Some individual organizational units within a company have their own business concepts; in principle they also have their own combination of products and resources. From a business point of view, each unit is a totality and represents a detached source of revenue and income. Such units are thus operationally separate from each other. They are often, but not always, built up around a product flow. We call them strategic business units or, more briefly, business units.

Business units are the fundamental components of a company. Information about them is also of fundamental importance when a company is analysed. For this reason we start our discussion of objects with this type of unit. Business units are frequently ordered in a hierarchy, where the highest levels are referred to as business areas, divisions, etc. We concentrate on business units placed directly below group management in particular, but most of the discussion is of a basic nature and also holds true for business units at lower levels.

OVERVIEW

Business units are sources of revenue and income, separate from each other and built up around individual business concepts. The structure of a business unit is characterized by:

1 its capacity, with regard to size and form, and the cost of this capacity,
2 the transaction-related costs of products produced and sold,
3 the sales volume, in monetary or other terms, and
4 the price level of products sold, in relation to transaction-related costs and capacity costs.

The structure of business units in these terms has decisive effects on cash flows. A business unit affects the company's cash flows as a result of its product or resource prices, minor adjustments to a given capacity and the implementation of operational activities.

Defining the responsibilities of business units in accounting terms is an important part of management control. Control, based on income and/or rate of return measures, is often an integral part of operations for such units, which may in many ways be regarded as independent firms with few business links. The way in which group management defines responsibilities in accounting terms and in terms of processes may have important effects on the actions of business unit managers. The rate of return on capital employed or the corresponding income measures are the main accounting measures. These kinds of measures, despite a somewhat negative reputation in academic textbooks, have been proved to function rather well in many control processes. Activities may often be analysed in several steps by describing them in terms of gross and net margins and capital turnover rates.

As has been shown in Part Two, measures of traditional income and rate of return on capital should be interpreted with caution and often supplemented with other information. Above all, supplementary information may provide more accurate and faster indications of the immediate state of a unit. There is a need for systematic information both about demand and the market picture, and also about internal resources in order to assess stability of income and rate of return tendencies, and possible changes. Financial and non-financial data, and additional purely qualitative data, are useful in this context. Sources of data collection may include the accounting system, the media, and special questionnaires or interview surveys. This type of information about business units is, in principle, useful for both internal management control and for public reporting.

Formal rate of return targets may have important effects internally but, at the same time, lack accuracy when applied. The main alternatives for defining such targets are requirements calculated from stock market yield requirements, internal financial needs or potentials of each business unit. The alternative chosen depends, in particular, on the type of dialogue senior management wish to have with business units.

13.1 STRUCTURE OF BUSINESS UNITS

Business units run current operations independently, mainly on market terms, but are not normally independent from a financial point of view. The actual level of autonomy enjoyed by a business unit should be observed in each individual case. The position of a genuinely independent company should be used as a benchmark in this context.

13.1.1 Business units as separate objects

Business units in a group perform various functions, which are necessary in current business operations, such as marketing, production, research and development. With regard to these operations, business units have in principle the same autonomy as independent companies, i.e. their business orientation is determined within the framework of the normal commercial rules of the game. Agreements with other parties are made on market terms. Unit managers themselves make all important operational decisions.

However, even if everybody's intention is to make units autonomous, group management must weigh up the advantages of decentralization in different areas against the advantages of co-ordination and economies of scale. In the interest of the whole group, it may be justified to use the opportunities available to the entire group, at the expense of the independence of business units. From a business unit's viewpoint, this naturally represents a restriction in comparison with the position of an independent company. On the other hand, without such constraints there would be less reason to place business units in a group framework at all. One example might be forest units producing logs, which they are obliged to deliver to industrial processing units within the group, even if there are alternative external markets for timber.

Business units seldom bear the full financial consequences of unfavourable results. On the other hand, business unit managers are exposed to the values, attitudes and intentions of a superior who is responsible for resource allocation in a way managers in an independent company would not be. Group management often needs to be convinced of the desirability of a particular project. Close relations with group management can affect the extent and orientation of a certain business unit in a positive or negative direction, as compared to an independent company. Access to funds will be better or worse: major expansion and current deficits may be easier to finance but, on the other hand, surpluses may be transferred. Some business units may have financial autonomy to a certain extent in the sense that group management believes that each unit should be developed with self-generated funds as its financial basis. The ability to generate financial resources will then determine the degree of freedom for business operation decisions in a manner which resembles the situation in an independent company. This is not normally the case, however.

13.1.2. Activities of business units

A business unit can be formed around one business operation and one business concept or consist of several small business units, which in turn are formed around one business operation and business concept. All such core business operations can be described in the following common terms:

- *Available capacity, in terms of personnel, buildings, equipment and working capital, and costs for creating and maintaining this capacity.* Some capacity costs are product-related, i.e. they concern capacity for a certain type of product. Other capacity costs are function-related, i.e. they have a tangible correlation mainly with functions rather than with a certain type of product.
- *Incremental costs of producing and selling a product in connection with the use of capacity.* We have already referred to such costs as transaction-related. One example is costs for materials.
- *Sales volume*, in monetary or other terms.
- *Price level of products sold*, in relation to transaction-related costs and capacity costs.

The structure of business units in these terms has decisive importance for cash flows. The form of capacity required in individual cases is very significant. There are many possible patterns. For example, as far as certain units are concerned, investments in buildings and equipment are required long before inflows. In other units, capacity means personnel and office premises. Costs may then occur at more or less the same time as sales.

Other units may have heavy intangible investments, e.g. salaries of marketing or R&D personnel will occur well before the corresponding sales.

In many business units net assets are small, either because activity does not require assets in an accounting sense or because liabilities originating from day-to-day operations are important. Other units may have formally disposed of their assets but they continued using them – an increasingly common practice in recent years (*see* internal renting of property in Chapter 10). Capital which is tied up is less significant as the primary basis for financial requirements in such cases. Risks are also associated with factors other than tied-up capital but visible signs of risk and increased risk, however, may sometimes be difficult to observe. Each future cash flow stream represents a certain residual risk to be considered when an income level is assessed *ex ante* and *ex post*. Compensation for residual risk is important and needed in cases like these, but not primarily compensation for book capital.

The scale-setting and orientation of a business is mainly decided at group level. Within this framework, a business unit can influence the short- and long-term cash flows of the company, and the associated risks, largely in the following ways.

Modification of capacity	This concerns how capacity is adjusted in either direction. Previous capacity decisions will prove to be more or less favourable and this represents a *capacity risk*; the main risk occurs at group level where structural decisions are taken. To some extent, capacity issues lie within the area of responsibility of a business unit at a certain point of time. Often there are minor adjustments, with given conditions for scale-setting as a restriction.
Price activities	These involve the relationship between the purchase price of resources and the selling price for products. In turn, differences of this kind may be further divided into two parts: one relates to purchasing (how actual purchasing prices relate to relevant current resource prices) and the other to selling (how sales prices relate to current resource prices). Business units manage *price risks* related to differences between purchasing and selling prices. The temporal relationship between quotations/sales agreements and decisions about resource acquisition, production, delivery and payment in relation to each other is of decisive importance in this context.
Volume activities	These involve product market activities and the use of actual capacity. Each business unit has a certain capacity at its disposal in the form of personnel, buildings, equipment and inventories, etc. It must compete on product markets to ensure that its actual capacity is used. The business unit manages a *volume risk*. Low sales volumes affect cash flows unfavourably, especially if actual capacity is not fully utilized.

Physical
transformation
from resources
to products and
cash inflows

Physical processes should be efficient in a broad sense. We label risks in this context *operational risks*. Outcome in this respect does not only have immediate effects. It also includes subsequent costs, for example customer claims and credit losses and effects on future suppliers/customer relationships.

Operation-
related
financing

Some financial sources occur more or less as a direct consequence of operational activities as such, e.g. accounts payable and liabilities related to wages and salaries. Operational activities affect volumes and terms. In this respect, business units manage an *operation-related finance risk*. Frequently, this risk cannot be distinguished from the price and volume risks mentioned above.

The above risks combine together to form *operational risk*. From a short-term perspective, the main scale-setting cannot be changed and independent companies and business units cope with similar operational risks. They face similar conditions in terms of products, prices and marketing policy, etc. Volume and price risks are essentially similar, and this also applies to the possibility of managing operational risks. Internal deliveries may give internal business units a more favourable position due to stable customer relations. After all, there must be very sound reasons for choosing an external supplier when corresponding products are available internally, within the group. In both independent companies, and in corresponding internal business units, one generation of managers must live with conditions established by predecessors, especially the capacity which has been built up and the capacity risks.

13.2 CONTROL PROCESS

Business units are important objects in several interrelated parts of governance processes:

- *the internal control process of a business unit*, with emphasis on the economic efficiency of the unit and how it can be improved;
- *the group control process*, with group management having the possibility of defining and monitoring the economic responsibilities of business units;
- *the public process*, in which major business units (often labelled segments) will be especially important, and will have a distinct external image, to some extent.

13.2.1 Business units and their managers in control processes

In a decentralized organisation, business unit managers have considerable responsibility and a great deal of freedom. In many respects, they often run their operations in an independent way. At the same time, group management has public profit responsibility for the group and the performance of major business units is extremely important in achieving this objective. The manager of a business unit thus plays a key role in relation to the group chief executive officer's (CEO's) obligations and commitments. A CEO must ensure that sufficient periodic pressure is felt at business unit manager level for the outcome for the group, at least from a reasonably short-term perspective. Close involvement and decisive actions are particularly important among those who are responsible for an entire, quite separate income source. Besides, business units are relatively homogenous, limited areas, for which a CEO primarily needs to have a dialogue about strategic opportunities, financial conditions, previous performance and possible action. Furthermore, resource allocation at group level involves a choice between such areas; the ability to satisfy the rates of return required by the market is thus the crucial guideline.

Degrees of freedom for business unit managers are normally limited both in purpose and time. They are often supposed to manage an operation within an existing business structure, but sometimes they also have the authority to change the structure. In many cases, scale-setting and the main orientation may be regarded as being determined from a short-term perspective by conditions laid down at group level. In this case, the main role of business unit managers will be the co-ordination of functional activities within this framework. Business unit managers may influence such a framework by taking initiatives and arguing for changes, but group management has normally the ultimate say.

Certain business unit managers can act relatively freely, but only within the framework of a time-limited action plan, e.g. a one-year budget, while others are not subject to such limitations. Likewise, contacts between levels will have an effect on what the actual boundaries are. Situations will vary from group to group. A range of relationships is possible:

- active day-to-day relations, normally including discussions of many things happening in the unit;
- a sparring relation, in which group management keeps sufficiently well informed to play such a role;
- a relationship in which group management have more of an investor perspective and no real ambition to get directly involved in day-to-day activities.

The need for answers to control procedure questions will be especially obvious when business units are operating as formal subsidiaries. In practice, a distinction may be made between two control philosophies.

1 According to the first philosophy, the independent role of subsidiaries is denoted by emphasizing legal realities. Unit members in that capacity discuss such issues normally handled by a board. When board members are appointed who do not come from group management, this is often seen as a sign that this philosophy applies.

2 The second control philosophy implies that the group is actually managed from a group management position and that the formal legal

structure is essentially disregarded, i.e. the board of the unit as such, and board meetings in general will be given scant regard.

The degree of independence may also be indicated by the way in which business units are presented publicly. Even if the conditions are partially determined in legal terms, there is some scope for signals about group management intentions.

Profit responsibility is normally an important ingredient in the business unit manager's brief. This is in line with the original profit centre concept, i.e. with clear similarities between profit centre managers and managers of independent companies. Business unit managers are given more or less the same mandate for operational activities as their counterparts in independent companies. Operational interactions between different business units are limited. As far as internal deliveries and other joint activities are concerned, other business units are basically looked upon in the same way as any other business partner. Business unit managers have a responsibility for income and/or rate of return. There are few other restrictions, providing the income level and the outlook is satisfactory.

Group management's confidence in business unit managers and in business activities determine the degree of freedom to a large extent. Group management's overall impression is influenced by previous experience and the steps taken by the business unit manager in the current situation. The fact that financial goals are not met does not in itself reduce trust. There may be natural explanations. Decisive action in a difficult situation may even tend to strengthen the manager's position and increase the degree of freedom. On the other hand, difficulties in meeting financial commitments may be followed by doubts about individuals and activities. One more negative budget deviation, in addition to a number of previous ones, may reinforce an image of a business unit manager who is not quite reliable. The way in which profitability problems are handled may be a burden for a business unit manager, especially when profitability problems as such are the basis for doubts about his competence.

Management control, based on income and rate of return measures, is thus a rough instrument for group management. Questions about the detailed calculation of measures are seldom posed, and details about accounting numbers and their development do not normally attract great attention. One essential reason is that most assessments require some predictions about the future. 'Certainly, profitability has been rather low so far, but now there is reason to believe we have reached a turning point'. Major projected values are bound to have a an element of uncertainty, which makes accuracy in accounting numbers seem less crucial. From a group management perspective, income and rate of return measures are basically instruments for expressing expectations for business units and for checking whether business units are developing in an acceptable manner. How individual accounting numbers perform is only one basis for overall group management assessments.

The possibility of defining responsibilities and meaningful targets is an outcome every single year. The fact that goals are so close in time is especially stimulating. 'The sum of the best possible incomes in the short run is the best income in the long run', is the main idea in the unit.

Immediate income and rate of return improvements for a unit may be in conflict with other interests of the unit itself in two types of situations:

● Orientation towards income and rate of return on capital may result in (perhaps indirectly) low priority for activities which have no positive consequences for income and rate of return until later. The classical examples are low investment in R&D and cutbacks in maintenance.
● Orientation towards income and rate of return may result in (perhaps indirectly) low priority for values and ultimate goals which are important in themselves but difficult to measure in monetary terms. This might occur for activities of certain direct value for employees or customers and corporate goals which do not affect future income and rate of return.

The danger that a business units' orientation is too short-term, even with regard to its own interests, has been discussed extensively in the literature, often combined with the view that short-term orientation is stronger at business unit level than at group level. The empirical basis for these two statements seems open to debate, at any rate in relation to the frequency with which they are cited. In our experience, it is difficult to state in individual cases that time perspective really distinguishes one player from another. Perhaps each is inclined to judge future consequences of a certain course of action in a different way. With an uncertain future, it may sometimes not be so easy to decide who is looking ahead – those who want to invest in a certain activity or those who do not. What may seem to be differences in time perspectives at first glance may perhaps be more a question of differences in terms of business judgements about the future.

Similarly, it is not self-evident that the priorities of business unit managers, in comparison with superior managers, involve a stronger emphasis on short-term financial goals in relation to long-term risks. Certainly, business unit managers may have good reasons for considering short-run goals. One reason might be that relations between the group CEO and business unit managers are at a more personal level than between the group CEO and owners of the company. Rewards/sanctions may therefore be more immediate, creating a stronger form of pressure. Furthermore, business unit managers do not have responsibility for long-term capital structure to the same extent as the group CEO; when income and losses are not carried over from one year to the next, long-term perspectives may be less bright. A business unit manager may even have time to move on to his next job, before problems are visible. On the other hand, business unit managers may also be less inclined than the group CEO to achieve short-run profitability at the cost of long-term risk: operational risks are more easily counterbalanced at group level than they are at the business unit level, which should make individual business units less inclined to take a certain risk. Moreover business unit managers often take greater personal (undiversifiable) risks than the group CEO when the risk level of a business unit is increasing. Close and immediate experience of daily operations and non-financial values may also make business unit managers focus less on short-run financial effects.

The risk that negative effects are passed on to others may be just as important as the danger of being too short-sighted. A strong focus on income and rate of return for a certain unit may have the following negative effects:

- *Group and business unit perspectives may be in conflict.* Negative effects are passed on to the group as a whole. Normally, however, an orientation towards short-term business unit effects seems to be in line with group interests.
- *The business partners of the unit (existing and future) suffer.* From a customer point of view, a deterioration in product quality and customer service is a negative development. Employees may be affected by drastic changes – some are dismissed and stress will probably increase when the workload becomes heavier, etc.
- External players will be affected, i.e. individuals, companies and other organisations outside the unit. Environmental effects are one obvious example, and increased need for government unemployment benefits is another.

Clearly, this description of control based on income and rate of return measures raises some crucial issues about how a market economy functions. In view of the fundamental importance of these problems, there are surprisingly few empirical studies of the positive and negative aspects of these effects.

13.3 MEASURES

To a great extent, practically the same information is of interest for both internal control and external purposes. When measures are publicly reported, verifiability and robustness are especially important, however. The possibility of selecting information in line with personal convictions varies, of course, from case to case, but hardly anybody has a totally free choice.

A business unit manager must consider group management ideas about business in general and about information systems. Group management, on the other hand, have to modify demands regarding detailed information in view of the risk of perceived undue interference in the activities of business units, both with regard to data collection in itself and the desirability of potential action as a result of the data collected. With regard to public systems, the discussion below serves primarily as a benchmark for an indication of possible changes.

The question of whether accounting numbers for business units should be relative or absolute, i.e. the choice between rate of return and income measures, has been the subject of much discussion. From a measurement point of view, the two methods are similar in many respects, but not with regard to how demands on financial performance are stated. Residual income means that a certain required level is built into the very income concept as a cost of capital, which presupposes a certain interest rate determined on the basis of capital composition. In addition, further demands may be expressed in a second step by requiring a certain level of income. Computation of the rate of return does not presuppose any defined required level. It is, however, possible to define a required level, which is equivalent to the sum of all partial demands related to residual income.

The distinction between rate of return on capital and residual income has played an important role in management control literature. According to quite a common viewpoint, ratios should be avoided as single measures, since they can result in inappropriate resource allocation and inhibit growth initiatives where capital is controllable. However, it has not been empirically proven that such inconveniences are a consequence of the fact that these measures are ratios. Many forces are common for income and rate of return measures. Still, rate of return on measures should not be applied without also taking the absolute numbers into consideration.

Another approach for dividing operational income and rate of return is computing value-added as a starting point, i.e. the difference between revenues and the cost of goods and services which are purchased. For simplicity, let us assume that other transaction-related costs refer mainly to materials and services bought. Then the formula for dividing residual income (Ri) and rate of return on capital (R_{CE}), respectively, can be modified in the following way ('capacity costs' does not include wages and interest costs):

$$Ri = \text{turnover} \left(1 - \frac{\text{material}}{\text{turnover}} - \frac{\text{capacity costs}}{\text{turnover}} - \frac{\text{wages}}{\text{turnover}} \right.$$
$$\left. - \frac{\text{capital x interest}}{\text{turnover}}\right)$$

$$R_{CE} = \left(1 - \frac{\text{material}}{\text{turnover}} - \frac{\text{capacity cost}}{\text{turnover}} - \frac{\text{wages}}{\text{turnover}}\right) \times \frac{\text{turnover}}{\text{capital}}$$

Value-added (VA) in relative terms is indicated by the expression:

$$VA = 1 - \frac{\text{material}}{\text{turnover}} - \frac{\text{capacity costs}}{\text{turnover}}$$

We regard depreciation as a cost for resources purchased. This has perhaps not been common in value-added computations. However, it appears to be reasonable given our general assumptions.

13.3.2 Supplementary data

Traditional income and rate of return measures for a period, and their main components, provide essential information about the earning capacity of most business units. A qualified judgement from a financial point of view may require supplementary information, however, for various reasons:

1 Traditional measures may give misleading indications, period by period, compared with a method which is theoretically more correct.
2 Data other than rate of return measures and their main components may give earlier indications about the state of a unit.
3 The risk that immediate, rather than long-term, rate of return is given priority raises the issue of whether and how, a set of goals can be expanded for business units.
4 Apart from earning capacity, effect of a business unit on company cash flows must also be considered.

The need for supplementary information with regard to each of these aspects is discussed below. Financial, non-financial or purely qualitative data may prove to be useful and sources may include the accounting system, the media or special questionnaires or interview surveys.[2]

Measurement errors and limitations have been analysed in Part Two. They sometimes make operations or business unit managers look unduly good or bad. It is important to create a broader awareness of this problem in specific cases. Supplementary information which can make circumstances somewhat clearer may be possible. With regard to how accounting information is actually used, the practical and lasting effects of such information tend to be overstated. Qualitative comments, to some extent based on figures, are often desirable as a guidance about the nature and approximate scope of possible measurement errors even as regards the sophisticated use of traditional measures. Some examples of supplementary information are:

- effects of a certain capital investment pattern on how traditional numbers develop;
- effects of specific prices and price level changes on traditional numbers;
- the main limitations from a matching point of view, and their effects;
- effects of depreciation and prudent valuations with regard to income numbers for each individual period.

Traditional income and rate of return measures reflect turnover and gross and net margins on a historical cost basis for sale realized during a certain period. To a great extent, they reflect the market conditions when the deal was agreed. The gap in time between agreement and realization can vary considerably – for construction companies the time lag is years, and for some retail businesses only a few days. Income and rate of return numbers for a period also reflect the internal resources available both for these special transactions and in the form of permanent capacity.

In view of this, more detailed systematic information about demand, the market and internal resources is important for judging the stability of the rate of return and the possible direction of changes. For individual business units, external and internal variables with the strongest impact on income and rate of return from different time perspectives should be identified. Preferably experience-based judgements about the nature of these correlations are also desirable.

Perhaps the most urgent requirement will be demand functions and market pictures for product and resource markets. The first step is obvious in companies with long-term customer agreements. A simple analysis of volumes and margins for ongoing orders, or perhaps for orders on which work has not yet started, will provide some guidance as to income and rate of return levels in traditional terms for accounting periods in the immediate future. In addition, the present situation and tendencies regarding various indicators may provide guidance for the future development of income and the rate of return. Specific indicators vary from one industry to another, but some main categories of demand and market variables are of common interest:

1 *The general demand picture in product and resource markets:* general economic conditions; short- and long-term buyer preferences; total market development; current price levels and trends for products and major resources. Particularly during inflation periods with continuous price changes for raw materials and other bought-in items, the information system should be able to quickly pick up such price changes as a basis for rapid adjustments in sales prices or other actions.
2 *Competitive ability (in the product market):* market share; production costs in relation to competitors; image in relation to competitors; exchange rates, if products are sold or purchases made abroad.
3 *Potential customer interest in buying:* tendencies regarding short-term inflows of orders; inventory levels for traditional customers and for their customers; the level of attention at exhibitions; the level of attention for certain specific campaigns.
4 *Ability to satisfy customers:* customer satisfaction according to surveys; proportion of customers re-purchasing; guarantee claims; complaints; guarantee costs.

The use of resources in internal operations will be reflected in income and rate of return numbers, e.g. in the ratio between capacity costs and turnover and in margin levels. In these respects too, both qualitative and quantitative supplementary data may provide indications of future development in accounting terms. One important indicator is the long-term trend for various cost items in relation to turnover. Another is attitudes among various personnel groups.

The question of whether supplementary information can also counteract the potentially negative effects of income and rate of return measures is open to discussion. Does a broader set of goals, including qualitative and non-financial variables, tend to weaken the possible risk of short-term actions on the part of a business unit? Sometimes the impression is that it should be rather easy to identify and counteract the risks of short-term action if group management is conscious of those risks and therefore realizes that a sufficiently broad set of goals is required. This is rarely the case, however. Both long-term and short-term perspectives are required. It is impossible to concentrate on today's problems without considering tomorrow's consequences. On the other hand, expectations about tomorrow can not always be pushed into the future without ever being tackled. In other words, a trade-off is needed between a keen interest in rate of return from a short-term perspective and other desirable effects, for example business and systems development. The academic literature tends to make this issue sound too simple while, in practice, it receives too little attention.

Ideally, the group management message should have a balanced emphasis on the short-term perspective and on more long-term interests. Both should be encouraged at the same time. This is easy to say, but well-balanced messages normally have difficulty in achieving an impact in the organization, especially through several organizational levels. Messages easily become over-simplified, stressing a strong focus on rate of return in the near future, or on customer views, or on internal product aspects, etc.

Even if business units are normally not independent in financial respects, it is still possible to associate liquidity consequences with each single business unit to some extent, for example by computing net cash flows, period by period. The cash control of business units is discussed further in Section 16.4, below, which discusses the financial responsibilities for different parts of a group.

13.4 TARGETS

Issues about targets as active control instruments primarily involve internal management control. Explicit targets for income and rate of return are often defined by group management. According to empirical studies, whether this takes place and how this takes place have proved to be very important factors.[3]

13.4.1 Targets with regard to need or potential

The definition of targets for rate of return on capital employed in a business unit may be based on either need or potential.

In Chapter 6 we discussed various alternatives for determining required levels (needs) for return on equity after tax for an overall group. This means that targets for capital employed for business units can also be defined.[4]

An alternative approach is to base targets on potentials. As the definitions in Chapter 3 indicate, such levels reflect what is regarded as possible, taking into account the specific conditions of the business unit in terms of the nature of product and resource markets, the stage in the product life cycle, the age of buildings and equipment, etc. Specific unit targets are then stated accordingly. Such targets are an instrument for judging whether a business unit is doing reasonably well or not, considering the current market and operational conditions. Some guidance about possible levels is provided by the achievements of other similar companies.

13.4.2 Choice between target concepts

In internal management control, the choice of target concepts may have repercussions on the real autonomy of business units. First, the nature of the target will affect how critical the target will be as a restriction for a business unit; e.g. a target based on requirements which can be relatively easily achieved does not demand very much extra effort in comparison with a level clearly above that attained at present. In addition, a high degree of autonomy is only consistent with a target concept which does not require detailed discussions and thorough detailed knowledge about business units on the part of group management.

Targets based on financial needs are natural instruments for group management if it wants only limited involvement in the day-to-day operations of business units, i.e. giving the business a high degree of autonomy. Such targets represent a fundamental condition for existence. If only one requirement is to be stressed in a highly decentralized group, such a level would be appropriate. At the same time, targets based on financial needs are advantageous for group management with regard to the division of labour and knowledge in highly decentralized groups. Even in groups with very independent business units, the funding and financial conditions of the group are mainly a competence area for central management: a dialogue about such issues does not normally arise between group management and business units.

On the other hand, dialogues about targets based on potentials can be relatively intensive. The basis of such targets are circumstances with which profit centres are very closely involved and which are well known to them. A target based on potentials can be a natural feature of a discussion of common objectives between managers at business unit and group level and may be a means for group management to initiate a dialogue about business conditions for individual business units. Defining such goals in terms of numbers can sharpen a dialogue, which has a value in itself.

Group management can refrain from a discussion with business units about targets based on potential for two reasons.

1 It does not want to get too involved in the day-to-day operations of the business unit. This issue concerns what constitutes a desirable form for contacts.
2 Group management wants thorough discussions with business units, but does not find quantification particularly meaningful.

Group management can thus choose from several strategies for targets. It may prefer a dialogue which results in the establishment of formal targets or it may prefer to avoid such quantification.

13.4.3 Accuracy of target systems

Needs and potentials are both meaningful bases for targets. An obvious question is whether it is convenient to apply both types in parallel. This idea has seldom been practised. Making distinctions between several target concepts and several stated levels is rarely in accordance with the not very sophisticated way in which target systems function in many companies. When day-to-day operations are being assessed, questions about the exact meaning of targets are seldom posed. Rate of return targets are often components in rather vague and inaccurate assessment processes. A system with several types of targets would thus in many cases require a remarkable change in the way formal targets are applied.

The important issue of whether return requirements should be differentiated or not is closely related to the choice of target concepts. Targets based on internal financial needs often involve group needs in general terms, without any differentiation between business units. Targets based on financial market demands should be varied with regard to risk. Targets could also be differentiated with regard to potential, which is the case when the individual prerequisites of business units are the determining factor. From a general, theoretical point of view, differentiation of market-based levels with regard to risk differentials is justified. In practice, however, the question of how risk differentials should be identified and considered is problematic. Empirical knowledge about such risk measurement is very limited. Risk differentiation in practice often seems to be based on the idea that risk differentials should be remarkable if they are to be considered. Accordingly, the same market requirements are applied for most activities. Levels for activites with especially large or small risks are sometimes modified by a few percentage points.

One special problem is represented by activities which are strongly dependent on the business cycle. How can meaningful comparisons be made between targets and outcome numbers for such activities? As mentioned previously, rate of return measures and targets are also important in such business units, and also often for judgements on a year-to-year basis. Clearly, a long-term target cannot be easily compared with budget or outcome data for a single year. In principle, there are ways of facilitating comparison:

1 Numbers are stated for a certain typical year in a longer cycle, e.g. a bottom year or a top year. Numbers for these typical years are in turn consistent with the experience of averages for such a cycle.
2 The evaluation period is made sufficiently long. An overall judgement for the next five-year period is made. Moving averages for five-year periods are subsequently computed. It is hard to believe that this kind of calculation could be of any practical value. Quite simply, the beginning of a five-year period would probably be conceived as too distant and of too little interest once the end of the period has been reached.

rules for the division of labour between owners and the board/senior management mean that internal management will have some scope for interpreting economic responsibility, including public profit responsibility. At the same time, such responsibility is a very powerful force. A group CEO and his closest officers are often strongly aware of the need to continuously live up to stock market expectations, as expressed in share prices and public information flows. However, at this level, short-term influence on day-to-day activities in the company is limited.

Traditional measures for income, capital, capital structure and rate of return on capital – the rate of return on equity, the rate of return on capital employed, liquidity measures and debt-to-equity ratio – provide important but incomplete indications of the financial strength and development of a company. A more complete picture of opportunities and problems as regards cash flows is also needed. In particular, supplementary and additional information are required to interpret traditional measures, e.g. about units which are not consolidated and the effects of acquisitions and off-balance transactions.

Targets for rate of return and for financial strength, in terms of liquidity and capital structure, are meaningful for a self-sustained company. Rates required by shareholders are ultimately determined by what alternative investments might yield. Both in principle and practice, such levels are difficult to transform into company targets. Nonetheless, the way in which the company rate of return on equity relates to rates required by the market is an important indication in the short and the long term.

14.1 STRUCTURE OF SELF-SUSTAINED FIRMS

Compared with managers of business units, the management and board of a self-sustained company have full authority over financing activities within the boundaries of normal legal and market-based rules. There is also full autonomy for operational activities, i.e. independent production and marketing decisions can be made within the frameworks permitted by commercial rules and market-based agreements with other parties.

14.1.1 A self-sustained firm as a separate object

In principle, cash flows to and from a self-sustained company only occur on market terms. This is also true for the transfer of resources to owners or to other companies with (in principle) the same owners. There are no formal guarantees as a result of ownership, and there are no operational relations with other units. In addition, resources are internally transferable without restrictions.

The possibilities of surviving and developing are thus exclusively dependent on the firm's *own* ability to generate cash surpluses and income, and the way in which this ability is regarded by players with different interests. Income after tax and market-based dividends are in themselves a source of finance. Accumulated income, retained and maybe growing year by year, makes it possible to cope with business risks. Generated equity is also the basis for attracting further equity and for creditworthiness. Possible losses will have reverse effects on equity and development opportunities. Liquidity and the need for a balance between equity and financial commitments consequently establishes limits for freedom of action. Given such conditions, the board and senior management can determine the total growth of a company, its business orientation and the use of various sources of finances.

Particularly in the case of groups, what should be regarded as an 'entire financial unit' is not self-evident. Preparing the accounts for a number of corporations with owner relationships involves a very important consideration. On the one hand, *the group of corporations* is in reality a target for financial market requirements, and therefore accounting should represent such a totality. In other words, accounting for the activities of these companies should preferably be made, as if they were executed within the framework of a single corporation. On the other hand, these activities are actually carried out in *a number of separate corporations*, which certainly have limited real autonomy but nonetheless constitute separate legal entities. Accounting for all this, as if there were only one corporation, is obviously a deviation from strict representational criteria. In a way, this is an insoluble problem; some fictitious analogy must be used and corresponding operational criteria developed.

The ability to transfer financial resources is the most fundamental factor in identifying an 'entire financial unit':

External transfers

Externally, i.e. in relation to owners, customers, suppliers, etc., flow of resources should be traded in accordance with normal market-based conditions. Cash flows to owners should be regulated with procedures similar to market-based dividends and the dividend amounts should be at an acceptable market level in relation to financial inputs. Resources purchased and products sold should likewise be priced in line with market conditions. Owner contributions and commitments should be scrutinized in individual cases with similar procedures and criteria as in the market.

Internal transfers

Internally, real possibilities of transferring resources preferably should be similar to those within a formal corporation. Transfers within groups naturally face obstacles. Mandatory legislation means absolute obstacles, and if certain types of action are permitted but regarded as unacceptable from an economic point of view, this constitutes an economic obstacle. There are also self-constraining obstacles if the control philosophy of the group allows group sub-units to lead a relatively independent life.

In particular, legislation may counteract the transfer of financial resources between corporations in a group. Civil law may stipulate what funds may be distributed, regardless of whether there is a group or not, and currency and tax legislation may stipulate what is transferable between countries and the tax consequences of such transfers. Foreign subsidiaries in multinational groups may, for this and other reasons, present a strong local

affected both through changes in structure as such and through actions in various fields of activities within this structure. Everybody in a company has some effect on short- and long-term cash flows, apparently with varying power depending on the organizational level involved.

14.2 CONTROL PROCESS

In Section 14.1, we described *what* is controlled. We now describe *how* governance takes place – the interaction between external and internal forces.

14.2.1 A self-sustained firm and senior management in the control process

There is a fundamental legal relationship between the company and its shareholders: shareholders have the right to compensation determined in a certain way and to exercise influence on company decisions in accordance with certain procedures. The company, as such, acquires rights and obligations as a special party, represented by board and management, e.g. group management in a listed company. Legislation aims at protecting certain interests of owners, lenders, the company as such, employees, government, etc. – various national laws have different primary aims in this respect.

The relationship between the owners and management is thus legally determined in many important aspects.[3] The forms of owner influence are actions in legal arenas, such as general annual meetings, and the election of board members. In principle, owners also exert influence through their decision to buy or sell shares. The owners' endeavours to achieve personal economic efficiency, and their buying and selling decisions, may have repercussions on share prices and hence also on group management and the company. According to the general concept of the market, such governing forces should play an important part. Each share price may also – as described above in Part One – be perceived as making implicit demands on the company rate of return and income.

With this market-based view, the mission of senior management is to be actively involved in courses of action which have positive effects on share prices. Players in stock markets may perhaps perceive management responsibility in this particular way. It is difficult to tell what is the specific and substantive basis for owner evaluation of management in individual cases. The effect of share prices in relation to company income and rate of return on equity is seldom very clear in practice when the position of management is called into question. The common factor in management dismissals may be described more vaguely as owner dissatisfaction with company's financial development and lack of trust and confidence. This pattern in practice typifies profit responsibility: unfavourable income development may have negative personal consequences, taking, in certain cases, rather drastic forms.

We term this evident and powerful, but not very well articulated, responsibility, *public profit responsibility*. It is public in two senses. First, it is based on a legal relationship and involves a purely legal responsibility, under civil and criminal law. In extreme cases, legal action can be taken against board and management, for example because they are considered to have caused damage in some respect. Second, well-known companies and managers are monitored very closely in a public process, and this is especially true in the case of listed companies. Owners only have access to public information. Owners and their representatives normally have limited influence on additional information provided. Public monitoring of companies often contains an element of drama. Reference to winners and losers sometimes seems more appropriate for story lines in TV-series, than what is justified in terms of the business process as such. Drastic switches from success to failure or vice versa seem to be especially appealing. An image of (continuously) demonstrated success for a company is important both for company and senior management in this context. Setbacks will mean an additional burden as a result of negative attention, taking up time and energy.

> After having written very negatively about me for several years, a business magazine put my picture on the cover and wrote about my revenge. That was one of the best days of my life.

Publicity plays a special role, because professional success and the social prominence of business managers are linked and are often an important basis for professional and private life. A common experience among former CEOs and their families is that their social life also changes:

> Rather soon you note that you are no longer on the mailing lists. You realize you have not been invited simply because you are nice and pleasant.

At the same time as a group CEO is exposed to such public pressure, his other ability to achieve short-term influence on outcome is very special and in many ways limited. The CEO is separated from each of the operations in the existing portfolio and this is especially true of an organization with a widespread and pronounced delegation to business units. Such delegation may have its advantages from a governance point of view, not least in motivational terms; the alternative is that business unit assignments would be more limited and require more detailed and frequent reviews. Extensive delegation, however, also means control risks for group management and significant restrictions on short-term controllability. Business unit managers, who enjoy considerable trust, have in fact an important degree of freedom; that is the idea, otherwise the relationship would rarely continue. Naturally, business unit managers may set their personal stamp on orientation and operations, but within the frameworks which are acceptable to the group CEO. At any rate, the group CEO cannot affect individual actions at a lower level directly, but may do so indirectly through governance activities as laid down.

To a large extent, therefore, the work of a group CEO involves giving structure to an organization, appointing subordinates and being a leader. The major opportunities to exercise control are:

- choosing organization and control procedures;
- affecting business orientation and frameworks for various business units;
- electing key officers;
- influencing attitudes in the company, through actions and statements about expectations, primarily at the highest organizational levels;
- keeping sufficiently well informed about development in various units, and acting on this basis.

An important task for group management is evaluating and modifying the entire company structure (see Section 14.2), i.e. weighing up strategic opportunities against operational and financial threats. Decisions about what lines of business should be included and what main sources of finance should be used are obvious examples. Decisions about the scale-setting and orientation of specific operations are also important – what the capacity should be and how it should be primarily employed. What group management basically affects is often group exposure to strategic business risks rather than the detailed actions when the risks have been taken.

Exposure to capacity risks (i.e. whether the chosen capacity will prove to be more or less favourable with regard to what happens in the future) is thus essentially determined at group level. A certain capacity may perhaps have no alternative use when important decisions have been taken. Similarly capacity is mainly a given factor at lower levels. At group level, it was at least controllable when the decision was taken, and similar new situations will probably occur. Group management's success in these respects is essential for long-term confidence in the business on financial markets. It is noteworthy that in many cases the effects of decisions taken by previous generations continue to be felt for a very long time and that, at any given point in time, a company has to cope with inherited conditions established by predecessors, for example as regards capacity levels in various business units.

When a business unit is developing very unfavourably, the question of the personal position of the group CEO naturally arises. When performance is evaluated from a controllability point of view, tasks and issues central to his or her specific role should be judged, i.e. the five areas of action mentioned above. When performance is particularly bad, there may be a tendency to emphasize the latest individual event on an isolated basis, discussing actions and omissions in particular from a relatively operational viewpoint. The following statements are certainly fictitious but still typical: 'Despite the fact that Mr. A has now been group CEO of the B-bank for almost six months, internal control is still not good according to the auditors' report.' 'Group CEO, Mr. C, surprisingly says he is not aware of the specific circumstances regarding the order in question.'

Working methods in relation to the CEO role, rather than the details of specific examples, should be the basis for evaluating performance from a control point of view. Another question is what role the ability to control should have at this level. One idea might be that CEOs should resign, even if they have done everything possible in the call of duty. However, considerations about ability to control should be given greater emphasis in legislation and, above all, in media reporting.

One point which is often discussed is how well informed the group CEO has been when problems emerge. There is an obvious risk that the CEO does not receive – or at any rate does not perceive – the clear signals he or she needs to be aware of emerging problems. Even if a reporting system is adequate in a formal sense, there may be an (often unintentional) bias, both in reporting and interpretation. It is by no means certain that dominant and perhaps visionary senior business leaders also have the ability to perceive signals from officers below. In addition, reported data may be adjusted tactically, level by level, before they ultimately reach the top of the hierarchy. The group CEO may have the ability to see through this, but still some uncertainty remains. Furthermore, extensive delegation may make the CEO too remote in information terms from the phenomena discussed in reports. Sometimes it is difficult to draw very specific conclusions and even more difficult to act on such a basis. These mechanisms are often even more evident in the case of the group board.

In practice, when a company has a dominant owner, represented on the board, there is a tendency for responsibility for group management to be close to what applies in ordinary internal relationships. In such cases, the relations of the owner with the group CEO may be rather similar to the relationship between group and business unit managers. Such owners may even regard legal forms as a kind of formal obstacle to rational behaviour. Experience is mixed as regards pressure on group management. Both the absence and the presence of a strong main owner have been referred to as the decisive factor when severe direct pressure on group management has been avoided in difficult situations.

14.2.2 Senior managers and the effects of public profit responsibility

In practice, many boards and senior managers will have considerable scope for interpreting their assignments. Their personal opinions about appropriate basic perspectives will also be aired. What weight should be attached to the interests of owners and the market value of shares in relation to the development of the company as such? What should the time scales be? What weight should be attached to other perspectives – the interests of lenders, employees, potential and present customers, society, etc.? From time to time, different emphasis is given to owner interests compared with corporate and management interests in a narrower sense. The relative power of the board compared with senior management may be significant in these trade-offs. The degree to which senior management hold shares in the company is an important factor. These are supposed to encourage senior management to regard their actions from a shareholder perspective to an increasing extent.

Nowadays, group CEOs and their closest officers commonly spend a

earning power and creditworthiness of a self-sustained, independent company. As a result, the structure of financial sources is an important indicator of financial risks, especially the relationship between debts and equity, measured, for example, by way of a debt-to-equity ratio. As a main definition of this concept, we choose interest-bearing debts in relation to equity. There are several reasons for this; for example, that a measure of this kind expresses the risks resulting from borrowing in a pure manner (not the risks involved in liabilities in general). It is also consistent with computing return on capital employed instead of total capital; when capital employed is computed, operation-related liabilities are deducted from assets and not aggregated together with interest-bearing debts.

Some conclusions can be drawn regarding key financial ratios at group level. When a group's operations are heterogeneous, only the most general and most financially oriented measures will have any practical value, such as return on equity, income after tax and debt-to-equity-ratio. Because a group is a totality with financial autonomy, development should be followed up in such terms. Corresponding key ratios for total operations may be difficult to interpret, or less meaningful, however, if there are a number of activities of very different character. Measures such as return on capital employed will have little practical value if they are used for very disparate activities. It may, for example, be questioned if such measures give any important information at group level for a group consisting of both a major industrial operation and a major financial operation.

14.3.2 Need for supplementary data

The traditional accounting measures mentioned above represent vital and comprehensive information for evaluating the earning ability and creditworthiness of a group. However, from an analytical point of view,[6] improved accounting numbers do not necessarily indicate actual improvements in these two respects. It is important to raise this point, particularly for measures at group level. Improved values for accounting numbers are only important if they mean improved cash flow streams, currently or potentially. When accounting measures are chosen and interpreted, the underlying realities are as they are. Understanding how different measurement methods supplement each other is more important than a fixation with the question of what is the correct measure.

An analysis of activity structure variables, both quantitative and qualitative, can give a perspective on accounting numbers. Naturally enough, neither the strength of a company (e.g. unrealized values) nor all the negative risk elements will be reflected in traditional accounting measures. The need to consider this has become increasingly obvious in recent years, not least for measures at group level. Business developments have to some extent produced conditions for accounting which are more complicated than in the past:

- There have been frequent acquisitions. It is no longer normal for groups to maintain essentially the same structure over a long period of time. In addition, group structures have become more and more complicated. Minority holdings just below the level of consolidation are common, and the same applies for strategic alliances with a shared ownership for relatively big corporations.
- Resources and obligations can give rise to future cash flows, either recurrently (in current operations) or non-recurrently, e.g. when significant resources are sold or a loan is taken. For many years, recurrent cash flows were the predominant feature but an element of non-recurrent amounts has become more and more common in income statements. As a result, an amended method of accounting may also be needed for many assets, including financial instruments. Traditional accounting is most suitable when resources are consumed on a continuous basis.
- In the case of financial instruments, the economic significance of transactions and positions is much more clear and quantifiable than for many non-monetary assets which dominated the financial statements of industrial companies for many years. Actual and expected market values govern company trading in financial instruments on a daily basis. Accounting based on market values for such instruments reflects the economic significance of transactions in the best possible way. Such accounting seems most appropriate not least among the players themselves. There would be no stimulus for transactions affecting accounting income through realization of holding gains.

Both internal and external users need supplementary information in relation to traditional measures, partly due to these tendencies. It is important to observe all activity structure variables at group level in a systematic way (*see* Section 14.1) and consider to what extent and in what way they are reflected in accounting measures. Likewise, information needs should also be defined in non-accounting terms, especially in the following respects.

Current operations

1 *Business development*, at quite a detailed level, for the most important business units:

- capacity;
- growth rates;
- financial strength of business concepts;
- stability of operational inflows, determined by market positions, competitors, market shares and hence price mobility within various product areas;
- capacity and investment needs for various operations.

2 *Effects of accounting allocations between periods.* Income and rate of return measures are more reliable for longer periods. For one thing, allocations, which are inevitably somewhat arbitrary, will have less relative importance. This issue will be less urgent at group level than at

business unit level (*see* Section 7.4). Moreover, it is often complicated to analyse and provide information about allocations, for example depreciation patterns for industrial equipment. It is possible, however, to provide certain information about allocation effects to those who want to evaluate the outcome for a certain year. If, for example, especially prudent valuations of assets or debts have significant effects on income, there are very good reasons for providing detailed information about this in a qualitative and perhaps even quantitative form. This is important both at the stage when the original prudent valuation is made and when possible positive income effects occur when there is a subsequent revaluation. These phenomena are natural in systems with a sharp focus on creditors; 'a strong balance sheet' is a virtue and allocation errors easily occur. A common example nowadays is costs for restructuring groups and companies.

Structural changes and their effects

Significant structural changes need to be described very thoroughly, both in qualitative and quantitative terms: mergers and acquisitions, sales of companies, sale-and-lease-back agreements and the closing down of business units. What are the main effects on the group as such? How are key ratios affected? How sensitive are these effects for choice of accounting methods? Data about individual, major transactions and accounting items may be important from several points of view.

- How are key ratio levels and allocations affected? Effects of significant acquisitions may need to be reported over several years. To some extent, such data may facilitate meaningful comparisons between companies and between years.[7]
- How should different items be classified and what are the effects of alternative approaches?
- Traditionally, accounting has been focused on continuous operations. Major realized capital gains have been typically labelled 'extraordinary'. This view is being disputed more and more.

Existence of separable resources

Supplementary information about separable resources may be useful, especially when financial statements are based on historical costs and the convention of prudence. Accounting at market values or discounted values would certainly have its problems with regard to measurement system criteria, such as verifiability and reliability. It might, however, be considered for certain assets (*see* Part Two); consequences may need at least to be discussed. For instance, such information is important for major holdings, in terms of current values, and how they have developed, or as regards more indisputable basic data of importance for these values.

Liquidity position

Certain liquidity ratios, based on financial statements, are made public and may also have effects on internal planning, especially if numbers are observed over time or compared with the corresponding values for similar companies. However, they are often inadequate as bases for internal cash budgeting. Ultimately, a company needs to judge what capital needs could occur in different time scales under unfavourable conditions, and what cash resources could be mobilized in the same time scales. It is very important to identify possible surpluses and deficits in this respect. Such estimates have no simple relation to items presented in traditional accounting. Events requiring cash must be identified, as well as different ways of making cash resources available, irrespective of what is visible in traditional accounting. A time dimension must also be considered. When might needs arise and when might cash resources be available?

Financial sources and risks

Levels of financial obligations and risks for the group should be described, irrespective of whether they are shown in a traditional balance sheet or not. In particular, the practice of employing off-balance financing has made this need very urgent. Own risks in part-owned companies should also be clarified, including holdings below the formal requirement for consolidation. This issue has also become more and more important in recent years; individual cases should be described adequately.

Market demands may be expressed primarily in real terms, while company accounting primarily employs (approximately) nominal values. To facilitate desirable comparisons, company rate of return on equity values may be related to inflation levels during the corresponding periods. For groups with a high level of activity abroad, data about inflation levels in important countries may be of similar interest.

Both external and internal users of accounting measures need various supplements for traditional numbers. For external users this represents a request for supplementary information. Internally, demands for verifiability and robustness may be less stringent; certain supplements can thus be available internally without being made public. The need to control a group from an operational point of view will also make the information needs of group management different. The information basis for cash planning serves as an example.

14.4 TARGETS

For a overall self-sustained, independent company, there are targets for rate of return on equity as well as for liquidity and capital structure.

14.4.1 Return on equity

Reference levels for most players take the basic form of *minimum* levels, which is natural for all those who have an interest in the survival of the company. Certain players, however, are interested in the *maximum* reasonable and acceptable levels for rate of return and wealth; income and wealth distribution in society is a major concern for them.

We will focus on the survival perspective and targets that board and group management need to define from this point of view. In Chapter 6, we

cost of equity capital is, however, a fundamental reference level for the rate of return on equity at group level.

14.4.2 Liquidity

Defining the liquidity reserve concept and determining minimum level are central elements in setting goals for group liquidity. The definition of a liquidity reserve usually includes funds which are (almost) instantly available as cash, i.e. not only liquid resources as such but also unutilized credit lines, certain marketable assets and so on. Minimum targets may be determined with regard to business activity volume, acceptable frequencies and the size of risks and costs for liquid resources with a low or even negative return. It is not meaningful to discuss these goal-setting problems in detail in this context; there is a fund of specialist literature in this field.[10]

14.4.3 Debt-to-equity

Targets for debt-to-equity level for a company may be decided with regard to a number of different possible effects:

- How will a higher debt-to-equity ratio increase variations in the rate of return on equity? What is acceptable in this respect?
- How will the debt and interest burden increase in absolute amounts, and hence the likelihood of losses? What is acceptable?
- How will the debt and interest burden increase and hence the strains from a liquidity point of view? What is acceptable?
- How do the stock and loan markets view an increased debt-to-equity level? How important is this for company choice?

These various aspects need to be considered when a certain target for the debt-to-equity ratio is defined. The effects of debt-to-equity-ratio on return on equity are an important issue. Expected outcome must be balanced against risks, where risks can be measured in terms of various expressions for variations in rate of return. A company has its operational risk, related to uncertainty in business operations as such. Loan financing adds a purely financial risk – additional variations in return on equity due to the fact that equity is not the sole source of finance. Loans mean a possibility of improving return on equity, to the extent that rate of return on capital employed will be higher than the borrowing rate. On the other hand, return on equity will be reduced, if the rate of return on capital employed does not reach the predetermined level of interest on loans. The significance of this leverage effect will depend on the debt-to-equity ratio. This can be expressed in the following formula (without consideration to taxes):

$$R_E = R_{CE} + (R_{CE} - R_D) \ D/E$$

where R_E is the rate of return on equity, R_{CE} the rate of return on capital employed, R_D the borrowing rate, D interest-bearing debt and E equity.

From a company perspective, expected outcome should be weighed against risks in the traditional way. It must be considered that increased debts may affect return on capital employed by facilitating the growth and business development of an operation that could otherwise have had a lower rate of return. It must also be considered that increased debt may mean a higher cost level for borrowing, in the manner described below.

From a stock market perspective, higher debt means a tendency for an increase in the company-specific risk premium, which in turn may lead to a higher cost of equity capital. That should be weighed against expectations about higher income and dividends, as a result of increased debt.

From a loan market perspective, increased debt means a tendency for higher risk premiums on loans. As shown in Chapter 4, this will be most apparent when ratings for a market-based loan affect borrowing rates. A pure evaluation of creditworthiness will focus on liquidity risks related to the loan, i.e. the risk that interest payments and instalments will not be paid when due. The question is thus how an increased or reduced debt burden for a company will affect ratings for a loan and hence possible cost of borrowing. At one extreme, general loan markets will not be available; the company will subsequently be referred to direct negotiations with various types of credit institutions.

As implied above, group management must satisfy demands from stock markets as well as loan markets, and therefore face goal conflicts. A certain level of debt-to-equity ratio, appropriate for return on equity and appreciated by the stock market, may possibly be a burden from a creditworthiness point of view. At any rate, there may be a conflict between the objective of attaining a high rate of return (e.g. as a result of the leverage effect) and the goal of having a low debt-to-equity ratio. Loan markets give considerable emphasis to a strong capital structure. In analyses from a stock market point of view, the balancing of expected outcomes against risks may be of a different nature.

NOTES

[1] Moonitz, M. *The Entity Theory of Consolidated Statements* (1951).

[2] For an explanation of each of these factors, *see* Section 13.1.

[3] Relations between a principal and agents expressed in laws and other similar systems do not reflect the same core problem as many applications of agency theory, where the interests of the principal are strongly emphasized.

[4] The analyses in Part Two have covered this in great detail with regard to fundamental measurement problems, e.g. changes in specific prices and price levels and accounting for groups.

[5] For a thorough treatment of this problem, *see* Donaldson, G. *Strategy for Financial Mobility* (1969).

[6] We here disregard the case where accounting numbers have legal importance, the so-called post-contracting role.

[7] This leads to the issue of different valuations at group and company level. See Chapter 11.

[8] *See* Johansson, S.-E. 'Growth of Capital, Capital Structure and Rate of Return', in Brockhoff and Krelle (eds.) *Unternehmensplanung*, 1981.

[9] *See* Donaldson, G. and Lorsch, J. W. *Decision Making at the Top: The Shaping of Strategic Direction* (1983).

[10] *See* e.g. Donaldson, G. (1969), for a classic description of these issues.

CHAPTER 15

Functional units

Sales units, production units and various forms of support units are not operationally separate from each other, but need to be co-ordinated within the framework of a business unit or a company. Defining goals at this level is directly related to working conditions and the setting of goals for those who have purely operational tasks. General issues about functional units are discussed in the first half of this chapter and this is followed by a study of specific issues for each type of unit.

OVERVIEW   Within the framework of a business unit or company, functional units have strong mutual operational interdependence, and therefore need to be co-ordinated. From a financial point of view, the output of separate functional units only has any real market value when it is combined with output from other units. The costs for each functional unit cannot be related to market-based revenues (which is normal for business units). In principle, therefore, the market-based rate of return target cannot be defined on a separate basis for each unit. Responsibilities at levels below that of business unit manager are functional and involve output and resources used within the framework of the total strategy for a business unit.

Evaluation of economic efficiency for functional units will involve the following steps:

1 identifying output in terms of type, volume and quality;
2 measuring costs for the unit; and
3 determining cost targets.

For functional units, two basic forms of accounting and goal setting are especially important:

- Cost measures and targets are directly related to distinguishable output units (e.g. products to be sold or internal projects).
- Cost measures and targets are directly related to functional units or sub-units, achieving output of a certain homogeneity.

For traditional production units, standard costs and flexible budgeting are important control instruments. Economic efficiency for sales units involves both effects on product markets in terms of volumes, turnover and margins, and the cost level for the sales capacity. The main issues for support units are what costs are acceptable for a certain capacity giving services on an itemized basis and/or certain sub-functions for which it is difficult to identify individual services.

15.1 STRUCTURE OF FUNCTIONAL UNITS

Functional units cannot be regarded as separate from the business concepts for units of which they are a part. By definition, each functional unit does not need to cater for any product market on its own.

15.1.1 Functional units as separate units

Output from various functional units has no real observable market value unless it is brought together. It is, in principle, not possible to measure relationships between activities of a certain functional unit and total cash flows of a business unit. Thus, it is not possible to identify fully how each individual functional unit contributes to such cash flows. Output must be evaluated in terms of costs and the role for the total activity of a business unit. It may, in fact, be difficult to evaluate output separately, especially when volume and quality are not easily identified.

Combining functional units is critical for the success of a business unit and as a result operational co-ordination is crucial. The entire process for individual products, from the very first stage until revenues are received, can be considered as a single coherent chain. Decisions in different parts of this chain need to be co-ordinated, both in terms of content and time. More complicated processes include several decisive functions such as marketing/sales, construction, purchasing and production.

15.1.2 Activities of functional units

We make a simple distinction between three functions.

- *Selling* is managing customer and product market issues in various time scales. Apart from direct sales, the conditions for future selling are shaped through various activities, such as maintaining relations with traditional customers, contacting potential customers, gathering information about markets, communicating such information within a company, etc.
- The core activity for *production* is providing products and semi-manufactured products at low costs and acceptable quality.[1]
- *Support units* support sales or production units or an entire business unit, either immediately or over a certain time period.[2]

An entire business unit thus requires output from several functional units:

- products to be sold to external customers;
- sales operations to be accomplished;
- support activities for these two types of output to be carried out; or
- internal output to be produced;

all of a certain quality. The relationship between volume and quality of output achieved on the one hand, and costs on the other hand, will deter-

Intraprofessional values rooted in various functions are important. Trade-offs between professional and private life may also be different, particularly perhaps at lower levels.

Ambitions for economic efficiency from their own perspective, however, are also often a strong force for functional units. Combinations of analyses and actions give effects, stimulated by continuous control systems or when special activity programmes are carried out. In many cases, the main analysis is considered as straightforward and consequently pure energy and drive are the decisive factors. Analytically, perhaps directing attention to critical areas is the most essential step towards achieving ultimate effects.

In many successful cases, reference levels have played a considerable role in analysis. Not least, comparisons between similar units have proved to have strong motivational effects. This has been experienced both in industries with many similar companies and in groups with many similar regional units; nowadays 'benchmarking' is a well-known term. According to this experience, representatives of units compared are often irritated by comparisons they consider unjustified with regard to differences in the detailed nature of activities.

In other successful cases, measures in physical, non-financial terms have been focused at lower organizational levels: the number of tons of paper produced, the number of rejects in a factory, etc. Such information has been supplied to supervisors and workers through daily announcements in immediate relation to the work carried out. Effects at this level will seldom arise primarily as a result of the availability of data from a traditional accounting system.

15.2.3 Functional responsibility: the risks of shift of burden

Solutions of a problem within one functional area may give rise to new or reinforced problems in another area, i.e. there is a shift of burden. Classically, each functional unit only takes into account what is happening outside its own professional area to a limited extent. Production units aim at low production costs without considering market consequences. Sales units differentiate offers to customers without considering repercussions on production. Functional units take emergency action with essentially negative effects on other functional units, in the short or long term.

There are always tendencies in this direction. They are reinforced if the accounting numbers of a unit attract considerable attention at the expense of factors which are more difficult to quantify or concern external parties. Effects will be especially unfavourable if the accounting numbers tend to reflect what is easy to measure, rather than core tasks and output. This happens easily in a functional unit when there is a natural objective to have measurable goals. The negative aspects of this effect must obviously be weighed against the positive effects. Accounting measures often encourage production and sales units to adopt a stronger economic orientation in their core activities.

15.3 MEASURES AND TARGETS

Core information for functional units includes output, resources/costs and reference levels; information should relate to narrow manageable areas. The design of measures and possibilities for determining targets are closely related and are be discussed in this section, first with reference to general aspects and then with practical examples from various functional units. We emphasize costs and other components of traditional income and rate of return measures. However, as has already been stated , non-financial and qualitative data are very important supplements at a functional unit level.

15.3.1 Targets

Evaluation of a functional unit will in principle involve three steps:

● identifying a certain output;
● measuring the cost of the unit;
● determining cost targets, possibly in relation to evaluation of output.

Two interconnected problems are clear: defining the type, volume and quality of output, and finding reference levels for costs. Every explicit target definition will therefore involve two steps, directly or indirectly:

● identification of output;
● identification of cost targets for each unit of output.

It is often difficult to find clear signs of size and quality of output. For a homogeneous product, produced time after time in a single process, the situation is relatively simple. Identifying output on a continuous basis is more difficult in other cases (e.g. for services with effects which are difficult to trace or for unique major products, such as construction projects).

Basically, two forms of accounting and goal setting are of importance.

1 Cost measures and cost targets are directly related to identifiable units of output (e.g. products to be sold or internal projects).
2 Cost measures and cost targets are directly related to functional units or sub-units that are achieving output of a certain homogeneity.

In the second case, output volume is denoted in one of the following ways:

● directly in the form of an explicit output volume;
● directly in the form of a qualitative description;
● indirectly when two units are supposed to carry out comparable output achievements; or
● merely implied.

Explicit targets in continuous information systems for functional units are often based on potentials. According to a common ideal, levels should be feasible but difficult to attain, given a certain time scale. The possibilities of defining such targets vary, according to the following factors:

primarily referred to a certain organizational unit or a process rather than to output directly. Many costs cannot be allocated to any output directly. Costs which are indirect in relation to products may be classified in the following way:

- *Certain transaction-related costs*, i.e. costs arising when capacity is used for a certain volume of a product, but which nonetheless cannot be allocated to products directly in the accounts. Energy costs and incidental materials may often be examples.
- *Function-related capacity costs*, i.e. capacity costs which cannot be allocated to any product unit or any type of product but normally to some function. Costs of quality control or a sales force may be examples. Tasks and output in such sub-functions are often very difficult to describe in a very precise manner. Sometimes output essentially involves capacity of a certain specialized kind which is available for some purpose rather than the itemized output which happens to be delivered in a certain period; a repair department may serve as an example.

Identifying areas in which output/cost relationships are not satisfactory is important. Thus, the way in which the costs of a functional unit should be allocated is an important issue. What output and functional sub-areas should be regarded as separate objects and how should costs be specified for each of them? In other words, the basic questions are the following:

- What partial objects, if any, should be used? What should the smallest object be?
- What costs should be referred to these objects?
- How should the costs be allocated to each object, either directly or by means of allocation indexes?

Distribution of costs should reflect the way in which certain factors determine cost levels. Costs should be grouped together with regard to how they can be affected. What dimensions should be used, and in what detail, depends on the possibilities of measuring resources/output and defining targets. Allocating costs to sub-objects in a relatively detailed manner often stimulates action. At the same time, identifying more than certain specific resources for output at a very detailed level is difficult; likewise identifying clear output for sub-functional units at low levels also presents problems.

15.4 PRODUCTION UNITS

Examples of the concepts described briefly in the last sections will now be discussed for various functional units, starting with production units. After the structure of a unit has been described, measures and targets are discussed. Sales and support units are analysed in a corresponding manner.

15.4.1 Structure of production units

In a production unit, two general types of resources are used:

- resources for building up and maintaining production capacity, i.e. plants, inventory and personnel;
- additional resources for utilizing capacity for a certain type of product.

Evaluation of output *per se* involves two dimensions:

- attributes and quality of products produced, given the framework of a production unit, i.e. other units are developing and selling the products;
- the treatment of operational risks, above all, risks for future cost increases or revenue decreases due to problems arising from recent activities.

The structure of production units may differ considerably within these frameworks. The following examples illustrate this.

- A single object is produced for a special customer, including considerable assembly activities. Costs for wages and material are important items (production of houses, ships or oil rigs may be examples).
- Many units of the same product are produced in a long production run. As in the preceding case, assembly activities may be an important component. Costs for wages and materials are important items. Production may concern standard or customer-designed products (production of cars and trucks may be examples).
- A certain volume of goods is produced in a coherent process; costs for using machine capital and raw material costs are important (typical examples are the heavy chemical industry, the forestry industry and the steel industry).
- A certain volume of goods is produced in a coherent process; plants represent a relatively small part of total costs. Costs for raw material and wages are important (some types of food production are an example).
- Services are carried out for external customers on a relatively standardized or tailor-made basis. Durability varies. Wages and salaries are often important cost items in these cases. Other costs may also be significant, e.g. costs for using capital and energy costs (airline companies may be an example). Obviously, it is not generally true that service companies demand little capital. On the contrary, some service companies have traditionally required considerable quantities of capital (e.g. telecommunication companies and airlines).
- Special projects are carried out when customers buy a system of goods and services – not only goods but also various services connected with the goods, including installation. Such projects often run over several years. Costs for technical personnel and for material are significant. Capital tied up in work-in-progress and sources for financing this capital are important issues (systems for power distribution are examples).

The conditions for reducing costs vary considerably in these different cases. First, the very production process itself determines the extent to which the amount of resources may be reduced. In what proportion and in what way are the resources used dependent on production volume? In what time scale can there be a decrease? What are the alternative uses of these resources?

Second, the possibilities and importance of affecting resource prices are different. Levels of wages, and therefore also wage negotiations, are critical for some types of production. In the case of purchases, market character, corporate production planning and ties with suppliers give varying scope for action affecting points of time, choice of suppliers, prices, quantities, etc. When material represents a relatively low proportion of total costs and lasting relations with suppliers are more important than short-run price advantages, negotiations about purchasing prices will be less important. However, when a large volume of resources is to be acquired, and prices vary strongly over time or between different suppliers, there is certainly good reason to focus on the price issue.

Typical examples are:

- activities which basically involve transforming raw materials with wide price fluctuations (e.g. raw coffee, certain metals and crude oil);
- activities which include sub-contracts for major projects (e.g. construction projects).

Some general areas for lower production cost per output unit are the following:

1 *Production is rationalized for resources strongly dependent on volume.* The potential for meaningful improvements varies; resource structure and previous rationalizing activities are the determining factors.

   Materials quantity per output unit is an important variable for some types of companies, not least in process production, where it is important to encourage low wastage. Special savings campaigns and more continuous reviews may take place. The content of the product itself may also be changed somewhat in order to use less of certain materials.

   Time used per output unit is also important for many companies, particularly when production involves much administrative work, e.g. pure service production. There are different possibilities for rationalization. Personnel are replaced and vacancies are left unfilled. Investments which minimize personnel costs are carried out. Reliance on external services is reduced, or increased.

2 *Periodic cost frameworks are more restricted for resources which are not clearly dependent on volume*, e.g. for supervision and quality control. Costs often mean wages and salaries, which may be somewhat difficult to change. However, through replacements, changes in work tasks, etc. results may be achieved, even in the short run. This type of action does not necessarily mean rationalization in the sense employed above; cost reductions can be made at the expense of increased operational and quality risks.

3 *Purchasing prices and wage levels may be affected.* This may be achieved

through the purchasing process but also through production planning in a narrower sense: the material qualities used, whether work is carried out at convenient working times or not, and whether manpower is hired for long periods as an alternative to permanent employment.

15.4.2 Measures and targets for production units

When economic efficiency of production units is evaluated, acceptable cost levels are one of the main issues if product quality and operational risks are given. Information about production costs contain three elements, which are interrelated:

- some measure for resources used;
- some indication of volume and quality of output; and
- some level for acceptable use of resources.

Direct costs

In the case of direct costs,[3] targets can be determined, outcome registered and deviations identified for the following factors:

- quantity of material for each product;
- price for each unit of material;
- working time for each product unit;
- wage rate for employees;
- amount of services purchased for each product.
- price for each unit of services purchased

Targets in these cases can be defined according to a standard cost calculation, i.e. projected product costs. Such a calculation can be used for some time when a certain type of product is produced. It may be used for several purposes; in this context, we only consider its function in establishing a cost target. The level of aspiration which standard values should express has been much discussed. Should the ideal level be very difficult to achieve? Should it be a level slightly better than a historical average? Or should it be an average level based on experience? A rather common idea is that standards should express a fairly high level but which, at the same time, can be reasonably achieved by a professional of average ability, i.e. in principle a target based on potential.

For customer-order products and other products not produced continuously, projected values must, in principle, be determined in each individual case; previous experience provides guidance to a varying extent. The classic example is a construction company, in which estimates for each order are the basis for production. This type of situation seems to have become more and more common as production has become increasingly based on customer specifications. On the other hand, as a side effect of information technology, work tasks are sometimes repeated over and over again in areas where there used to be more variation.

Indirect costs

In the case of indirect costs, budgetary values are a common form of target. Cost relationships determine how budgetary values are constructed. They

Cost level of sales capacity

Can costs be justified with regard to objectives and the outcome for turnover and gross margins? Information and control problems are similar to those experienced in production units as regards many capacity costs. In the case of costs of sales capacity 'internal benchmarking' is common and often effective; explicit comparisons between cost levels of regional sales units within a company, possibly after subdivision into homogeneous sub-groups with similar conditions.

Dividing up accounting numbers with regard to several parallel concepts is important when sales units are analysed and controlled: products, customers, sales districts, etc. Aggregates at different levels should reflect some pattern for how revenues, gross margins and capacity costs are determined and can be affected. If certain defined actions can be focused on certain objects, information about each of these objects is also appropriate. The possibility of allocating costs is an essential factor in choosing scales and levels. Accounting based on some hierarchy of objects is appropriate, with some principle at each level for handling indirect costs.[5] The level of detail required depends to a great extent on the possibilities of defining meaningful targets. Accounting data for objects without budgetary values are only of limited use.

15.6 SUPPORT UNITS

Support units assist group and business unit management or execute services for reasons of economy of scale, which would otherwise be done by line units. Examples are central departments for accounting, control, information systems, personnel, research and development and law. Operational advantages or risk sharing may be one argument for common activities in a group. In certain cases, activities can not physically be connected to separate, individual line units in a group.

Ultimately, support units should be of value to production or sales units or a total business operation, subject to a certain time scale. A dialogue between users of internal services and specialists in support units is needed, in particular with regard to development issues. From experience we know that it is not always easy to establish such contacts. First, users may give low priority to development projects with an uncertain outcome which do not originate in the user units and, at any rate, take up time which could be devoted to more urgent tasks. In addition, central units may be overloaded with work and therefore unable to establish the volume of the user contacts which they would like to have.

To some extent, support units have cost structures which resemble those of production units. The cost of invoicing is one example. The element of discretionary costs in programme activities is, however, considerable, i.e. costs determined basically as a result of established cost frameworks. To this extent, output is in principle different to that for production units:

1 The output of support units is normally not equally measurable in a

physical sense. Therefore, determining efficiency by relating output to use of resources is difficult. Evaluation of R&D units over relatively short periods is one common example.

2 Some services carried out centrally are actually development work and therefore investments; positive effects will only occur in later periods.

3 Services carried out are not normally identifiable elements of products sold externally (there may be some exceptions in the case of service companies).

4 Some support activities are company specific and are of strategic importance as is the case for many production and sales units. Support units frequently differ from this model, however. There would hardly be any strategic consequences for a company as an entirety if, for example, certain computer or legal services were carried out externally.

5 Intraprofessional norms are common within specialist functions and may be important in the internal operations of these units. This perspective may mean that managers of an R&D unit may, for example, focus more on intraprofessional aspects than is really justified with regard to the overall business operation.

Ideally, output of a certain quality, or, even better, effects of that output, should be related to costs of a unit. Determining quality of output or effects in a meaningful way is often very difficult. Costs of output of a certain quality, perhaps not easily identified, will be the main economic measures in line with the principle of controllability. Measures and targets may refer to either individual units of output (such as individual projects or use of computer power) or sub-functions embracing a whole battery of services not too easily distinguished on an individual basis.

The above description indicates that the possibilities of observing physical and individual output are rather limited in the case of certain support units. In many cases, output actually involves keeping a certain capacity available; how this capacity will be used in a particular period is somewhat uncertain. For a company lawyer, for example, one important part of his or her performance is to have an overview and general competence available when it is needed, rather than dealing with specific detailed questions which happen to arise. As in other forms of capacity costs control, cost levels which are acceptable for a certain capacity are the main issue, rather than costs for individual items of output.

15.7 FUNCTIONAL UNITS FROM A BUSINESS UNIT PERSPECTIVE

Managers of business units and functional units have a common interest in local efficiency for functional units. This has been the basis for discussing measures and targets for functional units. In addition, business unit managers have a further perspective, of promoting efficiency for all functional units, working together.

15.7.1 Co-ordination between production and sales units

The mutual dependence between production and sales units is strong. Hence, co-ordination between such units is often of great importance for the short- and long-term cash flows of a company. There are several matters of common concern.

1 *Product concept.* Levels of production costs and product and process development are crucial for selling possibilities in the long run. A production unit must consider the effects of its structure on later stages in the commercial process; at the same time, a sales unit must provide feedback about market experience which has to be taken into account in production decisions.

2 *Adjusting capacity and volume to each other.* In some situations, an attempt to increase volume in order to achieve satisfactory capacity utilization is a natural step. For this reason, it is particularly important that sales units take heavy capacity costs in previous stages into account. In other situations, reducing capacity, costs and production volume, on a temporary or permanent basis, are realistic alternatives. In a recession, adjusting production volumes and resources in line with demand in product markets is of the greatest importance for cash flow. Certain costs for work carried out may be eliminated, even if employment levels are maintained. Sub-contracted work and hired services may decrease. Recruitment ceases. Overtime and double-time working are avoided. Personnel are given different tasks. The conditions for reducing substantial capacity costs vary with the nature of the activity. This can be illustrated by the following two cases:

  ● activities consist of a large plant, managed by a small number of personnel and with limited variable operational and maintenance costs (a heavy process industry or a real estate business, for example);
  ● activities are strongly personnel intensive – employees, in principle, are only engaged in specific tasks, requiring very special competence (an engineering consulting firm, for example).

3 *Physical flow.* The flow of resources, from purchase through production to sales is, in the first place, very important for purely operational reasons, and, in the second place, co-ordination between consecutive stages is crucial for cost levels and competitive ability. Fast deliveries may be an important competitive factor.

4 *Capital tied up in inventory* for raw materials, work-in-progress and goods to be sold is a crucial issue in many companies (e.g. for large-scale production, trade or systems sales). Rationalization will, to some extent, involve flows *between* organizational units, which means special problems for management control, focused on responsibility areas.

Production units and sales units participate in most business risks to some extent: capacity and volume risks and total operational risk are all illustrated in points 1 to 4 above. They also share total price risk, in the short and long term, i.e. how resource and product prices develop in relation to each other.

15.7.2 Measures from the business unit manager's viewpoint

Business unit managers need to co-ordinate operations in terms of product concepts, production and sales volumes, pricing, logistics, etc. Co-ordination can be supported through various forms of cost allocations, transfer pricing, etc. In particular, business unit managers must select control instruments carefully; functional units should not be encouraged to achieve quantified objectives, and then pass on the negative effects to other functional units.

One essential co-ordination question is short- and long-term adjustment between the production cost structure and demand in the product markets in terms of volume and price. The roles of production and sales units, respectively, must be defined in this context and an information system must be chosen with regard to this. The roles of these units as regards external customer pricing are very important. Sales units can either be informed about prices set by others or cost information as a basis for more independent pricing. Such cost information may in turn consist of either projected data (transfer prices/ standard costs) or the actual production outcome for some period, possibly the period when the very products to be priced were produced. Information given to the sales unit may either show total cost of the product or more detailed data about various cost components.

Transfer prices – in the sense of predetermined total values for products – often function as an instrument for co-ordination between the cost structure and pricing to customers. Transfer prices may be based either on the company's production costs or product prices to ultimate customers. In the first case, transfer prices reflect production costs, perhaps at different capacity utilization levels, thus giving sales units guidance for decisions about external prices. In the second case, transfer prices are deduced from ideas about customer product price and a required margin level. Thus production units get indications about cost levels which are feasible with regard to the competitive situation in the product market.

One question is the actual responsibilities for production and sales units, given various forms of cost information, transfer prices and external prices. Many such forms are possible. For example:

- business units determine price to external customers; there are no transfer prices internally;
- business unit managers determine prices to external customer; there is a transfer price based on production cost;
- extensive cost information, perhaps outcome data, is given to sales units, which then decide the external price; there are no transfer prices internally;

16.1 GENERAL PROBLEM

Sometimes managers consider whether income – and perhaps even rate of return – should be used as measures for production, sales and support units. They may also consider whether business unit evaluations should be based on measures including effects on the financial function, not merely on the rate of return on capital employed. Below, we identify a common core problem and then discuss individual cases.

16.1.1 Traditional model of responsibility

According to classical conditions for income control, profit centres should be at arm's length from other units as regards business operations, but fully integrated with the group as regards the financial function. Traditional divisionalization into many groups serves as an example. Product areas in different divisions often had only weak links with each other, while group management determined inflows and outflows of financial resources. Economic responsibility in accordance with classical ideas is illustrated in Table 16.1 (based on Chapters 13, 14 and 15):

Table 16.1 Relationship between responsibility and measures in accordance with the classical control model

Manager/unit	Responsibility/task	Measures
Manager/entire company	Total activity	Return on equity
Business unit managers/business units	A multifunctional responsibility	Return on capital employed (or the corresponding income measure)
Functional managers/ functional units	Sales	Volume, profit margin, costs
	Production	Costs
	Support functions (R&D, computer services, etc.)	Costs

Belonging to a group always involves constraints for individual sub-units. Internal profit centres do not merely operate under different conditions to independent companies as regards the funding and finance function. Possibilities of choosing product lines, purchase sources, customer segments, etc. may also be more constrained. Limitations with regard to such business issues are often less visible and less evident than limitations related to the finance function, which may perhaps be expressed in formal routines and quantified rules. Limitations for business operations are sometimes even implicit, and in such cases particularly easy to underestimate.

In classical situations, the advantages of income control have often proved more important than the disadvantages, even if dysfunctional effects certainly may be striking. When the profit centre idea is applied in less obvious cases, the pros and cons are more ambiguous. The disadvantages tend to dominate more when the idea is applied at lower levels. The advantages which exist at high organizational levels can be lost. The real independence of sub-units can be more limited, which in the long run at least may have some negative side effects.

Thus, there is often a tendency for groups to allocate responsibility internally to a larger extent, and give it a wider interpretation than is justified with regard to the real legal structure. The opposite phenomena is consolidated accounting for groups: companies are brought together into groups in a way which is not based on a strict legal structure. In both these cases, which we can label segregation and aggregation respectively, accounting and control problems arise which are difficult to solve in principle.

16.1.2 Common reasons for deviations from classical ideas

Control issues in practice not only concern a choice between the pure categories shown in Table 16.1. Trade-offs as to forms in between are perhaps an even more important issue. After all, is it not more desirable to apply a measure which is formally more in line with assignments at a higher organizational level? Could there not be favourable effects on attitudes and decisions? Would there be an intensified and meaningful dialogue between different units? Are managers so sensitive to their formal responsibility that such effects do not occur? Do powerful managers find their independence sufficient, even if they lack formal authority to a certain extent?

It is easy to understand questions of this kind. Not even large sales units fulfil requirements for a classical profit unit, even if they are often perceived as having a great amount of freedom. Foreign subsidiaries in many multinational groups are examples. They are, on the one hand, responsible for a financial function within a relatively wide framework; they have, for example, their own contacts with local banks. From a business operations point of view, however, they are often strongly integrated with activities of the parent company through central decisions about product lines and production plans at group level.

Even for production units, effects of defining profit responsibility may be worth considering, as the following example illustrates. In a forestry industry group there is one division with the primary task of cutting timber and delivering it to an industrial unit which utilizes the entire volume. The division in question is thus a production unit, in the sense employed above. It is told what volumes to cut, and hence the internal sales volumes. Its impact on internal prices, if any, is debatable. The main task is thus to produce a by and large given volume, with an acceptable quality and at an acceptable cost. If economic responsibilities are defined with Table 16.1 as a starting point, the problem is simple: the main measures for production unit control are costs.

All the combined stages in an integrated chain of a company contribute to a certain income and handle certain operational risks. The degree of freedom for each unit within this chain, and conditions for internal transactions, determine how income and risks are allocated between different stages. The business risks of profit centres in an integrated chain may be higher or lower than for a corresponding company with similar activities. On the one hand, their actions can have certain limitations but, on the other hand, they may be facilitated by special opportunities due to integrational relations. The stronger the integration, the more the conditions for profit centres will deviate from the conditions for independent companies. Relations will, however, not differ too much from what is the case for two formally independent companies which enjoy a close and durable relationship.[1]

16.2.2 Alternative control models and their significance

Managers of business units and companies have certain basic alternatives for management control for a production and sales chain. They are summarized in Table 16.2.

Table 16.2 Main principles of alternative management control methods in a production and selling chain

Production unit	Sales unit
1 Costs	1 Contribution/income
2 Income or return on capital based on transfer price	2 Income or return on capital based on transfer price
3 Income or return on capital with commission paid to the sales unit as a cost	3 Income in the form of revenue minus sales costs
4 Income or return on capital on the basis of actual external revenues	4 Income or return on capital on the basis of actual production costs

1 A producing unit is regarded as a cost centre. A sales unit is evaluated in terms of income or contribution (a central issue is whether, and to what extent, a measure should reflect actual outcome as regards production costs). This alternative is in line with the traditional meaning of the controllability idea, and thus it is natural to regard it as the main alternative.

2 Profit responsibility is defined for each unit with classic profit responsibility as the ideal. Internal transfer pricing of product flows between units characterizes this form of control. Ideally, transfer pricing should lead to some market-oriented income sharing in the total chain. One important aspect of different variations of Alternative 2 is whether risk sharing and income opportunities are in line with each other in the same way as for classical profit responsibility, stage by stage.

3 Profit responsibility is defined for each unit but there are no internal transactions and pricing of products; internal pricing only involves services performed by a sales unit for a producing unit, regarded as mainly responsible for income. Profit responsibility of the producing unit covers the core of the business activity in the chain and fees to the sales unit are one cost item among several as far as the producing unit is concerned. For the sales unit, commissions are the main revenues to be balanced against costs, which are mainly a function of sales capacity.

4 Corporate management chooses a profit responsibility philosophy where both parties are credited for their common contribution to the total chain, and some further direct costs may be debited to each party. Consequently, no transfer price is utilized. Measures aim at promoting co-ordination between units in the chain.

We will primarily discuss the meaning of Alternative 2. Units in the *first stage* deliver their products to an internal 'captive market'. They may have a lower volume risk (than an independent company) to the extent that their capacity is used without any real marketing effort and market risk for them. They may also have a lower price risk if transfer prices are based on their costs which, in this case are actually passed on to subsequent units in the chain. On the other hand, units in the first stage risk being unable to deal with the roots of possible marketing problems, i.e. demand from ultimate customers in the chain. Moreover, units in the early part of the chain may be of strategic importance for the entire chain, which is perhaps not sufficiently observed in individual cases or reflected in transfer prices.

Units in the *second stage* will have access to an (internal) supplier who has built up knowledge of this particular chain in a way which is common within a company but not very common between companies. At the same time, such units may not have any direct responsibility for the capacity in the first stage which is a prerequisite for this advantage. From time to time it is advantageous for these units to bear only volume risk associated with their own capacity costs. The disadvantage for the second stage is inferior opportunities to improve competitiveness; ties to the production unit may mean a restriction.

If profit responsibilities in each stage in the chain are to resemble the classical ideas, business risks and income opportunities should be in reasonable balance with each other. In turn, the relationship between the two units should not be too different from a purely commercial relationship. A decisive factor in this context is that prices and other sales conditions are determined in ways which are not too unlike procedures in markets. This has two sides – the *conditions per se*, especially price, and *procedures* for determining such conditions.

It has often been thought that to determine whether a price should be regarded as a market price or not, one simply has to determine what the product in question would cost from an alternative external supplier. This is an unsatisfactory definition of the problem, sometimes even misleading. Products may possibly be identical from a physical point of view but prices

the same time no other control measures are considered either. A manager who is formally responsible for profit refers to his or her mandate, but it is practically impossible to distinguish any meaningful related income.

16.2.4 Effects of profit responsibility without internal trading

Two clear cases have been compared above; there are also two further alternatives (see Table 16.2). In Alternative 3 in Table 16.2, a sales unit is considered as an internal sales and marketing 'company' to be compensated for its special contributions by means of fixed and/or variable commission. The role of such a unit is subordinate to a producing unit with more comprehensive profit responsibility. On the positive side, production units will adopt a fairly complete business responsibility, while sales units will nonetheless acquire a relatively strong business identity. On the negative side in Alternative 3, it will be difficult to define market-based commissions although such commissions determine the income of a sales unit. Moreover, ambiguities and conflicts regarding marketing may arise.

In Alternative 4 in Table 16.2, each unit is basically credited with the combined income of both the production and the sales stages. Some advantages as regards profit responsibilities may thus be achieved at the same time as some potential disadvantages are avoided. Both parties will have their business attitudes and their interest in scale-setting and orientation reinforced, but will have a broader outlook which extends beyond the confines of their own unit. For instance, sales and price decisions in the second stage will not only be based on conditions for a particular unit but will focus on the cost structure of the total chain. In other words: the basic idea is to support co-ordination between two parties for which activities have a very close mutual dependence.

The disadvantages are obvious. When the income numbers for each unit are dependent on the performance of the other to a large extent, there will be an important lack of controllability. This will always involve control risks, e.g. measures are not accepted or that each unit will devote too little time to what can primarily be affected. In this case, measures reflect a product perspective rather than a functional perspective. There is a risk that production and sales managers will not feel sufficiently responsible either for the total product process or for their own special function. This is a major disadvantage if superior managers have delegated responsibility in the hope that managers with so-called profit responsibility are to be strong forces in the company.

16.3 SUPPORT UNITS

The possibilities of using the profit centre idea for support units can be judged from viewpoints which are similar to the above and which vary widely for different types of central services.

16.3.1 Comparing support units with corresponding independent firms

Many supporting units provide a certain capacity which can rarely be purchased externally. Limitations regarding alternatives will then be of the same kind as for many production units. In other cases, dependence between support units and their internal customers may be essentially weaker than between production and sales units. One example may be divisible services of a general nature, e.g. consulting services of no strategic importance.

In this latter case, there is a relatively good likelihood that corresponding services can be found externally, while the rationale for integration is not very strong. The more similar support units are to an independent company, the more they lack protection against external competition and the greater freedom they have to sell externally. For a client unit, on the other hand, the corresponding issue is whether it is permitted to purchase externally or not.

16.3.2 Alternative control models and their significance

The choice of measures for support units involves three alternatives, which are summarized in Table 16.3.

Table 16.3 The main contents of alternative control forms for support units

Support unit	Client unit
1 Cost	Increased income requirements
2 Cost	Costs allocated afterwards – reduces income
3 Income	Costs based on transfer prices – reduces income

1 Client units are not debited with costs of services used; group management will increase income targets.
2 Costs are allocated according to a certain basis (afterwards). Income targets can thus be lower than in the first case, but costs computed for client units have no immediate correlation with the services actually used.
3 Group management try to create a commercial relationship between supporting units and clients. Support units are regarded as profit centres and client units are debited on the basis of actual volumes and a negotiated transfer price.

More than one method is commonly applied at the same time in the same group. For some services, the conditions for commercialized control models are relatively favourable, as has been mentioned above. In such cases, internal products must be very carefully defined; it is not always so obvious what the transfer price should cover. Let us use systems development, which is an important example, as an illustration.

According to one view, a support unit develops products, processes and systems, and subsequently internal transactions occur, either on a single occasion or over a longer period. Development activities take place continuously in the supporting unit, with capacity and volume risks; such a unit can be compared to an independent company selling systems in various ways. Price is set in accordance with this idea. This model assumes that development activities are financially strong enough as a business concept for the supporting unit.

According to another view, client units buy development capacity from support units, either on a continuous basis or for special assignments. Single divisible services can also be purchased (e.g. computer time). Subsequently, consuming units pay continuously for these services. The supporting unit in such cases will be similar to an external consulting firm which sells development capacity at a fixed or variable price and works very closely with its client. This model assumes that support units are permitted to develop an ability to handle close client relationships in more or less the same way as an independent consultant. In this case support units will also have a capacity and volume risk, although to a different degree to those in the first view. If actual costs of support units are continuously transferred to client units, these units will *de facto* have capacity and volume risks.

Accounting for development costs may be conducted differently at group and unit levels, which is a disadvantage from a management control point of view. According to the first view – that the support unit first develops a product which is subsequently traded internally – meaningful income measures for support units call for allocations of costs for immaterial assets. This involves some special measurement problems and will probably also mean less congruence with income measuring for external purposes. As far as client units are concerned, revenues and costs will match reasonably well, period by period.

According to the second view – in which support units sell development capacity continuously – development costs will be a burden for client units prior to receipt of the corresponding revenues. Client units will have the same accounting problem concerning future revenues as any buyer of consultancy services. For support units, however, there will be fewer matching problems. Such units have costs and income which correspond to each other on a continuous basis. These figures are also rather easily related to public accounting cost figures.

16.3.3 Possible effects of profit responsibility

Commercialized management control will give a user-oriented evaluation of support unit activities. Horizontal control forms will be more important, at the expense of vertical forms. Users tend to give priority to relatively immediate positive effects. Traditional cost control, on the other hand, may mean a higher priority to the support unit, with a more important element of intraprofessional norms.

In the first stage, therefore, scale-setting and orientation can be affected by control forms, including the choice of measures. Transfer pricing systems will sometimes – but not necessarily always – stimulate a smaller scale of activities and perhaps a changed business orientation. Transfer prices may also be effective benchmarks for achieving operational efficiency, in principle by highlighting the market price level for alternative purchases, but also to some extent by indicating user views of values. As we have emphasized in Chapter 15, it may be difficult to measure operational efficiency on a continuous basis when costs are controlled in a traditional way.

Apart from the effect on support units, the choice of measures can also have an effect, *in the second stage,* on the general business attitude of internal clients. If clients feel that they have good opportunities to affect the volume and quality of services purchased internally, this may generally reinforce their feeling of real profit responsibility and their general business attitude. This is especially true if there is at least a long-range possibility of choosing external suppliers, who may perhaps be more competitive than internal suppliers.

It is not necessarily the case that client-oriented systems are the best. On the contrary, it is sometimes important from a development point of view to emphasize intraprofessional aspects. Client opinions need to be balanced against intraprofessional views represented by support unit specialists. One particular perspective may easily be exaggerated. From time to time, the overall balance must be considered. If overdimensioning (excess capacity) and lack of user orientation is the problem, commercialized transfer price systems may be an effective counter measure. If the absence of development based on intraprofessional competence is the problem, on the other hand, traditional approaches may be preferable.

One visible sign of the effects of management control is, as is often the case, the dialogue between the parties. Group management is responsible for co-ordination between support units and clients and therefore also for a meaningful dialogue. A successful organizational structure with profit centres will stimulate productive attitudes: support units perceive user viewpoints as important and users regard support services as a limited but important resource for the entire company. It should also be added that different control forms require different resources in terms of time and administration, which must be considered in a total evaluation.

16.4 PROFIT CENTRES AND RESPONSIBILITY FOR THE FINANCE FUNCTION OF THE FIRM

It has sometimes been regarded as important to give profit centres incentives to consider more fully the variables of the finance function. It is necessary, therefore, to establish how cash and finance functions related to profit centres should be organized and how mangement control should be designed in accordance with this.

16.4.1 Finance activities of profit centres in comparison with independent firms

Funding, cash management and allocation of generated funds have traditionally been managed centrally, even in groups with a strong decentralization of business operations. A central group treasury department is responsible for funding and the placing of cash surpluses. Capital investment in profit centres is approved without any formal links with where surpluses were generated. The financial risks of unfavourable outcomes are in fact borne by the overall group. In other words, the individual parts of a group are financially dependent on each other.

Profit centres – and also subsidiaries – will always have more limited financial autonomy than in an independent company, i.e. a unit entirely relying on its own ability to manage contractual obligations and generate equity.[2] Senior management, for very good reasons, often have a relatively centralized philosophy with regard to tax and capital investment questions. Differences between a profit centre and an independent company can therefore be very clear.

However, sometimes the idea of making profit centres participate more fully in purely financial function issues and thus of extending their responsibilities has been pursued. A common intention has been to encourage greater concern about the cash position, the level of capital tied up and lower interest expenses for the group. One instrument has been increased incentives for profit centres to encourage funding of their own activity, e.g. by giving them some authority to decide over the use of the income they generate and to allow them to accumulate income from year to year. The idea is to give profit centres conditions closer to those of an independent company.

16.4.2 Alternative control models and their significance

The main accounting measure for profit centres is the rate of return on capital employed (and the corresponding income measure), often excluding the cash aspect and return thereon. The direct consequences of the finance function are thus not included, i.e. no purely financial variables. An alternative approach to profit centres which share responsibility for financial issues has sometimes resulted in an alternative view of purely financial variables. In many groups, profit centres have been given more or less complete financial statements, including cash and a total credit side of the balance sheet. In some of these cases, the main measures have been changed and measures typical of independent companies have been given somewhat stronger emphasis: not only return on capital employed but also debt-to-equity ratio and return on equity have acquired a more prominent role.

A group management, which has the objective of letting profit centres share responsibility for purely financial questions, may strive towards an internal environment modelled on the external milieu of an independent company.

- *Internal bank.* An internal bank is given the task of taking care of cash and currency planning for the group, funding, etc. The profit centres normally place their cash surpluses in this bank at a market-based rate and will also borrow from this internal bank. Profit centres may be given the option of using their own channels for contracts with external finance institutions.
- *Internal taxation.* In some groups, there is an objective that the tax burden on profit centres should be roughly equal to that of self-sustained companies, even if profit centres participate in group tax planning. Internal accounting transactions are made with the aim of achieving similar results for an individual profit centre as for an independent company, regardless of the actual tax situation from a group point of view. There must thus be assumptions about what tax costs should have been, if the profit centre had been independent. Profit centres can be debited for an internal tax cost or credited with a corresponding positive item.
- *Owner requirements on a market basis.* Owners, represented by senior management, require dividends and allocate further capital on conditions which resemble a stock market.

Two relationships should be kept analytically separate in this context. One is the relationship between an internal bank and profit centres regarding operational routines, for cash management and funding, i.e. a horizontal relationship. This has reasonably good conditions for functioning on market-based terms. The second relationship is that between group management and profit centres, i.e. a vertical relationship in which group management, as a superior institution, has the ultimate power over resource allocation within the group. Rules for this allocation primarily set limitations on the meaningfulness of measuring and controlling with the same measures as for an independent company.

One key question, at least from the perspective of a few years, is the extent to which profitable profit centres have access to internal bank placements built up on an accumulated basis. Assume, for example, that a unit is referred to the normal, centralized capital investment routine, regardless of the size of the internal bank account. In this case, internal receivables and interest revenues will represent an increasing proportion of financial statements. Income and capital measures will then contain a large uncontrollable element. These mechanisms may certainly resemble those of an independent company which lacks attractive alternatives for investment within its traditional activity area. This phenomenon will, however, be more accentuated for profit centres which embrace only a single and perhaps rather narrow area of activity and, in addition, are dependent on what priorities superior management give to their long-term programmes in relation to other sub-units.

The debt-to-equity ratio – and thus rate of return on equity – is rarely (totally) meaningful for a profit centre with financial relations with other units. Such an accounting number can be influenced to a great extent by

not yet come into play. One argument is that the life of such a system should be no shorter than normal in any case.

From a group management point of view, increased financial autonomy involves both possible advantages and a number of risks. The credibility of senior management will decrease if profit centre managers ultimately perceive reforms as less far-reaching than was originally imagined. Previous measures will become less important unless new measures make a significant contribution. New measures may provoke sub-optimizing on the part of the profit centres. Our analyses lead to one obvious conclusion: the more regulation of resource allocation in a group is based on tax and capital investment considerations, the more difficult it will be to exercise meaningful control based on debt-to-equity ratio and return on equity for sub-units. Possibly such forms of control will be more powerful in the short term than in long term.

Group management may aim to create an internal environment modelled on financial markets for different reasons. Regardless of what the motives are, expectations within profit centres will often be that relatively significant changes will occur in these respects. Ambiguities in responsibility allocation and negative attitudes among key personnel may result, if the changes do not prove to be important. Clearly communicated motives are therefore particularly important in cases like this; perhaps such risks should even be mentioned explicitly as soon as system changes are planned and introduced.

16.4.4 Financial autonomy of subsidiaries

To what extent can a subsidiary be independent from a financial point of view? What are the limiting factors?

Individual subsidiaries will naturally always have a more limited role as regards finance than a firm with financial autonomy. How great these differences are will depend on how resource allocation and financial routines within the group are arranged:

- What are the obstacles for individual subsidiary growth in terms of turnover and capital employed?
- What are the mechanisms behind operational income in subsidiaries? To what extent, for example, is this income market-based?
- What are the mechanisms for allocating funds generated by subsidiaries themselves?
- How is taxation handled?
- How is debt-financing arranged and financing through normal business operations?
- How is the business orientation of subsidiaries determined and hence the structure of assets?

To some extent a subsidiary within a group will have different conditions in these respects to an independent company. How fundamental are such differences?

In an independent company, *total growth* and *asset structure* must be planned within frameworks permitted by the board and external providers of capital. Subsidiary managers must operate within the decision frameworks established by their board. These frameworks in turn are normally co-ordinated with group management views regarding capital investments in various companies. The more group management with its total authority affects subsidiary activities, with or without formal boards, the more the subsidiary situation will deviate from that of an independent company.

Operational income in a subsidiary will often be determined on the same market basis as in an independent company when activities are not integrated with other group units. When there is operational integration, the issue is more complicated. The framework for subsidiary activities will be narrower than in an independent company. There may also be a conflict between potential synergies as a result of group management, on the one hand, including re-allocation of financial resources, and, on the other, a strictly commercial view of transfer pricing.

The *debt-to-equity ratio* of a subsidiary will be determined by one factor which is difficult to control for subsidiary managers (apart from those which apply for an independent company), namely, the possibility for group management to make re-allocations which are not based on the market. Group management contributions may be in the form of loans or increased equity. The form of contribution is not so important as in financial markets, where various financial forms are associated with different legal claims. When group management give a wholly owned subsidiary access to funds, the form is less decisive. In groups where transfers on non-market terms are common, debt-to-equity ratio will be far less important than in a self-sustained company. Moreover, trade-offs for risk are different for a subsidiary in a group than for an independent company (*see* above).

It is sometimes, if not usually, the case that the pronounced ideal for group management is allocating available resources between subsidiaries with regard to its own priorities, legal frameworks being the only constraint. Resources will be allocated to the companies which are most appropriate from the group point of view, regardless of where funds have been generated. With this philosophy, it is hardly meaningful to control an individual company as if it were an independent company. When the pronounced ideal is financial autonomy for an individual subsidiary, however, such control may be more meaningful. Group management intentions to pursue such decentralization concepts may vary in strength and durability, however; moreover, the ideas must stand the test of the stress to which the environment and general economic development will expose them. There are many different technical variations. It is essential to identify the principal content of each technical solution.

● Are funds transferred from a *group* perspective? Is the need for re-allocation from a group point of view the primary concern, while effects on individual subsidiaries are secondary?

volume and value measures which are traditionally used are not very appropriate as allocation indexes.

The opportunity cost concept is the main basis for product evaluations, i.e. the opportunity value of resources and the related economic considerations. In practice, however, periodic accounting measures are also often important. There are basic differences between cost calculations and traditional accounting measures (e.g. for interest costs). Interest costs are to a large extent capacity costs which are sometimes product-related but much more often function-related. There is also a required rate of return for capital not directly referable to the object of calculation. At full costing, interest cost will be allocated to products in this respect too. When variable costs are calculated, the rate of return required should reflect capital not allocated. It is important that capital items can be directly or indirectly related to products. Defining the required rate of return for individual types of products and product areas is an important part of overall management control. These targets should basically have a relation to the rates required on financial markets, i.e. there is an element of vertical control. At the same time, product market demand and the competitive position set an upper limit on what can be achieved, i.e. there is an element of horizontal control.

Product and business areas (i.e. higher levels in the product hierarchy) will often be related to ordinary organizational responsibilities. A particularly important special problem is control of product-region matrices in business units and groups.

17.1 ACTIVITY STRUCTURE AND THE PRODUCTS

A company will of course strive to allocate surpluses and costs of a company to primary sources for revenues, especially products. One of the major problems is, however, that relatively few costs, and as time goes on, a decreasing proportion, have any specific correlation with individual product types.

17.1.1 Products as separate objects

The analytical perspective for products is different from that discussed in preceding chapters. The basic idea is that revenues should be matched to costs for a total product process, regardless of organizational classifications. In such a product process some, but not necessarily all, of the following type functions will occur:

1 *Procurement.* Involves purchasing goods, employing personnel, procuring services.

2 *Production.* Can in turn be divided into further sub-functions:

- Production phase 1. End result is work-in-progress to be transformed in an integrated process, finished goods which require packing, etc.
- Production phase 2. Involves further processing and refinement, packing, etc.

3 *Service production.* Either solely or in combination with goods sold (e.g. transport or administrative work, etc.)

4 *Selling.* Planning and execution, including bids and quotations.

5 *Logistics.* Involves raw materials, goods in production, goods to be sold etc. This function covers several others – procurement, production, selling – and very much involves co-ordination between them.

6 *After sales operations.* Invoicing, payment routines, customer complaints, etc.

7 *Support functions for functions 1 to 6 above.* Often carried out via central units. Some of these services can be regarded as development activities which do not affect revenues in the current period.

This description of how costs arise in a product process (incomplete in itself) is based on how functions were systemized in Chapter 15. Categories are not listed in chronological order but with regard to the nature of activities. Relationships between functions mentioned and specific product types/product units may be difficult to identify. At any point of time, there is a certain capacity as a consequence of decisions made previously; this capacity would not be changed automatically by certain product decisions. In addition, increased future resources for each function may be utilized for several product types and product areas. Common use of resources may be the result of economic, technical or market factors and is often an important prerequisite for each product type. These interrelations, however, set boundaries for the possibilities of judging each product type on a separate basis. Products are separate from each other only to the extent that special consequences occur on a certain occasion, consequences which will take place if a special product alternative has been eliminated.

A specific product or type of product is thus often, and increasingly, part of a greater totality. The proportion of resources and functions closely related to a single product or transaction has decreased sharply. Some of the underlying reasons are:

1 Due to automation and mechanization in plants and offices, the proportion of direct labour has decreased, in many cases to a remarkable extent.

2 An increasing number of companies have activities other than traditional production and as a result, a more complicated product and resource structure.

3 The proportion of costs for product and market development, for marketing and sales, etc. has increased in the business world. Generally, costs for such intangible resources have a weaker relationship with individual products sold than traditional production costs.

17.1.2 Products and individual activities

Relationships between single products and company activities give the following pattern for costs:

1 transaction-related costs which are simple to assign directly,

2 other transaction-related costs,

3 product-related capacity costs, and

4 function-related capacity costs.

1 *Transaction-related costs which are simple to assign directly,* e.g. materials for a certain type of product. The effects of a certain type of product on transaction-related costs are basically simple. If capacity is not used to produce and sell such products, the need for a transaction-related resource does not exist. Determining a relationship between product and resource/cost is a practical accounting difficulty, rather than a problem in principle. Some costs are simple to assign to some type of products directly – they are included in this first category. Information technology has improved the possibilities for direct assignment. This is of special interest because the meaning of 'direct cost' is often related to how actual registration is made, not a logical relationship in itself.[1]

2 *Transaction-related costs which are difficult or expensive to assign directly,* e.g. costs for certain incidental materials. Such resources are also added to capacity costs and they are preferably assigned to products by means of allocation indexes for practical (and economic) reasons. The means of influencing these costs is essentially similar to that for the first group, although there is probably a greater focus on organizational units and processes.

3 *Product-related capacity costs,* i.e. capacity costs which can be assigned directly to a certain product type, e.g. wages for work on production. On the one hand, there might be a close relationship between products and costs, and on the other hand, capacity as such will not change in the short run due to changes in production volume. Some possible relationships between production volume and cash flows are illustrated by the following examples:

- If the volume of some product or product type is reduced, capacity continues to exist for a certain future period and there is no opportunity value for this idle capacity.
- If the volume of some product or product type is reduced, capacity continues to exist for a certain future period and this available capacity has a certain opportunity value.
- If the volume for some single product or product type is reduced, there will only be surplus capacity for a short time.
- Capacity costs could be reduced without any decrease in volume for the product or product type in question.
- If the volume of some product or product type is increased, capacity costs could increase (because they can increase step by step).
- If the volume of some product or product type is increased, capacity costs could be unchanged.

4 *Function-related capacity costs,* e.g. costs for administrative services and research. These are capacity costs which can normally be assigned to some function required for a product type. Such costs may have complicated

relationships both with product concepts at different levels at a certain point in time and with various product volumes over time. This is not merely a question of mutual interdependence between product types. Furthermore, product processes are not limited in time either, and therefore the volume of a certain product during a certain period may have a complicated relationship with costs for previous, recent and even future periods.

In addition to the difficulty of identifing cost relationships for product-related capacity costs, there are further difficulties for function-related costs. Some examples are:

● Several product types have common, indivisible resources (e.g. for the development and operation of a computer-based production system). Reducing volume for one product type would not essentially reduce total capacity cost.
● Several product types have common divisible resources for certain functions (e.g. of an administrative nature). Reductions in volume for a product type can affect capacity costs, at least in the long term.
● Several product types have common resources for programmes without any direct relationship with the recent volume of the product (e.g. cost for development capacity).

Capacity costs and utilization of capacity can be primarily affected via the levels in the product hierarchy which are the direct cause of capacity requirements:

● product types;
● product groups;
● business areas;
● total product line.

Does, for example, the existence of a certain product group or a certain business area justify a certain sales or production capacity? It is not enough only to act when relationships are clearly visible. Logical relationships between capacity costs and products are often difficult to identify within a product group or a business area. It may nonetheless be reasonable to imagine relationships between capacity use and the product concept, at least in the long term and at some level of the total product line. Each marginal change regarding products may have only a negligible effect on such costs in the short run; but at a more aggregate level, however, the effects may be substantial if capacity can be made available when product volumes decline sooner or later. Demands on capacity often occur as an aggregate effect of actions for several types of products, rather than for any particular product.

17.2 CONTROL PROCESS

Profitability and cost measures of products are important for the scale-setting and business orientation of an activity and for operational efficiency. They provide a basis for decisions about what products are to be developed and marketed, and at what prices. Analyses of the sales, costs and profitability of products have traditionally been based on product cost calculations and sales budgeting.

Choices between products, both on a continuous and an *ad hoc* basis, basically involve choices between courses of action for product objects of various sizes. Alternatives which vary in how well they are defined often have to be treated in a routine way, but may perhaps have complex relationships with each other. Many choices must be made despite uncertainty as to what courses may be available in the future and relationships between recent and future decisions.

Thus, basically the evaluation of a product is a part of an analysis of a specific course of action which has economic consequences, given particular defined alternatives. Products are often evaluated on a periodic basis, however, more or less separated from such a context. Periodic values are important in the following cases:

- An organization is categorized with regard to product concepts. This is relatively common, especially at more aggregate levels (with labels such as product groups, business areas or similar); trading companies may serve as an example.
- Specific courses of action are explicitly evaluated with regard to the consequences for an organizational unit, as a supplement to an opportunity cost calculation.
- Calculations are made continuously for many small decisions and perhaps only highly standardized elements of opportunity costs are included, if at all.

When products are evaluated, it is products that are in focus, not persons and areas of responsibility. To this extent, information has a purely analytical function as a basis for decision and action. However, there are often also personal ties with products. Somebody may feel a strong sense of personal involvement in the outcome for a certain product or product type. This may, for example, affect attitudes as to how costs should be assigned. This mechanism is most obvious when product concepts appear at different levels in a formal organization. Personal responsibility may be very important, especially at more aggregate levels and for major product units. This means that non-analytical accounting functions may be more important (*see* Chapter 2).

17.3 MEASURES

The product dimension in economic analysis is a decisive factor which sometimes has been neglected in companies with a strong emphasis on organizational units. Both cost calculations and traditional accounting measures are useful. It is important to consider how capital is tied to products.

17.3.1 The product dimension

The starting point for a profitability analysis of products is causal relationships. What revenues and costs can be regarded as caused by products, product types or other defined product objects? In a way, products are the most fundamental objects of business activity: they legitimize the function of companies in society and they give companies their revenues and hence financial viability.

It is thus very desirable to analyse each product object separately. Product calculations fulfil this function and have traditionally had the following form in a manufacturing company:

● Direct materials
● Direct wages
● Direct services purchased
● Production overhead applied
● Sales and administration overhead applied

In many cases, a relatively complicated calculation technique has been required. Relatively demanding allocation techniques have been used, with extensive allocation of indirect costs on the basis of various indexes.

The conditions for separating product objects from each other have changed in recent years.[2] On the one hand, mutual dependence between products is more and more typical in company activities, as described above. On the other hand, information technology has improved the possibility of identifing relationships between products and costs. This means that it should be possible to formulate the problem of assigning costs to products in somewhat different and more general terms than in the past.

Real and observable causal relationships only exist to a very limited extent, or at least identification in terms of numbers is not economically justified. Consequently, approximation models with a varying degree of arbitrariness are inevitable if the bulk of the costs are to be assigned to product units, product types, product groups, etc. An important question in individual cases will thus be, what level in a product hierarchy should be in focus when possible actions are analysed:

● total product line,
● business areas,
● product groups,
● product types,
● product units.

The possibilities of assigning costs can be discussed from this viewpoint. There are relatively few basic problems in the case of transaction-related costs. Some costs will be direct, i.e. their relationships to products are clear and they are assigned to single product units or product types without allocation indexes. For example, in companies with physical production, the production of one product is separable from another, physically and in accounting terms, as well as in terms of the amount of resources for these products.

Normally cost relationships are more complicated. This is true especially of capacity costs. The first step is to refer capacity costs to organizational units or functions which have reasonably strong links with these costs:

- procurement,
- different forms of physical production,
- different forms of service production,
- sales operations,
- logistics operations,
- after-sales,
- support functions.

Each of these functions, or at least some sub-functions, are closely related to some level in a product hierarchy. It is thus easy to assign costs to this level. Subsequently, it is also easy to make analyses at the product level to which the main functions are closely related. Sometimes this may be appropriate and sufficient. When analysis needs to be applied at a lower product level, however, difficulties occur. How are various products connected to various functions? What are the cost- and capital-determining factors within units and functions ('cost drivers', 'variability factors')?[3] How can these in turn be related to specific products, so that costs can be assigned to products on this basis? Such factors need to be identified, function by function.

A detailed classification into sub-functions *may* be appropriate for a cost allocation based on causal relations. In order to have well-defined relationships between functions and products, it is desirable only to aggregate functional elements for which both cost- and capital-determining factors and cost relationships are reasonably similar. There is a need for trade-offs. In an extreme case, each sub-function might contain only one element for each product unit. On the other hand, this would mean that the assignment of costs to sub-functions in the first place would be more arbitrary. Another question is how small sub-functions with limited tasks can be identified at all.

With such an approach to assigning capacity costs, direct costs will have a less important role as a general allocation index. Moreover, working time, which used to be a very important index, will be largely replaced by machine time, due to increased mechanization and automation. In many cases simple volume and value measures will not be appropriate allocation indexes. Factors such as product line and order sizes will be important for selling and handling costs, for instance. Product costs based on such allocation concepts can therefore differ very much from product costs based on traditional methods, because allocation is based on specific cost relationships for each sub-function to a greater extent.

In the long run, a financially autonomous company needs to cover all its costs, irrespective of product/cost relationships. Both full cost and variable cost calculations can provide a basis for evaluations with this ultimate aim. With regard to allocation problems, we draw two types of conclusion:

1 Increasingly complex cost relationships call for a greater emphasis on what product objects can be separated from each other from a profitability point of view. Calculations for product groups, business areas, etc. are therefore likely to become increasingly important. At the same time, there is a need for calculations at product unit and product type level, particularly for pricing and inventory valuation.

2 For each level in a product hierarchy, decisions must be made about what costs to allocate; costs which are not allocated require an increase in targeted surplus. The choice of basic philosophy is important, especially at the lowest product level, i.e. for product units with the most immediate relationships with company revenues. Capacity costs need to be considered for product units in some way. If costs are not allocated, the surplus target must be increased to a corresponding extent. Thus, the target for product revenues is affected in turn, either through computed product costs or by the surplus target.

17.3.2 Main types of measures

The guiding line for choosing courses of action is economic measures, not traditional accounting measures. This is true for products too, of course. The main basis is opportunity cost concepts, the opportunity values of resources and related economic considerations, irrespective of the accounting conventions which are applied. Periodic measures, including traditional accounting measures, have an important function, however, in continuous evaluation of plans and outcome (see above).

In principle, economic measures involve specific courses of actions, while traditional accounting measures show plans and outcome for periods based on accounting conventions. This results in some basic differences in content:

1 One coherent economic object can be split up between several periods in accounting. The impression from accounting measures can be more negative or positive initially than justified in the light of the economic meaning of transactions. For instance, plans for a new product may mean that the first few years will provide smaller realized revenues than the accounting costs, while in economic calculations this might be regarded as an investment which yields reasonable rate of return from an overall perspective. Another example might be a construction company which needs a reference object for a newly developed technology; initially the company is prepared to accept an order at a loss, despite an accounting deficit. Future benefits from such an order are uncertain and, even if they

do arise, will not be reflected in the accounting numbers until later. A third example involves risks. Economic calculations, and sometimes also internal measures, can include a computed compensation for risks and at the same time corresponding revenues. Accounting, on the other hand, involves losses which in some sense have occurred; this kind of loss often appears in a later period than revenues, e.g. guarantee costs and credit losses.

2 Economic measures may include opportunity cost elements, which have no equivalent in accounting. Accounting, on the other hand, can include costs for capacity without any real opportunity value; they are therefore not considered in economic calculation. Interest on equity is often regarded as a cost in economic calculations and is sometimes taken into account in internal accounting measures, but not in public traditional accounting measures. On the other hand, costs for unutilized production capacity and development costs for future products are often included in public measures although it is far from clear that they should be debited as costs in economic calculations for products marketed during a certain period.

3 Some phenomena appear in both economic calculations and traditional accounting, but the valuation principles are different. It is important and common that product costing is often based on current prices for resources, while traditional accounting is based on historical costs.[4] The method for computing interest on borrowed capital in economic calculations can be close to an accounting method or may deviate rather significantly.

The relationship between economic and traditional accounting income for a period can be summarized in the following way:

Revenue for the period
- Pre-determined full cost of goods sold
- Indirect costs not allocated

= *Surplus on partial ex ante basis*
± Differences between *ex ante* and *ex post* calculations

= *Surplus on ex post basis*
± Valuation differences for resource prices
+ Interest costs for equity in economic calculations
± Differences as to costs for debts
± Differences as to costs for risks
+ Other special economic costs
- Other special accounting costs, except tax costs

= *Income before taxes*
- Tax costs

= *Income after tax*

Economic calculations assume certain production and sales volumes, often for a normal year. If outcome deviates from volume assumptions, the sum of allocated indirect costs will deviate from the corresponding actual indirect costs. The resultant adjustments are one aspect of the differences between *ex ante* and *ex post* calculations. Moreover, it must be considered that inventory changes may contribute to a failure to match revenues/costs and income/capital to the extent that product costs include items properly regarded as periodic costs. Costs which are not important for future revenues can be included in cost allocations and hence in inventory values. If inventory volume increases, accounting income will be improved for one period and at the same time capital will tend to increase particularly strongly. When inventories decrease in a subsequent period, capital is initially valued too high and at the same time accounting income will be lower than called for.

The distinction between traditional accounting measures and economic calculations is very clear if a traditional public accounting measure is compared with a specific calculation for a large object with specific opportunity costs. In the case of internal accounting measures and continuous product calculations, the differences are sometimes not so obvious. Furthermore, traditional accounting measures may include some opportunity values. Periodic reporting systems often include surpluses for products, possibly with economic cost items, i.e. periodic measures and product measures are integrated.

The differences between economic measures and traditional accounting measures will be especially evident when variable costing has been applied to individual product units. In this case, costs for available capacity will not be assigned to products in economic calculations but will be considered in traditional accounting even when opportunity values for function- and product-related resources are low. For instance, the capacity cost for fixed assets can be computed on the basis of historical cost, alternative use or future re-acquisitions adjusted to future volume needs.

17.3.3 Considering product capital demands

Under full costing, interest costs are assigned for products. Interest costs largely represent capacity costs for fixed assets and working capital, and are sometimes product-related but more often function-related. With variable costing, a separate rate of return target for product capital is the main option. Interest computations and separate rate of return targets require that capital items can be allocated to products. One major problem is the extent to which items of capital employed – machines, buildings, inventory, accounts receivable and operating liabilities – can be assigned to different product levels on a causal basis:

Machines are often common for various products. This is true for heavy machines in early production stages and also for light machines in later stages. In the case of operation time, there are often relatively good possibilities of stating use at low product levels, directly or indirectly. These

capital is not relevant. Such an interest rate represents a target based on potential.

In practice, calculated interest rates often express an average cost for the whole capital employed. Such an average may in turn be based on the cost of the whole loan capital and the whole equity, with proportions for these financing forms as weights. Assume that the cost of equity (at 5 per cent inflation) is 18 per cent before tax and the cost of loans is 9 per cent. Assume furthermore that the debt-to-equity ratio is 2 : 1. The calculated interest rate for capital employed will thus be 12 per cent (18 x 1/3 + 9 x 2/3).

An approach employing average interest rates can be given several interpretations:

● It reflects a satisfying philosophy with focus on major need-based requirements. Product calculations should primarily permit identification of products for which profitability is not sufficiently high in view of the general financial needs of the company as a whole.
● It can be conceived as an approximation to more long-term marginal interest rates.
● Companies avoid the use of more than one interest concept in management control. Average interest rates of the kind mentioned above are sufficiently close to accounting interest costs and accounting target rates. Relationships are rather simple and relatively clear between product cost calculations at a low level in a product hierarchy and more responsibility-oriented product concepts at high levels, for which accounting approaches are often regarded as reasonable.

An interest computation may also be based on levels previously attained on the average for all capital, rather than on the cost for forms of financing. In practice, some methods can be said to reflect this. Thus they represent a target based on potential.

Capital needs are relatively limited for many products, product groups, etc. An interest cost calculated in accordance with the above methods will therefore be low, perhaps negligible. There may, however, be other risks in financial terms which need to be considered in cost calculations: risks when different kinds of capacity are built up, as well as price risks and operational risks.[5] A consultancy firm project at a fixed price can serve as an example.

17.4.2 Calculated interest cost or required level of surplus

For a complete comparison between economic calculations and accounting measures, both measures and targets need to be taken into consideration. Levels required for return on equity and loans may be treated in accordance with one of the following main methods:

● In a specific full-cost calculation, calculated interest cost on capital employed is included, i.e. also a proportion for interest on equity.

- In a specific variable-cost calculation, no computed interest cost is assigned to products. When surplus targets are defined, compensation for capital should be included.
- In a specific full-cost calculation, some proportion of the return required may be excluded from calculated interest cost, and is instead taken into account in the surplus targets.
- In a specific variable-cost calculation, some capital is regarded as variable, and to this extent products are charged with interest cost. In other respects, requirements take the form of surplus targets.

These alternatives make it quite clear that a required rate of return can be represented either as a calculated cost or as an element in a separate surplus target. In terms of the real burden, the total levels required may be equivalent. There are, however, differences from a technical point of view. When outcome is reviewed, a calculated cost will normally be computed as a predetermined, interest rate (or possibly several differentiated rates) applied to *outcome* for the *capital* of products (determined through direct registration and/or index allocations). Even if a separate surplus target is determined with capital tied up in products as the sole basis for calculation, the result does not need to be equivalent in terms of real burden. Separate targets are often formulated in terms of predetermined estimations of capital per product, rather than subsequent outcome.

Furthermore, from a behavioural point of view the next question is whether a calculated cost gives the same impulses as a separate surplus target, even if they involve an equivalent burden. Small or negative surpluses tend to lead to strong reactions, regardless of measurement methods. The combination of high surpluses and high targets may give weaker impulses than a smaller surplus in combination with a rate of return requirement which is included in allocated costs. Short-term effects on sales prices and product line choices may occur, and possibly also a risk that capacity costs will increase unnecessarily, sooner or later.

From a strict causal point of view, not all capital components can be referred to the same level in a product hierarchy. Different forms of inventory may serve as an example. This phenomenon in itself involves a choice between principles:

- Causal allocations are made for each capital component at as low a level as possible; surplus targets will have to make up the difference for capital which is not allocated. Inventory should be assigned to each appropriate product level, as should the calculated cost for various forms of inventory.
- Each type of capital – inventory, accounts receivable, etc. – is assigned to the lowest level to which the main proportion can be attributed from a causal point of view.
- With an approximate method the entire capital employed is assigned to the same product level. This is the simplest way of comparing calculated cost components and surplus targets.

transfer pricing under quasi-market conditions (*see* Chapter 16). In this case foreign subsidiaries – at least the successful ones – will tend to become independent companies, and will cease to be purely distribution channels. This was a common situation, for example, in leading Swedish multi-national companies for a few decades, until the end of the 1970s.

Table 17.1 Control strategies for product divisions and local sales units

Product division	Local sales company
Independence strategies	
1 No consolidation, commercialized revenues for goods delivered	1 Commercialized cost for goods received
2 No consolidation, revenues based on predetermined standard costs of production	2 Goods received valued at production standard costs
Coordination strategies	
3 Consolidation	3 Goods received valued at some form of standard prices, determined on the basis of production costs or the market
4 No total profit responsibility	4 Goods received at production standard costs
5 Consolidation	5 Actual production costs are the basis for product values

Alternatives 3 to 5 are, in their various forms, more an expression of co-ordination between product and sales units. *Alternative 3* is relatively common and normally means that profit responsibility of product divisions involves external revenues and the cost of the total process, possibly with the exception of certain sales and administrative costs in the sales company which are common for several products and difficult to allocate. Profit responsibility for a sales company, on the other hand, has a local focus. Transfer prices have often been set as a co-ordinating instrument, without actually aiming at a degree of freedom close to that of an independent company.[9]

Alternatives 4 and 5 mean, in fact, that sales subsidiaries have a clear profit responsibility for the whole process, from the very beginning in the parent company country to the ultimate delivery to a local customer. At least in a formal sense, moreover, they have profit responsibility for their local profit, based on official transfer prices. For product divisions in these cases, there is either a pronounced, wide profit responsibility (*Alternative 5*) or a more classical functional responsibility (*Alternative 4*). Of course, transfer prices are not required in *Alternative 5*.

The independence strategy (especially *Alternative 1*) and the co-ordination strategies (*Alternatives 3, 4 and 5*) have their respective advantages. Independence strategies should primarily promote the recruitment of managers, motivation and local adjustment capabilities. Foreign subsidiaries will be more attractive as working places for managers who appreciate independence, which is often essential for handling local markets. On the other hand, a co-ordination strategy can support a globally co-ordinated performance in terms of marketing, logistics, production and development.

A multinational company needs both locally oriented actions and global co-ordination. Both perspectives need to be sufficiently represented. Therefore, at any particular point in time, the issue is whether emphasis needs to be changed or not. Is there a need for a stronger emphasis on regional units at the expense of business areas or vice versa? Changing accounting methods may be a powerful tool for influencing this emphasis. If incentives are needed for more decisive local action, *Alternative 1* and possibly *Alternative 2* may often be powerful instruments. If, on the other hand, global co-ordination needs to be strengthened, *Alternatives 3 to 5* are to be preferred at that particular point in time. Control philosophies of this kind are rarely appropriate for ever. They are appropriate for a certain period, for a few years, with regard to the current situation.

NOTES

[1] This will also affect valuation of inventory in public accounting in cases where valuation is related to the size of direct costs.

[2] For a description *see* e.g. Johnson, H. T. and Kaplan, R. S. *Relevance Lost: The Rise and Fall of Management Accounting* (1987).

[3] *See* Johnson, H. L. and Kaplan, R. S. (1987), and Madsen, V. *Regnskabsvaesendets opgaver og problemer i ny belysning* (1959).

[4] *See* Chapters 9 and 10.

[5] *See* Section 13.1.

[6] Changes in specific and general price levels in this context are discussed in Chapter 10.

[7] See Section 16.2.

[8] We use a form of terminology that is common in practice, even if the term 'consolidation' has a somewhat different meaning than in group accounting.

[9] *See* Chapters 15 and 16 regarding the profit responsibility of functional units.

CHAPTER 18

Capital projects

Capital investments give business operations their long-term, often decisive, and to some extent inevitable working conditions. Profitability targets for investments are highly important, not only for individual companies but also for the orientation and scale-setting of economic activities in society at large.

OVERVIEW

The evaluation of capital investments basically involves specific effects of certain courses of action which increase or maintain capacity. Durable resources are acquired, sacrifices and benefits are spread over time and capacity with limited alternative use is built up, at the same time as unavoidable financial commitments are made. Trade-offs regarding interest and risks are necessary. The economic value of new capacity is conditioned by its contribution to old capacity. Even if there is a positive contribution at the margin, the total effect of both potential and previous capital investments may be different.

It is important to consider all the consequences of an investment alternative throughout its whole lifetime, irrespective of periodic limits. Even evaluation from a periodic perspective is meaningful, however, at least as a supplement, due to the nature of the control process. Capital investment budgeting is thus the primary basis for decisions, but periodic accounting measures also have an important function, both in the planning and outcome stages. The perspective of periodic accounting measures is in practice relatively short term and may be contrary to a capital budgeting perspective, which is basically long term. Organizational designs and procedures emphasizing accounting measures at the expense of capital budgeting may cause somewhat stronger pressure in the direction of a short-term horizon.

There are several fundamental differences between capital budgeting measures and traditional accounting measures. Expected cash flows are the basis for the economic income concept, not the revenues realized. Economic measures express the effects of a specific course of action over several periods, while traditional accounting measures for a business unit represent an organizational totality, and are divided up into periods. Economic measures basically involve a marginal rate of return, while traditional accounting measures normally show an average rate of return on total invested capital. In principle, the rates of return required are marginal in an economic calculation, while targets for accounting measures can often be seen as average requirements. If both could be defined with regard to need, and if, in addition, risks could be considered in a similar fashion, there is no reason why a long-term difference should arise. The long-term consequences of 'defensive' capital investments on corporate financial statements should be considered. The most important capital investments in many companies nowadays are acquisitions. There is reason to make traditional acquisition calculations as well as analyses of the effects on accounting-based key ratios.

18.1 STRUCTURE OF CAPITAL PROJECTS

Capital investments mean commitments to financial sacrifices with the objective of achieving subsequent advantages. An essential element of risk taking in a company is inherent in this. Sacrifices, to some extent of uncertain size, will be followed by future positive effects, which are even more uncertain.

18.1.1 Capital projects as separate objects

In principle, capital investment decisions mean that courses of action are evaluated with regard to some reasonably well-defined conditions. Analytically, this is a different perspective to that involved in evaluating a continuous activity for an organizational unit on a periodic basis.

In essence, these alternatives will give a new permanent capacity, in the past often as a result of tangible assets but nowadays more and more often in other forms, e.g. as a result of research or market development. The contribution of new capacity will cause a number of specific effects in terms of risks and possible costs and revenues. At the same time, there may be ties to previous activities to a varying degree:

- A capital investment means a rationalization of previous processes but does not change product orientation, production volumes or markets
- A capital investment means a larger volume, basically of the same products in the same markets.
- It may be possible to introduce new products in old markets as a result of the capital investment.
- New sales capacity is built up in new markets for the old product line.
- R&D activity is initiated within a new field.
- A new company is acquired without any real operational synergies.

The economic value of new capacity is conditioned by what old capacity there is and what new resources contribute to this. Even if additional capital has a value at the margin, the total effect of new and previous investments may be different. It is not unusual for companies to make defensive investments, to counteract cost increases or declines in revenue, and thus achieve considerable marginal effects. Nonetheless, the total company rate of return on capital may shrink from period to period (but possibly less than would have been the case if defensive investments had not been made). A capital investment is a part of a total entity, for which the following type of questions should be asked. Can a better yield be achieved on corporate capital in some alternative use? Should defensive capital investments continue until other alternatives show up for the entity?

18.1.2 Capital project activities

Capital investments mean that capacity is built up or at least maintained. They create a necessary basis for future business opportunities, but may also mean new business risks. Liquid resources are exchanged for new business capacity, which is less liquid; resource use and effects on future cash flows are by nature uncertain. Inevitable financial commitments are made at the same time as additional business capacity has limited alternative use – this is important from a risk point of view.

In classical investment processes a basic investment is followed by possible further in- and outflows, either continuously or when the use of resources ceases. This pattern is not general, however. For instance, when leasing transactions are carried out, there is no single primary sacrifice at any one point in time but instead a time pattern of cash outflows and benefits which varies from case to case. It is however of fundamental importance that resources are durable. There are a few general significant considerations. Sacrifices and benefits are spread over time, making both interest payments and risk very important.

18.2 CONTROL PROCESS

Analyses of capital investments involve the scale-setting and business orientation of a company. Courses of action and their specific effects are under consideration, not the personal responsibilities of the type associated with organizational units. From this perspective, information may perhaps be expected to have an analytical function, without a personal touch. Personal ties to capital investments and capital investment calculations may, however, be very strong.[1] Professional convictions and ambitions and the uncertainties involved in building up capacity are important elements in the process in which capital investment decisions are made.

To some extent, decisions about capital investment projects are made separately from decisions about day-to-day operations. Decision routines will in any case be related to the organizational structure for continuous activities. Every manager responsible for day-to-day operations is given authority which is limited, for example, in the following way. In the case of minor investments up to a certain amount, functional or business unit managers are given an allocation of a certain size, which they can utilize without requesting permission on every specific occasion. Corresponding amounts are higher for every step upwards in the organizational hierarchy. Only the company board can make formal decisions above a certain amount level.[2]

In many cases, there is considerable uncertainty not only about future benefits but perhaps also about the size and amount of the sacrifices to be made. For a manager responsible for profit, new capacity represents both opportunities and threats, at business and personal levels. Those who are most involved in the future are obviously often the strongest driving forces behind a project. They need both to convince and inform others when real and formal decisions are to be made. Calculations will therefore be a tool for arguing a case as well as for actual analysis. In this process a superior manager attaches considerable weight to his or her other general confidence in a manager responsible for profit and to confidence in his or her activity. It is not an uncommon view that business unit managers 'qualify themselves' for investment funds. Those who have proved to be able to manage capital in the past, have an important advantage when project plans are scrutinized. In other words, accounting measures for previous periods will be important.

Traditional accounting measures for organizational units will also have great, if not the greatest, importance in practice for future following-up of operations. It is not often considered possible and desirable to separate and follow up the effects of specific investments. The future periodic income of a unit, including the effects of a specific capital investment, will certainly be most important for managers responsible for profit. Therefore, in practice the periods in which the effects of capital investments occur will be of some importance. The definition of accounting periods will therefore be of some significance when capital investments are made, despite the fundamental idea that the consequences for the entire life of the investment should be evaluated without regard to period boundaries. Sometimes, capital investments are also evaluated on a systematic basis from a periodic perspective.

In practice, certain capital investment decisions will almost entirely be period decisions, i.e. they are extraneous to capital investment project routines. Originally, such routines were primarily applied to physical assets such as machines and buildings. Other investments, in the sense in which the term is used here, were regarded as periodical. Initially, leasing involved some kind of ambiguity. The acquisition of tangible assets in such forms could be made within a day-to-day operation, without specific scrutinizing at different levels in accordance with capital investment routines. Over the years, intangible investments – such as research and product and market development – have become increasingly important. Decisions have to some extent been made within traditional investment routines, and have to some extent been related to periodical decisions about programme costs in day-to-day operations.

Resource decisions handled in accordance with formal routines are not necessarily the most important from an economic point of view. Formal routines may not be employed for more important decisions, for example regarding market development or recruitment, in which the company's future obligations may in fact involve substantial sums, in comparison with some investments in machines. Resource allocation systems may not be fine tuned with regard to the importance of the consequences. Especially in the case of business units, it is very common to find examples of decisions which have potential long-term consequences, but may be taken with less formality than a rather minor traditional capital investment decision.

18.3 MEASURES

Economic measures are a primary basis for decisions about capacity but traditional accounting income and rate of return measures also have a role to play. Economic and accounting measures represent two perspectives: (uncertain expectations about) the long-term outcome for individual major projects and short-term periodic outcome for organizations as a whole, respectively. Both approaches are justified in terms of the nature of the control process, for physical as well as intangible investments.

18.3.1 Main types of measures

In principle, estimates of future inflows and outflows, related to an investment, are required as a basis for the investment calculation. Moreover, a required yield must be defined as a basis for calculation. This reflects a minimum target required by the investors.

One possible criterion is discounted cash flow value, with the required rate of return as the discounting rate. If the discounted value of the whole series of annual cash flow surpluses is identical to the size of the primary investment, there will be a rate of return at the same level as the required rate. If the discounted value is higher (or lower) than the primary investment, the investment will provide more (or less) than the required minimum rate. Another criterion is the internal rate of return, i.e. the interest rate at which the discounted value of future inflows and outflows is the same as the primary investment.

Optimal capital use, in line with these views, is attained when capital is allocated to projects which are expected to provide the highest interest rate or the highest discounted value (or the most favourable value according to any other similar criterion). Measures of these kinds are the fundamental basis of investment decisions. From the owner's point of view, ideally investments should be carried out if they increase the market value of shares. Such investments give long-term cash flows with a rate of return which is higher than the rate required by the market (at a given risk level). Alternatively, investment calculations can be made, based on company or company management prerequisites rather than those of owners. In this case, too, the guideline will be long-term cash flows. In practice, alternatives which include benefits rather close in time will perhaps receive priority in calculations, simply because they are easier to envisage.

Traditional accounting income and return on capital measures are a reasonable basis for evaluating capital investments, both at the planning and review stages. It may be necessary to compute both the marginal effects of an investment and the total level for some organizational entity. This is particularly true for capital investment in the form of major corporate acquisitions. A periodic accounting measure with a relatively short-term perspective may of course provide a different picture to an investment calculation which takes, at least in formal terms, a long-term perspective. It is hardly astonishing that an accounting perspective sometimes tends to be described as an illogical obstacle to long-term objectives.

An accounting perspective is, however, meaningful in view of the nature of the control process:

- It is necessary to follow all business processes continuously, including those initiated by capital investment.
- It is important to judge business totalities, not only specific courses of action.
- Delegation to players with responsibility for day-to-day operations is common. Periodic review of their responsibility areas is essential. These players have often been strong forces behind an investment decision. At any rate, they are responsible for how added capacity is used.
- Most systematic review systems are based on periodic reporting of traditional accounting measures for organizational units. Subsequent identification of the effects of specific courses of action often involves considerable difficulties, both in principle and in practice.

There is thus a need for periodic reviews, which are based on measures that function in processes where rhetoric and strong personal feelings are natural elements. Both *ex ante* and *ex post*, the total picture of a company or a single area of responsibility must be clarified. Economic measures, based on expectations about future payments which are difficult to measure, are often insufficient, especially since they only cover individual projects. Traditional income and return on capital measures have an important advantage from a control and review point of view since they are based to a greater (and essential) extent on events which have occurred and been recorded, rather than on expectations. Certainly, as we have had cause to reiterate in this book, these measures are not always robust and unbiased with regard to persons. But nonetheless, they provide verifiable data which is most valuable in periodical reviews.

18.3.2 Economic measures in comparison with income and return on capital in traditional accounting terms

Economic measures are based on the economic value concept. Income arises when cash flows come closer in time and expectations about future flows change. Measures in accordance with some accounting convention will certainly also be based on expectations to some extent (e.g. the valuation of assets or calculation of depreciation). However, in traditional accounting, the main principle is that expectations about future values should be fulfilled – or at least have a high degree of probability – before income is recognized or depreciation adjusted. A clear example is the income concept based on historical cost and a prudent approach.

Accounting measures for organizational units and economic measures for single investment objects, for a given period, will also be different for other reasons:

- Economic measures should capture the consequences of specific courses of action, while traditional accounting measures should give a picture of a total organizational unit embracing several projects of different duration and age.
- Economic measures (when discounted value or internal rate of return methods are used) express a marginal rate of return for a specific course of action, while traditional accounting measures show average rate of return for total capacity invested at a certain point in time.

Relationships between accounting and economic numbers are complicated and vary with investment patterns, e.g. with regard to age structure and growth rates. We have discussed these issues thoroughly in Chapter 2.

18.3.3 Effects of economic and accounting measures on time perspectives

Control methods based on traditional income and return on capital measures, which are periodic by nature, tend to reinforce a short-term perspective to a greater extent than control methods based on economic measures which focus on alternative courses of action. A shift from a perspective where courses of action are in focus to a more periodical perspective or vice versa contributes to a change (planned or unplanned) in time perspectives. In recent years, many organizational changes have meant a heavier emphasis on periodic income and return on capital measures, and hence also a shorter time perspective for capital investments.

Resource allocation may thus be affected by a transition from a functional organization (with traditional capital budgeting) to an organization with a strong emphasis on profit centre responsibility. The need to review periodically an activity in accounting terms increases if authority is delegated; this is particularly true in the case of transition to profit centres. As a result, there may also be a shift in the time focus of management control – and the intention is frequently that observable user needs should receive greater priority.

'Periodic pressure' as a result of the stock market listing of shares, and the resultant effect on capital investments within a company, is a classic problem. On the one hand, the value of shares is a function of long-term cash flows. Therefore it should be consistent with shareholders' interest to implement projects which satisfy their rate of return requirements, even if the expected positive cash flows will not occur for a number of years. On the other hand, the stock market and information intermediaries focus on short period accounting measures to a great extent. At least two interpretations are possible:

1 The market attaches importance to the fact that promises are met and performance is manifested in numbers.

2 Levels and changes of levels expressed in short-period reporting, are regarded as signals about long-term development.

Both interpretations lead to the conclusion that a reasonably short-term perspective is important for senior management.

Not all business managers seem convinced that information about investments which are only justified from a long-term perspective will have the same strong impact on the stock shares as short-period yield manifested in numbers. Empirically based knowledge about the time perspectives of (recent and potential) shareholders and the possible reactions of senior management to these patterns is meagre, especially with regard to the crucial importance of this issue.

The choice of one accounting measure rather than another for periodic review purposes may affect the time perspective. Traditional income and return on capital measures will often give quite a different picture of the early stages in the investment process than economic income and economic rate of return. It is frequently said that major investments involve a heavy burden on income in the early years, and should therefore not be carried out. The reasons for this view may be largely traced to differences between measurement methods. One decisive factor is how inflation compensation included in the interest cost is handled in traditional accounting and the resultant allocation effects. The following example illustrates this.

EXAMPLE

The primary investment is 600. Expected gross income is assumed to have a constant real value of 100 for ten years. According to an investment calculation, the real internal rate of return will be approximately 10 per cent and the investment can be entirely financed by loans at a real rate of return of 5 per cent. The loan is to be repaid in ten annual instalments, which means that the annual instalment coincides with a 10 per cent yearly depreciation of the asset. It is assumed that there will be no inflation and it is decided that the investment should take place. Under such conditions the development of net income is illustrated in Table 18.1.

Table 18.1 An investment financed by a loan when monetary value is stable

Year	Gross income	Depreciation	Interest	Net income
1	100	60	30	10
2	100	60	27	13
3	100	60	24	16
4	100	60	21	19
5	100	60	18	22
6	100	60	15	25

Now assume that inflation is expected to be 10 per cent instead of 0. Assume, furthermore, gross income and interest costs are adjusted in line with this, first by means of 10 per cent annual increases in gross income, and second as a result of

the rate of best possible alternative use for the company, or as a weighted average of the cost for the possible additional capital. However, correlations over time are vital. The courses of action at a certain point of time cannot be evaluated without regard to the potential of future project alternatives. Furthermore, the acquisition of additional capital for a project has repercussions on future financing possibilities. Therefore, targets in terms of average rates may be meaningful in practice.

Empirical observations suggest that corporate financial targets for investment projects are often determined without any real degree of accuracy. It is not always easy to identify the theoretical basis. Rates are often determined with regard to the cost of acquiring capital and are based on needs. In principle, such targets should vary with the risk involved, but obviously the extent to which simplicity should dominate such considerations tends to be a matter of convenience. Risk adjustments can be made with regard to the targets of the company or its owners. For organizational reasons, targets are not easily adjusted to changes in the market value of capital – they are often maintained at a stable level over several periods.

Relationships between investment project targets and the traditional accounting rate of return required cannot be stated in general terms. If both types of targets are determined with regard to needs and, moreover, risks are considered in a similar way, there is no reason for a long-term difference. With other assumptions, differences may be justified. The potential rate of return for a certain project may be very high in relation to targets based on needs. This is often the case for defensive investments in activities with low average profitability (see Section 18.1). In addition, targets based on potential or future investment requirements, are frequently stated at higher levels than what is justified with regard to the combined potential for old and new capital. For this reason, targets in terms of economic measures will in practice sometimes be higher than those targets that are tied to accounting measures, which are averaged and involve all capital at a certain point in time, including old capital in line with its original prerequisites.

18.5 CORPORATE ACQUISITIONS AS CAPITAL PROJECTS

Capital investments nowadays often take the form of company acquisitions. It is important to supplement business evaluations, including acquisition calculations, by taking into account the effects on periodic measures. At least major acquisitions should therefore be evaluated with regard to the investment rate of return at the margin *and* the effects on financial ratios for the company as a whole. The fundamental problems of measurement when groups are formed and companies acquired were discussed in Chapter 11.

18.5.1 Relationship between acquisition values and accounting values

It is relatively common for the accounting principles employed in connection with corporate acquisitions to give rise to objections on the part of
managers, for example when acquisitions have unfavourable effects on
financial statements, despite the fact that the deal is considered to be
advantageous. There are thus good reasons for discussing the background,
based on our view that a company acquisition is an investment at group
level.

An ideal accounting method could be outlined, based on the economic
income concept. An acquired company represents a resource which cannot
be re-acquired (*see* Section 10.5). A group has acquired the right to future
cash surpluses at a certain price. Assuming everything thereafter will be as
predicted, the new investment would give a yearly rate of return equal to
the internal rate of return of the investment. Depreciation should reflect
changes in discounted values for future cash flows from the beginning of a
year to year-end. Of course, the effects on group return on equity will
depend on the relative size of the investment.

The effects in practical accounting terms can be described in the following way. We show rate of return on equity in the first year after
acquisition. We disregard possible integration gains, internal transactions
and minority interests. Basically, group income will receive a positive
contribution from the income of subsidiaries. On the other hand, the
financial costs for the acquisition must be taken into account and also
depreciation on the acquisition value for the group of the assets indirectly
acquired (to the extent this value is higher than the corresponding book
value in the subsidiary; depreciation on this book value will reduce the
income of the subsidiary). The financial costs include increased interest
costs, lower interest revenues or the cost of a share issue. In terms of a
formula, this can be expressed in the following way:

$$I_{Gn} = I_{Gk} - F_P + I_S - a(A - E_S)$$

where I_{Gn} = income in Year 1 of the new group (including acquisition of S)

I_{Gk} = income in Year 1 of the old group (without acquisition of S)

F_P = financing costs of parent company (after tax) in Year 1 for
acquisition of S

I_S = income in Year 1 for the new subsidiary

A = acquisition value of parent company for all shares in S, i.e.
book value in the parent company

E_S = equity in the subsidiary at the time of acquisition (beginning of
Year 1)

seldom develop in line with economic income. Furthermore, the combination of financial sources and financial costs for the individual acquisition may in practice be different from what is assumed when the interest cost level is determined in acquisition calculations, perhaps reflecting optimum capital structure from a group point of view. The proportions between debt and equity differ from the relative weights of the required rate of return. Actual financial costs may also deviate from assumptions in the calculation as regards interest cost level.

18.5.2 Accounting for company acquisitions

Accounting for business acquisitions is a vast and complicated area; nevertheless we will try to present some viewpoints in line with the discussion above. The aspects we wish to emphasize can be discussed also on the assumption that everything turns out exactly as was predicted when the acquisition was made.

Ideal accounting should reflect the internal rate of return period by period, based on group acquisition values, not on some value in the books of the company acquired. If goodwill values for the shares acquired, and the related depreciation on these values, appear to be a burden, this may be due to a number of circumstances, of which the following or possibly a combination of the following may be the most important.

1 The rate of return required for the capital investment was relatively low, and the price for the company acquired was subsequently relatively high in relation to future cash flows.

   Return on equity for a newly acquired subsidiary may in itself be rather high. This is not decisive for group return on equity, however. The buyer pays for the right to cash flows with a certain rate of return requirement. If calculations prove correct, precisely this rate of return will occur from a group point of view; any subsidiary return 'above normal' predicted at the time of the transaction should have been taken into account in the acquisition price and should not be a reason for any abnormal income for the new group. A new group should thus not be credited with all income in acquired companies after the date of acquisition. Depreciation of goodwill values is partly an expression of this. This is of interest, for example, to a group manager looking forward to continued high levels of profitability in a corporation which is about to be acquired.

2 Allocation problems may occur in relation to depreciation. Assume a subsidiary which is acquired provides a rate of return at the levels predicted in *ex ante* calculations and in line with book return on equity without an acquisition. Linear depreciations will normally be made. For individual years, such depreciations may be lower or higher than estimates of economic depreciations. Allocations of income between years will thus differ from the economic value concept.

   Justified depreciation patterns (according to economic income) will often deviate sharply from the most common forms of depreciation on goodwill. This is particularly true if there are integration advantages. As we have shown in Chapter 11, the first years of an acquisition are often characterized by low income.

3 To the extent that accounting is based on capital values from recent acquisition calculations, the income and return on capital values will be unfavourable in comparison with values for groups with older assets. There are several partial explanations, as in the case of other fixed assets. In older groups, a growth in value in real terms may have occurred over the years, which among other things will appear in the form of low depreciations. If changes in specific and general prices were fully taken into account, differences between old and new groups would not be that remarkable.

The price paid for a new company and the yield on this capital should be in focus when a company acquisition is analysed. Splitting up capital into a subsidiary component and a goodwill component is not particularly relevant from this point of view. In the group accounting area, there may be unusually large deviations between practical accounting and economic income/economic value. In addition, it is difficult to create meaningful series of numbers over time if group structure is subject to frequent change. Consequently, group accounting data is often an inaccurate, but necessary, basis for control.

NOTES

[1] For a thorough description of these processes *see* Bower, J. L. *Managing the Resource Allocation Process* (1970).

[2] *See* Section 16.4.

[3] *See* Chapters 9 and 10 for a more thorough analysis of effects of specific and general price levels.

CHAPTER 19

Towards theories for measuring and utilizing accounting information

The predominant theme of this book has been issues regarding measures and targets from a financial control perspective, especially periodic information needs. These should also be a core element in accounting theory. Other considerations must also be taken into account, however:

- Accounting information used for other purposes than financial control.
- Processes for the use of information and systems development.
- The possible effects of economic control instruments at various organizational levels, including society at large. To what extent is it possible to exercise control in practice and what are the effects of financial control, both from a company's and from a national perspective?

The descriptions and analyses in this book provide a basis for the conclusions and further discussion at all these levels. This is illustrated in this final chapter.

OVERVIEW

Information requirements in a market economy are very largely dependent on how financial markets function in practice. Certainly, verifiability and robustness must be strongly upheld in accounting. The convention of prudence of traditional accounting is a universal guideline, but it can nonetheless be discussed with regard to information needs for financial control. The manner in which traditional accounting measures can be combined with measures on a market basis and on a calculated basis is an important research question. It is rarely desirable that external and internal measures and targets should be kept quite separate from each other with regard to overall effects on society. From a research point of view, it would be interesting to clarify the interplay between internal and public measurement systems over the years and to see what tendencies have developed in recent years.

Behaviourally oriented theories of accounting information must include not only measures and targets, but also processes for systems use and the development and effects of information.

- The processes in the use of systems are of considerable importance for effects on attitudes and action. One fundamental issue is a balance between two interests – on the one hand, a commercially oriented offensive approach in which individuals and their inclination to act decisively in a business situation is stressed; on the other hand, a more systems-oriented approach where 'good and systematic order' are key words and in which accounting information routines are more important. The achievement of both these interests in themselves is valuable. How difficult are they to combine? What is required to achieve this?

- From an information technology point of view, there is considerable freedom of choice as to systems development for the future. The costs of data processing and control processes are important constraints, however. Basically, the issue is not what information everybody should have access to, but rather what a control process in society and in a company should look like. Information technology certainly permits freedom of choice but there will nevertheless be a tendency to concentrate accounting information on what is important to the functioning of financial markets. How should local data in an environment of decentralization be arranged, given these conditions?

- Research on management control with regard to effects has so far had too narrow a perspective to be able to determine the long-term, structural and dynamic effects of financial control. Thus is true both at company and society levels. This is a research area of fundamental importance for the future.

19.1 MEASURES AND TARGETS

The need for information for resource allocation and operational efficiency, in society and companies, has been the main impetus for our analysis of what is appropriate information.

19.1.1 Financial control and other uses of accounting information

Assessing the staying power of companies and sub-units on a continuous basis ultimately means judging future cash flows and determining whether and how conditions are changing period by period. Many people have a common interest in assessing the question of survival in the long term, and also in predicting a company's ability to meet payment and delivery claims from a narrower perspective. To this extent, there is a common information need. Essentially this need was our starting point in Parts Two and Three where we discussed what constitutes appropriate accounting information.

We have stressed that income and rate of return on capital period by period, in relation to cost of equity capital in the market, will give important indications about the probability for owners and other parties of having their interest met. Economic income is an ideal for the construction of income measures but the need to have verifiable and robust measures means that this ideal must often, indeed normally, be abandoned.

As we have already shown, traditional allocations between periods may give misleading indications. At the same time, there is considerable need for short-term periodic accounting. If targets are not modified with regard to changes in specific and general price levels, misleading indications may be reinforced. This dilemma is crucial, especially as traditional accounting numbers are on the 'bottom line' and in fact attract the greatest attention. Misleading indications may be of such a magnitude that there are practical effects; they frequently seem to contribute to an unduly favourable or unfavourable evaluation of individuals and business operations. Developing methods of collecting and communicating supplementary information is therefore important. Major measures in public information are important but need to be supplemented. The more complicated business activities and the standard-setting processes are, the more reason there is to interpret measures critically and to supplement them with regard to fundamental information needs.

Measurement principles in themselves can also be discussed from this point of view. Basically, the capacity to generate cash flow surpluses should be reflected in income and return on capital measures as soon as the important conditions of verifiability and robustness are fulfilled. The convention of prudence in traditional accounting may be questioned as a general guideline for at least two reasons:

1 Separable resources operations and market-related financial operations are becoming more common in companies. Verifiable market values are often available for the valuation of resources and obligations. If a common information need, period by period, is to be satisfied, related to cost of equity capital in the market, there are strong reasons for using verifiable market values where they are relevant. As we have emphasized above, in practice, international tendencies seem to be in line with this.
2 The convention of prudence in its traditional form means that assets and debts will be given excessively low and high values respectively. In periods of recession, the decrease of the reserves thus created may cause a delay before the impact of more recent tendencies affect income and rate of return measures. This causes additional uncertainty about the interpretation of periodic values and this is highly undesirable in view of the need to follow the performance of company and sub-units period by period.

Apart from common information needs, there are also special needs related to each particular claim on the company and the decisions called for in these contexts. One fundamental issue for each claim is the time scale and the cash flows which can be mobilized from various sources. What inflows are possible for resources which cannot be separated? Expected surpluses cannot automatically be the basis of loans and for this reason liquidity will also be an important dimension in companies with the prospect of favourable operations ahead. What inflows are possible for separable resources? Assets with a certain value in the long term, could, if sold, produce higher or lower inflows from a short-term perspective.

The viewpoints of many people on accounting information are not related to their own information needs in the senses discussed above. Other effects may be more in focus. Two special interests are mentioned here: protection of creditors and the need for a basis for taxation. One main issue is the extent to which demands on information systems for such purposes will deviate from common information needs with regard to financial control.

Accounting information may have direct effects on wealth, possibly favouring one party at the cost of another. Information systems may have been chosen with such a primary concern in mind. Protection of creditors is one example. The system has been designed to counteract excessive dividends. In this respect, the convention of prudence is in the interest of creditors. Information needs as to creditworthiness of borrowers will not be improved, however; the contrary is more likely. As long as the scope for dividends is directly shown on the balance sheet, creditor protection of this kind can not be combined with valuation which focuses more on information needs. When public information systems are chosen, there is thus a fundamental conflict of interest rather than an important difference between the information needs of different parties.

In addition, when accounting information is to provide a basis for taxation, demands are different from the information needs mentioned above, both from a representational and measurement systems point of view.

- The degree of liquidity has a greater importance for taxation than for evaluations of long-term survival and measures used period by period in relation to this.
- One single, and inevitably inaccurate, income measure will be the basis for taxation and have immediate effects on wealth. When inaccurate measures are the basis for decisions about resource allocation and use, they are only one part of the overall basis. What is acceptable to meet such a part of an information need does not have to be acceptable as an independent basis for taxation.
- The consequences of deficiencies in the robustness and stability of accounting numbers may be important and somewhat arbitrary when taxation is based on certain numbers at a certain moment in time and these numbers naturally fluctuate over time. When the ability to survive financialy is to be assessed period by period, such variations are taken into account in the interpretation of numbers, i.e. the method of determining targets may be modified.
- Data also need to be reliable and verifiable in detail for a taxation system. Trade-offs between representational and measurement systems requirements may thus differ from those where systems are intended to guide allocation and use of resources.
- The ability of the players concerned to predict the future design of a system should be of a different nature in a tax context because direct effects on wealth are involved.

With this background, the obvious question is how taxation and public information should be related to each other. In our view of the role of public accounting for economic efficiency in society, there is an apparent conflict of interests. The idea that there are more or less 'correct' values,

dominant role. As information providers, they had considerable influence over what information was supplied by the company to owners and other public players. With a central accounting department they also had internal systems design under their control, since they presided over centralized accounting systems. This dominant senior management role is, in fact, no longer so prevalent (we shall return to this below).

In the processes for the production, distribution and use of accounting information, two interests must be balanced against each other. On the one hand, the motivation and creativity of individuals should be stimulated without collectivistic compulsory restrictions, either as to business action or information search. On the other hand, more systems-oriented requirements must also be satisfied. Routines, including routines for accounting information, should function in a reliable manner. Data should be comparable. Both publicly and internally there is a conflict between these interests.

Maintaining a balance between these two factors has proved particularly difficult at the internal level in some companies. What are the underlying reasons? Why are these two interests so difficult to combine? Are messages that two interests need to be considered too complicated for an organization? In practice companies actually go from one extreme position to the other. To what extent is behaviour at the lowest organizational levels tied to personalities and to what extent is it affected by the influence of higher management? Is the nature of working tasks at the lowest levels ultimately the decisive factor? After all, when practical work is to be carried out minute by minute and day by day, it is difficult to make allowances between competing factors.

This balance between two interests is a researchable area of great practical importance. We will explore this issue to a certain extent by specifying two important demands which should be considered in this context.

19.2.2 Need to support input routines

In the past, accounting systems have been subject to a vast amount of reconciliation and checking procedures. It has often been pointed out that this 'accounting orientation' is not particularly business-like. Accounting is a 'Zahlenfriedhof', a 'numbers graveyard', to mention an often quoted expression from Schmalenbach. Accounting information was considered to appear with too much delay and often too late to be a basis for action.

Another important view has developed gradually and has perhaps tended to predominate: accounting data should be distributed quickly. This is more urgent than accuracy in detail. Actions and effects are important, not excessive attention to numbers as such. In many companies, the post of controller at different levels has become very common in recent decades, to some extent as a reflection of this view. For many years in the debate on management control, the tendency was perhaps to emphasize controlling at the expense of a more traditional accounting role. It was a natural over-reaction to the previous situation, when detailed checking and reconciliation operations predominated, perhaps sometimes out of all proportion to their practical importance.

Views of this kind shift from time to time. In recent years, it has been evident again on certain occasions that special – and perhaps unexpectedly great – attention needs to be devoted to qualities such as reliability of data and good internal control. This is particularly true in the case of many systems which are often regarded as pre-systems to an accounting system. Qualities of this kind are often a function of processes around a data system as such, not only the system structure itself. To what extent do various suppliers of information operate *de facto* in accordance with appropriate instructions? How do various units for checking and reconciliation function? One basic difficulty has been attitudes to this kind of work in relation to more controller-oriented work. Traditional accounting tasks have not always seemed attractive; appreciation of traditional accounting work has sometimes been given something of a lip service in a business-oriented environment.

Good quality in checking and reconciliation work is of decisive importance for total information and control processes, with regard to the future-oriented functions of the stock market and to internal processes. The internal order should affect external confidence in the numbers provided. Auditors must be able to see that unexplained differences are small in relation to reported income and return on capital levels and, if this is not the case, they should be able to state the contrary in their report. This is important for the whole economic system in the long term. What can be tolerated internally may, perhaps, be more focused on specific effects, in the short and long term. A reasonable degree of certainty regarding accounting data is a basic prerequisite for control processes in companies and societies, however, not least because many unpopular actions require very clear arguments. On some occasions, it has been shown afterwards that certain data about economic conditions have been lacking at critical points of time for companies faced with difficult decisions.

19.2.3 Need to support use of data

Working procedures and routines which support the use of output data are important, both for internal and public information. Decisions about these routines represent an important control instrument *per se*; internal processes are thus to some extent a parameter for senior management. Finding appropriate forms in this respect may be as difficult as finding appropriate measures. Senior managers in major companies describe their control and accounting problems remarkably often in terms of communication with managers and controllers in subordinate units, often labelling them 'training problems' (*see* Section 2.3). Possibly there are several explanations for problems formulated in such terms. We shall mention three mechanisms of different kinds: training problems in decentralized organizations, lack of clarity in controlling principles and routines for control processes.

Training problems

There may of course be important training needs in decentralized organizations, where many working assignments are similar to those at a high level in an independent company. It is still astonishing how often corporate representatives at higher levels describe their problems in these terms. A question of fundamental interest is to what extent this pronounced need for training actually expresses a difference in perspective between units at high and low levels. Subordinate units often believe they can function with their methods to solve the problems which they regard as urgent. Managers of superior units see other problems and other solutions from their point of view. Such a difference will, to some extent, depend on what degrees of freedom various subordinate units should have (we return to this below).

Lack of clarity in control principles

Stablility and clarity regarding allocation of responsibility are good bases for information and for discussions about actions in a decentralized organization. Explicit changes in accounting systems are a very effective pedagogical way of informing a great number of people about group management intentions. The choice of formal control instruments can be one important signal which a superior manager transmits to his or her subordinate units. This is often a very powerful tool; choosing such instruments carefully, is a very important way of expressing intentions to large numbers of subordinates with whom there is not even any direct personal contact. Many practical examples have occurred in recent years, especially in turnaround situations. On the other hand, ambiguities regarding formal control instruments can lead to a confused responsibility picture at lower levels, thus counteracting effective action. Confusion makes communication more difficult and reduces the possibilities of using accounting measures as powerful pedagogical instruments.

Deficient routines for control processes

This involves the way in which individuals work with planning and review data. For instance, traditional practical discussion about internal management control is often limited to what measures and objects should be registered and reported. Analysing all potentially important control instruments is urgent, however: choice of media, planning and review processes, forms for contacts with people, etc. When control problems occur, they are perhaps too often attributed to the formal aspect of control instruments, such as reports *per se*. Working routines receive less attention, which is perhaps natural. Reporting formats are easier to observe and discuss, are less related to individuals and are therefore more accepted targets for open criticism. In addition, they are often easier to change than the deeply rooted working habits of various players.

To illustrate, we can outline the following fictitious example. Management of the A Group have found that their picture of the group's financial position is not totally reliable; indications of problems in various profit centres show up too late. One question discussed is whether the reporting system can be changed so that early-warning signals can be received. When a comparison is made with other companies with similar structure, however, the reporting system as such appears to have basically the same type of content. Several other groups differ in another way. They have invested more in functions for interpreting and transforming data in reports received from profit centres. The important question is, then, whether group management should acquire increased capacity for interpretation operations or not, rather than introduce changes in reporting systems as such.

A key issue in this context is the design of the controller function, i.e. the function of players analysing material about various units and acting in the spirit of a line manager with such analyses as a basis. Most managers in subordinate units welcome constructive discussions with senior representatives of a superior unit. They look upon it as a kind of support, especially if there is an emphasis on issues which subordinate managers themselves perceive as important problems. In the worst case, however, contacts with a controller of a superior unit can be time-consuming, and dominated by questions of detail without much insight. Avoiding such a state is very important.

Selection of individuals for controller positions will thus be crucial. Ideally, controllers have a combination of attributes which are not too common: analytical capacity, power of action, social talent and a good background for understanding products, markets and the facilities of various organizational units. Some structural conditions as to organizational working routines may contribute. For instance, it is of fundamental importance that the controller makes his or her own observations to a considerable extent, and does not only rely on written material. Furthermore, facilitating a personal network is important; patterns of contacts with subordinate units should be uncomplicated, for example by making the real position of a controller very clear and by giving subordinate units contact with only a few people at superior level.

19.3 SYSTEMS DESIGN

The question on whose terms a company should be controlled has become increasingly important with radically improved information technology. In the past, most senior managers have had considerable real influence on public reporting and on internal systems. Is this likely in the future? Will pressure from external demands increase, backed up by new information technology, and will it perhaps be even more legalistic in design and use? Will the importance of local demands increase and be different from those of senior management?

19.3.1 Changed conditions for systems design

In the postwar period, public accounting had a limited role in many countries, since financial markets were relatively undeveloped. Financial accounting measures had little importance from a control point of view. Financial and management accounting could sometimes be co-ordinated from a systems point of view in so-called monistic systems, which were more common in certain countries than others. The main business problem was production, with cost efficiency as a guideline, rather than marketing and revenue generation. Reviewing the production cost of products was a natural step. Companies were organized functionally. The building up of groups had hardly started on any significant scale. Accounting and calculation systems were based on punch card machines or were entirely manual. Individual parts of company systems were perhaps not even co-ordinated with each other.

After some time public reports from companies began to be increasingly open. Even if there were some conflicts of interest between standard setters and companies providing information, standards were still relatively uncontroversial. From the late 1960s accounting information systems were usually computer-based, and undoubtedly offered operational advantages in relation to previous systems in terms of more details in registering, storage, calculation and improved routines for data processing. The new systems required more uniform definitions and increased co-ordination between reports. Information was managed and distributed by central bodies in companies, which had an obvious key role in information-provision processes, both for internal and external use. At the same time, there was a major wave of decentralisation in Europe; many companies were divided up into profit centres.

As time passed, external demands on company information were reinforced, particularly due to the development of financial markets and increased media attention. Business activity also became more complex. Standards of public accounting had more and more controversial elements; compliance decreased, which in turn created counterforces for an increased uniformity between companies. The development towards internal organization and control forms with increased decentralization continued. Accounting information systems required extensive resources for operation, maintenance and development. The importance of specialist knowledge about system issues as such – not only about activities to be supported by systems – became increasingly more evident. Systems cost in a wide sense attracted more attention. Questions were increasingly asked about systems value in relation to costs and what could be done to achieve rationalization. Those questions involved the volume of information and the systems structure in itself. Old core issues, such as what information needs are ultimately important, became more urgent.

From an information technology point of view, there are many possible choices ahead. In the long term, new information technology as such will mean few constraints for those who can decide over systems content.

Communication networks and computers will make many distribution forms possible, publicly as well as internally. Who should then be able to satisfy their own information needs and be able to provide information based on their own responsibility for data? Who should have their information needs covered by data supplied by other people who are responsible for sources of information? Or, more specifically, how will internal availability be affected at various levels? Will the information supplied by companies have electronic media elements, and how will this be achieved? Will companies, for example, report data to an electronic database to which the public has access? The changes in availability and access may have effects both on information use and content.

19.3.2 Role of control processes and systems costs for systems design

The idea that everybody should be able to satisfy their own information needs, adjusted to their own behavioural patterns, is undoubtedly very attractive. In a way, it also represents a kind of an ideal, and the technological conditions are excellent nowadays. The cost of data processing may, of course, be a restriction. But more fundamentally, the issue is not so much what information each player should have access to, but what control processes should there be in societies and companies. There are strong forces of integration and limitation built into a chain of measures and targets in society.

In the upper part of this chain, in the area of public information, standard setting in many countries is characterized by two objectives: increased compliance with norms and the increased acceptance of international norms. Two main streams may be observed, in a somewhat simplified way.

1 One may be called *legalistic*. Democratically elected bodies should ultimately be responsible for standard setting in this field of law as in others. Standards should be applicable in many contexts, including the courts. 'Internationalization', from this particular perspective, involves a process in which the legal systems of many countries are adjusted to each other in the accounting field, so that information from companies may also be standardized. Co-ordination within the European Union with its supranational legal function is the main issue in Europe in accordance with this approach.

2 The other main stream can be labelled *self-regulation on a market economy basis*. The needs of financial markets are stressed. In principle, private institutions are responsible for standards. In this perspective, 'internationalization' means adjustment to bodies setting standards which are important for financial markets, above all the IASC and the FASB.

The two main streams are not developing independently of each other.

At the same time in the lower part of the chain, in the field of internal information, there is an intention to have local systems with a heavy

corporate activities, as consumers, employees, tax payers, etc.?

These are fundamental issues in line with the interests which 'behavioural accounting' researchers have been increasingly pursuing. There has been a gradual extension from 'management control' to 'societal and management control'.

Conceptually, these issues are hardly new. From time to time it has been emphasized that accounting should be seen from an organizational and social perspective. For example, as early as 1939, this was formulated by a committee within The American Institute of Accountants; their view is close to ours.

> The committee regards corporation accounting as one phase of the working of the corporate organization of business, which in turn it views as a machinery created by the people in the belief that, broadly speaking, it will serve a useful and social purpose. The test of the corporate system and of the special phase of it represented by corporate accounting ultimately lies in the results which are produced. These results must be judged from the standpoint of society as a whole – not from that of any one group of interested parties.[2]

According to one kind of ideal for the functioning of a system based on a stock market, the price of a company's shares reflects expectations about company cash flows, which in turn reflect the expected utility for consumers of company products. Whether this really should be considered an ideal is open to debate. The strength of the model is obvious at any rate, as are its deficiencies: all the external effects of company activity are not reflected in company costs and revenues. Tax systems, measurement deficiencies and distortions in income distributions will also produce effects which differ from those in a model world. It is not obvious what the exact meaning of these deficiencies is for resource allocation and efficiency evaluations.

- What role do share prices and expectations about share prices actually play in the action taken by owner groups and senior management, with regard to effects on the allocation of funds between companies?
- What perceptions and ideas about interesting products and activity areas are such expectations based on?
- What are the bases for senior management expectations when decisions about resources are made? What is the role of documented outcome for relatively short periods, for example?
- What in turn will this mean for quality of output and for resource allocation within a company, between subsidiaries, departments, products and investments?
- What material needs tend to be satisfied through such a process and what needs will not be satisfied? Which goods and services attract financial resources and which do not?
- What detailed effects will arise due to such a process – also outside the natural scope of players at the highest organizational levels?
- What economic activities are appropriate for such a process? What are their respective characteristics?

According to a common principle of management control, reporting frequency should be adjusted to the nature of processes to be controlled. The more long-term the process, the less frequent the information and the evaluation. From this point of view, what will be the effects of financial market information and evaluation of cash flows which basically involve long-term processes?

The time perspective of owner actions and owner demands on an organization are important. Are there, for example, differences in the time perspective for owners who act according to financial logic on a stock market, according to political logic in state-owned activities or those who act according to an interest-oriented logic in a co-operative undertaking?

The possibilities of changes in ownership structure are a potential motive force in stock markets. Such forces are required for company development but companies also need stability. Where and how incentives are established in the owner-company-sub-unit chain to create change and development seem to vary from case to case. The question deserves empirical studies. There are numerous examples of change processes triggered by share price changes; thus changes in ownership structure seem to have had the function prescribed by the ideal model. On the other hand, there are also numerous examples of change processes in companies due to changes in ownership structure in which long-term utility is not that obvious. Furthermore, there are examples of processes, where the primary motive forces for a change can be found at senior management level in cases where it has proved difficult to change the ownership; this very stability has been mentioned as a reason for change. What general empirical conclusions could be made, if any?

Our book primarily discusses companies listed on a stock market. Problems of determining measures and targets at the highest organizational level for such companies are only typical for them. Many other problems, however, apply to other companies. For instance, a government agency financed via budgets will encounter many problems which resemble those faced by functional units within stock market companies. A relationship between senior management and divisional managers demonstrates striking similarity with the relationship between an owner and senior management if the company lacks financial autonomy.

Research about effects of economic systems is feasible even if research problems are especially difficult to handle in certain respects. It is particularly important that researchers are at a distance regarding their own doctrinal perceptions. There is certainly research which analyses related issues of great importance. Total control processes and total effects, however, have rarely been the object of empirical study to the extent justified in view of their fundamental and increasing importance. Furthermore, effect-oriented research about management control has (presumably inevitably) had too short a time perspective to capture long-term effects of a structural and dynamic nature. The importance of long-term perspectives makes work around the borderline between management control and economic history very fruitful.

REFERENCES AND SELECTED ADDITIONAL READING

PART 1

Argyris, C. *The Impact of Budgets on People*, Cornell University (1952).

Ashton, R. R. (ed.). *The Evolution of Behavioral Accounting Research: An Overview*, Garland Press (1984).

Beaver, W. H. *Financial Reporting: An Accounting Revolution*, 2nd edn, Prentice Hall (1989).

Benston, G. J. 'The Role of the Firm's Accounting System for Motivation', *The Accounting Review*, April, 1963.

Bromwich, M. *Financial Reporting, Information and Capital Markets*, Pitman (1992).

Cyert, R. M. and March, J. G. *A Behavioral Theory of the Firm*, 2nd edition, Prentice Hall (1963).

Dearden, J. 'The Case Against ROI', *Harvard Business Review*, May–June, 1969.

Donaldson, G. *Managing Corporate Wealth*, Praeger Publishers (1984).

Einhorn, H. J. and Hogarth, R. M. 'Behavioral Decision Theory: Processes of Judgement and Choice', *Journal of Accounting Research*, Spring, 1981.

Financial Accounting Standards Board, *Statement of Financial Accounting Concepts No. 1 Objectives of Financial Reporting by Business Enterprises* (1980).

Financial Accounting Standards Board, *Statement of Financial Accounting Concepts No. 2 Qualitative Characteristics of Accounting Information* (1980).

Financial Accounting Standards Board, *Statement of Financial Accounting Concepts No.5 Recognition and Measurement in Financial Statements of Business Enterprises* (1984).

Financial Accounting Standards Board, *Statement of Financial Accounting Concepts No.6 Elements of Financial Statements* (1985).

Gordon, M. J.'Dividends, Earnings, and Stock Prices', *Review of Economics and Statistics*, May, 1959.

Gordon, M. J. *The Investment, Financing, and Valuation of the Corporation*, Irwin (1962).

Gordon, M. J. and Shapiro, E. 'Capital Equipment Analysis: The Required Rate of Profit', *Management Science*, October, 1956.

Hendriksen, E. S. and van Breda, M. F. *Accounting Theory*, 5th edn, Irwin (1992).

Hofstede, G. *Culture's Consequences. International Differences in Work Related Values*, Sage (1980).

Hopwood, A. G. *An Accounting System and Managerial Behaviour*, Saxon House (1973).

Ijiri, Y. *The Foundations of Accounting Measurement*, Prentice Hall (1967).

Ijiri, Y. 'Theory of Accounting Measurement', *Studies in Accounting Research*, no. 10, American Accounting Association, 1975.

Jacobson, R. and Aaker, D. 'Myopic Management Behaviour with Efficient, but Imperfect, Financial Market', *Journal of Accounting and Economics*, 16, 1993.

Johansson, S. E. 'Growth of Capital, Capital Structure, and Rate of Return', in Brockhoff and Krelle (eds), *Unternehmensplanung*, 1981.

Johnson, H. T. and Kaplan, R.S. *Relevance Lost: The Rise and Fall of Management Accounting*, Harvard Business School Press (1987).

Jones, T. C. and Dugdale, D. 'Academic and Practitioner Rationality: The Case of Investment Appraisal', *British Accounting Review*, 26, 1994.

Jönsson, S. A. *Accounting Regulation and Elite Structures: Forces in the Development of Accounting Policy*, Wiley (1988).

Kahneman, D. and Tversky, A. 'Prospect Theory: An Analysis of Decision under Risk', *Econometrica*, 47, 1979.

Kahneman, D. and Tversky, A. 'Choices, Values, and Frames', *American Psychologist*, 39, 1984.

Libby, R. and Lewis, B. L. 'Human Information Processing Research in Accounting: The State of the Art', *Accounting, Organizations and Society*, 2 (3), 1977.

Madsen, V. and Polesie, T. *Human Factors in Budgeting: Judgment and Evaluation*, Pitman (1981).

Miller, M. H. and Modigliani, F. 'Dividend Policy and the Valuation of Shares', *Journal of Business*, October, 1961.

Schmalenbach, E. *Dynamische Bilanz*, Westdeutscher Verlag (1953).

Stedry, A. *Budget Control and Cost Behavior*, Prentice Hall (1960).

Swieringa, R. J. and Weick, K. E. 'Management Accounting and Action', *Accounting, Organizations and Society*, 12 (3), 1987.

Whittington, G. 'Corporate Governance and the Regulation of Financial Reporting', *Accounting and Business Research*, 23 (91A), 1993.

Williams, J. B. *The Theory of Investment Value*, Harvard University Press (1938).

Williamson, O. E. *Markets and Hierarchies: Analysis and Antitrust*, Free Press (1975)

PART 2

Accounting Principle Board (APB), Opinion No. 21, *Interest on Receivables and Payables*.

American Institute of Accountants, *Changing Concepts of Business Income*, Macmillan (1952).

Anton, H. R. 'Depreciation, Cost Allocation and Investment Decisions', *Quarterly Journal of Economics*, 1956.

Archibald, T. R. 'Stock Market Reaction to the Depreciation Switch-Back', *The Accounting Review*, January, 1972.

Ball, R. and Brown, P. 'An Empirical Evaluation of Accounting Income Numbers', *Journal of Accounting Research*, Autumn, 1968.

Baxter, W. T. *Accounting Values and Inflation*, McGraw-Hill (1975).

Baxter, W. T. *Depreciating Assets*, Gee (1981).

Beaver, W. H. *Financial Reporting: An Accounting Revolution*, 2nd edn, Prentice Hall (1989).

Beaver, W. H. and Demski, J. S. 'The Nature of Income Measurement', *The Accounting Review*, 54 (1), 1979.

Bell, P. W. *Current Cost/Constant Dollar Accounting and Its Uses in the Managerial Decision Making Process*, University of Arkansas – Fayetteville McQueen Accounting Monograph Series (1986).

Bertmar, L. and Molin, G. *Capital Growth, Capital Structure and Return on Capital* (only in Swedish), EFI Ekonomiska Forskningsinstitutet vid Handelshögskolan i Stockholm (1977).

Brief, R. P. and Lawson, R. A. 'Approximate Error in Using Accounting Rates of Return to Estimate Economic Returns', *Journal of Business Finance & Accounting*, January, 1991.

Brief, R. P. and Lawson, R. A. 'The Role of the Accounting Rate of Return in Financial Statement Analysis', *The Accounting Review*, 67 (2), 1992.

Bursk, E. C., Dearden, J., Hawkins, D.F. and Longstreet, V.M. *Financial Control of Multinational Operations*, Financial Executives Research Foundation (1971).

Choi, F. D. S. and Czechowicz, I. J. 'Assessing Foreign Subsidiary Performance: A Multinational Comparison', *Management International Review*, 23, 1983.

Czechowicz, I. J., Choi, F.D.S. and Bavishi, V.B. *Assessing Foreign Subsidiary Performance: Systems and Practices of Leading Multinational Companies*, Business Corporation (1982).

Derimag, I. S. 'The Treatment of Exchange Rates in Internal Performance Evaluation', *Accounting and Business Research*, Spring, 16, 1986.

Edwards, E. O. and Bell, P. W. *The Theory and Measurement of Business Income*, University of California Press (1961).

Elikai, F., Moriarity, S. and Ayres, F. L. 'The Impact of Current Cost Information on Investment Decisions: An Empirical Assessment', *Journal of Accounting, Auditing & Finance*, 8 (3), 1993.

Engshagen, I. *Finansiella nyckeltal för koncern versus koncern bolag* (Financial Ratios for Groups vs. Legal Entities) (only in Swedish), mimeographed research report, Stockholm School of Economics (1987).

Financial Accounting Standard Board, *Exposure Draft on Accounting for the Impairment of Long-Lived Assets*, Financial Accounting Series, No. 132-B, 29 November, 1993.

Fisher, J. *The Nature of Capital and Income*, Macmillan (1906).

Harcourt, G. C. 'The Accountant in a Golden Age', *Oxford Economic Papers*, 17, 1965.

Hopwood, A. *Accounting and Human Behaviour*, Accountancy Age Books (1974).

Horngren, C. T. 'How Should We Interpret the Realization Concept?', *The Accounting Review*, April, 1965.

Johansson, S. E. *Taxes - Investments - Valuation* (in Swedish with mathematical appendix in English), EFI Företagsekonomiska institutet at Stockholm School of Economics (1961).

Kim, M. and Moore, G. 'Economic vs. Accounting Depreciation', *Journal of Accounting and Economics*, April, 1988.

Lawrence, B. et al. 'A Test of the Reliability of Current Cost Disclosures', *ABACUS*, 30 (1), 1994.

Lev, B. 'The Impact of Accounting Regulation on the Stock Market: The Case of Oil and Gas Companies', *The Accounting Review*, July, 1970.

Lindahl, E. *Studies in the Theory of Money and Capital*, Allen & Unwin (1939).

McCracken, P. W. 'Inflation Profits and the American Economy', in Griffen, P. A. (ed.), *Proceedings of the Financial Accounting Standards Board: Financial Reporting and Changing Prices*, 1979.

Paton, W. A. and Littleton, A. C. *An Introduction to Corporate Accounting Standards*, American Accounting Association (1946).

Peasnell, K. V. 'Some Formal Connections Between Economic Values and Yields and Accounting Numbers', *Journal of Business Finance and Accounting*, Autumn, 1982.

Revsine, L. *Replacement Cost Accounting*, Prentice Hall (1973).

Ricks, W. E. 'The Market's Response to the 1974 LIFO Adoptions', *Journal of Accounting Research*, Autumn, 1982.

Salamon, G. 'Accounting Rates of Return', *The American Economic Review*, June, 1985.

Samuelson, L. A. *Models of Accounting Information Systems*, Studentlitteratur (1990).

Solomons, D. 'Economic and Accounting Concepts of Income', *Five Monographs on Business Income*, Study Group on Business Income (1950).

Stauffer, T. A. 'The Measurement of Corporate Rates of Return: A Generalized Foundation', *Bell Journal of Economics and Management Science*, 1971.

Swanson, E. P. 'Relative Measurement Errors in Valuing Plant and Equipment under Current Cost and Replacement Cost', *The Accounting Review*, 65 (4), October, 1990.

Terborgh, G. *Realistic Depreciation Policy*, Machinery & Allied Products Institute (1954).

Thomas, P. B. and Hagler, J. H. 'Push Down Accounting: A Descriptive Assessment', *Accounting Horizons*, September, 1988.

van Breda, M. F. 'Accounting Rates of Return under Inflation', *Sloan Management Review*, Summer, 1981.

van Breda, M. F. 'The Misuse of Accounting Rates of Return: A Comment', *American Economic Review*, June, 1984.

Windal, F. W. 'The Accounting Concept of Realization', *The Accounting Review*, April, 1961.

PART 3

American Institute of Accountants, *Accounting Research Bulletin*, 1, 1939.

Anthony, R. N., Dearden, J. and Govindarajan, V. *Management Control Systems*, 7th edn, Irwin (1991).

Boland, R. J. Jr. 'Control, Causality and Information Systems Requirements', *Accounting, Organizations and Society*, 4, 1979.

Bower, J. L. *Managing the Resource Allocation Process*, Irwin (1970).

Choi, F. D. S. and Czechowicz, I. J. 'Assessing Foreign Subsidiary Performance: A Multinational Comparison', *Management International Review*, 23, 1983.

Clark, J. M. *Studies in the Economics of Overhead Costs*, University of Chicago Press (1923).

Cooper, D. J., Hayes. D. and Wolf, F. 'Accounting in Organized Anarchies: Understanding and Designing Accounting Systems in Ambiguous Situations', *Accounting, Organizations and Society*, 3, 1981.

Dearden, J. 'The Case Against ROI', *Harvard Business Review*, May–June, 1969.

Demski, J. S. 'Uncertainty and Evaluation Based on Controllable Performance', *Journal of Accounting Research*, Autumn, 1976.

Donaldson, G. *Strategy for Financial Mobility*, Irwin (1969).

Donaldson, G. and Lorsch, J. W. *Decision Making at the Top: The Shaping of Strategic Direction*, Basic Books (1983).

Eccles, Robert G. *The Transfer Pricing Problem: a Theory for Practice*, Lexington Books (1985).

Engshagen, I. *Finansiella nyckeltal för koncern versus koncern bolag* (Financial Ratios for Groups vs. Legal Entities) (only in Swedish), mimeographed research report, Stockholm School of Economics (1987).

Galbraith, J. *Designing Complex Organizations*, Addison-Wesley (1973).

Hirshleifer, J. 'On the Economics of Transfer Pricing', *Journal of Business*, July, 1956.

Hirshleifer, J. 'Economics of the Divisionalized Firm', *Journal of Business*, April, 1957.

Hofstede, G. *Culture's Consequences*: *International Differences in Work Related Values*, Sage (1980).

Johansson, J. and Mattsson, L. G. 'A Network Approach Compared with the Transaction-Cost Approach', *International Studies of Management and Organization*, 17(1), 1987.

Johansson, S. E. 'Growth of Capital, Capital Structure and Rate of Return', in Brockhoff and Krelle (eds), *Unternehmensplanung* (1981).

Johnson, H. T. and Kaplan, R. S. *Relevance Lost: The Rise and Fall of Management Accounting*, Harvard Business School Press (1987).

Lawrence, P. R. and Lorsch, J. W. *Organization and Environment; Managing Differentiation and Integration*, Division of Research, Harvard Graduate School of Business Administration (1967).

Madsen, V. *Regnskabsvaesendets opgaver og problemer i ny belysning* (only in Danish), Gyldendal (1959).

Moonitz, M. *The Entity Theory of Consolidated Statements*, American Accounting Association (1951).

Östman, L. *Management Control Based on Accounting Measures* (only in Swedish), EFI Ekonomiska Forskningsinstitutet at Stockholm School of Economics (1977).

Solomons, D. *Divisional Performance Measurement and Control*, Irwin (1965).

Sundgren, B. *Databasorienterad systemut veckling* (Database Systems Development) (only in Swedish), Studentlitteratur (1992).

Vancil, R. F. *Decentralization: Managerial Ambiguity by Design: a Research Study and Report for the Financial Executives*, Dow Jones – Irwin (1979).

INDEX

Also available from Pitman Publishing ...

Accounting in the Business Environment

by John Watts

This textbook has rapidly established a reputation as a sound conceptual approach to accounting, particularly suitable for courses with a European orientation. This edition has been brought fully up-to-date with the latest accounting standards issued. Short questions for student's self-testing are now included in each chapter. Bookkeeping has been strengthened and the section on management accounting expanded.

The book contains a number of features that make it a good choice for those wishing to develop courses with a European focus. Differences in financial reporting practices within the EC and their evolution from common origins are addressed. Unusually for an introductory text, it takes the group as the most common form of business organisation and discusses the issues raised.

Worked examples are used throughout the text to clarify complex issues and questions are provided in the text and in a separate Instructor's Manual.

John Watts is Principal Lecturer in Finance and Accounting, Anglia Polytechnic University, Cambridge

0 273 61560 2

Financial Reporting, Information and Capital Markets

by Michael Bromwich

This important book by a leading academic is a scholarly study of contemporary accounting theory from a capital market perspective. Michael Bromwich adopts an informational perspective on accounting theory, necessitating a more than usually detailed consideration of uncertainty and capital markets. The book explores how accounting information facilitates the working of these markets and integrates with them according to their level of organisation. It sets out the arguments for non-market regulation and reviews how this can be achieved, including through the use of a generally accepted conceptual framework. The final part of the book discusses the implications of agency theory for financial reporting.

Michael Bromwich is Professor of Accounting, London School of Economics

0 273 03464 2

Advanced Financial Accounting

by R W Lewis and D Pendrill

This popular textbook has now been thoroughly revised to incorporate the latest legal and professional developments, including the most recent accounting standards. This book covers the latest issues in financial reporting in considerable depth and provides an up-to-date range of questions to test students' understanding and interpretational skills when analysing financial statements. Answers to the basic questions are given at the back of the book and the more advanced questions are published separately for the exclusive use of lecturers adopting the main text as a set book.

Advanced Financial Accounting
- is the leading comprehensive text on financial accounting theory and practice at second or third year level
- is a thoroughly revised edition of a well-established text
- covers recent professional and legal developments
- maintains the structure of the previous edition but with additional new questions

R W Lewis is Pro-vice Chancellor, Open University and **D Pendrill** is Esmee Fairbairn Professor of Accounting, University of Buckingham

0 273 60500 3

Accounting for Business Activity

by David Hatherley

The theme of this book is the relevance of accounting to an understanding of business. It provides insights into how business activity and accounting information are interlinked through the medium of a series of fictitious case scenarios, within which a wide range of operational functions are explored.

Accounting for Business Activity can be used flexibly in a variety of teaching situations where an integrative and interpretative emphasis is required, and is particularly suitable for tutorial work. It is aimed at students on MBA and business degree courses, and may also be of use on accounting degree and HND courses.

David Hatherley is Professor of Accounting, University of Edinburgh

0 273 60115 6